The Death of

IN THE SAME SERIES

P. Souvestre & M. Allain (adapted by Mark P. Steele). *The Daughter of Fantômas*

A. Bisson & G. Livet (adapted by Frank J. Morlock). *Nick Carter vs. Fantômas*

Arnould Galopin (adapted by J.-M. & Randy Lofficier). *The Man in Grey*

Rick Lai. *Sisters of the Shadows 2: The Cagliostro Curse*

P. de Wattyne & Y. Walter (adapted by Frank J. Morlock). *Sherlock Holmes vs. Fantômas*

David White. *Fantômas in America*

The Death of

by
Pierre Souvestre
and
Marcel Allain

adapted by
Sheryl Curtis

A Black Coat Press Book

Acknowledgements:

English adaptation Copyright © 2017 by Sheryl Curtis.
Cover illustration Copyright © 2017 Mike Shoyket.
Introduction & Afterword Copyright © 2017 Jean-Marc Lofficier.

Visit our website at www.blackcoatpress.com

TABLE OF CONTENTS

Ill. By Mike Shoyket

Introduction

The Death of Fantômas is actually comprised of the last two issues of the *Fantômas* pulp series, written by Pierre Souvestre and Marcel Allain, published by Arthème Fayard just before World War I. They are:

* No. 31. *La Cravate de Chanvre* (translated here as *The Hemp Necktie*), released on August 20, 1913; and

* No. 32. *La Fin de Fantômas* (translated here as *The Death of Fantômas*), released on September 20 1913.

These two stories were written at a time when Souvestre and Allain were concentrating on another series, the patriotic adventures of super-spy Nez-en-l'air (15 issues, released 1912-13). It is, therefore, more than likely that they used a ghostwriter (or ghostwriters) to lighten their burden on Fantômas. Certainly, *La Cravate de Chanvre* and its immediate predecessor, *L'Hôtel du Crime*, appear to have been ghosted, which would explain certain inconsistencies both in plot and characterizations.

Soon after Fantômas ended its enormous successful run, Pierre Souvestre died, quite suddenly, of pulmonary congestion on February 26, 1914, and we will never know what his plans might have been for an eventual return of the Lord of Terror.[1]

It wasn't until 1925 that Allain alone dared to resurrect Fantômas, but most everyone agree that the subsequent volumes he wrote have little left of the surreal horror and diabolical plots of the original series.

Meanwhile, Fantômas' fame grew by leaps and bounds, boosted by the brilliant Gaumont serials directed by Louis Feuillade which came out in 1913 and 1914.[2]

We have chosen here to present the last two issues of the original series because, for the most part, they form a complete story. However, because the format relied heavily on the "to be continued" principle, inherited from the old

---

[1] It was Souvestre alone who had been hired by Fayard to develop the character of Fantômas; Allain was initially his secretary, then his ghostwriter, before being granted co-credit, but Souvestre remained the driving force of the team during his life.

[2] *Fantômas, Juve contre Fantômas, Le Mort Qui Tue, Fantômas contre Fantômas* and *Le Faux Magistrat*, all starring René Navarre as Fantômas. These are reviewed in the article devoted to Fantômas in our book *Shadowmen: Heroes and Villains of French Pulp Fiction*, Black Coat Press, ISBN 9780974071138.

newspaper *feuilletons*, it is useful to give the reader a brief summary of the events that happened before the curtain rises.

The year 1912 opened with what might well be Fantômas' greatest criminal enterprise: the robbery of the Paris Mint, known as the Hôtel des Monnaies. In order to further his scheme, Fantômas murders the man-servant of the Director of the Mint, then his mistress, and frames him for both crimes. Impersonating a detective, Fantômas then seeks to gain the Director's trust by pretending to help him prove his innocence. In reality, he is trying to gain access to the gold bullion and steal it. However, the scheme is foiled, as usual, by his nemesis, Detective Juve, who has identified Fantômas. Still, the master criminal manages to escape in the nick of time, trapping Juve and his boss, Sûreté Chief Havard. (This is the subject of episode 28, *Le Voleur d'Or*.)

Meanwhile, Hélène, Fantômas' alleged daughter,[3] has been kidnapped by her father's gang and is being held prisoner aboard a semi-automated ship which eventually reaches the Bay of Campeche in Mexico. That ship—which can also travel underwater like a submarine!—was designed by Fantômas to carry his plunder, once a year, to his secret lair in Mexico. Rigorous instructions have been left with the locals, who serve Fantômas, to kill anyone aboard upon arrival. In this case, the only passengers are Hélène and the ship's captain, later revealed to be Vladimir, Fantômas' equally evil son.

Hélène, of course, manages to escape and eventually finds Fantômas' secret lair, hidden in a lost valley surrounded by foreboding mountains and hostile Indians. The Lord of Terror's treasure is safely stored under a torrent, whose bed hides an invisible safe.

Meanwhile, back in France, Fantômas is now impersonating Juve. Using this disguise, he frees M. Havard from his own trap, thus convincing the trusting Director that he is indeed Juve. Even better, Fantômas has the real Juve, committed to the Sainte-Anne lunatic asylum, and later succeeds in getting his hands on a reward of 10,000 francs promised by Havard for his own capture!

Fortunately, Juve manages to clear his name, but only to discover that, in the meantime, Fantômas has fled to Mexico. The indomitable detective follows. Fantômas arrives just in time to save Vladimir and Hélène from the natives. Eventually, Juve saves Hélène's life by shooting Vladimir, just as he was about to murder his half-sister. Fantômas escapes, leaving his son's body behind. (This is the subject of episode 29, *La Série Rouge*.)

We're now in April 1912. Journalist Jerôme Fandor, Hélène's fiancé, is at the Dermas sanatorium in Switzerland, watching over his dying mother. Before he left for Mexico, Fantômas had ordered his men to kill Fandor, because he wants to stop him from marrying Hélène. The Lord of Terror's agents fail and, instead, become responsible for the death of Fandor's mother. Seeking revenge,

---

[3] The story of Hélène is narrated in *The Daughter of Fantômas*, Black Coat Press, ISBN 9781932983562.

the journalist returns to the Sanatorium, disguised as attorney Paul Mazeran, to conduct his own investigation.

At that moment, Fantômas and Hélène arrive separately in Switzerland. Fantômas has decided that he can just as well sabotage the lovers' wedding plans by proving to Hélène that Fandor has been unfaithful to her. He does that by tricking Fandor into kissing Natacha, a young Russian anarchist who has repented her sins and is dying, and has asked Fandor for one last kiss. The chivalrous young Frenchman could hardly refuse! Watching from afar, Hélène is convinced of Fandor's betrayal and leaves Switzerland for parts unknown.

Meanwhile, Fantômas, after committing another murder, steals a large sum of money from the Sanatorium, before vanishing into the night. (This is the subject of episode 30, *L'Hôtel du Crime*.)

The curtain now rises, a few weeks later, in Saint-Petersburg in Tsarist Russia...

Jean-Marc Lofficier

PIERRE SOUVESTRE & MARCEL ALLAIN

FANTÔMAS

LA CRAVATE DE CHANVRE

LE VOLUME COMPLET
65
CENTIMES

A. FAYARD et Cie ÉDITEURS DU "LIVRE POPULAIRE" PARIS

BOOK ONE: THE HEMP NECKTIE

CHAPTER I
The Police Lieutenant

The oil lamp tumbled to the floor. The room, which had been bathed in the half-light cast by the lamp under its large lampshade, plunged suddenly into darkness.

It was a large room, heavily cloaked, in the Russian style, with thick tapestries. The air was hot, heavy, filled with the extraordinary scent of leather that permeates Russian homes, palaces and humble dwellings, along neighborhood streets and the main arteries of St. Petersburg.

Obviously, something terrible was going on. But, with darkness veiling the horror, it would have been difficult to make out exactly what tragedy was being played out. Yet, the sound of fighting filled the air.

Panting. Every now and then a rough voice rang out. Hoarse insults: "Scoundrel! Wretch! Murderer!" all followed by appeals to the holy icons, desperate entreaties to the Madonna, the Virgin, the Little Father since, in Russia, the Tsar is appointed by God in person!

Silence fell again, suddenly, interrupted by the same sounds, scuffling, furniture falling, chairs bumping, and yet again the heavy sound of adversaries trying to overpower one another, falling to their knees, getting up, falling again.

A horrible battle was being waged in the dark. It went on and on. Five minutes had already passed since the lamp had fallen and gone out. Yet, there was no sign that the fight was drawing to an end.

The combatants, obviously, were fierce adversaries, filled with a mortal hatred. They had to be brave, strong, powerful, fighting with the conviction that their struggle would come to a tragic end.

Yet, this house was the calmest one in all St. Petersburg. Everyone would have sworn that no such drama, no such battle could ever take place here. Boris Pokroff, a lieutenant in the secret police, the Tsar's man, lived there.

Boris Pokroff, in his forties, dark face, broad shoulders, a well-built colossus, was a major personality. His position with the police, a very senior one, made him a man to be reckoned with. His instructions came from the Tsar personally. Boris Pokroff was feared by the poor. He hunted down the nihilists, just as he tracked down common criminals. It was well known that, on occasion, he made personal sacrifices and that he was not a man to retreat in the face of danger, no matter how great.

As a result of his duties, it is true, Boris Pokroff was often the target of vengeance. With a grim sense of humor, people referred to him as the "gallows man". In fact, his activities kept the hangmen busy performing the executions that held Russia in the grip of fear and brought to mind the iron hand that governed the large, friendly country.

Naturally, each execution garnered new enemies for Boris Pokroff. The head of the secret police received threats constantly. In return, he was perpetually under guard, surrounded by a crowd of police officers, each one spying on the next, always on the look-out for a traitor, constantly fearing assassination, always on the defensive.

Obviously, the fight being fought in his house that night meant that the police lieutenant's adversary was a determined man, a scoundrel who, without a shadow of a doubt, had already sacrificed his life and wanted only one thing—to kill the police officer before being strung up on some terrible gallows!

Regardless of who this man was, he had, obviously, met his match, as the saying goes.

Boris Pokroff must have been surprised at work. He was, in fact, signing arrest orders when the man had rushed him. Immediately, the scene had transformed into a merciless struggle, a terrible battle that waged on and on, without an end in sight, in the dark.

But, then, a cry of anguish filled the room. One of the two adversaries had just suffered a serious injury. A cry of joy rang out at the exact same time.

"Ah, now I've got you...!"

Another cry, the terrible shriek of a man having his throat cut... followed by the sound of a body falling heavily onto the carpet.

Silence returned, impressive. A moment later, nothing more than ragged breathing, all too quickly replaced by a death rattle, a weak sound, almost a moan, the gurgle of drowning.

"He's done for!" a deep voice rings out in the heavy silence.

The man speaking, moreover, regardless of who he is, the police lieutenant or his attacker, has to have been an extraordinarily brave man. He had just taken part in an abominable battle. He had, of course, just taken considerable risk with his life.

Yet, the words were uttered in a firm, unwavering voice.

A few minutes passed. The victor spoke again, "Now, down to business."

His heavy, weary footsteps shook the carpet. He must have been digging through his pockets since the familiar clicking of a set of keys could be heard, followed by the scraping of a match and a flicker of flame.

"Let there be light!" the voice said.

Guided by the light of his match, he picked up the lamp. The glass had broken, but the wick was still intact and the lamp could still be used.

The man lit it.

Only then, did he turn his head.

"Just as I was saying," he murmured. "That imbecile is done for. I do believe that he is quite dead."

The man faced the most frightful of scenes. In the disorderly room, a room with the tragic look of murder, a man lay on the carpet, folded arms unmoving. A long dagger jutted up from the frightful wound in the poor wretch's throat. The blow that carried it had been wielded in a last-ditch attempt at violence. The carotid had been severed. Possibly the spinal column had been cut.

Then the voice repeated, "Let's get down to business. What time is it?"

The man took a gold watch from his pocket.

"Good grief! Five o'clock," he murmured. "Marfa will be down in an hour. I'll have to be quick about this."

For a second, the man seemed to hesitate. The battle he'd just waged, the drama in which he'd taken part, had without a doubt, despite his composure, despite his unquestionable audacity, rattled him somewhat, since he seemed to have no clear idea as to what to do...

"That body is bothersome," he murmured a short while later. "No one needs to know about this. A death like this would just complicate the situation. Why worry His Majesty?"

His words were strange, impossible to understand. Yet even harder to decipher, however, was the attitude of the man uttering them. He was rushing, in fact. To take on a strange task. He'd just headed toward a large earthenware stove, one of those enormous, monumental stoves found only in Russia, made necessary by the harsh climate.

"This burns with the fires of hell," he commented. "I couldn't hope for better."

He'd opened the door of the stove, bent over the fire, and clucked his tongue, almost joyful.

"Really, this is a bit of luck, since I wouldn't want anyone to find out..."

He didn't complete his sentence but, with a calm that demonstrated his complete composure, he returned to the cadaver. The living man lifted the dead one. Quickly he dug through his victim's pockets. Papers, a wallet, a letter... he picked up everything and placed it on the desk.

"It's always a good idea to keep documents. It makes the job easier."

And he continued to speak such truths to himself with the impressive sangfroid of someone trying to make the best of a delicate situation.

He showed no sign of embarrassment, concern. His search of the body completed, he looked at it for a moment, shrugged and uttered one word, the most terrible, the cruelest of epitaphs, "Imbecile!"

Then he muttered, "He should have used the revolver."

At that moment, standing in front of the stove, he appeared to think.

"This might not be the best means. Bah! I don't have any choice. And this assassination must be covered up."

Coldly, he pushed the body into the stove and closed the iron door. At that moment, despite himself, he shivered.

"Let's hope the body will burn."

He stood there, next to the door, listening. Soon, a smile swept over his face. The fire, almost dead earlier, kicked back into life with a new intensity. A rumbling rose up through the grille. The dead man's clothing must have ignited already. Then, something abominable occurred, a familiar sound, rendered tragic by the circumstances, the crackling, the sputtering of the flames as they licked at flesh.

Two minutes later, the man frowned again.

"Good grief! I didn't even think about this little problem!"

The problem he referred to was obviously, a moral one. The man who had killed, possibly in self-defense, the man who was just now burning his victim's body appeared to want to cover his recent actions with silence. Yet, circumstances were against him.

After deciding to cremate the body, to eliminate it, to make any search impossible, he realized that the fire would leave traces that, without a doubt, would draw attention. The room, in fact, was filling with acrid smoke, with the disgusting odor of burning fat and flesh.

"What a disaster!" he said. "I could be asphyxiated."

He showed no signs of shame, no disgust. He seemed put out by the turn of events, but showed no sign of any other emotion.

"That odor, that smoke!" he grumbled. "This could cause problems. Better take care!"

He turned off the lamp and walked over to the window.

A moment later, the curtain drawstrings squealed. The pallid dawn of a pale day penetrated the large room. The man opened the two inside windows, since Russian houses always have double windows.

"What a disaster!" he grumbled again.

Then he added, "It's terribly cold this morning and yet it's snowing."

It was snowing, in fact, with large flakes rushing down one after another, without end, without slowing, in dizzying swirls. And the cold was intense, 20 degrees below, not counting the wind, which was blowing fiercely.

With no regard for the cold, the man leaned over the sill. He looked out over the white panorama of houses buried under snow as far as the eye could see. Obviously, it was winter and St. Petersburg would look like this for another six months to come.

"No sleigh, no one about," grumbled the man. "It's still early. Good."

And he breathed in the air with a bored gesture.

"What a stench! What smoke! This is surely enough to rouse the neighborhood. Bah! It will take no more than a moment," he murmured.

At this point, as he leaned against the railing in front of the window, he jumped in surprise.

"Hey!" he said, "I've been injured. I didn't even notice it!"

He had just seen, in fact, a large drop of blood fall onto the ledge of the window. His face darkened. He looked eminently upset.

"Blood, blood! I don't need people to find blood in the office, particularly since that Marfa is such a gossip…"

In four steps, he strode across the room, coming to a stop in front of a mirror. He was rather seriously wounded and only the stress of the tragic moment could account for why he had not yet noticed that fact. His face had been gouged, a large cut running from his cheek to his throat.

"Honestly, it ended just in time," he complained. "A bit longer and that would be me in the fireplace…"

He must have found his comments entertaining since he burst out laughing. Yet, even as he continued to chortle, the man didn't waste a second. He quickly bandaged his wounds. He took a flask from his pocket and used its contents to wash his injury. The blood stopped flowing.

"Fine!" he murmured. "If I pull up my collar, no one will notice this little nick. It will heal quickly. In just 24 hours and no wagging tongues will bother me."

The fireplace continued to smoke, however. And the bitter odor persisted. Despite the wind rushing in through the windows, chasing billows of white snowflakes into the center of the room, the atmosphere remained oppressive.

"This is taking so long!" the man grumbled.

He walked back over to the fireplace and, noticing a large poker leaning against the wall, he prepared to stir up the fire. Yet, once the iron door was open he stepped back, despite himself. It was a horrible spectacle. As the fire burned, the cadaver contorted in a most horrible manner. The body was already three-quarters consumed, impossible to recognize, without a human face, its hair and beard burnt, the eye sockets empty, a gaping hole in the belly spewing foul materials that immediately disappeared up in smoke.

"Ah, I hope I'll finally be rid of that imbecile in 15 minutes!"

Enraged, the man continued to stir up the fire. The limbs of the cadaver twisted even more. For a moment, it looked as if the hands were waving, large fingers splaying, then clenching in a vengeful grasp.

"Damn!" the man grumbled, "That does look impressive!"

He slammed the door.

Despite the barely closed stove, the man was shivering. The wind had carried an arctic cold into the once hot room.

"This could be the death of me," the man thought. "And yet, no one must notice the odor, no one must notice the smoke."

Possibly to warm himself, but more certainly in an effort to remove the traces of the struggle, the man set to repairing as much of the disorder that reigned in the room as he could. He picked up chairs that had been turned over, straightened small objects on the desk, taking extreme care with his task.

It was impossible, however, for him to completely remove all signs that a bloody battle had taken place. One chair had broken a pane of glass and the foot of a delicate side table when it fell.

'I can explain that," thought the man.

But, when facing a large blood stain that marked where the body had fallen, he seemed somewhat more embarrassed.

"That's a lot of blood!" he grumbled. "Bah! We'll see!"

Although the smoke was waning, the odor persisted. Once again, the assassin poked at the fire, where no more than a few remnants of charred bones remained, slowly turning into ash, and then he walked over to the desk.

"There's no time to waste! I must get back to work!"

Just a few brief seconds after the man had taken a seat behind the desk, the door to the office opened suddenly. The man jumped.

"Since when do you come into my office like this, Marfa?" he asked.

An old woman had just entered the room. She might have been 50 or so, but deprivation, poverty and hard work had worn her down so that she looked like 60. Obviously, Marfa was a servant. Her white hair disappeared under a cap and she wore a large blue apron, both signs of her position. Hearing the criticism implied in the man's voice, she stopped short.

"Oh, your Excellency," she murmured. "I didn't think, as the Little Father is my witness, that you were there! You rarely work at this time, your Excellency. It's barely six in the morning.'

Hearing those words, the man shrugged.

"Marfa," he ordered, harshly, "You should know that I work all hours of the day and night. There's no rest for Boris Pokroff!"

The police lieutenant since, obviously, it was the lieutenant who had won the battle and was answering the old servant, spoke with a barely concealed anger.

Marfa, however, no matter how much she respected her master, must have been accustomed to dealing with his harshness since she showed no signs of dismay. Quite the contrary, she smiled and set about putting the little objects that lay strewn willy-nilly about the room back in their places.

The old maid grumbled, "In any case, perhaps you work all the time, but one thing is certain, your Excellency is not always reasonable. Opening the windows in weather like this! There's no rhyme nor reason in that!"

As the old maid headed over to the windows, Boris Pokroff ordered, "Leave the windows open!"

Upon hearing the order, old Marfa rolled her eyes in surprise.

"But this can't be!" she grumbled. "The snow is blowing in all over."

"Too bad."

"But it's 20 below!"

"Too bad."

This time, Marfa placed her hands on her hips and looked her master straight in the eye.

"You always say the same thing," she complained, "There's no hope for you! Twenty below and the windows open! No! And you're not even wearing your pelisse!"

She took three steps toward the stove and added, "What's more, the fire must be almost out!"

"Leave the fire alone," Boris Pokroff interrupted.

"But it's going to run out of wood, your Excellency!"

"Leave it alone, I said!"

Surprised, Marfa took three steps back.

"Fine," she said, in the familiar tone of old servants who can dare to make such comments. "I'm not even going to try to understand anymore. You don't want a fire? It will be the death of you!"

In an authoritative manner, ignoring the order she'd been given, Marfa turned back to the stove. Just as she was about to open the iron door, the man knew he had to stop her. Boris Pokroff stood up abruptly. He grabbed the old woman's arm, forcing her to stand still,

"Are you going to obey me? I told you to leave the fire alone!"

This was, obviously strange, so strange even that Marfa looked at her master, unable to hide her concern.

"Good grief, you're frightening me!" she said.

Then, taking a deep breath, she added, "You really are behaving oddly. And how this room reeks!"

Boris Pokroff didn't answer, seeming to consider the servant looking at her intently.

Marfa started up again, "And the entire house is filled with smoke...Obviously, you've been up to something again..."

But she interrupted herself in mid-sentence, to scream in fright.

"Oh! Holy Virgin, Mother of God," the maid said. "By all that's holy, what is that?"

Boris Pokroff had released her arm and she walked to the middle of the carpet bent over and added, "But it's blood! It's blood!"

And, suddenly Marfa turned around.

"Your Excellency, you're hiding something from me. Whatever happened here?"

Just then, Boris Pokroff took a thin yellow cigarette from a cup and leisurely lit it.

"I had a nose bleed, Marfa," he said.

The old maid clasped her hands.

"Oh! What a miserable day. And you didn't even tell me! Your Excellency, you must not move. You have to stay still!"

"That's what I'm doing, Marfa."

"But why didn't you tell me? I would never have bothered you with my idle chatter! You must have bled a lot!"

"Yes, a lot, Marfa."

The maid was pacing back and forth now.

"Too bad. I'm closing the windows," she declared. "I know that you need air but, anyway, that's no reason to get really, really sick!"

As she closed the window, the maid saw the broken pane of glass in a dark corner.

"And that?" she murmured. "My God! So many misfortunes today!"

Boris Pokroff shrugged.

"I had a nosebleed and then, as I was walking about in the dark, I struck that pain of glass and fell to the floor. That's all Marfa."

But there would just be one surprise after another that day for the old woman. Now, she was no longer listening to her master. Eyes wide, she started at a small table standing at the other end of the office.

"Your Excellency... Your Excellency," Marfa called.

"What now?" said Boris Pokroff.

"What's this, then?"

Already, Marfa's voice was changing. The old servant had turned pale and her hand, as she pointed at a piece of furniture, was shaking.

Boris Pokroff turned to look. There it was, forgotten by mistake, the dagger that he had plunged in his victim's throat a while earlier.

Without a moment's hesitation, Pokroff replied, "That dagger, Marfa, is a piece of evidence I need for a trial. Does that answer all your questions, now?"

Boris Pokroff pretended to lose his patience. The old servant noticed nothing. Still very pale and shaking violently, she nodded her head, enraged.

"Your Excellency, that's hardly possible!" Marfa uttered. "That dagger is still covered with blood and the blood is fresh..."

Marfa looked Boris Pokroff straight in the eyes. He suddenly lost his calm.

"You have no right to doubt my word," he ordered.

Then he lost his temper.

"Go get the mail for me. Hurry up! And come straight back!"

This time, Marfa, who was still quite upset, did not dare disobey her master's order. She left the room. As soon as she had gone, Boris Pokroff ran over to an electrical panel located close to the desk. He bent over the call buttons, checked the labels, and pressed one for a long time.

A second later, two men, giants, identified by their uniforms as members of the police squad responsible for security in St. Petersburg, entered the room.

"At your service, your Excellency," they said as one.

Boris Pokroff looked determined. He stared at the two strapping men who stood at attention, as motionless as statues. Without a doubt, the honest loyalty he saw in the two servants' eyes reassured him.

"I can count on them," he thought.

"Alexander Alexandrovitch!" he said.

"At your command, Your Honor."

"Fedor Fedorovitch!"

"At your command, Your Honor."

"You will pick up the person I tell you to and take him immediately to the chain gang. Is there a chain gang leaving for the mines this morning?"

"Yes, your Excellency."

"Fine, here's the arrest warrant."

Boris Pokroff scribbled a few worlds on a large sheet of paper, which he gave to the two policemen.

"Don't mention this to anyone."

"Yes, Your Excellency!"

The two men showed no surprise.

The Siberian mines are terrible places. Generally, they're reserved for people sentenced to death, people the government wants to get rid of. The people sent there never return. Many die along the way, from cold, fatigue, deprivation. The prisoners set out on foot, chained to one another. Others die in the mines, at the farthest reaches of the steppes, in an icy hell.

Moreover, it's quite easy to sentence someone to this slow death. An accusation of nihilism, a political smear, the whiff of a suspicion.... that's all the courts need to impose such terrible sentences. Perhaps even less. The Russian police, charged with maintaining security, for ensuring the safety of the Tsar, can freely, without answering to anyone, send anyone they want to the mines. Even today, the police enjoy the power once conferred by *lettres de cachet* before the Revolution. And the police lieutenant had, in fact, just signed such a letter. Who did it name?

A moment later, Marfa returned. The old servant carried the mail over to the desk.

"The mail, Your Excellency."

"Hand it over!" said Boris Pokroff.

He took the mail and added, "You can leave now, Marfa."

The servant headed for the door.

Boris Pokroff waved his hand.

"Take her," he ordered.

It took no more than a second. The elderly servant had no time to cry out in surprise. The two henchmen leapt at her, gagged her and dragged her out.

"To the mines," they yelled.

Boris Pokroff stood alone, smiling.

"That woman will never speak," he grumbled.

Then, the police lieutenant brushed his hand over his forehead.

"It is true, he added, "That those two imbeciles who just arrested her might say something... Bah! I'll take care of that"

He rang again. A moment later, four police officers listened as Boris Pokroff issued orders.

"You will find Alexander Alexandrovitch and Fedor Fedorovitch, your colleagues."

"Yes, Your Excellency."

"You will arrest them."

"Yes, Your Excellency."

Boris Pokroff realized that the two officers were dumbfounded. Without a moment's hesitation, he explained his conduct.

"I have information about them. They're nihilists..."

Then he waved his hand at the four officers, who seemed frightened.

"Go! I'm counting on you."

A moment later, Boris Pokroff was once again alone in his office. He seemed quite satisfied.

"Things are coming along just fine," he muttered. "One body, three people off to the mines...Now no one will say a word and the Tsar will know nothing. The Little Father will not be concerned!"

The police lieutenant went back to work.

CHAPTER II
The White Card

"It's snowing out, Ma'am."

"I don't care!"

"It's terribly cold out."

"So, I'll wear my pelisse."

"No one would want to go out, Ma'am."

"I'm going out anyway."

"But that's just careless."

"I can be as careless as I want."

"Well, may the Holy Saints keep you then. Will you be coming back early?"

"I have no idea."

"Madam won't leave the city at least, will she?"

"I don't think so."

"There are wolves this time of year, lurking about the city."

"Bah! Wolves don't scare me!"

"Really? You're not afraid of anything?"

"Nothing, Gregoria. Nothing at all!"

The young woman who was demonstrating such peace of mind, such surprising courage, an audacity so placid, was tall, possibly about 20, and should have been pretty. She had a fine figure, a pleasing voice and her slightest movements were filled with a particular grace, an innate distinction, a truly deep charm. Her face was hidden behind a very thick veil. It would have been difficult, even impossible, to recognize her. Yet, the sparkle of her large eyes, both energetic and soft, revealed the remarkable beauty of her very expressive features.

"Madam is not afraid of anything!" grumbled the elderly maid who, while working for the lodgers who occupied the furnished rooms in the house, was helping the stranger dress.

Gregoria, of course, would never have gone out in such weather. Since the morning, in fact, large flakes of snow had been falling, constantly doubling their violence, and the ground, blanketed in a thick carpet, was thoroughly frozen by the intense cold. Crossing herself, she watched the extraordinary preparations of the young woman who was audacious enough to want to face the rigors of the climate, at any cost.

Her preparations did not take long. Although the young woman did demonstrate a certain flirtatiousness while arranging the folds of her veil, which she bundled into her thick fur pelisse, it appeared that she had other concerns than elegance. She barely glanced at the mirror on the wall before slipping her hands into a thick muff and then left the room.

A second later, the foreigner, and she certainly had to be a foreigner since there was nothing Russian about the young woman, was in the street. Instinctively, she glanced right and left, as if afraid of being followed or possibly spied on. But that didn't prove anything since, in Russia, the police were so powerful that everyone was always afraid of being spied on, denounced, for the most futile reasons, the most insignificant incidents.

In any case, the young woman should have been reassured since the street she found herself in was deserted as far as the eye could see, cast into deep silence by the soft carpet of snow.

She walked down the street, reached the Nevsky Prospect, then continued quickly on her way, heading to a sort of station where five or six horse-drawn sleighs stood in a line, ready for hire. She walked past the sleigh station, looking carefully at the drivers, one by one.

Was she hoping to recognize one of the placid coachmen who, in keeping with fashion in the country all wore, in addition to the traditional Russian dress, enormous cummerbunds that gave them the paunchy shape considered the epitome of elegance for drivers in St. Petersburg?

"I don't know a single one of them. They all look so calm, I don't dare try!"

Walking past the past carriage, leaving the Nevsky Prospect, the stranger headed into a new street, broad as all streets in St. Petersburg are, just as deserted as well since all the streets are deserted at this time of day and in this kind of weather.

Two sleighs drove by. This time, the young woman hailed one of them.

"Stop, little father."

Immediately the driver reined in his horses and the sleigh stopped as he flattered his beasts with the most endearing of epithets.

"Gently, my little swallows! Stop my little lambs of God! Slower my winged arrows!"

The stranger walked over to the sleigh. Obviously, she was familiar with Russian ways since she had taken a few coins from her purse, which she held out to the man.

"Take this, little father. I like your cummerbund and I want you to drink your tea hot this evening."

The coachman was not surprised by this familiar expression of courtesy.

In France, people give tips when they get out of a carriage. In Russia tips are given when you hail a sleigh since, in this way, the driver knows how much generosity to expect from his client and can decide how cooperative he wants to be.

The young woman, however, after paying her driver a tip, frowned, seemed to hesitate a moment and then sent the sleigh off.

"Go on, little father! I've changed my mind. I no longer need you."

Although he was surprised by the client's sudden dismissal, the driver didn't hesitate long, happy to have pocketed a tip that had not been hard to earn.

Yet, if the driver was surprised at being stopped and then sent on his way, he would have been even more surprised if he had accompanied the young women for even a few moments. She did, in fact, stop a second sleigh. One after another, she stopped four in all, giving the drivers tips and then sending them on their way.

A fifth was more fortunate. Just as the young woman held out a few coins to him, he appeared to be overwhelmed with emotion.

"Ah! Pardon me," he said, jumping up and down on his seat. "I didn't understand…"

And stranger even than these mysterious words, were his actions as he reached out his hand to the young woman as if to give her a familiar hug.

The stranger was not the least bit offended. Perhaps she had paled a little, but that was her only reaction. She was most certainly a strange woman, with strange tasks since, without indicating any intentions, she climbed into this last sleigh and sat down without even giving the driver an address.

It would in all likelihood have been pointless to make the effort since, as soon as she sat down, the driver was already urging his horses into motion., He had three robust animals hitched side by side, heads crowned with the quaint bells so typical of Russia.

"Away my swallows! Run my little birds of the steppes! Faster, faster, my slender gazelles! We're working for Mother Russia. We have to hurry for the cause!"

This was all very odd and yet the stranger remained impassive. As the sleigh quickly accelerated, sliding at a dizzying speed over the snow, the three horses walking strangely, the one in the middle galloping as the other two continued to trot, the foreigner started to talk out loud. She must have been very worried, her mild filled with a serious concern since, despite herself, her voice sounded shrill.

"My God! I was so afraid!" she murmured. "I thought I'd given the wrong sign with my fingers… None of the drivers understood my hand signals. Only this one understood what I wanted… But where is he taking me?"

The young woman, as could be seen from her words, was not aware of the point of her race. It seemed, moreover, that she had chosen her driver, not at random, and based on his more or less good appearance, but for reasons she didn't explain in detail.

She had to have settled for a driver that acted in a certain way. Perhaps she was a member of one of those associations that were spreading through Russia? At least that would have explained the characteristic hand sign she had given the sleigh drivers, which only the last one had understood. In any case, the young woman now slumped in the back of the sleigh, warmly wrapped in the furs there.

The three horses raced like bats out of hell, driven on by the driver's voice, through the neighborhoods of St. Petersburg, covering large distances, then into the countryside where the sleigh slid even faster since the snow was deeper and frozen hard.

"Where are we going? Where are we going?" the young woman repeated from time to time.

The countryside looked almost deserted. The dawn revealed an infinite succession of large fields that disappeared uniformly under the mantle of snow and stretched as far as the eye could see with desperate monotony.

"Little father," the young woman soon asked, "Is it far?"

The driver looked over his shoulder.

"We've covered seven verste and we have three more to go."

"Good. Faster! God be with you!"

"God be with me, in fact."

The driver turned back to his horses and urged them on, "Gallop my little white hen! Walk my adored star! Trot my duck with the long wings!"

And the sleigh flew even faster.

Just a few minutes later, a sudden turn in the path, revealed a small pine stand, some way off, surrounded by a dozen tiny white houses, like those of the Russian peasants. In the middle of the hamlet, stood a sort of covered shed, which served as a church. The coachman pointed at it with his whip.

"That's it," he said.

The young woman shivered. When the sleigh stopped, she turned white and seemed to be overcome with emotion. Yet she stepped down from the sleigh immediately and walked over to the wooden door of the church.

It was close to eight o'clock in the evening and normally the building should have been empty and plunged in the deepest darkness. That was hardly the case. The stranger stepped through the door and into the nave alight with sparkling candles and filled with a silent crowd.

"There are a lot of them," she murmured.

Her teeth chattered with fright. Her entire body trembled.

"Bah! I'm doing my duty," she added.

The intriguing woman walked on. As she stepped over the threshold, a man dressed in black like a sexton approached her.

"Who are you?" he asked.

"She who comes…"

"What do you want?"

"He who will go…"

"How do you want it?"

"By all means…"

The man in black dipped his head and pointed at a register.

"Sign, my sister."

"Yes, my father."

The young woman picked up a pencil and wrote the name that was to be hers in large letters: Olga. Then she kneeled on the floor, close to the nave, against the pulpit where the pope would harangue the faithful a few moments later.

Were those people filling the church the faithful? What did the words exchanged with Olga, if that really was her name, mean? They appeared to have a secret meaning, to be some sort of password.

The young woman had only been kneeling a few minutes when a pope entered the pulpit. He made no gestures of piety. He was a strapping fellow, in his fifties no doubt, with large hands, a bushy face. He appeared to be somewhat drunk, a common condition for Russian priests. Once settled, the pope pounded his fist on the edge of the pulpit, imposing silence.

"Brothers and sisters," he started.

As the congregation fell silent to hear him, he pounded his fist against his chest.

"I have been sent here to you to replace our deceased brother, Pope Credo, hanged three days ago, by the order of the Tsar. None of you know me. I name myself: from now on you will be the brothers and sisters of Pope Alleluia. Is that what you want?"

The crowd filling the church shouted, "Yes!"

Then the pope, who had taken the name Alleluia, obviously a nom de guerre, clapped his hands.

"Brothers and sisters," he said. "I was very moved when I learned that I would head your section. What does this mean? I will do my duty! The one who must perish will perish and no one is better placed than I am to help you, when we will have to carry our banner at the head of the troupes and march against the enemy!"

These were, in fact, odd words for a priest. This pope had a strange way of calling the devoted to the love of God. He started to speak of murder and massacre.

"We will destroy everything, when the time comes," he proclaimed. "Our justice will start with universal destruction. We will make the void equal. Brothers and sisters…"

This strange pope was about to continue preaching in these terms when one of the flock suddenly stood up.

"Alert!" he cried out.

Panic filled the church. Those who were sitting or kneeling stood up. Weapons sparkled. A thousand frightened voices ran out.

"What is it? Cossacks?"

But just then, a man climbed up the long stairs to the pulpit. The pope backed off to give him room. The man indicated that he wanted to speak.

"Brothers and sisters. I am convinced that there is a spy among us. You all know the risks we are taking. You all know that the Tsar will soon have all the gallows he needs to hang us, the nihilists. Well, I ask you to make an effort this evening. Let us defend ourselves! Death to traitors! Let us judge the one who has come to spy on us!"

Silence fell, impressive. In that church, which was usually deserted, a crowd of men and woman had gathered under Pope Alleluia. They were no faithful believers but conspirators, ferocious, terrible conspirators, known in Russia as nihilists. Formidable terrorists, frightful politicians founding a political movement on a very harsh moral framework, akin to the stoics, utopians who are the cousins of the anarchists, the Russian nihilists cause a reign of terror in the largest empires. They are the personal enemies of the Tsar, the nobility, the rich. Prohibited by law, outlawed by decree, they simply deny the law. Force is used against them, they respond with cunning. They are dissolved, they reform. The authorities track secret associations, they prosper.

Russian nihilism is worse than the Italian mafia. Russian nihilists are exalted, sympathetic, convinced, rising from the flames like a phoenix, with their own martyrs. Each execution draws in more believers and one day the nihilists may well take on the Tsar, equal to equal.

The small chapel was filled with nihilists, who had taken over the building for their clandestine meetings. Pope Alleluia, like many popes, was a nihilist as well. Sent by the section president, he was responsible for maintaining order above all. As the clamor of voices swelled in response to the speaker's words, Pope Alleluia spread his arms.

"Brothers and sisters, silence!" he roared.

And, in a fierce voice, he added, "There may not be enough gallows to hang us all, but the Tsar will order us strung up on the first branches available!"

He laughed, somewhat sardonically, then questioned the man standing with him in the pulpit.

"Brother, you say that there is a spy among us. How did you recognize him?"

The man shrugged.

"Someone came in," he stammered. "Someone who certainly doesn't know the rites of our association. Someone who, I have just made sure, signed the book but did not place his token in the urn. There is one signature too many in the book. There is one token too few in the secret urn. The individual without a token is definitely a spy."

This was, in fact, a safety measure adopted by the nihilists. Always at the mercy of spies, always on the look-out for a denunciation, perpetually afraid of police brutality, hunted like wild animals, the nihilists invented a thousand ways to keep an eye on one another. At each meeting, for example, they voted on a new password. Only those who had attended the meeting could know it. As a result, only they could attend the next meeting, vouch for their nihilist credentials.

That evening, there had been two safety checks: signing the book was the first, placing a token in the urn was the second.

"Someone signed without a token," screamed the man standing next to Pope Alleluia. "That person is a spy! Let him be brave and step forward!"

At that moment, a voice called out, a voice filled with disdain, "Here I am!"

It was a woman. She stood up and walked steadily toward the pulpit. A fierce silence reigned over the church.

Nihilists are not people to forgive spies. Their justice is expeditious, their sentences are often capital. The woman walking down the nave was inevitably walking to her death. Everyone fell silent to watch her.

Yet, from the top of his pulpit, the pope asked, "Who are you?"

The woman did not answer.

"Where do you come from?"

She remained silent.

"Are you with the police?"

The unknown woman had reached the pulpit. She climbed the steps without trembling. When she was halfway up, in clear view of the crowd filling the church, she motioned with her hand, indicating that she was about to speak.

"I'm not from the police,' she murmured. "My name is Olga and you will recognize me by this."

As she spoke she waved about am extraordinary golden case, which flickered with a thousand fires. Voices clamored again in the church. It was as if seeing the golden case had galvanized all of the nihilists there. But they were not crying out in anger. There were no furious imprecations, no enraged curses. Quite the opposite. They sounded sympathetic.

"Who are you? How did you get that? Speak, sister."

Olga, since she was Olga, motioned for silence again.

"Natacha chose me," she announced. "She gave me the golden case you see in my hands. Of course, you realize the terrible meaning of that."

"Yes! Yes!" they responded.

Olga continued, "This case contains a terrible poison distilled a long time ago to execute the tyrant, the Tsar, who is oppressing the Russian people. Brothers and sisters, I have been denounced as a spy. If I were a spy, Natacha would never have entrusted this golden case to me. You wanted to know who I am? You will. I am the one who will kill the Emperor!"

Olga had barely uttered those words when emotion overwhelmed the congregation. The secret assassination, the murder of the Tsar, this political crime was ardently desired by all nihilists, convinced, like the fanatics they were, that once the Tsar was killed, Russia would be saved from the despotism of the noble classes.

All nihilists knew the secret of the golden case. The only one who could possess the magic case was the person who had agreed to assassinate the emperor. Natacha had held it in her hands at one time and when she passed it on to another woman, it meant that woman had decided to assume the tragic responsibility.

"Olga, Olga, you are our sister!"

Cheers erupted in the nave. Pope Alleluia had to intervene.

"Gently, my brothers," he grumbled. "If the police are watching, they will hear you."

But it was almost impossible to quell the crowd's enthusiasm.

Olga made a supreme gesture. The nihilist, since the young woman had to be a nihilist, suddenly declared, "If you still have a doubt, let that doubt disappear. I have the means to place myself at your mercy. You are all here. Veiled, your faces are impossible to recognize. You will all see me with my face uncovered."

Olga tore off her veil. The cheers grew louder, in a crazy acclamation for the young woman, an unbelievable ovation. And that ovation continued to grow until, a few minutes later, Olga spoke again.

"For example, if I intend to accomplish my mission, I want you to help me in any way you can. You have to swear that, as long as the golden case is in my hands, none of you will make an attempt on the Tsar's life. I want to choose the right time and he must not have any suspicions."

Olga, her face uncovered, remained motionless on the steps. Who was this young woman who had just claimed a colossal place in the midst of the nihilists, who was this woman who had been hesitant on her way to the meeting yet now looked prepared to command all of the fanatics around her?

This young woman, this so-called nihilist, was acknowledged by the world of heroes. If Police Officer Juve had seen her, if the journalist Jérôme Fandor had heard her, they would have been surprised, and they would have perceived that surprise as joy.

Juve would have yelled, "Hélène!"

And Fandor would have shouted, "My wife!"

Was this Hélène? Was this the daughter or rather the alleged daughter of Fantômas who, playing the role of Olga now found herself in St. Petersburg passing herself off to the nihilists as a nihilist herself?

That was the truth. Hélène was Olga. It was Jérôme Fandor's wife who was just now receiving compliments from Pope Alleluia, who had been transported in enthusiasm. But what was Hélène doing in St. Petersburg? More important, what was she doing with the nihilists? What was she planning to do with the golden case that sparkled in her hands?

Hélène would have responded with a single word. With the pride that comes with taking a courageous action, she would have simply stated, "I'm doing my duty!"

Yes, the young woman was doing her duty. When she had arrived in the Alps a few weeks earlier, to join Jérôme Fandor, Hélène was astonished to come face to face with Fantômas.

At the very moment when these formidable events were taking place, Hélène was still unsettled by an unexpected discovery she had made. In the mountain snow, the young woman had found a golden case. It contained compromising papers. As she read them, Hélène understood their significance, became aware of terrible secrets. Suddenly she found herself tracking down a formidable plot against the Tsar. She learned that the sovereign of all the Russias was in terrible danger, that he could be assassinated at any time.

Hélène was suffering at the time. She had every reason in the world to believe that she had been betrayed, to imagine that Jérôme Fandor had abandoned here, that he was in love with another woman. Yet despite her atrocious suffering, Hélène did not hesitate. She understood that, before she dealt with her personal problems, she had a duty to play a role in the terrible secret she had unwittingly uncovered.

Regardless of the sympathy she felt for the nihilist cause—she knew that many of the utopians' demands were legitimate—Hélène, like all honest people, disapproved of anarchistic assassination.

The Tsar was in danger. What should she do? Without hesitating and despite the fact she was alone, Hélène decided to try to save him! And truthfully, it was to save the Tsar, to prevent a political assassination, as horrific as any crime, that Hélène had come to Russia.

Like all valiant people, moreover, she obviously hoped that by dedicating herself to others she would forget her own suffering.

But would luck continue to be on her side? Would she ever manage to outsmart the nihilists? Of course! Hélène must be quaking and experiencing some intense emotions in the small chapel, buried under the snow, as she heard a powerful flow, an ocean of cries and exclamations well up toward her.

Suddenly, the clock rang out over the din. It hadn't yet finished ringing midnight when Pope Alleluia, quaked in turn.

"My brothers and sisters!" he shrieked

He pointed at the face of the clock, speaking quickly. "Today's meeting has been thrown into turmoil by the unexpected arrival of our dear sister Olga. My brothers, we have not had the opportunity to speak of urgent matters and we can only stay in this church for another half hour without getting caught. Does anyone have any messages for us?"

Pope Alleluia thought that surely no one would answer his appeal. Yet three people stood up.

"Yes, yes. Let us speak!"

Pope Alleluia waved his hand and an old, shaky voice started, "I'd like to report thefts that have been occurring for some time now. The police are blaming us, the nihilists. This is very harmful for us. We're revolutionaries, not thieves!"

The protestor had barely finished speaking when another voice spoke out, "I wanted to make the same complaint, to draw your attention to the fact that, according to the police reports prepared following each robbery, white business cards are left at the scenes of the crimes."

More voices rang out. From the back of the church, people yelled, "White cards like these ones…"

The faithful had, in fact mysteriously found real business cards, but completely blank, on several of the chairs. What do these mysterious papers mean?

"My brothers and sisters," Pope Alleluia yelled, "Let us go on our way. It's time. We will discuss this matter at our next meeting but, for the love of Russia, let us leave now!"

Anyone who had looked at the lovely face of the so-called Olga would have noticed her deathly paleness.

But, what was happening now? The church slowly emptied. The sleighs that had been waiting outside were carried off by galloping horses.

CHAPTER III
The Tsar of All the Russias

Once the four agents he'd summoned had set out on the trail of the first two police officers he'd assigned to take the old maid, Marfa, to the chain gang heading off to Siberia, Boris Pokroff took a deep breath. It seemed as if this extraordinary individual had been relieved of a great burden, that he was regaining confidence and that, after the terrible night he'd just spent, he was now prepared to enjoy, and understandably so, a return to calm. He dropped heavily into one of the enormous arm chairs that decorated his office.

"Umpph!" he murmured. "Here I am alone and master of the situation."

He walked about, while speaking, casting slow looks all around, considering the appearance of the room so attentively that one would have willingly imagined that he was seeing it for the first time and was trying to note all of the details.

"Fine. This will just make one memory more."

He smiled briefly, as if enjoying some secret thought that he would not express out loud, then stretched like a man who has slept badly.

Boris Pokroff paced up and down a while more. He stopped before the wood stove that had just served as a funeral pyre and, opening the iron door, made sure that the flames had completely destroyed to cadaver he had stashed there.

The door closed once again, Boris Pokroff stopped by the bloody stain on the floor.

"That is a bit more of a problem! Obviously, this stain could draw attention. Bah, a nose bleed can explain everything!"

He took in the window with the broken pane, the table with the wobbly foot.

"That`s nothing at all. No one will ever know!"

And this time he chuckled outright. Boris Pokroff was undoubtedly a very intelligent man, a refined man in a Russia that was still home to so many semi-barbarians.

He continued his monologue, "This is a truly curious country. The chief of police required to handle such manners on his own. His officers all busy spying on one another. Intrigues everywhere. Endless problems caused by the nihilists. And then there's His Majesty the Tsar, that timid young man who lives in fear of assassination while so many of his subjects have sworn to assassinate him!"

Suddenly, he interrupted his monologue, the monologue of the cynic he so obviously was, saying, "Back to work."

He went to sit down behind his large desk. Already, he prepared to search through the papers in an open drawer, seeking some important document when he stopped short, upset. A large drop of blood had just fallen in the desk blotter. Boris Pokroff picked up his handkerchief and wiped it over his face. It was covered with blood.

He stood up and walked over to a large mirror hanging on the wall, looked at it and frowned. The wound he'd received during the battle, the gash on his face, had re-opened. It was bleeding profusely. Obviously, if he wanted to stop this bothersome hemorrhage, he'd have to consult a doctor.

"Things are just getting worse and worse!" he grumbled.

He seemed to hesitate for a few moments then, making a decision, headed over to the ringer panel yet again. Once there, he hesitated again.

"This is abominable! I just had my maid arrested. I've had the people who arrested her arrested. All this, just to keep the situation secret, to make sure the Tsar has no suspicions. Yet, once again, I'm going to have to expose myself to the wagging tongue of that drunkard, my doctor!"

He stopped short and shrugged, "Bah! I'll take care of him."

He walked away from the bell panel, leafed through an address book, a sort of official directory, and walked over to the telephone.,

An hour later, Boris Pokroff stood in his room with a serious-looking young man. The doctor he had called. He was a young, recently returned to Russia, after earning a medical degree in Paris.

The young physician looked most surprised and, while washing Pokroff's wound, remained profoundly silent. And he was entitled to be surprised. He had been called out under strange circumstances. A telephone call, telling him merely that a car would pick him up at his door, that he had to get into it, that he would be taken to see a patient who needed his care. He had received no other explanation.

In Russia, however, there are so many highly placed individuals who for, whatever reason and under many circumstances have an urgent need to remain anonymous that he had not hesitated to follow the instructions he was given. A few minutes later, a sleigh stopped at his door. He got in. It took him to the home of the chief of police.

"Well," he thought, "What has happened here?"

He was very concerned and grew even more worried when, after he rang the doorbell, it was answer by Boris Pokroff in person.

"Strange!" he thought.

His amazement grew minute by the minute. Was he here to treat Boris Pokroff? And was Boris Pokroff hesitating to explain both the nature of his injury and the manner in which he had received it?

The physician had protested at first. He believed in his art and wanted to treat the man who had called in with a good conscience.

"I need to know what went on," he said. "I need to know if the wound is septic or aseptic."

But Boris Pokroff just shrugged, "You won't learn anything, doctor. Bandage my wound, that's all I want."

And the bandaging was just about complete. The doctor had just wound a long strip of cloth around the injured man's face. He attached it with a pin and stepped back.

Boris Pokroff asked, "Could you tell me, doctor, how long it will take this wound to close?"

"Yes," he replied, "It should take at least 48 hours."

"Thank you."

Boris Pokroff delicately slipped a bank note into the doctor's hand and stood up, indicating that the man was free to leave.

"At your service, sir," he said.

"Thank you, sir."

The two men nodded.

"You know the way out? I'm sorry but I can't accompany you."

"Don't worry, sir."

The doctor started to walk down the stairs. He had barely reached the middle landing when he heard a whistle. It came from the upper floor. What did the signal mean? The doctor barely had time to think. The whistle blew again as two men rushed him, gagging him tightly, tying him up like a package.

From the top of the staircase, Boris Pokroff shouted, "Off with him! That's the poor fool I told you about on the telephone. Take him back to the asylum and tell the manager, on my behalf, to keep a close eye on him!"

Boris Pokroff sniggered as he walked back into his office.

"Another one! Ensuring silence takes so much work!"

Then he turned thoughtful. "That doctor told me I should be free of this wound within two days. That's two days I need to find."

The head of the secret police picked up the telephone once again. He must have been contacting a highly placed individual since he immediately announced, "I have the honor of informing your Excellency that I will be away for 48 hours. I've dismissed my servants, given the necessary orders. Yet, as a result of the vengeance to which I'm exposed, I would appreciate it if Your Excellency would have his regular officers keep a discrete eye on my home. I want no one, absolutely no one to get into my house during my absence!"

Two days later, Boris Pokroff, faithful to the instructions he'd been given by the doctor, removed the bandage from his face. He chortled in satisfaction.

"Perfect. I've definitely been fortunate by deciding to be patient for once! It is impossible now to make out the injury I sustained. It has healed completely."

In fact, no trace of the knife wound he'd received that tragic night could be seen. The unfortunate doctor, sent to live with the insane, must have been a skilled man. He'd been able to stitch the flesh perfectly, preventing any scarring.

Boris Pokroff rubbed his hands in unabashed joy, "And now for a little expedition!"

It looked, in fact, as if he were commanding some sort of adventure. His face had transformed instantly. This extraordinary man looked truly impressive. A sudden light flashed from his deep, black eyes. Boris Pokroff remained like that. Staring, for a few moments then, suddenly shrugging, he smiled.

In the large office where the injured man had spent most of his time during the two days of his voluntary captivity, papers were piled high. He grasped one and read it with extreme zeal.

"Hearing today. Well, I won't miss that."

As he said that, a strange, surprised smile flitted across his face. This man always seemed to speak with enigmatic words, in double entendres. It was no doubt one of the sad privileges of his trade as a private police officer, a Russian police officer, who, as he lied and lied, grew incapable of the slightest sincerity.

Boris Pokroff dressed with extreme care that morning. He pulled on satin shorts, silk socks, a blue suit and then slipped an unlikely hat, his court hat under his arm.

The Tsar's secret police chief enjoyed a strange position. Although people generally supposed that no one knew his exact functions, that was not exactly true. The police officer was very well known. Although his face wasn't popular in the universal meaning of the word, there was not a single person at court who had not seen him walk by, who did not have a relatively good idea of just what he did, who couldn't guess that he was a man to be treated with kid gloves, a man you needed to be on good terms with.

Once he had donned his court attire Boris Pokroff checked the time on his gold, diamond encrusted watch, a princely gift from the Tsar, then used the telephone to call for a sleigh.

The chief of the secret police rarely used his own carriage. Obviously, he felt that it would be completely useless, given the public's general hatred for him, to attract attention by using vehicles that would be noticed. In a sleigh, however, he did not attract attention.

The chief of the secret police left his home with a light step. He crossed the sidewalk, after glancing furtively left and right, a man always on the lookout for adventure, then jumped in behind the driver of the old, hired sleigh.

"Where can I take you, Your Excellency?"

"To Tsarskoye Selo."

"Yes, Your Excellency."

The driver clacked his whip and the horses trotted off.

Tsarskoye Selo is both a village and a fortress, a palace and, above all a prison. There's no other word to describe the imperial residence of the Tsar of all the Russias, a sovereign reigning over the largest territory in the world.

The most respected and powerful of all sovereigns, the Tsar is condemned, despite everything to live in perpetual fear.

Russia, an immense state, could be compared to a giant vat in which the most varied ferments boil and foam. There are veritable castes in Russia and these castes are enemies. The nobility is hated by the people. The city worker is hated by the farm worker. The Siberians fight the Uralians and the Manchurians can't get along with the Polish.

There is better or worse.

While the various peoples categorized as Russias have risen up against one another out of racial hatred, while differences in wealth have created rival castes, it should never be forgotten that there are formidable political parties in Russia and that, in addition to these dedicated political parties, there are secret societies that draw formidable armies to their banners.

And nihilism floats over all these elements of discord.

The nihilists who are, in theory, the followers of a sublime philosophy, succumb in reality to practices that could only be considered criminal. They are invisible, indestructible. They are as dangerous as martyrs, people of faith, the illuminated.

The nihilists promote terror and Tsarskoye Selo was born out of all this. This palace with its thick walls, with its fortified enclosure, is surrounded by massive police forces; this palace which no one ever approaches was actually designed to protect the Tsar against the perpetual threat of assassination.

It is a palace with sumptuous apartments, splendid gardens and festive events. It's a city as a result of its scope and the resources at its disposal to protect itself against an uprising. It is a prison because the Tsar and his wife, the Tsarina, live there like prisoners.

The Tsar could easily be compared to the sultan. He can never go out with an imposing escort. He can never go into the street without being surrounded by armed protectors, without the police first sweeping the roads clear and ordering all windows closed.

At Tsarskoye Selo the most extraordinary distractions are needed to make up for such a sad existence. This prison has its own theatre, race track, game rooms. All of the luxuries that can possibly be imagined, all the specialties of modern life, can be found there, on a small scale, installed for the pleasure of the Tsar.

It was to this imperial residence, strange in so many ways, that Boris Pokroff was heading. Of course, as he gave the driver the address, he would have seen immense astonishment wash over the man's face. The brave driver was not in the habit of taking people to such a place.

If he had not had the typical Russian sense of obedience, if he had not had a resigned, Slavic soul, he would have protested that it was impossible to drive to such a place. To approach the imperial palace... What madness! What audacity! The police would be standing 200 yards in front of it, ordering everyone to turn around, and he would neither argue nor resist.

The driver must then have been doubly surprised when, as they approached Tsarskoye Selo, Boris Pokroff stood up in the sleigh. He must have been recognized by the police officers who stared at the vehicle since they were allowed through to the monumental door without problem. Boris Pokroff motioned at the officer guarding the door that he was to pay the driver.

Forty minutes later, the chief of police was taken into an enormous room. He stood motionless, with an excessively respectful posture, bowed, bent in two while to tell the truth there was absolutely no one in the immense hall.

Boris Pokroff, it is true, knew that, from one moment to another, the Tsar who had summoned him for his daily audience could make his appearance. Quite naturally, Boris Pokroff, respectful of the customs and rules of protocol, remained bowed so as to be able to greet the Tsar as soon as he arrived.

And he did not have to wait long. After fifteen minutes, the door opened wide.

A chamberlain, in a blue uniform covered with gold announced, "His Majesty!"

And, as the chamberlain backed away, fading into the background, a short, thin blond man with narrow shoulders, a sickly look, a beard that was too long, eyes perpetually moving, filled with worry, entered the room.

It was Nicholas II, the Tsar, the emperor of all the Russians, the formidable autocrat whose sovereign authority seemed to have survived, well beyond ancient customs, into our century of liberty and modernity!

Nicholas II took a few steps and turned around suddenly to make sure the door through which he had entered the room had been closed and that chamberlain who had heralded his arrival had withdrawn. Then, reassured, the Tsar walked quickly over to the police officer, who was still bent in two, motionless, as if frozen in respect, not daring to utter a single word. He walked to the middle of the room and spoke, "Come here my chief of police."

Docilely, Boris Pokroff walked over to the emperor. But Nicholas II shivered as he saw him stop again.

"Don't stay there Pokroff," he ordered. "You're right under the light. I know that those cursed nihilists have sworn to take off my head!"

Boris Pokroff, still silent, took a step to the side.

"More to the right! More to the right!" the Tsar begged "You're standing in front of a window. They can shoot you through the window!"

Boris Pokroff took another step.

"There, there!" said the Tsar. "I think we're risking nothing!"

The emperor of all the Russias had pulled out an armchair. He looked as if he was about to sit, but then abruptly stepped away from the piece of furniture.

"I'm being careless," he murmured.

And in a taut voice he gave another order, "You sit down, Boris Pokroff!"

The chief of police smiled and sat down. He remained there only a second and then got up abruptly, and the Tsar replaced him in the chair.

Boris Pokroff was not in the least surprised by all this activity. He knew exactly what it meant. Hadn't they once found a box, in a chair intended for the Tsar, which would have exploded if he had sat down? Since that time, the Tsar distrusted all chairs. He never sat down unless one of his underlings had already tested the seat.

Nicolas II ran his hand across his forehead, as he seemed to enjoy a moment's peace. Finally, he deigned to notice his chief of police. The Tsar stood up and in a bitter tone said, "What are you here to tell me Boris Pokroff? Who is going to kill me today?"

"Sire," Boris replied in a serious tone. "I'm pleased to tell your Majesty that, at present, you're in no danger at all."

"Really," the Tsar replied, in a skeptical tone.

"Sire," stated Boris Pokroff. "Thanks to your Majesty's magnificence I have been able to hang 78 of the most dangerous nihilists. Forty-two others are under lock and key at this very moment and will be executed shortly. I believe your Majesty is completely safe."

The autocrat deigned to smile. "That's what you always say. Meanwhile, where is the golden case?"

Boris Pokroff remained silent.

The Tsar lost his temper, "See! I'm not safe," he murmured. "As long as the golden case remains in circulation, I have everything to fear."

As he spoke, the Tsar wiped his handkerchief nervously over his face. The unfortunate dictator, this condemned man living such a pitiful existence, was dripping with fear. He knew about the existence of the golden case. He knew that the symbolic box contained a formidable poison, that the nihilists entrusted it to their most determined leaders, that any individual who was given the golden case for keeping promised, on their honor, to use it to kill the Tsar. Only his death relieved them from their mission. As long as the golden case was in circulation, the Tsar had no illusions at all. He knew beyond a shadow of a doubt that there was someone in the world who had sworn to kill him and that the killer would spend his life carrying out his mission.

After a moment's silence, the Tsar asked Boris Pokroff, "And you? No one has tried anything against you?"

"No," the police chief replied.

The Tsar lost his temper again, "You're lying to me! I know you're lying to me!"

That was one of his hobby horses. He trusted Boris Pokroff. He believed that the man was capable of protecting him, but he also knew that the chief of police was under constant threat from the enemy. The Tsar believed that Boris Pokroff took risks similar to his own. He feared that his police chief would be assassinated, not out of any pity for the man but because he needed him.

"You're lying to me!" he murmured, his voice growing softer. "I'm convinced that you're not telling me the entire truth. That's bad, very bad."

He panted, face red and congested.

Boris Pokroff replied with his usual calm, "I dare to tell your Majesty that he is making an error. Such audacity frightens me. Yet, your Majesty has no grounds to believe that I'm hiding the truth. Even if he were to have suspicions, he could imagine that I simply want to avoid useless alarms and, since I have sacrificed my life for him for many years now, I am prepared to die without saying a single word that could cause him pain!"

Just then, a fearful look crossed over the sovereign's face. He believed that he understood, at least partially, Pokroff's words.

"Ah!" he said in a heavy voice. I can see the truth, Boris Pokroff. You have been away for two days, so that's a lie... I'm certain..."

"Is your Majesty spying on me, Sire?" Pokroff asked.

With those words, the emperor stood up abruptly.

"No, no. I don't have anyone watching you," he swore. "I trust you completely. Don't worry about that, Boris Pokroff. I trust you and only you!"

"That's a great honor, Sire, and I'm profoundly grateful to your Majesty."

The Tsar started to pace up and down. He avoided walking in front of windows, he kept away from the furniture, he made sure he never stood under a light where he ran the risk, hypothetical as it was, of being crushed by enormous crystals.

Suddenly he turned around, "So, nothing new Pokroff?"

"No, sire."

"On your honor?"

"On my honor, sire."

"Well, go on then. I trust you and only you!"

Boris Pokroff bowed to the Tsar without replying. But as he bent over, the chief of the secret police frowned instinctively. He was thinking about his master and judging the Tsar.

"A poor man, an imbecile, a weakling. I was right to hide everything from him. He would have lost his head and that would have complicated things enormously."

Boris Pokroff backed out of the room since no one was allowed to turn his back on the Tsar. Once he was gone, however, the dictator took a golden whistle from his pocket and blew. He never used the electronic calling buttons since he was afraid that they had been tampered with and would explode if he used them.

In response to the Tsar's call, two men, two gigantic men, arrived. They were devoted servants, two brutes brought to the city from Caucasus to do God only what work. They came and went. Sometimes it seemed as if the Tsar was truly afraid of them.

As soon as they stood before him, he ordered, "Boris Pokroff has just left. Follow him. Spy on him. I want to know where he goes. Quick!"

As the two agents raced off, the Tsar looked even more concerned.

"My God!" he muttered. "If I could only be certain those two imbeciles won't betray me! I use them to spy on my police but who can I get to spy on them?"

Lost in thought, Nicholas II started pacing up and down again, starting at the slightest sound.

Once outside the private salon where he had been received by the Tsar, Boris Pokroff walked off down the imperial hallways unaware that two agents were following him. He was worried. That had to be the reason he cried out, startled, when a fabulously beautiful woman raced ahead to meet him as he turned a corner.

It was the grand-duchess, Ekaterina, a close relative of the emperor and the Tsarina's matron of honor.

Despite her pale face, the grand-duchess smiled at him charmingly.

"Ah! Boris, Boris!" she sighed. "These last two days have been so long without you. You don't love me anymore? You don't want to love me?"

Boris Pokroff stepped back suddenly. Automatically he reached into his pocket as if looking for a weapon. At the same time, his face tensed.

Yet the grand-duchess continued, "Listen, since that day I acknowledged the passion I feel for you, it seems as if you're distancing yourself from me. I'm suffering, I'm suffering you know. Do you love someone else?"

The grand-duchess gave a pain-filled laugh. She shrugged and added, "I'm dying from jealously."

Boris Pokroff smiled strangely in return. He approached the young woman, clasped her pale hands and kissed with passionate ardor.

"You're suffering and you are wrong," the police chief murmured. "You are jealous and you're getting yourself worked up for no good reason. I love you, only you. I've already told you that!"

"No!" the grand-duchess protested. "You've never told me that!"

Boris Pokroff shivered.

"That's true. I've never said it but you should have guessed."

He seemed to hesitate, searching for the right word.

The grand-duchess, unaware of his disarray, continued, "I undoubtedly should have guessed, but it's so nice to hear the words. Why won't you say them? I tell you that I love you. Why do you refuse?"

The Russian noblewoman quivered. She was deliciously beautiful, captivating. Love made her a woman capable of distracting even the most resolute man from his duties.

Boris Pokroff, however, stiffened. He seemed to make an effort of supreme will replying in a hesitating, trembling voice, "I'm afraid for you... Being the mistress of a man such as I exposes you to disaster. I protect the Tsar. I'm the one they'll kill first. I'm afraid of dragging you along my path. I don't want to expose the woman I love to the vengeance I deal with effortlessly when I face them alone. That's why I refuse to love you!"

Boris Pokroff did not need to add another word. The Grand-duchess Ekate-rina placed her beautiful blond head on his shoulder and sobbed.

Boris Pokroff would have been surprising to look at right then. He raised his head suddenly, an ironic, sarcastic, demonic smile playing over his lips.

CHAPTER IV
An Utter Imbecile

He went by his own name, Nirdinsko, and seemed excessively proud about being the last in a line that had sold preserves. Yet, his pride was not justified because, while the Nirdinsko family had been merchants, that had never brought them happiness and, during a riot one day, their shop had been pillaged, burgled, and sacked by local people, calling them monopolists, usurers and, to be perfectly honest, shameless Jews.

In any case, Nirdinsko was a fat man, happy with his lot in life. He had not gone into business, but had married a widow to his liking, although she was thirty years his elder, for her considerable dowry, which consisted entirely of a servant placement agency.

Nirdinsko, whose girth continued to grow, was, therefore, in all senses of the word, a prosperous man. He had not even realized that his wife, who had a definite taste for youth, got along famously with all the neighborhood children who were old enough to get into trouble. Furthermore, he had no idea that he was, in fact, his wife's first servant and that, despite the fact that he claimed to be a boss, he performed the tasks no one wanted to do, the tasks that would have discouraged the most persistent workers.

That afternoon, smiling as usual, his sweater unbuttoned as always to give his large belly some air, Nirdinsko was in the small placement agency office. He was locked in serious conversation with his wife, named Alexandra in honor of the empress, despite her lack of any resemblance to that enormous shrew.

Convinced of his insight, Nirdinsko stated, "I tell you, that boy will do the job. He's stupid, half deaf, three-quarters mute, completely obtuse, incapable of anything, thin enough to discourage a pope, and ugly enough to cause six women to miscarry at the same time!"

The fat Alexandra nodded, hesitating, and her husband continued, "I tell you, he's a superior servant! We won't find any better than him."

Yet, Alexandra remained unconvinced.

Running out of arguments, Nirdinsko proposed, "Do you want to interview him again? Do you want to see for yourself, if you don't trust me?"

Alexandra, who was an intelligent person and trusted no one but herself when it came to managing the placement agency, nodded in approval. It was obvious that nothing her husband said mattered. Moreover, perhaps she was not wrong and Nirdinsko himself, when he let down his guard, had no problem confessing that his wife was endowed with qualities far superior to his.

Nirdinsko, who wanted above all for his wife to take an interest in his favorite, pressed on a bell. The door to the small parlor opened and an old woman, the agency assistant, asked, "What?"

"Send Alexis in."

A moment later, the office door opened again and a tall young man, in his 20s, entered the room, clumsy and awkward, and walked toward the desk where Alexandra sat.

"Come in, young man," Nirdinsko ordered.

The young man took a step forward, an enormous hat still on his head.

Alexandra intervened, "Come on, now, take that hat off!"

The newcomer removed his hat and, with obvious satisfaction, wringing it this way and that.

"What's your name?" Alexandra started.

"Alexis."

"Alexis what?"

"No, not Alexis What, just Alexis!"

"I understand, but Alexis is your first name. What's your family name?"

No response.

The agency manager brightened up and winked in response when her husband clicked his tongue in satisfaction.

She started her interview immediately.

"What do you know how to do? Are you a cook?"

"No."

"Are you a valet?"

"No."

"Do you know how to drive?"

"No."

"So, you're a gardener."

"No."

"Well, then, what can you do?"

The extraordinary Alexis, who was laughing stupidly, seemed completely unaware of the irony hidden behind the question. Did he even understand the questions they were asking him? It seemed obvious that he did not, given the stupid way he continually giggled.

His face was both flat and bloated. Moreover, he wore an enormous bandage around his jaw, required no doubt as a result of some horrible toothache. His hair was uncombed, long strands hanging over his poorly shaved face with an extraordinarily bushy mustache.

Obviously, the unfortunate Russian belonged to the lowest class of people. He must have come to St. Petersburg by chance and no one was less qualified than he was to hold the sensitive position of servant in a large house.

"What do you know how to do?" Alexandra repeated.

Missing the point of the question, Alexis replied, "I want to make a lot of money."

His demand was so out of place that the agency manager burst into laughter. She regained her composure and asked, "How much do you want to earn?"

But the young man, who was obviously incapable of intelligent thought, of setting a reasonable figure, bypassed the discussion. Stubbornly, he repeated, "I want to make a lot of money."

Then, as if he had suddenly taken them into his confidence, the idiot launched into a monologue that seemed as if it would never end.

He came from very far away, the outer reaches of Siberia. There, people were dying of hunger. Farming was no good. So, the pope had told him to go to St. Petersburg, where people made money. And he did just that. He wanted to make a fortune in ten years. Then he would marry his cousin, who had a pair of cows that were perfect for pulling a plough.

Then, Alexis repeated again, "I want to make a lot of money!"

Obviously, they would have to get rid of him. Alexandra showed him the door.

"That's fine, young man. Away with you!"

As soon as he had left, Nirdinsko asked his wife, "What do you think? Isn't he perfect?"

"It would seem so," Alexandre said, thoughtfully. "He's a superior imbecile."

The placement agency manager opened a drawer in her work table and took out a letter.

"No one will be able to reproach us," she added. "That's exactly what they're looking for."

She read a letter out loud, demonstrating that she was never wrong:

Madame: I would appreciate it if you would find a valet for me since I am obliged to replace my own and have had to fire my old serving woman. I would like the boy you send me to be a complete moron. I need servants who are completely lacking in intelligence; otherwise they might be inclined to take advantage of the secrets they might overhear while in service. Select a perfect imbecile for me, with strong arms. I would accept someone who is one-eyed, deaf and mute. Moreover, you know what satisfies me since I have used your agency to hire servants on many occasions.

Alexandra read this strange letter, repeating the signature out loud, "The name is perfectly legible. It's signed: Boris Pokroff, head of the Tsar's secret police!"

For a moment, Alexandra remained pensive, re-reading the letter. She finally made a decision and it was in keeping with her husband's projects.

"You're right," she declared. Alexis is the perfect imbecile Mr. Pokroff needs. We'll send him over."

Most certainly, Alexandra would have been most concerned if, that very evening, she could have climbed up to the attic the extraordinary Alexis, the superior imbecile, had rented in the city. On his own, now, the young man had transformed. Slow and stupid earlier, he had become lively, nimble, even intelligent, a flame burning in his eyes. Once the door to his attic had closed, he became a totally different creature. Alexi danced a little polka. Then, standing before the washstand, he dipped a cloth into the water and rubbed his face vigorously with it. Soon, the cloth was stained with all sorts of colors: red, blue, black, a thick paste coating it. This simply showed that Alexis had been in disguise, something that was proven beyond a shadow of a doubt a few seconds later when he tore off the wig he had been wearing, along with the fake mustache that had rendered him unrecognizable.

Transformed, Alexis looked nothing at all like the sublime imbecile that had seemed to satisfy all of Pokroff's conditions.

So, who was Alexis?

Of course, if Juve had seen him he would have certainly recognized him.

If Hélène had only caught a glimpse, she would have been overwhelmed with painful emotions.

Alexis was Fandor and Fandor was in a fine mood!

"How perfect!" he told himself as he finished removing the make-up that coated his face. "What an excellent skill it is to be able to eavesdrop at doors. That's how I learned the kind of valet Pokroff needed. A superior imbecile! Of course, I've taken on all sorts of disguises so far. I definitely had to try this one. A superior imbecile. A perfect dolt. I've obviously taken a step up. Hey, nothing should discourage me. Perhaps, one day, I'll perform with the greats, while playing a dung collector!"

Fandor, who had finally washed the grime off, could go to bed with a clear mind. Once in bed, he took care to close his eyes. The journalist, who always found it very difficult to rise in the mornings, found it almost as hard to fall asleep at night.

Joking, he liked to say that he preferred not going to bed to having to get up early. And that was no lie, but profoundly true.

Jérôme Fandor, in bed, gave free reign to his dreams while smoking a cigarette something which, in his case, revealed a sense of profound well-being.

"Now," thought Jérôme Fandor, "I'm going to have to keep my eyes peeled, as my good friend Bouzille, whom I have not seen in a long time, used to say. Tomorrow, at Pokroff's house, I may have something very interesting to discover."

What was Fandor's plan? What projects did Juve's intrepid friend have in mind?

There was nothing mysterious or extraordinary about Jérôme Fandor's presence in St. Petersburg, for anyone familiar with the courageous journalist's most recent adventures, for someone who knew his deep sense of honor.

In fact, Fandor had been involved in the most tragic and moving of adventures. He had been there for the last sigh uttered by Natacha when, overcome by the cruel disease she believed she had caught, she fled to the top of the Alps.

At that time, Jérôme Fandor learned that Natacha loved him. He was all the more overwhelmed by this knowledge since, naturally, he felt nothing more than sympathy for the nihilist, as a result of the sincere love he still felt for Hélène. Yet, he had learned the dying woman's deepest secrets. She had asked him to announce her death to her father, Boris Pokroff, and, above all, to prevent, if he could, the attack the nihilists planned against the Tsar.

At that very moment, not knowing what had happened to Hélène, and the tragic disdain that had caused her to believe he had betrayed his oaths, Fandor had set out immediately for Russia. Fandor was far too cautious, far too familiar with police investigations to take such a mission lightly. He surmised that Boris Pokroff had to have close ties with the nihilist. The police chief had to know that his daughter Natacha, was a formidable political conspirator.

So, how would Boris Pokroff welcome him?

The journalist decided it would be an excellent idea to find out more about the situation before going to see Natacha's father. He spent a few days conducting a discrete investigation. Jérôme Fandor had already had a few opportunities during the course of his eventful life to enjoy the benefits of luck, he now realized that fortune was smiling on him once again.

In fact, Jérôme Fandor had no regrets about the time and effort he had spent spying on Boris Pokroff. He had made a few strange discoveries. He had uncovered a few surprising mysteries, alarming secrets, terrifying unlikelihoods, despite the fact that he usually worried about nothing. At that moment, Fandor had to wonder if he himself were not a victim, if he were not making some terrible mistake, if he had not gone mad.

"I'll have a clear heart," he said to himself.

Such a promise, made to himself, was a solemn oath for the journalist.

Fandor never gave up on an assignment once he had started. He never retreated from anything. Once he questioned something, he always managed to acquire an absolute certainty about it.

"I'll get close to him," Fandor thought. "I'll investigate that man."

And he would do everything it took to do just that. Good reporter that he was, Fandor managed, nine times out of ten, to find fantastic ruses to achieve his purposes. Consequently, without delay and knowing full well that Pokroff wanted to hire a stupid servant, he went to the Nirdinsko placement agency and played the fool.

Jérôme Fandor was such an excellent actor, had been so sublimely dense, that the agency had sent him to Pokroff's home the very next day.

Pokroff, obviously, had better things to do than waste time selecting his servants. After a brief interview, most similar to the one conducted by Alexandra, Jérôme Fandor found himself hired as a valet, a jack of all trades, by the redoubtable chief of the secret police.

"Young man," Pokroff recommended, "You have two functions to perform here. The first is to sweep my office, without ever disturbing my papers. The second is to open the door when the bell rings. Apart from that, since you don't know how to do anything, you will do nothing. Now, get to work!"

Jérôme Fandor had played his role as a superior imbecile perfectly during this little speech. He had managed to tip over an ink pot and clean up the ink with a corner of the silk curtain that flowed from the top of the window. That done, he had laughed stupidly when Pokroff had raised his voice and dabbed at his eyes when the police chief announced that he was hiring him.

Pokroff must have been delighted with his servant's stupidity.

On the other hand, was Jérôme Fandor pleased with his new employment?

As he left the office the expression on the new servant's face could only be called extraordinary. Jérôme Fandor, who had been playing the role of an imbecile just a moment earlier, now looked energetic and determined. Despite his wig and his fake mustache, despite all the make-up applied to help him play the role of Alexis, Jérôme Fandor had suddenly turned back into himself. Moreover, he grumbled in the throes of excitement.

Good Lord! Good Lord!" he muttered. "This is harder than trying to sneak up on an elephant, worse than trying to catch the moon in a fishing net. This is even harder than trying to find a police sergeant who is not an imbecile in Paris."

And just as he was expressing his utter surprise with the most unseemly of comparisons, Pokroff called him back.

"Alexis?"

"Sir?"

Jérôme Fandor's face once again bore an idiotic expression.

"Dear boy, hurry up," the police chief ordered. "You will sweep my office as I watch, after which you will man the front door. I'm expecting visitors."

"Yes sir."

"I'm called "His Excellency.""

"Yes, Sir His Excellency."

You don't say sir. You say 'Yes, Your Excellency.'"

Alexis remained silent and Pokroff did not insist.

Moreover, for a few minutes, the police chief had been staring intently at his new servant. What was his interest in Alexis? Possibly, despite his bravery and as a result of his particular situation, Pokroff might well be interested in knowing who entered his household as servants. Suddenly, Pokroff called his servant, who was limply sweeping his office.

"Alexis!"

"Yes?"

Pokroff chewed at his lip. For a second, he saw Alexis standing in front of him and his appearance seemed to have impressed him terribly. Pokroff said nothing, however. He appeared lost in some secret emotion.

Then he gently ordered, "My friend, take the poker and stir up the fire."

Alexis did not make the police chief repeat his order. He ran over to the stove, picked up the poker and, after opening the door, started to stir up the fire. Yet, as he perched over the fire, the face of the fake Alexis turned pale. What did Jérôme Fandor feel? What did he think? Did he have any idea of the tragic events involving Boris Pokroff a few nights earlier?

It was possible since Jérôme Fandor stood up and said, "Your Excellency! Why are there bones...?"

At that moment, Boris Pokroff literally jumped out of his seat.

"What did you say?" he asked.

Looking back down at the fire, Jérôme Fandor insisted, "There are bones. What looks like a skull."

And as he spoke, Fandor turned around. He looked at Boris Pokroff's face and saw that it had turned livid. The smile on Fandor's face at the very moment was extraordinary.

"That's it," he thought. "The other day, when I was on the roof, I recognized the characteristic odor coming from the chimney. And yet..."

At that moment, Pokroff stood up. The police chief walked over to the stove and rudely said, 'You're crazy Alexis! You see a skull in the stove? What does that mean?"

The two men looked at one another. The fake Alexis held his employer's eyes and Boris Pokroff appeared ready to pounce on the servant.

It was as if some terrible tragedy were about to take place. Anyone entering the room would have guessed that the two men would soon be involved in a terrible struggle.

Yet, Pokroff regained control once again. Just as the so-called Alexis stood up, he gently said, "The door bell is ringing. Go and let them in."

The order was formal, but would Jérôme Fandor obey? Smiling, the fake Alexis stood up.

"Yes, Your Excellency," he replied. But his tone of voice had changed and he no longer sounded like a superior imbecile.

"I'll open the door and come right back."

Of course," Pokroff replied.

The chief of police, however, kept his hand obviously in his pocket and his eyes on the servant. But the man had suddenly turned respectful and backed out of the room. Pokroff left his hand in his pocket.

Fandor, on the other hand, crossed the floor and walked down the stairs that left to the ground floor and arrived at the door.

Meanwhile, Pokroff walked quickly over to the window.

"Escape. It would be a better end!

47

He walked over to the stove. "What is this story about a skull and bones? I'm sure there's nothing left."

Boris Pokroff bent over the stove and stirred the red coals with the poker and stood back up, angry.

"Of course, there's nothing there. It was just a trap. The masks are off!"

Yet, while the chief of the Tsar's secret police was having this little chat with himself, what had become of Alexis, or rather Jérôme Fandor? The journalist was following orders and had gone to the front door.

"There's no danger. I can leave him alone up there. I destroyed the window bolts myself last night. I know he can't escape."

Jérôme Fandor, who seemed to consider Boris Pokroff a total wretch, reached the front door. He opened it wide. A woman stood there.

"What do you want, Miss?" he asked, concentrating solely on getting rid of the unwanted visitor.

Yet, as he raised his eyes to look at the young woman, he was overcome with an intense emotion.

'My God!" he muttered.

The woman standing in front of him was none other than Hélène. Jérôme Fandor could not know that Hélène had come to see the head of the secret police. But it was only natural that he should be surprised when he recognized her.

And the young woman was every bit as surprised. First, she had seen a servant who had looked at her with a complete lack of interest. Then he had spoken, making shivers run up and down her back.

"Good grief! I'm losing my mind," she thought, her heart caught in a vise. "This is Fandor. This is my husband."

Her husband! Under French law, Jérôme Fandor was not her husband. The marriage he had contracted was void and then again Hélène was not the type of woman to apply the letter of the law, to restrain a wandering husband by force. No, what provoked her suffering was the fact that, at that very moment, Hélène recalled a recent vision, an abdominal vision. In the Alps, had she had not seen Jérôme Fandor embracing Natacha? Yes, well then it was easy to guess what Fandor was dong in Boris Pokroff's house. Naturally, he was there as a suitor. Obviously, he was acting as a valet to visit his future father-in-law.

Such an idea was obviously crazy. Yet, things were happening so fast that Hélène had no time to recognize her own extraordinary blindness. She was suffering and, like any woman who is suffering, she was incapable of reason.

But Jérôme Fandor took stock of the situation. Far from realizing what could be going through Hélène's mind, he stood up, convinced that she had not heard him and asked again," What do you want, Miss?"

But at the very moment, vanity swept over Hélène. She stiffened, refusing to acknowledge that she recognized the man standing in front of her. In a dry voice, she replied, "I would like to see Boris Pokroff."

That was exactly what Fandor feared. Listening to the woman he adored, he clenched his teeth and replied, "His Excellency is not available."

Hélène insisted, "Give me paper and pen. I'll write a message and he'll see me."

"No, Madam." Fandor replied, closing the door on the dumbfounded woman.

Strength sapped, Hélène leaned against the wall on the other side of the door for a moment.

"He doesn't love me anymore. He pretended not to recognize me."

"My God! My God! Do I have the strength it takes not to go after her? To take her in my arms, tell her of my love for her? That would be so right."

At that moment, a voice rang out from the second storey.

"Alexis!"

It was Pokroff who had obviously heard the door close and was calling his valet.

Once again, Jérôme Fandor stood up with an effort of will.

"Do your duty!" he grumbled. "You have to do your duty!"

Like a madman, Jérôme Fandor climbed the stairs four at a time. How different this young man, fiery and raging, as he raced towards Boris Pokroff's office, was from the sublime imbecile the police chief was convinced he had hired as a valet.

Boris Pokroff, moreover, noticed the transformation. Sitting behind his desk, he asked in a tight voice, "What were you doing downstairs?"

The fake Alexis smiled. "I was celebrating my good fortune," he replied.

And since Boris Pokroff was looking at him, uncomprehending, Jérôme slowly repeated, "I was celebrating my good fortune since it allowed me to find you."

"Find me?" Boris Pokroff said, his voice trembling. "What do you mean?"

Jérôme Fandor took a step forward.

"No more masks!" he shouted abruptly, pointing a browning at his master. "No more masks! Boris Pokroff, I know who you are... You're Fantômas!"

Boris Pokroff simply shrugged.

CHAPTER V
Raining Telegrams

"Mr. Juve, no one would recognize you!"

"Why not, my good fellow?"

"Because you look like some wild man, if I may say so."

"That's really too kind of you."

Oh, Mr. Juve, don't take it the wrong way. I had no intention to offend you. It's just that you're all tanned."

"Well, I've become a knight and spend my days under the burning sun."

Juve was in Paris, in the Prefect's offices.

With his usual good cheer, he was chatting with one of the civil servants who, assigned to the Prefect's office, had known him a long time and could be permitted such pleasantries.

Juve, it was true, had changed a great deal. The extraordinary adventure he had just come back from in Mexico, chasing after Hélène, a trip that had ended in Switzerland, under the snow, pursuing Fantômas, had tired the excellent police officer somewhat and his face bore unquestionable traces of the hardships he had endured.

Juve, however, had not changed. He was still filled with energy, still lively and could hardly stay still, pacing back and forth, chain-smoking cigarettes, and grumbling over and over.

Juve had tracked Mr. Havard to the Prefect's office, after missing him by five minutes at his home.

Juve had not been in Paris long, only 24 hours since he had jumped off the train from Switzerland and, yet, he already seemed eager to set off again, giving his card to Mr. Havard two or three times, begging to see him for an emergency.

Unfortunately, as usual, Mr. Havard was bogged down with work. Moreover, his character had not changed during Juve's absence. He had not become any less conniving, any less ambitious and, that morning, as a result, he was even busier than usual since he had to draft a report to be submitted directly to the Minister.

All this meant that, for once, Juve had to sit in the waiting room. The police officer paced back and forth in front of Mr. Havard's office, grumbling naturally, saying, "This makes no sense whatsoever! I bet that Havard is busy drafting wordy sentences... What the devil! That's not his trade. It should be handled by some scribe. He should do police work since he is a police officer."

Juve, who had been following that rule for 20 years, had encountered the most extraordinary dangers, the most unlikely perils during his adventures in the police, did have some grounds for complaining.

He was so renowned, in fact, had played such an important role that, to put it simply, Mr. Havard could certainly have set aside his work for once and met with him. Yet, 20 minutes passed without the office door opening. Juve was still waiting. And he grew so impatient that, Juve, with his unbearable cheek, decided to shake things up. Despite the hostility of the clerk, who was already expecting the worst, Juve quietly walked over to the police chief's door, pressed a finger against it, opened the door quickly, and walked in.

Mr. Havard was at his desk. He looked up, in surprise.

"So, it's you?"

"It's me, Juve."

The police chief looked upset. Obviously, Juve was no tiresome intruder who could be sent packing. As soon as he had entered, he had to be welcomed. Mr. Havard regretted this situation believing, incorrectly, that it would be far better for him to quietly complete his report.

Juve for his part had fallen heavily into an armchair.

"So?" he started. "What's new, chief?"

"Nothing at all my good man. I should be the one asking you that."

Nevertheless, Mr. Havard found the opportunity to exact a little vengeance against Juve. He asked, "Did you arrest Fantômas?"

But Juve was not the man to take offence for so little.

"Good grief, no!" he retorted. "Once again, that villain was able to slip through my fingers. Yet, I sense that he's starting to run out of steam and he won't get much farther."

"Let's hope so!" said Mr. Havard, smiling.

At that moment, the police chief, resigned to having to put off writing his report, suddenly pushed aside the papers in front of him and asked, "So, Juve, what's new? Did you find Hélène?"

"Yes."

"Is your friend Fandor with you?"

"No."

"So, what happened?"

Juve slowly shrugged. He was not a man to feel embarrassed and not someone who would try to hide the truth.

He replied, "Well, Mr. Havard, what happened is very simple. I've had victories and defeats, more victories than defeats, moreover. I found Hélène but I let Fantômas escape to Mexico. After returning to France, I escorted Hélène to the Alps to meet with Jérôme Fandor, her husband, and we let Fantômas escape again. Unfortunately, I lost Hélène and Fandor in the struggle."

Juve said this as quietly as possible. Mr. Havard could not help but smile.

"Dammit" he grumbled. "You have a talent for this! You lost both Fandor and Hélène? How did you manage that?"

Obviously, the police chief's curiosity was piqued. Juve realized this. But what did that matter? He had no intention of hiding anything from his superior.

The extraordinary police officer did not hesitate at all. He quickly informed Mr. Havard about the most recent events. He told him about the extraordinary dangers he had faced in Mexico, he explained the risks run by Hélène and how he, Juve, had managed to save the young woman from a horrible death.

"Unfortunately, that bandit escaped. He fled to Switzerland and as Hélène and I were slowly returning, after taking some time to recover from our hardships, Fantômas was already hunkered down in the Alps, pursuing his dastardly deeds.

"When we arrived there, Hélène wanted to go and find Fandor on her own. She was a woman in love and I gave in to her. But, I was wrong to do so since, just a few hours later, I had to accept the obvious."

"The obvious what?" asked Mr. Havard.

"A sinister fact," confessed Juve. "That I had missed capturing Fantômas and that Hélène and Fandor had completely disappeared."

That was, in fact, the truth. At that moment in time, Juve had no idea where Hélène and Fandor were. The young woman had set out secretly, like a mad woman, for Russia, because she wanted to protect the Tsar and she had said nothing to Juve because she was suffering from a terrible jealousy that had overwhelmed her when she saw Fandor with Natacha.

Fandor, for his part, upset by Natacha's confidences, had decided, on his own, to intervene in Russia. He had no idea Juve and Hélène were in the country, since they had arrived there in secret, in order to give him a welcome surprise. He left without saying a word, merely sending Juve a telegram, which the police officer had received upon arriving in Paris.

The telegram was not explicit since Fandor had simply informed Juve that there was nothing to worry about, that he was setting off on a mission and that he would return as soon as he could.

Mr. Havard nodded as he listened to all these details, looking convinced. Despite his profound apathy, in fact, despite his indifference as a meticulous civil servant, Mr. Havard could not forego a certain sense of regard for the heroic Juve who always spoke of battles, who always risked his life and seemed to find it quite natural, entirely logical, to dedicate himself entirely to his profession.

Mr. Havard cast about unsuccessfully for a compliment.

"You... you've earned my admiration..."

Then he jumped up after glancing discretely at the clock and said, "Dammit, how time flies! So, Juve, what can I do for your?"

Juve had been waiting for this question. An ironic smile played over his lips and he said, "A little and a lot."

His response was so enigmatic, Mr. Havard asked, "A few more details, please, Juve. What do you want from me?"

Just then, Juve calmly removed his coat, folded it with extreme care and hung it over the back of a chair.

"Mr. Havard," he explained. "I'm quietly waiting for you to give me some money."

Obviously, this was an extraordinary request. Mr. Havard's eyes grew round in surprise.

"Money?" he protested. "Why?"

"Because I don't have any."

"What do you mean?"

"Traveling is expensive," Juve replied, voice dripping with judgment.

Since these aimless comments would easily have gone on for some time without any concrete progress, Mr. Havard decided to take charge of the matter.

"Well," he said. "You don't have any money. That's a problem, Juve, but it's not serious. Your appointments await you."

"I need more than that."

"Unfortunately, my dear friend…"

"I don't want to hear that."

"So, what do you want?'

Juve's smile grew broader and broader. He looked at Mr. Havard, eyes sparkling with intelligence, apparently amused.

"Well, now, the time has come."

Then he laughed, almost despite himself and continued, "My dear Mr. Havard, I have some extraordinary projects in mind, a complete campaign plan. I am determined to finish Fantômas off, in one way of another. I want to put an end to his truly legendary exploits. And to do that, I need money. Let me make myself perfectly clear. I don't need money for my personal needs. If that were the case, I would not be so insistent. The money I need will be used for my research. That's what I need the money for, Mr. Havard, so please give me some."

Never before had Juve spoken so openly about such matters, which usually left him quite indifferent. Mr. Havard had no idea what was going on and felt overwhelmed with surprise.

"But," he protested at the end of the tirade. "I have no problems with giving you money, but where do you think I'll get it? I can't do anything for you."

"Yes, you can," Juve replied quietly.

And, surprised as he was by this response, Mr. Havard fell silent, wondering where Juve was headed with all this. Juve, still calm, but displaying an authority that proved he was not speaking out of the top of his hat, was digging through his pocket.

Soon, he pulled out a newspaper, which was obviously a few weeks old. He rifled through it, looking for a page, running his finger over the columns and finally read this official notice:

For his good and loyal services and in order to facilitate his research which he is about to undertake, the Prefecture has voted to give Mr. Juve, Senior Police Inspector, a subsidy of…

Mr. Havard did not give Juve the time to finish.

"Well," he said, leaping up from his chair, "What are you up to Juve? I know full well that we voted to give you a subsidy. But you don't know what we did with it. We gave it to…"

It was Juve's turn to smile.

"We, actually you, you gave it to Fantômas, Mr. Havard, and Fantômas made a superb fool of you, convincing you that he was Juve. I know that, for a fact, but what do you want me to do? An error was made. You made a mistake. Too bad! I need money for the public interest. I'm merely claiming the amount that was promised to me and I did not receive. I repeat: I really need this money to try something. The Prefecture may be so poor that I have no doubt it would refuse to pay me if I were to ask for it. On the other hand, I have no scruples about requiring them to pay me what I am owed since I have decided to use it for the good of all."

As he listened to Juve, Mr. Havard turned red, then pale. He faced a terrible impasse. He knew full well that Juve was right, that they had voted to give him the money. Juve had not touched it since Mr. Havard had been stupid enough to let Fantômas steal it.

Everyone would support Juve if he claimed the money and Mr. Havard could not refuse to pay him. How could he avoid ridicule by claiming that he, the police chief, had been duped by Fantômas like an idiot?

"Juve, Juve" Mr. Havard said. "What you're doing is truly not very nice! I don't know how to handle this matter. I don't have any funds at my disposal and, on the other hand…"

Juve stood up. He took a small piece of paper from his wallet and handed it to Mr. Havard.

"Do you recognize this?"

Mr. Havard recognized the piece of paper since he had signed it. It was a service order that Mr. Havard had signed in a moment of pique, giving Juve a brigade of inspectors that would be kept busy on stupid tasks. It was clear that the order was inspired by jealously and that the purpose was to prevent Juve from continuing his pursuit of Fantômas.

Trembling, Mr. Havard asked, "Well, Juve?"

"Well!" said Juve, " this piece of paper bothers me. I have better things to do than track down minor criminals. As a result, Mr. Havard, this is what I propose. You set me loose for one year. You give me 12 months to handle the cases I find interesting. In exchange for that concession, I agree not to hassle you for the money you owe me."

Juve had no need to add anything else. Mr. Havard's face lit up. He tore up the order, which Juve had handed him, and threw the pieces into the wastepaper basket.

"Agreed!" he said. "You'll do what you want."

Juve left the police chief's office a moment later, smiling.

"What a strange turn of events!" he though. "Havard and I just played an amusing scene. I know he hates me. And yet, we exchange polite words. Another thing. We're both police officers and yet we behave like two villains. For my part, I admit that I gently blackmailed Havard. I tore my freedom from him by threatening to go after the money, something I never would have done since I know full well that he has already paid it!"

And, with that, Juve concluded his philosophical meanderings.

At that moment, Juve was walking past the docks along the Seine at a good pace. Despite himself, he enjoyed the charms of that incomparable Parisian landscape. Although it was still winter, the weather was superb, with a blue sky and brilliant sun. He leaned on the railing and looked around, thinking, "Good Lord! And to consider this the sinister truth! To think that this immense city, this admirable Paris, which reigns over the entire world... To think that this city, where exasperated civilization brushes against decadence, to think that this world, filled with pride in its inventions, its science, its wealth, its refinements, to think that all this is under the heel of a man, a man I know, a man I'm tracking, one I fight and can't vanquish!"

Juve held back a sob and, despite himself, thought he saw a fantastic vision appear before his eyes. A colossus, a giant, a character both legendary and superhuman! It was a man, dressed correctly in a black suit, wearing a tall hat and white gloves. Over his face, he wore a black wolf mask, a mask symbolizing his mysterious ways, his shadowy behavior, his criminal and evil royalty!

This man, this immense giant, seemed to dominate the city, to step over it with a single stride. One of his feet crushed the rooftops. The other leg disappeared into the infinity of the horizon! Genial and monstrous, the character dominated all of Paris, holding it at his mercy, under the threat of his dagger! He walked past, sowing misfortune, death and ruin. Laughing. He was the master, the master of all!

And Juve, despite himself, shivered as he recalled the fantastic character, naming him in a rage that made his voice tremble, "Oh, Fantômas, Fantômas. Evil demon, Criminal genius, Master of fear, malevolent inventor of the most frightful tortures. Is it true then, colossus, that I will never manage to overturn you one day, chain you up, deliver you to the executioner, to the immobility of the tomb, to the powerlessness of the grave?"

Then Juve stood up. A burst of pride filled his mind. Faced with the terrible, supernatural vision he had just seen, he answered his own questions.

No! It was not true. It was false. It was impossible! Juve was certain he would vanquish, that a time would come when justice would win and crime would be punished. He could not allow himself to be beaten. He must not fear the size of the task or its difficulties.

Juve gave that calm, ironic smile that made people say he was incapable of emotion.

"Victory without peril is a triumph without glory!" he murmured. "One day, people will tell their children: he was a monstrous criminal and a brave policeman rid humanity of him. Let's get to work!"

Juve had not spent more than five minutes there. When he stood up, however, something had changed inside him. He had suddenly forgotten the years spent fighting in vain. It seemed to him that a new phase in his life was starting. Success no longer seemed questionable and eventually he would achieve the triumph which had been his goal for so long.

"Fantômas! Fantômas! It's just the two of us!"

A carriage drove past. Juve hailed it. Suddenly, he was in a rush to return to his small office on Rue Tardieu. He needed to be alone and think.

A few minutes later, Juve closed the door to his favorite place. He picked up a cigarette and, seated in this armchair, stared ahead, seeing nothing, deep in thought.

"Where is Fantômas," Juve asked. "How can I find him? How can I interfere with his plans, upset his projects, and release the world once and for all?"

Of course, the problem seemed simple when put in so many words. He had to find the villain and stop him. The reality was much more complex. Would it be possible to find Fantômas if the man wanted to disappear? Was there the shadow of a hope? He seemed impossible to capture, always fleeing, always knowing just when to disappear, to take off, even when covered with blood and satisfied with his crimes.

"Let's sum this up," Juve thought, in an effort to avoid evoking everything that was swirling about in his mind about the fantastic legend of Fantômas. Juve wanted to focus on studying small, specific events, unquestionable acts, that were rigorously certain, that could provide a detail, a clue.

"Let's see, where was Fantômas last seen? I know. Near the Croisset Hotel. I know that he threw himself into a luge and set off down the mountain…"

Just then, a knock at the door interrupted Juve's thoughts.

"Jean" Juve shouted. "Leave me be. I don't want to be disturbed."

Unfortunately, Jean was a model servant. He knew when he should obey, but he also was aware that, on certain occasions, disobedience was acceptable. That morning, he ignored Juve's warning.

"Sir," he said. "There's a telegram for you."

"Slip it under the door."

Juve imagined that it was some unimportant bit of news. He frequently received telegrams. Usually they came from the Police department, for the most part indicating some stupid tip Juve ignored. Yet, he had to make sure.

Juve stood up, picked up the paper, and glanced at it. The expression on his face changed immediately.

"Good Lord!" he exclaimed.

He read the telegram out loud.

Come to St. Petersburg immediately. Stop. Need you. Stop. The Tsar's treasure is at risk. Stop. Fandor. Stop.

In all honesty, Juve did not believe his eyes. How could Fandor be calling him from St. Petersburg, Russia? And calling on him to save the Tsar's treasure? What did that mean? Deeply disturbed, Juve threw himself back into his armchair. He closed his eyes, thinking about this new mystery.

"Fandor needs me…"

Another knock at the door. Juve shuddered.

"Jean," he shouted! "Let me be!"

"But, sir, there's another telegram."

Juve leapt from his chair. Obviously, it was most likely that this telegram would be unimportant. But could he count on that? He tore it open, turning from pale to red. And read the telegram.

Urgent. Stop. Come to St. Petersburg. Stop. I know your reputation. Stop. You are my only hope. Stop. A woman in love beseeches you. Stop. Come to protect the chief of the secret police. Stop. I await you. Stop. Grand-duchess Ekaterina. Stop.

"I don't understand a thing," grumbled Juve. "Who is this grand-duchess? Why should I protect her lover, particularly if he's a police officer? Everyone wants me to go to St. Petersburg!"

Juve walked slowly back to his chair. He had barely sat down when the elderly Jean, still impassive and calm, appeared once again.

"Sir," the servant announced. "The flood continues."

"What flood," asked Juve.

"The flood of telegrams. Here are two more."

Jean carried two telegrams. By some strange coincidence, four telegrams had arrived at Juve's place at the same time. The first two had already upset the policeman. What would he learn from the two latest? Juve shook as he opened them.

The first telegram he read filled him with emotion:

Rush to St. Petersburg. Stop. You alone can save a human life. Stop. I hold terrible secrets. Stop. We have to protect the Tsar. Stop. Hélène. Stop.

"Hélène! Hélène!" Juve shrieked, bewildered. "Now, Hélène is summoning me."

He almost forgot the fourth telegram. It was a little longer than the previous ones. The message was so surprising that Juve had to read it over several times.

We trust you. Stop. We are nihilists. Stop. Our suffering is terrible. Stop. You alone can save us. Stop. Come to St. Petersburg. Stop. Come. Stop. You have to stop Fantômas. Stop.

Juve read a series of Russian names that meant nothing to him. His mind was elsewhere. His lips mouthed a name, a horrible name, over and over, "Fantômas! Fantômas!"

Was it true that he would have to face the terrible Master of Horror, yet again?

CHAPTER VI
The Rope-maker

In response to the monstrous accusation made by his servant, Boris Pokroff merely shrugged in scorn. He did not seem surprised, or upset by the accusation. He did not look like a man disgusted by such a suspicion. He did not look at all overwhelmed with fear at the thought of being recognized.

No, with perfect indifference, absolute calm, and complete peace of mind Boris Pokroff frowned. One would never have thought that he was the one being referred to, that he would be accused of being the formidable and terrifying Fantômas.

Fandor, however, was panting. The journalist was far from as calm as his adversary. Although he felt no fear at the danger he obviously faced, Jérôme Fandor shivered. He pointed his browning at Boris Pokroff, the man he accused of being Fantômas, his hand shaking.

"So!" thought Fandor. "The decisive moment is finally at hand. Will I have the honor of his capture?"

As he mastered his nerves, controlled the perfectly natural emotion that had swept over him, Jérôme Fandor repeated:

"Off with your mask, Pokroff! I recognized you! You're Fantômas!"

Then he coldly added, "Don't move. Don't count on the slightest weakness on my part. I'm determined to shoot. I'll put you down like a dog!"

Pokroff shrugged again. Maintaining his indifference, he said, "You're crazy, I imagine. Well, too bad for that. No one reasons with a mad man. What do you want from me?"

It was, in fact, a strange scene. Fandor himself, despite the seriousness of his predicament, realized that things were not going as they should have. He had expected rage. He had expected the villain he faced to betray himself through some gesture. Or perhaps furious denial? But there was nothing like that. His adversary's indifference was ominously out of tune, a false note that rang out strangely in the silence. Disconcerted by the superior composure of the man he threatened with his browning, Jérôme Fandor replied, "Fantômas, I want to take you in. I want to deliver you to justice, which will deliver you to the hangman. I've been fighting you for years, years during which you spawned evil, with impunity, without remorse, pity or mercy. Well the time has come. You're trapped. Be a good sport, Fantômas and surrender!"

Perfectly calm, Boris listened to the young man's speech, the choppy phrases he uttered with increasing nervousness. He made no move. He seemed unafraid of the browning pointed at him. He stood motionless, like someone completely unaware of the importance of the time passing.

In a completely calm voice, he replied, "I don't understand you at all. Your words are most puzzling. Surrender? To whom? It's stupid for you to claim that I'm Fantômas!"

Fandor interrupted him, "So you deny it then? Are you so base, Fantômas, that you want to discuss your personality with me? Are you such a rogue that you would try to avoid your responsibilities? Come on, that's just unworthy of you!"

At the moment, and despite himself, Jérôme Fandor was honoring the mastermind of crime. Suddenly, Pokroff seemed to be struck by the young man's words. Although Pokroff had remained impassive up to that point, his face suddenly turned pale and he appeared to lose his calm.

He said, "Well, that's it. Off with the masks. I am Fantômas and while you recognized me, I recognized you as well. You're Jérôme Fandor."

The journalist shivered. So he had not been wrong. He was facing the criminal mastermind, the monstrous torturer, the abominable genius who had invented so many nameless horrors. Fantômas was finally at his mercy!

"Yes, I'm Jérôme Fandor," he said.

Then he repeated, "And you're Fantômas?"

"Quite right!"

Boris Pokroff, or rather Fantômas, since Pokroff had just admitted his true identity, remained calm. A slight trembling of his lips barely revealed that he too was experiencing real emotion. But he did not remain perturbed.

He said, "So, we've recognized one another. Fine. But that's not enough. Fandor, you asked me to surrender. You're going too fast. Things just aren't that simple. Moreover, I have something to ask you."

Jérôme Fandor shook his head.

"There's no point," he said. "You've taken advantage of us too many times. You've escaped from us too often, Fantômas! I'm resolved. You'll get nothing from me!"

"Excuse me," said Fantômas. "I need some information."

"What?"

"Information that you can hardly refuse to give me. How did you recognize me?"

Fandor smiled. In truth, it was a strange series of events, a fantastic adventure that had led him to discover that Boris Pokroff and Fantômas were one and the same. While Jérôme Fandor had been investigating Boris Pokroff, a man he considered only as the father of the nihilist Natacha, who had died in his arms, he had been surprised to note the strange attitude adopted by the man.

One evening, Jérôme Fandor heard suspicious sounds coming from the room. He also observed smoke pouring from the chimney. He climbed onto the roof, collected some of the soot from the chimney, and decided, without a shadow of a doubt, that a body had been burned in the fireplace. But whose? Jérôme

Fandor would have spent a rather long time determining this if a multitude of coincidences had not put him on the right track.

He had noticed that Pokroff dismissed his servants abruptly. He learned that, after sustaining a minor injury, he had changed doctors. Moreover, he had spent two days locked up in his home. But all this meant little, proving only that Pokroff had committed murder. Yet, this initial discovery was followed by another, more important one. As Fandor was lurking discretely around the house, he learned that Boris Pokroff had had a package delivered to him from France and that he had declared to customs that it contained wigs. Jérôme Fandor was strangely troubled by this piece of news. So, he found a way to get into Pokroff's residence. He spied on Pokroff constantly. And while keeping watch over the man, Jérôme Fandor quickly made an extraordinary discovery.

Pokroff, Natacha's father, had been an honest chef of the secret police. However, a few days earlier, the unfortunate Pokroff had been killed. It was his body that had been burned in the fireplace, his bones that had been found in the traces of soot in the chimney. But who had assassinated Pokroff?

It easy to imagine! Boris Pokroff's murderer was another Boris Pokroff, the very man who had replaced his victim, the man who, skillfully made up, had fearlessly assumed the place of the dead man! Boris Pokroff was dead, but another Boris Pokroff still existed, usurping the other man's personality, titles and functions. Who other than Fantômas would have the audacity to do that?

Gradually, Jérôme Fandor had arrived at the conclusion, "Fantômas is posing as Boris Pokroff!"

Jérôme Fandor, with extraordinary courage, with well-thought-out audacity, had immediately decided to make the most of his discovery. Initially, and he was most likely not far off the mark, he decided that Fantômas had intended to rob the Tsar's treasury, which he was specifically assigned to watch over as part of his duties. That's when Fandor had wired Juve to come.

Yet, that was still not enough. While the certainty that Juve would soon arrive in Russia should calm Fandor a little, he still trembled at the thought that, from one second to another, something irreparable could occur. Such as Fantômas fleeing.

Jérôme Fandor strove to keep his prey in view. He knew that the so-called Boris Pokroff was looking for a servant. He was not unaware that the head of the secret police was looking for a particularly stupid servant, one who would not uncover Pokroff's machinations.

Knowing that, Jérôme Fandor did not hesitate a second. He would be that servant. Pokroff would hire him. Things had worked out very well. Jérôme Fandor had been hired. He would most likely have waited patiently, played his role, mastered his impatience until Juve arrived if a fortuitous incident, impossible to predict, had not caused him to take sudden action.

A few seconds earlier, Jérôme Fandor had been abruptly surprised by Hélène's arrival. He had felt afraid for the young woman who was asking to see the head of the secret police. Tortured by concern, he had lost patience. He rushed into the room where he had left Fantômas and, a victim of his legitimate anger, he cried out, "Off with the masks!"

This was all most surprising and could justifiably intrigue Fantômas, who could have no idea which clues had set Jérôme Fandor on his trail. So, Fandor was not surprised by Fantômas' question. It seemed natural to him. However, he was determined not to give him a satisfactory answer. At that moment, one thought filled Fandor's mind. "I've got my browning pointed at this wretch. He can't make a move without my permission. That's all that matters. I'm determined to show him no pity. I have only one thing to do. I must not let him go."

So, Jérôme Fandor replied, "You'll learn that at your trial, Fantômas. For the time being, I don't have to answer you."

Fiercely, Jérôme Fandor ordered, "Hands up, so I can cuff you!"

"No, "Fantômas replied.

The criminal's refusal was abrupt, categorical.

Jérôme Fandor had not expected that and was violently surprised.

"You refuse to obey me?"

At the same time, he armed his weapon, the safety lock snapping, ready to fire.

Fantômas appeared unmoved.

"I do," he simply said.

And as a spark burned in Fandor's eyes, as he prepared to shoot, Fantômas, playing with danger, scorning death, said, "You'll look ridiculous, Fandor. I'm not moving. Don't shoot. Listen to me."

Fantômas was truly a man in all meanings of the word. Regardless of the circumstances, regardless of the events that occurred, of the peril he faced, he still had a way of speaking, or being heroic, of forcing respect.

Although he was determined to shoot, Fandor did not.

"What do you have to say to me?" he said.

"I have a story to tell you."

Still calm, standing less than 20 cm from Fandor's browning, Fantômas closed his eyes for a second, like a story-teller mentally preparing an anecdote intended for an attentive audience.

"My dear Fandor," Fantômas started in a quiet, mocking tone. "I would like to bring a brief memory back to your mind. You've seen Juve recently. So, he must have told you what I'm about to relate..."

"You've got three minutes," said Fandor.

"That's much more than I need," retorted Fantômas.

Perfectly still, mindful of the death sentence imposed by the weapon pointed at him, Fantômas said, "Some time ago, I was being pursued by Juve. So, I played a role. As far as everyone was concerned, I was a personality and no one, other than Juve, suspected me. Juve, however, was wrong about one thing. He thought that I was not on my guard. But I always am. The result will prove that..."

"Excuse me," Fandor interrupted. "But what's the point of all this?"

Fantômas shrugged.

"Patience!" he said. "You'll see. One day, Juve decided to arrest me. So, he summoned Mr. Mix. At that time, I was posing as Mr. Mix and, bit by bit, while chatting with me, he allowed himself to wane ironic. Suddenly, Juve cast off his mask, removing mine as well. He shouted, 'You're Fantômas!' Good grief, Fandor, I must admit it had all worked a little faster than I had thought. I had not been certain that I would be arrested that evening. So, since I was surprised, I reached into my pocket to take out my weapon and kill Juve..."

"Wretch," Fandor roared.

Fantômas did not respond to the insult. Peacefully, he smiled. Yet there was something deeply disturbing about his smile. Despite himself, Fandor felt troubled. He knew Fantômas too well, in fact, to ignore the fact that his good humor meant no good.

Visibly, Fantômas was amused. Why? He had no reason to be cheerful. He had been caught! Jérôme Fandor stiffened, with a sudden surge of emotion.

"Enough!" he said. "Your three minutes are up. You've been stringing me along, but enough is enough. Hands up!"

"No!" said Fantômas.

And, as Fandor approached him face pale with emotion, ready to shoot, Fantômas shrugged.

"I said no and I'll say it again. Furthermore, I wasn't lying, Fandor, when I claimed that I had perfected Juve's technique. You have the means, don't you, to force my obedience, your revolver... That revolver makes you feel calm, convinced that I'm at your mercy. So, it was a good thing I let you keep it. Yet, I have a much more powerful reason for refusing. So, try to shoot!"

Jérôme Fandor grew livid. Given the criminal's extraordinary mockery, he knew something was up. He pulled desperately on the trigger. The weapon did not go off.

Fantômas said, "You see, I'm in control here. I let you keep the revolver, but I removed the bullets."

Then, with dazzling speed and marvelous agility, surprising Fandor, Fantômas leap, then rolled on the ground. He was so swift that Fandor, who rushed at him, grabbed at nothing but air as Fantômas stood up, on the other side of the room, and pushed a button.

Two men appeared almost immediately. And Fantômas, who was still Boris Pokroff in their eyes, issued an order.

"Grab that man. Bind him. He tried to assassinate me!'

It all happened so fast that Fandor had no time to protest. Just as he opened his mouth to cry out, to shout the truth at the two police offices, that Boris

Pokroff was in fact Fantômas, he thought of something that forced him to remain silent.

What could he do, in fact? Would the officers take him solely at his word?

If he shouted, "Boris Pokroff is Fantômas, they would certainly mock him. If he wanted to fight, if he tried to resist, one against three, he would no doubt make his situation worse.

Jérôme Fandor, moreover, did not want to lower himself to fighting in front of Fantômas. He was trapped. Vanquished. He would accept his fate with a dignity that would impress the wretch.

"Well played," Fandor said.

Fantômas smiled. "Thank you for the compliment," he replied.

The guards, however stared at him, dumbfounded and Fantômas realized he should not give them the time to wonder.

"Well," he said abruptly. "What are you waiting for? Don't you understand? He's an assassin and will be a rope-maker in three days?"

The guards turned pale. They rushed at Fandor, bound him tightly and carried him off.

Fandor looked back. One last time he looked Boris Pokroff in the eyes, as he stood in the middle of his office, and saw the wretch smile. Fantômas had triumphed yet again and had managed to outwit his valiant enemies. He was the master of all and of everything.

Fandor said, "Good day, Your Excellency!"

Fantômas replied, "Shut up, rope-maker."

Then he shrugged and turned away.

A Russian prison. In one of the neighborhoods of St. Petersburg. A large, ordinary building. It was flanked by four enormous towers and surrounded by a tall wall. The four towers were connected to one another by long corridors, with double rows of metal doors on each side that opened onto the cells where the prisoners were locked up.

At the end of each corridor, a heavy door. On the ground floor, the door opened onto a large, circular room that occupied the entire tower. The door was locked and the key was kept in the guardroom. The door was under constant guard.

Inside the room, no furniture, just a table and four chairs, which are removed at night. The window is small and heavily protected, running from floor to ceiling. The room has been built into the ground and is nothing more than a cellar where it is normally so dark that it would be impossible to read a newspaper there, even at noon.

At night, a small, weak electric bulb on the ceiling is turned on, so high above the floor that the light it casts is useless.

No bed. Anyone in the room would have to sleep on the floor.

That room—there are rooms like that in each prison, like a tomb, damp, cold, filled with shadows, where 20 or so men lie together—is called the rope-maker's room.

What's a rope-maker?

As Fandor was being carried off by Fantômas' men, he heard the villain call him a rope-maker twice.

"What does that mean?" the journalist wondered.

However, an epithet, no matter how intriguing it might be, could not hold his attention just them. Jérôme Fandor was thinking about something other than Fantômas' insults. He was already studying a plan for revenge.

Yes, of course, Fantômas had had the last word. He had managed to get rid of Fandor by ordering his arrest. It looked like he had won. Perhaps he had. That would not last, however.

And Jérôme Fandor told himself, "I will succeed!"

After all, what more could happen?

Jérôme Fandor was picturing the scene already. Of course, Boris Pokroff would accuse him of assassination. They had arrested him with a revolver in hand. Boris Pokroff would claim that Fandor had been trying to kill him.

"Well, well," said Fandor. "Others, like Juve when he arrives, would tell a different story. I'll be judged by a court. There are judges in St. Petersburg of course since, according to myth, even Berlin has some. So, I'll defend myself. And it will be a good fight. Fantômas hasn't seen the last of me!"

Jérôme Fandor focused on these thoughts, insensitive to the blows of the guards brutalizing him as a wagon carried him rapidly to the St. Jean Prison in St. Petersburg. Although the journalist acknowledged that his situation was no walk in the park, he managed to calm his fear. But, as they arrived at the prison, Jérôme Fandor experienced an unpleasant surprise.

They were not taking him to the court. As he stepped down from the sleigh, he took part in none of the formalities that usually ensued, everywhere in the world, when a criminal was jailed. Quite the contrary. They dragged him quickly down a corridor. The prison guards ran alongside, asking those who accompanied Fandor in poor Russian, "Who is this"

They replied, "A rope-maker.

Jérôme Fandor grew exasperated, "They're driving me mad with their rope-maker!"

Despite the brutality of the guards, he asked, "What's a rope-maker?"

The guard looked him up and down and replied, "A bare naked man."

The man appeared scandalized when Jérôme Fandor burst out laughing. "Rope-maker or bare naked man," he thought. "They've given me the most unusual titles."

His guards, however, did not ease up. They shoved him on vigorously. Once he had walked down the corridor, Fandor arrived at the door to the round room. A key grated.

The guard ordered, "Go in. Hurry up."

He entered. The door closed behind him.

And Jérôme Fandor, eyes blinded by the light, unable to see clearly, tried to get a feel for the surprising room in which he found himself.

There were about 15 young people there, soft faces, looking resigned, who stared at him in curiosity

Jérôme Fandor was about to question them when one approached the journalist and asked, "Brother, who are you? Why are you here?"

Hesitant, Fandor replied, "Good grief, for very complicated matters which I don't understand myself. But you can tell me, what a rope-maker is? What's a bare-naked person?"

The other person smiled weakly. "Rope-makers are those who are sentenced to death. We call them that because the government decided not to leave handcuffs on the torture victims. They merely tie their hands behind their backs with rope."

The explanation was sinister indeed. Jérôme Fandor grew pale.

"A bare-naked man is someone sentenced to swing from the gallows. By order of the imperial government, in order to save a little money, the clothes are stripped from the hanged man's body, everything is sold and the money goes into the Treasury."

The Russian provided these explanations in a mocking tone. Jérôme Fandor shivered as he listened.

"Good Lord!" uttered the journalist. "So, I'm sentenced to death!"

Without blinking, the other man said, "Without a doubt. You'll be hanged just as we all will."

Then, with the fatalistic soul of a Slav, the Russian man added, "But don't let that impress you too much. No one grows bored in this room. We have excellent musicians, fine singers to accompany us. Dying on the gallows is unpleasant, of course, but inevitable once you come here. So, there's no point in worrying about it."

Jérôme Fandor, despite his deep courage, despite his talent for brushing up against death, could not help but shudder. He wanted to live. He wanted to take vengeance. He wanted to defeat Fantômas!

CHAPTER VII
The Man with Ape-like Hands

"Shut up, in the tower! Shut up! If you start singing again, I'll tell the lieu-tenant."

The guard lost his patience. He tapped the butt of his rifle against the thick wall, but his impatience and exhortations were pointless. The tower continued to sing.

The tower was the immense room which housed the unfortunate prisoners who would soon have the pleasure of meeting the emperor's hangman. Jérôme Fandor's companions, Fandor himself. Executions were an everyday affair in Russia and the prison was full of people sentenced to death. There was no short-age of work for the hangman, who sent five or six people to the other world eve-ry morning. And that was just for one prison, not the entire empire.

Yet, those who awaited the death sentence in Russia naturally looked for distractions. And, since was the only leisure activity available to them, they would all sing some popular ditty or even a revolutionary hymn. They made the tower sing with extraordinary music, an unbearable concert that would rise from the sinister round rooms, causing even the bravest, the most indifferent to quiv-er.

Those who were sentenced to death in Russian prisons formed, as strange as this may seem, a sort of mysterious society, one in which the membership was constantly renewed. They had their habits, their customs, their way of doing things and they all spent the few days between the moment they entered the jail and the fatal instant when the guard came for them, in the same manner.

Jérôme Fandor was with these people, taking part in their activities, partic-ipating in their anguish, unfortunately, since it was impossible to hold onto the slightest illusion. He was a rope-maker and they were going to hang him one morning or another.

Initially, Jérôme Fandor had been chilled to the marrow when he learned of his unfortunate fate. He had not taken the arrest ordered by Fantômas seriously. He told himself that, even though he was under lock and key, he would find a way to defend himself and no one would prevent him from tearing the mask off that had enabled the abominable criminal mastermind to take the place of Boris Pokroff.

Unfortunately, his illusions did not last long.

Jérôme Fandor questioned his companions. They were all political prison-ers. They were in the cell reserved for those sentenced to death, waiting for their final minutes, for insignificant crimes, that were considered monstrous by the State. Some had chanted revolutionary slogans in the street; others had insulted the emperor; still others were suspected of "expropriation" a Russian term used to refer to those who stole, not for their own benefit but for a political reason, such as taking vengeance against the tax collector.

Although their crimes differed, the same punishment was reserved for all. The 20 men in the room would all strangle, hanged from the gallows, where they would spin slowly, until their feet stopped twitching.

Jérôme Fandor, who felt full of life, who was young, who adored his wife, rebelled at times, filled with rage and despair. Those with him, however, were resigned, calmly fatalistic to the point that they did not seem to understand the horror of their destiny.

"But, Good Lord, they're going to hang me!" Jérôme Fandor had screamed, when he learned why everyone called him a rope-maker.

The Russians around him merely nodded.

"Of course, of course. Unless you want to die by your own hand, if that could be possible."

And that was typical of all the men waiting for death in the cell. They felt like death's prisoners. They knew they would not escape. They had lost their hope for life, but they still wanted, with their meager means, to rebel against the law. Jérôme would see soon enough. Some of them desired above all to escape the hangman's death. They preferred to kill themselves!

Their greatest wish was to obtain a knife, to stab themselves in the heart, to latch onto some virulent poison that would send them into the other world, all to prevent the hangman from doing his job.

Jérôme Fandor realized all this during the first hours of his captivity.

Death was, in fact, the topic of all their conversations. The men overwhelmed him with their thoughtfulness, they provided information amicably. This brought a sad smile to his lips.

"Well," thought Fandor, "So I'm the man of the hour!"

It was true that all of the occupants of the lower room were always thrilled when a new prisoner arrived. It broke up the monotony of their day.

Jérôme Fandor thought he was living in a nightmare at that very moment. It seemed impossible that his adventures could be real. Was it true that all of those surrounding him, those Russians, with their thoughtful expressions, those ardent revolutionaries who dreamed of a society in which everyone would be happy, those 17 and 18-year old children, were really sentenced to death?

And Jérôme Fandor, who had been on the point of giving in to the horror, felt ashamed by his emotions when he noticed how those around him remained absolutely, rigorously calm, the calm of those who knew that they were irrevocably in the hands of fate.

The first night, however, was truly horrific for Fandor. He saw the condemned men lie down next to one another on the ground and, as they closed their eyes, they exchanged joyful good nights.

"Sleep tight," they said.

No one could be certain that the hangman would not come in a few hours to take them

Jérôme Fandor learned that there was no regular procedure. Some had been waiting for the fateful moment for over 50 days; others were hanged at the end of their first week of incarceration. It all depended on the paperwork, an administrative quagmire no one understood.

"Plus," added the Russian who had been explaining things to Fandor. "There's really no point in thinking about it since there's nothing you can do to change it," said, maintaining that supreme logic, invoking a crazy fatalism, a horrific and incomprehensible resignation.

Jérôme Fandor lay down like the others and thought.

His neighbor looked at him and said, "You're looking thoughtful. You must not give in to bad thoughts. You have to forget everything, to sing..."

And the Russian hummed a few bars of a popular song. The entire tower started to shriek. That was their habit. When one of the convicted men shivered, as the frightening vision of the gallows rose before his eyes, the others forced him to sing. That would always change his mind, at least that's what they all claimed, and perhaps they were right.

Lying on the ground, sleep unattainable, Jérôme Fandor was unable to calm down. After a moment of understandable defeat, he felt overwhelmed with a wild rage. At the very moment that he had thought he'd defeated Fantômas, the criminal mastermind had invented a radically new strategy.

"I'm going to be hanged," Fandor said.

And he preferred to think about that, about his painful death, than about his poor Hélène who was all alone in St. Petersburg, exposed to the monstrous cruelty of the man who had passed as her father.

The night seemed interminable to Fandor. At about 11 pm, a feverish agitation overtook the man next to him. The convicts who had seemed to be sleeping up to that point were moving about. Some rushed, at the slightest sound, to the door of their cell, and placed their ears against the openings. What were they so eager to listen to?

Were the noises they heard, in the distance, those that usually accompanied the preparations for an execution? Were those footsteps that approached, those of the hangman looking for his prey?

When silence returned, Fandor noticed jagged breathing, quiet moans. The candidates for death included poor wretches who had pleasant dreams and others whose nightmares were filled with torture.

The next morning, Jérôme Fandor was still when he awoke. He had barely closed his eyes all night, going over and over the circumstances of his arrest in his mind.

"Of course," he thought. "Since they've already placed me in with the men who are sentenced to death, since they already consider me a rope-maker, there is no chance that I will be brought before a court. Russia is an arbitrary country.

Pokroff, or rather Fantômas, now has the authority of the police and must have arranged for my execution. Fantômas will not go easy on me. He must be in a rush to get rid of me. My time will come soon."

Yet the next morning held a surprise for the journalist. The guards came to the cell for him and took him to see three individuals in a small room. One of them was an enormous man. He appeared to be the leader. To his right sat a very old individual, humble and respectful. In a corner of the room, Fandor saw the back of a very strange man, oddly thin and twisted. He kept his face turned carefully toward the wall, but he held his hands, with enormous, contorted, incredibly hairy fingers, like those of an ape, in clear view, clasped behind his back.

"What the devil does this mean?" Fandor wondered. "Are these men judges? Are they going to interrogate me? Have I had the good fortune of being referred to a regular court?"

He was, in fact, appearing before a court. The tribunal was meeting in keeping with Russian law, but it was nothing like ordinary courts, the courts in other, more civilized countries.

Fandor was asked no questions. When he attempted to speak, he was ordered to remain silent.

The large man, probably a judge merely read a document, reading it so quickly, pronouncing the words so poorly that the entire text became unintelligible. Yet, Jérôme Fandor guessed at the meaning. He was being read his sentence. He understood one thing only, that he had been convicted of attempted murder and would be hanged by the neck until dead.

The enormous man was completely indifferent as he read. His neighbor, the small old man, a clerk, or so Fandor thought, seemed to be occupied with something else, carefully cleaning his nails. The man with the ape-like hands did not move.

When he understood, Jérôme Fandor stood straighter and shouted, "I'm French, I demand a meeting with my ambassador!"

But his interruption produced no effect. No one listened to him and five minutes later, Fandor was taken back to his cell. He no longer had any illusions. The parody of a hearing had been carried out and he was truly sentenced to death. There was no hope.

"Well," thought Jérôme Fandor. "Since I have to die, I must accept my fate. And if Fantômas is curious enough to ask about my final moments, I don't want him to hear that I lost heart."

And that day, Jérôme Fandor was the most cheerful of all the dying men. He understood the true secret behind their indifference. They were political prisoners, revolutionaries. Many of them must have been nihilists. They faced death bravely. Obviously, they had no desire to tremble before the authorities they refused to accept. Jérôme Fandor grew calm after accepting his fate.

"They did say," he grumbled, "That I would come to a bad end. I was sentenced to the garrote in Spain. Here, I'll be going to the gallows. That's not quite as good. After all, with the garrote you sit, but you stand for the gallows."

It was grave humor. But in the worst of moments, the most abominable situations, Fandor had the energy he needed to react, to find a word, a witticism, to use typical French irony to hide his deepest feelings.

The fatalism of the men around him took over. It was obvious that his fate was set in stone. There was no point in trying to escape. There was nothing he could do to stay alive. He might as well face death bravely and look it in face without fear.

The days dragged on, monotonous. The prisoners were strangely calm, subdued by destiny. They talked politics, religion and philosophy. Some played cards. Others sang tirelessly. When one of the men turned inward, seeming to want to be alone, the others instinctively drew closer to him, forcing him to sing, trying to cheer him up. The idea of death was everywhere, weighing down on all of the men, but not a single one spoke of it.

One morning, however, emotion swept over the room.

"Adieu, adieu…" The cry rang out through the cell. Jérôme Fandor, who was still sleeping, pale dawn barely breaking, sat up suddenly.

"What is it?" he called out.

They told him.

"The escort is at the door. They've come for one of us."

"Who?" asked Fandor.

The others shrugged.

"Impossible to know. But it can't be you. You haven't been a rope-maker long enough."

Just then the door opened. Jérôme Fandor, who was standing in the middle of the room, arms crossed, felt his heart pound when he saw the uniforms.

The large corridor that led to the lower room was crowded with people. First the prison guards, then the Cossacks followed by the officers and then by the authorities, laden with furs and braided hats, faces pale, drawn with the emotion that overcomes everyone when they go to get a sleeping and take him to his death.

"Damn!" Fandor thought. "Look at all those people."

His mind was clear and lucid at that moment. Jérôme Fandor experienced a strange feeling, thinking, "It's not my turn today. But tomorrow it will be. I have to get used to the performance so I can play my role properly."

And he repeated that thought to himself over and over, since there are times when one's mind is overwhelmed with a single concern, moments of supreme anguish, when insignificant details suddenly seem colossal.

And, a moment later, a moment that lasted a second but seemed longer than a century, Jérôme Fandor saw two prison guards approach, protected by four Cossacks with their sabers drawn. And in his confused mind, the death penalty, the supreme penalty on which all modern societies are based, suddenly seemed vile and grotesque to him.

How could people come, in the middle of the night, to kill another! They hid in the shadows, they were protected by soldiers! Then, when they had given free rein to their cowardice, they said, "In the name of the Tsar…" and they carried their victim off, bound, to assassinate him in the name of the law!

"The death penalty… infamy," thought Jérôme Fandor. "A barbaric remnant of past times, something unworthy in our civilized period, rejected by philosophy, refused by the human heart. Obviously, if I were not sentenced to death myself, I'd write a book about this one day!"

Jérôme Fandor was thinking incredibly quickly at that moment. One idea chased after another in his mind, as if wound on a gigantic reel. Then suddenly he stopped thinking.

The guards walked over to him and placed their hands on his shoulders.

"Come!" they ordered.

Fandor's heart stopped for a second. They were coming for him? He was the one being executed that morning? Then, in the extraordinary throes of rebellion, he threw himself to the side. Would a fight break out? Would he try to escape? Jérôme Fandor abruptly fell silent. Calm swept over him. There was no point fighting… There was no honor in resistance. If it was his fate to be hanged until dead, then hanged he would be. He was ready!

He recognized those around him. The large man shivering was the judge. The bailiff blowing in his hands to warm them was the old man he had seen before. Without a doubt, he had completed his manicure. Behind him came the pope. An elderly man who walked slowly, clasping the doctor's arm, with the look of an imbecile, asking him for information about liver problems.

"Come!" the guards said again.

And Jérôme Fandor went with them docilely.

The prison corridor was jammed with soldiers. As he walked past them, they raised their weapons.

"They are so very afraid," Fandor thought.

It all seemed the more grotesque, to him, since he was not dangerous, he was unable to do anything; he was alone against everyone, and they were taking him to his death like a lamb to the slaughter.

When they reached the office, Fandor thought, "The longest part is over. In ten minutes, at most, it will be done…"

He was getting used to the gloomy idea. As he attempted to think things through, he realized that he was more overwhelmed than frightened. He felt as if he had been struck on the head with a hammer. His thoughts were muddled.

"This feels strange," Fandor told himself, standing straight, refusing the help of a guard, walking all alone.

At the office, the assistants continued to talk and Jérôme Fandor realized that everyone seemed uncomfortable. They were embarrassed to be there. None of them would have wanted to relinquish their place.

All eyes were on Jérôme Fandor. He felt them staring at him, examining him and he wanted to shout, "So, there's something amusing about a man who is going to die?"

But he said nothing. They were taking care of him. Someone, the clerk, read a long sentence.

"By the authority of His Imperial Majesty..." and since he was still cold, he stopped to blow on his hands.

Jérôme heard nothing of his sentence. His mind was elsewhere. Hélène... Juve... the two beings he loved most in the world. Their memories haunted him. He would never see them again! He would never again enjoy Juve's cordial and abrupt handshake. He would never lose himself in Hélène's lips again.

"Well!" thought Fandor. "I should stop thinking about them. That will just make me feel emotional and I don't want that!"

And events were raced on.

"Do you have anything to say?" asked the pope.

Fandor stared at him and said, "A cigarette."

He smiled since everyone was visibly pleased that he had expressed a wish. The people there were certainly not his enemies. They were simply doing their duty. Although they all felt the horror of their situation, they truly wished to execute him since not doing so would have started a revolution.

Twenty cigarette cases appeared. A guard took one out and placed it between Fandor's lips as they attached his hands behind his back.

"A match!" demanded the journalist.

As the doctor lit his cigarette with a poker, Fandor focused on the grotesque details. At that very moment, he heard the physician talking with the substitute, "Tobacco," he declared, "Is very bad for one's health."

"Fine," thought Jérôme Fandor. "One less thing I'll have to worry about."

"Come now," the guards said. "Outside with you."

Jérôme Fandor found it hard to walk. He was wearing irons. The chain was heavy, rubbing against his ankles. Yet he did not want help. He made an effort and followed the guards. Behind him, all conversation stopped and the audience rushed to follow, not wanting to miss a single detail.

Jérôme Fandor shivered. They led him into the prison courtyard. It was terribly cold and the snow whirled about.

"Surely, I'll catch my death of cold," Fandor joked out loud.

But no one smiled.

Death was there, listening like the others, and his presence made them all fall silent from fear.

"The blacksmith?" a voice orders.

'Yes, Your Honor.'

At the order of the prison warden, one of the guards walked away. Then he came back followed by two people. One was the blacksmith. Jérôme Fandor paid him little attention. The other made him shiver.

He was a small creature, thin, deformed, legs twisted, head bony, neck stretched by a goiter. Jérôme Fandor recognized him immediately. He was the man who had turned his back during his appearance before the extraordinary tribunal.

Why had he been looking at the wall like that? Fandor guessed the reason easily enough. Furthermore, he was dressed strangely. He wore a large red shift tucked in peasant's pants and a black cloth mask covered his face. Certainly, the man did not want to be seen.

Jérôme guessed the truth, "That's the hangman!"

Then he repeated, "That's my hangman!"

However, the blacksmith was working about Fandor. He placed the chain that bound his Fandor's ankles on a block. The blacksmith's hammer flew through the air tossing shards of steel about. He rained blows down, the links fell and the chain broke.

"Too bad," thought Fandor, stretching. "It looks like freedom, but it's really death."

And it was.

Once the chain had been broken, the procession set out again. They left the first courtyard and entered a second. Fandor, his arms and legs free, walked proudly, without shaking, without hesitating.

When he entered the second courtyard, the journalist looked up. There was still a crowd, a great many people were waiting for him, important personalities, choice guests, an entire audience that had had to scheme their way into the prison.

But Fandor saw no one. He saw only one thing, standing in the middle of the courtyard, the gallows. After examining the courtyard, he turned his head. A few steps away, a loud racket rose from a hole that four or five men were digging. The cold was so intense that their spades made the dirt sing.

"My grave," Fandor guessed.

At that moment, the official went over to the workers and asked, "Is it the legal depth?"

They indicated that it was and events proceeded.

Fandor suddenly noticed that everyone had stepped away, leaving him all alone. He stood still, waiting.

"Juve… Hélène…" he thought.

Yet, one man had stayed next to the journalist, the man with the ape-like hands. He seemed perfectly resigned. He knew full well what he had to do and he did it without rushing, without hesitating, performing usual task that was not of much interest, standing next to a large, empty crate. He bent down and tore off the cover. The box appeared to grow larger. It contained the infinity of the tomb, the unknown void.

"Not much of a coffin," Fandor smiled.

The journalist was still in control of himself. He felt no fear. From time to time, barely perceptible, his shivered with rage at the thought of this ignominious death, a superb victory for Fantômas.

From the depth of the box, the hangman pulled out a large white sheet. As he unfolded it slowly, it rustled.

"What's that?" Fandor asked, then answered his own question. "My shroud!"

Second by second, action by action, Fandor noted the details of his death. Yet, the hangman did not rush. He unfolded another white bag, a smaller one, which he simply took from his pocket. And, a few seconds later, he walked over to Fandor and placed the bag over the journalist's head. The journalist remained patient as the poorly made bag slipped awkwardly over his face.

Yet Jérôme Fandor continued to think. At that very moment, the intrepid young man felt an irresistible desire to tell a joke.

"I must look like a ghost, a white monk. They've put the bag over my head to avoid seeing the grimace I'm about to make."

The hangman pushed him by the shoulders.

"Come, come, come."

And Jérôme was filled with disgust as he felt the ape-like hands take his arm. He took a few steps.

"Farther back," shouted the hangman. The gallows are behind you.

Docilely, Fandor stepped back. A few seconds passed. Finally, he felt a rope winding around his neck.

"This is it," the young man decided.

Yet the hangman continued to fidget around him.

"What can he possibly be doing?" Fandor wondered. "Hurry up, hangman, how long does it take to tie a noose?"

The other man merely said, "Pull!"

The workers standing behind the gallows pulled on their end of the rope, which tightened suddenly, and Jérôme Fandor felt himself pulled up from the ground.

A few seconds later, his body swayed in the void...

CHAPTER VIII
Interrogation

Jérôme Fandor's body swayed ominously in the air. Hanging from the crossbar of the gallows, it looked like a scarecrow. The shroud fell below his feet; the bag covered his face, hiding the poor man's grimace.

No one said anything. They could barely make out the horrible death that must have been taking place under cover of the shroud. The swinging feet seemed to claw at the air, looking for something to grasp. There was very little wind and the body spun only a little. No convulsions. Quickly, it stopped moving. The man had to be dead.

The doctor approached. He held a gold watch in his hand and he watched the hands turn.

"Wait," he ordered. "We have to wait ten minutes after the hanging."

That was the law. The law that governs executions went into the most macabre detail. People who had been hanged had to remain on the gallows for ten minutes. Those ten minutes seemed like centuries to witnesses, the privileged who had maneuvered to be allowed to watch the execution.

No one moved. They all appeared to be dumbfounded. For a second, death reigned over everyone. The spectacle of the hanging man was horrific, gloomy and grotesque. The poor body swinging in the breeze seemed so pitiful that no one dared to break the silence.

The least courageous and the most nervous, feeling their legs about to give way beneath them, allowed themselves to fall back against a large pile of wood that had been stacked some distance away. The others, standing, remained there, arms dangling, eyes staring, watching the body swing like a white rag at the end of the rope.

At that moment, all of the workers climbed out of the pit. They had been told that they were free to go, that they were no longer needed, but they stayed. The blacksmith remained as well. That was a curious thing. Everyone was shivering, yet they all remained in place, immobile, frozen in astonishment, completely incapable of moving.

The doctor watched the hands on his watch. After a moment, he declared, "The ten minutes are up."

Then he did his job. He walked over to the hanged man. He grasped the feet under the shroud and made sure they were not moving. Quickly, he brushed his ear against the shroud. The man was so obviously dead that his inspection was most cursory.

"Fine," he said. "Do your duty, hangman!"

The man with the ape-like hands, the man who wore a black cloth mask over his face to make sure that no one recognized him, so that no one, in the future, could be tempted to take the revenge that his horrible traded merited, the hangman walked quickly.

He took a saber from an unsuspecting Cossack and pulled it from its sheath. The blade shone for a moment in the air. The hangman swung it, cutting right through the rope and Fandor's body fell heavily to the ground. In keeping with the law, the official declared, "The body belongs to you hangman. You're free to take the clothing…"

The hangman nodded. He grabbed the body by the shoulders and without removing the shroud, he dragged it over to the pit and abruptly shoved it in. The spectators heard the body land. Then the hangman picked up a shovel and slowly started to fill the grave.

Just then, the spectators seemed to wake up, as if from long nightmare, shaking off their immobility one after another. Time seemed to have passed horribly slowly. But, finally, the man was dead and the hangman was throwing dirt on the body. It was over. The poor wretch was dead and buried and they could go, leave the horror of this courtyard behind, run from the frightful vision, forget the work of justice.

They were already exchanging their goodbyes. And since it was horrifically cold, they rushed to return to the warmth of the furs left behind in the sleighs at the prison doors. It would be good to go back home, as well. Yet, the warm tea in the samovar would have a bitter taste.

Within fifteen minutes, all of the spectators had left.

After that, close to the gallows, which still appeared new, looking as if he were waiting to be given other men to kill, the hangman continued his work. He shoveled large amounts of dirt into the pit and given the speed with which he worked it would not take him long to finish.

Soon, in the prison courtyard, people would see nothing more than a small heap in the place of the pit, then, with the next storm, the snow would level everything and freeze it, leaving no trace of the frightful drama.

Jérôme Fandor, dead, would not even be given the honor of a tomb where his loved ones could go and kneel. The brave man, thrown into a hole, would rot without the homage of a memory, a tear, a prayer…

That same day, in one of the outlying houses in St. Petersburg. In a cold room, with poor walls, and no ornament, a room where light barely entered through a narrow spy hole meagerly carved in the stone walls and where even less air penetrated, the low door was sealed. The persistent odor of smoke reigned in the shanty. There was an old stove that always smoked a little. Throughout the winter, black soot escaped through at an elbow in the chimney. It spread over everything and was never cleaned. It fell in a thick, soft blanket and appeared to be part of the atmosphere.

In that room, however, darkened with smoke, in that room where twilight barely penetrated, a human figure came and went. It looked like a ghost with an extraordinary shape. But, a closer look revealed that it was not a ghost but a woman, an old woman, wrapped in a black mantle from head to foot, walking about barefoot, wearing a large bonnet tied with ribbons, black as well, that looked like the fluttering wings of a dark night bird.

The old woman walked from the stove, where the open door cast a red light, to the back of a sort of alcove hollowed into the wall, which contained a bed. The old woman bent over the bed, mumbled something that seemed to make no sense. "He'll make it or he'll die. The rum is strong… I think they'll come this evening, moreover… He's young and strong. Yes, there he is, opening his eyes."

In the poor room, the silvery tinkle of a spoon stirring a drink, rang out. The scent of rum mingled with the odor of the soot.

The old woman grumbled, "Drink, son, drink. It's just what the doctor ordered."

After a moment, a voice, a resonant voice, warm but still weak, still trembling, asked, "Where am I mother?"

"In my home. Safe."

"Who are you?"

"Marfa Berena. Vassili's mother."

The weak voice said, "Vassili's mother. But who is Vassili?"

"You'll find out later. Sleep now."

Silence reigned for a moment. As the old woman came back from the stove and approached the alcove, the feeble voice asked again, "Where am I? Prisoner? Free?"

"You're alive," replied the old woman.

In the alcove, plunged into total darkness, something moved slowly. An unknown shape. A white ghost. A long mass, wrapped in the folds a rough fabric. Nothing else could be seen.

The old woman clasped her hands and said, "Good grief! What are you doing? Sleep!"

"No, mother, I'm getting up."

"Sleep son. You have to rest."

The voice, although weak, grew clearer, "Dammit! I'm fine."

The old woman rushed over. One moment, the white shape shook, then the fabric was pulled off. What was this mystery and how could it be possible?

A dead man got up from the bed in the alcove. And it was a dead man, since Jérôme Fandor was dead, he had been hanged, he had been buried, with the dirt already weighing down on his chest. Yet, here he was, and he had to be alive, since dead men don't usually return from the grave.

Old Marfa watched without fear as this extraordinary apparition got up from the bed.

She begged, "My son, believe me. Stay in bed. You'll be better off there than elsewhere."

Jérôme Fandor or the shadow of Jérôme Fandor protested, "Mother, I can't stay still. It's not in my nature."

"Well then, come."

"Where?"

"I have orders."

The old woman got up. She took the extraordinary creature in the white shroud by the hand and guided him to a small door, black with soot, which she opened with difficulty.

"Come," repeated Marfa Berena.

He followed her. They both walked down a dark staircase, the brick walls sweating.

A few minutes later, Marfa Berena opened the door, very thick, very solid, to a large cellar.

"Go in," she said.

The man went in and asked, "Are you going to leave me here?"

"I have orders."

Obviously, Marfa did not want to give anything away, did not dare give the man questioning her the information he wanted, since she closed the door abruptly.

But what was this mystery?

The man who had just entered the cellar, the man who looked like Jérôme Fandor, stayed there alone, and sat down on a crate. He placed his elbows on his knees and rested his head on his hands. He seemed most surprised and very weary.

"All right now," he murmured. "Where am I?"

He barked a laugh and added, "I don't know if I'm dead or alive, if I'm on the earth or down in hell…"

The man was, in fact, Jérôme Fandor. But wasn't Fandor supposed to be dead? The man wondered. The adventure that he had been caught up in was so fantastic, so impossible to understand, so unexpected that he did not know what to believe. That left room for doubting, hesitating, waiting.

His mind overwhelmed, he found it difficult to understand what his senses showed him. He remembered the tragic execution of that morning. The chain of his memories continued until the moment when the hangman had placed the fatal noose around his neck.

"Pull!" the man had shouted. The rope tightened. Fandor felt as if he had been pulled into the air. But what had happened next?

Marshalling all of his memories, striving to find a fleeting truth, Jérôme Fandor gradually reconstructed what had to have happened. Yes, that was it. As the rope tightened, as he felt himself being pulled into the air. As the hangman pushed his feet in order to finish him off faster, Fandor recalled that he had experienced an extraordinary surprise.

Of course, he felt bruised, grazed, wounded by the terrible hanging. Yet, he breathed freely. Nothing blocked his throat. The air continued to flow into his chest. Nothing hampered his lungs.

Everything Jérôme Fandor felt, was a suffering like a wound, like a very hard object that pressed under his chin, at the back of his neck, around his face. At that moment, in a flash of though, Jérôme sent a final kiss to Hélène, saying, "I'm going to die, but Juve will avenge me some day."

Yes, he was not suffering. Unquestionably, he had been hanged. His body floated in the air. His feet, which kicked against the air despite himself, could find no foothold. Yet, he continued to live. He was in perfect control of himself and that surprised him.

"What's going on? What's going on?"

Fandor quickly guessed. It was unlikely, yet quite simple. The shroud that the hangman had placed on him, the cloth shroud that wrapped around him like a bag, contained a steel frame, a frame Fandor could feel around his neck. It was like an infinitely resistant piece of armor that fit like a detachable collar.

What was it used for? Initially, Jérôme Fandor thought this was some plot hatched by Juve or perhaps even some police officer who wanted to save him. The iron necklace he wore did, in fact, prevent the noose from doing its job. And Jérôme Fandor owed his very life to that iron necklace. The rope tightened, but not around him since the rigid armor did not give way under its pressure.

A moment passed and Jérôme Fandor felt hope wildly rising. If they had prevented him, even against his will, from being hanged by the hangman's noose, then obviously someone was watching over him, someone who could save him.

Jérôme Fandor had no doubts. And, given his usual presence of mind, he found the strength to resist the desire to shout. He had enough self-control to remain absolutely silent.

"They'll cut me down, but let's hope they do it quickly," he thought. "This is unbearable."

The unfortunate man's situation was, in fact quite terrible. Although the rope was not strangling him, it was painful. The iron necklace held the journalist, resting on his chin and the back of his neck. His entire weight was supported by his neck. He could feel his spinal column stretching and felt as if it would break at any moment.

Despite himself, he beat at the air with his feet. People being hanged usually did. No one watching the hanging would have the least bit surprised. It was a conscious movement, but they all considered it a reflex. Moreover, at that point Jérôme Fandor was not in any condition to control the disorderly movements of his limbs. Blood raced to his head, his heart pounded and he was on the point of losing consciousness.

The last thing he heard clearly was the doctor saying, "We have to wait ten minutes."

"I'm lost," thought Fandor, and he fainted.

A few moments later, the unfortunate victim felt himself fall, painfully, not once but twice, once when they cut the rope and then when the hangman threw him into the pit.

It was all so painful, so unexpected that Jérôme Fandor fainted again. That, at least, meant that he did not feel the shovelfuls of dirt thrown on his face. He did not see the hangman, the man with the ape-like hands fill the pit. Jérôme Fandor was not even aware that, once the authorities had all departed, the same hangman worked even faster, removing the dirt he was supposed to be shoveling into the pit, dragging the so-called dead man out of the pit and over to a sleigh where he hid him.

Jérôme Fandor woke up at Marfa Berena's place He did not know the woman. He did not understand how he had arrived at her place. He did not understand why he had been rescued. Yet, there was one thing he did realize. He was alive, fresh air entered his lungs and he was free to talk and walk

Jérôme Fandor, his strength gradually returning, was once again as energetic and valiant as ever and could not stay down for long. He paced furiously back and forth in the cell where he had been locked. And his curiosity was piqued.

"Why did they save me?" he thought. "Who saved me? Where am I?"

And, he came up with all kinds of crazy stories.

"They must have caught Boris Pokroff," he said to himself. "They figured out that he was Fantômas and they overturned my sentence... I'm certainly in the hands of the police and they will come to question me. They'll release me..."

As he strode about, however, he noticed that next to him, in a neighboring cellar, since he was certainly in a cellar, there was someone else, pacing just as he was.

Who could that be? Another prisoner, no doubt. Perhaps another of Fantômas' victims? And Jérôme Fandor felt like hitting his head against the wall.

"My neighbors, who must be prisoners, might be able to give me some information. I could find out from them where I am and who that Marfa Berena is and if they'll hang me again or let me free."

Juve's friend, however, did not have long to think. The door to his cell opened suddenly and Jérôme Fandor spun around, filled once again with fear, and stared at the man who came in.

He was a large man, strangely dressed, in a manner that inspired terror. He wore a large black coat, like those worn by French priests, collar reaching to his chin, along with a large, soft hat that hid his eyes. His face was covered by a black mask.

Who was this man? What business did he have with the dead man who had escaped the gallows?

Jérôme Fandor waited impatiently for the man to speak. Yet, the newcomer did not appear rushed. He proceeded slowly to close the door. And, without glancing at Fandor, he headed toward the back of the cellar. There was a cask there. He used it as a desk, placing a series of papers on it. Then and only then, did he decide to speak.

In a gentle voice, he said, "My friend, I know you don't know how you managed to come here. And, in any case, that's not important. All you need to know is that, if I decide to, I can save you, free you, and that, also if I want to, I can send you back to the gallows and hang you again."

Jérôme Fandor said nothing.

He was most surprised, wondering where this was all headed and if he had not been deluded when he thought he was actually about to be saved.

The man, however, continued, "You will answer me honestly. Your fate depends on that. We know a great many things, but not everything..."

Jérôme Fandor decided to speak up, "I will answer you honestly," he said. "Because I don't ever lie. Yet, I will admit that I don't know everything myself. If you want to know, for example, how I was saved from the gallows, I have to admit I have no idea. I thought I would die this morning and I'm as surprised as anyone to see that I'm still alive."

As he spoke Jérôme Fandor was obviously telling the truth. He had no idea about the mysterious manner in which he had been rescued. He suspected that the hangman had carried off his body, or rather his alleged body, but he did not know that for a fact. If he had known, however, he would never have betrayed the man.

What actually happened?

At that point, the journalist had a glimmering of the truth. Someone must have wanted him alive and they must have paid the hangman to arrange that. He had not been strangled, although things could have ended badly.

"When they freed me," Fandor thought, "They must have noticed that I wasn't dead. Those who carried me off, deprived of all feeling, must have been arrested. The man in front of me is a judge and the best I can hope for is to convince him that I am perfectly innocent."

That would be quite some job, though.

Jérôme Fandor thought it was highly likely that he would be sentence to death again. But, the man standing before him did not give him much time to think. He smiled when he heard Fandor state that he had no idea how he had been taken from death. Then his expression grew serious again and, in a rough voice he said, "Your name is Jérôme Fandor. Is that true?"

"Yes," replied Fandor.

"You came to Russian on police business. Is that true?"

"Yes."

"And you went to Boris Pokroff's house on police business?"

"Yes," Fandor said again, starting to feel somewhat reassured.

The interrogation, in fact was going well. It seemed that the judge knew about his case. At least, he knew his identity and was not unaware of the reasons he came to Russia. Without a doubt, he would believe Fandor, in a few minutes, when He told him that Boris Pokroff was actually Fantômas. Yet, a few seconds later, Fandor started to worry once again, as the voice of the Russian who was interrogating him grew more and more serious.

He said, "Jérôme Fandor, you were aware of the functions performed by Boris Pokroff? You knew, no doubt, that he worked as the chief of police?"

Jérôme Fandor nodded.

"So, you realized how important this individual was?"

Jérôme Fandor smiled.

"I knew perfectly well. All the more so since..."

"Wait!" interrupted the judge.

The man seemed to collect himself. He was shivering visibly, as he continued to question Jérôme Fandor.

"Tell me," he said. "You can speak later, but first I want you to answer all of my questions accurately... Tell me, is it true that you were hired to work as a servant for Boris Pokroff?"

Jérôme Fandor did not hesitate. Did he need to hide the truth? Of course not. Moreover, it was not in his nature to do so.

"That's true," he admitted.

"So, you clearly intended to get close to the man?"

"Yes," Fandor said again. "But I did so because..."

"Wait!" said the judge.

Jérôme Fandor was starting to lose his patience. He was burning to tell the man that Boris Pokroff was Fantômas.

The judge continued, "Is it true that you intended to kill Boris Pokroff?"

Fandor stood taller. He crossed his arms over his chest and stared at the other man with shining eyes.

"Sir, you insult me! I'm not an assassin. I'm not even an executioner. I did not want to kill Boris Pokroff. I wanted to unmask the man. I was doing the work of justice because..."

Jérôme Fandor was about to continue speaking. He stopped suddenly because the judge stood up abruptly.

Furious, the man asked, "You swear on your honor that you did not intend to kill Pokroff?"

"I do!" said Fandor. "He was..."

"You did not go into his service in order to assassinate him?"

"Not at all. I wanted to prove that..."

"So, you had no intention to kill the chief of the secret police."

"Not at all," Jérôme Fandor repeated. "I intended to prove that Pokroff is Fan..."

"Wretch!" interrupted the judge. "We saved you. So, we were mistaken? You're not a nihilist?"

"Of course not," replied Fandor.

Then something strange happened. The man questioning him suddenly reeled back.

"Oh! Holy Virgin!" he shrieked. "He's not a nihilist. He said so.! He boasts of it!"

Jérôme Fandor had not yet recovered from the legitimate surprise that this exclamation caused when two vigorous hands grabbed him. Assuredly, another individual had entered the cellar without him noticing. Upon a sign from the judge, this man threw himself at Fandor, who could do nothing at all, as he was bound hand and foot and gagged.

But what did all this mean?

CHAPTER IX
The Revolutionary Tribunal

Jérôme did not understand a thing. Yet, precisely as a result of his extraordinary bravery and unshakeable nerve, the young man was much less worried about the series of adventures he seemed destined to get involved in without ever truly being able to unmask the truth.

Yet, the events of the past two hours had surprised him. If Jérôme Fandor raged, he truly did have to be brave so that this bad temper would not simply transform into incredible fear.

At the very moment that Jérôme Fandor was energetically denying the nihilist's accusation, an accusation he did not merit, since he simply was not a nihilist, he felt himself grabbed from behind then quickly gagged and bound so that he was completely incapable of fighting.

"Well, what does this mean?" the journalist wondered. "Exactly what is going on here? I don't think I'll ever understand. So far, I've been in prison, with people who were nihilists and who had been imprisoned for that and now people are jumping on me specifically because I'm not a nihilist…"

It took an extraordinary amount of courage, at that moment, for Jérôme Fandor to think that clearly. In fact, his current situation was about as inappropriate for rational thought as it could be for the excellent reason that blows were raining down upon him and he ran the risk of having his skull bashed in at any moment.

"Gently, my friends, gently!"

But his protests fell on deaf ears.

Jérôme Fandor did not utter another word. His was on the point of fainting when suddenly a loud voice rang out, "Don't kill him. You must not kill him! First, he has to be tried!"

As if by magic, the blows stopped. Yet, for all that, his situation had not improved. Although they were no longer hitting him, they had tightened his bonds and he could feel the thick rope digging into his skin.

A few seconds later, Fandor felt himself grabbed by the feet and shoulders. Obviously, they were carrying him. But where were they taking him? The journalist did not have the slightest idea. Yet, the trip was not long. All too soon, Jérôme Fandor was thrown roughly to the ground, skinning his face.

He groaned and muttered, "Trials, trials! Since this morning people just keep dropping me. I'm starting to get tired of these clowns. If this keeps up, I'll make a complaint…"

Jérôme Fandor, to be perfectly truthful, was attempting to make a joke. He belonged to that race of brave men who, when danger presses in, know how to face it with a smile on their lips. He still did not really understand exactly what was happening to him, why they had saved him and how, after tearing him out of death's arms, they were now after him. One thing, however, was certain; the people who held him prisoner wished him no good. Obviously, they would not hesitate to kill him within a few minutes.

"They said they were going to judge me," Fandor thought. "Damn! I'm starting to get an idea about trials in this primitive country. They are most certainly quick and not terribly impartial."

Lying on the ground, Jérôme Fandor struggled and managed to turn around. As soon as he lay on his side, he started to grimace under his blindfold with such perseverance, such wild energy, that he managed to free his eyes.

"Damn," he grumbled." I may be free to see but that gets me nowhere. I'm completely in the dark."

He was in the dark, in fact, in absolute blackness. Without a doubt, he had been pitched into some sort of windowless cubbyhole. Would he be there long? Would they come quickly to release him from this horror?

"I would prefer it if they rushed," Fandor decided.

But he avoided making any other wishes. He was so powerless to try anything, to change his situation, that making wishes would have served no purpose.

"Let's look at things as they are and wait!" he grumbled.

Yet waiting seemed profoundly horrible, particularly if he were to die that evening.

And the unfortunate man sighed. At that moment, despite himself, he pictured Hélène and the thought of that young woman, his beloved, waiting for him hurt him.

Hélène! Hélène! She was so far away. She must be worried. She must be surprised by his attitude. Oh, without a doubt, time would pass before she would learn, if she ever did, what had happened to the man she loved more than anything and who had not loved her as he should have, as she deserved.

Jérôme Fandor made a colossal effort to control his mind. He chased the tender image of Hélène from his mind.

"Let's get ready," he thought. "Ready to appear before the judges."

Hours passed, endless, and monotonous. Moreover, remaining still was starting to be quite painful. They had not untied his bonds and they were eating into his flesh.

Jérôme Fandor thought, "These Russians are wretches. If Juve ever manages to arrest Fantômas in this god-forsaken country, he will most likely get into trouble trying to keep them from torturing his prisoner!"

Despite himself, Fandor smiled. The idea of Juve having to defend Fantômas against those that arrested him, was amusing. Yet, despite the effort that the journalist made to not let his thoughts weigh over his fate, he was starting to wonder if he had not been sentenced to die of hunger in the horrible cell where he found himself, when voices rang out. And sure enough, men were approaching his cell. Soon, the door grated.

"Ah!" thought Fandor, shrugging. "Is this some new torture? Or has the moment of justice arrived? But what does it matter after all. Although I have no idea what's going on, I'm sure I'm already lost!"

Those who arrived, however, lifted Jérôme Fandor without causing him too much harm. The journalist could not see their faces, since they all avoided looking in his direction.

"It's curious," He thought. "But these people seem to be afraid of being recognized. Since they are police officers, they shouldn't be so timorous. They're just doing their duty and…"

Jérôme Fandor stopped his monologue just then. Those carrying him had just entered a large, plain room. It was an enormous room, completely bare, with no furniture except for a large table covered with a green tablecloth. Behind the table, there were five chairs and in front of each chair a piece of white paper.

Jérôme Fandor noticed strange writing. Names, Russian names, each followed by a date and preceded by a small black cross.

"Damn, that's strange," Jérôme Fandor said, and he shivered as he looked around the room. "It's like being in a cemetery or a mortuary."

As he wondered what they planned to do with him, the Russians dropped him onto the floor, throwing him there like a package, a few yards from the large table.

"What am I doing here?" Fandor asked. "Is this a torture room or a tribunal?"

He did not have to wait long for an answer to his anguished question. Those who had been carrying him took a step back and five individuals entered the large room and took their places behind the large table.

Jérôme Fandor immediately recognized one of the five new arrivals. It was the same man who had questioned him at Marfa Berena's house a few hours earlier. It was the man who had lost his temper when Fandor had stated he was not a nihilist. The four other individuals, however, were complete strangers. Fandor was unable to see their faces since they all stubbornly kept their heads lowered

One alone stood out. This individual, located at the end of the large table, was rather far from Fandor. He had entered last and the journalist did not have a clear view of him, since the light was behind him. Despite that, the man instinctively turned his head to the side.

"That's strange!" Fandor thought. "That's very strange! I could swear that last one is a woman. For a moment, I thought…"

Fandor's eyes filled with tears. The brave, intrepid man was overcome with emotion at that very moment. He did not have the courage he needed to complete his thought.

What had poor Fandor believed? Of course, he had been the victim of a hallucination. And that hallucination, under the circumstances, took on a tragic nature. Jérôme Fandor thought he had recognized Hélène! He thought that the woman, whom he could barely see, walked and looked like the woman he loved above all.

Obviously, he was crazy to even imagine that Hélène could be there! The young woman would never have been involved with this type of crowd. It was just impossible for her to be there.

The journalist turned his head away. He did not want to maintain such a cruel illusion. He did not want to think such mad, such impossible thoughts.

"I'm losing my mind," he grumbled. "Hélène cannot have any idea what has happened to me. And if I die, I'll die without having seen her again…"

Die. Was he really going to die? Would he not be able to convince, the triumph, to persuade those who were to hear him that he was innocent of everything they charged him with?

"Come on," he grumbled. "It's now or never. I must control my nerves. I will not allow them to assassinate me! They have to hear me."

At that very moment, one of the five people who had just entered the room, the man who had interrogated Fandor, slowly stood up.

"My brothers," he declared in a deep, solemn voice. "You know why we are gathered here today. You know why you have been summoned here. We have to judge a man. We have important decisions to make."

The extraordinary speaker paused and pointed at Jérôme Fandor, still lying bound on the ground and quite incapable of moving.

"This man," continued the Russian, "This man has played us for fools. I'll make him repeat his last words briefly, however. I don't want the shadow of a doubt left in your minds. I ask your permission to interrogate him again."

Jérôme Fandor, who had not missed a word of this speech, saw the four others nod at the judge in approval. That latter stared at Fandor.

"I've already asked you a question," he declared. "I will ask you again. Are you a nihilist?"

Jérôme Fandor grated his teeth. He found the question intolerable. He had spent enough time in Russia, in fact, to understand that just being suspected of being a nihilist would certainly result in a death sentence. He was not a nihilist. He didn't even know the entire nihilist doctrine. So, wasn't it stupid of them to persist in reproaching him for feelings he did not share?

Through his gag, Jérôme Fandor shouted, "I don't know who you are. I don't know what you plan to do with me. But one thing I do know is that there are five of you and I stand alone. You don't have to be afraid. So why do you leave me bound and gagged as I am? Remove my bonds and then, and then I'll answer you!"

The judge shrugged and said, "We don't free miserable wretches that may be dangerous."

He was about to continue speaking when the woman, the only woman in the group of five judges, suddenly interrupted, "That's just. The accused is entitled to defend himself freely. And if it pleases my comrades, I'll release him immediately."

She stood up and walked toward Fandor. At that moment, the journalist was even more upset than before.

The voice of that woman, of the woman who had interceded for him, who had asked to have his bonds removed, how strangely had that voice resonated in his being, as if re-awakening painful echoes in his thoughts! That voice, that gentle voice with its musical intonations, seemed familiar to Jérôme Fandor.

"My God, my God," he said to himself. "That's Hélène's voice."

Yet, at the same time, Jérôme Fandor thought that, under the sway of emotion, given his fright, which was completely natural, caused by his successive adventures, he had to be very mistaken.

Obviously, Hélène was not there. She could not be there.

Despite all that, however, Jérôme Fandor could not help but look at the young woman as she prepared to free him. But, just then, one of the other judges stood up quickly. A young man, trying to look gallant.

"No," he protested. "Don't move sister Olga. I will free the prisoner."

Jérôme Fandor would have cheerfully cursed the interloper, but he restrained himself. He was in fact, relieved that they were removing his bonds and the gag and, despite everything, this simple gesture gave him renewed hope.

He stood up slowly, took two or three deep breaths, looked at the chief judge and said, "I'm all yours, now. Speak. Question me. What do you want to know?"

The judge glared and asked, "Are you a nihilist?"

"No," Fandor replied. And the journalist shivered.

As he finished speaking, the judge raised a vengeful hand in the air and shrieked in rage, "In that case, may you be cursed, you and all your descendants."

Dumbfounded at first, Fandor regained his composure and proudly repeated, risking the ire of those who had the power of life and death over him, "I am not a nihilist. I know nothing about nihilism. It is possible that the philosophical theories that provide the basis for this doctrine contain some kernel of truth but one thing is certain, and that is that I hate direct action, I do not tolerate assassination, even for political reasons. Now, if you don't believe me…"

He did not have time to continue.

The anger that he had already noticed on the judges' faces seemed to grow more intense. They all stood up. Only the young woman named Olga, the young woman who looked and sounded like Hélène, remained seated and calm.

The chief judge said, "Shut up wretch. Shut up!"

Fandor lost his temper and said, "I'll shut up if I feel like it! I've had enough of these interrogations! Who are you! Are you regular judges? What kind of court do you hold?"

"Shut up!" the judge repeated.

But Jérôme Fandor ignored him and said, "You want to find me guilty, at any price, of something. Well, too bad for you. I won't take part in this farce. I am innocent. If you want me dead, then kill me, but don't look for excuses."

With that Fandor fell silent. He was out of breath. With his vehement outburst, he had unloaded all of the rage that had accumulated in his heart.

"Now," he thought. "These people will certainly do away with me. Too bad! I've given them some of their own medicine. I've been accused of being an assassin for so long that now I shall scream!"

At that moment, the intrepid young man felt that he had reached the end of his life. Since he could no longer do anything to save his life, he decided that it should end quickly, without glory, without panache, by defying the judges and throwing their cowardice in their faces.

Jérôme Fandor was stunned by the response he received.

The chief judge stood up. The serious man seemed to be quivering. He seemed to be overwhelmed with rage. Only his superb willpower kept him from throwing himself at Fandor, although he must have wanted to punish him for his insolent behavior.

"Listen," he said slowly. "You don't know what you're saying. You're just talking off the top of your head. That's why you're uttering such stupidities. So, you say you're not a nihilist? Well we thought otherwise, but we were wrong. And that's most unfortunate for you. You want to know who we are? We're exactly what you see before you. We're nihilists."

Jérôme Fandor was dumbfounded. How, after being hung by the Tsar's civil servants, after being sentenced to death for being a suspected nihilist, had he now had the misfortune of falling into the hands of the nihilists just as he was boasting at the top of his lungs that he did not belong to their party?

Overwhelmed with emotion, Fandor said nothing.

The judge continued, "We are nihilists and it is precisely because we are nihilists that everything that happened occurred. Do you understand?"

"Of course not!" roared Fandor.

"You will."

Crossing his arms, raising his eyes as if looking for some radiant vision overhear, the conspirator continued, "We are nihilists. We all want a society in which even the humblest can attain happiness. We fervently believe in a universal event, which will eradicate the strong, the powerful, the rich, the leaders and will eliminate all iniquities that arise out of strength, power, wealth and authority. We do not believe in God, the Tsar or laws. We are the enemies of all those who take part in the sacrilege of order or defense. Do you understand?"

"Well..."

Despite himself, Fandor was interested. It was very obvious that the man speaking to him was convinced and inspired.

Of course, Fandor had read, in many books discussing the Russian social situation, that the nihilists were, above all respectable. He knew that the conspirators could occasionally commit excesses, but he also knew that their theory was based on profoundly respectable principles. Despite, himself, Fandor respected the judge.

"Damn!" he thought with his Parisian sense of humor, "Hats' off to this man!"

The nihilist continued, "Guided by these feelings, we learned that you had wanted to kill a police chief. We don't know everyone who is a nihilist, but we do recognize actions. What did we think? Don't try to understand. We decided that this man wanted to kill Boris Pokroff, he dreamed of destroying a wretched police chief, an agent of the Tsar. He must be a nihilist!"

The judge paused and Jérôme Fandor asked, "So?"

"So, since we were convinced that you supported our cause and knowing that you had made a courageous gesture, we realized that you ran the risk of becoming a martyr, that the authorities would not be lenient with you, and we understood that you would be sent to the gallows and that you, who had dreamed of freeing people, would be hanged like a criminal."

"That almost happened," said Fandor.

But the people in the room did not hear his interruption.

The judge continued, "We could not support that. We have access to a great deal of intelligence. Our cause attracts new supporters every day, has won over civil servants who seem to be most attached to the State. Listen and you will understand."

"I'm listening with all my soul,' said Fandor. "I find this most interesting."

He was still jeering but he wondered, in reality, what was going to happen and how this scene, in which he played a very important role, would end.

The nihilist continued, "The hangman who executed you is a nihilist. He hates his work and does it only to soften the final moments of those sentenced to death. We asked him not to execute you. We looked for a way to save you and we found one. An iron ring was hidden under the shroud to prevent the rope from strangling you. And it worked. You fainted, looked dead, and were thrown into a grave. Then, when the authorities left, you were pulled back out."

"Bravo," joked Fandor.

But the judge continued on, "We were all overcome with joy. We were convinced that we had saved one of our brothers. We might not have suspected otherwise except that, by chance, the hangman informed us about certain conversations that took place in the prison, in which people stated that you had spoken out against nihilism. So, we grew suspicious and we interrogated you."

"Perfect, perfect."

Jérôme Fandor grimaced as he listened to the judge's final words and when the man stopped talking the journalist asked, "So you obtained information. You know that I'm not one of you. I'm far too honest to take refuge in a lie. And I'll tell you the truth. Not only am I now a nihilist, but I went to the house of the chief of the secret police with a goal much different than assassination in mind."

"What goal?"

Jérôme Fandor hesitated a moment, thinking. Should he announce that Boris Pokroff was Fantômas? Should he reveal that information to total strangers when such a revelation could have such heavy, tragic consequences? He hesitated and then made his decision.

"That's my secret," said Jérôme Fandor. "I cannot tell you."

But that simple declaration aroused the wrath of the judges once again.

In a mocking tone, the Russian who seemed to be presiding over the strange tribunal said, "Do you have such terrible secrets?"

"Perhaps…"

"Are you implying that you cannot disclose these confidences to anyone?"

"Without a doubt."

"In that case, you will be surprised by our verdict."

"Why?"

Jérôme Fandor felt fear wash over him again. The situation was clear. There had been a misunderstanding. He had been saved from the gallows because they thought he was a nihilist. And he had just confessed that he was not. What could happen? What decision would they make?

Jérôme Fandor asked, "What are you going to do with me? You saved me by mistake, but I thank you any way. I'm not a member of your party, but I respect it. What will you decide?"

The judge shrugged, "I don't even need to consult my colleagues before telling you. Your own words, your own feelings should be a clue for you. There are things that are secret by nature. There are incredible mysteries that no one can reveal. You said as much yourself. Things that have to be kept hidden. You decide what is to be your fate now, you who have seen our faces, you who could recognize the nihilist leaders, you who would do us so much harm."

Hearing these words, Jérôme Fandor grew pale. Yet, he did not want to admit defeat. He just wanted to keep up a good appearance and, if there was any means in which he could save himself, he wanted to try it since he considered it cowardly to give up without trying.

"I don't have to decide my fate," Fandor said. "Yet, I still have a few things to add. It is true that I now know terrible secrets about you. It is true that I could harm you. Yet it is also true that you saved me from death. That should reassure you as to my conduct. I'm not a member of your party, but I demand you give me the same respect I have decided to give you. I give you my word of honor, and you can believe this, that no one will ever learn what I have learned, through surprise and error…"

Jérôme Fandor stared in the eyes of the nihilist. He thought that he had touched him, moved him, convinced him

The nihilist slowly shook his head and said, "I'm not the leader, but I do have heavy responsibilities. Personally, I would take you at your word, but in my official capacity, I have to doubt you."

Then he uttered the sentence, "You will die. You will die slowly."

CHAPTER X
The Replacement

"You will die. You will die slowly..."

The inexorable sentence, the mortal verdict, resonated in the large room where the extraordinary nihilist revolutionary tribunal judged the unfortunate Jérôme Fandor, who remained impassive as he heard it.

In fact, he had foreseen the obvious outcome of the proceedings. He knew that, unless some miracle occurred, nothing could save him. The death sentence did not surprise him and only surprise could have forced some response from him. But Jérôme Fandor could not be touched by fear.

"Well!" he simply said, bowing to the judges. "If I have to die, then let your will be done. Yet, why do you want to torture me? And what do you mean by a slow death?"

The chief judge smiled calmly.

"A slow death is one that leaves no traces. Your body could be bothersome for us. By taking your life, we are taking a security measure to prevent dangers of all kinds. Under these conditions, we have to consider everything and that is why we will make sure that your death will not set the police on our trail."

Jérôme Fandor shivered when he heard this.

While the void did not frighten him, while he had long prepared for the eternal night of the tomb, he could not keep his flesh from reacting to the idea of torture.

"And," he asked, "What will this slow death entail?"

"We'll decide."

The judge, who had remained standing throughout his discussion with Fandor, suddenly sat down. He turned to look at the other judges, their serious faces, completely motionless, were as hard as steel.

"What is your decision?" he asked. "In keeping with our laws, I have to pronounce a sentence, but I don't determine the means of execution. That is your role."

Just then something strange happened, something the nihilist had not planned.

The young woman who, up to that point, had remained almost motionless, appearing to take no notice of the discussions, suddenly stood up.

"Brothers," she said, in a voice that quivered while revealing a strong will. "Brothers, what we are about to do is unjust."

Naturally enough, these words provoked a sense of scandal. The revolutionary judges sat up, looked at their sister, eyes filled with questions.

The young woman repeated, "What we are about to do is monstrous!"

"What do you mean?" the chief judge asked.

His pale face flushed. Most certainly, he hated the words of pity that he expected the young woman to utter. All the members of the tribunal were filled with emotion. But, as they watched their colleague stand up to speak, they experienced a violent emotion mingled with anger. Jérôme Fandor was as upset as all of them.

Oh, that woman's voice, that voice he was hearing for only the second time, yet which brought back so many memories. Was it possible for him to be so wrong? Was it possible that all of his senses were mistaken?

Jérôme Fandor felt tears well up in his eyes. He who remained so calm when his death sentence was pronounced shivered now as heard this woman's voice, that voice that resonated in his heart like music.

"That's my beloved Hélène's voice," he said to himself, and he stared at the young woman everyone called Olga, trying to make out her features.

At the same time, he forced himself to think logically. And with cold logic, he forced down the crazy thoughts that swept into his mind. No, that woman could not be Hélène. No that was not Hélène who was about to speak.

Jérôme Fandor thought, "Hélène is not a nihilist. She cannot sit on a revolutionary tribunal and all the more so, if I understand correctly, since the tribunal is made of up the party heads!"

And it was mad for him think that Hélène sat on the other side of that table with its repulsive green tablecloth. No, his beloved could not have joined such coarse people, who had sentenced him to death, without scruples, knowing full well that he was innocent, and only because they could not trust his word of honor.

Jérôme Fandor clenched his fists and nervously dug his fingernails into the palms of his hands, drawing blood. But he felt no pain. His soul was filled with a single thought, Hélène, as he strove not to get lost in the final adventures in the drama that would end in his death.

"What do you mean, Olga?" the chief judge asked the young woman, who looked very calm.

With an elegant, feminine gesture, she took a golden watch from her bodice and said, "It's late. Twenty minutes are all that separates us from a nameless horror. Will we commit it?"

"What do you mean," the chief judge asked again.

The young woman, Olga, was obviously convinced of what she was saying but, just as obviously, those who were listening to her did not understand her words or her attitude.

"Yet," the Russian woman continued," in 20 minutes, my brothers, just a few steps from here, a frightful misfortune will fall on the head of an innocent woman. Did you not know that?"

The chief judge shook his head and said, "I don't understand what you're saying. Explain yourself, sister!"

The young woman took another step. She placed one of her delicate hands on the table. That hand seemed to tense as if under the sway of a terrible emotion. Yet, the nihilist continued in the same, calm voice, "A woman, a very poor woman, Marfa Berena, lives just a few yards from here. You all know her, my brothers. Well, do you know what is about to happen to her?"

Everyone remained silent. No one dared reply.

Vehemently, the young woman continued, "The unfortunate woman has a son, Vassili Berena. Do you know what dangers Vassili Berena faces?"

The silence continued.

In a vibrant voice, Olga spoke again, "Vassili Berena was one of ours. Vassili was one of the most faithful of our followers. He dedicated himself body and soul to the cause, to nihilism. Well, brothers, you can hardly say you don't know what has happened to him?"

And without giving anyone time to interrupt, the Russian woman continued, "Vassili Berena has been betrayed, his name given to the police. The executioner appointed by the Tsar was told to condemn the man and he did just that. Vassili Berena is sentenced to 10 years of forced labor in the Siberian mines."

Just then the chief judge interrupted the young woman, asking, "Olga, why are you reminding us of such cruel matters? We can't do anything for Vassili Berena!"

But Olga ignored the interruption and ardently continued, "Marfa Berena saw her son arrive a few days ago. Vassili could not go a long time without embracing his mother. He went to her house, tracked down like a wild beast. Unable to trust even his own shadow, he feared denunciation, fled from traps, slipped through the dark of night to Marfa Berena's house. My brothers, the son and the mother were embracing one another..."

The chief judge, interrupted impatiently, "That is no doubt all true, Olga, but once again, what can we do?"

"They had," she continued, "one minute of happiness. Old Marfa clasped her son to her bosom, imagining that she was once again living in a time when she did not have to fear the police. Yet, although the moment was happy, it was brief. When Vassili Berena wanted to leave, flee, start a wandering life running from the Tsar's Cossacks, it was already too late. A spy had reported him. The police surrounded his mother's house. She hid him, down in the cellar, where he is right now, crouching in the darkest corner..."

"Olga, Olga," the chief judge interrupted.

The young woman opened her arms. "In 20 minutes," she shrieked, her voice filled with rage. "I know that the police are going to come. I know that they will attack that little house in 20 minutes. They will search Marfa Berena's house from top to bottom. She'll be blessed if they don't torch it! In any case, one thing is certain. Old Marfa, who is a nihilist, will see her son Vassili, who is also a nihilist, dragged off to the mines, in the depths of Siberia, a country from which he will never return."

The young woman sobbed. Overwhelmed with emotion, she was a fright to see.

"And I," she continued. "I will live in peace! And you, my brothers, you will also live in peace. And that crime will be committed. No, no, the nihilists must not give up, Vassili Berena was one of ours and, on our honor, we must save him!"

These wild words, this violent declaration moved the tribunal.

Jérôme Fandor recalled many things at that moment. He thought of poor Marfa's sad face. He also remembered that, during the first few minutes he had spent in the good woman's cellar, he had heard discreet sounds nearby. The discussion, however, could not go on forever.

The chief judge asked Olga, "This is abominable, of course, but what can we do? Do you know how we can save Vassili Berena?"

Olga replied, "Yes, I do know how to save Vassili Berena! Blood buys blood. A human life saves another human life. For every crime, there is expiation."

Then she turned suddenly to look at Fandor and fiercely added, "You blasphemed early, convict. You blasphemed against nihilism. That's your crime. And that's why I would have applauded the death you deserved. Yet, your life will be saved, at least if that's what you want. You heard what I said, isn't it true?"

Jérôme Fandor nodded and replied, "Perfectly."

His voice trembled. Since Olga had turned to look at him, since she had approached him, since the young woman had spoken directly to him, he was filled with the most extraordinary sensations.

Was it true? Could it be possible? Was it Hélène? But as soon as he felt certain, doubt washed over him yet again.

"No," he said to himself. "It could not be his beloved."

Jérôme Fandor, to be truthful, heard the words addressed to him, distant, indistinct sounds, as if through a fog.

Olga, however, continued, "You realize that one of ours, a nihilist, an honest man, is being tracked by the Tsar's police? You heard me say that the poor wretch has been sentenced to 10 years in the Siberian mines? Listen to me. You were supposed to die a slow death and I'm offering you a chance to be saved. Would you agree to replace Vassili Berena? Those who plan to arrest him do not know what he looks like. Will you take his place in the chain gang? Do you want to go to the mines? If you agree, you might live, that is if the Tsar's guards don't kill you as they do so many others!"

Naturally, Jérôme Fandor did not hesitate and replied, "Fine! I'll go in Vassili's place."

He did not hesitate for two reasons. First, he still wondered anxiously if this Olga, if the woman speaking to him, was actually his wife Hélène. And he was unable to make up his mind on that matter.

He was still too far from the young woman and there was too little light in the room for him to see her face clearly. And Hélène, if it was her, would have had to change a few details in her dress and her hairstyle, to play her role as a Russian nihilist. Perhaps, in order to stay safe, to avoid recognition, she had even had to use make-up.

But, while Jérôme Fandor did not know if Olga were Hélène, and that only would have made him accept the young woman's proposal, he knew other facts that meant he would never hesitate.

"If I refuse to go to the mines," Fandor told himself, "These people will quietly kill me right away. If I agree, on the other hand, I'll have a chance at getting away. After all, not everyone dies in the Siberian mines and some deportees do manage to escape."

Jérôme told the young woman, "I agree."

The house of a Russian moujik. A very poor room that Jérôme Fandor immediately recognized. Was it the same room in which he had opened his eyes, astonished to find himself alive after having been hanged a few hours earlier?

There was a woman in that room. Marfa Berena. She came and went, hurrying to serve a meager meal to Jérôme Fandor, who ate hungrily.

Marfa Berena chattered like a magpie. "Take some of this roast, son!" she said in a loud voice. "Take some, Vassili! I'm sure you haven't eaten so well in a long time."

Jérôme Fandor did not reply. Without the slightest scruples, the journalist took a copious serving of meat, glancing at his hostess without the slightest recognition.

Marfa Berena continued to shower him with thoughtfulness.

"Wait, wait, Vassili!" she said in a shrill voice. "I'll get you a bottle. I'll bring it up from the cellar you were hiding in.'

Still, Jérôme Fandor said nothing.

Marfa Berena suddenly crossed the room, calling, "Vassili! Vassili!"

Then, since Jérôme Fandor stubbornly refused to reply, she continued, "Vassili! You'll have to get up early tomorrow, to get away, if they don't arrest you tonight. I'll open all the double windows. Then, when dawn comes, you'll wake up on your own."

And Marfa Berena opened the double windows, roughly shoving aside the shutters that had covered them.

"Vassili! Vassili!" the old woman called again. "It's hard to see. I'll turn the lamp up."

Still Jérôme Fandor said nothing and the loquacious old woman was not satisfied. She walked quickly over to Fandor and this time, whispered in his ear, "Listen. Do you know how to sing?"

Hearing that question, Jérôme quickly abandoned his silence. He seemed to be overwhelmed with impatience. He turned toward the Russian woman.

"No, he declared," furiously. "I don't know how to sing. When I sing, the birds cry."

Jérôme Fandor used a little humor to cover up his bad mood. In fact, the journalist was justified in not feeling terribly cheerful. There was nothing particularly joyful about his situation. This is what had happened to him. The revolutionary tribunal had taken Olga's advice under consideration. They had decided to take Jérôme Fandor to Marfa Berena's house. There, he was to pretend that he was Vassili and turn himself over to the police when they came to arrest the nihilist. And Fandor would be arrested and sent to the mines and the audacious subterfuge would save old Marfa Berena's son. For lack of any better idea, Jérôme had accepted.

Yet, despite his respect for the arrangements, Jérôme could not keep from cursing old Marfa Berena who, since she was eager for the strategy to work, was doing everything in her power to attract the attention of the police, to make sure they would arrest the man posing as her son as quickly as possible. Marfa Berena called Vassili. She opened the window, she turned up the lamp.

Damn!" thought the journalist who, despite everything, had retained a shred of hope, "I have no illusions left. There's nothing to be done for it. This crazy old woman will get me arrested!"

And Jérôme Fandor was not wrong. Marfa Berena's comings and goings had not gone unnoticed by the police who, as Olga had said, had surrounded the house in order to arrest Vassili. As Jérôme Fandor was finishing his slice of roast, someone violently knocked at the door.

"Open up, in there. Open up now."

Marfa Berena hurried over to the door. She grew pale and shook all over.

Good lord!" she moaned. "Who can that be knocking at the door?"

The pounding intensified.

"Open!" yelled a deep voice. "Open up, old lady, or I'll knock the door down!"

Marfa Berena did not want to give in too quickly. That would surely raise suspicions. She wailed, "I'm just a poor old woman and deserve respect."

"Open up! Open up!" the deep voice replied.

Marfa Berena did as ordered. A she did so, she glanced at Jérôme Fandor. Obeying the oath he had sworn, he stopped eating. He opened the door to a large cupboard and hid there, just carefully enough that people would think he was trying to escape, yet clumsily enough to let the police discover him. And they did.

A moment later, a Cossack lieutenant, face rough, movements awkward, pushed Marfa Berena violently out of his way.

"Your son?" he asked. "Where is your son?"

The old woman clasped her hands and replied, "I don't know."

The Cossack lost his temper, yelling, "You know very well where he is. Go and get him."

Just then, Marfa Berena truly did lose control. She was a nihilist. She was terribly afraid of the police and she completely forgot the role she was to play.

"My son is not here," the old woman stated. "Have pity on me!"

But the sinister Cossacks who had entered the humble dwelling had no use for mercy or pity. The officer stomped his foot.

"If you do not turn Vassili over to me," he said. "I will take my vengeance. Your house will be tossed, your furniture will be burned and I will have the soldiers whip you."

As he spoke, he raised a large crop to poor Marfa.

He said, "Do you understand me? Do you want me to give you a good whipping?"

The crop whistled through the air. Yet, just as the terrible whip was about to strike the old woman's shoulder, a surprising event occurred, something no one could have suspected. The officer suddenly turned about. He tripped over his large boots and his forehead struck the wall. At the same moment, the crop he had been brandishing was torn violently from his hands, broken in two and thrown to the ground.

A firm voice stated, "Here I am. You're looking for me, so go ahead and arrest me. But you have no right to hit my mother!"

What a strange thing! The man who turned himself over, the man who said, "Here I am." The man who had shoved the officer and firmly stated "You have no right to hit my mother." That man was not Vassili Berena, but Jérôme Fandor!

Jérôme Fandor had, in fact, just become a glorious victim to his knightly habits. Of course, he had no tender feelings for the Berena family, mother or son, who through sheer selfishness had placed him in such an unfortunate position. Yet, Fandor could not ignore the officer's brutality.

Marfa Berena was a woman. Marfa Berena was old. The young man's heart had skipped a beat when he saw that the brute was about to hit her. Instinctively, Jérôme Fandor felt no anger against the old Russian woman. Was she not trying to save her child? To protect him? Was she not trying to keep her son out of the Russian penal colony? That terrible Siberian mine to which so many young people were sent, never to return?

"Here I am," Fandor yelled.

He crossed his arms to keep from throwing himself on the officer who had recovered his balance and was rapidly walking in Fandor's direction. And, as is always the case when a brute is justly reprimanded, the officer was enraged.

"Wretch!" he shouted. "You dare raise your hand to me? I don't know what's holding me back!"

Jérôme Fandor cut him off with a single word. "Fear," he said.

And, since this extraordinary reply left the officer flabbergasted for a moment, Jérôme Fandor continued, "You have orders to arrest me. You must take me to the chain gang or face the consequences. Make sure you don't kill me. You won't outlive me for long."

Obviously, Jérôme Fandor was just talking off the top of his head. In fact, he knew nothing about the officer's orders or responsibilities. Yet, Fandor spoke with assurance and easily convinced the other man.

The Cossack stepped back. He glared at Jérôme Fandor, eyes burning with hatred.

"Fine," he said in a hoarse voice. "You're right. I'm responsible for your life until I've taken you to the chain gang. But once the chain gang has set out, anything can happen! The papers are signed, there's no longer any control. Listen to me, dog. I'll be the one accompanying that bunch of deportees to Siberia and I don't want you to finish the trip. You'll die along the way."

The officer was panting, voice filled with rage, as he waved his fist in front of Fandor's face. Fandor did not look concerned. He cast a mocking glance at old Marfa Berena who, frightened, pale as a ghost, did not dare say a word.

Calmly, Jérôme Fandor continued, "Do your duty. Arrest me!"

Valiant and courageous, when he should have been frightened, Jérôme Fandor commanded his torturers. The officer motioned with his arm. The brutal Cossacks fell into step behind him, prepared to take the unfortunate Jérôme Fandor.

"Take him!"

They all took a step ahead.

Just then, Fandor had a sudden thought, "Good grief! I should have warned Juve."

Thinking to ask the old woman for a favor, the fake Vassili Berena asked, "Will you allow me to embrace my mother?"

"No," the officer said. "Come with us now!"

Jérôme Fandor shrugged.

"I'm lost," he thought. "But before I give up, I must find a way to take care of that beast. I broke his crop. Too bad! I would have enjoyed dusting his ribs with it!"

CHAPTER XI
Russian Penal Colony

"Obviously, my tribulations are not over. To date, my time in Russia has brought me nothing but misfortune and I greatly fear that it will continue to do so."

Jérôme Fandor conducted this conversation in his mind as the Cossacks escorting the brutal officer quickly dragged him in the direction of the St. Jean *ostroghi,* where the convicts to be sent to the Siberian mines were gathered. He was gripped by fear.

"Either one of two things will happen," he supposed. "I'll get out of this situation or I won't. But, truly, if I do get out of it, that will be very lucky, since it seems as if everything is in league against me.'

Everything was, in fact, in league against the courageous young man. The officer dragging him along was particularly hostile and his anger could have serious consequences. Moreover, the direction in which the escort was heading was significant for Jérôme Fandor. Although his knowledge of the neighborhoods of St. Petersburg was imperfect, he was convinced they were taking him to the St. John prison. And Fandor was known at that prison. He would be at the mercy of the slightest incident, the slightest hazard. There, a fortuitous encounter, a careless word could bring about the worst catastrophes.

If, by some misfortune, one of the guards assigned to the men sentenced to death passed by just as Jérôme Fandor was in the prison courtyard, there would be a terrible scandal. Whether he was a brute or a timid man, the guard would be most surprised that one of the convicts who had been executed the previous day was once again a member of the prison population.

It was clear that, if Jérôme Fandor were recognized and if they noticed that the man who had been sentenced to death the previous day was still alive, an investigation would be ordered. And the investigation could not fail to determine how Fandor had been torn from death. They would realize that he was not Vassili Berena and he would be rushed back to the gallows.

Jérôme Fandor grimaced.

"Hmm," he concluded, "I think it would be a good idea to avoid grumbling and stay quiet. It would be best I were to pass unnoticed."

Jérôme Fandor stopped thinking about his own fate, although that fate was indeed horrible, and returned to the last scenes that had played out. How was he to interpret that? What should he conclude? Was it really Hélène who had played the role of Olga on the extraordinary revolutionary tribunal that had just determined his fate? Was it Hélène who had, to a certain extent, so skillfully intervened on his behalf? Strangely enough, Jérôme Fandor was unable to arrive at a decision. Of course, he thought he had recognized his wife. He thought that the woman who had stepped between him and his jailors was, in fact, Hélène. And it would have been natural for Hélène to do so. If Olga was Hélène, the young woman had done everything in her power to save Fandor. And she had done it most skillfully. It would have been impossible for anyone to obtain mercy for the man who had just insulted the nihilists. She had saved him from imminent death.

And, despite himself, Jérôme Fandor felt obliged to say, "Obviously, being sent to the mines is better than a lingering death."

And yet, although Jérôme Fandor said that, if in fact he had noticed that it was Hélène and that Hélène had done her duty, he still felt very hurt by the young woman's attitude. Despite his courage, his valiance or his manly energy, Jérôme Fandor was, in fact, a sentimental poet. He thought that, while saving him, Hélène had remained remarkably calm in his presence. He thought that the young woman he had seen on the revolutionary tribunal had remained completely indifferent to his fate and that, as a result, she could not really be his beloved.

"No!" said Juve's friend. "If Olga had been Hélène, she would have betrayed herself, at least by her eyes. She would have given me a look, a word... No, I was mistaken. That woman did not recognize me!"

Jérôme Fandor preferred to believe that he had been mistaken and that he had not seen Hélène than to admit that his beloved had been completely cold with respect the perils he face. It would have hurt her; she would have found it extremely painful.

But, Jérôme Fandor would have viewed the situation from a completely different perspective if he had known that, for many long weeks, Hélène had carried the most painful, the cruelest, of injuries in her heart. After all, when she had returned from America, had Hélène not seen Jérôme Fandor apparently courting the unfortunate Natacha? Had she not, as a result of Fantômas' cruel infamy, witnessed the kiss Natacha gave Fandor?

Yet, there was more.

Jérôme Fandor did not believe that Hélène had recognized him when, disguised as a servant, he had opened Boris Pokroff's door. Yet Hélène had indeed recognized her husband. She had very clearly seen that Alexis and Jérôme Fandor were one and the same, and that had brought new pain to her heart since, at that moment, she decided that Jérôme Fandor was at Boris Pokroff's house to ask for the hand of Natacha, who he appeared to love, although Hélène had no idea she was dead.

Since Jérôme Fandor could not guess Hélène's feelings, he told himself, "I was wrong. Hélène has no idea of the situation in which I find myself. Hélène is staying peacefully in St. Petersburg. Juve will come. Juve will find her..."

Then Fandor added this unfortunate thought, "Juve will console her..."

The young man had, in fact, little hope of escaping from his terrible fate. As the escort dragged him toward the *ostroghi*, where he would be chained to some other poor devil to be sent like him to the mines, he decided that Siberia was a voracious killer of men. According to the official statistics, in fact, of all those that head out only three percent come back.

The Russian penal colony! Despite himself, Fandor shivered at the thought. He felt lost, lost in the vast world, so far from his loved ones, so far from those who could comfort him, who would at least be interested in his fate, that he felt there was no point in calling on them for help.

Of course, Jérôme Fandor had traveled considerably. On many occasions, he had found himself in terrible circumstances and had had many brushes with death, but his situation had never been quite so bad as at this very moment, as he was about to set out for the Russian penal colony.

Walking for weeks before reaching the goal, putting up with the terrifying closeness of the most degraded assassins, the most infamous wretches, shoulders bruised by the heavy chain that bound the men in the gang together, ankles bleeding from the rubbing of the heavy rings. That was his immediate fate and it would not improve once he reached the penal colony, if he did not die from fatigue and exhaustion along the way.

The Russian penal colony! The pestilential mine from which they took copper. Jérôme Fandor had read descriptions. He knew what kind of hell it was. He could already imagine the narrow winding tunnels the miners had to descend, risking their lives. And he knew that there was a machine gun at the end of each tunnel. He knew the orders. If a single miner rebelled for a single moment, the machine gun would immediately spit out bullets, gunning down entire ranks of convicts.

And that was not the only form of death that hung over the heads of the unfortunate convicts. There were also the guards' clubs and the pestilential fevers.

It was true, as a sadly informed Russian writer had dared to shout in the face of the world: the Russian penal colony was horrific; those sent there are, without fail, condemned to go mad, unless death puts an end to their suffering.

Jérôme Fandor shivered at these thoughts. He trembled with disgust and anger. He wondered how long he could withstand the terrible voyage, the horrible imprisonment. Above all, he was furious at the thought that he had done nothing to deserve such treatment. If he had been able to talk for a few moments with an honest magistrate, not only would he have been absolved, but they would have fallen at his feet, to thank him for unmasking the terrible Fantômas.

Suddenly, Jérôme Fandor stood taller. Up to that point he had walked with his head down. Yet now, he hastened his pace, stood proud and said, "It doesn't matter. I wanted to do my duty. I have no right to complain!"

It took the escort 20 minutes to take him to the *ostroghi*. There everything was in turmoil and the courtyard was filled. Just as people had traveled far and wide to attend Fandor's hanging, there were many curiosity-seekers who wanted to watch the tragic departure of the Tsar's chain gang.

His escort led him over to a group of convicts.

"Stay there!' the officer ordered.

Jérôme Fandor, who realized that all resistance was futile, respected the order. He stood still and looked about at the tragic scene. The departure of a chain gang is always accompanied by horrific details. The atmosphere is uncomfortable, the breeze filled with tears. Those who are leaving know they will not be coming back. Those who watch the men depart know that they will all die.

The convicts instinctively try to maintain an air of pride. They do not want to acknowledge their fear. Among the spectators, there is an involuntary movement of pity and, sometimes even a horrible tendency to crack jokes.

This was the time for society to take its vengeance, the time when honest people, who grew stronger, to take pride in their strength and use it abusively. The convicts who were leaving for Siberia were brought into the courtyard in groups of ten, where they were placed in groups, without much concern for the reasons for their convictions. Simple political prisoners, nihilists being sent to die in Siberia for their opinions, were brought in side by side with murderers who have been saved from the gallows by imperial clemency. They were all very pale. Yet they all tried to smile.

But there came a moment when the most intrepid turned serious, when the most courageous could not help but shiver. When the convicts were brought out of the prison, they were made to stand in rows in front of a large log. It was time to link the chains, to bind the wretches like evil beasts. Each convict was required to place his right foot on the log. The blacksmith would then choose a large iron ring, roughly the size of the man's leg, and heat it until it was red, then white hot. It would be struck with a chisel and opened. Then the man's foot would be placed in the ring and it would be riveted shut.

It was a frightful operation. The blacksmith had to work while the ring was still hot. If the man being chained made the slightest movement, he would be seriously burnt. If he merely trembled, if the blacksmith missed his target, the heavy hammer would pound down on the wretch's ankle, breaking it. Accidents were common. Every time a chain gang set out, four or five men were horribly injured. Many men were crippled for life. Some even died.

Jérôme Fandor knew all this. The horrors that took place before his eyes were not new to him. Yet he could not help but shiver as he watched. Of course, he had never imagined that one day he too would be a convict and that he would have to face the terrible torture of the chain.

It was his turn. The guards called him. His bit his lip and stepped forward. He told himself, "Don't move! My word, this is much more important than having a photograph taken."

To master his nervousness, to dampen his natural fear, he counted the hammer blows.

"One… two… three…"

The blacksmith must have been a skilful man. In any case, he seemed to have a talent for this sinister type of work. His violent blows were regular. Sparks flew from the hot iron and the ring gradually took shape. Just then, suddenly, Jérôme Fandor shivered. A light flashed in his eyes. He frowned, and shrugged imperceptibly.

What was Jérôme Fandor thinking? What extraordinary idea had just run through his mind? The journalist did not move.

In a very low, persuasive voice, he said, "Blacksmith!"

The blacksmith turned his head, hesitating and looking surprise, and said, "What?"

What was Fandor's goal? Why had he spoken to the worker? During the few brief seconds that the blacksmith had stopped working, Jérôme Fandor quickly bent down over the iron ring that would attach him to the chain of men and spit on the iron. Was this a simple gesture of disdain? Was it bravado? Without a doubt the jailers had to think so since they paid it no attention.

The blacksmith trembled, paused for a second, and muttered, "Ah."

His heavy hammer shook in his hands. He looked Jérôme Fandor straight in the eyes. The journalist did not look away. It was an extraordinary moment. But only Jérôme Fandor and the blacksmith knew how tragic it was.

The blacksmith, who had grown pale, shouted, "Stay still!"

And his hammer started to spin in the air and once again fell on the ring.

Jérôme Fandor regained his composure. He was even, if that could be possible, calmer than before and anyone who observed him closely would no doubt have noticed an ironic smile tugging at the corners of his lips.

"So, it's not all over," murmured Fandor.

But what did those words mean? Of course, it was not all over. The chain gang had not even set out.

Jérôme Fandor, his iron ring on his ankle, the ring through which the heavy iron chain had been pulled, was shoved by the guards toward a group of convicts. They were in the same gang, chained to one another, chains slipped through the rings on their right ankles, making them one, linking them to the main chain that connected five such groups.

Naturally, these chains were very heavy. To keep from injuring themselves while walking, the convicts had to carry the chains by hand. Although the burden seemed less heavy if everyone supported a part of the weight, the first few days were still completely exhausting. An abominable torture.

Jérôme Fandor, firmly chained to his group, remained motionless.

Those on the chain looked at him and asked, "Comrade, you're not Russian?"

"No," Fandor replied.

"Comrade, you seem indifferent about your fate?"

"What's the point of complaining?"

"Comrade, you'll be singing a different song in two weeks! We're going to hell!"

Jérôme Fandor shrugged. He had just realized that he had unfortunately been chained to a gang of common criminals. No doubt they had guessed that he was a political deportee and they would add to the torture of the guards by letting him carry most of the chain. It was just another of the cruelties of this terrible trip that was about to start.

The chained men were forced, unfortunately, to put up with the traveling companions the guards gave them. As a result, convicts who hated one another deeply were obliged to travel side by side. The stronger one would oppress the weaker. Every day, bloody dramas played out between people on the same chain.

Jérôme Fandor was not mistaken. Fandor, who generally got along with everyone, who was pleasant to everyone, had the misfortune to be chained to a total wretch, one of those horrible individuals who do not seem to have any redeeming features.

The entire time the departure ceremony lasted, the horrid man sang terrible songs or made obscene jokes. Jérôme Fandor did not pay him too much attention. Yet, when the chain started to move to the beat of the drums that pounded out the departure order, a frightful torture started for the journalist for, in fact and quite naturally, Jérôme Fandor knew nothing of the art of walking on a chain gang. He did not know how to carry his chain; he did not know how to walk without injuring himself. One hundred yards from the prison, Jérôme Fandor's feet were already slick with blood. And that was when his partner cruelly invented a frightful joke.

Just when Jérôme Fandor least expected it, in fact, the brute stopped. He dropped his chain which meant that Jérôme Fandor, who was trying to walk normally, suddenly had a formidable weight to drag. He stumbled; he fell. The guards were never far, always ready to strike with their whips or their guns.

And this might have continued if Jérôme Fandor, who was energy itself, had not suddenly decided, one day, after a certain time, to set things right.

Jérôme Fandor turned around, in fact, and looked at his companion who seemed to take pleasure in harassing him.

"Listen to me," he said with extraordinary calm. "I give you my word as both a prisoner and an honest man. Try to understand. This is serious."

The other man laughed and said, "What? The gentleman wants to preach?"

"No," Fandor replied. "I simply want to warn you about something."

And looking the other man straight in the face, Fandor slowly said, "In exactly five days from now, I will escape. At the moment, my good man, one of two things will happen. Either you continue to act like an imbecile and, in that case, I won't leave here before I bash your head in or you'll be quiet and I'll spare you. You've been warned. Think about it!"

"In five days, you claim to be escaping. But…"

Jérôme Fandor cut him off, "In five days, I'll be leaving."

"How?"

"That's my secret."

"You're crazy."

"Why?"

"There are wolves!"

"I don't care!"

"You'll starve!'

"I don't care!'

"There are the guards…"

"I'll trick them!"

"You won't be able to break your chains."

"Yes, I will!"

"Are you serious?"

"Do I look like I'm laughing?"

The prisoner looked at Jérôme Fandor and fell silent. He did not feel like playing tricks on him. He did not understand, but he admired the dark energy shining in the young man's eyes.

CHAPTER XII
A Profitable Error

The column of convicts was already far from Saint Petersburg. Although, for economic reasons, Russia had kept the system by which prisoners were taken, on foot, to the penal colony, a horrible system which all civilized nations had abolished, it was no less true that the penitentiary administration would, as needed, adopt other processes.

After many lengthy steps, the men had been loaded into miserable cars coupled to the end of a freight train, which had rolled for two days without stopping. With the passing miles, the nature of the landscapes they had traveled through had changed so abruptly that it was impossible to ignore the distance traveled. They had left behind the laughing, wooded plains that surrounded the Russian capital and moved into the deserted, monotonous steppes. The prisoners presumed that icy, deadly Siberia was close at hand.

The cold, which had been tolerable when the chain gang set out, had intensified abruptly, bringing winter, with its horrible pains, procession of suffering and frightful tortures. Snow fell continually, piling up in the convicts' wretched clothing, freezing on the men and forming sharp needles of ice on their hands and necks, without the slightest compassion or pity.

Jérôme Fandor bore with this procession of misfortunes and calamities with his usual carefree attitude. Perhaps, because he was European—and French at that—he felt the cold more than his sinister traveling companions. He let nothing show, however, and took pride in not complaining.

In the train cars into which they had been packed, the men, soaked, half dead, seemed to have fallen into a silent, beast-like stupor brought low by famine and winter.

Only Jérôme Fandor, it should be said, seemed to retain a little bit of energy a presence of mind, a sense of courage. He alone, did not give up. The fire in his eyes revealed that he continued to dream of escaping as he had done so many times before when caught up in tragic circumstances.

His renown, moreover, was starting to spread among the convicts, who seemed to share a strange sense of solidarity. All too often, convicts hate one another. Brawls are not uncommon, murders are even frequent. Yet, the prisoners settle their quarrels among themselves. Certainly, no prisoner has ever called on a guard for protection against another prisoner.

The solidarity of the chain gang lies in the fact that the prisoners join forces when it comes to fooling the guards and Jérôme Fandor was well aware of this. He had even used that feeling, which is common to all galley salves in all countries, to impose silence on his ferocious chain partner, who could not help by be very favorably impressed when he heard the mysterious words Jérôme

Fandor had uttered. Although he had said nothing at the time, he had returned to the matter over and over again since then.

"Is it true," he asked, "That you're going to escape?"

"It's true," Fandor replied.

"You're certain you'll succeed?"

"I am."

"You've calculated the thickness of the shackles?"

"The solidness of my irons is of no interest to me."

"You have ways for dealing with hunger?"

"I will."

"You have weapons for fighting the wolves?"

They had had the same conversation hundreds of times and the entire gang had grown aware of it. Everyone knew that the convict walking in the second group, the cheerful-looking blond man, planned to escape.

The men on the chain gang started to admire Fandor. In any setting, bravery, energy, courage are enough to impose respect and instill admiration.

As soon as Jérôme Fandor posed as a future escapee, those around him started to consider him a leader. And the journalist had no qualms that they would betray him. Although he had plans to escape, there was no danger involved in telling those nearby about them. Prisoners do not betray one another, knowing full well that the slightest betrayal would be punished immediately by death.

The days passed.

Already, 24 hours had passed since they had left the train, and the chain gang found itself in the middle of a dessert, in a country where solitude increased the wild beauty. It was an immense plain, rigorously flat. Snow covered it as far as the eye could see and the horizon was absolutely, blindingly, monotonously white.

At seven each evening, the chain gang stopped. Then, as the harassed men slipped to the ground, with the sole hope of letting their chain rest, of no longer feeling its weight, those who guarded them climbed down from their horses, set up their tents, distributed the meager bread rations to the convicts and then settled down to a good dinner.

Every night, the guards slept in the same tent, taking turns setting it up. They also took turns at guard duty, something they spent little time thinking about since they all agreed that it would be impossible for a convict to escape and that even if one did he would not go far.

Jérôme Fandor had noted all these details. Every night, the people on his chain questioned him. They all knew about the prison colonies in Siberia and were familiar with the bloody history of the chain gang. They provided Fandor with information.

"You want to escape?" said one. "Fine, but take care. Leaving here is not easy. Breaking your chain and escaping is almost impossible. Yet, that's not even the most difficult part. Think about this, comrade. You have to eat and there's nothing in this plain that surrounds us. You have to defend yourself and you have no weapons. Dozens of wolves will hound you."

Jérôme merely smiled his usual ironic, determined smile in response.

"Fine. Thank you. I said that I would leave on the fifth day, so I will!"

They were all filled with curiosity and continued to question the young man, but he remained discreet.

"How will you do that?" they asked.

"You'll see!"

"How will you break your leg irons?"

"That's simple."

"Do you have a saw?"

"No."

"A file?"

"No."

"A chisel?"

"No."

"Some sort of tool?"

"Nothing at all."

And when the questions grew too insistent, Jérôme Fandor merely smiled.

"Comrades, let me sleep. I don't have long before I have to go and I need to save my strength."

Then the hardest scoundrels surrounding the young man would fall silent religiously. They looked at one another, devastated. They were all convinced that their courageous companion was heading for certain death and would have liked to dissuade him.

But Jérôme Fandor was stubborn and, in response to all objections, all comments, simply replied, "I want to leave."

The fifth day arrived. It was even colder than usual and the snow had fallen all night.

Painfully, the column set out. Yet, a fever ran through all of Fandor's companions in misery. They looked at one another, furtively, eyes filled with questions.

All of the convicts felt like Fandor's accomplices, waiting for extraordinary events. They nourished the hope that something unexpected would benefit each of them.

"Will you take someone?" one asked Fandor.

The journalist shook his head and said, "No because I will not be able to break his shackles."

"Yet you can break your own!"

"That's not the same thing."

The column proceeded painfully. Whispers spread through the rank and file.

"When will you leave?"

"Tonight."

"During the night?"

"During the night."

The news raced from one end of the column to the other.

The walk dragged on. They would have to wait to find out how the young man would leave, but waiting seemed intolerable. The skeptics chuckled.

"He lied," people started to say. "You'll see. He won't leave."

And they always brought up the same arguments.

"Good grief, he won't be able to break his shackles. They searched us too carefully at the start. No one has any tools. Not even him. Plus, he'll die from hunger and cold, if the wolves don't get him."

At about noon, one convict roughly said to Fandor, "Look. Don't you know Russia? You'll understand. White plains and still more white plains. Thousands of miles to travel. Snow... cold... that's what will stop you. I once found myself alone, when I was free, in these solitudes. I thought I would die. Stay."

Fandor shook his head and said, "No, I'm going to leave!"

Night fell. The sun had set a long time ago, disappearing below the horizon. The cold and snow intensified. That day, the column set camp early because the guards, despite their warm furs, despite the alcohol they drank, despite the horses that carried them, were broken by fatigue.

The guards set up their tent. They invited the convicts to lie on the ground in groups, then threw a heavy tarpaulin over them. The snow piled up on it, covering them like a blanket.

"Are you leaving?" someone asked Fandor.

Fandor replied, "Soon."

As the minutes passed, each one the same. Fandor gave no hint yet, instinctively, each of his companions in misery knew how to behave. They fell silent, remained still, did not to attract the guards' attention.

At about midnight, however, Jérôme Fandor raised himself part way and said, "Farewell, comrades."

His voice did not shake. Those around him were much more emotional than he was.

"Do you know what you're risking?" they said, yet again.

"I do."

The journalist shook the hands that reached out to him. He was determined and did not hesitate. He preferred death over the torture of the penal colony to which he was headed. Yet the difficulties of escape were just starting.

His chain partner asked, "How will you break your shackles?"

"Like this," Fandor said.

He bent down, lifted his right ankle a little and grasped the ring of iron riveted around his ankle with both hands.

"I'll break it," he said.

But the men around him shrugged since they all knew that the iron rings were solid and that trying to break them was mad. Yet, Jérôme Fandor seemed certain. He held the ring with his hand and struck it sharply with his shoe. Those watching were dumbfounded as they realized that he had barely hit the iron. Yet it was opening! Jérôme Fandor merely had to pull it. How had he broken the ring?

Jérôme Fandor appeared perfectly calm

"Easy as pie," he said.

And he explained: "When the ring was welded around my ankle, I took some precautions. While it was still cherry red, I spit on it. The iron was suddenly cooled by my saliva. I managed to temper it somewhat, making sure that at one point my iron ring was not as solid as it should have been. The slightest blow could break it. Moreover, the blacksmith saw what I did and he said nothing."

No one responded. The young man's explanation was very simple. Yet, it showed an uncommon presence of mind and the convicts instinctively realized that their fellow traveler was much more intelligent than they were. After a few minutes, however, they started questioning Fandor again.

"But, if you were certain that you could free yourself, why did you wait so long before breaking your irons? You could have escaped the first night!"

Jérôme Fandor chuckled and replied, "No. Because they would have set the St. Petersburg police after me. Here, the guards won't think of looking for me. Everyone will presume that I'll die from hunger. I'll be reported dead and that's what I want."

The men fell silent again. Obviously, the other convicts admired the young man.

Yet, one of them asked, "But are you really certain you won't die? How will you deal with hunger, the wolves and the cold?"

Jérôme Fandor smiled and said, "You don't understand the means at my disposal."

"What do you mean?"

"I have a name."

"A name?"

"Yes, a woman's name: Hélène."

Leaving his companions deeply dumfounded, Jérôme Fandor made the most of the night and slipped from under the tarpaulin, crawling through the snow, escaping. He had not lied when he said that, once he was free, all he had to fight against the dangers he faced was Hélène's name. But thinking about his wife, thinking about the woman he adored, he would be able to fight, to conquer, if victory was possible. And Fandor quickly realized that his battle was a colossal one. Yet, luck smiled on him. Just as Fandor slipped out from under the tarpaulin, he had the good fortune to bump into one of the sleighs that accompanied the convoy, filled with provisions.

Jérôme Fandor instinctively thought that it would be a good idea to fill his pockets with a few supplies. He bent over the sleigh, hiding behind it to avoid being seen by the guards watching over it. He managed to climb into the car and there he discovered a crate filled with boxes of tins.

"Hooray!" thought Fandor. "I've got boxes of preserves. The journalist picked up two. He was about to pick up a third when he realized that he had unfortunately made a noise of some kind and a guard was approaching. Remaining near the sleigh any longer would not be a good idea. Jérôme Fandor rushed away

"Well," he thought. "Two large boxes of tins mean I have at least four days of supplies. Well, within four days, I will either have reached a city or been eaten by wolves."

In fact, wolves were turning out to be Fandor's biggest worry. No more than two hours after leaving the chain, Jérôme Fandor turned back and saw the shining eyes of several of the ferocious beasts following him at distance. He shivered.

"So," he thought. "It's started.

Yet he swept away his own fear and continued on his way. He walked five hours without stopping, following the stars, into the steppe. Then he stopped, half paralyzed by the cold. His feet hurt. The injury the shackles had caused to his ankle had opened and was bleeding.

"Let's take a break," Fandor said to himself. "Let's eat and rest."

He sat down in the snow, throwing rocks at the wolves who dared to approach. He opened one of the large boxes of preserves he had carried so painfully since the time of his escape. But after prying a lid off one of the tins, the young man shrieked in anger. Fortune had abandoned the young man. The tins he had carried contained no preserves, just black soap. At that moment, Jérôme Fandor seriously considered hitting his head against the frozen ground in to the put an end to his agony. He knew what had happened. He knew that each sleigh carried large boxes of black soap to be used to grease the blades and prevent snow from building up, which would have made traction much more difficult. Although the explanation came easily enough, it did not advance Jérôme Fandor's cause.

Yet, a few minutes later, he was once again calm, his unlikely courage had returned. He pitched the two boxes of soap into the snow and headed off.

He said, "I'll keep on as long as I have the strength to do so. No one will be able to say that I didn't die fighting."

And five hundred yards from there, Jérôme Fandor was suddenly filled with joy.

"Good grief," he said. "What is that?"

He started to run, like a crazy man. In the smooth snow, he had just noticed a long, characteristic swelling. Like an undulation of the soil, it ran across the entire plain, from one side of the horizon to the other. Jérôme reached the swell and fell to his knees, exhausted.

"My God! My God!' he murmured. "So I will be able to get out of this hell!"

Luck smiled on the young man once again. He had reached the Trans-Siberian track. Yet, this did not guarantee that he would escape. Many, no doubt, would have even thought that escape was still impossible. Jérôme Fandor did not share their opinion. Soon, he stood up and waved his arms like a man in the throes of delirium.

"Saved!" he murmured. "Saved! I have to climb aboard the first train. I have to find a way to hide in the cars. I'll manage!"

Yet, as he uttered those words, his joy suddenly evaporated. As he put his project into words, Jérôme Fandor suddenly realized the difficulties he would encounter. Of course, the train would pass by. He would most certainly see one of the Trans-Siberian trains. But how could he climb on board? How could he jump onto the train that would be speeding past him?

Jérôme Fandor thought. The intrepid journalist recalled that he had once tried to stop a racing train. He was with Bouzille at the time, pursuing Fantômas. Unfortunately, the circumstances were quite different and Fandor could not use the means he had used then. With Bouzille, Jérôme Fandor had operated a siding and signaled the locomotive engineer. This time, there was no siding and not only could Fandor not signal the engineer, he had to avoid catching his attention.

The journalist thought for a long time. He was about to despair when he suddenly started rubbing his hands.

"Well," he said, "I'm about as stupid as they come."

And Jérôme Fandor raced off to pick up the two boxes of black soap he had discarded a few moments earlier. What did he plan? What crazy idea filled his mind?

Jérôme Fandor was perfectly reasonable. He had simply recalled that, in America, bandits had stopped an express train once by greasing the rails with black soap. The wheels of the locomotive slipped and the train stopped. The bandits made the most of the opportunity to rob it.

Jérôme Fandor said to himself, "I'm a lot less demanding. All I want is for the train to slow enough that I can jump on board."

And then Jérôme Fandor spent two long hours coating the rails with black soap over a distance of 150 yards. Once he had finished this exhausting work, he merely had to wait. The waiting seemed long. Night was falling when the whistle of a locomotive tore him from the state of sleep he had gradually fallen into. Jérôme Fandor was on his feet within a second.

"Will I succeed?" he wondered.

The train sped ahead and the journalist's mind filled with doubts. But he was wrong to worry. His plan had been a good one. As the train reached the soaped rails, the wheels of the locomotive started to slide this way and that. Surprised, the locomotive engineer applied the brakes. The train slowed. Fandor could not hope for better.

He ran along the ballast, grabbed on to a freight car with two hands, allowed himself to be dragged, almost fell under the wheels and, with a desperate effort, managed to climb aboard. The car contained freight of all kinds. It was covered with linoleum Jérôme Fandor slipped beneath it.

At that moment, the intrepid young man made a joke, as he usually did in such situations.

"This is fine," thought Fandor. "But I forgot to ask the employees. Which way are we heading? Is the train heading to St. Petersburg or to China?"

Jérôme Fandor did not complete his joke. He had run out of energy. As the train accelerated, he collapsed in the car.

CHAPTER XIII
By the Order of the Tsar

While Fandor, who had miraculously climbed aboard the Trans-Siberian, was traveling in the speeding train, not knowing whether it was taking him to the Russian border or to the distant regions of eastern Asian, other trains throughout the world were crisscrossing countless other tracks. Other trains came and went, slowly or rapidly, carrying an important portion of humanity, constantly in motion. One of those trains that day was the large, weekly convoy, known throughout Europe as the Nord Express.

The Nord Express, which had left Paris the day before, had crossed the Russian border, in the middle of the previous night. The passengers had had to change trains. French railway cars could not travel on the tracks of the Russian empire, since the track gauge was larger in Russia than the rest of Europe.

Yet, this inconvenience, which took place in the middle of a cold, dark night, was more than overcome by the fact that the passengers had entered Russian territory ensconced in comfortable cars where they could end their night in comfort. Day came and the icy, deserted steppes they had crossed, steppes so uniformly white that they filled the surrounding landscape with a poignant touch of monotony, gradually made way for modest-looking houses, followed by small villages and finally towns.

Several people had gathered in the aisle of a first-class car and were looking curiously at the landscape that flew by. Young men and women, elegant, joyous, animated, whose professions were obvious. The men were carefully shaved and their slightest gestures portrayed scope and appeal. The women, with their expressions, figures and graceful, yet seemingly studied voices. Anyone who questioned their profession would have quickly corrected their opinion after glancing at the numerous suitcases and gigantic packages the passengers had accumulated at the ends of the car. Each bag bore a small label, with red letters: Imperial Theatre. It was a troupe of French performers who had come to spend the season in Russia. Most of them had never been to that distant country and they listened, dumbfounded, with a certain amount of respect as one of their colleagues, Mr. Melchior, who usually performed dramatic roles for the Comédie Française, explained, rolling his r's dramatically, how they could manage to live well in Russia.

Turning to the actresses, Mr. Melchior recommended, "And, above all, ladies, take care with respect to the cold. The temperature in St. Petersburg goes down to more than 30 below and the newspapers have predicted a harsh winter."

A pretty blond with delicate skin, Miss Luce, from Vaudeville, looked frightened.

"Good grief!" she said. "I fall ill with the first freeze in Paris. What am I going to do in this frightful country! I already regret signing my contract!"

Melchior started to laugh and said, "I'm exaggerating a bit. The wind is what determines the cold. There's never any wind in Russia and people can withstand very low temperatures without difficulty. You just have to avoid traveling in open carriages or sleighs and you'll make it through the winter without freezing the tip of your nose!"

Melchior stopped talking. A man had just stepped out of a previously closed compartment into the corridor to join in the conversation. He looked jovial, satisfied and enthusiastic.

"My children!" he shouted. "Just another half hour and we'll be in the capital of the Tsars, in St. Petersburg, a city renowned throughout the world. We'll see the magnificent Kremlin, that architectural masterpiece..."

"Excuse me, maestro," Melchior interrupted, smiling. "But the Kremlin is in Moscow!"

The man stopped speaking and looked at Melchior, with an expression that was both dismayed and furious.

Then he continued, "That's not important. St. Petersburg has its own monuments and artistic treasures. We just need to spend time admiring them. Plus, I know what I think of them and I do believe that I'll discuss that matter in my lecture, in a truly new and original manner."

"My dear maestro," Melchior observed again. "Allow me to point out that we'll arrive at the station in 10 minutes and that you are still in your pajamas. It might be a good idea to get dressed. Otherwise, we'll lose a great deal of time when we arrive."

The enthusiastic individual immediately retreated back into his compartment. The performers looked at one another, smiling.

"What a character!" said Madam Aurelia, an elderly actress who had traveled the world for over 40 years and played all of the noble mothers in the repertory.

Melchior, who was obviously the leader of the troupe, replied, "Yes, what a character, no doubt, but what a skillful man!"

"Well, who exactly is that Roger Darmont," Miss Luce asked.

"Oh, that's quite simple," Melchior replied. "A man of letters without any literary baggage, like so many others found on the sidewalks of Paris. He doesn't dare plagiarize the works of others, by appropriating them, because the written word remains and printed materials do get noticed. But, since he has no ideas of his own, he steals those of his colleagues, learns them by heart, and manages, when he can get the right financing, to travel about and repeat them as if they were his own, to any more or less willing, sleepy or snobbish audience. Roger Darmont is an opportunist, everyone's favorite speaker. He has turned speaking into a veritable profession. And unwilling to settle for France and Paris, he has now set out to dazzle foreigners with his avalanche of words. Needless to say, Roger Darmont makes a lot of money doing that!"

The actor was interrupted by the arrival of a newcomer, who listened for a few minutes, smiling through his graying beard. He was another traveler from Paris who had discretely mingled with his compatriots during the trip. He was pleasant to the performers, behaving modestly and correctly, unlike the people who usually revolved around the theatre world. A few hours after their departure from Paris, the gentleman had introduced himself to the actors. His name was Mr. Pol and he was a civil engineer on his way to Moscow for a study trip.

He must have been about 50 at most, although his thick gray beard, made him look older. Yet, the sparkle in his eyes and his lively facial expressions made people think he was a decade younger.

Mr. Pol responded to Melchior's comments, saying, "You're quite hard, dear sir on that poor lecturer! It's natural for someone with the gift of speech to use it."

Melchior protested, "You've never heard him speak? That Roger Darmont replaces oratorical talent with a skill for elocution that has nothing to do with the talent that made Cicero and, more recently, Lachaud so renowned. But you can judge for yourself if, as I presume, you are to be in St. Petersburg when he'll give his famous lecture for which he is to be paid 4000 rubles."

Mr. Pol shook his head and replied, "Unfortunately, I won't be able to attend his conference. I have to leave for Moscow this very evening and it is for that reason that, before I leave the train, I have come to bid you farewell."

This was a real surprise and the entire troupe was desolated.

What? Mr. Pol wouldn't even spend 48 hours in St. Petersburg! They would not enjoy the pleasure of seeing him at the Imperial Theatre! He was about to disappear suddenly! To head deep into the heart of Russia!

The women, in particular, were devastated. During the trip, Mr. Pol had been so pleasant, gracious and respectful toward them, charming them. A few of them even nursed secret hopes of developing more intimate relationships with him at some later point.

In vain, Melchior attempted to convince the engineer to delay his departure by 48 hours. But Mr. Pol, who appeared sincerely upset by having to refuse, stuck to his plans.

At that moment, Roger Darmont came back out of his compartment and walked over to shake Mr. Pol's hand. The speaker had dressed as he saw fit to face the rigorous temperature. He had placed an enormous astrakhan hat on his head and tossed three or four fur-lined cloaks on his back, along with a cape, which was also fur-lined. Sweat rolled down his scarlet face.

"So I won't be cold," he shouted.

The group smiled as they looked at him.

Melchior placed a hand on the man's shoulder and said, "Really, you exaggerate dear fellow!"

Only after he had been assured that two cloaks were enough did Roger Darmont decide to go and remove the rest of his clothing.

"That's it," he said, confiding in Mr. Pol, "It's essential that I avoid catching cold. My voice is like Sarah Bernhardt's, worth its weight in gold. Can you imagine they are paying me 4000 rubles to speak for an hour! It's true that I have an audience unlike others. His Majesty the Tsar will hear me speak along with the entire imperial family. I'll be seeing the Head of Protocol about that matter this afternoon. I'll also meet with the French ambassador. Can you imagine, Mr. Pol, speaking before the emperor is an extraordinary, formidable opportunity! I'll try to make the most of the circumstances to get him to invite our pleasant traveling companions, who are to join the Imperial Theatre, to perform in his private theatre."

The train had slowed and, as they saw numerous tracks and cars on either side of the train, the group realized they were approaching the station.

"We're here!" shouted Melchior.

And, in the general hustle and bustle in the car, the actors exchanged warm, hasty handshakes with the engineer who was about to leave them. Roger Darmont clasped Mr. Pol's arm.

The speaker hastily scribbled a few lines in pencil on his business card, then handed it to the engineer, saying, "Here's my address in St. Petersburg. I hope to hear from you. Since you're going to Moscow, why don't you try to organize a little conference for me there? Tell the gentlemen in that city that I have some very interesting things to say and that I'll come for 1000 rubles. Naturally, there will be 200 in it for you."

Mr. Pol thanked him, laughing, and said, "I don't handle that kind of business. But if the opportunity arises, I'll willingly perform that service."

Finally, the train headed into a large, glass covered hall and slowly stopped at the edge of a platform. Curious heads peaked through the door as the corridor was invaded by a series of individuals with long, blond beards and square shoulders. The station porters.

Once again, they exchanged warm farewells, promising to meet again, and then each person set out to take charge of their luggage and prepare for their imminent departure from the train and the trip to the hotel.

Mr. Pol, who was traveling with nothing more than a small suitcase, quickly obtained permission from the customs authorities to leave the station where the Nord Express had deposited him. Yet, in the station, he seemed to hesitate for a few moments, walking back and forth.

Then he said to himself, "The performers are going to the French Hotel. I must not go there."

He dug through his pocket, took out Roger Darmont's business card and continued, "That imbecile said he was staying at the Neva Hotel. Why shouldn't I go there after all? The important thing is for him not to recognize me!"

So, Mr. Pol was not heading to Moscow as he had announced and was planning to stay in St. Petersburg? That was, in fact, true.

Once he had decided to stay at the Neva Hotel, he waved for a carriage, gave the address to a large, potbellied driver who understood only a few words of French and stepped into the cab.

If the driver had paid any particular attention to the passenger who had climbed into his vehicle he would have been most surprised. At the station, he had picked up a man in his fifties, face hidden behind a gray beard. Yet, when they reached the hotel, a much younger, clean-shaven man climbed out.

The man who arrived at the station ordered the door man to pay for the carriage, then headed directly to the office and asked to speak with the manager. After a few moments of conversation, the hotel manager escorted the guest personally to his room.

After settling the man in, the manager said, "Rest assured, Mr. Juve, that your privacy will be respected. I'm registering you under your real name, because that is required by law, but the personnel will know you only as the man in room 22."

That's fine, my friend," the new arrival said. "Don't worry. I won't forget you, if you ever need the protection of the French embassy or myself."

The man who had arrived in St. Petersburg in this manner, who had traveled with a fake beard, who had told everyone his name was Mr. Pol and that he was an engineer traveling to Moscow, was none other than Juve, who had taken the precaution of hiding his identity from the time he had left Paris and had firmly decided to remain in St. Petersburg!

"Would Her Imperial Highness, the Grand Duchess Ekaterina do me the honor of seeing me?"

It was four in the afternoon. Juve, who was shivering despite his cape since he had traveled a long way by sleigh, stood in front of the gate of a superb property built in the middle of a garden in the luxurious neighborhood of St. Petersburg, next to the islands.

A gigantic doorman, wearing a superb uniform, who could have been mistaken for a division general, replied to Juve's question in French.

Shrugging, he chuckled and said, "Her Imperial Highness does not deal with peddlers and if you want to see her you will need a letter for a hearing."

"You my dear man," thought Juve, "You're a little sure of yourself. I'll deal with you!"

Juve took a sealed letter from his pocket, threw it at the giant and said, "Take this to your mistress, moujik, and hurry because I don't intend to spend long standing here in this snow."

The tall giant understood Juve's order, particularly since Juve had slipped a few rubles into the doorman's palm. The man bowed low, stammered a bit as he looked at Juve and said, "Forgive me, Your Excellency!"

Then he ran as fast as he could, entering the property through the servants' door.

A few minutes later, the main door to the elegant home opened. Two lackeys stepped out, walked toward Juve, and invited him obsequiously to enter the house. The policeman did not have to be asked twice. Although there was no wind outside, he was shivering, chilled by his sleigh ride. The servants took Juve's cape, wiped the polished boots he wore and escorted him into a vast parlor where a large fire burned in the hearth.

One of the men bowed low and said, "Her Imperial Highness, the Grand Duchess Ekaterina, will be with you immediately.

"Tell her not to rush," said Juve. "I have time."

The policeman was most interested in the décor of the room in which he found himself. The parlor was furnished with the best of taste, in an 18th-century French style. Masterpieces hung on the walls and, with the exception of two or three minor mistakes which indicated they were in a foreign country, Juve found the elegant and distinguished influence of French taste in the home of the Russian duchess.

The policeman did not have time to observe the details of the room further. A door opened, followed by the rustling of skirts, and a woman entered. Juve bowed to her, astonished by her radiant beauty. It was the Grand Duchess Ekaterina.

Graceful, charming and simple, she walked over to the man, hand outstretched. She was smiling and looked very Parisian. With a wave of her hand, she motioned him to sit on a small sofa opposite her. She sat in a Louis IV chair that suited her fine and distinguished figure perfectly. She spoke French perfectly and talked with Juve about his trip and Paris for a few moments.

"When did you arrive, sir?" she asked.

"This very morning, Madam," replied the policeman. "I took a brief time to settle in and then came over here immediately, at your service."

Up to this point, the conversation had been banal and ordinary like all those conversations that take place in so many parlors around the world, in the early evening. But, suddenly, when she heard Juve say that he was at her service, the Duchess Ekaterina seemed to recall why she had summoned the policeman. She frowned, the expression in her eyes grew wild, and her cheeks turned a pale red.

Then she looked down and murmured, "I must have had absolute trust in you, Mr. Juve, to have sent you such telegram, using such clear and open language!"

Juve nodded without replying. He shared her opinion. He recalled that the telegram he had received, in which the Grand Duchess Ekaterina demanded that he come immediately to protect someone she loved more than life itself.

However, Juve replied, "I hope that your Highness will not come to regret the trust she has shown in me. I rushed here as soon as I received her invitation, but I do wonder just how I can be of use to Your Highness since I know little about Russia, having only been here once before for a few days. Yet, I'll do my best to ensure your satisfaction, madam."

The duchess walked over to Juve.

In a low voice, she explained, "For some time now, my existence has been no more than an existence. I'm always worried, always concerned. I'm afraid, not for myself but for the man I love. He has the most renowned, the most exposed position in the empire. He is hated by many and a good number of his predecessors have perished at the hands of fanatics. People in Russia say that when His Majesty does you the honor of appointing you to be the chief of his secret police, he is signing your death sentence. Sir, the man I love, the man who is my lover, Boris Pokroff, is the chief of the secret police. Now you understand why I constantly worry for his life, which is perpetually threatened, why I want to do everything possible to ensure that he is protected. Please tell me that you will help me?"

"You've used the right word," said Juve. "I will help you. By that I mean that I will give you my full support as long as you will give me yours in return. The protection I must provide for Mr. Boris Pokroff, in order to be effective, must be secret. Even he must be unaware that I am watching over his life."

"You may be right," said the duchess. "But how will we proceed? He is always on his guard and if he sees anyone lurking around him the first thing Boris will do is to have that person arrested!"

"So," continued Juve, "I will have to follow him without being seen."

"Is that possible?" asked the duchess.

Juve looked her straight in the eye for a few moments, as if trying to peer into her innermost thoughts. Then he said, "It's possible."

"Oh!" said the duchess, dumbfounded, and then she pressed on and asked, "How will you do that? What is your plan?"

"Well," said Juve. "That's my little secret. And since you have granted me your trust, madam, give it to me fully and allow me to act as I see fit."

Disappointment swept briefly over the face of Boris Pokroff's mistress, but she did not insist. She was already very pleased that Juve had responded to her call. She trusted in him, knowing his reputation and skill. Despite the fact that she was a grand duchess, she would never have considered giving orders to a man such as Juve, a man who she could count on to protect the man she loved so ardently.

Juve questioned the Duchess Ekaterina for a long time, obtaining information about Boris Pokroff's private and public life, about those around him, about his relationships. Although he asked a great many questions, Juve provided little information about himself and did not even give the duchess his address. Juve had decided to be cautious.

Was the duchess sincere or was she setting a trap for him? What did she really want with respect to Boris Pokroff?

"What a strange man this Boris Pokroff is," Juve thought. "A police chief who needs to call on other policemen for protection."

Once he had obtained the information he needed, Juve changed the direction of the conversation.

"Your Highness," he said suddenly, "During your conversations with Boris Pokroff, have you heard anything about a certain mysterious matter that is upsetting the authorities of St. Petersburg?"

The duchess smiled vaguely.

"There are many matters," she said. "Many matters that disturb the Russian police."

"Let me be more specific," said Juve. "Is there something about the theft of a necklace made of extremely rare diamonds and pearls that belongs to someone very highly placed in the court?"

Juve, who had only the vaguest idea about the famous treasure that was to be protected, based on what Fandor had said in his telegram, had asked the question purely by chance and was exceedingly pleased with the response to his question.

As the last words left his mouth, the Duchess Ekaterina jumped up and said, "But that's the Tsarina's necklace!"

"Excuse me," said Juve, who thought he had heard incorrectly. "What?"

The duchess continued, "The Tsarina. That's how we refer to Her Majesty the Empress Alexandra, the emperor's wife, the Tsarina, if you prefer."

"Perfect!" said Juve.

The duchess asked him, "But how did you know about that? How did you hear the mysterious and secret rumors that have barely traveled beyond the walls of the imperial palace?"

Juve merely cocked his head and said, "A policeman must know everything, madam and I'm pleased that I brought up this matter since you already know about it. Can you provide a few details?"

"My God," said the Duchess Ekaterina. "I hardly know what's happening! The only thing I do know is that His Majesty the Tsar has informed Boris Pokroff on numerous occasions that he was concerned about the empress's necklace. An audacious thief let people know, I have no idea how, that he intended to steal the necklace, at any cost!"

"Ah!" said Juve. "And, of course, no one knows that name of that thief."

"Well…" the duchess said, hesitating.

"Yes?" said Juve.

"Well," continued Ekaterina, "The bandit did not give his name, but rumor at court has it that he would be Fantômas!"

"That comes as no surprise," Juve said calmly.

Then he asked, "Where is the empress' necklace?"

The duchess replied, "Boris Pokroff told me that the royal family always takes it with them whenever they travel. And the Tsar and his wife travel constantly out of fear of attacks. They're currently at Tsarskoye Selo, I presume."

Juve interrupted, "Then that's where the necklace must be.

It was night when Juve returned to the Neva Hotel and slipped quietly into the room he had reserved. As soon as he entered the room, his attention was caught by an envelope with a large black seal, placed in clear view on his table. Nothing was written on the envelope and Juve hesitated to open it. He called for a servant.

"Who brought this envelope here," he asked when the servant had arrived.

"I don't know, sir."

"I had left instructions that no one was to enter my room," Juve replied, tersely.

The valet protested, "I swear, sir, that no one entered your room. I never stepped out of the hallway all afternoon."

"Fine," said Juve, dismissing the servant.

A few minutes later, he turned the enveloped over and over with his fingertips, then suddenly broke the seal. It contained a single piece of blank paper. Juve smiled enigmatically.

"Good grief," he said. "I should have known."

He did not appear to be overly surprised by this strange document and simply carried it over to the radiator. Gradually, the paper contracted under the effect of the heat and writing appeared.

As he read the letter, Juve clenched his hands:

Juve, you're too late and I'm so certain of victory that I will let you know what is going on. Tomorrow evening between 11 pm and midnight, I will take the empress' necklace despite everything you might to do prevent me.

The outrageous document was signed: *FANTÔMAS.*

Despite everything, Juve was moved and very impressed by the letter he had just received.

Fantômas seldom corresponded with Juve in ordinary times and this new technique, essentially a declaration of war, was not one commonly used by the criminal mastermind.

"What trap is he hiding?" Juve wondered.

And, purely out of a sense of contrariness, he was almost tempted to doubt the authenticity of this declaration, except for the fact that it confirmed to a certain extent the conversation he had a few hours earlier with the Duchess Ekaterina, about the necklace in question.

Juve thought about the situation for a good hour before concluding, "I have to go to Tsarskoye Selo tomorrow between 11 pm and midnight. But how will I be able to get into the heavily protected palace without revealing my identity?"

Of course, Juve could have easily obtained permission to enter the famous palace, but that would have involved revealing his position, something he did not want to do. He had to find some subterfuge to reach his goal.

"What should I do?" the policeman wondered.

Suddenly, the hand he had plunged into his pocket, to pull out a pack of cigarettes, encountered a small card, which Juve automatically pulled out. It was Roger Darmont's business card.

"That imbecile," Juve grumbled. "I had forgotten all about him."

He threw the card across the room, sighed and said, "That man has all the luck. He's going to Tsarskoye Selo tomorrow! He'll be in the palace between 11 in the morning and midnight. He won't have any problem getting in. Whereas I..."

But Juve suddenly lost his usual calm and violently struck the table.

"What an idiot, I am!" he said, smiling. "And to think I never even considered this solution. It may be a bit brutal, but the end justifies the means!"

With that Juve rushed over to his suitcase, took out a large metal box that held make-up, wigs, and fake beards and then walked over to the washroom.

An hour later, a traveler, who had been sleeping deeply in one of the rooms in the Neva Hotel, awoke suddenly. Someone was knocking at the door.

"Who is there?" he asked, voice thick with sleep.

"Open the door," came the reply.

The traveler, none other than the lecturer, Roger Darmont, leapt from his bed and headed for the door, asking, "What do you want and who has sent you?"

"By the order of His Majesty the Tsar!" a voice replied.

Roger Darmont opened the door immediately.

A man stood there, wearing a large cape, and a Russian hat pulled down over his eyes. A long blond beard flowed over his chest.

The man touched the visor of his hat and said, "Get dressed immediately, sir and come with me. By the order of the Tsar."

Roger Darmont was dumbfounded. He knew that one had to be prepared for anything when you made yourself available to the autocrats, but he was somewhat mortified that such a boor had come to wake him in the middle of the night. He attempted to question the man, but he pretended not to understand much French. When Roger Darmont was ready, the mysterious man took him by the arm.

"Let's go down right away," he said.

And since Roger Darmont continued to hesitate, he repeated the magical words, "By the order of the Tsar."

They jumped into a cab and the mysterious man ordered the driver to take them to the station.

"That's what I thought," the lecturer thought. "We're obviously heading for Tsarskoye Selo."

In vain, he attempted yet again to question the man with the blond beard, but he was a terrible brute and it was impossible to drag anything out of him.

Roger Darmont fell into a scornful, snobbish silence, promising himself that he would relate the strange tale of being roused in the middle of the night and of his even stranger trip to the Paris newspapers once he returned to France.

The coach stopped at the station, which was almost deserted at that time. Yet, a train was preparing to leave and Roger Darmont, who was pacing up and down the platform while waiting for his traveling companion to obtain tickets, learned, from reading the signs, that it was an express train heading for the German border.

"That's not our train," he thought.

But, to his great surprise, the man with the blond beard returned just then and invited him to enter a compartment in the train. Whenever Roger Darmont asked for explanations, the mysterious man replied, "By the order of the Tsar!"

The locomotive whistle blew. The lecturer was in the car and his traveling companion was standing on the step.

Roger Darmont lost his temper and said, "But what does all this mean? I want to know where you are taking me. You're always talking about some order from the Tsar, but what exactly is that order?"

Then and only then the man with the blond beard took a piece of paper from his pocket. He handed it to the lecturer without saying a word.

It read:

Order of the Tsar, given to all representatives of the police of the Russian empire, to expel, as quickly as possible, outside the borders, French lecturer Roger Darmont, who harbors wicked thoughts about Their Majesties! Any resistance on the part of Roger Darmont must be met with force. Signed...

Roger Darmont was unable to read anymore.

"But that's not true!" he shouted. "I never thought anything bad about the Tsar and the empress! I protest!"

However, as he spoke, he backed further into the car, as the man with the blonde beard took a revolver from his pocket and aimed it at him. Roger Darmont collapsed on a seat in the compartment.

"These savages are crazy!" he grumbled. "Well, they can rest assured that I will not resist. I won't make any effort to stay here! And I fully intend to head for the border. I will only feel at ease once I've left this abominable country."

The locomotive whistle blew again and the train set off. On the station platform, the man with the blond beard watched the train for a long time, until it disappeared on the horizon. Then he slowly walked off.

"I do believe that I handled that rather well. Our man took fright and will not try to come back, at least not within the next 48 hours. That's the important thing. I don't need more time than that."

CHAPTER XIV
The Diamond Necklace

It was 9:30 in the evening. Colonel Sarkov, the great chamberlain of the imperial palaces, was standing in an antechamber when he suddenly straightened up, raised a hand to his astrakhan hat, and remained perfectly motionless.

The Tsar had just entered the hallway. He was coming out of his private apartments where, after a dinner that had taken place in absolute privacy, he gone to put on the uniform of a division general.

Nicolas II was in town clothes and was wearing, with a certain amount of elegance, the dark, sober uniform of the Don Cossacks

He turned to Colonel Sarkov and asked, "Is everything ready?"

"Yes, sire!" the officer replied. "I prepared His Majesty's sleigh and my secretaries are writing telegrams to be sent to the newspapers to confirm what has already been written up, namely that our Little Father will not attend the conference to be given this evening by the French man of letters at the Tsarskoye Selo private theatre, before the performance by the Imperial Theatre troupe."

The Tsar looked satisfied.

"Fine," he said. "Go and give the order to my sleigh to set out and tour the park for two hours."

Colonel Sarkov looked surprised and said, "Your Majesty..."

But the Tsar interrupted him, "You must understand that if I make an announcement to the St. Petersburg press telling them that I am going to tour the park all night by sleigh, that's because I have no intention of doing so. I told them that I would not be going to the theatre so that is where I will be going."

The colonel was used to the sort of the decisions the emperor occasionally made when he was afraid, as he so often was, that he was the victim of some plot or some conspirator. Moreover, the emperor had quickly disappeared while the colonel was following his orders. He walked into a room where a few ladies in waiting waited for the empress. They all stood up when they saw the Tsar come in and curtsied deeply.

Nicolas II responded with a slight nod of his head, then waved at one of the ladies. She walked over.

"Countess," he asked, murmuring in her ear, "Which box is reserved for me in the theatre?"

The countess replied, "As usual, I reserved the front imperial box for your Majesty. The ladies and the grand duchesses will be able to sit there."

The emperor interrupted her, saying, "The grand duchesses can sit there on their own. I will sit alone in the gated proscenium."

"Your wish is my command," said the countess, bowing to the ground.

The Tsar, however, who was thoroughly familiar with all of the hallways in the palace, opened a door hidden in a wall, and entered a small room where three men were working around a table.

Nicolas II tapped one of them on the shoulder and the man leapt up.

"Michel," the Tsar said. "Go and make sure that Colonel Sarkov ordered my sleigh to drive around the park for two hours, without stopping. Come and give me your report in the theatre."

The man, an agent of the emperor's secret police, immediately left the room. His two companions seemed to have heard nothing of the conversation.

As he was leaving, the Tsar called out to one of the two remaining men, saying, "Petroff, go see the countess in charge of the theatre. Instruct her to reserve the box to the left, opposite the gated proscenium, for me when I go to attend the performance in ten minutes."

Petroff headed out and the Tsar returned to the room. Sitting next to the man who continued to work, he murmured in his ear, "What attack is being planned against me?"

No one would have recognized Boris Pokroff, the head of the secret police, in the individual, who had been working at the agents' table. Boris Pokroff was an expert in the art of disguise and his subordinates, when they saw him seated next to them, had no idea he was in fact their chief.

Boris smiled and said, "Your Majesty has no need for concern. There will be no attack against him. The only thing you have to worry about is the empress' necklace, in case some audacious thief plans to steal it."

The Tsar hesitated a moment, thinking, then said, "I want to believe you. But I advise you to pay closer attention. Don't forget to watch over my private office, where the necklace is being kept. Also, promise to keep an eye on Michel and Petroff."

"I trust both officers," replied Boris.

"You can never trust anyone," said the Tsar. "Be careful!"

He left, walked back across the hallway, where he had met Colonel Sarkov a few minutes earlier, and slowly head toward the theatre, taking an inner passageway.

He entered a type of lounge where a number of guests had gathered. Everyone fell silent when the Supreme Sovereign of all the Russias appeared. Then an absolutely beautiful woman appeared, walked over to him, curtsied and kissed his hand.

The Tsar helped her up with a friendly smile.

"Good evening, Ekaterina!" he said. "You look particularly lovely this evening. I congratulate you on your ability to remain eternally young."

"Your Majesty, is really too kind," said the duchess. "I'm happy that I've pleased you. Of course, I haven't suffered from the passage of time much since I haven't turned 30 yet."

A chamberlain approached, bowed very low and asked, "Should I order the performance to start as soon as your Majesty is present?"

"Order them to start," declared the ruler. "I'll go to the theatre when it pleases me and I don't want anyone to notice my presence there."

As the chamberlain walked away, the Tsar offered his arm to his cousin the duchess and asked her, in a voice filled with emotion, "What do you want to say to me Ekaterina? You indicated that you wanted to talk with me?"

The guests left the room, entered the theatre and the curtain rose, revealing the actors who had been waiting for more than two hours for the performance to start. They had been instructed to be ready for 8:00 that evening and it was now 10:00. They were not surprised by the delay knowing full well that, in the case of performances given before sovereigns, the starting time, as well as the ending time, were determined by those who attended.

The Tsar, after hesitating, finally decided to sit in a box, renouncing his earlier plans. Nicolas II was driven by caution and the perpetual fear that some assassin would find out where he was and attack his august person. The man, a powerful man among other powerful men, was constantly overwhelmed by the thought that he could not trust anyone and that, in order to ensure his safety, he had to have his police force continuously monitored by a counter-police force and that the counter-police had to be watched by other policemen!

As he entered the box, which he had selected at the last minute, he spoke to a tall lackey who stood in the doorway, murmuring, "Above all, don't forget to find out what Boris, the colonel, Michel and Petroff are all up to!"

The large lackey was also a member of the Tsar's police force and he left, to keep an eye on his colleagues, knowing full well that he too was being watched.

In the box, alone with the emperor, the duchess said, "Majesty, that policeman, Juve, has finally arrived in St. Petersburg."

The Tsar sighed in satisfaction.

"I'm very pleased," he said. "I have been assured that this inspector from the French Sûreté is very competent. And I am reassured by the thought that he may be able to support the efforts of our police force which is sorely overworked since we have been threatened by Fantômas' sinister proclamations."

The duchess agreed with her august cousin and said, "His Majesty can be at ease. Moreover, I have a good piece of news for him. Juve, with whom I spoke this very afternoon, is in the theatre this evening."

"Here?" the Tsar said, surprised.

"Here," the duchess replied.

"That's impossible," said the Tsar.

"May His Majesty forgive me for contradicting him, but Juve is not a boastful man. He promised me that he would attend the performance and he will certainly be here."

The Tsar turned pale.

"So," he stammered, "We have been betrayed if Juve is in the theatre! I checked the guest list myself. There is no one in the group of people present this evening that I do not know, at least by sight."

Maliciously, the duchess found the Tsar's concern amusing.

"Don't worry, your Majesty, Juve is here."

The Tsar leaned over the edge of the box, looked through his opera glasses and grumbled, "I wager, Duchess, that Juve is not here and that he will not appear here this evening."

The duchess did not insist. The curtain rose, revealing a table covered with a green tablecloth. The traditional glass of water stood on it. The audience waited a few minutes in silence and then burst into applause. A man in a suit had just appeared. He bowed respectfully to the audience, sat down behind the table with the green tablecloth and started to speak.

"August Majesty, Imperial Highness, ladies and gentlemen."

They murmured his name.

It was, in fact, the lecturer, Roger Darmont.

The topic he spoke on did not want for originality and entailed no danger. He spoke about the effect growing flowers had on the public mind. And the lecturer proposed to demonstrate that the profession an individual practiced, whether rough or gentle, determined whether they would be violent or stable. He intended to conclude that if everyone set about growing flowers, all mankind would be more peaceful, gentler.

The Tsar was not listening.

Opera glasses glued to his face, he examined the faces in the theatre one by one. That task lasted took him about 20 minutes, after which, Nicolas II, satisfied with his work, turned to his neighbor and triumphantly declared, "I've won my bet, duchess, and I can assure you that your Juve is not here!"

The duchess was starting to lose her assurance. She too had realized that Juve was not there. She was quite vexed that she had backed the promise given by a French policeman to the Tsar. Ekaterina was also worried for herself and for her lover. If Juve was not there, that was the first failure. Should they continue to trust in a man who had failed as of his first appearance at court? She grew anxious. Initially she had listened to the lecture with only half an ear. Yet, gradually, she took in the man's words and seemed dumbfounded by what she heard.

"Well," said the speaker in a voice both inspired and convinced. "What a pity it is that our wishes have not been fulfilled, that in the large empires, which serve as the keystone of the civilized world, we simply have not started growing roses. I know more than one sovereign who would benefit enormously from taking up this inoffensive and relaxing activity, while those same rulers, who settle for developing their armies, increasing their fleets, taxing their people, deserve to be called tyrants!"

As soon as the word had been uttered, a deadly, icy silence fell over the theatre. The Tsar made a motion with his hand and two enormous guards, who had been standing on either side of the stage, rushed over to the lecturer, pulled him up from his chair, and carried him backstage as the curtains fell.

The speaker had just committed a serious mistake. People in the audience murmured that he had committed treason and were concerned about the consequences his subversive comments would certainly have.

The Tsar, who had grown quite pale, turned to the duchess and said, "Truly, your Juve would have done well to have been here, if only to close that boor's yap."

The Tsar stood up and left the box. The duchess, who had also grown pale, followed. Suddenly the agent, Michel, appeared before the furious emperor.

"What is it?" the Tsar asked, quivering. "Have we been betrayed?"

"By all the holy images," the agent stammered. "I swear to the Little Father that, if he has been betrayed, it was not by me and that I would deserve to be hanged a hundred times if the thought even crossed my mind."

"So, what have you come to tell me?" asked the emperor.

"I dare not say," Michel said.

"Speak!" Nicolas II ordered.

"Well, your Majesty," the agent said, trembling. "There's a Juve who wants to speak with your Majesty."

"Really!" said the Tsar. "Well have him taken to my private office."

"But that's impossible," Michel replied.

A glance from the Tsar silenced him and the police officer turned about, a panicked expression on his face.

The crowd of guests had spread to the lounge, but not quickly enough to meet the Tsar who had returned to his private chambers and headed for his private office, still followed by the duchess. Yet, as he walked along the hallway on his way to the room where he was to meet June, he heard a great hubbub. He retreated, slipped behind a tapestry and eavesdropped.

The two guards, who had arrested the speaker, were dragging him down the hallway by his collar when Michel appeared in front of them.

"Order of the Tsar!" he declared. "Juve is to be taken to the Tsar's private office.

The guards shrugged, laughing, and said, "You've had too much to drink, Michel, and giving an order you most certainly have not received could cost your dearly."

But Michel insisted, "The Little Father ordered it. I swear!"

Then, as the guards realized that Michel was not drunk, they hesitated a second, before abruptly setting off with their prisoner once again.

The Tsar realized that they were taking the man to his office. Justifiably worried, he glanced at the duchess, who was standing nearby.

"Are you afraid, Ekaterina?" he asked.

The duchess protested, "No! I'm never afraid when I'm with your Majesty, even along the road to death…"

"We all travel that road," the Tsar replied. "But come with me anyway."

Agent Petroff appeared at that moment.

"Majesty," he started. "I did what was needed."

The Tsar interrupted him impatiently, saying, "You're not supposed to do what's needed. You're supposed to handle the unexpected!"

Then he murmured in Petroff's ear, "Petroff, I put you in charge of watching Michel who must be planning to betray me. Give me your report in an hour."

An awful din greeted the Tsar when he entered his private office. Two guards were pummeling the unfortunate lecturer who, without retaliating, was trying to escape from their brutality.

The duchess had entered the cabinet first and as soon as he saw her, the lecturer cried out, "Madam! Please! Get these men away from me."

When she heard that voice, the duchess trembled, turned to the emperor and said, "I beg you, Majesty, order these men out of the room and let us stay alone with this man."

Although the duchess' request seemed odd, her tone of voice was so convincing that the Tsar ordered the two guards out.

As they left, he ran over to them and instructed, "Stay behind the door and at the slightest cry from me, grab the duchess and take her to prison."

The Tsar turned back to his cousin. Up to this point, he had trusted her. She was perhaps one of the only people in his entourage with whom he could speak openly. But, suddenly, the Tsar was filled with terror at the idea that even his own relative might want to betray him. As a result, he had taken the precaution of ordering the officers who had brought the audacious lecturer to his cabinet, to keep a close watch.

The Tsar had accompanied the guards to the door and when he turned back, he cried out in surprise. The man standing before him was no longer the old lecturer with his curved back, limp legs, and thick beard, but a strapping, robust, clean-shaved, energetic man with a lively and sincere gaze.

The grand duchess, who was once again serene, bowed deeply and said to her cousin, "Your Majesty, allowed me to present Inspector Juve."

Stunned, the Tsar said, "Juve! And what about the lecturer?"

"They were one and the same, Majesty," the duchess hastened to say. "Mr. Juve has just explained to me that, in order to get into Tsarskoye Selo, this evening, he had to take the place of Roger Darmont, the lecturer you authorized to speak here."

"What an interesting subterfuge," the Tsar said.

Frowning, he continued, "It is obvious that Mr. Juve is not used to speaking and that his comments are so subversive they deserve an exemplary punishment!"

Humbly, Juve replied, "I sincerely apologize, your Majesty but I uttered those subversive words in order to force my arrest and interrupt both the lecture and the performance."

"You wanted to be arrested?" shouted the emperor.

"I did, sire. Time was passing…"

"What does this mean," asked the Tsar.

"It means that since your Majesty had been warned that Fantômas would steal the empress' necklace which is hidden in the office, between 11:00 pm and midnight, I had to find some reason to get into the office before 11:00 pm. I'm here now and it is only 10:55. I promise your Majesty that Fantômas will not steal the necklace if it is still in its hiding place at this moment!"

"Bravo!" shouted the Tsar. "You've done well, Mr. Juve and I acknowledge that you deserve to be the king of policemen."

The emperor took the key from his pocket, opened a safe hidden in the wall. He noted with satisfaction that it contained the Tsarina's superb necklace. He was about to close the safe when Juve intervened.

"Allow me," he said. "Leave the safe open. In that way, we will be able to keep our eyes on the necklace until midnight."

The duchess was satisfied with the turn the discussion had taken and addressed the Tsar, "Does your Majesty believe that we can trust in Mr. Juve's skill, in his genius if I do say so?"

"I do," replied the Tsar. "Moreover, the manner in which Mr. Juve obtained an audience with me was most original. I might just hire the newspapers to relate it tomorrow. That would make Fantômas think, teach him that if he continues to attack us, we will deal with him harshly."

"Don't do that," said Juve.

"Is he joking?" asked the Tsar, who did not like to be contradicted.

Juve realized that and apologized, saying, "I merely meant, your Majesty, that I have a plan to present. After You Majesty hears it, you might not want to reveal anything to the press."

"So be it," said the Tsar. "I'm listening."

This time, in order to show just how much he trusted Juve, the Tsar indicated to the duchess that she was to leave, and, as she was on her way, he murmured to her, "Find Colonel Sarkov and instruct him to watch over the door to my office, not the one the guards are watching, but the other one. He is to be prepared, at my call, to arrest this Juve. He may be a traitor, after all."

That was exactly like the Tsar who constantly saw everyone in his entourage plotting against, him, planning to assassinate him, preparing to usurp his power. At Tsarskoye Selo, as in St. Petersburg, as at Peterhoff, the situation never changed. The emperor's entourage was given secret missions and police investigations. Everyone had to be watched. Of all of the jumbled information the Tsar received, there was really nothing he gave credence to.

Juve explained in a few words, "The situation is serious, your Majesty, and I am convinced that Fantômas, who is growing exasperated by the obstacles I constantly place in his way, will do anything to attain his goal. And I will do everything to fight him, I will do the impossible to defeat him but, your Majesty,

I believe that if I am to serve you well, I must remain strictly incognito. I am afraid that since I am at Tsarskoye Selo, I may be recognized by Fantômas, since he is certainly here as well. Your Majesty, I am sure that you agree that you must announce that you have expelled the lecturer."

"That's right," said the Tsar. "I think the same as you do, Juve, but will people really believe that I have expelled the lecturer?"

Juve was about to respond when there was a discreet knock at the door. At the order of the Tsar, the policeman hid behind a curtain. Colonel Sarkov entered.

"May your Majesty forgive me for interrupting," he said. "I have received a telegram from the personal service of the imperial cabinet which no one understands…"

"Hand it over!" said the Tsar.

Nicolas II read the telegram, made no comment, and merely waved the colonel out of the room. Once Sarkov had left, the Tsar called Juve.

"Read this telegram," the Tsar said.

Juve read it and could not keep from smiling. It was an outraged protest, sent from Berlin by Roger Darmont, the real one, complaining that he had been rudely chased out of Russia for no good reason.

Seeing that Juve was smiling, the Tsar questioned him.

The policeman replied, "Everything is fine, your Majesty. I must admit that I am the one who chased Roger Darmont from the empire."

Then he told the Tsar how he had chased the lecturer away, since it was Juve, in fact, who, in order to take the speaker's place and get into Tsarskoye Selo, had gone to Roger Darmont's room the previous evening, disguised as a Russian police office, and forced him to take the first train leaving the empire.

"This telegram is excellent," Juve shouted. "All we have to do is confuse the dates, and publish only the telegram tomorrow evening and Fantômas himself, if he thinks I'm here this evening, will be convinced that I have been expelled from the empire."

"So be it," said Nicolas II. "I'm starting to understand your goal… you want no one to know you are in the imperial palace. You can count on me to do everything possible to see that is so."

Juve bowed respectfully. Obviously, things were going as well as possible and he hoped he could kill two birds with one stone. He had to guard the empress' necklace while also protecting that Boris Pokroff, the duchess' lover, in order to keep the promise the French policeman had made to that grand Russian lady.

Juve obtained permission from the Tsar to spend the entire night in the cabinet.

"Tomorrow, however," he said to the Russian emperor, "I will ask your Majesty to have me replaced since I have another mission to perform, for which I will need your august assistance."

"Of course," replied the emperor. "Tomorrow morning, I will have Boris Pokroff replace you!"

"Boris Pokroff!" Juve murmured, a mysterious gleam in his eye.

CHAPTER XV
Old Riga

All was quiet in the imperial palace. The hours passed, slowly, silently, monotonously, that night. Juve, in keeping with the promise he had given the Tsar, kept watch in the darkness, in the emperor's small work study, keeping the chest containing the necklace close at hand.

The police officer was both satisfied and vexed. He had completed a good portion of his program; he had met Fantômas' challenge with triumph, with victory.

Fantômas had, in fact, been so daring as to inform Juve that, despite the precautions the policeman might take, the empress' necklace would disappear between 11:00 pm and midnight. Juve, however, had arranged to save the necklace. From time to time, using a flashlight, the policeman would check on the precious item. And as he looked at it he understood why Fantômas was interested in taking it. It was, in fact, a remarkably beautiful piece, a magnificent necklace worthy of an empress. The pearls and diamonds were set in platinum and gold mounts. In addition to the value of the gems, there was also the historic worth of the necklace since a large number of the stones had both a name and a history. The necklace was certainly worth a fortune and that would have been enough for Fantômas to want it.

Juve had managed to prevent Fantômas from putting his plans into in action. The policeman, who had been mysteriously summoned by Fandor, had been able, within less than 12 hours, to get a personal audience with the Tsar and earn his trust. Moreover, Juve had assured the sympathies of the Duchess Ekaterina, who spoke with authority at the court. He had worked skillfully, all the more so since he was adventuring into terrain that was unfamiliar to him, working almost blindly, knowing full well that he could be discovered and unmasked and was unaware of where his enemies and adversaries were hiding.

Even better, Juve, who had been drawn to Russia by Fandor's appeal, had had no news of the latter and did not know where he could be reached. Finally, although the policeman had been informed that Fantômas was in St. Petersburg, he was displeased by the fact that the people that denounced Fantômas were the same people he was tempted to consider a formidable adversaries and dangerous enemies, since Fantômas had been denounced by the nihilists.

Juve thought about all these things as the night passed. He decided that he would not be upset, the next morning, to make the acquaintance of the man the Tsar had designated to take his place guarding the necklace. He had heard the man's name. His Imperial Majesty had said that Juve's successor in the small office where the treasure was locked up would be Boris Pokroff.

But who was the man? What role did he play at the imperial court? That's what Juve did not know.

In principle, it appeared that the chief of the Tsar's secret police would be a man above all suspicion. Juve had barely seen him in the hallways of the theatre and was barely able to hold onto the opinion he had forged. But Boris Pokroff had made a bad impression on Juve and, despite himself, the policeman felt that he should not trust the man.

Was that instinct talking? Juve could not have said. When he thought of Pokroff, if someone had told him that the man was none other than one of Fantômas' accomplices or even Fantômas himself, he would not have been that surprised.

In any event, Juve waited impatiently, for the time when Boris Pokroff was supposed to come and get him.

He no longer thought that Pokroff had to be unaware of his presence at the palace or that Juve had promised the duchess to watch over Pokroff in secret and protect him, without the other man's knowledge, against the numerous murder threats that, in Russia, always hung heavily over a highly-placed police chief.

Of course, following the evening's events, Juve was not thinking about that detail, but someone was and that person was the Duchess Ekaterina.

When morning came, when it was time for Juve to retire, someone, accompanied by a group of Cossacks, showed up at the entrance to the imperial office. That person knocked discreetly four times, as agreed. Juve leapt up.

"Finally," he said. "I am going to see this Boris Pokroff and we will have a chance to talk."

He rushed over to open the door, but when he saw the individual standing there, he was greatly disappointed. It was not the chief of the secret police, but the brave colonel Sarkov, in full dress uniform. He seemed to be quite pleased with the mission he had been assigned. He did not seem to know Juve by name, but he had no doubt been told that he was a policeman since he greeted him respectfully, with the instinctive sympathy given to those are in the good graces of sovereigns.

And, in order to exonerate himself in advance from any accusations that could be made against him in the future, Colonel Sarkov said to Juve, "By assigning me to watch over the empress' necklace, he does me a great honor and proves that he believes in me. His Majesty is right. Anyone who would attempt to take the piece without a written order from my masters will have to do so over my dead body and those of my Cossacks."

Juve took his leave of the courageous military man and, finding himself in the hallway, met a chamberlain and two servants who walked him through the palace for 30 minutes and took him into a small room at the very top of the castle. There they invited him to get some rest.

Juve could not ask for more. He was very pleased to have an opportunity to sleep.

Yet, as he lay down, Juve wondered, "Why didn't Boris Pokroff come to replace me, as we had agreed last evening?"

If Juve was asking a question like that, it meant he was not taking the Duchess Ekaterina into account. She had witnessed the events of the previous evening and had clearly heard the emperor declare that Juve would be replaced by Boris Pokroff.

"And the minute that happens," the duchess told herself, "Juve and Boris will meet and my lover will immediately know that if the French policeman is in the palace it is because I summoned him, to protect him. He will be vexed and my goal will not be achieved."

The duchess cleverly convinced the Tsar to give a counter order. And, at about three o'clock in the morning, His Imperial Majesty had a message taken to Colonel Sarkov, informing the man that he was assigned to the mission previously give to the police chief.

Once that order was given, the duchess had retired. She had taken care to call her lover and was overjoyed to find him at her home when she arrived there. They took part in a tender demonstration of their love that lasted until dawn.

However, while the duchess slept, Boris Pokroff, or should we say Fantômas, who lay next to her without sleeping, kept watch, worried. For the last 48 hours, the terrible bandit felt as if he had been walking on top of a volcano and that singular, mysterious events were taking place all around him, one after another.

Fantômas had absolute trust in his mistress, the Duchess Ekaterina. He did not suspect that she had summoned Juve to St. Petersburg and, even if he had known about her telegram asking the policeman to come, he would have understood her purpose and would not have been angry.

But Fantômas knew nothing of all that, since the duchess had discreetly not wanted to inform her lover that she was having him watched for his own protection.

Fantômas, however, had learned about Juve's arrival in Russia through the reports he received from the secret police. He had quickly set out to find where the policeman was staying in St. Petersburg and, out of bravado and convinced that he was the better man, he had sent Juve a challenge. Yet, Fantômas was unable to gloat as he had planned. The incidents of the evening had prevented him from taking the necklace.

Fantômas had not seen Juve in the lecturer, but he had no doubt that the policeman was not far. He had to act quickly, or his reputation as a criminal mastermind would be tarnished. It was important for Fantômas to savor victory, if only to prove to Juve that Fantômas was always the stronger of the two.

Dawn had barely arrived and Fantômas, who was not sleeping, was developing the most extraordinary plans in his mind, when the telephone suddenly rang, breaking the intimate and discreet silence of the bedroom where he was resting next to his beautiful mistress.

The so-called chief of the secret police picked up the telephone on the bedside table. The call was from his valet, who knew where Boris Pokroff was spending the night.

Fantômas leapt up. He was to come to the imperial palace immediately to confer with the empress herself. This was the first time that the chief of the secret police had received such an order. The empress did not usually get involved in police business and, above all, it was the first time she had expressed a desire to speak directly with him.

Fantômas did not hesitate to obey. He informed his mistress, in a few words, of the empress' wishes and dressed quickly. An hour later Fantômas was at Tsarskoye Selo.

His car had taken him to an interior court that provided access to the private apartments of the Tsarina. He was received by a group of giants dressed in red, standing on the steps of a marble staircase, armed to the teeth, ready to pounce on anyone who appeared suspicious.

Fantômas, who played the role he had usurped as the police chief quite successfully, still experienced palpitations from time to time, particularly since he knew Juve was in St. Petersburg. He was constantly worried. Was he about to be suddenly surprised? Unmasked? Would the giants in red, who respectfully made way for him, receive a sudden order to arrest him? That's what Fantômas did not know. Why had the empress asked for him? What was she going to say to him? Who would be there? He was convinced that the empress would not talk directly with him.

In that respect, Fantômas was wrong.

He reached the top of the marble staircase and, although it was only seven in the morning, a lady waited for him, fully dressed. She walked over and curtsied. Fantômas bowed in return.

This woman, one of the empress' senior ladies in waiting, asked, "Do I have the honor of addressing Mr. Boris Pokroff, the chief of Their Majesties' secret police?"

"Himself," Fantômas replied.

"Please follow me," she said.

Fantômas obeyed and, for a good 20 minutes, walked without interruption through the hallways and secret chambers of the portion of the palace reserved for the empress. Finally, the lady in waiting stopped in a sort of small lounge filled with extraordinary, gilded furniture, where the walls were completely covered with white bear skins. The room was empty. Fantômas was invited to wait there. He was alone for 10 minutes, after which a door opened and the empress appeared.

The Tsarina was dressed very simply that day and wore a light-colored morning dress, decorated with English lace. Her hair was styled in the Russian manner into a halo around her head, ready for the imperial crown. The low neck on her morning dress revealed the harmonious and pure lines of her neck. Yet, what struck Fantômas was the fact that the empress was wearing the famous necklace that had been so carefully guarded.

Fantômas bowed to her, placing one knee on the floor.

The empress signaled that he was to stand up and said, in a voice that was as harmonious and gentle as her husband's was nervous and strained, "Sir, I've had you brought here to give me some advice."

"Your Majesty," said Fantômas," You do me a great honor..."

The empress interrupted him, smiling as she said, "Advice that I will follow if that suits me."

Then, changing tone, she suddenly said, "I had this necklace which I am wearing taken from the safe about 15 minutes ago. It is the object of such covetousness that the very presence of this necklace in the imperial palace represents a danger, in my opinion, for my husband the emperor. Although I do not want to get rid of this item which belongs more to the history of the imperial family than myself and yet, this necklace fills me with horror and dread. Mr. Boris Pokroff, please advise me and suggest a plan for keeping this necklace while ensuring the safety of my husband and children."

Fantômas bowed and declared, ironically, "Where, Majesty, could the necklace be safer than on your august person? I'm certain that no one would dare..."

Smiling sadly, the empress said, "I know that Fantômas covets this necklace. His reputation is so great that I have been assured that not only does he always get what he wants but that there is no one in the world so sacred that he would not hesitate to strike if he felt the need."

"That's right," thought Fantômas who, finding himself alone with the empress wondered if he should simply throw himself at her, grab the necklace and run off without any further ado. But, as he imagined that hypothesis, he considered the giants in red, standing on each step of the marble staircase. Plus, a new idea was germinating in his mind.

Unsuspecting, the empress, as she had asked him the question, had made the sinister bandit think of a way in which he could make off with the necklace.

Adopting a humble expression, Fantômas suggested, "Your Majesty will not be able to keep the necklace without risking great danger. A bandit like Fantômas would not hesitate, to place his sacrilegious hands on a sovereign's shoulders. Therefore, Majesty, you must abandon the necklace, which will never be safe in the emperor's private office, and give it to someone else, turning Fantômas' attention away from you and toward that other person. Moreover, if that person dies he will only have done his duty and there will be 1,000 others like him willing to fill that perilous position."

The empress appeared touched by this chivalrous language and asked the man she thought to be Boris Pokroff, "Who, in your opinion is the man who is noble enough, courageous enough to take charge of this necklace, who would protect it and defend it, at the risk of losing his life?"

The man pretending to be Boris bowed once again and said, "If it pleases your Majesty to give me this necklace, I will fulfill the mission in question. I own a property in Gatchina and I ask your permission to go there for a few days. I will leave this afternoon. If your Majesty entrusts me with the necklace, I assure you that it will remain in my possession as long as I live."

The empress held her delicate white hand out to Fantômas and said, "I trust you Boris Pokroff! And once my august husband has authorized me to do so, I will give you the necklace that could well be fatal for us in a most conspicuous manner."

The empress appeared to be reassured and was smiling as she left the room. Fantômas smiled as well as he left, but there was something dreadful about his expression.

It had been agreed that the necklace would be given to Fantômas at three in the afternoon and it was barely eight in the morning. The bandit, whom everyone thought was Boris Pokroff, left the empress' private chambers without any problems, returned to his vehicle and was immediately driven to his offices in St. Petersburg.

He spent an hour there studying the urgent files, ordering a few random arrests, demonstrating unexpected leniency toward certain criminals, after which Fantômas went into a private room and completely changed the style of his beard and hair, replaced his elegant clothing with miserable rags and left on foot, taking a secret passageway.

Fantômas jumped into a rental cab and was driven for about 15 minutes, until his vehicle stopped at the entrance to a narrow, repellant alley, surface covered with waste, bordered by tumbledown dwellings. Children played noisily in the dead-end street, which never saw the light of day and was perpetually cold, causing people to say that it knew only one season: winter.

Fantômas seemed perfectly at home in this type of miserable neighborhood. He noticed an old woman sitting on a stone doorstep, face blotchy, bloodshot eyes, wrapped in bags, old furs and animal skins.

Fantômas bent over the old woman and asked, "Is your brother home?"

A quiet groan escaped from the old woman's bluish lips. It could have been interpreted in any way but since, it is easy to believe what one wants and Fantômas wanted to meet the brother of that wreck, he understood that the brother was at home. Fantômas went inside, not without first covering his nose with a handkerchief, as protection against the nauseating smell.

He walked up a poor and miserable staircase with slippery, broken steps, filled with the odor of hot grease and filth. Despite the repugnant horror of the shanty, Fantômas climbed up to the second floor, the top of the house, and kicked in a worm-eaten door. He found himself in an attic with a skylight, broken panes replaced by pieces of cardboard long ago. The inside of the attic seemed surprising, strange, like the shop of an old-fashioned alchemist. The rotting tables, stools and shelves were covered with all kinds of flasks. An odd liquid simmered on a cast-iron stove, giving off bitter steam while blue and pink salts melted in boiling water on the floor, crackling without cease.

In the back of the attic, a pale, old man with sunken eyes and a beard that had once been white but was yellow in places and black in others, lay huddled on a bed of straw. The man's eyes seemed to be the only part him showing any sign of life. He looked at Fantômas as he entered and, in a broken voice said, "Who are you brother? And why are you bothering an old man who is biding his time until he descends into his grave and samples the unspeakable joys of the eternal void?"

"Enough," said Fantômas. "Don't play games with me Riga, I need you."

The old man immediately stopped whining. He got up with a surprising agility for a man of his age and stammered, "Pardon me, Boris Pokroff. I didn't recognize you. Of course, you're good with disguises."

"That's my trade," Fantômas said, coldly.

He considered the old man and said, "You scoundrel, despite the grace I have shown you and the fact that you served only 15 years of a 30-year sentence, I imagine you're just as unrepentant as ever and that the nihilists have no one better to keep them supplied with bombs than you?"

The old man grew pale and fell to his knees, saying, "By the Holy Images and in the holy and sacred name of Maria Alexandra Fédérovna the august wife of our Little Father, I swear, Boris Pokroff that I no longer work for anyone and I don't even know how to make a bomb!'

"Ah," said the supposed chief of the secret police, disappointed, "That's really too bad because, my dear Riga, I have an excellent opportunity for you to earn a half-dozen rubles."

The old man, still on his knees, clasped his hands and stammered, "Virgin Mary! If what you say is true, Boris Pokroff, I want my memory to come back to me. Miracles do happen, you know."

"They do, my good man, they do," replied Fantômas. "And I'll give you five minutes to reach an agreement with Paradise. And if you still don't recall how to make bombs after that time, I will go back to the police station and send a dozen officers who will remind you about the joys of the knout!"

"Sir," the old man said, trembling. "I feel something coming back. The Holy Virgin is inspiring me and in a few minutes I will remember how to make one of those time bombs a brother nihilist wanted just the other day."

Fantômas frowned and tapped his foot.

"Hurry up he said and stop this nonsense. I'm not in the mood."

Who was this strange old man and what was Fantômas' business with him? Since he had replaced the real Boris Pokroff and gone unpunished for that crime, Fantômas had taken the place of the chief of the secret police and had been studying the files on all kinds of people. Fantômas decided to make good use of the information available to him and, in order to ensure that he had sympathizers in all camps and to avoid betrayal, he had punished or pardoned at random, liberating criminals and incarcerating the innocent. In fact, he had suddenly ordered an extremely dangerous nihilist, who had been sentenced to death on five occasions and mysteriously pardoned five times, a man Fantômas had finally found in a prison where he had spent 15 years, at the age of 80 years old with 15 years left to serve, he had ordered him to be released.

Fantômas had released the old bandit from prison in exchange for his services.

The old man, terrified of the supposed chief of the secret police, had promised to do everything he was asked and he left prison to return to his shack, back to his explosives and flasks, since he actually was a chemist.

Fantômas quickly realized that he had been wrong to liberate the old man in exchange for the information he could provide. Old Riga no longer had any contacts with the nihilists and could not inform Fantômas about what they were up to. Moreover, since he had been pardoned repeatedly, his former comrades no longer trusted him and Riga, plunged into the darkest misery, abandoned by the nihilists who suspected him and the police he provided no information to, almost regretted giving up the room and board he had enjoyed in the prison hospital.

Boris Pokroff's visit and the promise he had made represented an unexpected blessing and Riga stopped playing his games and asked, "Boris Pokroff, what do you want me to do? Give me your orders?"

"It's quite simple," said Fantômas. "I'm in a real rush. I need a bomb for three o'clock today to blow up the police chief's car."

"Excuse me," said the old man. I'm a bit hard of hearing and my mind is not what it used to be. If I'm not mistaken, you're asking me to make a bomb to blow up the police chief's car? But you're the police chief?"

"I am," said the supposed Boris Pokroff. "And I want to blow up my car."

"You're being fired? Replaced?" the old man asked.

"I'm still the chief of Their Majesties secret police," said Fantômas.

For a few minutes, old Riga looked at him, dumbfounded, then the light suddenly came into his eyes. He chortled, nodded his head, and said, "Now I understand! You want a bomb, Boris Pokroff, to blow up your car, without you getting hurt. A fake attack. You will make the most of the inoffensive explosive to arrest some of my former brothers and throw them into prison. In other words, nothing has changed and those miserable police officers are still stirring everything up."

The old man grew animated as he spoke. All of the hatred he had accumulated throughout his entire life burst out in his bitter words. He clenched his hands and his eyes blazed.

The supposed Boris Pokroff interrupted him, in a harsh voice, saying, "Come on, you scoundrel. No one asked you your opinion. I'm just ordering you to obey. I will do as I please once the carriage has blown up. Meanwhile, make your bomb and give me the information I need to blow it up when I want to. I want the car to blow up and I don't want to get hurt as I'm sitting in the back seat."

The old man did not reply. But he had got up from his pallet and walked over to a table where a few pages of yellowed paper lay. He took a pencil out of a pocket and drew the outline of the police chief's vehicle on it. He knew it well; it was after all quite famous in St. Petersburg. An old-fashioned looking carriage, armored, driven by a coachman sitting on a raised bench, drawn by four horses. He showed the drawing to Fantômas.

"That's your vehicle," he asked.

"That's it," replied Boris Pokroff.

Old Riga pointed at a spot, next to the front springs, with the tip of his pencil.

"That's where you have to place the bomb that I'll give you in a bit. Be warned, though, that the explosion will be violent. Plus, in order to make the attack look real, the explosion will have to cost the lives of at least two horses and the coachman, and maybe even three or four people nearby."

That's not a problem," said Fantômas. "People have to believe that I have been the victim of an attack, a serious attack."

For another hour, the two men spoke. Then, after all of the conditions were met, the old man got down to work. Under Fantômas' watchful eye, he prepared his explosives. It was noon when the bandit left the hovel, carrying everything he needed to blow up half the imperial palace if that was what he wanted. What were Fantômas' plans? Why did he want people to believe an attack was planned against him?

CHAPTER XVI
The Recalcitrant Coachman

While Fantômas was hatching this shadowy plan which, if it succeeded, would deliver the empress' necklace into his hands once and for all while making everyone believe that he had risked his life to defend it, the Duchess Ekaterina, who had requested a private audience, had been received in the greatest secret by the emperor and the empress.

Obviously, she wanted something strange and surprising from them, since the interview lasted a long time, much longer than usual in the case of a conversation among members of the imperial family, whose time is counted and who work so hard, day and night, to manage State affairs.

After 20 minutes, however, the duchess left the sovereigns and returned to her carriage with a triumphant air. She had the driver take her to the station, where a train was preparing to set out for a country estate in the outlying areas of St. Petersburg, which she shared with her lover. The duchess had barely sat down when she smiled with satisfaction and nattered out loud.

"My God! Thank you for suggesting that marvelous idea to the emperor. In this way, Boris Pokroff will be under the constant protection of the subtlest policeman in the world and he won't suspect a thing."

Following the conversation with the duchess, the emperor and empress had remained alone for a short while.

The Tsar looked at his wife, shrugged and said, "That duchess is growing more and more romantic. Now she's worried about the life of our friend Pokroff and she wants that policeman Juve to protect him. I don't see anything inconvenient in that, but there must be something more to it!"

The Tsar could hardly suspect what that something else could be since he was unaware of the private, romantic intrigues of those in his entourage. The Tsarina, on the other hand, often received confidences from the family princesses. People knew that, given her generous and discreet nature, they could confide in her fully. As a result, she was well informed about a number of romantic secrets and knew who was seeing whom and what was always going on among those who lived in the palace. Discreet as always, the Tsarina did not inform her august husband about why the Duchess Ekaterina was being so solicitous with respect to Boris Pokroff.

The emperor had orders to give and was about to leave. Before going her own way, the empress said to him, "Sire, don't forget that, within a few hours I must make a great show of giving the necklace which has set so many tongues wagging to the chief of the secret police and that Boris Pokroff must leave with the necklace, in formal attire, to go to his estate in Gatchina, where he will keep it securely and that he will be the official guardian of the crown jewels from now on."

"Madam," replied the Tsar, "You want me to let everyone know about Boris Pokroff's chivalrous decision?"

The Tsarina replied, "Personally, I find paying so much attention to the departure of our generous servant is dangerous for him but, with your approval, I will not hesitate to do so knowing full well that is Boris Pokroff's wish."

The Tsar smiled bitterly and replied, "All I have to do, madam, is utter a few words about the matter in the corridor we are about to walk down, where the courtiers are gathering. In order to make sure the news spreads like wildfire, I'll pretend to tell you about it in a confidential manner. After all, there is no shortage of spies and traitors at court!"

The empress did not dare contradict her husband. No one knew better than she did about the weaknesses of her entourage.

The emperor did as he had said. While the courtiers bowed low and the yeomen preceded him, he bent his head close to the empress and murmured, "I wish to inform you, madam, that in order to eliminate all danger from the Tsarskoye Selo, Boris Pokroff, the dedicated chief of our secret police, has decided to take the historic necklace to his estate in Gatchina, this very day, and keep it there until he receives new orders."

Less than an hour after the Tsar had uttered these words, the entire city of St. Petersburg had been informed about the upcoming trip of the chief of police. Moreover, when Boris Pokroff had returned to the palace, he'd decided it was necessary to prepare for his trip with a great deal of show and pomp. He had scolded all of the palace staff, sent the Cossacks throughout the royal residence, given contradictory orders and he had done this so effectively that, when it came time for him to set out for his estate in Gatchina, most of the courtiers and the palace staff had gathered either in the courtyard or at the palace windows to see the chief of the secret police leave with the crown jewels, the necklace that everyone rightfully considered one of the most valuable items in the imperial treasury. Furthermore, the necklace was turned over to the police chief with a certain amount of ceremony. The steward of the imperial palace, wearing his dress uniform, had handed the necklace over, in the presence of both the emperor and the empress, to Boris Pokroff, who had signed a receipt for it.

It was a curious ceremony since it involved moving the object coveted by the audacious bandit known as Fantômas, in order to keep it out of the hands of the renowned criminal mastermind. Someone who seemed upset, very emotional during that ceremony was Boris Pokroff, namely Fantômas himself... When he received the priceless necklace from the steward, his hands shook and it seemed as if it would take little for Fantômas to tear off his mask and race off, carrying off the necklace that had been given to him with so much trust.

But Fantômas would never throw caution to the wind like that. Having the necklace was not enough. He had to be able to keep it. He must never be suspected of having stolen it so that he could do with it as pleased afterwards, selling as he wished.

Fantômas had pulled off a stroke of mastery by having the item he planned to steal voluntarily handed over to him. But, this was by no means the end of the matter. Quite the contrary. He had to be able to keep it without being accused of stealing it, by making it seem as if someone else had stolen it...

Of course, Fantômas was far from winning the game, but he was so satisfied with this initial success, so pleased that he had the magnificent treasure in his hands, that, once the ceremony had been completed, he could not keep from racing over to the armored carriage that waited for him at the palace gate, jumping into it and locking the door. The vehicle immediately set off at a gallop, crossing through the gardens of Tsarskoye Selo and, once the magnificent avenues that surrounded the imperial residence lay behind it, the carriage headed for Gatchina.

Once the carriage had disappeared, the Tsar turned to the empress and murmured, "May God keep him and the treasure! And I hope that he will feel a little calmer. Did you notice, madam, that Boris Pokroff seemed a little emotional? As he climbed into the carriage, he didn't even notice the royal gift I gave him!"

The empress, always willing to see the best in others, replied, "You must forgive him, sire, for that involuntary inconvenience. I'm certain that Boris Pokroff is so preoccupied with his mission that nothing could take his attention from that!"

Fantômas hunkered down in his armored carriage, clasping the priceless treasure that the Tsar and Tsarina had given to him to his chest. The sinister bandit chuckled as his carriage raced through the busy streets.

"Obviously," he said to himself, "My imagination always comes up with wonderful plans and if my friend Juve learns what I've done to get my hands on this necklace, he will most certainly die of shock. Of course, he would never expect to see Fantômas disguised as the chief of the secret police of an empire such as Russia!"

But, after admiring his own skill, Fantômas thought about the course he should take, saying, "This is not the end, only the beginning."

And, with a certain amount of emotion, he looked at his feet, at a small wire that poked through the floor and trembled with the movements of the carriage on the pavement. Fantômas knew that all he had to do was pull on that little wire sharply to explode the bomb manufactured by Old Riga. The master criminal had attached that bomb himself to the front of the carriage. It had been arranged so that it would explode toward the horses, which would be pulverized, along with the driver. But Fantômas, positioned in the armored portion of the car, would be unhurt.

The faked attack would have two benefits for Fantômas. Not only would it be easy to blame the nihilists for assassinating him and making the most of the confusion caused by the explosion to steal the necklace, but Fantômas could also conduct investigations intended to cast suspicious on the nihilists, arresting and executing many of them without judgments.

Showing no sign of gratitude to Old Riga for supplying the bomb, Fantômas decided that the old man would be among the first to be arrested and that, in order to ensure his silence, he would have him shot on the pretext that he was fomenting rebellion, the first chance he got, without even charging him.

Fantômas looked out the window at the route they were taking. They were approaching a square surrounded by a group of modest houses occupied by workers and ordinary people.

"A real neighborhood for nihilists," Fantômas said to himself, looking with disgust and scorn at the dumpy houses that stood on either side of the winding alleys as his carriage drove by.

After catching sight of the square that stood about 150 yards away, Fantômas made up his mind.

"That's where I'll pull the wire. That's where the bomb will go off... And as soon as that is done, I will pretend to escape as if seriously injured and people will run over to look at my carriage. Later I'll tell the newspapers that, after a fierce struggle, the empress' necklace was taken from the courageous Boris Pokroff following a fierce battle by a gang of frenzied nihilists headed by a masked man, which the chief of police clearly recognized as Fantômas!"

The sinister bandit had barely worked out this plan when his carriage, skillfully driven by an enormous coachman, headed into the square. There was a large crowd there, since it was a fair day, and several large tents had been set up on the road.

Fantômas thought, "It's almost as if the Bohemians had gathered here specifically for me!"

Abruptly, Fantômas pulled the wire and immediately hunkered down in the back of the carriage, covering his face with his arms, waiting for the explosion. The coachman had been obliged to slow on his way through the crowd. Fantômas counted the seconds... To his great surprise, there was no explosion!

"Now, now, now," thought the bandit. "It just isn't possible that the bomb has not gone off."

But nothing out of the usual occurred. Fantômas would have to pull the wire a second time in an effort to set off the bomb. Nervously, yet vigorously, he grasped the end of the wire in his robust fingers and pulled until it felt as if the wire would break. He released it and once again hunkered down in the back of the carriage.

"This time..." he thought.

Fantômas remained in that position for a few moments, a few seconds, a few minutes. The carriage had left behind the square long ago, driven through the suburbs and was heading into an immense white plain on the roughly paved road that led to Gatchina. And the carriage continued to drive on and the horses continued to gallop driven by the coachman's whip. And the bomb did not explode! Fantômas sat up. Clasping his chin, he thought, attempting to understand what was happening, to figure out why the bomb had not detonated.

"Yet I planned things well," the bandit said to himself.

His face grew very pale as large drops of cold sweat pearled on his forehead and Fantômas hammered his knee with his fist.

"Damnation!" he grumbled.

An atrocious thought had just slipped into his mind. Fantômas felt as if he were suffocating, as he crossed his arms over his chest.

"I'm an imbecile," he proclaimed in desperation. "I'm as naïve as a child and more simple minded that a moujik! Obviously, that old scoundrel Riga has tricked me and this may very well be my final hour."

In fact, Fantômas was thinking that the old man he had ordered to make the bomb, despite his apparent sympathy and acknowledgement, had suddenly decided to kill him. Fantômas believed that Riga had made a device that would explode when he thought fit and that all of the information he had given the apparent chief of police about how to set off the bomb when he wanted to were inaccurate.

"I've been had... I've been had..." grumbled Fantômas, adding, "I have no problem dying if I do so at the hands of worthy adversaries. But what I can't stand is the idea of dying for no good reason after being taken in by an old nihilist. The entire world will laugh at me. Juve will be wild with joy... No, no, no! I'll do everything possible to avoid such as stupid death."

He broke through the small square of wood that separated the coachman's bench from the interior of the carriage and shouted, "Nick! Nick! Good old Nick! Stop right now. I have to get out!"

Nick was the name of the coachman who usually drove the armored carriage of the chief of police. Nick was in fact a former security agent who had grown so corpulent as he grew older that he was no longer able to work as a police officer but was perfectly capable of serving, with honor and dignity, as a coachman for an almost official vehicle. Nick was completely dedicated to his master, obeying him like a dog. However, Nick barely knew that very master by sight. For the six years, he had been in his service, he had only seen him face to face three or four times and, of course, he would have been one of the many who would have been unable to distinguish the real Boris Pokroff, now dead, from the murderer who had replaced him. Fantômas.

But fat Nick did not need to be able to recognize people in order to serve them with great dedication. He was under the orders of the chief of police and if the man had ordered him to throw himself into the Baltic Sea with his carriage and horse, he would have done so without blinking, without hesitating.

Fantômas did not know how dedicated his servant was, but he had had an opportunity, on several occasions while playing the role of Boris Pokroff, to test the driver's devotion.

So Fantômas was stunned, dumbfounded when he realized, after repeating his order twice, that the coachman was not obeying him. There was no way he could not have been heard. Fantômas had shrieked.

But, when he had heard Fantômas shout, "Stop right now!" Nick had whipped the horses into a gallop. The carriage tossed about on the rough road that leads to Gatchina. On both sides of the road lay a white plain, the immense white steppe. And Fantômas suddenly felt as if he had fallen into a trap and would most certainly have to work very hard to save his hide.

Was it deliberate or an unfortunate coincidence? He did not know, but one thing was certain, contrary to the orders he had been given, instead of slowing the carriage Nick was urging his horses on, faster and faster.

Fantômas grew more and more certain that he had not only been trick but even worse, betrayed by old Riga, but that he had no control over the bomb made by the old nihilist and it would explode sometime, anytime, tearing the horses, the coachman, the carriage and even Fantômas into a million bits. The criminal clenched his hands and fumed, but he felt powerless...

The doors of the carriage that he had locked had also been closed from outside by means of a latch that only the coachman could operate, preventing Fantômas from leaping out onto the road.

Fantômas slipped the muzzle of his revolver through the broken square of wood and shouted, "Nick, Nick, if you don't stop immediately I'll shoot you through six times to teach you to obey me!"

Nick did not answer. His only response was to whip the horses on. Drunk with rage, Fantômas was about to shoot when he realized that if he shot the coachman the horses would run on and maybe take the carriage head first into a ditch, or a river, or a ravine. The moats that ran along the road were deep and deadly. It would be better to leave Nick on his bench and see what would happen.

In the distance, possibly fifteen hundred yards ahead, Fantômas noticed the pointed turrets of the small castle at Gatchina, where his mistress waited. Furious that he did not understand what was happening, Fantômas once again hunkered down in the back of the carriage, pressed back to keep from being jolted from one side of the carriage to the other, closed his eyes and waited.

CHAPTER XVII
A Strange Discovery

What had happened? Why had the bomb provided by Old Riga not exploded in the crowd, in keeping with Fantômas' plans? And why had Fat Nick, usually so obedient, refused to stop the horses when his master had ordered him to do so?

That same morning, Juve, who had experienced a certain amount of disappointment when he saw that Colonel Sarkov was to take over from him and guard the imperial necklace instead of Boris Pokroff, whom he would have liked to meet, had nevertheless the accepted the offer to get a little rest.

Juve slept for a few hours, in a private apartment at the palace and, as soon as he woke, as soon as he was ready to go downstairs, he was visited by a chamberlain who invited him to go and see the emperor immediately.

His Majesty declared, "Mr. Juve, I've been told by people who have followed your exploits how audacious and dedicated you are. I have been told that your greatest desire would be to live incognito in the entourage of those who help us and defend us. Is that true?"

Curious to know what the Emperor was thinking, to find out where he was headed, Juve nodded and replied, "It is, your Majesty."

The Emperor apologized, "The Duchess Ekaterina asked you, Mr. Juve, to protect someone to whom she has given her well-meaning affection. That is our chief of police, Mr. Boris Pokroff, is it not?"

"That's true," said Juve.

"So," continued the Emperor," You would like to be in constant contact with Boris Pokroff without him suspecting your true identity?"

"Absolutely," said Juve.

The policeman was thrilled with this turn of events. The Tsar, moreover, added some information that fulfilled a wish Juve had not dared express.

"I want," declared the Emperor, "To recognize Boris Pokroff's dedication by giving him a present that will please him. I have decided to take two handsome horses from my imperial stables. I assign you Juve to deliver these wonderful animals and offer them on my behalf to Boris Pokroff. You will tell him that you are the groom responsible for maintaining the beasts and Boris Pokroff will most certainly hire you so that you can continue to provide the care you usually give to these horses. Is that acceptable for you? Would you agree, Mr. Juve, to perform such a lowly role for our excellent friend?"

Juve bowed deeply and replied, "Your Majesty may rest assured that I do not feel any role is lowly or superior when taking on a mission."

Thirty minutes later, Juve went to the imperial stables and took charge of the two horses the Tsar had decided to give to the chief of the secret police.

The Emperor had not been lying when he said that they were superb beasts. They were magnificent with their shiny, silky coats, well-defined muscles, and perfect, impeccable lines. They went by the names of Mars and Bellon, which were well chosen since the two proud steeds, judging by their martial look, clearly embodied the two mythological deities for whom they were named.

Juve, disguised as a groom then headed, a few moments later, to the stables which, although more modest than those of the Tsar, were still luxurious, where the teams for the various individuals assigned to live at Tsarskoye Selo were housed. He located the buildings reserved for Boris Pokroff's stables and suddenly found himself face to face with the enormous Nick, who looked at him in dismay.

Juve tried in vain to engage the enormous coachman in conversation, but the man was completely incapable of the slightest thought or movement. Nick had, in fact, drunk a formidable amount the previous evening and was now paralyzed, incapable of the slightest movement. Juve had found him in the middle of a pile of hay in a stall. Yet, as he noticed two other stalls that were empty, he led the two horses there and, wondering what was to happen to him, he had decided to wait and see, when he heard someone at the door to the stable calling for Nick.

At the threshold to the stable, Juve barely saw the silhouette of one of the red giants who served as military domestics at the palace of Tsarskoye Selo and he walked over to the man, taking the place of the fat coachman. As soon as he saw Juve, the red giant gave an order to the policeman, whom he took for a groom.

"You have to couple Boris Pokroff's armored carriage to the horses," he said. "Tell the coachman. Nick had better bring oats and supplies since they'll be heading to Gatchina."

"Perfect," murmured Juve who had suddenly come up with an idea and replied to the orders of the man in red with a question.

"When is the carriage to be ready?"

"In an hour," the man replied.

Juve's idea was certainly audacious, but also quite ingenious. He had examined the situation quickly. Nick, who was incredibly drunk, was in no shape to drive. At the same time, the coach was ordered for three o'clock and it was obvious that Boris Pokroff was planning to set out for his estate. Juve had been informed by the Tsar about the intentions of the police chief who, under the pretext of guarding the Empress' necklace, had announced clear and loud that he was going to take it with him to Gatchina. Juve felt that there was something mysterious about all this and now he was being given an opportunity to take Nick's place, an opportunity he could not pass up.

What did he have to risk, after all? If anyone noticed that he was not Nick and just a simple groom, he would say that he took the man's place to help a colleague who was a little bit under the weather. Yet, if no one noticed, that would be even better and he would be in a better position as a coachman than a groom to protect the chief of police as he had promised the Duchess Ekaterina he would.

Yet, Juve did not have a minute to waste if he wanted the carriage to be ready on time. He asked around in the stable to find out where it was kept and was told that it was kept in a shed a way off, at the very end of the service buildings.

First, the supposed groom went through the pockets of the enormous Nick, taking his keys, then he headed over to the shed. As soon as he opened the door, he spotted the carriage he was to drive. Juve never liked to get involved in anything without first finding out exactly what he was supposed to do or the nature of the objects he was to handle. When he took the carriage out of the shed, he looked at it closely, examining it.

Suddenly, the policeman called put in surprise. He had noticed a strange, unexpected device under the front end of the carriage. Someone had attached a small object under the front of the carriage and a wire ran from that object into the carriage, as if to serve as means to activate the mysterious package.

"Oh! Oh!" thought Juve, "What does this mean? Here's a device that has no place on a carriage!"

For a moment, he thought about pulling on the wire to see what would happen but, when he noted a metallic flash in the package, he had a premonition that stopped him from putting his plan into action. Juve cautiously removed the package from the coachwork.

He took a close look at the heavy object and cried out, "Good grief! It's a bomb!"

The explosive device looked familiar to the policeman. In France, he had had the opportunity to seize similar devices from Polish and Russian refugees. He was well aware of the danger, but he also knew how to render such terrible devices inoffensive. All he had to so was tear off the capsule designed to trigger the explosion to make it inoperative.

The bomb that Juve had found under the carriage was in fact, not a time bomb but a percussion bomb. Juve calmly placed it in his pocket, convinced that it no longer posed any threat and then, thinking about the discovery he had just made, he set off to hitch up the horses the horses offered as a gift by the Emperor.

"So, now I'm a coachman," thought Juve, "And I work for a police officer that someone wants to assassinate. This isn't really bad for starters. All the same, the Duchess Ekaterina cannot be as cowardly as people may think. She was right to entrust the protection of her lover to me. I do believe that if I had not been here this afternoon, Boris Pokroff would no longer be in this world tonight!"

Juve, in fact, was far from realizing that if a bomb had been placed under the carriage of the chief of the secret police, it was precisely the police chief who had placed it there. Yet Juve was so intelligent that this idea gradually made its way into his mind. And as he hitched the horses to the carriage and since he was intrigued by the discovery of the bomb, Juve returned several times to verify the position in which he had found the device. Then he realized that the wire was the only means for detonating the bomb. And since that wire ran into the carriage, Juve logically concluded that the person responsible for the attack would, obviously, be sitting in that very carriage.

Satisfied with this simple train of thought, Juve declared, "Well, when we know who is to board the carriage, we'll know who is supposed to set off the bomb!"

Juve then came up with a highly inventive plan. Placing the wire in its original location, namely allowing the end to emerge, he placed the other end on the coachman's bench.

"I'll attach the end to my foot," Juve said to himself. "When the would-be assassin wants to blow up the device, he will merely tug on my shoe!"

Thirty minutes later, the armored car of the chief of police, headed into the courtyard of the imperial palace. There was an enormous coachman on the driver's bench, who resembled Fat Nick from a distance. Yet the coachman was none other than Juve who, when taking place of Boris Pokroff's phenomenal servant, who was still dead drunk, had put on the man's clothing and packed it with straw.

Juve had coupled the new horses, the gift intended for the chief of police, and expected the surprise Boris Pokroff would experience when he saw them.

"He'll most likely question me," he said. "I made a mistake and I should have used the regular horses."

Juve barely had time to think before he saw the chief of the secret police walking down the main staircase, carrying the chest that held the valuable necklace. Oblivious to the new horses, he dove into the carriage and gave the order, "To Gatchina!"

He'd noticed nothing different about the horses.

Juve did not have to be given his instructions twice and, wrapping his horses with a masterful flick of his whip, he set out from the imperial palace, heading through, and along the avenues and streets. With the remarkable precision that he owed to his natural gift to get his bearings marvelously no matter where he was, and to know a region in depth after merely examining a map for a few moments.

Juve knew Tsarskoye Selo, St. Petersburg and the outlying areas as he knew Paris, having spent his entire trip from France to Russia carefully studying the map.

He was on his way, surprised to note that there was only one man in the carriage and was telling himself that, in all likelihood, the man who had planned to travel with Boris Pokroff had not been able to tag along when he suddenly felt the iron wire that he had attached to his foot tense just as they were approaching a large busy square.

"It can't be," said Juve. "I must be mistaken. No one can be pulling on the wire!"

Juve felt like a puppet. He shook his foot and felt nothing more.

"I was wrong," he said. "Furthermore, it cannot possibly be Boris Pokroff trying to explode the device."

Yet, after the carriage had traveled a few more yards, Juve no longer had any doubts. Someone was actually pulling on the wire, violently, from inside the carriage and Juve furiously exclaimed, "Well, I'm a complete imbecile! I should have realized! This Boris Pokroff is much stronger than I am!"

Juve, in fact, was developing a hypothesis and it was the right one. He'd noticed, without coming to any certain conclusion, that the bomb, when he had discovered it, was arranged so that it would destroy everything at the front of the carriage and spare everything at the rear when it was detonated. He thought about this and the light immediately turned on in his mind.

"Good grief!" he said. "Now I understand why Boris Pokroff took the Empress' necklace with him, with such an ostentatious show. He's organized a little attack on his person and was planning to escape unscathed after sacrificing his driver and horses. An explosion always upsets things for a certain distance. Boris Pokroff wanted the bomb to explode here, in this square, in the crowd. I can picture it all. Some people would have been killed; others injured. When Pokroff would have regained consciousness, because he would have certainly been knocked out, he would have noticed that the necklace had disappeared, that he had been robbed by his attacker. Well played! No one would ever have thought that the man behind the attack was actually the victim. Unfortunately for Boris Pokroff but fortunately for the Empress, Juve is the one sitting on the bench and he has the bomb in his pocket. Boris Pokroff's plans would fail."

So Juve, instead of obeying the order given by the man inside the carriage, who was supposed to be his master, whipped his horses on and did not stop. Juve never paid heed to threats and the more Boris Pokroff threatened him, the more he was convinced that he had the guilty party in his carriage. He wanted only one thing.

"Let's get to Gatchina as quickly as possible," he said. "Then we'll explain things!"

CHAPTER XVIII
At the Bottom of a Well

Gatchina is located about 20 verste from Tsarskoye Selo. It is a small village inhabited by moujiks and a few municipal civil servants and surrounded by fields of crops and forests. A river filled with fish runs at the foot of the hamlet, providing a rather large quantity of fish for the inhabitants, who either eat it or sell it in the Tsarskoye Selo market.

There is one single large and luxurious property, located at the top of the village, next to a large pine forest. The park is surrounded by walls. People entered through a large gate, open in a welcoming manner. This property belongs to the chief of the secret police, Boris Pokroff. It is a unique dwelling where, for many years already, the veritable chief of the secret police came to rest from time to time. And, after Fantômas replaced him, he could hardly avoid the place.

The circumstances under which the assassinated chief of police usually traveled to the property made things easy for Fantômas. In fact, the real Boris Pokroff never made himself known when he traveled to Gatchina and always kept out of view. People in the area barely knew him as a result and Fantômas found it extremely easy to pass as the real chief of police. And he had done even better than that since he had even managed to trick the rulers and their entourage into believing that the man who replaced the real Boris Pokroff, after assassinating him, was none other than Boris Pokroff himself.

That day, a carriage pulled by two robust horses, galloping easily over the snow, had appeared like a black dot on the horizon then gradually drew nearer to the village of Gatchina, running the risk that it would crush the peasants and children playing in the street. The driver of the vehicle whipped his horses on, rather than slowing, until they were covered with sweat, as they pulled through the gate and came to a stop at the foot of the stairs.

Juve, who had managed to pull off the masterful stroke of locking the chief of the secret police in the carriage, after realizing what the man was up to, was more certain than ever that his captive had not only decided to steal the empress' necklace but also fake an explosion to make people believe that while trying to protect the valuable piece of jewelry he had been the victim of an attack, during which the item in question had disappeared.

Juve told himself, "The first thing to do is get my man to his destination. He'll be greeted by people from the police or the army and will have to admit that he has the famous necklace with him. The fictional attack did not take place and he will have to come up with something else and, since I know exactly what he's up to, it will be easy for me to keep an eye on him!"

So, Juve had managed to kill two birds with one stone and was congratulating himself. He was going to keep an eye on Boris Pokroff, a man he had long ago lost trust in and someone he felt might be a villain. And he was going to be able to inform the Duchess Ekaterina that he was tracking the chief of the secret police and that he was prepared to protect him in the event anything happened.

Juve, who had initially planned, as soon as he arrived at Gatchina, to seize the necklace from the chief of the secret police and have a frank talk with the man, decided to do nothing of the sort. He would wait to see what happened, to see what this man would do once the carriage stopped and he got out.

If Boris Pokroff complained that he had not stopped, as he had been ordered to, Juve would have no trouble playing the imbecile and claiming that either he had not heard the instructions or that his horses had run away.

The door was closed from the outside and when the carriage stopped in front of the front porch, two enormous Cossacks rushed over to open it and Boris Pokroff leapt out. Without responding to the obsequious greetings addressed to him by a delegation of moujik, headed by the village mayor, he spoke to the mayor, while motioning for the Cossacks.

Juve noted that, while listening to the chief of the secret police, the three men glanced at him out of the corners of their eyes. And he wondered what they could be discussing.

However, the two Cossacks immediately leapt up onto the bench beside the French policeman. One of them instructed him to lead his horses on. They showed him where the stables were and Juve rejoiced at this turn of events.

"Well," he said. "My man had a fright. He didn't dare complain since he realized I had uncovered his plans."

The policeman imagined that the Cossack had climbed up beside him to show him where to uncouple his team. Yet, they had barely arrived in front of the stable when the large officers, as if obeying an unseen signal, pushed him hastily down from his seat and tied him up.

"Well," thought Juve, "Things are not going well. What are these two types going to do with me?"

He did not resist, knowing that it would be futile and settled for waiting. The two Cossacks remained still, standing next to their prisoner, until a small man, wrapped in a large black coat, came over to join them. It was the man who, a few moments earlier, had headed the delegation of moujiks.

"What's your name?" he asked, looking at Juve suspiciously.

The policeman replied, "I'm Nick, the driver…"

But the mayor interrupted him, saying, "That's not true. We know Nick. He's fatter than you are and always drunk. Boris Pokroff has had you arrested because you disobeyed a while back. You'll probably be sentenced to fifty lashes of the whip."

Juve tensed. The possibility of such a punishment did not exactly fill him with joy. Yet, on the other hand, he figured that if all they punished him for was disobedience, he could consider himself lucky.

He asked, "Then what will happen to me?"

The mayor answered quietly, saying, "Once you have been whipped, you'll be free, like any other man who has paid his debt to society."

While speaking, however, the mayor had walked closer to Juve and, taking a closer look at the policeman's attire. He was wearing a coat four times too large, which he had stuffed with straw. The mayor started patting the large pockets in his coat when, suddenly, he shivered and withdrew his hand from the pocket into which he had plunged it. He pulled out an object, dropped it immediately to the ground and ran off, followed by the two Cossacks, all three men shrieking.

"What's up with them?" Juve wondered.

He looked down at the object that had caused this sudden terror and burst out laughing. It was the bomb, the famous bomb, which he had discovered before setting out from Tsarskoye Selo, the bomb that was in fact absolutely inoffensive.

"Really, these people are getting all into a dither and I will have to show them that without any trigger the device cannot explode."

A few seconds later, Juve watched as the mayor returned, accompanied by moujiks, Cossacks and even Boris Pokroff. The little herd advanced with a certain amount of trepidation as if they had been told not to approach the bomb. Boris Pokroff, however, was braver than the others. He walked right up to Juve, picked up the explosive device at his feet and glanced at it quickly, making sure that it was inoffensive. Of course, he knew better than anyone that it was harmless, but, in order to pull the wool over the eyes of everyone around them, Boris Pokroff picked the bomb up gingerly and threw it into a bucket of water. Only then did the moujiks, the mayor and the Cossacks decide to approach.

Juve suddenly turned very pale. Not out of fear, but surprise. In fact, his glance had just caught that of Boris Pokroff. It had only lasted a moment, but it was enough time for Juve to make a sensational deduction.

Had Juve recognized Fantômas?

In any case, after his initial surprise, the policeman decided that he would not let anything show although his conviction was so strong, as the other men discussed his fate for an hour.

After their initial surprise, the Cossacks were furious. They waved their arms, thrust their fists in Juve's face, slapped the pistols hanging from their belts. The policeman understood enough Russian to realize what they were saying about him.

"He's foreigner, an assassin. He wanted to blow our master up. He must be killed."

"Yes!" cried the moujiks. "Death! Without any further type of trial!"

Batons were raised over Juve's head. Pistols were taken from the Cossacks belts.

The policeman, who had believed that he was in no danger just a short while earlier, thought, "I do think I'm lost this time. There's no point in trying to explain anything at all to these brutes. With the slightest movement on my part, any word of rebellion, they'll all jump on me!"

The mayor, however, intervened, placing himself in front of the men who were threatening Juve. With a strong, powerful voice, that was astonishing from such a little man, he said, "You have no right to put the prisoner to death. Of course, he's a wretch, but he must be sentenced in keeping with the law. As mayor of the town, I'm responsible and the chief of the secret police will not contradict that."

Boris Pokroff hid a grimace. It seemed to Juve that, despite the fact that it was illegal to do so, the police chief would have willingly allowed the crowd to massacre the prisoner. Yet, challenged by the mayor, Boris Pokroff had to give up.

"The mayor is right," he said. "There is no doubt that this man, on whom we found the bomb, wanted to assassinate me, but he must be judged, sentenced and executed in due course, out of respect for justice."

The mayor immediately took charge, saying "The man will be taken to the prison in Tsarskoye Selo this very evening. It's the closest prison to the town."

But Boris Pokroff frowned, as a brief smile flitted over Juve's lips. Juve felt as if he had just escaped from a great danger. As long as he was not executed immediately, assassinated on the spot, he would find a way out of this jam.

When he would appear before the Tsarskoye Selo judges, he would merely have to identify himself, to call on the Duchess Ekaterina and perhaps even the emperor and the empress, to testify. He would explain what he had discovered and then it would be Boris Pokroff who found himself between a rock and a hard place. Moreover, Juve had the impression that Pokroff was perfectly aware of this.

When the mayor had announced that the prisoner would be taken to Tsarskoye Selo, Boris Pokroff asked, "Is there no prison closer than that one which is at least 20 verste away?"

"No," replied the little mayor, who was quite imperious despite his small stature. "I know, police chief, what I have to do. I will make a call in a while from my office and asked for cavaliers to be sent to accompany this man, who will make the trip on foot, in chains."

"But, in the meantime?" Boris Pokroff asked.

"In the meantime," said the mayor, "the Cossacks and the peasants will guard the prisoner in an office at the town hall."

Already, despite his bonds, Juve was trying to take a few steps. He was worried about staying at this place and the idea of being transferred to the town hall was satisfactory to him.

But Boris Pokroff made one last effort, saying, "There is no need to burden your town hall with this prisoner. Moreover, the building is not suitable. I propose that you leave him here, in this shed, under the Cossacks' guard. Then we can rest assured that he will not escape."

The crowd accepted Boris Pokroff's proposal and Juve, who was most dissatisfied with the outcome, walked into the shed and was about to sit in a corner as the Cossacks took up their positions outside the door, joined by a few peasants.

Juve examined them one by one and, convinced that they were fierce but brave jailers, thought, "As long as I keep these guards, I will have only my adversary to fear."

The adversary was most perplexed and upset. When he had stepped down out of the carriage and had glanced in amazement at the extraordinary coachman who had been driving his carriage, he had been struck by the latter's appearance. Fantômas had shivered from head to toe when he recognized Juve on Nick's bench. As of that moment, he had had only one thought in mind: to capture the policeman and hold him at his mercy. He figured it would be a simple matter. By accusing his driver, in front of the drivers, of showing a lack of respect and of disobeying him, he would be able to have him bound and punished with 50 lashes of the whip.

After that, Fantômas would step in and give Juve, devastated and broken by the punishment, the final blow. It would take place between the two men, one on one, but no one would ever know how or why Boris Pokroff's fake driver had died.

Unfortunately, the Mayor of Gatchina searched through Juve's pockets and discovered the bomb. As of that moment, the prisoner's case became much more serious. From a simple disrespectful driver, Juve had been transformed into a major criminal, an assassin. It was no longer a matter of giving him 50 lashes of the whip, he had to be tried and hung. In the name of the municipality, the mayor took charge, and Juve escaped from Fantômas' clutches.

For that reason, his heart full of rage, Fantômas was obliged to declare that the mayor was right and that the man could not be put to death without going through the formalities of being judged. This all took about ten minutes and Fantômas, putting off any decision as to how he would put Juve to death until later, despite the mayor, despite the Cossacks and the moujiks, went inside the house.

He walked up to the first floor and had barely stepped onto the landing when two arms wrapped around his neck, two lips sought his. Duchess Ekaterina, who had been waiting for him in the shadows, now caressed him tenderly.

"Oh, Boris!" the duchess murmured, pulling her lover close. "I'm so happy to see you here. I've been waiting for you for two hours already and I was wondering why you were so late. Your profession is so dangerous, so formidable that I constantly fear for you."

Fantômas returned the duchess' passionate embrace, then walked with her into the small, brightly lit drawing room. A table had been set in the middle of the room. Dinner time was long past and night was, in fact, falling.

The duchess looked at the so-called chief of police and was astonished by his distraught air.

"By all that's holy," she said, clasping her hands, "What has happened to you, Boris? You look upset."

Fantômas responded, starting to smile, and said, "Nothing, well almost nothing…"

Then, out of bravado, in order to make himself look good to his mistress, he nonchalantly said, "People tried to assassinate me two or three times on my way, but I managed to get away and now I've put it out of my mind."

The duchess turned quite pale and sought Fantômas' eyes. For a few moments, since her lover had arrived, the duchess had felt perplexed. She had watched as the carriage arrived in front of the house and, when she saw someone on the driver's bench who was not Nick, her intuition told her that it had to be Juve. Had Juve not protected her lover? And why had she heard shouting from the stables just a few moments after the coach arrived?

The duchess asked, "You're telling me Boris Pokroff, that someone wanted to harm you? What happened to your attackers?"

"I don't know," Boris Pokroff replied evasively. "The local police are looking for them."

"Was no one arrested?" the duchess asked.

"No one," Fantômas said sharply and, in an effort to turn the conversation in another direction, he walked over to his mistress, kissed her hand and said, "You look lovely tonight, Ekaterina."

For a moment, the duchess wondered if her lover were telling her the truth, if nothing had actually happened when he arrived by coach at Gatchina and if there were no prisoner under guard in the sheds. But she had no opportunity to ask any more questions. Looking quite festive, her lover invited her to sit down at the dinner table and then they both dug into the meal, honoring the dishes that the servants had served in advance, in the Russian fashion.

They spent two hours eating, during which time a joyful Fantômas told his mistress about the dangers of his profession, concluding, "And none of that matters as long as I love you Ekaterina and you love me."

For some time, the duchess had concluded that if she managed to get her lover to agree to Juve's protection, it would be much better for both the policeman and the chief of the secret police. Although she had not mentioned the famous French inspector she had sent for to Boris Pokroff, she had done so just to spare his sensibilities. She decided that that evening would be an excellent time to speak to Boris Pokroff about Juve. She walked over to her lover, placed her head tenderly on his shoulder and murmured, "Boris, I see a cloud in our heavenly sky. And that cloud is large and black, full of menace. I would like your permission to chase it from my horizon."

Fantômas was filled with curiosity as he listed to his beautiful mistress and said, "Your words are filled with filling and poetry but, like a poet, your meaning is not clear. Please tell me what you mean."

"Oh, it's quite simple," the duchess said, with a smile. "I'm afraid for your Boris. I feel that you don't have the protection you need to practice your profession."

The so-called chief of police shrugged and replied, "How could I find anyone better than myself to protect me? You know, Ekaterina this unfortunate country is full of felons and traitors."

"I know," replied the duchess. "That's why if you agree to have a reliable and devoted protector at your side I would not look for one in Russia, but elsewhere..."

"Really," said the so-called Boris Pokroff, amused by the conversation. "And where would you go to find such a rare pearl?"

"To France! To Paris!"

"Paris!" Boris Pokroff repeated. "And who would you select in Paris?"

Sharply, the duchess replied, "I would choose the famous French policeman, Juve, since Juve is honest and clever. Juve is brave and incorruptible."

Well, if the duchess had known the true identity of the man to whom she was praising Juve, if she had suspected for one moment that Boris Pokroff, her lover, was none other than Fantômas, she would have been dumbfounded.

But the duchess did not suspect a thing and, taking her lover's silence for approval, she spent another 10 minutes insisting that he hire Juve to protect him, as soon as possible.

Women find it hard to keep secrets and, in order to finish with a firm proposal, the Duchess Ekaterina announced, "Juve is in Russia, in St. Petersburg. For several days now, he has been protecting you without your knowledge, Boris Pokroff. And he is doing so at my request. I'll tell you something else. Juve was your coachman this afternoon. He's the one who brought you here and he's busy taking care of your horses in your stables this very minute. Do it for me, sweetheart. Agree to let Juve protect you officially. He'll be more efficient like that. Boris Pokroff, do you want me to have him brought here?"

Considering the circumstances, considering the Duchess' anxiety, Fantômas thought for a few moments. Although Ekaterina suspected nothing, it was quite clear that he did not have to consider the strange coincidence that she was offering to have Fantômas protected by Juve at the very moment that Juve was at Fantômas' mercy. Yet, the sinister bandit wondered if the duchess was not playing some sort of game, confronting him in this manner to determine her lover's exact nature...

"You never know, just what these Russian men and women are thinking!" thought Fantômas, who had no idea of making his own thoughts known.

He adopted an impassive expressive and appeared to be touched by his mistress' proposal. He took her hands and clasped them, pulling the duchess into the adjacent room while planting a paternal kiss on her forehead.

"Ekaterina, your proposal touches me enormously. Unfortunately, I cannot respond right away. I'm exhausted and you are as well. I can see your beautiful eyelids drooping. Get some sleep. We'll discuss matters tomorrow."

The duchess realized that she should not insist. She obeyed her lover and immediately went into the dressing room next door to undress.

Fantômas immediately left the room and snuck down the stairway. He managed to make his way outside without being noticed by the servants, most of whom had already gone upstairs to be. He headed straight over to the shed.

The Cossacks were there alone with the prisoner. The peasants had stood guard for a while and then had gone home, leaving the soldiers alone. When he saw this, Fantômas shivered with excitement. For close to two hours, he had been wondering how he could get rid of the unbearable guards and he had found no way since he had no authority over the moujiks. Yet they had taken themselves home and all that remained were the soldiers. He could easily have his way with them

They were veritable robots, never thinking, never reasoning, satisfied with rigorously obeying the orders they received. When he saw them, on the threshold of the door to the room in which Juve was kept, bound, the so-called Boris Pokroff pretended to be furious.

"How can this be, you sinister brutes," he said. "What are you still doing here?"

One Cossack stood up, touched his hat and respectfully said, "Master, we're still guarding the prisoner. We have not been relived."

Fantômas shrugged and said, "You're just a bunch of donkeys. You see no farther than the tip of your nose! Other men came on duty 45 minutes ago and are guarding the prisoner, just as you are, but they're doing it from the other door to the shed."

And since the Cossacks did not understand the explanation they had been given, Fantômas kicked them and punched them, chasing them away from the door.

"Go back to your barracks," he roared. "We don't need you!"

And, in order to pull the wool over their eyes, recalling that the soldiers were paid one kopek for each additional hour on duty, he scolded them imperiously, saying "Miserable wretches! I know what you're up to! You're extending your guard duty to make a little money. I don't know why I don't report you all to the station chief!"

Dumbfounded, the Cossacks fled. When they had disappeared into the night, a triumphant expression swept over Fantômas' face. He had Juve all to himself and Juve was bound. He walked slowly into the shed, lit only by a smoky lamp hanging from the ceiling. In a hoarse voice, Fantômas, who no longer needed to hide his identity, greeted his prisoner in a triumphant voice.

"Well, Juve," he said. "So here we are, once again face to face.

Fantômas waited for a response, but received none. The policeman held his gaze without wavering. He was still rigorously bound, unable to move at all, barely able to stand, unable to take a step in any direction. Jubilantly, Fantômas walked around him.

"You're all trussed up, Juve," he said. "You've been rendered powerless and your life is in my hands."

Juve still did not answer and Fantômas grew exasperated.

"Oh" he continued, "I see your disdain and your mistrust, Juve, but we could have a lot to say to one another. It might be worth our while to provide a few explanations. Do you acknowledge that you are in my power, that I have beaten you? Fine, you could beg for my mercy, but you aren't doing that and that's your right. Your silence is just one more insult. I will be so magnanimous as to not take any further vengeance. If you held me captive as I hold you, you wouldn't hesitate, Juve to kill me. I'm the stronger one, so I'll kill you."

Juve still had not uttered a sound. Perhaps his lips a turned a shade paler, perhaps he had clenched his fists under his bonds. Fantômas, however, searched through his pocket and was pulling out his revolver, when they heard the sound of footsteps approaching. Fantômas quickly turned out the light and settled down to listen. Two Cossacks arrived and took up their position in front of the door, which stood ajar.

"Did we get it right?" asked one.

"I hope so," said the other. "I mean, our two comrades came back just now and told us that we were on duty so that means we're on duty!"

"But, weren't we at our station?" asked the first man.

"Most likely," continued the second, "They forgot to tell us... Fortunately our comrades came back to warn us. Otherwise, we'd have been in a real jam. When a chief forgets to give his subordinate an order and then he notices what has happened, it's always the subordinate that suffers!"

"Should we step inside?" asked the first Cossack.

"No," replied his companion. "We've not been given any orders in that respect and we don't even know what we're guarding."

"Those imbeciles," thought Fantômas. "They've arrived at exactly the wrong moment. How can I get rid of them?"

Fantômas thought for a moment and realized that, based on the conversation he had just overheard, nothing in the world would convince the Cossacks to abandon their station. At the same time, Fantômas could only kill Juve with his revolver, since he had no other weapons with him. But a revolver makes noise and when they heard the destination, the Cossacks would certainly rush in. However, Fantômas knew that the shed had a second door.

"Juve will die in silence," he said, as he came up with a horrific new plan for assassination.

Groping about, he approached the policeman, took him by the arm and pushed him forward. Juve obeyed automatically, only because he felt that each step helped loosen his bonds a little more.

"If only," he thought, "I could get Fantômas to make me walk two or three hundred yards, I could free my arms and legs. And then we'll see what happens!"

Fantômas pushed Juve across the threshold of the door at the back of the shed that opened onto an inner court, at the foot of the house. Up to this point, the night had been dark. But at this very moment a small ray of light pierced through the clouds. Fantômas halted his prisoner. The rays of the moon concerned him, since he did not want anyone to see that he was putting his formidable enemy to death.

Despite his precautions, Fantômas had made a bit of noise while walking. The Cossacks were concerned about what was going on inside the shed they were guarding. Then, since the noises had subsided, they fell back into their torpor.

Yet, as Fantômas entered the inner court, lit by the rays of the moon, he had noticed a thread of light escaping through the curtains covering one of the windows and he realized that it was the window of the dressing room occupied by Duchess Ekaterina. That room, where the bandit's mistress was undressing, looked out onto the inner court and the duchess must certainly have heard an unusual noise, since she must have been the one who opened the curtains and looked out into the court.

Fantômas was quite perplexed and wondered what he should do. He did not want the brutish Cossacks to witness the crime he was about to commit since they would certainly talk about it. At the same time, he didn't want to assassinate Juve in front of the Duchess Ekaterina since he would then have to account for the murder. He could not use his revolver since he did not want to make any noise and he had no dagger.

Fantômas ground his teeth and clenched his fists. Of course, it would be easier enough for him to pit himself against Juve, who was defenseless, and strangle him, but the criminal feared that the policeman would resist, that Juve would cry out for help. He had to find another means to take his prisoner by surprise.

Suddenly, Fantômas felt his heart pound and a deep sense of satisfaction filled his mind.

"Why didn't I think of this earlier?" he wondered.

He had dragged Juve out of the shed, in the direction of the inner court, without thinking about what he was going to do. But he had just noticed, on the ground, barely ten yards away, the moss-covered stone coping, blanketed with ice, of a deep well from which the estate's stable hands came to get water each morning, after first breaking the ice. He did not hesitate. All he had to do was shove Juve, who was still bound.

Fantômas' mind was made up. He grabbed Juve by the shoulder and, pretending to look in the opposite direction, he forced him to walk once more. Juve graciously agreed and took a few steps. He had the impression that his bonds were coming undone. Yet, as Fantômas had not noticed a thing, Juve pretended to have difficulty walking so that he could surprise the thief when his ropes were sufficiently loose that he could use his arms and legs. At one point, Juve felt as if one of the slip knots, that held his right arm to his thigh, had come completely undone. The ropes around his knees were coming lose as well.

"Just a few more steps and I'll jump on Fantômas. The battle will be brief, but decisive!" Juve thought.

Juve's eyes shone with hope since Fantômas seemed completely unaware. But, suddenly, Juve cried out in fright, surprise and anguish. Fantômas had shoved him violently backward. Juve stumbled, feet slipping on the frozen snow, hip striking the edge of the well, the weight of his body dragging his legs along. The unfortunate man collapsed into his future tomb with a heavy thud.

Fantômas, however, kept on walking slowly, eyes riveted on the window of the Duchess Ekaterina's washroom.

He sighed deeply in satisfaction and murmured, "The curtain has not moved. She heard nothing."

Then Fantômas rushed into the house through a service entrance.

CHAPTER XIX
Magnanimity

"Boris Pokroff, is that you my friend?"

As Fantômas was dragging Juve toward the fatal edge of the well into which he planned to shove him, Duchess Ekaterina, pleased to know, or so she believed, that she had almost convinced her lover to allow himself to be accompanied by the policeman, in whom she had complete confidence, had walked into her dressing room, where she quickly disrobed.

On her way back to the bedroom, she had called for Boris Pokroff, imagining that he had gone to prepare for bed as well and supposing that he was ready to join her.

To her great surprise, Boris Pokroff did not respond and, when she walked into the bedroom, the duchess found that her lover was not there.

She called again, in a louder voice that betrayed a certain degree of surprise.

"Boris Pokroff! Boris Pokroff!"

Silence reigned around her. Dumbfounded by this absence, Duchess Ekaterina suddenly thought she heard unusual noises coming from outside. Instinctively, she walked over to the window that looked out onto the garden and, pushing the curtain aside, she noticed, in the weak moonlight, the characteristic silhouettes of two Cossacks. It was the men who had taken over for the comrades standing guard at the door to the shed.

Undoubtedly, the duchess found the presence of the soldiers reassuring and yet, she grew worried as she saw the men running.

What was going on? Was there an alert?

She tilted her head, listening, after first opening the window, fearing that she would hear the sound of battle. But silence fell again and, reassured for the time being, although she still had no idea what had become of Boris Pokroff, she went back into the bedroom, walked across it. Suddenly she hastened her pace and headed once again to her dressing room since she once again heard furtive noises that came, without a doubt, from the inner courtyard of the property.

That was when the duchess had pushed aside the curtain through which a thread of light glowed, the thread of light that had concerned Fantômas so as he was dragging Juve.

Yet, after opening the curtain for a second, the Duchess let it fall back and did not touch it again. Silence fell yet again and, hesitating, perplexed, not knowing where to look, the Duchess turned back and sat down on the foot of her bed, worried, waiting.

She heard a dull sound and, although she did not know where it came from, her chest grew tight. Ekaterina was afraid, strangely afraid. She had the feeling that she was surrounded by mysteries, that she had plunged into the middle of a frightening, disturbing unknown.

Then the door opened and the man the young woman knew as Boris Pokroff entered the bedroom.

Fantômas was very pale and unable to hide the shivers that ran up and down his body. The terrible bandit had the clear impression that, this time, he had got rid of his adversary, that Juve had fallen into the depths of the well. If ever anyone pulled him out, they would be bringing a cadaver back to the surface. Juve's cadaver! Fantômas could not believe this turn of events and yet, it was obvious, indisputable, Juve had clearly plunged into the well, tightly bound, immobilized, incapable of offering any resistance!

His face grew peaceful.

"Definitely," thought Fantômas, "the god of victory is with me. A few weeks ago, I trapped Fandor and today I've reduced Juve to nothing. The way ahead is clear."

Fantômas was radiant... In the same manner as, up to now, he had never felt any remorse at the thought that he had caused the death of the noble journalist with the well-meaning heart—since Fantômas truly believed that Fandor was dead—he did not experience the slightest twinge of regret at the idea that Juve was now dying, was even most certainly dead.

Fantômas was thrilled with the idea of this double success. His trembling gone, face filled with triumph and tenderness, he walked over to the duchess whose bosom heaved. He hugged her tightly, surprised at her icy body.

"What's wrong, dear heart?" he asked.

She snuggled against him and murmured, "I'm cold. But above all I'm afraid."

Everything was sleeping or, to be more accurate, seemed to be sleeping, in the sumptuous house in Gatchina. Someone, however, was waking before dawn, since it was not yet three in the morning. That someone was the Duchess Ekaterina. She thought she had heard a cry, a dreadful groan, an agonizing shriek and she had leapt out of bed. Was it a dream? Was it real?

Ekaterina could not say, but she did not feel that she was hallucinating. She tried to go back to sleep, to snuggle down under the blankets next to her lover, who was sleeping soundly, but sleep eluded her.

The cry that had wakened her continued to resound in her ears and the duchess felt as if someone were calling her and that if she did not respond she would be responsible for a man's death. With that thought, the duchess leapt out of bed.

She stopped abruptly at the entrance to her dressing room to make sure she had not roused Boris Pokroff. He continued to sleep. The duchess walked into the adjacent room, dressed hastily, pulling on thick, fur-lined boots and a heavy mantle, then opened the window.

Once again, the cry of anguish rang out. This time, there was no longer any doubt that someone outside was calling, someone who was suffering, who was on the point of dying and that cry came from the inner courtyard of the estate.

At that very moment, three bats, spinning in the air, struck the duchess' forehead, as she leaned out the window, and an owl could be heard shrieking in the distance, in the forest.

"What tragic omens," said the duchess, who was indeed most superstitious.

As a deep sense of alarm washed over her, she felt an urgent need to ward off bad luck by going, even at the peril of her own life, to help the dying man who was calling her.

Walking down a hidden staircase, the duchess quickly reached the inner courtyard. The monotonous and persistent moans she heard took her in the direction of the old well. She leaned over the edge, looked down into the black hole and saw nothing. Yet, as she leaned in that position, she realized that the rope, which was used to lower the bucket into the well, was trembling slightly. Obviously, someone or something at the bottom of the abyss was pulling on the rope.

There was a handle and all she had to do was turn it to pull the cord at the end of the rope, up from the bottom of the well. The duchess struggled to turn it, wanting to respond to the call she felt was addressed to her. She turned the hand two or three times, and then, from the bottom of the well, she heard a voice cry out, "Be brave. Don't give up! You can save me!"

The duchess turned the crank feverishly. Large drops of sweat beaded on her forehead. Two or three times, she had the impression that she would have to give up, that the job was too much for her. She stopped, placed the rope on the notch to prevent the bucket from slipping back down, caught her breath and set about turning the crank again.

As the work continued and grew more painful, the duchess felt that the load she was pulling up was growing heavier and heavier. The voice, however, continued to encourage her. She felt that the burden she was pulling was heavy, possibly a man's body, the body of a human being of course...

For a second, she thought of calling out, of calling out to Boris Pokroff, telling him to come down, but a sense of foreboding, instinct, held her back, and her woman's intuition made her believe that that was the right course of action, that it was preferable not to wake her lover.

After resting for a few minutes, the duchess set back to work. She continued to turn the crank, until her arms grew exhausted and her hands grew bloody. Finally, just as she was about to give up, unable to enjoy the benefits of this hard labor because she was no long able to hook the rope on the notch to prevent the bucket from tumbling down inside the well, a human form appeared and, with a supreme effort, leapt out of the bucket and fell to the ground at the duchess' feet.

This human being was in a frightful, pitiful state, clothing frozen stiff, hands and face covered with blood, large ropes binding his arms to his chest.

Nevertheless, demonstrating extraordinary vigor, the man managed to stand up, making his frozen bonds crack, He exclaimed in surprise, and the duchess, who had fallen to the ground, cried out in astonishment. The man had recognized her and the duchess, overcome with surprise, cried out the name of the rescued: "Juve!"

It was Juve, in fact who had miraculously escaped from the frightful death Fantômas had planned for him. As he fell down the well, Juve had managed to prop his back against the walls of the frightful abyss and descend slowly to the bottom. The water in the well was frozen. Juve had been able to stand on the ice and for a good half hour had remained immobile, fearing a new attack. Then, he had tried to climb up the wall of the well, after first making sure he heard no suspicious sounds in the vicinity. But, despite his efforts, Juve had fallen back two or three times, unable to climb out of the well on his own. He experienced such violent pain when he landed heavily on the surface of the frozen water that he was unable to stop from calling out. It was these cries that the duchess had heard, that had drawn her to the well to rescue the policeman. The duchess and the policeman stood facing one another, bewildered. Juve had not known that the duchess was at Gatchina. And the duchess could not understand how Juve, the extraordinarily skillful policeman, had fallen so low, risking death if she had not intervened.

"How did you get down there?" the duchess asked.

Juve was about to tell her everything. Fantômas' name came to his lips. Instinctively, he was about to say that Fantômas had thrown him down the well, that Fantômas was none other than Boris Pokroff, but he thought better of it and abstained from making such an accusation.

He knew that the duchess was blinded by love!

Telling her outright that her adored lover, Boris Pokroff, was none other than the frightful bandit who saddened the entire world with his despicable crimes would not convince the duchess of her lover's infamy, but give her every reason to believe that Juve was totally mad. Instead, Juve explained what had happened without telling her the entire truth.

"Madam," he said, as he removed his ice-covered coat, "Boris Pokroff made a frightful error, took me for a criminal, tied me up and threw me into the well!"

The duchess was dumbfounded.

"Boris Pokroff did this to you?" she asked.

"Yes, madam," replied Juve. "But it doesn't matter since you rescued me."

The duchess clasped her hands, and said, "My God! My God! Blessed be the Holy Images that inspired me to come to your rescue! I would never have forgiven myself if you had died. I would have felt responsible! Mr. Juve, I'm sure you realize now the difficulty of the mandate I have given you..."

She questioned him in a hesitant yet audacious manner, self-centered in her love, "Despite everything, will you continued to protect Boris Pokroff?"

"You can count on me," Juve replied in an enigmatic tone.

Then abruptly changing the topic, he asked, "Madam, where is your protégé at this moment?"

The duchess replied, "Boris Pokroff was tired and is resting at this moment. He is sleeping in our bedroom. See how delicate he is? He worried me so much, not mentioning a word about the attack on his person."

Despite the horror of his situation, Juve was unable to an ironic smile from his lips. Obviously, fate got him into the most unexpected situations! And now, to please this woman, he was obliged to go into raptures over the delicate nature of the man who had just pitched him into a well, who was counting on him to die there in great agony, and who had not uttered a single word to anyone, all in order to maintain his mistress' peace of mind.

Sarcastically, Juve said, "Boris Pokroff is, in fact, a very tactful man!"

The duchess looked at Juve anxiously and said, "You're not angry with him?"

"Oh! Not at all," Juve replied. "However, I would be pleased to have a word or two with him in a bit."

"Let him rest a few more minutes," the duchess asked. "His work is so hard and he is so often tired that I hesitate to wake him."

"Being in love is a wonderful thing," thought Juve who, with a pang in his heart, realized that he was tired too and that, unlike Fantômas, he did not have the luxury of sleeping in a bed. And he also thought about the fact that, barely out of the well that might have become his tomb, he would now have to take part in the ultimate battle, and conquer or die! For, in just a few seconds, Juve had decided that he had to finish his business with Fantômas, that he would surprise him while he slept, that their roles would change…

Juve had made up his mind. He would not attempt to wring an explanation from the bandit! He felt for his belt, where he had hidden a dagger, a dagger he planned to thrust, without further ado, into Fantômas' heart, if Fantômas did indeed have a heart.

Teeth chattering, the duchess said, "Let's go inside."

These words tore Juve from his thoughts and he prepared to follow the pretty woman.

"She has just signed a death warrant," he said to himself.

And, while Juve felt no pity at all for Fantômas, the thought of the pain this woman would experience, in a few minutes, when she saw her lover die, troubled him a great deal.

"Poor wretch," Juve thought. "Love is such a sad thing when you love a criminal like Fantômas!"

The duchess was walking over to the small door from which she had left the building when she suddenly stopped. She reached out for Juve with a trembling hand and then, leaning against the policeman, Ekaterina murmured in a voice filled with anguish, "Did you hear that?"

"Yes," Juve replied.

"What can it be? Could it be the Cossacks?" she asked.

With a finger, she pointed at the shadows moving along the wall, appearing from behind the rocks, from out of the dark corners, flowing out over the ground in the pale rays of the moon.

Two or three strident whistle calls rang out then and Juve and the Duchess felt as if they had been surrounded by a troupe of admirably well-organized people, with a mission to kidnap them!

Juve suddenly felt as if he weighed less than a feather. He was being carried at arm's length and a gag had been placed in his mouth, but his eyes were not hidden and he could see. He saw that, like him, the duchess was being carried off. The audacious kidnappers that had rushed over, no doubt obeying orders, quickly walked away from the house and carried them into a sort of shed at the edge of the property.

The two captives were placed on the ground, side by side, and, as no one took notice of Juve, who once again found himself bound, they removed the ropes that had kept the duchess motionless. Voices around them whispered.

"It's her! It's Ekaterina!"

People spoke animatedly. Then, after placing the duchess under guard, they turned back to Juve. Someone quickly removed his gag. With a kick, they forced him to his feet. Juve fumed in anger and decided to make the kidnappers pay dearly, but the words he was about to utter died in his throat. The policeman was dumbfounded by what he heard.

"It's not him!" said someone standing in front of him. That individual was, apparently, neither a soldier nor a criminal. Quite the contrary, he inspired respect and confidence. He wore a long black robe and there was some sort of miter on his head. He must have been a monk, possibly even a pope!

"What is this animal doing here?" Juve asked, unable to stop smiling as he looked at the large, dumbfounded religious man. Someone walked over to the pope. It was a woman. In a broken, wavering voice that revealed her great age, she asked "So, you didn't take Boris Pokroff? Answer me Alleluia. You can see that I'm burning with impatience to take my vengeance and carve that monster's eyes out with my knitting needles!"

The pope nodded and replied, "No, Marfa Berena, we did not kidnap Boris Pokroff yet, and this is extraordinary since this is his house and that is his mistress standing there."

As he heard this conversation, Juve experienced great fear along with a sliver of hope. The name of the pope, uttered by the old woman with the bloodthirsty intentions, told him immediately what his aggressors intended to do. Juve had just been captured by a band of nihilists, possibly the most famous and feared band in all of Russia, the band once headed by Natacha, the daughter of the real Boris Pokroff.

Juve wondered what he was to do with these people. Should he let them know who he was? There was one way in which to earn their good graces and that would be to denounce where Boris Pokroff or, more accurately, Fantômas, was hiding, it would be to tell them where he was sleeping. But, Juve found that behavior repugnant. A loud cry rang out. It was the duchess who had just realized whose hands she had fallen into and the danger faced by her lover. She addressed a supreme appeal to her companion, crying out, "Juve! In the name of God save me!"

This supplication reminded Juve about the solemn promise he had made to the duchess to protect the chief of police, her lover, to the death. This was a decisive, yet poorly chosen moment.

How could Juve prevent the nihilists from massacring Boris Pokroff, after they quickly found him in the house? They had acted gently, silently. He could feel that there were a large number of them, perhaps 20 or 30. Most likely they were not all in the shed and a large number of them must be watching the edges of the Gatchina property to make any escape impossible.

Juve's situation was quite extraordinary. Obviously, he wanted Fantômas to die more than anyone else, but the idea of stirring up the nihilists against the bandit and using them to kill the criminal mastermind, masquerading as Boris Pokroff, was unacceptable to him. Juve's soul was so great, and his concept of conscience and duty was so rigorous that he could not behave in that manner.

"Between Fantômas and me, it will be a fight to the end, a duel without mercy, but that will only happen after we have come face to face and have both taken off our masks. At present, for these people, and for the duchess as well, that is not Fantômas up there in the house, but simply Boris Pokroff. And I made a promise to Boris Pokroff's mistress that I would protect her lover. I must do my best to keep my oath."

Once again, the policeman heard Ekaterina begging, murmuring words that only Juve could understand, "Save us Juve! By all the Holy Images, save us!"

As the nihilists continued to whisper quietly, the policeman remained silent, forehead furrowed, trying to come up with a plan. Suddenly, he looked up and in a clear voice called out, "Alleluia!"

The pope turned to him. He walked over to Juve and looked him in the eyes, saying, "Do you know me?"

"Good grief," Juve replied. "Aren't you Alleluia, the pope who officiates in the heights of Valdai, where your church is located?"

"That's right," the religious man acknowledged. "But you…"

Juve continued, "Aren't you Alleluia, the famous leader of the right and good cause, the man who commands the empire's nihilists, and whose sect grows stronger every day than all of the Tsar's armies combined?"

"All that is true," the pope replied, unnerved. "But you…"

"Are you not," continued Juve, "The man who, justly indignant to hear people say that the nihilists are committing theft and larceny for profit, discovered that such thefts were committed by a bandit by the name of Fantômas?"

"That is perfectly true. Are you Fantômas?" he replied.

Juve shrugged and continued, "Are you not Alleluia who, disdaining to search for a criminal yet wanting to get rid of him had, at the instigation of a few of his followers, addressed a telegram to the most famous policeman in all of France, inviting him to come and capture that Fantômas whose actions reflect so dishonorably on the just actions of the nihilists?"

"Ah, now..." hesitated the pope.

Juve interrupted him once again, reached out his hand and declared, "Now you recognize me, don't you, Alleluia? You realize that the man standing before you is Juve."

The nihilists had gathered at the pope's sides and, as Juve raised his voice, they heard his last declarations. A murmur ran through the crowd.

"Juve! It's Juve," someone said and the whispering grew.

The duchess, however, surprised and despairing at discovering that the policeman was pacifying the nihilists, rolled about on the ground, overcome with emotion.

"My God!" she said. "Juve is betraying me..."

Fortunately, she was speaking French and the nihilists did not understand what she was saying. But Juve jumped at the insult.

"No, madam, I'm not betraying you. Quite the contrary as you will see..."

The pope clasped Juve's hands warmly and declared, "We had no idea what had happened to you. Why didn't you warn us?"

"A policeman," Juve replied, "is always under cover. He only appears when not expected. But I'm ready to follow you now. In fact, it's even rather important that we leave as quickly as possible, since this place is dangerous. I know that Boris Pokroff left Tsarskoye Selo an hour ago with a troupe of horsemen to go to Gatchina. He'll be here soon, with men who are armed to the teeth. And you won't be able to withstand them."

"Boris Pokroff," exclaimed the nihilists. "So, he's not in the house we've surrounded?"

"Of course he isn't!" replied Juve.

The policeman uttered this lie with a certain amount of apprehension. If they did not believe him, if they decided to search the building, they would most certainly discover Boris Pokroff and massacre him. And Juve, who would be considered a liar and traitor, would not escape the supreme punishment.

Juve realized that by making his claim, he was playing rough. He needed an argument, some proof to back up his statement, to convince his audience of the truth of his words. They did, in fact, seem only half convinced.

One stated, "We were almost certain, however, that Boris Pokroff had arrived in Gatchina this afternoon to join his mistress. And his mistress is here. We've captured her!"

Juve suddenly came up with an idea… It was crazy, wild, but was he not risking everything and wouldn't something unlikely and unexpected seem more logical and plausible?

"You're thinking is faulty," Juve grumbled.

"Why?" a man asked. "Explain yourself!"

You have just noted that the Duchess Ekaterina…"

They interrupted him.

"There is no duchess here. We do not accept that title of nobility!"

"So be it," Juve replied, shrugging. "But that is of no importance! You have noted, as I said, that Ekaterina is here and you have concluded that Boris Pokroff must be with her. But what about me?"

"You?" asked Pope Alleluia, "What about you? We don't understand."

Juve drew the man closer and replied, "Listen, it's quite simple. I'll tell you in a low voice but you must not spread this around. I wouldn't want to embarrass this lady. Later, you can tell your companions after we have left, since I will be leaving with you. So, this is where we stand. I'm Ekaterina's lover. Do you understand me, Pope? I'm cuckolding Boris Pokroff with his mistress. So, it's quite certain that if I am here with her tonight, Pokroff cannot be!"

Pope nodded and said, "As a religious man, I'm not really aware of the customs of adultery. Yet, I suppose that you must be right. In fact, if this woman's lover caught you with her, he would not hesitate to kill you…"

"That's obvious," Juve replied derisively. "Either he would kill me or I'd kill him. In any case, one of us would be dead… but since we're both alive you have to admit that I'm here and Boris Pokroff is not!"

The pope nodded, agreeing with the policeman's logic.

First, when she had heard Juve's declarations, the duchess had jumped in indignation. What? This policeman was claiming to be her lover. His lie to the wretches was so vile. She was about to protest, but, fortunately, she abstained. In fact, she quickly realized that, although Juve was boasting about a good fortune that existed only in his imagination and was compromising her reputation, it was to save her lover's life!

The pope quietly told some of the nihilists surrounding him what Juve had just said. They appeared to take the ingenious policeman at his word.

Juve waited, understandably anxious, for the outcome of the secret conversation. What would they decide?

Finally, the pope approached him and said, "My friends are of the opinion that you must be telling the truth. They understand love and respect your feelings. Since you love her, no harm will be done to Ekaterina, as long as she swears on your head not to reveal that she has seen us here this evening. Moreover, we will not take her with us. She can go back inside her house and stay there quietly. As for you, Juve, we are counting on you to come with us. It is agreed that this is just a truce. It does nothing to change our plans for Boris Pokroff. Since he's coming here with the horsemen, we'll leave this place immediately, but we will be back! His time, the time of his punishment, is coming!"

Juve applauded the pope's words and said, "Brave! Bravo! Let us leave together. While you come up with a plan to take care of Boris Pokroff, I'll be working on one for Fantômas!"

Silently, slowly, fading into the dark walls, the nihilists left as they had come, invisible.

Juve quickly bade the duchess farewell, and disappeared in the company of the nihilists. After a few moments, there was no one left in the park at Gatchina, which was blanketed in silence.

The duchess remained motionless as excitement coursed through her veins. Ah, Juve had definitely given her extraordinary proof of his skill and dedication. The policeman had just saved her and her lover, and he did it just a few moments after Boris Pokroff had made a near fatal mistake and killed him.

When she was certain that there was no one in the garden, the duchess raced into the house and up the stairs to her room, where she thought she would find her lover still asleep. She was preparing to tell him about all the dangers he had risked without knowing it. When she walked into the room, she found the man she knew as Boris Pokroff up and dressed. He looked quite pale.

The duchess threw herself into his arms and stammered, "Oh! Boris, Boris, you have no idea of the great danger you have missed!"

The duchess' lover nodded his head, gravely and replied, "I know that something terrible has happened, duchess, but I do not know what. I suffered during your absence and did not dare make a move, for fear of compromising a situation I did not understand."

"Listen!" said the duchess, throwing her arms around her lover's neck.

Then, in a halting, quavering voice, Ekaterina who had no idea as to the true identity of the man she was confiding in told him everything, as she understood it, as Juve had presented it to her.

After half an hour, she concluded, saying, "Boris Pokroff, you will never love this man enough, this man who, after being thrown into the well by you, felt no bitterness toward you and saved you from the nihilists! This man, I have not told you his name yet, but you need to know his name."

But to her great surprise, Boris Pokroff interrupted her and uttered the name, "Juve! Juve is the man!"

"And how do you know that?" asked the duchess.

Fantômas was filled with emotion by his mistress' question, but recovered quickly and replied, "Am I not the chief of police? Don't I know everything?"

The duchess, who was still overwhelmed by the idea of the formidable danger that her lover had just avoided, knelt down at the foot of the bed, in front of the Holy Images and asked, "Would you like us to honor heaven for its clemency in our respect and call on the All-Powerful God to protect Juve?"

And then something happened, something that neither Juve nor Fantômas could ever have imagined seeing one day. Fantômas knelt down, clasped his hands, and pretended to pray to God to protect his enemy. However, as the duchess was praying ardently, Fantômas felt touched to the bottom of his heart and thought, "What Juve did there was really quite clever!"

CHAPTER XX
Underground

It was still night. At the end of the tree-lined Skobeleff Avenue that runs along the Neva in St. Petersburg, a street cleaner seemed to be busily cleaning garbage away. The man, bent over his broom, was attempting to make an enormous pile of waste disappear down a drain inlet that was far too narrow. And he was constantly being interrupted in his work. People appeared out of the shadows and walked over to him, appearing to brush up against him, stopping for a few seconds. It looked like the sweeper would murmur something in their ear, then the people would disappear and the man would continue his work.

Two policemen appeared, their heavy footsteps on the sidewalk troubling the silence of the night.

One of them, seeing the old worker, greeted him politely, "Good evening, Michel."

The sweeper grumbled, "Good evening. It would be better to say good day, though, since dawn will be here soon. But it's all the same. Whether it's night or day, this is hard work!"

"Bah!" said the police officer, as he continued to walk. "It's either this or something else when you're not rich."

"Of course!" grumbled the sweeper. "Of course."

He watched the policemen for a moment, as they walked off, then continued to grumble, "It's just that better days will be coming and then those who struggle will rest and those who do nothing right now will work in their place."

In any case, the sweeper went back to his work and, with a nervous fury pushed the garbage toward the sewer. The officers had just disappeared around a corner when an old woman, who had been hiding behind the trunk of a large tree, walked over to the sweeper.

"Michel, where is the meeting?" she asked in a bitter, grating voice.

The sweeper did not reply. He placed his finger on her lips, indicating that she should remain silent. Then, making sure that the officers had disappeared, he decided to speak.

"You shout too loudly, Marfa Berena! You'll compromise all of us! Those policemen were chatting with me barely a few seconds ago and cannot be far off."

It was, in fact, old Marfa Berena who had just walked over to the sweeper.

"By the Holy Images," she said. "I'm so impatient to get justice that I neglect the most elementary precautions!"

"I know," replied the sweeper. "I know that you asked for our tribunal to convene. Is it something serious?"

"It's incredible," the old woman replied, frowning. "I'll explain everything to you in a bit, along with the others. Tell me, Michel, where are we to meet?"

"You're almost the last one," he replied. "All of the others have passed by, on their way to the meeting. Here's what you must do. Walk down the road to No. 1465. In front of that house, in a nook, there is a metal plate that hides an underground staircase. All you have to do is lift it. Go down the stairs, walk in the darkness, making sure you always stay to the right. You will come across a brave man installing electrical wires in the sewers. He'll say 'Good evening' to you and you'll reply 'Natacha.' That's the password. Then the man will tell you how to go through the labyrinth underneath the city to get to the meeting."

"Thank you, Michel," the old woman replied. "Will I see you there in a bit?"

"Yes," he replied. "I plan to be there."

Marfa Berena followed the instructions the mysterious man had given her. She lifted the iron plate hiding a staircase, walked down the stairs that led into the entrails of the city. She met the electrician, gave him the password and was taken by the man, after walking about 10 minutes, into a vast, cold, poorly lit room, a true basement, walls dripping with humidity, and buried so deep in the ground that it seemed like some sort of tomb.

That room or rather that cellar, was an old, abandoned quarry that had been covered over when it came time, 25 years earlier, to build the Skobeleff. Most of the engineers who had been involved that project were no longer in St. Petersburg. Some had been sent off to work elsewhere; others had simply died and a few rare ones were municipal employees who had remembered the vast crypt hidden under one of the most important avenues in the capital.

When people stood in the gigantic cave, they noted, not without a certain sense of surprise, that there was a sort of spring at one end where water dripped from the rocky ceiling. When, by chance, a newcomer arrived and asked where the water came from, he would be told that it leaked in from the Neva and that, moreover, the intermittent inhabitants of the sinister place had to work hard to protect it from flooding.

Inside the cave, however, in the light cast by lanterns hanging on the walls, people came and went, people with very different appearances, their social standing obvious from their clothing. Yet they all wore some kind of black veil over their faces.

There were moujiks with trimmed furs, long greatcoats worn at the elbows and back, a few soldiers, civil servants of all kinds, particularly municipal workers.

There were a fair number of women in the room, a few of them young and pretty, others elderly and wretched, poor or disinherited.

When Marfa Berena arrived, she wore no veil and was in no apparent haste to put the black cloth over her face, triggering a flurry of emotion.

People rushed to her sides, asking, "What's happening?"

The old woman, trembling with emotion, clasped the hands that reached out to her and replied, "You'll know in a moment. Has Alleluia arrived?"

The pope was there. He came over to join the old woman, clasped her hands and, glancing around him declared, "We must all be here and it is time to start our meeting."

"Excuse me," a voice interrupted. "Could you tell us, Alleluia, what happed to the expedition sent out to capture the chief of police in Gatchina? It does not appear that that wretched Boris Pokroff was put to death as it had been decided."

The pope turned to the speaker and replied, "Providence has its own secret plans and we men cannot always do as we wish. But rest assured brother Boleslas, everything comes to he who waits."

Boleslas shrugged and went over to a corner to sit down.

Marfa Berena climbed up onto a sort of podium and silence fell over the participants. They knew that she had something important to say, that they had been summoned at her request. They just had to listen to the old woman to find out what was going on.

Pope Alleluia murmured a few words, inviting the people to remain calm and silent. When he had finished, he asked the old woman to explain herself.

"My brothers," she said in a hoarse voice. You know that a few weeks ago, in order to save my son Vassili from the claws of the police, since they wanted to take him to Siberia, another man, one who had been condemned to death by our tribunal, was released from that sentence as long as he took Vassili's place and left under his name."

Someone replied, "We remember it clearly, Marfa Berena. That man was not one of our brothers. His name was Jérôme Fandor and he was French."

"That's not important," Marfa Berena continued. "Last week, I was quietly sitting in my humble abode and as I labored, since that is what the poor do, I saw two men from the police walking toward me, accompanied by the village mayor. I pretended not to notice anything, but my heart started pounding since I always fear a visit from such people. The mayor spoke to me, saying, 'Are you Marfa Berena?' I replied that I was and asked him what he wanted with me. Then one of the policemen stepped forward and asked me where my son Vassili was. I replied that his masters had condemned my son to ten years in Siberia and that his kind had taken him off in the direction of the mines three months earlier. I assured them that I had had no news of my unfortunate son since that time. And I was trembling as I spoke those words since, as you know my friends, Vassili was saved as a result of you and is currently working in a plant that he will blow up one day, but where he is quiet and well paid for the time being."

"Then the policeman acknowledged that I was telling the truth but told me that he knew more than I did about recent events. He told me that my son in Siberia had broken his chains and escaped. I looked dumbfounded. And I told the three men that by all the Holy Images that could not be possible. I said that my son had ten years to serve and that if he escaped he risked hanging."

As she recounted these events, the old woman was overcome with emotion. She turned to the pope and, shaking a fist at an imaginary adversary, she shrieked, "So, that's where things stand. Do you all understand what has happened? That Jérôme Fandor that we spared, who we allowed to live as long as he went to Siberia in the place of my son, has escaped from the mines. Since he was passing for Vassili, they're looking for Vassili now and if they find the real Vassili, my son, they will hang him... Do you understand how anguished I am? Do you realize how much I'm suffering? I regret that Vassili didn't just head off for the mines. He could have done his ten years then come back. He wasn't risking a death sentence and now, if they find him, what kind of explanation can he give them? He'll hang!"

The participants muttered; lively conversations broke out among the nihilists gathered there. After all, Marfa Berena was right and it did seem that Jérôme Fandor, who have benefitted from a measure of indulgence, had not recognized the friendship they had shown him. From the time he had stepped into the shoes of Vassili Berena, he had to remain in the Siberian mines for ten years, so that the real Vassili was not disturbed.

"Unfortunately," someone said, "It's fine and dandy to lament, but what can we do? We all know, through our friends, brothers, and parents who have been deported, the fate that awaits anyone who escapes. One out of a hundred manages to succeed, the others perish in the steppes, killed by the cold, wolves, hunger. We should presume that the escaped prisoner found death immediately after his departure. So, after all, he has been punished in keeping with God's law, but it is regrettable that his death does not serve the interests of a living man. He would have done better to stay..."

The pope sought to impose silence, saying "As our brother said, there is no point weeping over spilt milk; let us look at what we should do."

Old Marfa Berena got back onto the stool from which she had climbed down and said, "I have a request."

The audience fell silent. The old woman tore off her veil and they were able to see her eyes, shining cruelly in the shadows. Most of the participants also uncovered their faces. In actual fact, this precaution was intended to ensure that no one would recognize anyone else and also to unsettle the police if ever an officer joined a meeting.

Old Marfa saw the impression produced by the grimace on her face and chortled, saying "It looks like you're afraid of me. Yet, you know I'm not evil. All I'm asking for is justice!"

"So, tell us what you want," some said impatiently.

The old woman replied, "When you want to heal a wound you look for the cause so that you can treat it. When a river is poisoned, you don't examine the water at the mouth, but you go back to the source. So, if you want to help me to avenge Vassili, and to save him, we don't have to consider what is going to happen, but think about what has actually happened!"

"You talk like some obscure book and I don't understand a thing," said one of the military men, mouth agape.

Another man, who looked like a municipal civil servant, interrupted, saying, "I understand clearly. Marfa Berena wants us to track down Jérôme Fandor."

"No," replied the old woman. "For now, I don't care what happens to that man. But there is someone who was behind the indulgence that was shown to him. Brothers and sisters, do you remember that woman, Olga, a stranger if I'm not mistaken, who came and begged us to send Jérôme Fandor in my son's place to the Siberian mines? That woman got what she wanted, and she made fools of you all. Naturally, as soon as her protégé left for the mines, she thought of only one thing: getting away, telling him to flee, without giving a thought to what would happen to my son, not caring that as soon as Jérôme Fandor, the man passing for my son in the mines, escaped, the police would be looking for my son. That woman betrayed us and I demand that she be judged!"

Marfa Berena's declarations were met with icy silence. In principle, the nihilists did not like disputes and internal wars, but it seemed to all as if the old woman was right.

Boleslas stood up and said, "This proves, my brothers and sisters, that we are always punished by what we preach. You showed yourselves to be indulgent and generous with respect to one of our adversaries but in fact you were weak and this is the punishment! As a result of your attitude one of our brothers, and one of the best at that, Vassili, is currently sought by the police, while his mother laments. Perhaps they're arresting him right now! If things go like that, Vassili will be dead by nightfall. And who is really responsible for that murder? You, my friends, you who were weak enough to let the man you had sentenced to death live!"

Boleslas' words were welcomed enthusiastically.

"Bravo! He's right!" the participants shouted, making such a din that Alleluia's efforts to obtain silence were in vain.

"Judgment! Judgment!" they cried. "The person responsible is that woman, that Olga... We must capture her..."

The pope waved his hand, indicating that all of the masks, all of the veils covering faces were to be removed. Then, as if taking part in a drill, the men went to stand along the wall, side by side, lined up like soldiers. The women did the same. Armed with a torch, Pope Alleluia strode up and down the ranks of this strange group, examining each face.

He stopped in front of a woman and said, "I think I recognize you."

The woman took a step forward. She was pretty, her face was a bit pale, but her eyes were extraordinarily bright. Her appearance, elegant, fine and distinguished, stood out in contrast to the rough, heavy look of the people around her.

She said to the pope, "I'm Olga... I came to you, don't forget, at the request of Natacha, who gave me the golden case."

The pope seized the opportunity to question the woman known as Olga, who was in actual fact Hélène.

"How did you get that golden case, which belonged to Natacha, the daughter of Boris Pokroff?"

Hélène replied sharply, "I already told you Alleluia that I could not tell you about that. It doesn't matter how the golden case came into my possession, as long as I didn't steal it and it didn't come to me as a result of a crime!"

Everyone had remained silent during this conversation. Old Marfa Berena who could hold still no longer rushed over to Hélène and, threatening her with a fist, grumbled, "In any case, if my son Vassili is hanged, no one will say that you were not responsible for his death! It will be all your fault. In order to save a man who must be your lover you sent him off to Siberia in Vassili's place so that my son would be punished harshly!"

This interpretation of the facts was profoundly inaccurate, since when they had suggested to Marfa Berena that Fandor be sent off to the mines instead of her son, she had applauded the offer with both hands.

Hélène realized that any discussion was impossible, and merely shrugged. Moreover, the young woman had sacrificed her existence. She bitterly regretted having returned to this wasps' nest of nihilists, when nothing had required her to do so. In fact, since the day when she had saved Fandor, Hélène had left St. Petersburg. Her goal had been to join Juve to find out where he was hidden. She had also sought to unmask Fantômas, but the young woman's efforts had been in vain and she had been unable to get to any of the places where she thought she would find the people she was so ardently looking for.

Changing her plans, Hélène decided to go to the mines in Siberia and share Fandor's unfortunate fate. Of course, she'd had no time to talk with him. Of course, she was more and more convinced that Fandor had betrayed her and that, caught in the net of the beautiful Natacha, he had fallen madly in love with the other woman.

In any case, regardless of how Fandor felt about her, she was now resolved to take back the man who was her husband, with all her soul and heart. She had saved him once and now she had to save him a second time! So, she had set off for Siberia, but on her way she had learned that the prisoner Vassili had escaped.

Hélène knew what that meant.

If the prisoner Vassili, namely Fandor, had escaped, he was far away by now. Would he stay in Russia? Would he set off for another country? For France? Hélène did not know. So, abandoning her plans to go to Siberia, she had returned to St. Petersburg and fell back into the midst of the nihilists, the only place where she was known, and helped, since she had introduced herself with the golden case once owned by Natacha.

Moreover, Hélène had to fulfill her mission. Had she not promised to watch over the Empress' treasure and to do her best to keep Fantômas from stealing the priceless necklace?

When she had returned to St. Petersburg, Hélène had hoped to see Fandor again, to meet Juve once and for all. That would enable her to play a more useful role in the battle against Fantômas who, certainly, would make the most of the free time they had given him to come up with the most audacious plans, to prepare the most incredible skirmishes.

After learning that a secret meeting was to be held a few days later, in the sinister and mysterious caves hidden under the Neva. Hélène went there, filled with hope. And now she realized how horribly the situation had turned against her. She felt forced to admit, in advance, that she was lost.

In fact, the unfortunate woman found herself in an impossible situation and the events swirled about her with implacable logic. As a result of Fandor's escape, the authorities were looking for Vassili and the real prisoner would eventually be discovered and they would realize that he had been replaced when he was sent off to the mines. As someone at the meeting had said, what was to be done? What had happened had happened.

Moreover, Hélène had quite another concern. She'd heard, during the meeting, that anyone who managed to escape the mines in Siberia most certainly exchanged captivity for death. Anyone fleeing from the guards inevitably fell victim to the cold, hunger or wolves.

So Fandor had to be dead. Fandor's fate must have been the same as that of anyone who escaped. And if that were so, there was no point in Hélène living if Fandor was no longer in the world. So, wishing to hasten her end, Hélène shrieked in anger and despair and fiercely said, "After all, your stupid judgments and idiot courts are of no importance to me! Do with me as you will! Rest assured that I despise people like you who criticize the organizations of civil society and who, nevertheless, rush off to create their own courts, judges, jailers and executioners... Give me death without any further trial!"

Inarticulate shouting hid Hélène's voice, growing and growing in the cave, despite the frightened shouts of the pope, as he said, "Silence! Silence! We'll make so much noise that the police will come!"

Men rushed over to Hélène. Boleslas was the most enraged. He took the young woman by the arms and, with a sudden jerk, threw her to the ground and forced her to her knees.

"You wretch," he shouted. "You think you can die without a judgment, without a trial? Fine. All I want to do is spill your aristocratic, treacherous blood since I guessed who you were from the start. I clearly saw that you were not one of us. Oh, you can bravely spit out your anger. In just a while you'll be like all of those who have been punished before you. You'll scream in pain and beg for mercy. But it will be too late. I want them to hand you over to me! I'll make you die bit by bit. It will last for hours and you'll suffer incredibly."

Hélène remained hunched over, her arms twisted by the blood-thirsty man who was already preparing to take his dagger out of his pocket. But suddenly he moaned and collapsed to the ground. Someone had struck him in the forehead with such forced that he had toppled over and lost consciousness.

The man who had struck him then leapt out from the middle of the crowd where he had gone unnoticed. He grabbed a stool and, arms windmilling about, he cleared a space around Hélène in order to protect her.

"You wretched dogs!" he shouted. "You, who claim to be more just than the imperial justice, are you not ashamed of torturing a woman. Try to live up to your stands. You're not nihilists. You're not worthy of that name. You're nothing more than wild cats, rats or snakes."

The young man's energetic words turned the audience around.

"He's right," someone murmured. "We shouldn't kill, not even our enemies, without a judgment. We have to take this woman before the Tribunal!"

But the man continued to shout, to the amazement of all, saying "You won't take her before the Tribunal alone. You will take me too and I only hope you treat me the way you want to treat her. She's the one who saved your prisoner, Fandor, from death by sending him to the mines in Siberia. Fandor escaped and even came back. He stands before you. I'm Fandor!"

And as he uttered those words, Hélène stopped shivering, stood up and looked him in the eyes.

"Fandor!" she said.

And the young man, overcome with emotion, opened his arms to the young woman who fell on him sobbing. The spouses, the eternal lovers, had found one another and joined in a long kiss in the face of death.

The death, in fact, was imminent since, once their initial astonishment had passed, the crowd turned angry.

What, this man who had just intervened was none other than the man they had spared one time, that they had sent off to Siberia in Vassili's place, instead of putting him to death, and who had returned that favor by escaping and putting Vassili into such danger! And now he had come back to face the judges! He deserved no pity!

Metal flashes shone out in the darkness of the cave. Almost all the revolvers had been taken out of the pockets where they had been kept. The meeting, which had started in discussion, was about to end in a bloody massacre. Already Boleslas, brought back to life by the care of an old woman next to him, was inciting his companions to take vengeances.

"Shoot!" he screamed. "Shoot and finish these wretches off!"

The sound of guns being armed filled the space. All of the nihilists had withdrawn into the depths of the cave, leaving Hélène and Fandor facing them, standing along the wall, indifferent to their surroundings, arms entwined, hugging tightly, face to face, lips to lips. Their last moment was upon them and, without trembling, happy to be reunited, they waited for death...

Pope Alleluia's intervention postponed that moment. With difficulty, the religious man shoved the crowd aside and stood between the revolvers and the intended victims.

"Stop! Stop!" he shouted. "If you do this, if you assassinate these people, you will be covered with shame and dishonor."

"That doesn't matter," someone replied. "They deserve death..."

"They must be judged first!" the pope said harshly. "And if you do not do that, God's wrath will fall on you in a rain of curses."

That threat seemed to have a certain effect on the audience and the pope continued, saying "Like you, I believe that an exemplary punishment is required and that it must be rigorously determined. But, the harsher the sentence it is, the more important it is that we follow the rules. My friends, today, we have a guest that we have called to our aid to help us get rid of the man who has discredited us so much, so that he can capture Fantômas. This man, this policeman, the famous Juve is in the room today and is taking part in our deliberations. What do you believe this good man will think of us if we behave like this in his presence?"

The pope's words stilled the fierce crowd. The name of the famous and popular Juve had traveled by word of mouth and was on everyone's lips. But, of course, no one was more surprised by this revelation than Hélène and Fandor.

Although they were prepared for anything, they had never expected this. They had never imagined that Juve could appear at the very moment when they were counting the final seconds of their existence. Joy flashed over their faces. The two young people, who had bravely accepted their fate, were filled with hope at the idea they would live.

They went from one extreme to the other since, although it was wonderful to know that Juve was there with them, there was no guarantee that the policeman would be able to save them.

However, the pope continued to speak, "I've been speaking with this honorable policeman about the situation of the two accused that we are about to judge... First, Juve did not want to meddle in our affairs but, at my insistence, he agreed to preside over our tribunal, which will meet any time now. We will respect the sentence he renders after consulting the audience, won't we?"

The astonishment provoked by the pope's words suddenly transformed into frantic enthusiasm. Juve's name was well-known and all the nihilists loved him. Many of them, who had lived in Paris, were familiar with the man's reputation for bravery and loyalty. They knew that he had come, simply and bravely, at the first appeal from the nihilists. They were convinced that he would serve them loyally in searching for and capturing Fantômas, as he had promised.

"Let Juve preside over the hearing and we will carry out the sentence," people in the room shouted.

People in the room bustled about, picking up a few ladders, making a desk, a table where Juve would sit. What did the policeman plan? It was impossible to tell by looking at his face.

The accused had been positioned in front of him, two lanterns shining on their faces. Juve had stared at them, first one and then the other, without blinking, with giving the slightest hint that he knew the couple.

Hélène and Fandor, moreover, had realized that it was essential for them not to give the impression they knew Juve.

The investigation started.

"Do you acknowledge the facts for which you have been accused?" Juve asked, seeming visibly concerned and not just trying to save time.

Hélène and Fandor had decided how they should behave and for close to 30 minutes, they talked with the unusual man presiding over the supreme tribunal, getting lost in insignificant details. Juve helped them in this, wanting only one thing, to extend the debates in the hope that it would have to be put off to another time.

Initially, the audience did not notice this strategy. But, over time, people started to lose patience and Boleslas suddenly interrupted Juve, shouting loudly, "None of this matters. What matters is we get on with this. Are the two accused guilty or not? If they are, don't they deserve death since death is the only sentence the nihilist tribunal can render?"

Juve tried to alleviate the considerable effect produced by this declaration.

"The nihilists' tribunal is better yet than an impartial and free tribunal," he said. "When it condemns, it can obviously render a death sentence. But it can also absolve, acquit!"

This unfortunate pronouncement was greeted by shouting in the cavern. Boleslas walked over to Juve, waved his fist at the policeman, and roared, "Our tribunal is nothing but play-acting and you know it. People wanted to respect the formalities for sentencing Fandor and Olga. Well those formalities have been respected. Since you're presiding, sentence them!"

Juve look desperately around him, trying to find some support, but no one seemed to understand him. The crowd grew belligerent, spurred on by Boleslas' words.

"Sentence them, sentence them!" they shouted.

Hearing these ferocious cries and realizing that those the crowd wanted to put to death were none other than Hélène and Fandor, namely the two people he loved most in the world, he saw red… for a moment, he considered taking out his revolver, motioning for Hélène to stand next to him, and defending them until their last drop of blood, but he regained control of himself.

Acting like that would certainly condemn them all to death. Juve, even in the most desperate circumstances, always kept hope, believing that as long as the body held a spark of life there was a smidgen of hope!

Acting like that would merely precipitate the fatal end. It was essential, since they had started out by respecting the rules, respect those rules until the very end, and in that way gain time.

"Sentence them, sentence them!" the crowd shouted.

Juve realized that it would be impossible to render any other sentence and that he would be disavowed, that he would see those he was trying to save murdered before his very eyes.

To the astonishment of Hélène and Fandor, who heard Juve speak without understanding their friend's intentions, the policeman uttered the fatal words, saying "Following the debate, which was conducted in due form, the head of the nihilists court sentences his brother Fandor and his sister Olga to death!"

This decision was greeted with shouting and applause. Yet silence fell yet again since the judge had not finished speaking. He still had to state how the punishment would be enacted.

"The condemned will be hanged! The execution will take place at this time tomorrow!" he said, in an authoritarian and energetic voice.

CHAPTER XXI
Juve's Trickery

It had been about one hour since Juve had sentenced Hélène and Fandor to death. The crowd of nihilists who had been summoned to the meeting which had ended so tragically, had almost entirely departed from the secret cave, in which the most ardent and most notorious members of the formidable group of government adversaries.

These people, who practiced various professions, could not, in fact, stay away from their work for long. Workers, employees, soldiers or civil servants… they had to perform their duties. Juve was counting on just that when, completely by chance and in order to gain time, he had set the date and time for the horrible sentence, which he had found himself forced to pronounce, having done so solely in order to keep Hélène and Fandor from being murdered immediately by the crowd of nihilists who were exasperated by the young couple's attitude.

Yet, since the execution could not take place before the next morning, those who were sentenced to death would be guarded carefully until that time.

As soon as the sentence was pronounced, the most ferocious of the nihilists had volunteered to guard the prisoners until the time of their execution. And, before Juve could intervene, or even exchange a few words with the unfortunate victims, they had been separated and dragged off, Fandor to one end of the cave and Hélène to the opposite one. Then, their guards had taken up position around them and it was clear they intended to remain them until the sentence was executed.

Juve was uncertain as to how he should behave. He clearly saw that Fandor and Hélène would have wanted to speak with him since the two young people, most astonished and then overcome by their fate, would have wanted to know, before dying, how it had come about that Juve had been the supreme judge of the tribunal that was to judge them and why he had felt obliged to sentence them to death. And while Fandor and Hélène were overcome with curiosity, to the point that they forgot about the sad fate that awaited them, Juve was every bit as curious.

The previous night, he had met the nihilists for the first time, after being miraculously rescued from a hideous death by the Duchess Ekaterina. A gallant man, Juve had in turn saved her from certain death while also saving her lover from the nihilists' attack. Following that, Juve had been obliged to accompany the nihilists and he returned to St. Petersburg with the aid and protection of Pope Alleluia, an extraordinary man, a veritable visionary, who incarnated both the desire for murder and the principles of religion, unable to understand, despite his thorough knowledge of sacred texts, that one thing above all is intangible and respectable: life!

Juve had quickly earned the pope's trust and Alleluia, who never given up, who developed the most extraordinary plans with the policeman for tracking down Fantômas, had invited Juve to the famous cave under the Neva that evening, to attend the nihilist's meeting scheduled to take place at dawn.

Juve had no further intention of getting involved in the intimate existence of such formidable people, he did not want to know or have to keep their secrets and he had no desire, in the event of a surprise, of being arrested by the regular police for plotting against the life of the Tsar, the man he was actually supposed to protect. Juve merely believed that, by going to see the nihilists, he might have a chance of hearing Fantômas speak, if not actually meeting him.

But the turn of events had dumbfounded the policeman when he suddenly found himself in the cave facing the two people he had been searching for in vain for several weeks, without finding the slightest trace. Juve had found Hélène and Fandor!

He was about to walk over to them, to make himself known and ask what had happened to them when the meeting started with the recriminations of old Marfa Berena and Juve's joy had immediately transformed into mortal anguish and frightening concern.

He did not understand that the famous Olga everyone was hurling abuse at was actually Hélène. And he had no idea why Fandor had set off for the mines in Siberia in the place of Vassili, the old woman's son, but he was very certain that his poor friends were in a most unique situation and that all they could hope for was that they would not be murdered right away.

To make matters worse, Pope Alleluia had asked Juve to judge the accused and Juve understood that this formality was just a comedy and that if he did not render a sentence in keeping with the crowd's wishes, the execution would still take place.

That is why Juve rendered his sentence and declared that the execution would only take place the next morning. He hoped that, within 24 hours, he would manage to save Hélène and Fandor...

As the guards were keeping the pair clearly in view and the crowd was slowly dissipating, all agreeing to return the next day, Pope Alleluia took Juve aside.

"My dear friend," he declared, "There's no need for us here. Moreover, we have to come to an agreement about tracking down Fantômas... I'm sure you realize that the nihilists' organization is the most powerful one in the civilized world right now. As I already explained, we are men of justice, not wrong-doers. We support death without failing, but we cannot accept people spreading ignominious rumors about us, saying that the nihilist steal or kill for riches like vulgar robbers. No! Our victims are not true victims. The people we execute are justly sentenced. For some time now, there have been many thefts and crimes in which money disappears. Fantômas is responsible for such evil deeds. The rumor has spread, in the population that the nihilists wanted to steal the precious jewels of the Tsar's wife... The nihilists don't want that, but Fantômas is the one planning this heist and is trying to make us take the blame for it. And, in order to avoid that, Juve, we called you. Time is of the essence. Since we have the day before us, would you like to study the problem with me, to find a plan for taking care of Fantômas?"

Juve hardly wanted to take care of Fantômas that very day, believing that he did not have nearly enough time before the execution to find a way to save his friends.

"Later," he said to the pope. "Later we'll have an opportunity to talk!"

Ingenuously, Alleluia declared, "You have a few hours free and I would have preferred to spend them with you. But it that does not suit you, too bad!"

The Pope and Juve had arrived at the entrance to the sewer hallway through which light filtered in. In a low voice, the Pope told Juve, "That's how we get in and out. The sewer worker, Michel, serves as a doorman for us..."

Alleluia shook the policeman's hand and added, in a confidential tone, "I am counting on you to attend the execution of the two criminals tomorrow. It is common practice among us for the judge to make sure that his orders are executed."

Juve shivered and said nothing,

Alleluia continued, "I'll be in the cave as of 2:00. I have to say the usual prayers. At three o'clock we'll hang them."

And with those words, the pope walked away from Juve and, without a thought as to what would happen to the policeman, he exited the sewer, walking up the staircase that led to the Skobeleff.

Juve turned heel and quickly walked back the way he had come. He was extremely agitated and wondered how he would manage to save his friends. All in all, it was a very simple matter. Juve had, in fact, turned back to note the exact route he would have to take to get from the road to the quarry in which the nihilists would gather, in just a few hours, to witness the executions.

Although the very idea disgusted him, Juve had decided that he would notify the police and have everyone arrested. Juve was noting the details of the route in his notebook when suddenly a robust, massive silhouette stepped in front of him. He stepped aside to let the man pass and quickly hid his notebook in his pocket. The individual, however, stopped and stared at him.

"Well," he said after a moment. "It's the judge from earlier. Good evening comrade."

"Good evening," Juve replied, frowning, since he had just recognized the person who had been among the most vociferous when demanding the execution of Hélène and Fandor.

It was Boleslas.

The man was carrying a long piece of wood and, with a ferocious smile, he waved it at Juve and said, "You see, comrade, we don't waste time!"

"I don't understand," said Juve looking at the piece of wood with an instinctive terror.

Boleslas chortled and said, "I'm carrying a piece of the gallows. We're about to set it up in the very center of the room and we'll use it tomorrow morning!"

Juve jumped. So, this wretch was going to add to the horror faced by Hélène and Fandor, by setting up the instrument of their death several hours ahead of time.

Juve could not keep from shouting, "But that's abominable!"

Boleslas, however, shrugged and continued on his way, muttering, "I don't trust that man."

Juve followed him from a distance and, for close to two hours, he wandered through the secret corridors of the underground sewers that ran along the famous quarry, under the Neva. Juve had prepared a very detailed and complete plan of the premises and he was quite pleased with the idea that, in all likelihood, he would be able to bring an entire army of policemen into the labyrinth without anyone knowing until such times as they rushed the nihilists and prevented the execution of his two friends.

Juve voluntarily abstained from entering the quarry, fearing that he would betray some sympathy for Hélène and Fandor. After completing his arrangements, he walked back towards the exit, stopping at an intersection along the way to fine-tune his plans.

"We will have to position six officers here," he thought, as he wrote the number 6 in his notebook followed by the word "officers".

Just then, a loud voice shouted and an enormous wrist threatened to strike Juve on the head. He had barely enough time to step back before turning around and finding himself face to face with the man who, a few hours earlier, had announced that he was carrying the gallows.

"You again!" said Juve "What do you want?"

Boleslas dragged Juve into an underground corner. He approached him hands clenched, and hissed, "Do you think I'm as stupid as I look, as stupid as all those around me? Do you think I haven't seen you coming and going, that I don't realize that you're going to betray us? I know why you've been surveying all these underground passages. It's so you can bring the police in and save those damned foreigners that you only condemned because you had to! Fortunately, I was watching. I'm telling you two things. First, you won't be leaving here until the execution is over. In that case, you won't be able to warn the police and you won't post six at the intersection as you've planned to do. Second, I've demolished the communication system that enabled people inside to call Michel, the sewer man, to have him open up. From now on, people can come in but no one can get out."

Juve listened, distraught, as Boleslas spoke. What would become of him? What would he do? Was the game over?

"One thing is certain," Juve thought, filled with an icy anger, "Within ten minutes one of us will have defeated the other since we can't both remain standing here. But that won't save Hélène and Fandor!"

Boleslas, however, grew more and more animated as he spoke, "You tried to trick us, you wretch, but you're the one who will lose. I'll tell our friends and will have a third hanging tomorrow morning. You!"

Calmly, coldly, Juve continued to say nothing. He was thinking, trying to decide what attitude he should adopt and how he could get out of this situation. Boleslas took his silence for resignation and fear.

In a cheerful voice, he added, "After all, I should have let you come in with your policemen. They would be dead as well. The only reason I spared them is that their deaths would have caused the deaths of most of our members!"

Since Juve, despite everything, was staring at Boleslas, eyes filled with astonishment, the man explained, "You see, you wretched traitor, these underground vaults are not only controlled by the entrance at which old Michel stands guard, but the tumultuous Neva flowing over head, kept out by a simple valve… Did you notice the small metal doors here and there in the walls? They open onto the river. If one or two are opened, the caves will fill… If you had arrived with the police, I would have opened these doors. I have the key. And everyone would have drowned."

This time, Juve understood and, taking advantage of a momentary lack of attention on the part of Boleslas, Juve rushed the other man, grabbed him by the throat and started to throttle him.

"Help! Help" the nihilist said.

But Juve had rushed him so violently that he held him still. Boleslas resisted less and less and, half strangled, lost consciousness. It took Juve no more than a minute to tie him up firmly, and push him into a dark corner of the deserted underground. Feverishly, the policeman dug through Boleslas' pockets. He took out a wallet in which he found a key.

Filled with joy at this discovery, Juve shouted, "Dying for death's sake, we will die defending our existence!"

In his hand, Juve held the key that could be used to open the doors and flood the underground case with water from the Neva. Indiscreetly, Juve glanced at the papers in Boleslas' wallet. He could not contain his surprise. Written in red ink in a corner of the wallet, he had discovered a name, a name that certainly belonged to Boleslas, a name that, despite everything, made the policeman shiver with emotion. Juve had just discovered that the ardent nihilist was none other than a close relative of the Tsar!

The pope, wearing his religious attire, stood mournfully in the middle of the room in which the prisoners Hélène and Fandor had been held overnight. In the centre of the quarry he had set up a sort of table on which he had placed colorful images and a variety of small objects. He had had two large candles carried in and was preparing to light them when, suddenly, someone touched his shoulder. The pope turned around, indignant.

"Who dares place a sacrilegious hand on a priest wearing his sacerdotal vestments?"

It was Juve who had touched the pope. Alleluia recognized him.

"Ah, there you are," he said. "That's fine. I was afraid that you would not attend the executions and the ceremony that is to precede them. I'm pleased that you came. As for the rest, you'll see, it's interesting…"

Up to this moment, an hour after midnight, Juve had never shown his face in the vicinity of the prisoners, who were looking at him. Yet, he had not wasted his time and, judging by his weary look and his dirty, torn clothing, he'd been hard at work throughout his absence. What had happened to him? After looking at him from head to toe and noticing that his clothes were stained with mud and torn in many places, the pope naively asked him just that.

"None of your business," said Juve. "Am I not a free man?"

"Of course!" said the pope, raising his arms. "It's fine to want to do things in a normal manner, but everything is always poorly organized. That Boleslas, who'd volunteered to set up the gallows… well he brought the wood but he didn't assemble it. I don't know what happened to him. He must be dead drunk in some bar somewhere!"

"That's highly likely," said Juve, who recalled this Boleslas and knew full well that as he spoke with the pope Boleslas was tied up and hidden in a dark corner of a passageway where no one would ever think to look for him.

The pope paced back and forth, agitated, and said, "The comrades will start arriving soon. We have to be ready to execute the convicts, as soon as they get here. We can move the executions up in order to get done with this. It will take me just a few minutes to say my mass."

"Your mass?" asked Juve. "What mass?"

The pope seemed stunned by his question and replied, "Oh, the French are such an impious people. Have you not noticed my clothing, Juve? I'm wearing my sacerdotal vestments and I had set this table up like an altar in order to say the mass for the dead…"

"My God!" Juve said, as he realized the purpose of the sinister instrument placed in the middle of the room. He guessed the purpose of the candles that were being lit. The nihilists were about to add to the tortures of the unfortunate wretches they planned to execute. This abominable pope was going to say the mass of the dead before them. … They were going to hear the *De Profundis* said on their behalf!

Was there any way Juve could oppose this ceremony? No, that would be impossible!

"After all," he said, repressing his feelings, "That will give us more time."

The pope was already kneeling before the altar, in the weak light cast by the two candles.

Hélène and Fandor, torn from the drowsiness into which they had slipped, grew fearful as they witnessed the preparations. They realized what was happening and they understood that, once the mass had been pronounced, they would certainly be executed.

Although they could not touch one another, they could hear. Hélène cried out, expressing all her tenderness, all her love, saying "Farewell Fandor."

Fandor replied, "Farewell Hélène!"

But a third voice rose over the silence and the semi-darkness, clearly saying, "Be brave children, don't despair!"

Who could have said those words?

The pope, who had been praying, stopped immediately, stunned, as he heard the words. But he saw no one in the room apart from the guards, apart from himself, apart from old Marfa Berena who, assisted by another ancient shrew, was attempting to set up the scaffold that Boleslas had abandoned.

"Be brave!" the voice had said.

Hélène and Fandor suddenly felt as if they had been electrified, since they recognized the voice. It was none other than Juve.

People were swarming into the room. Nihilists appeared from everywhere and the pope, rushing through the ceremony was about to finish up when suddenly he was interrupted in his prayers.

He was kneeling in front of the altar and grumbled furiously, in a low voice, because he did not want to look as if he'd interrupted.

"What is that? What does it want with me?"

He heard someone speaking with him, speaking from the other side of the altar, someone who was certainly hidden under the black sheet, littered with the silver tears he had thrown there.

"How much longer are you going to take?" the voice asked the pope.

Alleluia realized that it was Juve speaking.

"No more than five minutes, then we'll hang them!" he declared.

To his great surprise, Juve retorted, "That's too fast. Your ceremony has to last another fifteen minutes!"

"But it won't take me more than five minutes to finish the mass," declared the pope.

"So, make your prayers longer," Juve suggested.

"But that's impossible," said the pope.

"In the name of God!" the policeman shouted, in exasperation. "As sure as my name is Juve, I'll strangle you this very minute if you don't make your mass for the dead last another quarter of an hour!"

"I'm dealing with a mad man," thought the pope, terrified, as he continued to mutter his prayers. Yet he could not disobey Juve.

"Fine," he said. "I can't extend my mass, but I can start it over. "

"Good!" Juve said, satisfied, as he continued to hide under the black sheet.

197

He slipped the barrel of his revolver through a tear in the sheet and as the pope started his *De Profundis* over again and he said, "Don't stop, continue without interruption. If you end before I tell you to stop, I'll shoot you right away!"

But why would Juve want to make the ceremony last longer?

The pope did not understand.

He started his mass over a second time. A quarter of an hour passed and Juve ordered him to start over a third time.

The pope was distraught.

"Honestly," he thought while muttering his prayers. "It's impossible to conduct a mass under these circumstances. I've never seen anything like this and I'm convinced I'm not saying my prayers properly, upset as I am by that gun pointing at me!"

Catching his breath, Alleluia begged Juve, "I beg of you. Let me be. Let us hang the guilty and get it over with. I can't start my mass over again a fourth time…"

The pope heard no reply, but a frightful shriek rang out from all directions. The nihilists in the room had leapt up and were shouting in terror, "The Neva! The Neva!"

At the same time, a cold, damp wave suddenly swept over the congregation. Water sloshed over the ground that had been dry until then, and suddenly flowed in.

The initial moment of surprise over, the nihilists understood without a doubt and cried out.

"We're being flooded! The underground caves are filling with water from the Neva! We'll all going to die. We'll drown!"

The water had been flowing in for some time without anyone noticing and now suddenly rushed into the large room. A section of the wall had collapsed under the pressure of the water and it now rushed in with the violence of a whirlpool. Within the space of a second, the pope's altar had been carried away. Darkness fell in the room and the screams that had announced the cataclysms had been replaced with moans of pain, the cries of the dying.

What frightening coincidence, what tragic will had caused the river to invade the nihilists' underground chamber?

CHAPTER XXII
Mysterious Disappearance

Seventy-five brothers and sisters, members of the group of nihilists, once headed by the defunct Natacha, had just been washed under the metal plate that hid the staircase leading to the sewers and from there to the quarry carved under the bed of the Neva River.

Old Michel who, in keeping with his duties and habits, had come on duty at one o'clock in the morning on Skobeleff Avenue, had managed to let all of these people into this world in the entrails of the city without anyone being noticed by the police officers who patrolled the neighborhood.

Once the 75 members of the fierce association of nihilists had descended into the underground passageway and Brother Michel was convinced that no one else was coming, he closed the door and locked it with a special key.

"They'll figure out how to get out on their own," he thought to himself, completely unaware that Boleslas had demolished the device that served to open the entrance from the inside and that no one would be able to get out of the sewers until he returned.

Michel felt some regret as he walked off. Not only was he somewhat concerned because, despite all his precautions, he had noticed suspicious shadows in the distance, but he was also saddened by the idea that serious, important, tragic things would be happening that morning and he would not be there to witness them.

"They're going to hang people this morning," he repeated over and over. "They're going to hang people this morning and I won't be there…"

During the course of his long career as a nihilist, Michel had attended many executions. He was familiar with all forms of death, having witnessed them. He had seen a man die after his chest had been riddled with dagger blows; he'd seen gagged women strangled, he'd seen men of all ages hanged… And despite all that, the old nihilist experienced a bloodthirsty sense of regret whenever he missed one of those spectacles. He dreamed of being an executioner and, on this day, when his work duties kept him from being in the quarry with his comrades, he envied Boleslas, saying "He's the one who will hang the traitors… He'll place the ropes over their heads and will take them down once they're stiff and cold. He's so lucky!"

Of course, Michel had no idea that, at that very moment, Boleslas was writhing about on the floor, filled with the most violent anger, unable to undo his bonds or to tear off the gag that prevented him from calling for help.

So, old Michel was walking off, filled with regret, when he suddenly stopped in the middle of the road to listen. It was still very early in the morning. The sun was barely peaking over the horizon and, in the silence of the night,

Michel heard a strange, long sound, a sort of sinister grumbling of unknown origin.

"What's going on?" he asked.

Instinctively, he walked over to a sewer grate beneath a sidewalk. He knelt down in front of it and listened again. The most profound expression of amazement washed over the face of the old nihilist. He knew that the sewer grate in front of him connected to a pipe that, after many twists and turns, ended up in a large underground room where, at that very moment, his companions were about to execute the traitors. And Michel had the impression that a sort of anguished clamor was rising up toward him, hidden by some strange, powerful, continuous noise he could not identify.

"What can that be?" he asked himself again.

Suddenly, the street cleaner struck his hand against his forehead and said, "For God's sake! I know what it is, but I don't understand. It's like water boiling... and yet that can't be!"

An imperious, harsh clamor called out in the distance.

People were calling, "Michel! Michel!"

The street cleaner stood up. He looked at the horizon, at the far end of Skobeleff Avenue and saw no one.

"That's curious," he said. "I could have sworn..."

Suddenly he fell silent. An automobile suddenly appeared on a side street, turned quickly and rapidly came to a stop next to him. A young, elegant man wearing a green tunic stepped out of the car. It was one of the municipal engineers, the district deputy manager of sewers, Michel's supervisor. The engineer appeared to be overcome with an unspeakable rage. He walked over to the old nihilist, grabbed him by the shoulders and shook him so brutally that the old man fell to the ground.

"By the Holy Images and the Little Father," old Michel muttered. "What is happening to me? What did I ever do to you, Mr. Engineer, to be treated like this?"

"Wretch," shrieked the district deputy manager. "Have you no idea what's happening?"

Michel turned pale. He feared that he'd been discovered, an hour earlier, when he was letting the nihilists into the underground tunnels.

He tried his hand at luck and said, "I know nothing, I saw nothing..."

Furiously, the engineer replied, "You may be blind but deaf you're not!"

"What do you mean sir?" replied Michel, as he painfully got back to his feet, stumbling like a drunkard.

Exasperated with the man's attitude, the engineer boomed, "Didn't you hear anything? Don't you hear anything?"

"No, by the Holy Images," Michel swore.

The engineer grabbed him, shook him again and said, "Imbecile! Moujik! I'll tell you what's happening then! A blunder has been made. Either that or a crime has been committed. The valves in the underground sewer that runs along the Neva were opened, barely an hour ago. The water seeped in gradually and now it is flooding the basement since the wall must have cracked. I've just come from the office, you know where it is, next to the first set of locks. The floor collapsed suddenly and was replaced by a flood of boiling water and it didn't take us long, those of who are familiar with the lay-out of the basement, to figure out what was going on. It's crazy! It's mad! In an hour, if no miracle occurs, all of the sewers in the neighborhood will be under water. It will, be a catastrophe. Houses will collapse, foundations will be destroyed and, who knows, maybe even the course of the Neva River will be changed! And to top it all off, I will be held legally responsible. I should kill myself right now!"

However, the engineer, having pulled his revolver out of his belt, was not aiming it at himself. He looked Michel straight in the eyes and said, "But before I die I want to know if you're responsible as well. Did you keep a close eye on the valves? Did you check, as the regulations state, that they were closed last night? I'm convinced you didn't..."

Michel looked at his superior, his face haggard. No, of he hadn't checked the valves. He never checked them and there had never been an accident before. Moreover, he didn't care if the sewers were flooded or not. But he was devastated by the thought that, just as the flood was occurring, 75 of his brothers and sisters were locked inside the underground cave. That was terrible, horrible! They would all die, suffocated, drowned...

Suddenly a terrible anger washed through the old nihilist. He looked at his superior and, in a strange voice he bellowed, "I'm not responsible for the accident that's happening, but I'm pleased about it. It's heavenly vengeance against civilization... This will teach you, you engineers, those who want to confine nature and its invincible forces in your narrow and pusillanimous walls. When nature gets fed up, she makes an effort and all your puny narrow-minded, man-made, structures are swept away by divine power. So much the better if the course of the Neva River has just been changed! Let's hope that it will carry away all the masters and supervisors, that it will drag the Tsars and their servants to the distant sea!"

"Wretch!" shrieked the engineer, dumbfounded by this declaration. "Have you suddenly gone mad or are you a..."

He stopped as Michel once again bellowed, "I'm one of those who desire the destruction of everything! I'm one of those who want to see the world end and who will only be satisfied when the last man has given up his wretched soul to the god who tempted him with its presumptuousness and vanity. I'm a nihilist. Do you get me? And if I'm emotional, if I weep, it's because in the midst of the water boiling under our feet, at this very moment, 100 of my brothers and sisters are rendering their healthy, proper justice and planning reprisals. Unfortunately, at this very moment they may already be victims, cadavers. But that doesn't matter! Others will come after them..."

Michel stopped speaking, took a step back, shrieked loudly, then fell backwards, screaming, "Damnation!"

On the ground, his body twisted and writhed than fell motionless as blood from a gaping wound in his throat.

As soon as he realized what the man was, the district sub-manager of sewers had aimed his revolver at Michel and shot him down like a dog. And, at the very same moment, a frightful detonation rang out. The engineer staggered as the ground vibrated, as if an earthquake were taking place. A column of water gushed under his feet with such force that the civil servant was thrown more than five yards into the air and then fell back into the midst of an unimaginable chaos of stone, loose soil and water.

At the same time, a large crack, 50 yards long, appeared in the road and the entire sidewalk tumbled into the void, replaced by a lake of black, muddy water.

Human bodies, living beings bobbed to the surface of the water. These people, half drowned, driven by an instinct for survival, struggled to escape the cataclysms and made their way to the edge of this extraordinary lake that had just formed in the middle of the street. People screamed from all directions.

The engineer, however, who had been projected onto a clump of shrubs and lost consciousness for a few moments, recovered. When he opened his eyes, the appearance of the road had changed so much that he thought he had been carried to another place. But his memory returned and, after managing to stand up, he ran off, yelling, "Nihilists! Nihilists!"

A few seconds later, he ran into a flock of police officers running toward the noise, followed by a company of infantrymen, from a nearby barracks. These experienced soldiers, remarkably brave, were rushing to rescue the drowning people. Yet, as a measure of caution, they also grabbed them and put them under guard in an out-of-the-way place at the corner of a deserted street.

The fatal cry had been uttered, the tragic denunciation had been stated: "Nihilists! Nihilists!"

And, after an hour, they came to the realization that they had saved more than sixty people and all of them were taken prisoner. They questioned them, asking them where they came from, who they were and each and every one of them, realizing that lies would serve no purpose, proudly declared, "We are nihilists. Death to the Tsar!"

Juve had just entered the Tsar's private office. The policeman was still completely overwhelmed by the frightening events that had occurred. He had managed to change his clothes, thanks to the kindness of some chamberlain and, after quickly cleaning up, he had been taken to the private cabinet of Nicolas II who was supposed to join him there.

Juve had been in the room no more than a few minutes when the Tsar appeared. The ruler was pale and his hands shook. He looked at Juve in fear. Then, collapsing into an armchair, while making sure that two gigantic Cossacks remained at his side to protect him if needed, he interrogated Juve in a feeble voice.

"What happened?"

In a few words, the policeman explained the extraordinary adventure in which he played the role of hero. He told the Tsar how he had entered the nihilists' cave by chance, then gave the Tsar a detailed account of how he had been required to sentence two honest people, Hélène and Fandor, to death.

The Tsar frowned when he heard those names, but Juve noticed nothing.

"What happened then?" the Tsar asked.

"If your Majesty will deign to listen to me for a few more seconds he will know," Juve replied. "Since I wanted to do everything possible to keep my two friends alive, I decided that I would have to find a way to provoke a cataclysm to prevent the nihilists from carrying out their execution. I had learned by chance from one of the group that, if the valves in the underground walls were opened, the water from the Neva River would flood the cellars.

"I did not hesitate to do, this deciding that even though we might all be drowned there was still a chance that we would be saved. If we had to die then die we would, but we would die together and I would not have to watch the two beings I love most in this world perish before my very eyes.

"I managed to delay the execution until the water, acting like a battering ram destroyed a wall and rushed into the cavern with unexpected violence. At that moment, I believed that we would all drown, but then something strange happened. As it raced into the large quarry, which had no opening at the top, the water compressed the air there and the air pressure prevented the water from rising.

"We did not drown, but we were trapped under a granite vault and destined for a more horrible, slower death. We were surrounded by darkness and, as the water reached shoulder-height, we felt as if our veins were about to burst.

"That's when I called for Fandor and Hélène and was overjoyed when they called back, although the nihilists were screaming all around us. Suddenly, a violent explosion occurred and I lost all my senses. It was only an hour later, when I found myself alive in the police station, that I understood what had happened. Giving way under the pressure of the air that had been compressed by the water, the ceiling of the cavern had exploded, tearing a great rip in the soil overhead and, as the water surged, we were all projected into the road.

"That, your Majesty, is what I can tell you. That is what happened."

The Tsar remained stunned. Although he realized full well that Juve was not making anything up, he was dumbfounded by the unprecedented events that had taken place.

After a long silence, he said, "The nihilists have all been arrested, according to what the chief of police told me. They will all be tried in 48 hours and their sentence will be merciless. They will all be executed."

"Juve, I'd like to thank you for telling me this. I appreciate your honesty. Ordinarily, everyone in my entourage hides the truth from me and I am the most ignorant man in my empire. Yet, although I do not doubt what you say, I do, to a certain extent, doubt your perspicacity, Mr. Juve. It's almost certainly impossible that things occurred exactly as you said. I like to think that under all of these events, there were some horrific machinations on the part of Fantômas.

"I say this without any attempt to reproach you, Mr. Juve. You have handled your own affairs quite admirably, but I don't think you have concerned yourself with my business. Let us look back over the past few days and you tell me why you had me appoint you to serve as the coachman for the horses I planned to give to the chief of my secret police, to Boris Pokroff. What has happened to him since? And what do you intend to do to protect the Tsarina's treasures?"

It was Juve's turn to be dumbfounded.

The horrific explosion that had occurred, the arrest the nihilists meant nothing at all to the Tsar. What did interest him was knowing what Juve planned to do about the Tsarina's necklace! What the Tsar wanted to know was why he had joined Boris Pokroff as a coachman! For a moment, Juve was about to confess everything to the Tsar.

He was about to shout, "You wretched emperor! Believing Boris Pokroff is an honest man! Don't you know that Boris Pokroff was assassinated a long time ago and that the most formidable thief in the entire world, Fantômas himself, Fantômas in person, has taken his place, admirably disguised, mimicking his voice."

Distraught by the Tsar's blindness, Juve merely said, "Does your Majesty trust the chief of his secret police?"

"Excuse me," the Tsar interrupted haughtily. "We will not discuss that matter and if your role is to slander the man, we will go our separate ways immediately!"

The Tsar gave his large Cossacks a meaningful glance and Juve realized that if he persisted in saying that Boris Pokroff was none other than Fantômas, he would soon join the nihilists in the depths of the Saint-Jean prison where they had been locked up a few hours earlier along with, and this did concern Juve, Hélène and Fandor.

Juve realized that he would have to very cunning with the Tsar and said, "Far be it from me, your Majesty, to suspect Boris Pokroff of any evil intentions. But I must say that I fear for him, living alone as he does in his home in Gatchina. The nihilists have already tried to kill him. Bandits, no doubt led by Fantômas, are certainly planning to steal the necklace, your excellent servant will face certain death and you will lose your priceless treasure if both are allowed to stay at Gatchina. Moreover, I have seen the house and anyone could get into it. It is impossible to protect Boris Pokroff there and watch over the necklace."

"My God! My God!" said the Tsar. "We will have to seek divine intervention!"

He looked so overwhelmed and so unhappy that Juve decided it would be a good idea to make a suggestion.

"Sire," he begged. "Please listen to the plans I have just made. I swear that, within 24 hours we will catch Fantômas, while protecting Her Majesty's necklace."

"Speak," replied the Tsar. "What do you want?"

Juve said, "Order Boris Pokroff to return here, to Tsarskoye Selo, immediately. Tell him to bring the necklace with him and inform him that, as soon as he enters the palace with the necklace, he will be relieved of all responsibility for watching over it."

"And if I do that, what will happen?" asked the Tsar.

"I've just told your Majesty that, within 48 hours, Fantômas will be unable to do anything."

The Tsar sighed deeply. He looked at Juve for a long time, doubtful, wondering if he were dealing with a traitor, almost ready to believe it, accustomed as he was to suspecting those who were most dedicated to him. Finally, with a weary air, the Tsar rang a bell and an aide-de-camp appeared.

Nicolas II quickly wrote on a piece of paper.

"Take this order to Gatchina immediately and give it to Boris Pokroff," he ordered.

The aide-de-camp bowed deeply and disappeared into the countless hallways of the palace. A few minutes later, the Tsar indicated to Juve that the audience was over and the policeman left the room, taken by the two Cossacks to the private apartment reserved for him in Tsarskoye Selo.

Alone in his room, Juve rubbed his hands and said, "I do believe that things are going quite well. Never before, have we had such as close brush with death! Never before has Fantômas made things so difficult for us! Yet, I do believe that I have handled things quite well. Fantômas, who has no idea I have unmasked him, must be quite bothered about having to watch over the necklace at this moment. He'll be delighted to bring it back here, to be relieved of that responsibility and he will not hesitate to steal it. And that is exactly what I expect. Once Fantômas had been caught and unmasked, the Tsar will no longer be in any position to refuse me anything. What could I ask him for?"

Juve smiled, burst into laughter and thought, "A dowry for Hélène and Fandor maybe… if they are still in Russia when Fantômas is caught. I can't imagine that they're still in prison and that self-centered Tsar hasn't even told me when he plans to release them!"

Juve looked at the time.

"Six o'clock in the evening already? I know that at exactly nine o'clock the Tsar will go to the large gallery of busts. I'll prepare a decree for him. I'll meet him on his way and give it to him. He can sign it and Hélène and Fandor will be released immediately."

The aide-de-camp, however, had galloped to Gatchina and, without climbing off his horse, knocked at the door to the house which, after some time, opened slowly.

A voice asked, "Who is there?"

"The aide-de-camp, your Majesty!" the officer replied. "I have an order for Boris Pokroff himself."

The door opened wide. The man showed himself and said, "I'm Boris Pokroff."

It was, in fact, the so-called chief of the secret police who had come to open the door himself. He read the letter that the officer handed him and a flash of joy lit his face briefly.

Juve had guessed accurately when he decided that Fantômas was finding it difficult to steal the necklace.

When he received the Tsar's order to take the necklace to Tsarskoye Selo, Fantômas was more than pleased since he realized that, once he was no longer responsible for the jewel, it would be easy for him to steal it right away.

The fake chief of police whistled and two moujiks appeared.

"Keep this officer's horse," he declared, as the aide-de-camp dismounted.

Gallantly inviting the man to go before him, he said, "Come into my home, sir. We'll pick up the necklace together and it will never leave our hands until we are back in Tsarskoye Selo.

The two men walked up to the first floor and Fantômas guided his companion into a large lounge with luxurious furnishings. Then, he pressed on a button hidden behind the wall hangings. A door opened, revealing a small lead-lined cabinet. It contained a large chest.

As Fantômas opened it, he declared, "This is where I placed the necklace."

But as soon as the chest was opened, both men cried out in surprise. The chest was empty. The necklace was not in it. The aide-de-camp was dumbfounded. Fantômas swore.

The officer, who recovered from his surprise first, said, "By the Holy Images, the necklace has disappeared. What could have happened to it?"

Fantômas who, following his initial explosion of anger, had grown remarkably calm, allowed an ironic smile to flit over his lips, then repeated the officer's words in an enigmatic tone, "The necklace has, in fact, disappeared. By the Holy Images, what could have happened to it?"

Yet, Fantômas did not look particularly upset. However, he was not the one who had caused the necklace to disappear. What extraordinary thought lay behind his incomprehensible and mysterious smile?

CHAPTER XXIII
Supreme Attempt

"Boris? Boris, my love, are you there?"

The Duchess Ekaterina, quite pale, trembling from head to toe, had just knocked on the door to her lover's office, which was located on the first floor, not far from the duchess' room.

The so-called chief of the empire's secret police was coming up from the ground floor where, he had just noted, in the presence of the emperor's aide-de-camp, the disappearance of the famous necklace entrusted to his care.

Despite the real or faked emotion he felt, Boris Pokroff, or better yet Fantômas, put on a calm face and smiled as he answered his mistress, saying, "There you are my dear Ekaterina. I'm here. As a faithful, devoted lover, I appear as soon as you start to worry about what has become of me. The faithful little lap dog approaches his..."

When she saw her lover, the duchess started to smile and a blush washed over her cheeks as she threw herself into Fantômas' arms.

"Ah!" she stammered as her bosom heaved with emotion. "You may tell me that I'm silly, fearful, possibly even mad, but I'm always afraid for you when you go away and just now, as I knew you were meeting with a stranger, the darkest foreboding came over me."

Fantômas replied gently, "That was no stranger who came to see me. It was Prince Andrieff, his Majesty's aide-de-camp."

"Oh," said the duchess. "And what did he want? As I saw him ride into the courtyard I had the impression that he had pushed his mount hard the entire way. The horse was white with foam when the prince got down from his saddle."

Evasively, Fantômas replied, "His Majesty had a rather urgent message for me, in fact."

Affectionate and curious, the duchess asked her lover," Nothing upsetting, I hope. We're still going to be able to stay here for a few more days, aren't we, and enjoy some quiet, peaceful time together?"

The duchess stopped, upset, concerned, when the man in front of her shook his head.

"Unfortunately," said Fantômas, "We will not be granted that happiness. Contrary to what I had hoped for, I have to return to Tsarskoye Selo as soon as possible."

"I have to return... don't you mean we have to return?"

"If that doesn't frighten you, Duchess," Fantômas replied.

"Why wouldn't I return? Are you in some terrible danger?"

"Possibly," said the bandit.

"Well then," said the duchess, her face and voice filled with love, "That's one reason why I won't hesitate to accompany you."

Fantômas, too, was overcome with emotion. He pulled his mistress to him and embraced her slowly.

"My poor dear," he murmured. "It's so painful that you love a man like me, whose days are always numbered, whose existence is always threatened! I had hoped to have some leisure time, to spend a few happy days with you. To be peaceful for a while... and now I have to return to our emperor."

The duchess was more and more troubled and said, "Oh, I don't regret loving you. For me it's just another part of my love, knowing that you constantly need to be protected from your many enemies. I would like to be powerful, to be able to protect you myself. I was afraid again just now and I will always be afraid. Everywhere! For you! If you wanted to, we could escape, leave this country and you could once again be just Boris Pokroff. And I would no longer be the duchess and the emperor's relative, but a simple, unknown middle-class woman, ignored by everyone, your mistress, your wife?"

"That cannot be," replied Fantômas. "We have our duty to perform, no matter what it costs, and we have to keep on..."

"That's true," Ekaterina acknowledged after a moment's silence. "We do not belong to one another. Everything for the Tsar, everything for Russia!"

Fantômas replied, "Within an hour, Ekaterina, the armored carriage that is to take us back to their majesties will be ready. Go and make your preparations while I do the same. Let us leave this house in Gatchina without regret. We have enjoyed some peace here!"

"Recall the unusual adventures that took place during the night following our arrival. Perhaps, for us, safety lies in returning to Tsarskoye Selo."

Concern swept over the duchess' face as she said, "My God! When I hear you say that, Boris Pokroff... Are you afraid of something?"

And, since Fantômas did not reply, since he continued to look worried, anxious, the duchess pummeled him with more questions.

"Something is threatening you. I'm convinced of it! Some danger that Prince Andrieff came to inform you about, a danger you won't mention to me so I won't be frightened. Boris, confide in me. Tell me your concerns so I can share them with you!"

But Fantômas gave her a forced smile, shook his head, and said, "No, I have nothing to fear, nothing in particular, at least. Yet, I cannot hide the fact from you, without being able to tell you any more, that we must both take every precaution."

Putting the discussion to an end, Fantômas withdrew. The duchess slowly returned to her apartments. Her lover's mysterious words, filled with innuendo, had upset her.

"Oh," she said as she placed a trembling hand on the bell to call for her people. "I'm not afraid for myself, but for him. For him. As result of his position he faces so many dangers. He is constantly menaced by the nihilists. As the chief of the secret police he is always in someone's sights. What can I do? How can I protect the one I love, the one I love more than life?"

And, bit by bit, as she was thinking, an old idea once again took root in her mind and she said, "I absolutely must make sure that Juve provides protection for Boris Pokroff. Was I right to do what I did? Was I right to act as I acted? I can't believe it, although I want to convince myself, but I must confide in Juve and get his opinion."

Hearing a knock at the door, the duchess called out, "Enter!"

It was a servant. And just then, setting aside her mysterious problem that so concerned her, Ekaterina prepared to leave.

What had the duchess done? What initiative had she taken? Why did she fear the consequences? What was she hiding from her lover? And why was she hiding something from him?

Fantômas, on the other hand, when he had arrived to talk with Ekaterina, after his chat with the Tsar's aide-de-camp and their joint discovery that the valuable necklace had disappeared, had taken on a strange attitude, that would not have surprised anyone who really knew what had happened. Fantômas did not believe that he had to inform Ekaterina that the precious necklace for which he was responsible had disappeared from the secret chest in which he had hidden it. Surprisingly, it seemed that Fantômas had been robbed, and that this theft both upset him and amused him.

Once the aide-de-camp, frightened by the answer he had to take to the Tsar, was once again mounted on his horse, Fantômas, very calmly, bid him farewell and instructed him to inform the Tsar about the disappearance of the necklace immediately. He had not seemed terribly emotional about the situation and it was only as he was walking up to his office, when he found Ekaterina there, that he had shown any signs of concern, as if he wanted the duchess to think that, possibly, at that very moment, he was in even greater danger than before.

Why had Fantômas adopted such an attitude and what was he hoping to accomplish?

When the armored carriage had been brought to the front door, Fantômas made sure that it was actually driven by the fat coachman, Nick, and conducted a careful inspection of the vehicle along with the Cossacks who were to accompany him. Only then did he invite the duchess to climb aboard with him.

Yet, before that, the so-called Boris Pokroff gave the village mayor, who had come to see the couple off, a coded message that he was to transmit to the Tsar at Tsarskoye Selo, immediately.

Meanwhile, as the four horses galloped over the deserted, snow-covered road, Juve was sitting in the Tsar's private office, smoking.

Since the previous evening, the policeman had definitely earned the emperor's sympathy and favor. In fact, the Tsar was conversing quite familiarly with him, had invited Juve to sit down and had even offered the French man the cigarette he was now smoking.

For the past 20 minutes, he had been chatting with Juve, smiling at the policeman's words. By times, however, he would look startled, troubled by Juve's audacious words, but he immediately recovered and encouraged Juve to continue the conversation. And, although Juve was on excellent terms with the Tsar, he was deeply concerned.

The evening before, he had expected them to release Hélène and Fandor and, out of a sense of discretion, he had not asked the Tsar directly. But this morning he had learned that all of the nihilists arrested following the explosion on Skobeleff Avenue had been judged by the martial court and were to be executed in eight days. He had learned that Hélène and Fandor had been lumped in with the accused and were now sentenced to death!

Overcome with emotion, he had sought out the Tsar and thrown himself at his mercy.

"Majesty! Majesty!" he shouted, "A frightful judicial error has been committed. Two innocent people have been sentenced along with the guilty. I have come to beg your grace and tell you about them."

Then he explained that he was referring to Hélène and Fandor. He was most distressed when Nicholas II replied.

"It is most regrettable, Mr. Juve, that I did not know these things beforehand. But at this late hour, despite my omnipotence, I cannot change the decision made by the martial court. The law allows for no exceptions and I cannot intervene on behalf of your friends."

"But that's abominable! That's frightful!" screamed Juve.

"It is," replied the Tsar in a tone that brooked no comment. "The only thing I can do is pardon everyone and you know that is impossible."

These words, however, cast a glimmer of hope into Juve's mind. Of course, the task he was about to undertake was formidable, but why wouldn't it succeed? Since the Tsar could pardon everyone then he would insist that the man pardon everyone who had been arrested after the Skobeleff explosion. And Juve, with unparalleled ardor, pled for all the poor wretches. He had been fortunate to find the Tsar in a good mood and, because of that, a strange, extraordinary scene played out between the four walls of the office in which the two men, the Tsar and Juve, chatted.

The emperor of Russia listened kindly to the words of the French policeman and the French policeman, championing the prisoners held in the Saint-Jean prison, attempted to win the Tsar over to the nihilists' cause. That, in fact, was the formidable task Juve had set for himself. He told himself that, since he had to convince the Tsar to pardon all of the miserable wretches condemned to die along with Hélène and Fandor, the only way to do that would be to show the

Tsar that those people were right in their thinking and that they had to be released.

Juve argued, "Your Majesty should be the first to preach the holy theories of nihilism! Your Majesty should chase that useless and treacherous horde of lords from another time from his inner circles. Those people have backward ideas and prevent you from being touched by the mysteries of progress, of understanding the benefits of freedom, of seeing the blinding light cast by civilization."

"But," said the Tsar, "the nihilists are miserable assassins!"

"They are apostles and martyrs," retorted Juve. "What is more beautiful than giving up your life for an idea?"

"Nothing, of course," the Tsar replied in an ironic tone.

And, seeing that the Tsar was in a good mood and was allowing himself to be won over bit by bit, Juve added, "There is something more beautiful than the act of an apostle immolating himself, it is the act of the master, of the god, who prevents that sacrifice! That act, your Majesty, will be yours. I am not pleading for the cause of my friends, Hélène and Fandor, here. I'm pleading for the cause of modern humanity in its entirety, for progress, for universal happiness that can only be attained through indulgence and goodwill!"

Juve stopped, atrociously perplexed, wondering how the Tsar would take the audacious words he had just uttered.

"I've placed all my cards on the table," he thought. "And one of two things will happen. Either I'll win or the emperor will order me to join my friends in their dungeon."

Juve waited, panting. The Tsar stood up, paced back and forth in his office, as he did whenever he studied a problem.

He suddenly stopped in front of Juve and said, "You've convinced me. Well almost. The arguments you presented have touched me and it will not be said that the Tsar of Russia will behave like a savage. Juve, I'll pardon all of the convicts. Every single one of them! Even that abominable pope Alleluia, old Marfa, that sordid old hag, Vassili her son, who is still on the run, and Boleslas, who once held such a large place in my heart. Needless to say, your friends, Hélène and Fandor, will also be released, but..."

The Tsar stopped.

"But?" asked Juve, panting, already prepared to agree to all of the emperor's conditions.

But he received no reply. There was a discrete knock on the door of the private office. The Tsar and Juve looked at one another, stunned, concerned, fearing that it brought bad news, or at least news that was important, since the palace rules prohibited anyone from bothering the Tsar once he had retired into his private office. He was only to be disturbed for a sensational event. What were they about to learn?

The Tsar went to open the door and Prince Andrieff stood before him. The officer was drenched in sweat. His clothing was covered with snow and he had galloped wildly on the road from Gatchina to Tsarskoye Selo, for 20 consecutive verste, without allowing his horse to catch its breath.

When he saw the officer, the Tsar immediately knew that something extraordinary had happened.

"Did you see Boris Pokroff?" the emperor asked.

"Yes," the officer replied, out of breath.

"Is Boris Pokroff coming back?" asked the Tsar.

"He will be here in two hours at the latest," came the reply.

"Good," said the emperor.

And, pausing, after a brief silence, the Tsar added, "And I suppose that, in keeping with my orders, he will be bringing back her Majesty's necklace?"

Then the aide-de-camp looked at his master in fear. He raised his hand to his helmet and declared in a trembling voice, "No, Majesty, Boris Pokroff will not be bringing the necklace back."

The Tsar shouted, "He's not bringing the necklace back? Despite my orders? Why?"

"Because," said the aide-de-camp bowing his head. "Because, the necklace has disappeared. It has been stolen from Boris Pokroff!"

"From Boris Pokroff!" the Tsar said, staggering.

"From Boris Pokroff himself," the officer repeated.

Juve listened to this conversation in silence, as it grew more and more serious. The policeman felt overwhelmed and did not understand why the necklace had disappeared. Had Boris Pokroff, namely Fantômas, been unable to resist the temptation to steal the valuable piece of jewelry? That must be what happened, but it was a clumsy move on the part of Fantômas. Yet, Fantômas' mistake cheered Juve.

"Saying that the necklace was taken from him is like saying that he is unable to serve as the chief of the secret police. Boris Pokroff, or rather Fantômas will be fired, I suppose."

Juve already started considering the possibility that he would be appointed to replace the sinister bandit. He savored the thought that his first act in his new position would be to arrest Fantômas. But, as Juve was dreaming of these wonderful projects, a red Cossack appeared at the end of the hallway and walked, his back bowed, toward the Tsar. He held a document that he gave to the aide-de-camp who in turn passed it to the Tsar.

Nicholas II read the message, his face growing pal, his eyebrows furrowing and he yelled in anger, "Damnation! Those miserable wretches! It's always them! When I think that I listened to you, Mr. Juve! Do you want to hear about the latest crime committed by your nihilist friends?"

And as Juve, distraught, remained silent, the Tsar threw the message down at his feet and shouted, "Boris Pokroff has informed me that the necklace was stolen from him by the nihilists and that pack of scoundrels is now in possession of the most beautiful piece of jewelry in the royal treasure chest!"

"Majesty," Juve started.

But the emperor was beside himself.

He turned to the aide-de-camp and said, "Prince Andrieff, the martial court has condemned about 20 nihilists to death and they are to be executed in eight days. Got and instruct the prison, on my behalf, to execute them tomorrow morning!"

"Majesty, Majesty..." Juve started.

"Back off, get away from me or I'll hang you along with them," the emperor raged.

The aide-de-camp had withdrawn and was running to transmit the emperor's orders.

The Tsar was about to leave his office when Juve intervened, blocked his way, and said, "Pardon me!"

The Tsar grew even paler, believing that Juve would risk death instead of giving way, and said, "You dare...!"

"Yes," said Juve somberly. "I dare, Majesty, because I have nothing to fear and you have everything to fear."

"You're going to assassinate me?" the Tsar asked, growing even paler.

"Possibly," Juve said abruptly. "If you do not grant me what I ask."

"This is blackmail" said the Tsar, trying to get closer to the electric bell.

But Juve blocked his way, saying, "Majesty, I'm proposing a gentlemen's agreement to you. I want you to pardon the nihilists that the court sentenced to death and you want the Tsarina's necklace..."

"It's possible," replied the Tsar. "So?"

"Well," said Juve. "You scratch my back and I'll scratch yours. I find the necklace and you pardon all those miserable wretches!"

The Tsar thought for a moment and declared, "Fine! But if the necklace is not found by tomorrow morning they will all hang, and you with them!"

"That's your final word, Majesty?"

"That's my final word!"

"Fine," said Juve. "Agreed."

In the park at Tsarskoye Selo, a man walked, bareheaded, impervious to the cold, indifferent to the snow that fell slowly around him.

That man was Juve, appalled, devastated.

He had taken his leave from the Tsar an hour earlier. It was three o'clock in the afternoon and he had until dawn to act, in order to save his friends by finding the necklace.

Although he had won some time, Juve was not certain that he would triumph. Quite the contrary. The Tsar would most certainly not change his mind and Juve had to find the necklace.

How would he do that? Where would he look? If only Juve could get to Fantômas. If only he knew what had happened to the so-called Boris Pokroff. He had heard something to the effect that he was supposed to return to Tsarskoye Selo... But when? Juve had no idea!

The policeman went back into the wing of the palace where the apartment that had been reserved for him was located. His fists clenched with rage, he felt powerless to act, cold drops of sweat pearled on his forehead and he was barely able to refrain from sobbing when he thought that by this time the next day his friends, Hélène and Fandor, would be dead, hanged.

As he reached the floor where his apartment was located, a feminine silhouette suddenly appeared before him. A graceful, gentle voice, yet a voice filled with anguish greeted him, "Good day Mr. Juve. I'm so pleased to see you."

Juve stopped and shivered. The Duchess Ekaterina stood before him.

"The duchess is here," thought Juve. "Let's hope Fantômas is not far off!"

CHAPTER XXIV
Love Pledges

"They're nihilists!"

Just as the rescuers managed to tear the unfortunate wretches from probable death, as they were buried by the sudden explosion, a great cry rang out.

"Nihilists! They're nihilists!"

The revolutionaries made no effort to claim otherwise. Realizing, perhaps, that any effort to lie would be in vain and that cowardice would not save them, they took up their courage and proclaimed the truth, shrieking, "Yes, it's true, we are nihilists!"

Things occurred rapidly after that. The rescuers turned away, as did the troops that had gathered at the site of the catastrophe. A moment earlier, the survivors had been viewed as unfortunate victims and they enjoyed the sympathy of all. But now, everyone considered them assassins, terrible criminals, people who deserved neither pity nor compassion.

An order rang out. A battalion of Cossacks arrived, called by a few passersby who had sounded the alarm.

"Form a square! Surround these people! Take them away!"

Immediately a new horror fell over the poor nihilists. The sky suddenly grew dark and thick snow poured down, as is common in St. Petersburg. The ground was covered in white, traffic slowed, and the poor wretches were hauled off in a gloomy procession to the Saint-Jean *ostroghi*, followed by the shouts, gunshots, and the cracking of whips, the *knouts* the Russian army officers carry so often.

Who were these poor people who were being dragged off in this manner? First, there was a large crowd of those who believed in nihilism. And then there were the two people who had been sentenced by the nihilists, two innocent victims, Jérôme Fandor and Hélène.

To be truthful, when Juve had set off the explosion, he had torn his two friends from certain, immediate death. But had he really saved them?

That, unfortunately, was questionable since fate seemed to be against them.

They had faced the harsh revolutionary tribunal. Now they would no doubt face a regular court. Arrested with the nihilists, considered nihilists, they were going to answer for a crime that all Russia considered the most abominable crime, one for which there was no justice.

No doubt, they would be taken to face some martial court immediately and the sentence was already obvious, without any defense, without any opportunity to explain.

Jérôme Fandor, stunned by the misfortune that dogged his heels, asked, "How long before we die? When will they execute us?"

Recalling what he already knew about Russia, he shivered and thought, "We'll be precipitated into the void before the week is out no doubt."

He looked for Hélène. The young woman was a few feet away. She was walking bravely, in the middle of a row of prisoners, which protected her from the brutality of the Cossacks.

Once Jérôme Fandor saw Hélène, he could think of nothing else. With all his might, he would find a way to join her. He wanted to slip over toward her, to make his way to her side. Unfortunately, that was impossible! He had to stay quiet. The slightest movement would be punished by the cruel *knout*. Fandor shivered as he thought about trying anything at all. He would only draw attention to his beloved and expose her to cruel punishments.

Fandor remained still. He forced himself to a lack of action required under the circumstances. He docilely followed the procession that was heading to the prison, to the slaughterhouse that awaited there. The young man's sole consolation was that he managed to see Hélène's pretty face from time to time.

Fantômas' daughter was admirably brave and courageous. Despite the death that lurked around her, despite the certainty of the terrible fate that awaited her, she still managed to smile and that smile was for Fandor!

To the journalist, it felt as if the walk to the *ostroghi* took an hour. In actual fact, the horrible calvary took just a few minutes. Unfortunately, at the *ostroghi*, a new pain lay in wait for the young man. He had first supposed that all of the nihilists would be locked up together and he hoped that he would be able to join Hélène, that he could talk with her one last time, that he could hold her in his arms.

That was not the case.

No doubt as a security measure, the prisoners were separated. Some were taken down into the lower rooms and others, no doubt considered particularly dangerous, were thrown into cells. Jérôme Fandor had no idea why he was one of those thrown into a dungeon. And all too soon he would be more than familiar with the tortures a valiant soul would endure in such a dark place! The night passed. A night of horror and fear, during which Jérôme Fandor felt madness brush against his mind. He felt as if he had been crushed under the weight of the colossal, thick-walled prison. He felt as if he were in a tomb. Was he not a living dead man, incapable not only of trying to find deliverance, but also of providing any consolation to the one he loved so tenderly and who was spending a similar night of horror a few steps away.

The morning finally arrived. Jérôme Fandor was in a state of exhaustion when he was taken, along with three other condemned men, before the martial court. Everything happened quickly. A harried clerk muttered a few incomprehensible words in Russian. Three judges presided and gave the accused no opportunity to present their defense. Despite his obstinate energy, Jérôme Fandor was unable to get a single word in and, less than five minutes later, he was once again taken away.

"That's fine!" he said to himself. "I didn't understand the sentence, but I have no illusions. I'm sure I've been sentenced to death!"

Fandor was taken back to his cell. He had to spend another entire day in horrible isolation, thinking about death that was so close at hand, with all the suffering of his poor heart that raced in his chest when he thought about Hélène.

As night fell, the dungeon grew even darker and the prison seemed to slumber, footsteps rang out in the corridor.

Jérôme Fandor stood up quickly and murmured, "Already?"

He thought he knew what was about to happen. His frightened mind dredged up the final horror, the inevitable horror. Assuredly, they were coming for him, they were going to take him to the gallows. Before the door opened, he brushed his hand over his forehead as if to dismiss any problem, as if to chase away all extraneous thoughts.

"So be it," he said. "If I have to die, then I am ready."

Then the door opened suddenly. An officer, surrounded by Cossacks, stood there with a lantern in his hand, which he pointed at Fandor, ordering, "Come!"

There was no point in resisting. Jérôme Fandor shrugged and went with those who had come for him. Yet, they did not return to the courtroom. Jérôme Fandor soon realized that they were not taking him to meet death. Obviously, they were just taking him to a new cell. This transfer was significant, however, since there was no mistake about it, Fandor was being taken to the circular rooms that held all of the convicts who had nothing left to do but wait for death.

Resigned, Jérôme Fandor heard the guard play with the locks that opened the way to his last prison. The doors opened and he was shoved into the cell.

But, at that very moment, as the guards were closing the door behind him, a cry of joy rang out, "Fandor!"

And Fandor's lips trembled as he replied, "Hélène!"

Fate had, it seemed, decided to show some favor to the two unfortunate lovers. Sentenced to death, Hélène and Fandor were reunited in the round room, the waiting room for the gallows, where all of the nihilists had been placed. The two young people hugged and embraced with all the violent passion of their love.

At that moment, nothing else existed for them. They forgot about the Russian prison, their imminent deaths. They no longer thought about being prisoners, they had no idea they were in the sinister circular room and that other prisoners surrounded them and that they were all pressed up against one another, unfortunate wretches that no one could save.

At that ineffable moment when, after a lengthy separation, after such cruel tortures, they were finally together and Jérôme Fandor and Hélène thought of none of all that, no longer understanding anything. They only knew one thing, they only felt one thing, that they loved one another and that they adored one another.

Long hours passed as quickly as a minute. They had so many things to say, to many secrets to confide, so many unfortunate, frightful, horrible misunderstandings to explain!

Hélène was the first one to find the courage to bring up confidences. It was the young woman who, with her instinctive uprightness, her natural frankness, wanted to know the truth at any cost. So, Hélène questioned Fandor about the sinister adventures she had been part of at the time of her return from Mexico, when she arrived at Montreux, in the neighborhood of the Hôtel Croisset, which was apparently nicknamed the Crime Hotel.

"That Natacha," Hélène asked, "Did you love her?"

At that moment Fandor stood up, his voice filled with an expression it was impossible to mistake and said, "Ah! How could you have believed that, Hélène? How could you believe that I could love someone other than you? Do you think I'm capable of betrayal? I swear on my honor that there was never any love between me and Natacha. I had barely heard her touching confidences and that was when she was dying in my arms, at the fatal moment when jealousy blinded you, making you believe that I was embracing my mistress…"

And with that Fandor told Hélène, with his usual brevity, with great openness, everything about the death of the unfortunate Natacha. He told Hélène how the young woman was both pitiful and sinister. He related how the nihilist had been the extraordinary victim of her passion for the infamous and merciless Dr. Loeutch.

Then, suddenly, Fandor stopped talking. He no longer had any need to defend himself. He felt that Hélène believed him, that the young woman no longer doubted him. And what good would it do to poison their last few moments with a defense that was unneeded. They embraced again; their lips met once again in a lingering kiss.

And, yet again, Hélène was the one to bring up the frightening mystery.

"Fandor," she asked. "Do you know when we are to die?"

He nodded his head slowly. Unfortunately, at that moment, abruptly roused from his dream, as he returned to reality, Jérôme Fandor felt as if he had fallen into an abominable nightmare.

In the prison, around them, the nihilists around them were remarkably calm and resigned. They sang as they waited for death. Some talked. Everyone seemed to accept their destiny calmly, in the absolute certainty that they were irremediably lost and that nothing could be done to save them.

Dawn was coming. Jérôme Fandor and Hélène, shivering, looked at their cellmates, admiring their fatalistic resignation that is so much part of the nature of the Slavic soul, and that even the most courageous French people could never attain.

At that very moment, footsteps approached the cell. The singing stopped.

One of the nihilists asked "Whose turn is it?"

He asked the very question that had to be asked. The door opened, revealing the guards, the soldiers and a priest. They had come to take the first batch of prisoners to take to the gallows.

Hélène, growing pale, moved closer to Fandor. He took her in his arms as his listened to the guards shout the names. He dreamt, at that moment, of impossible things, a sudden rebellion, last-minute protests, a crazy battle. No, if they called Hélène he would not allow her to go, he would fight for her. They could not kill her! That was horrible! Mad!

The six nihilists called bid farewell to their comrades and then, with no apparent trouble, accompanied the guards.

The door closed.

The condemned man who had called out earlier, made another sinister comment, saying, "We have five minutes of peace and quiet. I think they'll take us all this morning!"

Jérôme Fandor, eyes hard, repeated, "Five minutes. Five minutes left to live. What miracle could occur in five minutes?"

He thought only of Hélène, filled with love and tenderness.

CHAPTER XXV
To Paris!

The day before that terrible morning, as Juve, who had been chased out of the Tsar's office, fleeing the great leader's anger, went into the gardens at Tsarskoye Selo to consider the measures he should take, the armored carriage that carried Boris Pokroff and his mistress traveled at full speed along the deserted road that ran from Gatchina to the imperial palace.

Sitting close together, Fantômas and his mistress did not exchange a single word during the first part of the trip. The bandit maintained his sarcastic and mysterious expression and the duchess grew more and more alarmed, fearing that something terrible would happen to her lover, sitting silent as her concerns and fears grew.

She was the one to break the silence.

"Listen to me Boris," she said in a pleading tone. "The life we've been living since we became lovers, since a crazy and sincere passion brought us together, is becoming more and more frightful every day. Just a while ago, in a spurt of enthusiasm, we declared that we do not belong to one another, that our existence, that our fate is linked with those of our sovereigns... Unfortunately, I'm just a poor woman, too loving to be heroic and I want this to change! You have performed your duty, Boris Pokroff, you had dedicated enough of yourself to the cause of the Tsar, and you are entitled to live your life now and to find happiness in a peaceful and quiet retirement. Do you want to prove your love for me?"

Fantômas listened to his mistress, took her hand and clasped it tenderly.

He responded with a question, saying, "How do you want me to prove my love for you Ekaterina?"

The beautiful woman hugged her lover and said, "This life of constant worry is killing me. I want you to resign as the chief of the secret police. Promise me that you will do that. Then, Boris Pokroff, we will go away together, this very evening, tomorrow morning, we will go and live our love in distant sunny countries where people say perfect happiness exists."

Assuredly, Duchess Ekaterina was not counting on a favorable response. She thought that her lover would refuse outright to provide the demonstration of love that she requested. Yet she asked for it anyway, promising to repeat it again at a later time, and convinced that she would eventually get Boris Pokroff to leave the Tsar's service.

Yet, to her great surprise and amazement, Boris Pokroff, pretending to seem weary, slowly said, "Unfortunately, Ekaterina, what you are advising me to do is not worthy of a man like me, but your proposal comes at a good time for my state of mind. It is germinating there, developing... I admit that I'm tired of these perpetual struggles and the constant anguish that you feel for me. So be it! As soon as we get to Tsarskoye Selo, I'll tender my resignation to the Tsar. This evening we'll be free and tomorrow we'll leave."

"My God! Is it possible?" the duchess shouted, unable to believe her ears.

"I swear it is," Fantômas said.

Then he gently added, "Are you convinced now that I love you more than anything in the world since I'm sacrificing my own self-esteem for love?"

"Tomorrow," the duchess said, her voice filled with joy. "Tomorrow we'll leave! But where will we go?"

As if wanting to speed matters up, Fantômas said, "The Northern Express leaves the St. Petersburg station at 11:55 tomorrow morning. We'll take that train, we'll go abroad, to France, then we'll see…"

The two lovers remained thoughtful, embroidering their dreams in the silence with a thousand details that were geminating in their minds.

The duchess was most surprised, not only because she had so successfully obtained what she wanted, but also because Boris Pokroff seemed so eager to organize their departure as quickly as possible.

In this state of mind, they arrived at Tsarskoye Selo. The duchess was entitled to personal apartments in the imperial palace. She set of for them quickly, while Boris Pokroff left her to go and see the Tsar.

She was waiting anxiously in her parlor for the authorization Pokroff had gone off to get from the Tsar when Prince Andrieff was announced.

"What is it?" the duchess asked, alarmed.

The distraught aide-de-camp explained what had occurred between the Tsar and her lover, declaring, "His Majesty was not pleased with Boris Pokroff. The Tsar criticized him for letting the nihilists steal the Tsarina's necklace. Pokroff was removed from his functions and invited to leave the empire as quickly as possible.

Pokroff chased out of Russia! Pokroff accused of letting the necklace be stolen! What did all this mean? The duchess was dumbfounded. Up to that point she had known nothing about the events that had taken place at Gatchina a few hours earlier. Fantômas had told her nothing, had mentioned nothing about the disappearance of the necklace.

She paced back and forth nervously. Her bosom heaved, her entire body was feverish.

"My God! My God!" she stammered. "What should I do? Which side should I take?"

She collapsed into an armchair and thought.

And then she uttered mysterious words, "What should I do? Should I tell all? Reveal the truth about the necklace. That would be so easy to do? Or hide everything, even from Boris Pokroff?" On the one hand, my lover will be rehabilitated in His Majesty's mind, but then he will be obliged to remain in the Tsar's service and he will most certainly die, sooner or later because his enemies will assassinate him. On the other, he will leave, covered in shame and disgrace. But that doesn't matter at all since I'll be keeping him alive and we'll be able to love one another for the rest of lives, without fearing his adversaries and enemies. My God! My God! What should I do? What will become of me?"

The duchess was still lost in thought when she suddenly got out of the armchair she had collapsed into.

"I cannot keep the secret for myself," she declared. "I have to share it with someone. I'll have to confide in Boris Pokroff, unless…"

Just as she was about to leave her apartments, the duchess stopped on the threshold. She had seen a man at the other end of the corridor. Juve. And the sight of the French man stopped her in her tracks. What secret could the beautiful Ekaterina be keeping?

A few moments later, Juve was with the duchess in her parlor.

"You want to talk with me? About what?" Juve asked.

"First," said the duchess. "Can I trust you absolutely?"

"Yes, madam."

"Can I trust you to keep the conversation we are about to have absolutely confidential?"

"Yes, madam."

Can I be certain, Mr. Juve, that if I do a service for you, you will do one for me, without discussion, without bargaining?"

"I'll see," Juve said, suspicion suddenly gnawing at his mind.

The duchess knew how to strike the policeman in the heart.

"At present, Mr. Juve," she said. "I know, since Price Andrieff told me, that you are in a terrible situation, the most terrible situation in which an honest man can find himself."

"That is true, madam," Juve acknowledged.

"You must find the missing necklace before tomorrow morning, or you will be hanged…" the duchess continued

"That is true, madam, but death is not important to me! What fills me with despair is that two innocent people, my friends, Hélène and Fandor, will be hanged with me…"

"What would you give to find that necklace?"

"Everything in my power, madam!"

"Would you protect the human being I tell you to, no matter what happens?"

Juve grew pale. He looked the duchess straight in the eyes, trying to understand. He suspected what Ekaterina was about to ask him. She was obviously going to ask him to protect her lover which, for Juve, meant sparing Fantômas! The only thing the policeman needed to know was whether or not the Duchess Ekaterina knew that Boris Pokroff was none other than Fantômas. But how could he ask her?

Juve asked, "Are you certain that you can find the Tsarina's necklace for me?"

"Yes, on my honor," the duchess replied.

Juve's mind was made up. As long as the duchess was not lying, and he would have proof of that within a few minutes, he would be able to save Hélène and Fandor, as long as he let Fantômas go. Juve hesitated to promise what the duchess asked of him.

She said, "Here is what I want. You will swear on everything that you hold sacred that, until noon tomorrow morning, you will protect Boris Pokroff against everyone that may approach him and wish him ill. Better yet, if you feel the need to raise your hand against him, you will refrain from doing so. That is the price for finding the Tsarina's necklace!"

This time, Juve could not keep from yelling at the duchess, "Curses, madam! Don't you know that Boris Pokroff is none other than Fantômas?"

The duchess turned pale. She looked Juve in the eye and said, "I've had my suspicions for some time. Now, you've just confirmed that Boris Pokroff is Fantômas!"

"He's a wretched, terrible bandit, the most formidable criminal mastermind," Juve said.

The duchess interrupted him with a wave of her hand and replied, "He's my lover, Juve and I... I love him!"

These words were followed by a long silence and then the duchess asked, "Do I have your word, Mr. Juve?"

The policeman bowed his head and as a large tear drop welled up under his eyelid, he said, "You have my word, Madam. I swear that, until noon tomorrow, I will not only protect Fantômas against any and all attacks against him, but I will also keep him from getting arrested. After noon, however..."

The Duchess rushed over to Juve and clasped his hands warmly.

"After noon," she shouted, "You will be as free as we will. Thank, Juve, thank you... I'll never forget what you have done for us."

"For you, madam, for you," Juve corrected.

"Fine, for me," the duchess said, smiling. "I must admit that one man alone seems capable of protecting my lover, just as one man alone seems capable of defeating him. You!"

Juve frowned and said, "Let's cut this short, madam. I've given you my word. The necklace if you please?"

The duchess hesitated for a second.

"Please, madam, don't dither about, don't waste a minute or I'll start to regret my promise!"

He stopped and looked at Ekaterina, dumbfounded. With an abrupt gesture, she tore off the light scarf that covered her bosom and shoulders and, uncovering her throat, she revealed, fastened around her delicate neck, the magnificent, sparkling necklace that Juve had promised to get back for the Tsar!

"The Tsarina's necklace," the policeman shouted. "You had it!"

"Yes," replied the duchess. "Allow me to explain…"

Ekaterina then told Juve that, fearing an attack against her lover and concerned that he was solely responsible for the superb necklace, she had taken it, that morning, from the secret chest in which it had been stored for safekeeping. She acted without Boris Pokroff's knowledge and she had not had an opportunity to tell him that she had the necklace in her possession since Boris Pokroff had neglected to tell her that the Tsar's aide-de-camp had come for it.

The duchess slowly took the necklace off and handed it to Juve, saying, "You see, sir, I'm keeping my promise. For heaven's sake, keep yours."

Juve bowed to her and slowly replied, "I will."

"Juve!"

"Fandor!"

"Hélène!"

The two young people and the policeman hugged passionately.

It was the morning after the tragic evening when Juve, after promising the Duchess Ekaterina that he would spare Fantômas, had received the famous necklace to be returned to the Tsar. The Tsar had lavished Juve with congratulations and thanks. Immediately after that, the Tsar had pardoned all of the nihilists detained in the Saint-Jean prison and the next morning, Juve, Hélène and Fandor had been reunited.

They had barely finished congratulating one another when Juve, who had turned somber, declared, "This is no time for us to relate all of the adventures we have had. The Tsar's pardon comes with a condition. You must leave Russia immediately. The Northern Express leaves St. Petersburg at 11:55 this morning. You have to be on that train!"

"And what about you, Juve?" Hélène asked.

"Unfortunately, I can't come with you," the policeman replied. "But I'll follow soon and we'll meet in Paris."

"And what about Fantômas?" Fandor asked, timidly.

The policeman's face grew dark and he said, in a mysterious voice, "Don't say that name to my face, unless you want to fill my heart with pain."

Without further explanation, Juve bid the couple farewell and, five minutes later, certain that Hélène and Fandor would take the train, he left the hotel where they had spent a few moments and headed back to Tsarskoye Selo.

Juve found the Duchess Ekaterina dressed for travel. She greeted him with a radiant smile.

"Juve," she said, "You have fulfilled your mission admirably. I know that you spent the night outside the door to Boris Pokroff's room and protected him…"

"I committed that crime, madam," Juve replied. "And I swear that, many times, I had to clasp my hands to keep from strangling that bandit!"

"Juve," continued the duchess. "In just two hours you will be free to continue hunting Fantômas, but you must keep your promise until then. Will you?"

"I will, madam."

The duchess took a step closer and said, "I'm leaving Russia, Juve. A train, the Northern Express, will be taking me to Paris in a few minutes. My carriage will come to take me to the train station. I'm counting on you to accompany our vehicle."

"Our vehicle?" replied Juve. "You're not leaving alone?"

"No," said the duchess.

A few minutes later, his heart filled with rage, Juve had to climb into the duchess' sumptuous limousine. She was accompanied by Boris Pokroff, who glanced at the policeman, eyes filled with scorn.

Juve needed exceptional strength to keep his oath! But he had given his word of honor and he would keep it until the very end! It was 11:40 in the morning. The travelers in the Northern Express were settling into the compartments. Furious, Juve paced back and forth on the platform.

"I can do nothing!" he screamed. "I promised to stay in St. Petersburg until precisely noon! I didn't see the trap! The duchess connived to help her lover escape. And I can't even warn Hélène and Fandor that Fantômas is nearby on their train!"

Juve had seen his friends settle in the compartment. He did not reveal himself to them, fearing that he would not be able to keep his secret. Then he had watched as the duchess settled in a reserved car, along with the fake Boris Pokroff, Fantômas, the man who had assassinated the real chief of the secret police.

Juve will overwhelmed by anguish and rage! He must not lose track of the bandit.

Suddenly an idea came to him and he raced to the stationmaster's office.

"Sir," he declared, in a voice that was both beseeching and authoritarian. "I find myself in a most extraordinary situation. I absolutely must take the Northern Express. But the train cannot leave the station until precisely noon. Can you arrange to have the train leave eight minutes late? I'll be responsible for any costs this might entail."

The stationmaster looked at Juve, dumbfounded. Then after a moment of silence, he replied, "Sir, I understand full well what you expect of me and there will be no cost. I'll delay the departure of the train for a few minutes."

Juve stopped, surprised that his request had been granted so easily.

"Are you certain, sir?" I can count on you?"

"But, of course," the employee replied, coldly.

Juve returned to the platform, heart pounding, as he watched the time pass. It was 11:55 and the minutes felt like centuries to the policeman. Suddenly a violent emotion washed over him. Usually, the train would leave in two minutes and all of the preparations seemed to indicate that the departure would take place as scheduled.

"Yet, the stationmaster promised me..." said Juve.

Then, he suddenly winced as he heard two employees whispering.

"You see," one said, pointing at Juve. "That man is crazy and the stationmaster reported him to us. He wanted to delay the train, no doubt for some extravagant reason! The stationmaster promised, because he didn't want to upset him, but he's scheduled the train to leave a minute early, just as a precaution!"

The train whistle blew. That was the signal.

"Curses!" Juve exclaimed, his face twisted in anguish.

What could he do? How could he keep the train from leaving? The policeman raced over to the locomotive, jumped onto the platform, landing next to the engineer.

"One hundred rubles! One thousand rubles to delay the train until noon!" he shouted as he held a wad of bank notes out to the man.

The locomotive engineer, initially surprised by the policeman's unexpected appearance, waved to his fireman, a giant covered with black coal dust, who threw Juve to the sidewalk.

The policeman landed so hard that he felt dizzy for a moment. Yet, two seconds later Juve was back on his feet. Before his eyes, the train shuddered slowly, silently sliding along the rails. It was exactly 11:51. Juve stayed there a moment, appalled, as he watched the heavy train move along the platform. Through one of the windows, he saw Fantômas, smiling at him ironically.

Dismayed, exasperated, Juve screamed, "A locomotive. Prepare a locomotive for me!"

And unable to resist the fear that had been torturing him, the fear of losing Fantômas, he was racing for the running step on the last car, as it passed by him, when hands grabbed his shoulders.

"Let me go!" shouted the policeman.

But the hands held firm.

"Are you Juve?" someone asked.

"Yes, I'm Juve," the policeman shouted. "Let me go! You can see that I have to catch this train, the train carrying Fantômas!"

Two voices laughed stridently. Juve looked at the people laughed. Guards.

"That's all fine and dandy," one of them said. "But you're not about to take the Northern Express for the border just now!"

"Why?" Juve asked, furious.

"Because," said the other guard, "We have orders from the Tsar to arrest you."

Distraught, Juve grew pale.

"Orders from the Tsar to arrest me! But why?"

"Come on," said the first guard, shrugging. "Don't try to make us believe that you know nothing about this! You know full well that the necklace you returned..."

"Yes!" said Juve, impatiently.

"Well," the man continued. "The necklace you returned is a fake. What did you do with the real one?"

"My God! My God!" Juve stammered

Distraught, overwhelmed, the French policeman collapsed, half conscious, as the two guards dragged him off.

CHAQUE VOLUME FORME UN RÉCIT COMPLET

PIERRE SOUVESTRE & MARCEL ALLAIN

FANTÔMAS

LA FIN DE FANTÔMAS

A. FAYARD ÉDITEURS DU « LIVRE POPULAIRE » PARIS

BOOK TWO: THE DEATH OF FANTÔMAS

CHAPTER I
The Trap

"In the name of the law, we arrest you!"

The Cossacks surrounded Juve suddenly and the policeman who, obviously, did not expect such an end to his adventures in Russia, could not keep from shuddering as he heard the words that indisputably announced new problems and difficulties. Yet, Juve recovered his composure.

In a calm voice, he asked, "You're arresting me. Fine. But that doesn't tell me anything at all. What are you arresting me for?"

The commanding officer replied, "You're accused of giving His Majesty the Tsar a fake necklace instead of the real necklace."

"Ah!" said Juve, and refrained from adding anything else.

Although, at the time of his arrest, he understood little about the reasons for it, he realized full well that there was no point in protesting to the Cossacks and that it was highly likely that, speaking at random, answering without knowing, could eventually expose him to more serious proceedings and greater problems.

Despite his composure, however, Juve grimaced. His arrest was so sudden, so unexpected that he initially wanted to consider it a mere formality. Yet, he quickly concluded that was not the case. They were not arresting him on a whim. They were completely serious, which became even clearer when they placed handcuffs on his wrists as four soldiers, four giants, kept a close eye on him.

"Well," sighed Juve, phlegmatically. "This trip to Russia is coming to a very bad end. What will happen to me now?"

At that moment, despite himself, Juve could not keep from glancing, with regret, at the Northern Express which, in a few minutes, would leave St. Petersburg, in a cloud of steam, heading for Belgium and France.

Assuredly, Fandor and Hélène had to be on the train, waiting for him. They would have no idea that he had been arrested, they would leave and Juve would be all alone in Russian, a large country with strange traditions and extraordinary customs where he felt so terribly foreign, misunderstood, alone in the middle of the crowd, abandoned by all.

A moment later, Juve recovered, saying to himself, "Well, we'll see which of us, Fantômas or me, has the last word. What is happening to me is obviously the consequence of one of that wretch's many tricks. He may have won this match, but I will have my revenge."

Juve docilely followed the soldiers as they escorted him out of the station and pushed him toward a sleigh. He was perfectly aware that protesting would serve no purpose. The soldiers who had arrested him were merely following orders, ignorant of the grounds. What did they care about Juve's recriminations, his complaints?

"All right," thought Juve. "He who laughs last, laughs best!"

The sleigh, surrounded by Cossacks on horseback, raced through the streets of St. Petersburg.

Juve, just a while earlier, as he headed for the station, had hoped, to tell the truth, that he would be leaving Russia for once and for all. Despite himself, he was unable to hold back a strong sense of disappointment as they took him back, a prisoner. Yet, thanks to the deep philosophical beliefs he always adhered to, he made the most of this unpleasant adventure to note, yet again, the picturesque nature of Russian customs. In France, the passage of a prisoner, in a vehicle surrounded by guards would obviously have aroused public emotions, a lively curiosity. But nothing at all like that happened in Russia. No one turned to look at the Cossacks, no one glanced at the prisoner. One more, one less, who was keeping count? There were so many arrests each day that onlookers had grown blasé.

"There's no reaction," Juve said to himself. "I can't even enjoy the satisfaction of hearing brave people call out, as they would in France, 'He looks like a bandit!'"

Juve, already reassured, started to joke. His gaiety, however, did not last long. The direction in which his escort was headed was filled with meaning.

"Good grief!" said the prisoner. "Are they taking me to Tsarskoye Selo?"

The sleigh did, in fact, sop at the Tsar's palace a short while later. At that moment, the officers of the escort that were accompanying the sleigh invited him to get down. Juve set foot on the ground.

"Will I be thrown into some dungeon?" he wondered. "Stood against some wall and shot? Or will I be lucky enough to be interrogated?"

A very brightly dressed officer, obviously some important dignitary, stepped out from the palace. He murmured a few words in the ear of the commanding officer of the escort that had just arrested Juve. The officer nodded and walked over to the policeman.

"What does he want?" Fandor's friend wondered.

At that very moment, the Russian stopped, bowed deeply to Juve, and introduced himself, saying, "His Excellency Gourochtsky, His Majesty's aide-de-camp."

The policeman was most surprised. People didn't usually introduce themselves to prisoners. What did this mean?

Not wanting to be impolite, Juve in turn bowed, bending double, then declared, "Juve, French police officer, from the Sûreté de Paris!"

He had barely finished speaking when the other man held out his hand. Juve, naturally, clasped it and shook it. At that moment, however, the excellent Juve's surprise reached extraordinary proportions.

"They're shaking my hand!" he said to himself. "First they arrest me and then they give me an almost official reception. These Russians are crazy!"

But he barely had time to think about the sudden madness that taken over the inhabitants of the imperial palace.

With exquisite manners, the Russian added, "Please follow me sir. I have rigorous orders in your respect."

"How could I not follow him," Juve grumbled to himself, adding out loud, "Your wish is my command, Your Excellency."

A moment later, Juve found himself alone in one of the large parlors at Tsarskoye Selo. It was a vast room, with truly remarkable architecture. It was, in fact, a rotunda. It was completely circular and there were no windows. Daylight flowed in through the ceiling, a ceiling of frosted glass on which human shadows appeared to be strolling back and forth. Juve noted all this with a glance.

He thought, "My word, this might just be the Tsar's personal parlor. No windows... because he's always afraid of being assassinated and thinks people will shoot at him through the glass... a glass ceiling with armed guards... that would be it!"

But, at the same time, Juve could not keep from smiling at that presumption.

"Damn, I'm a prisoner!" he grumbled. "And a prisoner suspected of robbing the Tsar of all the Russias... I suppose that, after all that, the Tsar won't be giving me an audience! The excellent Nicholas II must be convinced that I'm an abominable criminal and must be scared stiff of me!"

This thought had just passed through Juve's mind when his presumptions were proven wrong. The door to the parlor, the only door in the round room, opened wide.

An usher called out, "His Majesty, the Tsar!"

And the Tsar did, in fact enter. Nicholas II, blond, puny, looking like a young man, despite the fact that he was in his forties, appeared. He was wearing a military uniform and carried an enormous saber in his hand, which he used much like a cane. The Tsar was smiling.

He walked over to Juve, held out his hand, and said, "Good day Mr. Policeman."

And, for possibly the first time in his life, Juve was so dumbfounded that he was unable to answer. In fact, after he had been arrested in the manner in which he had been arrested, and now finding himself suddenly in the presence of the Tsar, who was holding out his hand, Juve found the situation so unlikely, so startling, that he remained silent.

The Tsar said, "Mr. Juve, are you cross with me? Are you furious with me?"

"But Majesty..." Juve said, then stopped and crossed his arms.

"Good grief, Majesty, if your Majesty would authorize me to speak openly, I would admit that I wonder if I'm dreaming."

"And what makes you think that?"

"Damn," replied Juve, who was starting to neglect the rules of protocol, something which had never really been his strong point.

"Damn, Majesty, because I'm surprised and astonished... and over-whelmed by everything that is happening..."

At that moment, the Tsar collapsed onto a low chair, overturning it.

"Really, Juve," he murmured. "You're astonished? Please tell me why."

"Willingly, sire."

And Juve, who was starting to feel his normal good mood returning, quickly and clearly explained why he was so astonished.

"I was about to leave," he said. "I was about to return to France... I was quite certain that I had given you the real necklace and then, all of a sudden, they tell me that it was a fake necklace and then they arrested me... Naturally, I was upset by the situation. I was expecting, Sire, to be punished for a crime I had not committed. I was afraid your Majesty was angry with me. Yet, now, it does not seem as if your Majesty is all that irritated with me, since your Majesty honored me with a handshake!"

The Tsar had watched Juve closely as he spoke. When the policeman stopped talking, however, the other man burst into cheerful laughter.

"My dear Juve," he murmured. "This simply proves that you don't really know me yet. I'm a man of the moment."

"Which means?" asked Juve.

"Which means," confirmed the Tsar, "that when I discovered that the necklace you had returned was a fake one, I ordered my men to arrest you."

Juve lowered his head and, without wondering if he were being too bold, asked, "And now, Sire?"

"Now?" said the Tsar. "Well, now I've considered the matter. You certainly can't be the thief so I'm not arresting you any longer!"

Juve did not move a muscle when he learned that he was free. He was always calm, extraordinarily calm, in good times and in bad. However, he did not feel particularly satisfied.

"I'm free," he replied. "So much the better. I don't really have a taste for prison! Plus, it's annoying to be considered a thief. But can your Majesty tell me what is really going on? The necklace I returned to you is not the real diamond necklace that was stolen?"

When he heard these words, the Tsar shook his head and said, "Unfortunately not. Just a bad copy with no value at all."

Then the Tsar told Juve what had happened following his departure.

He informed the policeman that a chance incident had revealed the error, Fantômas' swindle. He told Juve how, in a moment of fury, he had ordered his men to race to the station and arrest Juve.

The policeman, for his part, did not take long to realize what had really happened. He uncovered Fantômas' trickery, figured out how the bandit had been able to deceive him. It took him no more than a second. Unfortunately, it did not seem as if it would be easy to remedy the situation.

"I've been conned," Juve concluded, who never minced his words when talking about unpleasant matters. "I've been conned by Fantômas like a fool. It's time to take up the fight!"

Juve stretched his arm out, as if to make a solemn oath, and said, "I had hoped that your Majesty had the authentic necklace in his possession. Since that is not the case, I will have to set out immediately to find it."

Juve was about to say more, possible to ask permission to leave immediately and set off on his new investigation, when the Tsar stopped him with a wave of his hand.

"Juve," murmured the imperial sovereign, in a tone that had suddenly grown serious. "I have to find that necklace. I absolutely have to!"

As Juve looked the other man straight in the eyes, the Tsar insisted, speaking each word distinctly, as if to highlight their importance, "I have to Juve, because I'm going to need it... because, in a short while, in less than a week perhaps, the empress and I will be going to France and, in keeping with protocol, it will be necessary for her Majesty to wear the necklace during the festivities organized in our honor... And you, Juve, have to find it since I must admit, despite myself, that if the necklace is not found, I would continue to have some suspicions in your respect..."

The Tsar's voice was filled with emotion as he spoke.

Juve, despite himself, was touched, and replied, "Your Majesty can rest assured that I will do everything in my power to satisfy his wishes. But I will need my freedom if I am to act. Am I free, Sire?"

The Tsar hesitated. Nicholas II was assuredly, as he had just told Juve, torn between two emotions. When he took the time to think about it, he realized full well that it was completely ridiculous to suspect Juve of theft. Yet, just as the Tsar decided that Juve was innocent, he realized, despite himself, that everything pointed at the policeman and that it looked almost certain that he had been Fantômas' accomplice.

Yet, Nicolas II could not have any illusions about Juve's request, Juve had to conduct an investigation to find the necklace and, to do that, the Tsar would have to free him. Juve could hardly investigate while languishing in prison or being required to remain in Russia, or even by being kept under police surveillance.

Abruptly, the Tsar made up his mind and said, "You will be free, Juve."

Then he corrected himself, saying, "You're free immediately!"

Juve had watched the hesitations and uncertainties flit over the Tsar's face. And Juve was far too good a psychologist to be mistaken when it came to the Tsar's reasoning.

He replied, "I thank your Majesty for not letting himself get carried away by such unworthy emotions. And I fully intend to provide evidence of my good faith. I would appreciate it if your Majesty would accept the oath I am about to make. Sire, I give you my word of honor that I will do everything possible to find your necklace. If I find it, we will be quits. If I don't find it, I will turn myself over to your police lieutenant. I imagine that this will mean that your Majesty will no longer have any doubts about me!"

Juve's words were clear and definitive. The Tsar saw this. He lowered his head and asked, "Juve, do you have any orders to give? Do you want to take the measures you consider necessary right away? I, of course, will make sure that everyone here is at your disposal."

"Your Majesty is too generous," replied Juve.

The policeman thought for a minute, then lifted his head, and said, "I do have orders to give, in fact, sire. But first I'll need some information.

"What information? Can I provide it?"

"Without a doubt, if your Majesty allows me to question him."

"Go ahead, Juve. Ask away! What do you want to know?"

"What is the name," Juve asked, "Of that border town where the Northern Express leaves Russia and heads into Germany?"

The Tsar replied, "That's the little station at Eydtkuhnen."

"Are there any policemen stationed there?"

"Of course."

"And how do the travelers disembark?"

"As they do in any other border station, Juve. They get off the train. Russian trains are not allowed to enter Germany because of the difference in track gauge. Then they go through Customs, they greet the Holy Images, and they get back on the train. That's all."

"Fine," said Juve.

The policeman looked lost in thought for a moment, then asked, "Where is the one place where it is certain that all of the travelers, without exception, will pass by?"

"The Holy Images sidewalk," replied the Tsar. "No one can enter Russia, no one can leave Russia, without greeting the icons located at the border station. The passports, moreover, are checked right next to that icon."

"Fine," Juve said again.

And, since the Tsar was looking at him, no doubt expecting some sort of indication as to what he was about to do, Juve stood up coldly, without a word.

"I'll go and issue orders, Sire. Do I have your permission to leave?"

"Go!" said the Tsar.

The train from St. Petersburg arrived in a cloud of steam at the small border station at Eydtkuhnen. Russian trains are usually deplorably slow, but the Northern Express, exceptionally, had pushed its pace as it approached the German border. Employees were already busy at the station.

Dressed in picturesque outfits that made them look like butchers, the station employees, with their large aprons flapping in the wind, stood in a line along the platform. It was obvious that, as the train was about to stop, they would race off to attack the compartments and convince the travelers to confide their small hand luggage to them. They would then carry it off to the Customs, hoping for tips.

A few minutes later, in fact, the entire station was filled with the noisy hustle and bustle of the crowd as everyone strove to complete the various formalities involved in crossing a border, formalities which are all the more complicated in Russia since passports are still required.

The travelers, naturally, all raced in a disorderly manner along the platforms. Each individual wanted to be the first to go through Customs and they fought hard to make their way into a narrow corridor that connected the Russian border station to the German border station, a narrow corridor where the Holy Images that all travelers had to greet when entering or leaving Russia were located.

Yet, while the hustle and bustle was at its peak, while everyone rushed this way and that, a man deliberately, slowly climbed down from the train that was parked along the platform, the Russian train that was about to head back to St. Petersburg.

Who was that man?

If Juve had seen him, if Fandor or Hélène had merely glimpsed him, they would have most certainly shuddered. Unfortunately, Juve was in St. Petersburg and both Fandor and Hélène had rushed to disembark. The young people, concerned because Juve had not joined them, had been eager to get to the German station where they hoped to find a telegram waiting for them.

Did the man know any of this? Was he aware that Juve was not on hand, that Fandor and Hélène were concerned? That was possible, considering the ironic smile on his lips.

"No one!" he said. "No one bothersome! All the better! I'll leave Russia as easily as I got in. Obviously, the police are quite stupid! They can't even guard a border station properly!"

He carried no baggage. Yet, from time to time, almost automatically, the man would reach his hand into the fob of his waistcoat, seeming to make sure that an object he prized was still there. The man walked a few steps on the platform. In the distance, he watched the crowd attacking the Customs employees.

"Imbeciles!" he murmured. "Imagine the panic I could cause if I were to shout, "Hey. Take notice! I'm here! Fantômas is here!'"

And he burst out laughing.

"Fantômas!"

Was the man getting off the Northern Express at Eydtkuhnen really Fantômas? Was it really the terrible bandit who was walking slowly along the platform, glancing cautiously, carefully, left and right, clearly aware of the formidable gamble he was taking by trying to cross the border unnoticed?

It was, in fact, Fantômas.

Once again, Fantômas had been the supreme victor. Once again Fantômas had trumped Juve. Fantômas had managed to steal the real necklace. It was the precious diamonds that he had automatically sought in his pocket a few moments earlier. And if Fantômas, despite everything, was worried, after such a major victory, it was because he was thinking, "This victory is too wonderful to be final. Juve will never accept his defeat and, out of a desire for vengeance, that damned policeman will try to find me!"

Yet, he had to act. At that moment, Fantômas was fully aware of what he needed to do. If he could get into Germany, if he could get out of Russia, he would be safe. If, on the other hand, he was unable to cross the border, he would fear the worst since Fantômas had no illusions about the matter. Juve had probably set all of the Russian police on his heels.

Yet, despite his concerns, Fantômas remained calm.

While Juve was, at times, capable of retaining a surprising presence of mind, Fantômas mastered his nerves marvelously. Anyone who crossed his path, as he walked calmly along the station platform, would never have suspected the emotion that tormented him.

The master criminal looked left and right. At first, he noticed nothing suspicious. But all too soon he shuddered. On the other side of the train, he saw Cossacks cordoning off the entire train. What did this deployment of troupes mean?

Fantômas frowned and said to himself, "My word, the station is under guard. Could Juve have sent a telegram notifying them of my possible arrival? Have they set a trap?"

He took a few more steps and muttered, "This is abominable! Soldiers on all sides. The station is completely surrounded. Obviously, I won't be able to get out. I'll either have to stay in the train and head back to St. Petersburg or risk everything, face Customs, head down the corridor filled with policemen, make my way to the German station!"

He stopped for a moment, pretending to read a poster, and asked, "What am I to do?"

Obviously, Fantômas had to think for a moment. Going through Customs, exposing himself to a painstaking search, letting the authorities see him up close, it all involved a terrible risk. Should he retreat from this danger? Remain in Russia? That might involve even greater danger.

"Well, let's try this!" Fantômas murmured.

Then bandit walked straight over to one of the station employees and asked, "Customs, good man?"

The man stared at him and replied, "Straight ahead, to your right, sir. But first you have to have your passport stamped."

"Is that obligatory?"

"Yes sir."

After a moment of silence, possibly without realizing the whirlwind of emotions he had set off in the other man, the station employee added, "And today, sir, there's more. We've received telegrams, and you don't just have to go through German Customs. A special service has been arranged. All travelers have to be searched."

"Searched?" Fantômas said, startled. "What do you mean?"

"It's simple," explained the man. "You have to get undressed. Special employees, policemen I believe, will examine your clothes before you put them back on."

"Thank you," replied Fantômas.

He took a few steps in the direction indicated by the man, then as the other man turned his head, Fantômas turned right, and walked into a large hangar.

"Good grief!" thought Fantômas. "What the devil will I do?"

Then he thought out loud, "Curse Juve! Sooner or later, that infernal policeman will have to pay for the anguish he's causing me just now!"

Overwrought, Fantômas collapsed onto a bundle, a large crate that stood nearby. He had no illusions about what he had just learned. Troupes surrounded the station, the close scrutiny of passports, the search, the painstaking search, all proved that Juve had already given orders to mobilize the police and that all the travelers crossing the border at Eydtkuhnen were under surveillance.

Despite himself, Fantômas shuddered, muttering, "If they search me, if they search my clothing, they'll certainly find the necklace...On top of that I don't have a passport... Will my adventures come to an end here? Will I stupidly allow myself to be caught by the idiotic Russian police?"

He ground his teeth.

Fantômas was still thinking when, suddenly, he leapt to his feet, instinctively taking a dagger from his pocket. He had heard a noise. Close by.

"Is someone following me?" he murmured.

But, at that very moment he smiled. Obviously, fear was driving him mad! What had startled him was the commotion, coming from a large crate, the very one he had been sitting on, caused by a dozen black hens.

Fantômas shrugged and stared fixedly at the poor creatures, lost in thought.

CHAPTER II
A Mysterious Threat

"So, Mr. Havard, what's new?"

My goodness, not much dear friend!"

"Everything quiet in your department?"

"Good grief, everything is quiet."

"No upsetting matters?"

"No, none."

"No political surveillance?"

"Not for the time being."

"How happy you must be, Mr. Havard!"

"You've got that right, dear friend."

The two civil servants burst out laughing.

Mr. Havard had responded in a rather ironic tone and the man speaking with him, the man he called 'dear friend' did not seem particularly upset about that, fully cognizant of the advantages of his position and prepared to concede that, in fact, chance had given him a most enviable life.

His name was Mr. Peyroussin. He could not claim to have done anything remarkable. He had never done anything in his life and, yet, he was on his way to becoming an interesting personality and, what was even better, one of those handsomely paid bureaucrats found in such abundance in the Third Republic.

Mr. Peyroussin, a minor lawyer had not yet considered the possibility of either making a fortune or even adding a bit to the heritage that his worthy father had left him when he had learned, unexpectedly, while reading a newspaper in the Café du Commerce, in Bayonne, that one of his cousins, who had left for Paris a long while ago, had just wrangled the portfolio of Public Education, through political maneuvering.

When he had first learned the news, Mr. Peyroussin had felt profoundly jealous of his relative. He had, in fact, experienced the same feelings as all those who have failed when faced with the good fortune of another and asked himself, without understanding, "Why him? Why not me?"

Yet, this feeling was quickly replaced by another. His bile exhausted, his jealousy given free rein, he had immediately thought that, although it was undeniable that his relative had become a minister by luck, it was also just as undeniable that, unless he, Mr. Peyroussin that is, was a complete idiot, he should make the most of the good fortune enjoyed by a family member.

People from Midi, in general, have no doubts and have a serious advantage over other provincials, because they seriously believe in blood ties.

When he learned that one of his cousins had been appointed Minister of Public Education, Mr. Peyroussin quickly told himself, "A minister is a powerful man… a powerful man is someone who grants favors… Good grief! If I feel like it, I can be a sub-prefect!"

And, with that, without a moment's hesitation, he went home, packed his suitcase and took the first train to the capital.

When he arrived in Paris, Mr. Peyroussin did not even take the time to find a hotel. He simply called for a coach and shouted out, "To the Ministry!"

And, with that boastfulness that is typical of people from Gascony, he decided, in order to attract the coachman's admiration, to add, "The minister is my cousin!"

If Mr. Peyroussin had not been from Midi and, above all, if his cousin had not been born in the sunniest region of France, matters would have most certainty taken a turn for the worse. Ministers in general like to grant their favors to those who can be of service to them, not their provincial cousins. They are even less inclined to grant favors to relatives who turn up in the evening, suitcase in one hand and hat in the other, and who hand over their calling card to the clerk, saying "Tell you master not to keep me waiting. I'm famished."

But, fortunately, Mr. Peyroussin was from Midi and so was his cousin. And, although he might have felt a little embarrassed, the Minister was not the least surprised. Five minutes after reading his cousin's card, he opened the door to his office and discovered Mr. Peyroussin in a friendly discussion with the clerk, smoking a cigarette in the waiting room. Grounds for firing the clerk! But the minister didn't even blink. However, he just might have thought, "Obviously, my relative is straight out of the country. He's still unabashedly shameless!"

Yet, hand out, he walked over to his cousin, saying, "Well, well. Here you are! In Paris! What's brought you here?"

Mr. Peyroussin did not even wait until the door to the office closed, before saying, "Good grief! I've come to see what you can do for me… I need to be decorated first, then I'll want a sub-prefecture…"

In all truth, though, Mr. Peyroussin did not obtain everything he asked for. He was not decorated, although he was given an agricultural honor. They did not give him a sub-prefecture, but they did find an extraordinary position for him in the department, without giving him a precise title, which involved bothering everyone, under the pretext of providing supervision, for which the public purse paid him 15,000 francs per year.

And, since that time, just by chance, Mr. Peyroussin had not said a bad word about his cousin. He experienced not the slightest bit of hatred for his relative. He was not angry with him for finding him paid work. Mr. Peyroussin had not received any increase, but he was considered one of those immovable, hopelessly incompetent individuals, that swarm throughout the various ministries.

His cousin had, naturally, been defeated and numerous ministers had replaced him in power, but Mr. Peyroussin was still in his position, forgotten by all, unknown to the cabinet bosses, taking up as little space as possible, failing to go to his office, giving no sign of life, to be perfectly honest, except at the end of the month when it was time to go to the treasury to draw his wages.

Naturally, this type of life gave Mr. Peyroussin time for his leisure activities. He spent his days, as pleasantly as possible, visiting friends, for the most part other civil servants, taking part in lengthy discussions intended solely to kill time.

At this time, Mr. Havard was one of Mr. Peyroussin's closest friends. In fact, as a result of his duties, the head of the Sûreté most often had the most fascinating anecdotes to relate. He knew all about the most recent scandals, the latest gossip, the most malicious scandal-mongering that would scandalize all of Paris.

Mr. Peyroussin would chat with him and then, once informed, he would quickly don his hat, hastily take his leave and run to take care of his business, as he liked to put it. Generally, he would go to see another friend and pass on all the juicy news, playing the role of a well-informed man.

Now this day, in fact, Mr. Peyroussin had not been lucky. He had pushed Mr. Havard, interrogated him with the skill of a court judge, but he had obtained no information, nothing.

There was nothing to be learned from the Sûreté. Everything was calm.

No sensational crime, no half-smothered scandal, no politician found in a compromising situation, not even an elegant woman arrested in a large store for stealing!

"Well," sighed Mr. Peyroussin, stretching his arms. "Life is quite boring..."

Then, suddenly he had an idea.

"What about Juve?" he asked "Do you have any news about Juve?"

Mr. Havard roused himself from his torpor, shook his head furiously, shrugged, and said, "Juve is still in Russia. The last I heard he was on close terms with the Tsar. Juve will come back to us a decorated man!"

Mr. Peyroussin smiled ironically, as if to protect such as supposition and replied, "Now that's a good one! Juve decorated? Come now! He'd do better to arrest Fantômas!"

"Obviously," conceded Mr. Havard in a tone that was somewhat venomous, "But that's more difficult."

"No news of the thief?" Mr. Peyroussin asked.

"No... well..."

"Meaning?"

"Meaning that we know nothing for sure and people always talk about the Master of Fear in vague terms."

Although Mr. Havard continued to talk in pleasant tones, he provided no suggestive details. Perhaps the head of the Sûreté did not particularly want to discuss Fantômas.

Fantômas was, in fact, not only the King of Frightful, the Master of Fear, the Criminal Mastermind, the Unparalleled Torturer, he was also the Uncatchable. Fantômas was the legendary thief that all of the departments within the Sûreté had been trying to catch for years, without ever succeeding.

Fantômas was Mr. Havard's remorse, his shame. The newspapers joked about the head of the Sûreté; the magazines satirized him for his failure to stop the sinister criminal.

Unfortunately for Mr. Havard, Mr. Peyroussin, who had nothing to do, was far too curious to settle for a flat refusal. Of course, although he had not learned anything, he still suspected nothing and he had the feeling that Mr. Havard was hiding something from him.

The few words the head of the Sûreté had uttered, served as bait. He would have given everything in the world to force the policeman to provide more details.

Mr. Peyroussin made another attempt, saying, "Well, what do people say about Fantômas? Why do they only talk about him in vague terms?"

The question was clear and there was no way to step around it. Mr. Havard grimaced but gave in to the need to reply. Mr. Peyroussin, who enjoyed the security conferred by his nonexistent and useless sinecure, was someone to be handled with kid gloves. It was a good idea to flatter him, to satisfy his curiosity, and it was perilous to send him away unsatisfied, not sated with news.

"Bah!" said Mr. Havard. "People talk vaguely about the Master of Fear because they relate things that are not certain."

"Such as?"

"I received a report this morning, indicating that Fantômas had passed through the station at Eydtkuhnen. That's on the Russian-German border..."

"How do they know that?" asked Mr. Peyroussin.

"I have no idea," replied Mr. Havard.

But that response, which was quite natural, exasperated the civil servant.

"You don't know? But you're the head of the Sûreté! That's unbelievable! Of course, you're just trying to be discrete; you're hiding something from me."

"No, no, of course not!"

"Yet, if they're submitted a report on Fantômas, that means he made himself known some way or another. What did the report say?"

Mr. Peyroussin could hardly sit still. He was burning with curiosity, avid to learn something unexpected, something sensational.

Mr. Havard understood that and wanted inasmuch as possible to satisfy the man.

"After all," thought the head of the Sûreté, "I've said too much to shut up now. If I don't give this old gossip what he wants, if I'm not indiscrete, he'll leave here furious. I'll have to dot the I's and cross the T's for him..."

Mr. Havard searched through a stack of papers in a large folder on his desk.

He was looking for a document and said, "My dear Mr. Peyroussin, I'm going to prove to you that you demand too much too soon. In fact, I simply received a telegram, a telegram containing just a few words, one that was not even signed, and that told me very little... Ah, here it is."

Mr. Havard had located the document in question which had been hard to find, buried as it was in a heap of paperwork.

"Listen to this Peyroussin, you'll see..."

To the head of the Paris Sûreté. Fantômas must have crossed the Russian German border at Eydtkuhnen. He is returning to France, without a doubt, with great projects in mind. Be on the look-out!

As Mr. Havard read the telegram, Mr. Peyroussin opened his eyes wide, dumbfounded.

"I don't understand," he said. "I don't understand what this means... Is this a threat?"

"No," said Mr. Havard, quietly. "It's a warning."

And, without raising his voice, without revealing the slightest hint of distress, the head of the Sûreté continued, "It is likely, at least I think so, that this telegram is from Fandor... you know who I mean, Juve's friend... the famous Jérôme Fandor..."

Mr. Peyroussin was about to reply that he knew perfectly well who Fandor was and that he, like all Parisians, admired the intrepid journalist when there was a discrete known at the door of Mr. Havard's office, interrupting the two men.

"Enter!" ordered the head of the Sûreté.

A clerk entered and said, "It's the mail, sir."

"Hand it over!"

Mr. Havard automatically took the letters the clerk had brought him, spread them over his desk, glancing at them with a skill acquired over long years of practice, which enabled him to determine if a particular letter was of interest or not.

'Nothing new?" asked Mr. Peyroussin.

"I don't think so..."

At that moment, Mr. Havard was thinking that his indiscrete visitor would no doubt leave and give him an opportunity to go through the letters in peace. But that was not the case and, given that line of thought, Mr. Havard was completely unaware of the other man's real faults. In fact, since the mail had arrived, Mr. Peyroussin had been unable to hold still. He thought that it was more than likely that one of the letters would be of interest. Was he finally going to learn a bit of news, a juicy tale that he would be able to pass on? He gave a very friendly wave of his hand.

"But, don't let me interrupt you, Havard. Open your mail... Read your letters... I'll wait... I'm in no rush."

Mr. Havard smiled and replied, "You're too kind."

Yet, at the same time he thought, "May the devil take him! Is that man nailed to his chair?"

Once again, however, he did not have the means to resist. Mr. Havard took a letter opener and started to sort through his correspondence. As he had suspected that his curious visitor was in quite a state, he did everything to satisfy his curiosity, without seeming to do so.

"A letter reporting a theft by servants," he announced. "A banal affair... Ah, this one contains a denunciation of a gambling den... It doesn't look serious, a little blackmail... Well now, here's a letter from a crazy man who writes me every day to ask me for 50 million francs or he will blow of the Palais de l'Elysée..."

Mr. Havard opened another dozen or so letters and pushed the papers away with a weary gesture.

"Nothing, nothing at all!" he said. "How exceptionally boring."

And, after uttering this declaration, he was about to settle back into his chair when Mr. Peyroussin leapt up, saying, "But you forgot a letter. See, this one..."

He held a brown, rather elegant looking envelope, which had escaped Mr. Havard's notice.

The chief of the Sûreté glanced at it, saying, "Oh that can't be all that important. The paper is good quality. I suppose it is from some snob, informing me that his mistress wants to castigate him... I get about 20 of those a day and, nine times out of ten, the signer doesn't earn my sympathy..."

Mr. Havard, indifferent, opened the letter. He pulled out a sheet of paper, with strange writing, original, intent, obviously masculine, writing that would certainly draw attention.

"Look at this," he murmured, glancing at the paper.

Mr. Havard had barely started reading, when his face changed. Abruptly, he stood up, moving so quickly that he turned the large chair in which he had been sitting over.

At the same time, he swore, "In the name of God! In the name of God! In the name of God!"

The usually phlegmatic man's behavior was so strange, in fact, that Mr. Peyroussin exulted. Obviously, the letter was not unimportant. The news it contained was not unimportant. If that had been the case, Mr. Havard would never have been so upset, so distressed.

Anxiously, Mr. Peyroussin asked, "What is it? What does it..."

But Mr. Havard did not reply right away. The chief of the Sûreté seemed to have forgotten all about the visitor in his office. He continued to mutter, and seemed to be caught up in the throes of fury.

"Well, look at this… And everything had been so calm… In the name of God! What is he planning now? And Juve isn't here!"

All of this was most unclear and did nothing to satisfy Mr. Peyroussin's curiosity.

The civil servant insisted, "Answer me, man! What is it? What has been reported to you? Tell me whatever you see fit. Is it serious?

"Yes, it's serious!" said Mr. Havard. "It's frightening! I'm frightened! I must be losing my mind! I wonder…"

But Mr. Havard did not complete his sentence. Once again he swore, saying, "In the name of God! In the name of God! What should I do? What decision shall I make? How can I get out of this hornet's nest? And Juve isn't here!"

Twice, Mr. Havard had expressed the same distress, demonstrating the confidence he placed in Juve, despite the fact that he did not always express it.

Mr. Peyroussin, however, was growing more and more agitated. Mr. Havard's attitudes, his curses convinced him that the situation was very serious. Yet, he still knew nothing… Honestly, that was disappointing!

Mr. Peyroussin placed his hand on Mr. Havard's shoulder and, with an unshakeable composure that seemed somewhat grotesque, he said, "Well now, my friend, confide in me. Something is troubling you, isn't it? Are you afraid of something? That's it, isn't it, you're afraid of something."

Mr. Havard looked the other man in the eye and shouted, "Yes, I'm afraid of something. And I'm not the only one who will be afraid. All of Paris will be afraid if the information in this letter is made public. My God! Things were going too well. I should have known it could not last!"

"But what is it?"

Mr. Peyroussin was overcome with curiosity. In actual fact, if Mr. Havard did not give him the news, he would just grab the letter, the letter that the chief of the Sûreté kept reading over and over without telling him anything.

Mr. Havard seemed to rouse himself as if from a dream. He passed his hand over his forehead, as if trying to shake off a terrible nightmare, and said, "What? What do you want? You want to know what it says? Well, then, here's what the letter says, Mr. Peyroussin."

Mr. Havard's voice trembled. It seemed, at times, as if the words caught in his throat, and that he would be unable to articulate clearly. Yet, making a supreme effort, he managed to read:

To the chief of the Sûreté:
I don't enjoy bad jokes and your forces have just played one on me that I consider detestable. I had set off for Russian and you did not have to concern yourselves with me. But your subordinate, that policeman, took it into his head to hunt me down and it was only by chance that I escaped from his interfering activities.

Sir, my motto has always been 'an eye for an eye, a tooth for a tooth'. You meddle in my business, I'll meddle in yours. Moreover, you won't be my only target. All Paris supports Juve when Juve harasses me. So, I'll attack all of Paris!

You can, as a result, sir, inform the people living in the capital, that I am back and that I intend to chastise the city as it deserves to be punished, with a series of formidable attacks.

Please excuse me for treating you like a messenger and please accept my irony.

"It's signed?" Mr. Peyroussin asked, dumbfounded.

"It's signed..." said Mr. Havard, in a low voice, "It's signed.... *FANTÔMAS!*"

At that moment, in the large office where so many discussions had concerned the legendary bandit, it truly seemed as if something strange, stupefying, unsettling was upsetting the atmosphere.

Fantômas' name, all on its own, was the source of the problem.

The tragic syllables had, as usual, a terrifying resonance. They re-awakened echoes, they sounded the death knell, they embodied something darkly mysterious.

"Fantômas! Fantômas!"

As he repeated this name, Mr. Havard bowed his head, thinking that Fantômas was impossible to catch.

Mr. Peyroussin, for his part, was trembling. For him, Fantômas was above all a mad torturer whose refined cruelty rendered all those he captured quite mad.

"Fantômas!" Mr. Peyroussin repeated, in a quiet voice. "Fantômas is the one who wrote to you..."

"Who wrote to threaten me," Mr. Havard replied. "How can he be so certain, so filled with impunity, that he dares to warn me?"

Instinctively, Mr. Havard and Mr. Peyroussin fell silent, thinking, shivering.

Fantômas!

The sinister name absorbed all their thoughts, petrifying them. After a few seconds, both civil servants shuddered.

The door to the office opened and the indifferent voice of the clerk announced, "Mr. Janvial, sent by the Deputy Chief."

A visitor entered at the same time. Obviously, it was an important individual who had come to the Prefecture for a rather serious matter since the Deputy Chief who had received him was now sending him to Mr. Havard.

Mr. Havard, however, was in no state to receive guests. He welcomed Mr. Janvial, as he would greet some unwelcome visitor.

"Well, what do you want, sir?"

And he never even thought of asking Mr. Peyroussin to leave and that gentlemen did not even make the pretense of showing such elementary discretion.

Mr. Janvial, however, greeted the head of the Sûreté with the perfect amount of correctness.

He started by declaring, "I apologize for disturbing you, sir, but it is all the fault of your Deputy Chief, who asked me to come and see you. Does my name mean anything to you?"

"Not at all, sir."

"Then allow me to introduce myself. I'm the manager of the Jardin d'acclimatation here in Paris and the president of the International Agricultural Exposition, which should open its doors soon."

"Excuse me," Mr. Havard interrupted. "But what exactly do you want? I'm in a bit of a hurry."

Mr. Janvial smiled scornfully, indicating that he had clearly noted the other man's lack of manners, and said, "I've come to see you, sir, about a robbery."

"An important one?"

"Worth about 60,000 francs."

"Well, sir," replied the chief of the Sûreté, "Go and see my officers. I'm not the one who handles complaints."

Mr. Janvial smiled ironically again and said, "Your officers have sent me to you."

Mr. Havard, who was tapping his foot by now, protested, "Well, now, I can hardly do everything myself! What did they steal from you? Shares?"

"No, sir, chickens."

Dumbfounded, Mr. Havard replied, "Chickens? I don't understand. Ordinary chickens? Chickens that lay eggs?"

This time, Mr. Janvial smiled openly and replied, "My chickens lay eggs like other chickens and they are ordinary because all animals are ordinary. Yet, if I understand what you're thinking, you are astonished by the value I've placed on them. So, I'll tell you that these are extremely rare chickens intended for the upcoming exposition. I'm not exaggerating by placing their value at 60,000 francs."

Mr. Havard recovered from his surprise and replied, "Good grief! I understand your situation, but I still don't see what I can do about it. A thief who steels chickens of this kind is a very audacious thief who will not allow himself to be captured easily. Well, we will try. Where did this robbery take place? In Paris?"

"No sir. In Russia."

Mr. Havard lost his patience and yelled, "In Russia! What do you mean in Russia! What exactly do you want me to do now? I'm not a member of the Russian police forces. You have to be reasonable!"

Mr. Janvial remained calm despite his reception, which had been rather abrupt and not at all in keeping with police etiquette.

Yet, he did protest, "I simply came to the Sûreté to inquire into the matter. After listening to me, your inspectors told me to see your Deputy Chief and your own Deputy Chief told me to come and see you. I'm not to blame!"

Mr. Havard calmed a little and said, "Well, I accept that. But, once again, what do you want me to do about this matter, this robbery that took place in Russia? Where, in fact, in Russia? Russia is a large country!"

Demonstrating remarkable patience, Mr. Janvial replied, "My chickens had arrived at the border. They disappeared at the Eydtkuhnen station."

Mr. Janvial had barely finished uttering that name when Mr. Havard rushed at him like a mad man.

"In the name of God!" he shrieked. "But why didn't you say so? A robbery at the Russian-German border... where Fantômas was... Yes, that does interest me! Go on, go on... What do you know?"

Such enthusiasm, following on the heels of such indifference, most likely surprised the excellent director of the Jardin d'acclimatation.

"What do I know?" he repeated. "Well, not much, just that my hens have disappeared, that's all. The police are the ones who should be finding the information!"

Discouraged, Mr. Havard fell back into his chair, distraught.

"Ah, the police... the police..." he murmured. "Well they are in wonderful position to provide you with information."

And he sounded sad as he said that.

CHAPTER III
Black Hens

Just a bit afraid, despite his extraordinary audacity, realizing that the station was under surveillance from all sides and that it would be impossible for him to go unnoticed, Fantômas, wondering how he was going to extricate himself from the unfortunate situation he found himself, had entered one of the large freight terminals and sat down on a crate, staring fixedly at a flock of black hens locked up there, obviously being shipped to some distant recipient.

Fantômas remained in the hangar for a long time.

What was he doing there?

Only those who might have had the audacity to watch the Master of Fear would have been able to guess.

Fantômas, in fact, was able to act mysteriously, cautiously, to erase all traces of his actions, and anyone who had never seen him in action would be incapable of guessing what he thought, what schemes he dreamed up.

An hour passed.

The Northern Express had already left, carrying its passengers, carrying Fandor and Hélène. All that remained in the small, deserted station were a few employees going about their usual business, along with a few travelers waiting for the next train, an omnibus train, that was headed for Berlin.

Moreover, no one had any business in the hangar where Fantômas had taken refuge and the bandit stayed there in peace, without fearing any surprises.

Yet, what was Fantômas thinking about and why had he remained there, alone, seemingly waiting for something to happen? Had he come up with a plan to hide long enough that the surveillance would be removed so he would no longer have to fear immediate arrest?

Twice, the miserable wretch had stood up. He had walked over to the hangar door, glanced anxiously at the station platform then, shrugging, had returned to his place.

Fantômas could hardly hope that the police would abandon their surveillance quickly. The troupes sent to the station, in fact, had formed groups. People were now distributing mess tins containing soup to the Cossacks, who were setting up tents. Assuredly, the battalions were planning on camping there; assuredly the orders they had been given were harsh. The government would not stop its surveillance until Fantômas had been arrested or until they had made sure that he had managed to leave Russia.

"Obviously, they've decided to take me dead or alive, this time!"

But he burst out laughing.

"Juve hasn't caught me yet. I haven't quite made my mind up to make my acquaintance with Diebler's knife!"

Then, he hunkered down in one of the darkest spots in the hangar. Had he decided to fight the police with patience? Was he planning to wait there until the police left? Did he want to hide like an evil beast in the deserted hangar?

That, obviously, was Fantômas' secret and nothing would give it away. The man remained motionless, fading into the shadows, so stiff that he looked like a statue, except for the occasional wild gleam, the fiery spark, that flashed from his eyes.

Then, Fantômas soon abandoned his immobility.

"What's there?" he murmured. "Is someone coming... could it be the guide?"

But he provided no further details about the person he referred to with that mysterious term. Soon, there was no longer any doubt. Someone was definitely coming into the hangar. His footsteps could be heard. It was no doubt a station employee. In any case, it was someone who was taking no precaution to hide his arrival and who, believing himself to be alone, whistled a popular tune as he walked.

Fantômas, who had remained seated, knelt down behind a crate, taking care not to be seen. The person who was approaching could, in fact, be an enemy. He must take care not to reveal his presence unless it was necessary.

The man who had entered the hangar kept advancing. Soon, Fantômas could make out his silhouette. It was a tall, thin man wearing a helmet. He had both hands in his pockets and an unlit cigarette dangled at the corner of his mouth. He walked with the shambling gait of someone who was up to no good. The man walked on and on and Fantômas, eyes burning, did not miss a single movement.

A breath of terror washed over the large hangar, the dark hangar, with its insufficient lighting, provided by two feeble oil lamps... The man who had been walking calmly might have felt it. He stopped suddenly, turned about, and looked in every direction. He was no longer whistling. He had suddenly fallen silent, then said, in a strange voice, "Damn, this is not a cheerful place!"

A few moments later, he added, "And that's not all! Where are my hens?"

The individual took a few more steps, then turned right. A row of bulky bundles hampered his progress. He climbed onto them nimbly, then started to walk over them.

Fantômas continued to watch him.

The hangar was completely silent except for the noise made by the walker. Soon he stopped.

"Well, here you are my chicks. How are you my black girls!?"

He bent down over the crate that Fantômas had looked at earlier, the crate containing the black chickens. Now, as the man looked at the birds, as he took pleasure in kicking the crate with the tip of his foot, moving it, the stranger was suddenly overcome with wild terror.

His feeling was, in fact, quite justified. At that moment as he bent over the crate, he felt a heavy hand, a nervous hand press on his shoulder and grasp it, forcing him to stand up.

"Good God!" he cursed.

And a voice replied, "Good day."

The man, however, suddenly escaped from the grip that had so startled him. He was furious.

"Well, pal," he said. "You've got some strange manners. What's up with you? What do you want with me? My ticket? You a controller? They're a dime a dozen in this country!"

As he spoke, the chicken man was searching through his pockets for his ticket. It was so dark, in fact, in the hangar that he could not see the face of the other man, who stood completely still, arms crossed, and stared.

The chicken man, who had finally found his ticket, looked up and saw, in the black silhouette of the man who had accosted him, two eyes, burning like coals.

"Here's my ticket..." he started to say.

The other man interrupted him, waving the ticket away and saying, in a deep voice, "Good day."

Suddenly the chicken man shuddered. He took three steps back. He was no longer thinking about his ticket. Arms dangling, head bent forward, he said, "No, but... sometimes... What have I got myself into?"

For the third time, the other man said, "Good day!"

The chicken man, hearing the voice again, that deep voice, literally started to tremble. Words caught in his throat and he had a great deal of difficulty saying, "Who are you? Who are you?"

"Guess!" said the man.

"I don't dare."

"So, look."

The man who was speaking took an automatic lighter from his pocket and clicked. The small wick caught fire and a bright flash lit up his face for a second.

"Do you recognize me?"

The chicken man's teeth chattered as he said, "Fantômas! Fantômas!"

He stammered the name, overcome, dumbfounded by fear.

After a moment, and appearing unable to believe the truth, he asked, "Surely, I must be having a nightmare. It can't be you! You're not Fantômas!"

He received an answer filled with scorn.

"Imbecile! Do I have to prove my identity? Don't you recognize your Master? Will I have to throw you to Juve just to get rid of an idiot like you?"

The other repeated, "Fantômas!"

Since silence fell between the two men. Fantômas suddenly seemed to arrive at a decision.

"Listen," he started. "I knew you were stupid but not to this extent! You had no idea I was here?"

"No, Master, no."

"And why exactly did you think the station is being guarded by soldiers? Tell me!"

"Master, I didn't know."

Fantômas shrugged and replied, "You never know anything!"

Then, voice dripping with scorn, he asked, "But what are you doing here? How did you get to Russia?"

The chicken man seemed to be finding it difficult getting over the terror that had filled him when he faced Fantômas, the man he dared call master.

He replied, in a voice that still trembled, "Well, now... that's quite a story... And it will take some time to tell... It's all because Dégueulasse [4] broke his pipe, dismantled his stove, took off his shirt, turned over his innards... in other words, he kicked the bucket, slipped into the bottom of the hole poor Dégueulasse did!"

"What?" asked Fantômas.

"Well, continued the chicken man, when I saw my comrade turned into a carcass, I said, well I'll have to see about this, old Fumier,[5] it might be time to retire. I have a job."

"A job?" Fantômas scoffed. "Who would want to hire you, Fumier?"

And Fumier, since that was the name of the man, who had been the inseparable companion of Dégueulasse, who had recently died of *delirium tremens*, the man who now found himself in Russia, explained, "Well, it's not a very lofty position, of course. Not like being a minister! But, it's a job that doesn't mess up your mind. So, now, I'm what could be called the butler for the animals at the Jardin d'acclimatation."

Fantômas shrugged.

"A farm butler!" he said. "That's what you've become. Obviously, my pour Fumier, you were hardly worthy to serve under my orders... For a former criminal, you've come to a sad end."

Fumier did not respond.

Fantômas asked, "So, you're an employee of the Jardin d'acclimatation? Well. But why are you in Russia?"

Fumier replied, saying, "That, boss, is a most entertaining story. It concerns those hens that you hear clucking like a band of politicians. Black hens are rare. They're to go to the Exposition that is to be held. Mr. Janvial sent me to Russia to get them."

Fumier grew more reassured as he spoke. After all, or so he thought, he no longer had to fear Fantômas. He no longer had anything in common with the

---

[4] *Dégueulasse*: Filthy.

[5] *Fumier*: a pile of manure.

bandit who kept the whole world in fear. He no longer had to take orders from the man. Fumier was telling the truth when he claimed that he had gone straight. For the time being, in fact, Dégueulasse's former companion had honest intentions. He had been employed by the Jardin d'acclimatation, as he has just recounted, he was earning his living and he was free.

Yet, as he listened to the other man, Fantômas burst into laughter. It seemed that the abominable Master of Fear found Fumier's repentance and new life most entertaining.

Abruptly, he asked, "So, they sent you so far from Paris, simply to accompany these chickens?"

"That's right, boss."

"And you think you're going to take them back there?"

"Damn," Fumier said, taken aback.

"You're wrong," declared Fantômas.

The bandit gave Fumier no time to protest. With a wave of his hand, he interrupted the exclamation uttered by his former accomplice.

He asked, "How tall are you?"

"5 ft 6 in.."

"Do you have your passport?"

"Of course! Why?"

"Because..." Fantômas replied, in an enigmatic tone.

The bandit had just extinguished his lighter. The two men once again found themselves in the dark. Fumier could not, as a result, see the sinister expression on Fantômas' face.

Still, he said, "Master, I don't understand... You ask me questions, in all due respect, that make no sense. And what does it matter to you that they sent me to Russia to pick up some chickens?"

At that moment, Fantômas took a step forward He placed his mouth next to Fumier's ear and in a low, gentle voice, he said, "My friend, you're wrong. They didn't send you to Russia to pick up your chickens."

"Why did they send me here, then, boss?"

Abruptly, in an authoritarian voice, Fantômas said, "They sent you here to die!"

And the unfortunate Fumier had no time to do anything, had no time to move. He fell back, his throat ripped open, possibly dead...

Fantômas assuredly was still the terrifying assassin whose misdeeds had spread around the world. He was still the skillful murderer who never trembles, who never hesitates, who kills without fail, without pity and with mercy!

In the fortunate darkness, he had raised his right hand, armed with a thin knife. The unsuspecting Fumier had met his maker. With a rapid movement, Fantômas struck him and, with a single blow, had inflicted one of those terrible blows that he mastered so well.

He slit the other man's throat, cutting through the carotid artery. Then he dug through the bloody opening with the tip of his dagger, reached the top of the man's lung, tore through his larynx. Fumier died without making a sound…

Fantômas showed no emotion. Quietly, he spoke to himself, as he usually did, saying "Now that's a good deed. If I believed in God, I would thank the Lord for looking on me favorably. I won't have the slightest difficulty… Now, I must act quickly."

Fantômas lit his lighter again. He knelt at the feet of the motionless man and, meticulous as always, he wiped the blood coated blade of his knife on the coat worn by the still warm cadaver.

"No point leaving any compromising traces behind me. It would be just as pointless abandoning this dagger. I may still need it, after all…" he murmured as he placed the knife back in his pocket.

And Fantômas set down to a horrible task. With complete indifference, in fact, the wretch started to take his victim's coat off and then searched through the pockets. Naturally, there was a bit of everything in those pockets. Sugar cubes stolen from restaurants, cigarette butts picked up in the streets, broken matches, a pipe without a stem, a bread crust. Fantômas even discovered a bit of rotting, stinking meat, wrapped in paper.

"Nothing in the coat," said Fantômas, throwing the macabre cast-off on the ground. "Where the devil could he have hidden what I need?"

He suddenly slapped his forehead and said, "I'm such an imbecile. He was holding it in his hand!"

With a kick of his foot, Fantômas pushed the body of the unfortunate Fumier, which continued to spill blood, along the floor.

"As long as it's not soiled!" Fantômas grumbled. "I have nothing with me to remove compromising stains. Well, when it comes down to it, I could simply cut my hand and mix my own blood with that imbecile's."

As he spoke, Fantômas seemed to be searching for something on the ground.

"Ah! Here's what I was looking for!"

In the circle of light cast by his small tool, he had just noticed a greasy notebook that had fallen to the ground. Most likely Fumier's wallet. It had fallen there, quite naturally, just as the unfortunate man's throat was cut since Fumier, at that moment, was still holding the ticket he had had initially wanted to give to Fantômas, presuming he was a railway employee.

Fantômas, however, had already picked up the greasy wallet. He leafed through the bills, and then took out two papers, which he examined with satisfaction.

"Better and better!" Fantômas murmured. "Here's the waybill for the chickens. Oh, now here's something interesting… Here's Fumier's ticket…. And, and this is his passport. Luck is with me!"

Fantômas rubbed his hands in delight. His plan was a very simple one. Didn't he always carry a few make-up accessories with him, tools of the trade that he used so successfully? In just a few seconds, he would transform himself, until he looked like poor, dead Fumier. And, that done, he would have no problem escaping from the station. Fumier was his size. He would take his place. The description on the passport, vague as all such descriptions are, made his task easy.

"I'll pass," murmured Fantômas. "I'll pass without any difficulty and all Juve's precautions will be worth nothing…"

The bandit, however, could not spend any more time in the hangar. He would be exposed if an employee chanced by. If someone entered, they would discover Fumier's body, see the blood on the floor, and the situation would become very complicated.

But Fantômas was not a man to worry for so little. Skillfully, with surprising strength, he managed, in fact, to move some of the voluminous bundles that filled the hangar. And once he had done that he had no difficulty hiding Fumier's body under a stack of materials. He used crates, dragged by force over the traces of blood, to cover everything and hide it from all eyes.

Fantômas congratulated himself, saying, "They'll only discover this tomorrow, or the next day… or the next. And I'll be far away!"

Then he started to apply his make-up. He started with a wig to change the look of his face, applied a foundation to imitate Fumier's muddy complexion. Varnish, a few wisps of mustache, completed with a few fortunate lines drawn with a grease pencil completed the transformation. And, without a hint of repulsion, indifferent to the macabre aspect of his disguise, Fantômas put on the dead man's coat, congratulating himself on the precaution he had taken earlier, wiping his dagger on the lining of that piece of clothing.

"Obviously, I'm ready," Fantômas said.

He seemed to pause for a few seconds.

But Fantômas did not wait long. Chance, once again, seemed to smile favorably on his criminal plans.

The wretch had barely completed his transformation when a train arrived at the station. It was the omnibus train people had been waiting for. Droves of travelers disembarked and raced toward Customs, toward the Holy Images, toward the corridor that led to the German station.

Fantômas stood up.

"Now is the time," he said. "Now is the time to risk everything… Well, let's go!"

And he did something strange. Fantômas shouldered the large crate containing the chickens. Obviously, it was the final element in his disguise. It made him look like he was a porter, carrying the cage. Had he not also taken the waybill from Fumier? He walked through the hangar door without difficulty. The crowd was milling about in front of the Customs office. Fantômas walked by.

"No luggage?"

"Yes, this crate."

The two tax collectors placed their chalk mark on the crate.

"And the search?" one of them asked. "Have you been searched?"

Fantômas dared to lie, saying, "And how! What a strange matter, little father!"

He looked so at ease, so quiet, that the Russian customs clerk did not insist. Moreover, the surveillance was easing. The guards were much less severe with the travelers from the omnibus train that they had been with those from the luxury train.

"Go on! Go on! Hurry up!"

Along with the other travelers, Fantômas headed into the corridor where they all had to greet the icon.

An officer approached him saying, "Your passport?"

"Here it is."

At that moment, possibly the bandit might have experienced a slight emotion. He was obviously at the mercy of the slightest incident. If the officer noted something strange about the paper he had been given, if he noticed a difference in the description, no doubt the most terrible complications could arise at any moment.

But Fantômas was not a man to take fright for so little. He had prepared his plan. In the event of danger, in the event of surveillance, he would leap at the officer, stab the man, then jump over the barrier and run off through the fields.

They would chase after him, of course, that was inevitable. But how many times had he escaped from similar manhunts?

But nothing like that happened.

The officer who had been examining passports since the morning was starting to feel somewhat blasé. So, he looked at Fantômas' passport quickly, making sure the stamps were in order, then ordered, "Move on!"

And Fantômas moved on.

He was no longer in Russia, but in Germany. He no longer had to fear the trap set by Juve.

Despite himself, perhaps, he sighed, saying "Well that was a bit unpleasant, but I got through it just the same."

He was still carrying his crate of chickens. He calmly had it checked for the trip to Berlin. Then he climbed into a car.

And Fantômas, who was once again an ordinary traveler, who had completely forgotten about the murder he had committed, started leafing through the notebook he had stolen from Fumier.

He said, "What the devil could Fumier be noting down? What mindboggling discovery will I find in the memoires of that alarming individual?"

In actual fact, Fantômas thought that he would find some picturesque detail in the greasy notebook. All he saw was a single comment. It was not actually written in Fumier's handwriting. It was not as insignificant as Fantômas might suppose.

The bandit read it over and over again.

"Oh," he murmured. "This is interesting to know... La Toulouche is getting out of the central prison in Rennes in three days. I'll have to see her."

And, in a mysterious tone of voice, he added, "Good grief. La Toulouche will be an excellent nanny for some of my students!"

CHAPTER IV
Chicken Coop

"You there, try to arrange your baggage and follow me to the office, without causing any scandal!"

"Fine, fine, don't worry, I don't feel like grumbling today..."

"That will be a change for you, then."

"I don't know if it will be a change for me, it's quite natural. Do you think I'm going to risk getting extra time? Well, I'm not grumbling. But, dear sir, your wish is my command. If I have to embrace you, I've decided that's what I'll do, just to get things over with faster."

This was Mère Toulouche demonstrating extraordinary good will. Moreover, the old woman, just as she had said, seemed uninclined to raise her voice against anyone or anything at all.

She docilely obeyed the order that had just been given to her, she wrapped the few rags that lay on the floor around her in a large piece of dark brown paper.

But what was happening? Who was Mère Toulouche talking to and who was she offering to kiss, a truly desirable favor?

Mère Toulouche was in a narrow, dark room, a dark cell, walls oozing with moisture, in the central prison of Rennes.

That was easy to explain.

Mère Toulouche had been arrested many times. She had already been implicated in a number of shady affairs. She had been convicted of receiving stolen goods, associating with criminals and, on many occasions, the authorities had been able to prove that she did not turn down her nose at a little robbery.

Justice had not hesitated. As Mère Toulouche said herself, she'd been shown no mercy. She'd been sentenced to three years in the central prison and had just finished her time.

But, even for the most hardened criminals, arrangements can be made with the law. La Toulouche had served part of her sentence in isolation. Then she had earned the right to be transferred to a cell which, by rights, had reduced her entire sentence by half. And, finally, Mère Toulouche, a good negotiator, had managed to develop a good relationship with the prison staff. Not only had she managed to obtain some of those small favors that made her stay in prison more bearable, but everyone had agreed to put her name of the list of the convicts who behaved well and were, as a result, entitled to a reduced sentence.

There had been so many reductions in fact, that just 10 months after entering the central prison in Rennes, La Toulouche was being released on parole! And the word parole caused her no concern. La Toulouche had spent far too long in prison to take umbrage over the restrictive meanings of the word.

Good grief! It cost the State so much to keep prisoners locked up that it had no desire to hold them any longer than necessary.

And as La Toulouche said to herself, proving that she was quite familiar with the current customs, "When they kick you out of prison, there's no danger that they'll haul you back in, unless you get caught!"

Furthermore, she had no illusions about being arrested again, within a relatively near future.

La Toulouche did not pretend to be repentant as she left the central prison. She left the jail filled with shame that she had been stupid enough to have been busted and filled with the hope that, in the future, she would be able to avoid such a misfortune, despite that fact that she would deserve it.

Moreover, despite everything, La Toulouche was quite pleased. The idea of leaving the central prison, of no longer being restricted, the thought that she could, when she felt it, take a little nip made her heart truly light.

"No more," she repeated to the guard who was waiting to take her to the office. "I won't grumble anymore. Good grief, You're all good guys here. But that doesn't matter. I'm leaving the hotel without any regrets. Being locked up just isn't for me. A temperament like mine needs fresh air..."

La Toulouche accompanied these words with a short, satisfied chuckle. She finished folding her rags and finally said, "That's it. My bags are packed. Let's go to the office!"

And a few minutes later she found herself in a bright clean office where papers were signed and prisoners were brought in and later released. Once she reached the office, La Toulouche's attitude changed.

She wasn't comfortable with the quality of the employees. To a certain extent, like all authorities, they intimidated her somewhat. La Toulouche assumed a stupid expression, adopted the manner of a suitable woman, and behaved appropriately. Moreover, the formalities did not take a long time. They started by having her sign a receipt for her effects, which had been placed in the locker room. Then, they gave her the wages, the nest egg she had earned by working in the prison, about 38 francs. Finally, they gave her a form, suggesting that she read it carefully.

"It contains instructions you have to follow," the guard said in his monotone voice. "You'll notice that you are forbidden to go to Paris. At the same time, you will be under police surveillance. You'll see that, if you want to work, the form contains instructions about the patrons that will be responsible for finding work for you. Understand?"

"Yes, sir. Of course, sir."

La Toulouche folded the paper respectfully, despite her determination to disregard it completely.

They forbade her to go to Paris! They gave her contacts for finding work! What else? Was she going to be obliged to go to confession?

Yet, as she thought these subversive thoughts, La Toulouche bent over, in an ultra-long bow.

"Am I free to go?" she asked.

"Yes, the guard will lead you out."

La Toulouche bowed again, saying, "Goodbye gentlemen. It's been a pleasure."

She couldn't help but laugh at those words. Honestly, it was such a joke, saying goodbye as she left her jailers...

Of course, she hoped she wouldn't meet them again immediately. They could all die... She didn't care.

But once again, La Toulouche said nothing. The guard walked ahead of her, holding a form in one hand. He took her to the caretaker's room, spoke with the doorman, and had the door opened.

"That's it," he said. "You're free. Be off with you."

"I will, old man."

And, despite her large frame, La Toulouche was suddenly as agile as a young girl. She stepped through the door and found herself in the large square at Rennes.

"Ah! Freedom!" she said. "I've got 38 francs in my pocket. What a binge I'm going on tonight!"

And she immediately looked around for some bar where she could order a thick absinthe without sugar.

Now, La Toulouche had barely walked 20 yards across the square when she noticed a superb closed vehicle, parked a short distance away. A man was leaning out of the window, calling and waving.

"Drat," La Toulouche chuckled. "If I had just a dash of vanity, I could almost believe that he wants to see me. But that can't be right. I have no high-placed connections."

And she was about to continue on her way when the calls rang out again. La Toulouche stopped short, dumbfounded.

"But what does that man want?" she asked out loud. "Who the hell can it be?"

She walked over to the car.

Yet, as she reached the vehicle and was close enough to see the individual who had settled into the back of the seat, she was overwhelmed with amazement.

"Oh! Good grief! Fantômas! Can he have come to pick me up?"

She reached for the door.

Trembling, and with a slobbery smile on her lips, she asked, "Is that really you, boss? What do you want with me?"

"You'll know soon enough, replied Fantômas. "Get in."

La Toulouche got in.

Fantômas was alone in the car. The engine was purring slowly, quietly, smoothly. With a push on the pedal, Fantômas accelerated.

"What do you want with me?" La Toulouche asked again.

"Shut up!" retorted the Master of Fear. "You'll know soon enough. Sit down."

The Master of Torture shifted into gear just then. Fantômas was an excellent driver. His audacity and composure served him marvelously well when it came to automobile sports which, more than any other, requires energy, skill and the ability to think quickly.

So, the car was speeding down the streets, tacking back and forth through the neighborhoods of Rennes, winding through the peasants' carts. Then it left the city, traveled through the suburbs, headed past La Guerche de Bretagne and raced past fields, along the deserted route, devouring space at a crazy speed.

Up to that point, La Toulouche had not said a word, mute with amazement First of all, she had been deeply surprised when she recognized Fantômas. Then, she was further amazed to find herself sitting in a such a luxurious vehicle.

But, another problem caught her attention.

In front of her, at her feet, there was a crate. A rather large crate, sides pierced with holes. Fantômas had instructed her not to jostle it.

What could be in that crate?

Obviously, it had to be some kind of animal since it jiggled now and then. La Toulouche was still wondering what all this meant when Fantômas suddenly changed his attitude.

Nervously, the Master of Fear applied the brakes. He did so violently, like a wealthy man who obviously doesn't care for the expensive damage he is causing to his pneumatic system. Immediately after that, Fantômas spoke to his passenger.

"La Toulouche?" he asked.

"Yes, Master," the old woman stammered.

"I have two pieces of news for you."

"Fine. What?"

"First, you're going to have to head for Paris right away."

"That's not news," La Toulouche grumbled. "That's an order."

Fantômas smiled when he heard that comment.

"The second is that Fumier is dead."

La Toulouche opened her eyes wide. Of course, she knew both Dégueulasse and Fumier. She also knew that Dégueulasse had already passed away and she was not particularly surprised to learn that Fumier had given up the ghost as well. No, what surprised her was that Fantômas was the one giving her this news. What was his interest in the matter?

And La Toulouche, who always spoke her mind, even with Fantômas, dared to ask, "Fumier croaked? Fine! What's that to do with me, Fantômas?"

Fantômas could not help but smile again. And, although he was driving a full speed, he was quite at ease conversing, and he deigned to explain, "It means, La Toulouche, that it is dangerous not to obey me blindly. Fumier has been killed, by my own hand... Understand?"

This time, La Toulouche looked down. She understood full well. If Fantômas was talking like this, it was obvious that he was trying to ensure her obedience; that he was about to give her an important order and that he wanted to make sure, in advance, that she would follow his instructions faithfully.

"Fine, fine," grumbled La Toulouche. "I understand, Master. So?"

Fantômas frowned and said, "Well, I've got a mission for you."

"What is it?"

Fantômas smiled enigmatically and answered, "I don't like people asking me questions."

After a brief silence, he continued, saying, "La Toulouche, we're five miles from a railway station. I'll take you there. You'll catch a train and you'll go back to Paris."

"That's fine with me," grumbled La Toulouche. "Although I would have liked a drink this evening."

"Shut up!" interrupted Fantômas.

The Master of Torture gave La Toulouche such an evil glare that she did not dare say anything else.

He said, "You'll take the train, but you won't take it alone. You will take this crate with you."

"Fine, Master."

"In that crate there are two hens, two black hens..."

La Toulouche looked at Fantômas, eyes filled with wonder, and said, "Two black hens? But what am I supposed to do with them?"

At that moment Fantômas stopped his car. He leaned over toward La Toulouche, stared her in the eyes, in that imperious manner so characteristic of him that inspired his accomplices to follow his slightest order to the latter.

"You will do nothing with the chickens," said Fantômas. "You will do nothing at all. You will keep them, you will raise them..."

And since La Toulouche was so surprised she could think of no reply, Fantômas continued, ironically, "These chickens are a souvenir from Fumier... Do you understand that they are more valuable to me than my own eyes? They must not be stolen. They must not disappear!"

As he opened the car doom, he said, "Listen to what I'm saying, La Toulouse. They must not..."

Then he waved his arm at a bunch of trees nearby.

"Go now. The station is just beyond those trees."

La Toulouche got down onto the road carrying the crate holding the black hens. Fantômas disappeared well before she got over her surprise. He accelerated his car suddenly and the car raced off, its engine joyfully purring, raising clouds of dust and dead leaves in a whirlwind.

At five o'clock in the evening, three days later, the excellent Thibault, sole owner, manager and sponsor of the large Folies-Françaises theater, got out of a car, smiling as he usually did.

Mr. Thibault was an optimist. He had done nothing with his life, but had still managed to make a nice fortune. He had, in fact, enjoyed the unexpected opportunity of inheriting successively from two rich uncles he had never met. This double inheritance had enabled him to marry a young girl with a large dowry who had passed away after three years of marriage, namely after living just the amount of time it took to bury her own parents and inherit their estate!

Mr. Thibault, who was not the least bit crushed by these successive fortunes, had invested his money as a good father would, although he had fathered no children and could make no claim to that title.

Yet, luck is blind and Mr. Thibault's fortunes were enriched through lucky draws. The first time, he won 300,000 francs and the second time, 250,000.

Obviously, the honorable man could, after these successive bits of good fortune, well believe that money was easy to earn and that only imbeciles failed to die millionaires.

However, despite his beliefs, Mr. Thibault was no longer on the path of the future. In fact, this man whom luck had smiled on, was well on his way to ruin. After winning a tidy fortune, without lifting a finger, he had spent the past six months, working like a man possessed, to become penniless. His misfortune arrived on the day that he had discovered an unexceptional bit of information and decided that he was good at business. Mr. Thibault came from a modest background. He had earned a degree with difficulty and proudly showed off a first in gymnastics that he had earned about 15 years earlier.

But that did not prevent Mr. Thibault from being convinced that his knowledge was universal. He claimed to be looking for good deals like a dog tracks down game. He judged the government ministries, organized the future war and, above all, despised the Académie française, which he believed was made up of 40 hopeless men who had achieved fame through their wives.

Mr. Thibault did nothing. He was bored. When he grew excessively bored, he went to the theater. As a result of going to the theater, he knew a certain number of swindlers who immediately sensed in him what could only be called an excellent "sucker".

Immediately, they convinced Mr. Thibault, that he was exceptionally intelligent. Then, things went quickly. The swindlers recognized one another, organized and set up a company to take charge of the sucker.

At that point, Mr. Thibault stunned those close to him. This was a time when he started to judge playwrights, to treat them like dear colleagues, to treat them like close friends and to demonstrate that they were all quite inferior to him.

His close friends, naturally, gossiped. They accused Mr. Thibault of being quite mad. Then one day, wagging tongues fell silent. The media had published a sensational bit of news and Mr. Thibault was the man of the hour.

Quite simply, the imbecile, pushed by his board of directors, had purchased the Folies-Françaises!

The Folies-Françaises was one of those theaters, like so many in Paris, that seemed perpetually destined to drive their owners to ruin. Regardless of who managed them, regardless of the plays they put on, regardless of whether the spectators came to hoot or applaud, their financial results were always deplorable.

Moreover, this was easily explained by the fact that the operating costs were enormous and it was essentially impossible to make a profit.

Mr. Thibault should have noticed this.

After the first year, the self-made theater manager, in fact, should have been most upset when he saw the deficit created by his unfortunate management.

Another man would have been discouraged; he persevered.

"I'll work twice as hard," he said.

The result was that he lost twice as much money since he produced twice as many plays.

Yet, Mr. Thibault's activity knew no limits. He never stopped working. He stunned theater goers with the events he took on. And, quite naturally, the Folies-Françaises lost a little more money each year.

The game continued for three years.

Mr. Thibault was starting to be a little short of income, yet he continued to smile. On the other hand, the swindlers that surrounded him were almost all very rich and advised him to sell the business thinking, no doubt, that they would share in the assets that would become available.

Nevertheless, Mr. Thibault continued to smile.

He kept on smiling as he arrived at the Folies-Françaises, and raced joyfully over to the employee who handled ticket sales.

"Well," he asked. "Is the house full? Lots of spectators for this evening?"

The employee looked at him quietly and replied, "No one, sir."

Despite his optimism. Mr. Thibault grimaced as he said, "No one? Really? That's impossible! No one has bought tickets?"

"Yes, sir. But there's really no point talking about it, I've got six reservations."

Suddenly, Mr. Thibault relaxed.

"Well, six reservations, that's something already. You said there was no one. Good grief, we've already got six reservations!"

And the ineffable theater manager walked off to his office, smiling. He was particularly fond of his office. All of the walls were covered with portraits of actresses, with warm dedications. And that was easy enough to understand. Mr. Thibault always paid three times more than other theater managers.

Moreover, the room was comfortable, discrete, silent. There were excellent sofas for sleeping... And it was so easy to doze off in this room. As soon as he arrived, Mr. Thibault immediately threw himself onto a chair, while contemplating a difficult calculation.

"Let's see!" he thought. "I have six people in the room... How many more people do I need so that I can make money?"

But that was a difficult, perhaps impossible, calculation and Mr. Thibault gave up.

The manager of the Folies-Françaises gave up all the more willingly since someone knocked at his door. A stage manager poked his head in.

"Are you the boss?"

"Yes."

"Someone is asking for you."

"An author? Send him packing!"

"It's not an author."

"An actor then? Tell him we're not hiring."

"Not that either, boss."

"A friend perhaps? Give him two fold-up seats and tell him we're sold out."

The stage manager did not respond this time for the excellent reason that he had disappeared, violently pulled backward by someone who familiarly opened the door and stepped into the manager's office.

"It's my honor, sir..." he started to say. But he did not continue.

Mr. Thibault, outraged by the inopportune indiscretion of this fellow leapt to his feet, asking, "Who are you? What do you want?"

The other simply replied, "I bring you fortune, sir!"

At that, the manager of the Folies-Françaises gave a friendly bow and said, "That's fine. I was waiting for you... Sit down."

A moment later, Mr. Thibault and his visitor were excellent friends.

The man who claimed to be bringing fortune used words that immediately won Mr. Thibault over.

"Sir," said the stranger. "I have come to see you because I believe that you are the most intelligent of all theater managers..."

Mr. Thibault bowed his head at that.

"And the one that makes the least profits..."

Mr. Thibault looked up.

"But, most certainly the one who will make even more!"

Mr. Thibault bowed low again.

However, the individual who expressed such words was sinking deeper and deeper into his chair as he said, "So, sir, you are going to make a great deal of money because, based on my own calculations, there are 200,000 young people in Paris at least who are running after an heiress' dowry!"

At this point, Mr. Thibault stood up, concerned.

"I'm dealing with a mad man," he thought.

His visitor reassured him.

"These 200,000 young people," he continued. "I have an infallible way of bringing them to your theater. Do you want me to present my plan to you? I would like to add that if, as I promise, I find the means to bring 200,000 people to your facility, namely if I organize a full house night after night for close to a month, it will only be fair if I receive a certain percentage... I will ask you for one and a half percent of gross earnings. Is that too much?"

Mr. Thibault was dumbfounded.

"You will have two!" he replied, generous as always. "However, I don't understand you at all... How will you do this?"

"Child's play," continued the individual. "Read this."

He took a piece of paper from his wallet and handed it to Mr. Thibault.

A young girl with a dowry worth one million, fairly pretty, truly intelligent, independent but as strong as required, raised by a guardian whose name alone guarantees good morals, would like to wed a young man, even a poor one, but truly intelligent, a young man with a good heart, sentimental. To avoid the banality of a mundane marriage, this young girl, accompanied by her tutor, will be in Box 22 at the Folies-Françaises theater, every evening. All young people likely to be interested in this announcement may view her discretely before writing to K.B., General Delivery, Station 22.

Mr. Thibault read the paper without understanding.

"And?" he asked.

"And, his visitor replied impatiently. "It's as clear as the nose on your face! There won't be anyone in Box 22. But I guarantee that the day after this announcement is published, your theater will be packed. First, there will be the naïve types who believe the announcement. Then there will be the vicious ones who expect some sort of swindle... There will be the curious who, out of boredom, will come to see what's going on. There will be the revelers who will drop by in the hopes of taking part in an entertaining encounter... Finally, there will be everyone who is anybody in Paris, most of whom are imbeciles, and who will, quite naturally, act as a single man. Do you agree, Mr. Thibault?"

"Completely!" replied the manager of the Folies-Françaises, who was an exceptional speaker. "I agree completely! Your idea is marvelous! The month will be a great success!"

"You must pay me 50 francs," replied the individual. "That's the price for the announcement. I'm an ingenious man, but I don't have a cent…"

Mr. Thibault paid him.

CHAPTER V
Report from La Capitale

"All the same, they're going to be a bit impressed when they see me! I did, in fact, drop them, the excellent comrades… It's been some time now since I went over to the newspaper."

Fandor was talking to himself, smiling, as he climbed, with his usual haste, up the stairs that led to the editorial room of *La Capitale*.

Jérôme Fandor was not wrong in supposing that his arrival could result in total amazement at the newspaper.

Times had changed, in fact, since the time when Jérôme Fandor had been a star reporter who, every day, with amazing punctuality, went to the office to get his orders from his chief of information.

Life had upset that orderly existence. Fandor had taken part in the most surprising, the most unlikely adventures and, while continuing the fight against Fantômas, he had been forced to give up his regular activities with *La Capitale*.

Fandor was, however, still a journalist. He still belonged to the same large newspaper that had been founded and managed so successfully by poor Mr. Dupoint de l'Aube who had since been assassinated by the terrifying Fantômas.

The only difference was that, instead of being one of the regular reporters, the journalists who, day in and day out, submitted their reports, Fandor was considered an independent reporter, which gave him all the freedom he needed.

He didn't take orders from anyone, he did whatever he saw fit, he investigated topics that interested him and he brought his reports back, when he thought of it, to the newspaper.

It was moreover accurate to say that Fandor had benefited, even monetarily, from this arrangement.

Bit by bit, in fact, his adventures had earned him a great deal of renown that clung to his name and gave him a halo of celebrity.

The public did not consider Fandor merely a skilled journalist; he was above all, as a close friend of Juve, the relentless adversary of the Criminal Mastermind and that meant that at *La Capitale* they truly wanted to retain his services.

Since the best way to keep people is to remunerate them generously, no one skimped when it came to Fandor. The reports prepared by Hélène's husband were paid for generously and, as a result, the journalist was able to live easily, without worrying about the next day, and without having to work his fingers to the bone, which is the usual fate of those who slave for the daily newspapers.

Jérôme Fandor, moreover, only brought *La Capitale* for its articles about Fantômas and this had been the case for some time.

Since he had married Hélène, in fact, events had taken place so quickly, so feverishly, that he had had no time to take care of anything else.

Increasingly, he was Fantômas' reporter and he accepted that role, not as an apologist, but as a conscientious writer, preparing a formidable repertory against a wretch and nailing a being that deserved no pity to the pillory of public opinion.

And Jérôme Fandor had no illusions about the importance of his job.

He had no doubt that one day or another he would win a definitive victory against Fantômas. And that day, they would arrest the monster and take him before the courts and no doubt the jurors, like the members of the Court, would find it useful to leaf through the collection of his articles to document that many facts for which the accused would be required to pay dearly.

However, that morning, as he headed to *La Capitale*, Fandor was not thinking about Fantômas.

He had arrived a few days earlier in France with Hélène. And had been very occupied settling in the young woman who, suffering a little, had not wanted to remain in the heart of Paris and had already undertaken many steps to finally straighten out his marriage with Hélène since that marriage had to be considered non-existent in the eyes of the law.

Fandor's heart had been filled with a terrifying concern for several hours at least.

He had been overwrought when, at the St. Petersburg station, just as he jumped into the train with Hélène, he realized that Juve was not with them.

Fandor had wondered what misfortune could have arrived, if the policeman was the victim of vengeance or had been delayed by some accident.

Fandor, in fact, could have no idea of what actually had happened.

Nothing would have allowed him to guess that Juve had returned the necklace to the Tsar and that the monarch, furious, had ordered his arrest.

Fandor's concern, which grew over time, had been abruptly calmed however, by a telegram Juve had sent him from St. Petersburg.

The policeman had used the coded language developed by the two friends, not so much to ensure the secrecy of their communications as to authenticate the sender.

Juve had written: Don't worry, I'm staying on in Russia for a while but will be back soon.

Feeling calmed by Juve's message, having completed his urgent errands, having settled Hélène in and tasted with her the first days of happiness that they had had in a long time, Jérôme Fandor had naturally decided to make a trip down to the newspaper. He wanted to shake his friends' hands, find out what they had to say for themselves, what was being said in the well-informed circles, in a word, take the time to hear what his friends had to say about Paris.

At the top of the stairs, Jérôme Fandor found, sitting behind a black wood table, spotted with ink, the office boy who for the past 20 years had introduced strangers to the writing staff, who wanted to speak with someone from the firm.

"Bonjour Eugène!" Fandor said in a familiar tone.

The other jumped. "Now then," he exclaimed. "Mr. Fandor! I'm ever so pleased to see you. We were just talking about you the other day. I heard Mr. Mirat say, just like that, that of course you had to be dead since you had shown no signs of life..."

"Food for thought," Fandor commented, smiling.

As Eugène laughed, without understanding, the door to the editorial room suddenly opened and De Panteloupe, the secretary, made an appearance, carrying stacks of papers, angry, as usual.

"Good grief, Eugène! Where are the Havas telegrams? I've asked you for them a dozen times."

Eugène, naturally, remained unconcerned. He was too used to Mr. De Panteloupe's constants fits of anger and he knew, better than anyone, that they were inconsequential and never resulted in sanctions.

De Panteloupe stopped short.

A cheeky voice had interrupted him, saying, "Calm down old man. Don't get yourself in such a bother. It will make your hair fall out."

De Panteloupe, who liked to live it up, was always concerned about going bald. With an automatic gesture, the editor ran his hand over his hair, making sure that his hairline had not suddenly receded.

At the same time, he exclaimed, "Fandor! What are you doing here? So, you're not dead after all? What a surprise! It's been such a long time since we've had any news of you? Where have you been?"

"From over there," Fandor replied who, with a vague wave of his hand, seemed to indicate a very distant horizon.

De Panteloupe, however, returned to his usual activity.

"Well good grief," he said. "Since you're here, we'll have to open the champagne. This comes at a good time, I was dying of thirst. Get on with you, Eugène. Run over to the bistro downstairs and come back with four bottles... You can put them in my office."

Then he turned to Fandor, saying, "Will you join me?"

"In a moment," the journalist replied. "I never turn down a glass of champagne, but first I want to visit my colleagues in the newsroom."

"Off with you, then!"

De Panteloupe, a busy man, strode across the vestibule, reprimanded a messenger laden with telephones, smiled at Clément, the telegraph man, then quickly kicked open the door to his office and walked in.

Fandor headed toward the newsroom. The large room had not changed. It was still painted white, and decorated with the most fantastic inscriptions provided by the pens of the journalists. It housed a succession of small desks along the walls and in the middle there were two enormous tables where the 40 or so reporters employed by the newspaper worked, under the orders of the various section editors.

Anyone who had walked into this room, without knowing just how free reporters are in their manners, would no doubt have been very surprised by the usual chaos that reigned there. Often, someone could be seen bicycling around the tables, while others roller-skated and some fenced and others exchanged blows, hands wrapped in enormous boxing gloves.

That day, however, as Fandor entered the room, the usual atmosphere was gone. All of the journalists in the room had abandoned their posts and had gathered, jostling, around the small desk that belonged to Chien-Écrasé.[6]

Chien-Écrasé, as usual, was bedecked with jewelry that was as flashy as it was fake. He was the editor in chief of the important human interest column.

He was always the one who wrote about what went on in the streets. It was Chien-Écrasé who would write about the pitiful death of that poor woman crushed in the middle of the street, the humorous tale of the drunkard picked up from the middle of the sidewalk just as he thought he was in his bedroom, slipping his boots under his bed, while he was in fact throwing them into a voracious sewer!

Always in a cheerful mood, always smiling, convinced that he was a major man of letters, Chien-Écrasé was the newspaper's clown.

That was so true that Fandor, as he stepped into the room, and saw the agitation of his colleagues, had no doubt whatsoever as to what was going on.

"Well," the young man muttered. "That's it! I'd wager that Chien-Écrasé is once again preparing that formidable bedlam he is so famous for!"

Jérôme Fandor shoved his way through the crowd, trying to see what Chien-Écrasé was up to.

Yet, the reporter, sitting at his desk, was excessively grave. He was perfectly serious as he questioned an old woman and noted her answers. She was seated in front of his desk and seemed overcome with rage.

With a wave of his hand, Fandor silenced his colleagues who were about to shake his hand, He listened.

Just then, Chien-Écrasé asked, "How old are you, madam? I have to know your age...Obviously, I realize that my question is indiscrete, but I truly do have to know!"

And, although the old woman had to be at least 60 years-old, Chien-Écrasé added, in a serious tone, "It is true that, at your age, madam, people are no longer shamed to confess to their age! So, how old are you? Fifteen? Sixteen?"

That calmed the woman somewhat.

After hesitating for a second, she replied, "I'm 24 years-old."

---

[6] The "run-over dogs" column of a French newspaper gathers miscellaneaous minor items with no conmnection with the rest of the news of the day.

"You don't look it!" Chien-Écrasé replied. "Are you single? No? Married? I regret that I don't know your spouse. I would set about wishing you away from him!"

"Oh sir!" the woman protested with a pout.

"I would set about deceiving him," Chien-Écrasé continued graciously, "I would deceive him if, as I suppose, he has a pretty little mistress..."

Naturally, the woman scowled.

Chien-Écrasé continued," But, let's us get to the point of your complaint. Why are you making a complaint, madam?"

This time, the complainant, since that is what she was, stood up suddenly, saying, "Sir, I thought that a newspaper like *La Capitale*, which is written by quality men such as yourself who are always prepared to defend great causes, would not want to allow the people living in a six-storey house to be molested by government carelessness."

After that lengthy declaration, the woman huffed and puffed.

Chien-Écrasé made the most of the opportunity to agree, saying "You are right, madam to come to us. We will defend the six-storey house. We will defend it even if it has only five stories, or four or three, two and even one or less!"

The woman caught her breath and said, "Here are the facts. I live at 228 *bis* Boulevard Haussmann."

"That's a nice neighborhood, madam!"

"Yes, sir, it is, and it should be a quiet neighborhood."

"It should, madam."

"Well, it isn't, sir. At least it isn't anymore and hasn't been so for a few days. And that is why I am complaining to you."

"Madam," Chien-Écrasé said. "Let us get right down to the events that are upsetting you. They're announcing a flood in the year 2000 and you absolutely must tell me your secret before then!"

At the moment, the brave woman looked at Chien-Écrasé, her eyes filled with concern. She was starting to wonder if people were mocking here Yet, the serious expression on the reporter's face reassured her.

"Well, sir, here's what has been going on. Can you believe it? for the last seven or eight days I have been awakened every morning at dawn, by hens."

"By hens?" the reporter replied, astonished. "Where would one find chickens on Haussmann Boulevard?"

"In the poster column across the street from my place!"

This time Chien-Écrasé jumped. After having properly made fun of his elderly visitor, he was starting to seriously wonder if she was actually the one making fun of him.

Harshly, the reporter asked, "What are you telling me, madam? That there are chickens in one of the Morris columns on Haussmann Boulevard?"

"Yes, sir."

"Are you absolutely certain?"

"Absolutely."

"And they sing?"

"Every morning."

"And how do they sing, madam?"

"Well, like chickens sir... They cluck, cluck, cluck..."

Unfortunately, the perfect imitation the old woman tried to provide inflamed the zeal of the reporters who were present.

For half an hour, they had been enjoying themselves as they listened to Chien-Écrasé interview this visitor who had come in to complain after the installation of a chicken coop inside a Morris column on Haussmann Boulevard.[7]

General hilarity swept over the room in a storm of cooing and crowing. The 50 or so journalists clucked and chuckled, jumped onto the tables and all spoke out loud.

"Watch out for my egg, there!"

"Go and sit on your chicks."

The crowing and clucking was so loud it threatened to shake the entire building.

The lady, naturally, could not take any more. Seriously frightened and believing that she had fallen in to the clutches of a band of mad men, she stood up quickly and fled, followed by the crowing of her joyous torturers.

The visitor had barely disappeared when someone in the editorial room, which De Panteloupe had just entered, uttered a battle cry.

"To the windows, for goodness' sake! To the window! We must give her an ovation!"

The editorial room did, in fact, look out over a courtyard which the unfortunate plaintiff had to cross.

All of the *La Capitale* reporters gathered at the windows, ready to pursue the poor old woman with their crowing.

"Attention!" ordered Chien-Écrasé. "On the signal, men. One, two, three!"

But no crowing ensured. They all seemed to be paralyzed in bewilderment.

Chien-Écrasé summed the situation up with an extraordinary thought, "Well, well, well, he must really like fresh eggs!"

But what could have surprised the entire staff of *La Capitale* to such a degree?

The old woman had in fact walked out the door of the newspaper, and she was heading across the courtyard, but she was not alone. Someone had taken her by the arm, someone was listening to her. And that someone was Fandor.

"Madame, are you quite sure about what you're saying? You regularly hear chickens clucking in the Moriss column opposite your house on Haussmann

---

[7] Cylindrical outdoor sidewalk structures used for advertizing, named after Gabriel Morris, a printer, who held the concession in 1868.

Boulevard? And it has been going on for four or five days? You're not mistaken? Not deluded?"

"No, sir, I am not. I'm certain about what I'm saying."

The old woman had calmed a little. She found Fandor to be a polite, patient listener, respectful of her age. And since that was all she had expected, she thanked him profusely when Fandor tipped his hat and left her a few moments later, after assuring her that he would do everything necessary.

Yet, while the old woman was pleased with Fandor, she was also intrigued.

As always, in the midst of the gaiety, the journalist had listened seriously to the words being uttered before him. He had guessed that the woman addressing Chien-Écrasé was an unusual woman, perhaps a little mad, but he had also understood that she did have some common-sense and that, as a result, there must be an element of truth in what she was saying.

"A chicken in a Moriss column!" Fandor said to himself. "That's uncommon! Maybe I can cast some light on this matter?"

He had hurried out after the old woman, caught up with her in the stairwell, and he was now determined to find out this adventure could well mean and perhaps even get an amusing article out of it.

Jérôme Fandor was one of those men who liked to complete all of the tasks they take on. He immediately jumped into a carriage and headed for Haussmann Boulevard.

There was, in fact, a Moriss column there. Naturally, it was papered with posters and although Fandor walked all around it he did not hear a single chicken cluck.

"Strange!" thought the reporter. "The old woman must have been hallucinating... and yet..."

Then, Fandor had a stroke of genius. He struck the column with all his might, then listened. And, just as he leaned his ear against the column, he clearly heard something moving about inside the structure. Only, he did not hear anything that sounded like a chicken, but rather a groan, a human groan.

A wave of enthusiasm swept over the journalist.

"Good grief! I know what this means! I'll come back this evening!"

That very evening, at close to midnight, Jérôme Fandor returned to the famous Moriss column. At that late hour, since there were no passersby in the street, he would be able to work in peace. As a precaution, he had donned a large white shirt and carried a large metal bucket on his back. Disguised as he was as a poster man, it was completely natural for him to place a ladder against the column, which he planned to climb to the top where he was able to slip his head in under the cap and look down.

It took him no more than a few seconds to reach the top of the ladder and look inside, which was lit by the gas streetlight at the top of the structure. He had not even had the time to look down when he heard a voice from inside the column.

"No... You there, posterman, have you come to disrupt my peace? Well, try not to disturb Josephine. That will make her miss her egg tomorrow!"

Jérôme Fandor cried out in surprise," Good God!"

He felt an overwhelming urge to laugh. A frightful odor of cheese rose up from the column. A resounding crow rang out.

The voice, however continued to mutter, "Well, what's with you posterman? You're not going to betray me, are you? I'm not doing anything wrong! I'm quiet. I'm not bothering the government!"

Fandor shouted, "Shut up you animal. You don't recognize me, Bouzille?"

And at that moment Bouzille, since it was him inside the column, was surprised in turn and said "Well, well, Mr. Fandor. How did you get here? Well, I'm pleased in any case, despite my life in hiding."

Then Bouzille added, "Come in, come in. Don't fall on Josephine!"

"Who is Josephine?"

"My chicken!"

With that Bouzille pointed at a superb black hen sitting on a perch made from a stick.

Ten minutes later, Fandor was inside the Moriss column, crouched down on the ground next to Bouzille.

"What are you doing here, Bouzille?" Fandor asked.

"Well, you see, I'm in hiding. Because of a cheese."

"A cheese, Bouzille?"

"Yes, that's it," Bouzille replied, pointing at a superb skull on which he was sitting.

"I don't understand," said Fandor.

"Yet, it's perfectly simply" stated Bouzille. "One evening, I saw these guys that had stolen this cheese. The officers were running after them. Well, there was this ladder leaning against the column and one of these guys climbed up it and dropped the cheese inside. After that, they ran off."

"And then, Bouzille?"

"Well, then, I climbed in to protect the cheese. Like I said, I'm hiding here like a hermit in order to return this cheese to its owners when they come back. Only, they would do well to hurry up since their cheese is really quite good. And I've been eating it."

Fandor paid no mind to the fact this all seemed quite incomprehensible. Finding Bouzille who had turned into a hermit and was hiding in the Moriss column did not surprise him all that much since Fandor knew, better than anyone perhaps, the unlikely incarnations Bouzille was likely to take on from time to time.

Yet, the young man, amused as he was, continued to question the old tramp.

"And that chicken, Bouzille, what are you doing with it?"

Bouzille, who had been crouching stood up and replied, "Well, this chicken, well, it's because of my chick."

"Eh?" said Fandor.

But Bouzille tried to steer the conversation in another direction saying, "Don't you think we're fine in here? The gas streetlight provides light for us, heating too, we get all the latest literary news outside. It's heaven!"

"In fact," Fandor agreed. "But about that chicken, Bouzille?"

This time Bouzille frowned and replied, "Well, this chicken, I told you, if she's here, it's because of my chick."

Jérôme realized that he wouldn't get any more out of the old man without taking stronger measures.

The journalist looked Bouzille straight in the eyes and, in a severe voice, said, "Bouzille, you don't want to answer me? Take care! Don't be stupid. What is with this chicken?"

Bouzille looked very bored and said, "Well, this is my chick's chicken."

"Who is your chick?"

Bouzille sighed deeply and replied, "Well, my chick is La Toulouche..."

Then Bouzille looked scandalized as Fandor burst into laughter. The journalist could hardly retain his amusement as he imagined the extraordinary couple that the hilarious Bouzille and the abominable shrew La Toulouche must make.

Yet, Jérôme Fandor, noting Bouzille's bored look, guessed that the man must be hiding something from him.

He insisted, saying, "This chicken belongs to La Toulouche? So why do you have it?"

"Because, Mr. Fandor, because."

"Because why, Bouzille?"

"Things...," said the tramp.

Fandor frowned severely and said, "Oh, I see Bouzille. I'm going to have to get angry."

Bouzille thought about this. Abruptly, he decided to confide in Fandor.

"Mr. Fandor," he started to say, "That will cost you 40 cents..."

"Here!"

With that Bouzille closed his eyes, as if concentrating on his thoughts, and entrusted Fandor with a strange confidence, saying "All I know, you see, Mr. Fandor, is that La Toulouche came from Rennes where she had spent a few months in the company of this chicken... It seems that she values it more than her life. Seems above all that. She does not want to keep it at her place. So I'm in charge of taking care of it. I know more about this chicken than about my chick!"

Bouzille coughed, and added, "For something else, it will take another 40 cents."

Fandor felt as if he were involved in some mystery. Naturally, he didn't hesitate. He paid Bouzille again with another coin.

"Out with it, you wretch!"

But Bouzille swelled up and said, "You don't have to insult me, Mr. Fandor. Sometimes, I give you good information. Here, let me tell you something that is worth its weight in gold... Look where I've put my finger..."

Bouzille placed his ginger on the edge of the column. There was nothing extraordinary there.

Jérôme Fandor asked, "Well, Bouzille?"

"Well, Mr. Fandor, outside there's a poster, a theater poster. Are you following me?"

"Just fine. Get on with it Bouzille."

"So, the other day, these two guys were talking on and on about this theater. Naturally, I hear everything from inside my column."

"And, Bouzille?"

"Well, it's like this, Mr. Fandor, these two guys were going on and on, saying that in this theater, the theater on the poster there, a dreadful catastrophe will take place..."

This time, Bouzille seemed to be serious.

Fandor, despite his calmness, could not keep from shuddering.

What did all this mean? What did it mean?

He asked, "But you didn't understand right away, Bouzille... They were possibly talking about a play that would fail... You don't know who they were, the two men who were talking?"

At that moment, Bouzille picked up his black hen and caressed it lovingly.

"Well... yes... no..." he said quietly. "All the same, I think that one was Fantômas and the other, well the other was Le Bedeau!"[8]

---

[8] *Bedeau*: Beadle.

CHAPTER VI
Tragic Error

Fandor, naturally, was overcome with emotion when the extraordinary Bouzille, a hermit in the Moriss column on Haussmann Boulevard, told him, with his peaceful smile, that he had heard Le Bedeau and Fantômas talking about sinister projects, announcing a terrifying catastrophe that was to take place in one of the theaters in Paris.

At that moment, of course, the journalist did not consider the chicken, the first reason for his investigation all that important. Instead, he peppered Bouzille with questions, anxious to learn details that would enable him to determine what the terrifying Fantômas was up to.

Unfortunately, Bouzille was unable to add anything at all to the information he had already given Fandor.

The journalist could take out as many large bills as he wanted and wave them under Bouzille's nose, supposing that they would definitely ensure a certain degree of loquaciousness, but Bouzille remained mute.

His eyes burned with a flame of cupidity, yet he had the honesty to refuse the money he was offered.

"Impossible, Mr. Fandor," he replied to the offers made by the former *La Capitale* reporter. "Impossible to satisfy you this time. Just imagine if I were the most beautiful girl in the world, I could only give you what I have… and all's fair that's fair. At this time, I've given you everything I know. You can't ask for more. I know nothing more."

And knowing himself, Bouzille added with a chuckle, "And if I were you I wouldn't insist, I'd tell myself, this damned Bouzille is fully capable of making things up, just to take my money!"

Fandor had not felt like laughing since he'd learned that Fantômas was back in Paris and was planning some tragic project. Yet, the picture that Bouzille gave of himself was so likely that he smiled a bit.

"Well," he agreed. "Thank you, Bouzille. Keep this money in any case. You're a good guy. Yet, you are going to do something for me. I'm going to leave your home and you will hit the wall to tell me which poster Fantômas was standing in front of when he was speaking with Le Bedeau."

Bouzille, amazed by Fandor's generosity, a generosity he had clearly counted on, hurried to agree and the reporter climbed out of the Moriss column.

He was barely outside when he heard Bouzille angrily hit the same column.

Jérôme Fandor easily found the place where the tramp was tapping inside the column. There was a large, light blue poster from the Menus-Plaisirs theater pasted there.

"Fine!" Fandor said to himself. "Fantômas is planning an attack on the Menus-Plaisirs."

And, a few moments later, after saying good night to the hilarious Bouzille, he set off for home. Fandor walked with his head down, worried, nervous, concerned. Fandor knew Bouzille too well not to know that the other man had told him everything he knew. And he did not doubt the truthfulness of his words. If Bouzille said that an attack was being planned, then an attack was really being planned.

What should he do? How could he prevent it? How could he foil the plans of the Master of Fear? Fandor was all the more concerned since, in an effort to reason calmly, he had to struggle against an emotion that overwhelmed him.

"I can't do anything," he declared. "If I warn the police, they'll just laugh at me. If I warn the management of the Menus-Plaisirs, they'll think I'm crazy. Of, if only Juve were here!"

But Juve was not there and Fandor had no idea how to prevent the Menus-Plaisirs from becoming the scene of one of those diabolical tragedies the Criminal Mastermind enjoyed so thoroughly.

Jérôme Fandor, moreover, despite his dilemma, despite his concern, did not take long to come to a decision.

"Obviously" he declared, "There is nothing I can do officially. Unofficially, however, I will find the means to make myself useful! If Fantômas goes to the Menus-Plaisirs, he'll find someone to give him a talking to. I'll be there!"

Fandor was one of those stubborn men who never back away from a fearful project, He was quite resolved to watch every performance given at the Menus-Plaisirs.

Yet, just as he was arriving at this conclusion, Fandor realized that, by attacking Fantômas, he would inevitably cause Hélène painful anguish. Most certainly the young woman would fear for her husband when she learned that he was thinking about facing the Uncapturable.

"Good grief! How will I handle this?" Fandor thought. Yet, at the same time, he smiled.

Of course, he had hidden nothing from Hélène. He was not one of those men who believed that lying to his wife was not really lying. Moreover, he would never had agreed to do anything without letting her know, since he adored her above all else.

Yet, no matter how deep his adoration went, Jérôme Fandor told himself that there were cases when lying was not lying and that if the lie was made with a very specific goal, it was not a bad one.

"I'll handle things," Fandor decided. "I won't say a word to Hélène and I'll tell her everything once my mission has been completed!"

The very next morning, in fact, Fandor started his campaign.

He planned to go to the Menus-Plaisirs himself... He told Hélène that he was going to the newspaper to work and suggested that the young women go to the Folies-Françaises, promising that he would try to meet her there at the end of the evening.

Hélène did not really like the theater when it meant going alone. Yet, the thought that her husband would be joining her helped her to make up her mind.

"That's fine," she agreed. "I'll wait for you at the Folies-Françaises."

Yet, that evening, when she arrived at the theater, supervised by the excellent Mr. Thibault, Hélène must have been very surprised.

Like everyone else in Paris, she knew full well that the Folies-Françaises was a veritable oasis of solitude on the Boulevard. Generally, there were few passersby and the plays performed there went unnoticed.

Yet, as soon as she arrived, Hélène noted that hall was full with a cloud of spectators. Men in suits, women in ball gowns and superb jewelry.

"What's going on?" thought Hélène.

Then she burst into laughter. While walking behind a most elegant woman, who leaned slightly on the arm of a very pretentious gentleman, she learned of an amusing adventure.

Apparently in Box 22, there was a rich heiress to be married off. Notices had been placed in all of the large newspapers. And while the Folies-Françaises was sold out, it was the in-crowd that had come to mock the eccentric individual who had, to some extent, been put up for sale in the daily newspapers.

For her part, Hélène had very modestly taken a seat on the lower floor of the hall. She entered the theater, dressed soberly, drawing no attention, discretely taking her seat next to another lady, also dressed soberly. After a glance at the other woman's face, Hélène took an immediate liking to her. Then she most naturally did what everyone else in the theater was also doing. She turned around, looked for Box 22 and burst into laughter. It was completely empty. There was no one there. It looked strange and gloomy in the midst of the large theater where all of the seats had been taken that night, each for a small fortune.

"Well!" said Hélène. "It's either a joke or an ingenious form of advertising. In any case, let's watch the play!"

At that very moment the curtain rose and the most fantastic melodrama, the most unbearable agglomeration of commonplace tirades that had ever been invented.

"Well," sighed the young woman. "Is it actually true that the Folies-Françaises is completely incapable of putting on anything that could be considered even slightly good? Or will I have to ward off boredom the entire evening?"

Yet, while Hélène was feeling bored, there were other people in the audience who seemed to be wildly amused. First, there was the joyful band of young people who, having come to the Folies-Françaises to catch a glimpse of the heiress in Box 22, quite naturally realized that they had been duped and took it all in stride, laughing.

Finally, and above all, there were a few ladies on their own, quite alone, who, with a good sense for business, had decided that the notice would draw a large number of single men to the Folies-Françaises and that it might, in turn, be interesting to go there as well.

Quite naturally, these women were delighted that Box 22 was empty. They came and went in the theater, making the most of the intermissions to stroll about the corridors or take up a position in the walks, in the lobby, provocative, enticing, bumping the men with their elbows as they walked past, and audaciously staring at the unfortunate gentlemen that seemed likely to be up for a profitable conversation.

One of them, in particular, was truly entertaining with the perseverance which she sought after an admirer. There had already been two intermissions and she had started conversations with very few people. She had barely exchanged pleasantries with a sort of giant when he finally confessed that he was a boxer and was used to all women fighting for his favors.

The elegant woman quietly walked off.

"My dear sir," she posted with a lack of consideration that immediately revealed her roots, "People do not fight over my favors. I do regret that since it would please me enormously. A boxer or some other type, I don't care. What I want is someone, someone interesting, this evening…"

Yet, that young person, with her outspoken manners, finally found satisfaction. Her seat was on the lower floor as well, some distance from the central aisle, and the seat next to hers, which had remained unoccupied up to that point, had suddenly been assigned to a large individual, with dark skin, black hair and fingers covered with rings.

The elegant women immediately made her decision.

"He's a Brazilian. Perhaps even an Argentinian. Those people always have cash. I'll have to light his fire."

And, without further ado, she bent over her neighbor's seat and struck her powdered shoulder against the seductive gentleman's morning coat.

Brazilian or Argentinian, the large man was obviously easy to move. After only four minutes of such attentions from his neighbor, his face grew flushed and he felt the need to run a handkerchief—so strongly scented with perfume that it could give a migraine to anyone sitting in the vicinity—over his forehead.

"It's quite…" the Brazilian said softly, starting the conversation. "It's quite warm, madam."

"I was about to say the same to you."

"And yet, I'm used to the heat."

"You are, sir?"

"I'm from Brazil, Madam."

The elegant woman chanced a compliment, saying, "I could have guessed as much from your beautiful eyes, sir!"

The large man started to suffocate. Joy stifled him; pride made him dizzy. Obviously he was one of those social upstarts who come to Paris to party and spend the few golden coins they might have while trying to look like millionaires. Her was above all one of those enlightened souls that seem to have been born in Brazil or Argentina to serve as prey for small women in Paris.

"You guessed correctly, madam," he replied, forgetting all about the play and bending outrageously over his neighbor.

"You have guessed correctly since I am in fact from Rio de Janeiro itself. Moreover, my name is a sure sign of that. I am called Manoel Palatello."

And with the wild vanity of an ill-mannered child he added, "In Paris, I live on Rue Prony."

Obviously, the elegant woman decided that his confidence deserved another and she said," My name is Adèle, Adèle de Rivoli, and I live on Rue La Bruyère."

And quite possibly the conversation between the excellent Brazilian with the look of a *rasta* and Adèle de Rivoli, would have continued to be so interesting, so remarkable, if a strange event had not suddenly occurred.

The play being performed on the stage was in fact a military play with ultra-patriotic overtones. It related the truly remarkable accomplishments of a captain who, all on his own, took back Alsace and Lorraine, killing 100,000 Germans and, what was even more prodigious, putting Napoleon I himself back on the throne.

The entire audience, initially overcome with fear when faced with such an inconsistency, grew agitated. They clapped their hands thunderously, they called from box to box, interrupting the dialogue, shouting "Vive la France!" making the candles on the large chandelier shake.

No one was even listening to the performance anymore. What did the grotesque declarations of five or six actors on the stage matter? What did the adventures of the hero who, despite his truly supernatural bravery, wound up being a traitor carried off by 20 soldiers, matter?

And Hélène, gentle Hélène, who burst into laughter by the stupidity of the plot, was laughing all alone, despite her efforts to remain serious.

Then, suddenly the scene changed. For no reason at all, the actor who had been playing the hero walked over to the steps and turned back to the soldiers who had been surrounding him and ordered, "Shoulder your weapons! Aim! Fire when ordered!"

Then he turned back to the audience and said, "Ladies! Gentlemen! Hands up! Don't make a move. The first to move will be shot dead!"

And, since the audience did not seem to understand, this extraordinary actor added in an ironic note, "My collectors will pass by…"

And the audience murmured in astonishment. Adèle de Rivoli stopped chatting with Manoel Palatello. What was happening?

Following the announcement about the collectors, five individuals with dark expressions, five abominable savages entered the main floor of the theater. They went from row to row, bending over the terrified spectators.

"Come on now, no grumbling." They ordered. "Your jewelry, chickie. Your wallet, man… and your gold… and your watch!"

In less than an instant, the entire audience was overcome with panic.

Was this serious? Were they dreaming? Were they the victims of some crazy hallucination, a nightmare as stupid as it was extravagant?

The first spectator who was encouraged to give up his belongings by the sinister collectors, tried to rebel.

"But I don't have anything… I don't have anything."

Pointlessly.

The men were armed and, come what may, he had to obey.

At that moment, Hélène clenched her jaws, digging her fingernails into the palms of her hands.

"Drat!" the young woman thought. "I understand… I understand…"

Hélène recognized the man, the collector who had just come over to her, who no doubt intended to rob her like the others. It was Le Bedeau, Fantômas' sinister accomplice, the abominable individual who, in this crime, had claimed his share of blood!

At that very moment, Le Bedeau approached Hélène's neighbor.

"Your jewelry!" he ordered. "Be quick about it."

The young woman resisted, saying, "This is crazy, senseless…"

"Don't put on airs!" Le Bedeau interrupted her.

Hélène saw the savage's hand brutally tear the heavy diamond earrings from the unfortunate woman's ear.

"Don't touch me! Don't touch me!" shrieked the terrified young woman, her face covered with blood.

Shaking, Hélène leaned toward her and whispered, "Shut up! Don't resist. Fantômas is behind this attack!"

"Fantômas!"

Goodness, Hélène could not have any delusions left after this.

The man who was on the stage. The man who was watching the sinister collectors who had just swarmed over the theater at his orders, who were flowing through the aisles and up and down the rows, that man was Fantômas!

And Fantômas was laughing!

The bandit must have been planning this unlikely assault for a long time.

And despite her fear, Hélène remained clear-headed, reconstituting the entire drama in a minute.

Fantômas was obviously the author of the fallacious advertisement that had brought the crowd to the usually deserted Folies-Françaises, and Fantômas had brought all of his accomplices to the theater. Using surprise, they had encountered no difficulty controlling the ticket takers or the two guards standing at the top of the stairway. Floor managers and actors must have been locked up and killed during the intermission. After that, Fantômas had free reign and the ten companions that surrounded him, weapons aimed at the audience ensured his impunity.

What should she do? What should she try?

The slightest movement meant certain death. Escape wasn't even possible. Calling for help was pointless. Who would come? Who could come?

And as Hélène was thinking these thoughts, the extraordinary collection continued. Le Bedeau's men continue to rob the spectators, collecting immense fortunes, valuable jewelry and wallets stuffed with bank notes.

Absolute silence reigned over the audience, which was frozen in fear. Not a sound, not a single exclamation. Nothing but the orders shouted by the wretches.

"Come on now, sissy, get your hand out of your pocket... Are you hiding something, you old...? Do you want a punch in the face?"

And everyone handed over their valuables.

The scene was horrible, unlikely. The attack surpassed the imagination and yet, it all seemed so easy, lasting barely ten minutes.

For ten minutes, the 3,000 spectators who had rushed to the Folies-Françaises had to live under the threat of the guns aimed at them.

Then, suddenly, a whistle blew.

On the stage, Fantômas gestured with his hand. And something terrible happened. With a single wave of the bandit's hand, the lights turned out everywhere. The theater, which had been brightly lit just a moment earlier, was plunged into the semi-darkness maintained by the poorly operating emergency lights. And the spectators, more relieved than frightened by the darkness, stood up quickly, shouting curses.

Unfortunately, the poor wretches' suffering was not over.

A cry, and order, rang out.

"Fire!"

Flashes lit up the room. Detonations rang out.

Then, among the shouts and cries of the injured, the groans of the dying, panic swept over the crowd.

People raced to the exits crushing others on their way. Frightened men punched this way and that to force their way through. Panicked women struggled, moaning inarticulately.

And slowly, slowly while Fantômas and his entire band should have reached safety long ago, the Folies-Françaises emptied and the unfortunate spectators, half mad with fear, ran down the boulevard, sowing panic throughout Paris.

While the panic continued inside the theater and people crushed one another in their efforts to escape, what had happened to Adèle de Rivoli? What had happened to her friendly companion, the gleaming Manoel Palatello?

They had both been visited by Fantômas' collectors. Yet, their attitude had been quite different.

Manoel Palatello, trembling with fear, had hastily handed his jewelry over to the sinister savages. The Brazilian, who was rather wealthy, was much more eager to suffer a loss, even an important one, than to risk a scrap.

Adèle, for her part, had refrained from protesting. She had even, at the time, made an enigmatic comment that might have possibly caught the attention of Manoel Palatello if the poor man had been in any condition to pay attention.

Adèle de Rivoli had said, "Here, here, have my trinkets. I don't care about them, understand. They're meaningless. I'll find a way to get them replaced by real jewels."

What did that mean?

At that moment, Le Bedeau found it quite difficult to keep a serious expression on his face. The extraordinary bandit had, in fact recognized Adèle de Rivoli and her words were perfectly clear for him.

Adèle de Rivoli was simply Adèle, the former mistress of Oeil-de-Boeuf and the Bec-de-Gaz.[9] Suddenly overcome with pride, she had left her two lovers to take up her place, as she put it, as a woman of luxury, in the corridors of the music halls.

Adèle de Rivoli, as a result of the eventful life she had lived was obviously not a woman to be embarrassed, even in the midst of extraordinary adventures. When the panic started, she found a way to be one of the first out of the theater.

Since she had become of woman of luxury, Adèle de Rivoli had also become an excellent business woman and, as she was leaving through an emergency exit, she pulled the fat Manoel de Palatello behind her, holding him by the wrist.

She immediately said to him, "Well, old man, this has been quite the evening. We'll certainly remember it. Just as I'm sitting down to chat with you, they interrupt my work... And now look at you...Bah! Don't get all upset... You look like a serious man to me... I'll give you credit!"

That very evening, in fact, Manoel Palatello, who was not yet quite recovered from his emotional turmoil and was even more dumbfounded by Adèle as she dragged him forcefully through a series of bars where he drank strong liquor, always on credit, finally arrived at the apartment on Rue La Bruyère where the young woman lived.

Manoel Palatello was very much in love.

"You please me," he said. "You please me enormously... You'll be my little woman. Is that what you want, my sweet chick?"

"No! Not my chick. Don't call me your chick!"

"Why?"

---

[9] *Oeil-de-Boeuf*: asmall, round window as one mayt find in an attic; *Bec-de-gaz*: a street gaslight.

"Because!" said Adèle de Rivoli.

And since Manoel absolutely wanted to know why she refused to accept this term of endearment, Adèle de Rivoli explained, saying "Well, my featherless wonder, it just wouldn't do... Not that you're not a good old rooster but even then, there would be two hens in the house and that would be too many. Come and see."

And at that moment, Adèle opened a door into a dark room. Immediately a large hen rushed at them, wings spread, beak ready for battle.

"What is that?" Manoel Palatello asked, backing up in fear.

Adèle de Rivoli explained, "Oh, don't get all in a huff. It's a bird that doesn't come from France. I have to keep a close eye on it for a friend."

"What? Who?" asked Manoel.

And she dragged in her new lover, who was starting to wonder if he was dealing with a mad woman.

If Adèle de Rivoli, however, had been able to escape from the Folies-Françaises without being injured, the same could not be said for all of the spectators!

At the time of the shoot-out ordered by Fantômas, at the very moment when the bandit was coldly calculating that causing a wild panic was the best way in which to sure his escape, 17 people were shot, more or less seriously.

One of the most pitiful victims was certainly poor Hélène. The young woman, of course, had escaped death, but she was most grievously injured. A bullet had struck her shoulder causing a painful injury.

They were carrying her on a stretcher as all of Paris was already buying up special editions relating the catastrophe.

They were carrying her off, injured, and Fandor, his eyes filled with tears and his heart with despair, unable to understand why Fantômas had gone to the Folies-Françaises when he had threatened the Menus-Plaisirs, had been obliged to give consent for her to be taken to a hospital at the other end of Paris.

At this moment the unfortunate young man took his head in both hands and, despite his great courage, sobbed in despair. Was this the truth? Would he never be able to enjoy a few weeks of happiness? Would Fantômas always cross his path?

Yet, Fandor, who had been filled with despair, lifted his head in pride.

"I will get vengeance! I will get vengeance!" he shrieked.

And he no longer wept. His eyes, eyes filled with the flame of desire, were dry.

CHAPTER VII
Disobedience

An hour later, Fandor felt a bit more reassured about Hélène's fate.

He had summoned a doctor who examined the injured woman and waved away Fandor's concern, saying, "It's nothing at all, sir. The injury is clean, small and the patient has very little fever and will most likely heal soon and after two weeks of rest will be no more than an unpleasant memory."

Two weeks of rest! The doctor was talking to his beloved! He felt that two weeks was very short indeed and there was no need to mention it.

Jérôme Fandor was not convinced. Deep down, he was still concerned and wondered whether the medical man might perhaps be wrong. What if some unforeseen complications arose, aggravating the situation?

And then, finally, Fandor thought about Hélène's suffering and about the despair the young woman must be feeling, as she lay, motionless, on a chaise longue. She was so active that she could not sit still.

"Two weeks of rest? The journalist grumbled. "That's fine for him to say. Will we ever be able to rest?"

At that moment, Fandor was on the telephone, asking to be connected to Juve's home. But, the young man knew full well, unfortunately, that it would not be his friend, it would not be the excellent policeman who would answer at 36-0 North.

When Juve was not in Paris, in fact, old Jean had instructions to sleep in the apartment. He was to answer telephone calls and he was the one Fandor wanted to ask to help care for the young woman.

Jean, in fact, Juve's quiet servant, the man who was never disturbed, who could never be pulled from his usual calm, felt a great deal of friendship for Hélène.

Once before already, he had nursed the young woman and Fandor knew that he would go to marvelous lengths to find ways to distract her, to relieve her suffering as much as possible.

If it had not been for old Jean, Fandor would never have been able to leave Hélène's side, even for a second. Yet, now more than ever, he felt the need to be free, the desire to come and go.

Fantômas' latest attack, his most recent crime, had been most terrible. Fandor could not accept that it would go unpunished. He could not allow Paris to remain under the thrall of the terror that the tragedy at the Folies-Françaises would indubitably cause. On the contrary, he had to strike Fantômas and his band, hunt him down mercilessly. Fandor felt quite anxious at the thought that he was the only one who could take up the battle, in Juve's absence.

The elderly servant raced off in response to the young man's call and, once he arrived, Fandor gave him very specific instructions.

Old Jean was not to leave the side of the injured woman, who was now sleeping the deep sleep of the ill.

He stood there, motionless, attentive, ready to ward off any danger. If need be, he would throw himself into the fire since, in Fandor's eyes, he was responsible for Hélène.

"Off course, sir. I will obey the gentleman! The Master can count on me."

Jean replied in his quiet voice to the nervous recommendations made by Fandor. He never viewed things as tragic; in any case, he was always able to hide it if they upset him.

Fandor, pleased with the guard he had installed at Hélène's bedside left hastily.

At that very moment, the blood was pounding in the journalist's veins. He was quite mad with rage and, of course, had no hesitation as to which path he would take.

He hailed a taxi and called out the address, "To the Madeleine! Be quick! There's A hefty tip in it for you!"

Spurred on by the generous offer, the driver who was chauffeuring our friend Juve, naturally worked miracles. He drove at full tilt, tires squealing, weaving among the passersby as if they were bowling pins, drove over curbs, grazed the gas lamps and scraped the few vehicles he encountered, all to deliver his client to the Place de la Madeleine a few minutes later.

Fandor climbed out of the car, paid the driver, and headed for Haussmann Boulevard.

The entire time of the trip, quite naturally, the flames of the young man's rage burned ever brighter and he started to swear, words with no meaning, threats. Yet, he fell silent. He strode down Haussmann Boulevard like a mad man, causing the few rare night-time passersby on the aristocratic street, to turn around.

Soon, Fandor reached the Morris column where he had once met Bouzille.

He wasted no time. Fandor started to pound on the column, calling out at the same time, "Bouzille! Bouzille!"

And, at almost the same time, a voice, the voice of the old tramp, answered peacefully, "Well, well, who is making such a nose? I hear you. I'm here but if you keep up this you will wake Joséphine."

That was that. Of course, Fandor paid no attention. He shrieked even louder to the hermit in the column, "Get out here Bouzille! Get out here right now. I need to talk to you!"

Unfortunately, Bouzille was not a man to take matters lightly.

In a grating voice that seemed to come from underground, he replied "What do you mean get out? Do you want me to leave my column to take a stroll at this time of night? No, no, I'm having none of it. I've got arthritis and I can't even stand up."

"Get out here, Bouzille!" Fandor repeated. "I order you to get out here."

This time, Bouzille did not respond. The old tramp was a stubborn man. Obviously, he wanted nothing to do with obeying Fandor's injunctions.

"You can simply climb in," he finally grumbled, as the journalist continued to insist. "And don't keep making so much noise or my landlady will scold you. That's for sure!"

It was obvious that Bouzille was about to refuse to leave his extraordinary home for quite some time. Jérôme Fandor, of course, must have had his reasons for not wanting to join Bouzille in his Morris column, as he had that first time.

What was the journalist trying to do?

Then he had a formidable idea.

Abandoning his angry voice and talking in one of well-thought-out decision, Jérôme Fandor said, "Bouzille, you don't want to come out? Too bad for you. I'll get you out of there anyway. There's a water hose here and I'm going to spray you in the column. I imagine that will get you out…"

Of course, in fact, there was no water hose near Fandor and he was lying through his teeth because even if there had been a hose nearby he would not have been able to turn it on without attracting the attention of two distant shadows who were melancholically pacing up and down, and those shadows belonged to none other than two city sergeants.

Bouzille, however, was frightened by the young man's threat.

Bouzille, in fact, knew full well that Fandor was quite capable of the vilest tricks, the craziest deeds. He decided that it was more than likely that he would be turned out by a spray of water and he did not want to run the risk.

Yet he complained, "Truth be told, it's not very nice what you are saying there, Mr. Fandor. You just can't be doing things like that. These chickens have sensitive lungs! Come on, come on, don't get angry… Here I am after all."

Bouzille, in fact was arduously moving about in the Morris column. Meaningful cracking sounds rose to the surface and even Joséphine clucked loudly, disturbed on her perch by the gymnastics Bouzille performed as his head emerged. He had barely glanced out the opening of the Morris column, he had barely seen Fandor, when he suddenly stopped climbing out.

"Oh, but you tricked me!" Bouzille grumbled. "That too, Mr. Fandor, is something you just must not do. It shows a lack of respect for a man of my age… to a man with a white beard… Good grief! You'll burn in hell for three more days, at least."

And Bouzille added in a furious voice, "Why did you mention a water hose since there is none? My word, I almost feel like climbing back down inside."

Bouzille, who was holding on to the edge of the Morris column as if leaning against a balcony railing, pretended to head back down.

Fandor stopped him.

"Stop joking! I have to talk to you."

"It will cost you!" Bouzille replied seriously.

But Fandor was in no mood for joking.

"Which poster did you show me?" he asked. "Show me where it was. Here?"

Fandor was pointing his finger, touching the poster of the Menus-Plaisirs, of the theater where he had been and where nothing had happened. Whereas Fantômas had gone that very evening to the Folies-Françaises, where he had launched a most formidable attack.

Bouzille responded without hesitating to Fandor's question, "That one there!"

And the tramp was most surprised by the effect his words produced.

Increasingly nervous, Fandor was no longer joking at all.

"You're lying!" the young man screamed. "Nothing happened at that theater. As a result, that's not the theater Fantômas should have been talking about when you overheard him. You're lying to me Bouzille! Or you're deliberately trying to deceive me and, in that case, you will pay for it. Or perhaps, you were just playing with me and, in that case as well, you'll never go to heaven."

Obviously, Fandor was sincere. He clearly thought that Bouzille, with his usual recklessness, had given him false information. Yet he wanted to know, beyond any possible doubt, because he was filled with remorse at the thought that he had gone to the Menus-Plaisirs where nothing was supposed to happen while he had sent Hélène to the Folies-Françaises where she had had the most unfortunate experience.

Bouzille, however was struggling like a maniac at the top of his Morris column.

"What are you saying, Mr. Fandor?" he protested. "Are you saying that I lied? Well you're not being nice at all today! First of all, lie is not a nice word at all. I'm calling you out on that."

Then Bouzille, set outside his outraged sensitivities and in a completely neutral voice said, "First, I don't understand. If you're in such a snit because of the poster, well that's not my fault. It was the one you showed me that Fantômas was pointing at. If it indicates the Menus-Plaisirs then something was supposed to go down at the Menus-Plaisirs. But, there's always the chance that he changed his mind."

Jérôme Fandor shrugged.

Bouzille's hypothesis was, in fact, completely unacceptable. Fantômas was not a man who changed his mind. Fantômas never spoke lightly. Once he had decided to do something, he always did it. He was master of everyone and everything. He said so himself and there was no obstacle that could sway him once he had made up his mind.

"Bouzille, you're lying to me!" Fandor repeated.

Yet, at that moment, there was a great uproar. Bouzille, in a burst of indignation, had wanted to pound on his chest to affirm his perfect sincerity.

Unfortunately, Bouzille was balanced precariously at the top of the Morris column. Suddenly, he lost his footing and tumbled back inside the column, creating an even more extraordinary racket when his extraordinary hen, Joséphine, roused abruptly from her sleep, started to cluck desperately and beat her wings.

"Bouzille! Bouzille!" Fandor ordered. "Come back here this second!"

But, inside the monument, Bouzille rubbed his sides cautiously.

"Never again... I'll never start that up again. No, no! You make me catch cold, you insult me... and I don't care for that at all. Not at all. What have I got to do, Mr. Fandor, with your adventures? I give you information and you're still not happy. Then you make a racket at my door! What kind of manners is that? I live a quiet life and I don't want any nonsense. If I became a hermit it's because I want to be left alone. So, it's time to go to bed. You take care of your chickens and I'll take care of mine."

Bouzille, who was a chatty type, could have gone on for some time, shouting at Fandor in this manner, half furious, half mocking, when he suddenly heard a loud shout.

It was just Fandor, who was starting in again, swearing like a soldier.

"In the name of God! In the name of God!"

"Quiet!" shouted Bouzille. "What's up with you?"

But Fandor was no longer listening to the old tramp's questions.

"I'm so stupid! What's happened to me is so stupid! It's true, Bouzille wasn't lying. It was right here on the column that Fantômas was looking when he announced his abominable intention. But someone changed the posters! The other day, when I saw the Menus-Plaisirs poster, I never thought that it had been posted on top of one for the Folies-Françaises!"

As Fandor was talking to himself, furious, he was interrupted by Bouzille who, curiosity gnawing at him, had to started to climb back up and once again emerged at the top of the column.

"Mr. Fandor for all the time I've given you, I truly do deserve a drink."

But Bouzille was definitely playing with misfortune.

In order to attract Fandor's attention, he wriggled about like a mad man and fell a second time. Fandor, who was leaving, heard abominable shrieking. It was the chicken that Bouzille must have hit on his way down. She was clucking desperately and Bouzille was trying to calm her.

"Now, now," he said. "Don't go on about things like that, Joséphine. It's not like I broke your eggs. You have to be gentle. Am I complaining? And yet, my giblets are bleeding..."

Then Bouzille called out, "Mr. Fandor! Mr. Fandor, you owe me!"

But Fandor was long gone.

That very night, when such tragic events took place, mingled with such comical adventures, that very night when Hélène was injured at the Folies-Françaises, when Fandor was investigating the Morris column in which Bouzille was struggling with his hen, Joséphine, other adventures took place, events that demonstrated the extraordinary will of the one who, once again, had spread fear throughout Paris.

Once the horrible attack on the theater had been completed, Fantômas' companions had, naturally, rushed off on their separate ways.

The master's orders were quite clear.

"Everyone go home!" the Criminal Mastermind had shrieked. "You'll all be paid tomorrow"

Naturally, they had hastened to follow his instructions, since Le Bedeau, Bec-de-Gaz and Oeil-de Boeuf could never have resisted the Criminal Genius.

Fantômas had jumped into an automobile and hastily disappeared, taking with him the incredible loot his men had just given him.

While some of accomplices disappeared, racing away, slinking along walls, disappearing in Paris, where the news of the formidable crime had barely had time to spread, Bec-de-Gaz and Oeil-de-Boeuf, the cheerful idiots that they were, naturally head off to Les Halles, where they planned to have a drink before going home to bed.

Le Bedeau, who was much more audacious and, no doubt, also better informed, did not rush in the least.

Taking large strides, without rushing, he walked down the boulevard, both hands in his pockets, strolling with that sinuous pace of someone up to no good.

Le Bedeau went home. At that time, he was living in the infamous Tivoli alley, next to the Saint-Lazare station. He went home, as he said, with his mind at peace, like a good worker who had just completed his day and was in no rush to enter his miserable abode.

Yet, that evening, Le Bedeau was sad.

His sadness came from the jealousy that washed over his mind.

"In any case," he thought. "It's disgusting. It's always the same ones who have butter on their plates and the same ones who eat dirt! Right now, Fantômas has us working like dogs. Pick up everything he says. Do this… Do that… But I'll pocket what I want and you'll have what's left!"

A few seconds later, Le Bedeau swore, "Good grief. I'm fed up!"

Le Bedeau had, in fact, just played a major role in the attack so successfully undertaken by Fantômas at the Folies-Françaises.

First, he had hired the men who, at Fantômas' sides, had controlled the theatre with their weapons. Then he had supervised the thieves and he figured that this double role earned him a large part of the proceeds.

Thinking about Fantômas, Le Bedeau said, "I wonder what kind of booty he picked up. My hat was filled with diamonds and all kinds of luxurious trinkets! And then there were those blue bank notes. I stuffed my pockets. And isn't that a pity. That Fantômas could have slipped me a few tonight!"

All in all, Le Bedeau was experiencing the feelings normally felt by all those who serve as accomplices for criminals. Those who, even before the loot is divided up, find their share too small.

Le Bedeau, nevertheless, knew full well, that there was no point rebelling and clamoring for more.

Fantômas was not a man who could be moved by fear, not one who could be touched.

People had to accept his decisions with no hope of being able to change them at all. He was jealous, above all, of his authority and did not tolerate contradictions or advice. You either obeyed him or got out!

"Fine, fine," grumbled Le Bedeau. "We all obey. But, still... his day will come."

Le Bedeau, at that moment, had just walked into the abominable hotel where he lived. He had walked up a frightfully filthy staircase and, tiptoed down a stinking corridor, heading for the small door that opened into his room.

"Well, here I am. Let's go in and take a look," he said.

He pulled his key out of his pocket and placed it in the lock.

He walked into the room.

Just then, in the darkness, there was a rustling, a sliding, an imperceptible yet clear sound.

Le Bedeau was immediately overcome with rage.

"In the name of God!" he cursed. "It's starting all over again. Don't I get to sleep tonight?

Standing motionless in the dark room, Le Bedeau swore, "Well I'm fed up! I'm terribly fed up!"

But, in the dark, the noise continued...

Just then, Le Bedeau took off his coat. He grasped it by one sleeve and threw it, with all his strength, toward the corner of the room.

"Shut up, chicken!"

But, who was he talking to?

The jacket, its pockets stuffed with heavy objects, struck the wall noisily. A cry rang out, a strong cry, a clucking.

"I'd cheerfully wring the necks of all such beasts!"

And he kicked out at the dark.

Then he continued to undress.

He unrolled the red belt that held up his pants.

Suddenly he stopped, saying, "I'm hungry. Work kills you."

He seemed to hesitate. Then, in a low voice, he muttered, "Well, the guy told me to keep them. What's with this now? I'm to be a peasant now? I have to keep care of his animals? Goodbye, sir!"

Le Bedeau sat down on his bed. He had taken off his boots and was banging his heels on the tiled floor.

"I'm hungry!" he repeated.

Then he stood up suddenly, shouting, "And when you're hungry you eat! Good grief! I've got food tonight…"

Le Bedeau chortled sinisterly. He stood up, took a box of matches out of his pocket. And struck one of the wooden sticks.

"Where's my candle. Here it is."

Then he called out, "Where are you, you filthy beast?"

And something extraordinary happened.

At the other end of the room, in a corner, prepared or so Le Bedeau thought, to fight off any attack, there was a chicken, a black chicken, identical to those that Adèle de Rivoli and the excellent Bouzille had.

What was the animal doing in this dump?

Who could have entrusted it to Le Bedeau's care?

Why was the wretch sharing his room, which looked like a den, with this animal that could be of no use to him!

Le Bedeau looked at the creature fiercely. He laughed, as if something funny had just occurred to him.

"Chickens," he muttered. "Chickens, don't you play with me. Some I'll hit and the others I'll eat!"

Then he added, "I'm going to eat you little one."

He took three steps, then jumped on a terrified chicken that had no time to escape. He wrung its neck in a few minutes.

Le Bedeau, moreover, seemed to be enjoying himself quite a bit. He watched the final convulsions of the poor creature as it writhed on the floor.

"That's it, then. Die, little friend…It doesn't matter that I've been given orders to take care of you… I don't care about any orders! That's just how I am. Plus, I'm fed up!"

Le Bedeau was a stubborn brute.

Soon, he picked up the chicken, which was not quite dead yet and started to pluck its feathers without realizing how horribly cruel the act was.

"I'll eat you," he repeated.

Then laughing cynically, he pulled out the feathers by handfuls, throwing them on the floor of his dump.

Le Bedeau had plucked three-quarters of the poor chicken when, suddenly, he stood up.

"In the name of God!"

He had grown very pale.

Abruptly he threw the chicken on his bed. Then he ran to the door and placed his ear against it.

"Good lord, those are his footsteps.…"

He could, in fact, hear the quite steps of a man approaching in the corridor.

Le Bedeau threw himself back. He was white as a sheet, his face was covered with sweat. He clenched his fists as if he were about to throw himself forwards.

The steps, however, continued to approach.

Le Bedeau quivered all over.

After a few moments, he could no longer hear any sounds. The man who had been coming had stopped and must certainly be on the other side of the door.

Le Bedeau listened, panting. And it was all very simple. A key turning in the lock, a door grating as it opened.

Le Bedeau backed up against the wall.

"Good evening," a deep voice said.

"Good evening," Le Bedeau repeated in a wild voice.

The man stepped into the room, closing the door carefully behind him, and walked into the middle of the room.

"Well," he said, "What are you up to?"

"Nothing," said Le Bedeau. "What do you want?"

And Le Bedeau looked at his visitor, eyes filled with hatred and fear.

The man glanced quickly around the room.

No gesture betrayed his thoughts. He seemed impassive. The candle, placed on the tiled floor, did not light up his face. It was impossible to see more than his silhouette, tall, large, supple, trim.

Suddenly, the man turned around. He took a step toward Le Bedeau, standing close to the miserable, panting wretch.

And slowly, in a voice that bode no good, he asked, "Le Bedeau, where is my chicken."

Le Bedeau's teeth chattered.

"I... I don't know," he said.

And the man bent down. He picked up a handful of black feathers from the floor, waving in the current of air.

"You don't know?" he asked. "You're lying! Where do these feathers come from?

Le Bedeau did not answer.

Quietly the man placed his hand on Le Bedeau's shoulder, and grabbed him by his collar.

"Le Bedeau, answer me. Where is my chicken?"

And since Le Bedeau continued to say nothing, he insisted, "I told you to be careful, to keep her for me at any cost, to treat her as the apple of your eye. This was a mission of confidence that I gave you. Now, tell me, where is my chicken?"

Le Bedeau remained stubbornly silent.

The man, almost immobile, seemed to shiver.

"Le Bedeau," he continued in a lower voice, "You disappoint. How can you, an old colleague, a man I've known for 20 years, how can you have betrayed me like this? Do you know what this behavior deserves?"

At that very moment, Le Bedeau seemed to shake and quiver, as if run through by an electrical current.

"Mercy! Mercy!" he murmured. "Forgive me Fantômas!"

But the man standing before him, Fantômas, since it was Fantômas, smiled as he heard those words.

"I don't understand you," he replied. "I never show mercy. What's the point? Pity is a sign of weakness. Le Bedeau, you are going to die..."

A moan, an inarticulate groan, rose up from the thief's throat. It was indistinct, incomprehensible, a supreme invocation for pity.

Fantômas continued to laugh.

And it was a frightful thing. Le Bedeau seemed to sag at the knees. It was if he were making an immense effort to get free from the grasp that held him. Pointless. Fantômas did not even move. His hand, resting on Le Bedeau's shoulder had simply shifted over to the miserable wretch's neck. Agile fingers, strong fingers, muscled fingers, dug into Le Bedeau's flesh.

The thief did not cry out; his death rattle was smothered in his throat.

And while Fantômas seemed to be making no effort at all, using one hand, slowly, knowingly, as if trying to make the pleasure last, Fantômas strangled the man who had disobeyed him!

There came a time when Le Bedeau's body was a soft, limp thing, a horrible, disgusting wreck, face violet and eyes rolled back, nothing more than an ignoble mask of horror.

Then, Fantômas, still laughing, released his grip.

The strangled man's body fell heavily to the floor.

Fantômas pushed it with his foot, shrugging, amused.

"Definitely," he said to himself, "I'm finding it most difficult to retain my accomplices! Sooner or later, they always turn bad. What imbeciles!"

But Fantômas was not a man to take pity on a cadaver for long.

He seemed to completely forget the crime he had just committed. He had no more time for the man who had served him for so long, the man he had so pitilessly eliminated, at the first sign of disobedience.

No, Fantômas simply said, "What the hell did he do with that chicken? Could he have eaten it, by chance?"

But, then he thought to bend down.

Under the bed, Fantômas saw the bird's body and he picked it up with a satisfied smile.

"I got here just in time!" the bandit concluded. "I certainly haven't wasted my night!"

Fantômas quietly wrapped the bird in a newspaper and slipped it under his arm. He put out the candle, left the room, stepping over Le Bedeau's cadaver, closed the door then went on his way, a black shadow, slipping through the night, which passersby skimmed past without recognizing, and whose name, however, was displayed on the special editions, screamed out by newspaper boys, the name of horror, the name of blood, the name which, once again, had just sent a frightful shiver of terror around the entire world!

CHAPTER VIII
New Horror

"Speech... sandwiches... magazine... music... drumroll... decoration... another speech and another decoration... decidedly, I've got a lot on my shoulders!"

The man who was carrying on like this, talking to himself, was none other than Juve and Juve was expressing his innermost thoughts all the more sincerely since he was talking to himself, and no one was there to laugh at his bad mood, to tease him about the way in which he summed up his most recent accomplishments.

It was just as well that Juve, as he said so himself, believed that he had largely finished with the stupidly feverish existence that he had been living for four days.

Juve, in fact, had just come from taking part in the official procession, accompanying the Tsar of all the Russias, and the Tsarita, who had come to France for the most official of trips.

The policeman had embarked on the imperial yacht, had accompanied it to Dunkirk, had attended the naval review, suffered through an official reception at the City, endured the special train that took the sovereigns to the station at the port of Dauphine. Now, off to the side, he was considering the comings and goings of the official personalities that were responsible for talking the Tsar and the Tsarita in the carriages surrounded by an escort of cavalrymen that would ride to the Palais d'Orsay.

Juve was not a man who enjoyed protocol. Quite the contrary. He had deep disdain for all official ceremonies and that fully explained why, at this moment, swaying between duty and pleasure, Juve was wondering if he would continue to accompany the sovereign or if he would simply sneak out, get lost in the enthusiastic crowd and forget, for a moment, that he had just been given the honor of being included in the immediate entourage of His Majesty, Emperor Nicolas II.

Juve, in fact, had been unable to leave the sovereign since his mysterious adventures in Russia.

After sending the dispatches organized by surveillance, which had produced no results, to the border station, Juve had quite naturally manifested the desire to leave.

Yet, the Tsar wanted to hear nothing about that.

While he still claimed, out of vanity, that he could not trust Juve, he had, in fact, the most absolute confidence in the policeman's intelligence. Under the circumstances, Tsar Nicolas had, to a certain extent, sequestered Juve and ordered him, almost threatened him, to accompany him and the Tsarita on their official trip to Paris.

"Since we're going," said the Tsar," Then you will come with us. And if it is true that Fantômas is in Paris, well then we'll find the famous necklace that the wretch stole from us in Paris and we can get it back on our way."

Juve had to give in, but he did so with poor grace.

And now, precisely when the procession was getting organized in Avenue du Bois, Juve said to himself, "The Tsar made me promise to accompany him to Paris, but no farther than that... So here we are in Paris, inside the fortifications. So, I'm free. I'm going to get out of here and quickly at that!"

Juve was, in fact, walking away, when he saw Mr. Havard in the first row of the stewards.

The Head of the Sûreté was anxious, nervous, worried.

Every time sovereigns visited, moreover, he experienced numerous difficulties. On these occasions, he never relaxed for a second, fearing an attack, a scandal, an unfortunate demonstration, some of those incidents that are impossible to prevent, although people call the police useless when they unfortunately occur.

Juve walked over to Mr. Havard.

"Good day! How are you?"

Mr. Havard jumped and replied, "Ah! Juve! Where did you come from? We had no news whatsoever about you. Did you come back with the Tsar by any chance?"

"Yes."

"You're not joking?"

"Not in the least."

Mr. Havard was dumbfounded.

He knew Juve too well, however, to continue to be surprised about something he considered an adventure. And he would never admit that he was astonished. Good grief! Juve was a man of the strangest and oddest incarnations! He was with the Tsar. Fine! Mr. Havard nodded his head, indicating simply that he had no intention of trying to understand the reason for that fact.

And with that, still just as furious and still unable to back down, Mr. Havard grumbled, "So, you're with the Tsar! Well, you could have just as well have told him to stay at home. France is a Republic and not a country where we cheer on kings and emperors! Those wretches never give us a minute's peace!"

Then Mr. Havard jumped on another idea.

"What about Fantômas?" he asked.

Juve's face turned red.

A dark expression of fury passed over his features.

"Fantômas," stammered Juve. "Well, I haven't caught him yet, but I will! The fight between us drawing closer and closer. Moreover, I've always told you, Mr. Havard, that it will be him or me. It's a fight to the death for us!"

Mr. Havard nodded his head silently and did not reply immediately.

In the past, he had allowed himself to tease Juve, and joke about his misfortunes, his difficult investigations. Now, on the other hand, he grew serious, not joking at all, having finally come to the realization, despite his narrow mind, of the tragic side of battle Juve had been waging for so many years, risking his life each time, to release the world from a man who terrorized it.

Mr. Havard said, "Are you aware of his latest attack? Have you read about his mad attack on the Folies-Françaises?"

"Yes," replied Juve, clenching his fists. "I'm aware of it. The newspapers I read on my way from Dunkirk provided the information. Yet, there are details I'd like to discuss with you."

"At your service," said Mr. Havard.

But the Head of the Sûreté bit back his words immediately.

"Rather, I'm not. We can't discuss that here. Somewhere else. The procession is about to set off and I insist on accompanying it. Would you like to meet me at my office in two hours, Juve?"

"Of course, chief."

"I'll see you then."

The two men went their separate ways and Juve jumped into a carriage, calling out the address for his personal home.

"Rue Tardieu, driver. No. 1. You don't know where that is? Of course! Place Saint-Pierre... You don't know that either? The place where you catch the funicular for Sacré-coeur... Now you see? Fine."

Juve sat back on the cushions, savoring the joy of being alone, of no longer having to take part in the insipid conversation of the upper class trying to be likable, of being able to smoke one of the wonderful French cigarettes which he had missed for such a long time.

"It's going to be so nice to go home. Old Jean will jump out of his skin when he sees me. I can bet on that. As always, he will be occupied waxing the floor in the dining room. What a rare pearl he is! I can arrive at any time and he will always be there, and always in a good mood!"

Juve congratulated himself as he was making these relative suppositions about old Jean's occupations as he entered his apartment.

Juve, in fact, did not have his key with him and had rung the bell at the door to his home. No one answered.

He tried pounding on the door with his fist, but that produced no better results.

"What does this mean?" Juve wondered.

Obviously, Juve had absolutely no idea that Old Jean had been requisitioned by Fandor to care for Hélène. He was so very far from that supposition that he hesitated for a long time before deciding what to do.

"Good grief," Juve said to himself. "What am I to do? Yet I wanted to go home."

Then he burst out laughing and said, "To think that if I were standing in front of any other apartment, I wouldn't hesitate a minute .... I'd just put my shoulder to it and break the door down! Yet, here I am, at my own home and like any brave member of the bourgeoisie, I'm concerned about the vindictive complaints of my excellent landlord!"

Once again, Juve started knocking, ringing, making an incredible din.

Suddenly, he headed back down the stairs.

"I'm such an idiot," he thought. "Jean is a simple man. He wasn't expecting me to come back. I'm willing to bet that he stepped out, that he went to cheer on the Tsar and the Tsarita and their procession."

Pretending to be angry, Juve added, "For example, he won't be carried into paradise. I'll put him out. That would be the 530th time, if I'm not mistaken."

After walking down five floors, Juve called a carriage.

"To the Sûreté!" he ordered.

Thirty minutes later, the policeman found himself in the office of Mr. Havard, who had just raced in, overwhelmed.

"What a filthy job!" Mr. Havard murmured, hanging up his hat and throwing his gloves on the fireplace mantle. "What a filthy job! And the Tsar is demanding his necklace right away... The police prefect sent me a note. His necklace! What necklace? And what's his necklace to me?"

As Mr. Havard was grumbling, Juve couldn't help but smile.

"Oh that," he murmured. "But you don't seem too caught up with the most recent events, Mr. Havard. Didn't Fandor tell you?"

"No," Mr. Havard said, abruptly. "Fandor is with his wife. He has his hands full with her. I barely spoke with him..."

Juve stood up at that moment, smiling.

"Excuse me, but I have a question, Mr. Havard. Do you have the hens?"

As he heard those words, Mr. Havard stared at Juve, eyes round, mouth open, completely bewildered.

"The hens?" he repeated. "What hens are you talking about? What is all this about hens?"

And Mr. Havard, who was not a patient man, pounded on his desk, enraged.

"It's unheard of!" he declared. "It's as if people are always playing charades here... And now Juve, who's just come back from Russia, is talking to me about hens... How am I supposed to understand anything?"

"Everyone is talking about hens in Paris. There's that complaint lodged by Mr. Janvial, the manager of the Jardin d'acclimatation, who says that someone stole hens... in Russia for that matter, at the border train station... I even thought that it might have had something to do with your Fantômas... And, another thing, there's a police report stating that there are hens on Haussmann Boulevard... People can hear them clucking. Nonsense. And, even better, I received a complaint from a woman who lives on rue de Prony, who claims that a certain Manoel Palatello is raising chickens in his apartment! It's enough to drive one mad! And now Juve asks me if I have the hens. What hens? I don't know. White hens, black hens! Out with it man."

Juve stood up suddenly.

"Mr. Havard, he said, in that quiet voice which was ordinary for him. "Everything will be explained in the simplest way possible. The matter of the necklace, and the story about the hens, they're related. Moreover..."

"You're mad, Juve," Mr. Havard interrupted.

"No I'm not. Why?"

"What are you trying to tell me, that the Tsar's necklace and the chickens on Haussmann Boulevard are connected?"

"Obviously," Juve declared. "And it all points back to Fantômas. Fantômas!"

But Mr. Havard felt madness overtaking him. This precise, clear, categorical man, could not accept that he did not immediately understand what someone was saying to him.

"Explain yourself," he said, sounding wounded. "I hate puzzles. Tell me about the chickens... What do they have to do with Fantômas?"

"Mr. Havard..." Juve started to say.

But it was unlikely that Mr. Havard would obtain the explanation he wanted quickly. In fact, just as Juve was about to provide an explanation, the telephone started to ring.

Naturally, the chief of police picked up the handset and shouted "Hello!" into the device.

Mr. Havard's correspondent had barely uttered a few words before the head of the police department suddenly stood up. Holding the telephone to his ear, Mr. Havard grew strangely pale.

"Oh! Good grief! Good grief!" he said.

And suddenly, he dropped the device and collapsed back into his chair.

"Juve! Juve!" he panted. "It's horrible! It's abominable! In full daylight! In the heart of Paris. Fantômas!"

Juve grew nervous in turn.

That morning, Jérôme Fandor woke in a cheerful mood. He had received excellent news about Hélène, who was convalescing normally and who, most certainly, would soon be able to get up with nothing more than a bad memory of the tragic evening at the Folies-Françaises.

And Jérôme Fandor had another reason to be satisfied. In fact, two months earlier, he had written to the management of one of the largest amusement parks which, in keeping with the fashion in America, had grown popular in Paris, to request information about a scenery trick that he was particularly interested in. And, in his mail, Jérôme Fandor discovered a letter from the managers of the

Féeric City, asking him to go and see them that afternoon, about an interesting business matter.

"I don't know what these people want from me," Jérôme Fandor said to himself, "But I'll go and see them. I think all these large amusement parks are stupid, but I do admit they seem to please the common people. Who knows? Perhaps they'll ask me to do something interesting, since I don't presume they want to discuss the information I asked them for, so long ago."

Jérôme Fandor, to be truthful, had not revealed his personal hope. In actual fact, given his prodigious activities, his fertile imagination, he had created a rather entertaining invention and he hoped to be able to sell the secret to the management of Féeric City.

At three o'clock that afternoon, Jérôme Fandor arrived at the large amusement park and, since he was early, he started to stroll through the crowd that filled the circular alleyways.

One by one, Jérôme Fandor visited the dizzying roller coaster, where pretty women enjoyed themselves screaming in terror, the toboggans, where visitors came out covered with bruises, the rotating plates when people ran the risk of sprained ankles, the strange animals that smelled incredibly bad, the swings that creaked in lamentation, namely all of the dangerous attractions that provided the show at Féeric city.

"All those machines are so stupid," Fandor said to himself.

But he continued on his way, laughing at the enthusiasm of the crowd that had paid the admission fee and continued to pay for each attraction, in order to earn the right to be maimed, to vomit or to tear their clothing.

Strolling about like that, Jérôme Fandor suddenly saw the crowd in the large park flow toward the heart of Féeric city. There was some sort of arena there, a large circus tent which they piled into.

"Fine!" Fandor said. "What else have they come up with! A canon that will shatter our eardrums? A powder that will make us sneeze? Or a shower of icy water that will give us pneumonia?"

But, both and idle onlooker and a Parisian, Fandor could well complain about the American nature of the spectacle, he still followed the crowd and took his place in the circus tent.

He immediately realized what was about to happen.

An immense circular net had been installed at the top of the tent and above that net, swung flying trapezes, smooth ropes and rings.

"Perfect!" he said. "A change in program. Now they're going to show us the acrobats!"

And Jérôme Fandor was impressed with the fact that they had taken pains to install the net, in order to avoid accidents.

"This changes everything," he decided. "When the spectators are running the show, they're allowed to kill themselves. But when it's the performers, they put up a net!"

Jérôme Fandor, however, was wrong to grumble. A few minutes later, when the tent was filled with people, a troupe of acrobats made their appearance and climbed up the ropes.

For a few minutes, the performance was marvelous, enthusiastic.

The Féeric City troupe performed miracles. The men were consummate gymnasts. They seemed to push back the limits of the possible, flying through the air, and the vision of the supple bodies swinging from one ring to another, flying from the trapeze to a fixed bar, catching one another by the ankles, sliding dizzyingly along smooth ropes and, like elastic balls, bouncing back onto the highest structures, was incomparable.

The crowd went wild, clapping their hands, shrieking in delight.

Carried away, even Fandor, stood up.

"Bravo! Bravo!" he shouted.

But, suddenly, he cried out, he cried out in horror, "Oh God! Oh God!"

Then he cried out again, "Be careful. Every man for himself! Every man for himself!"

What had Fandor seen?

What led him to cry out in panic?

The journalist had just seen a frightening vision!

Suddenly, at the back of the tent, an acrobat had arrived. He was dressed, or rather draped, in an enormous cape, with the hood pulled down over his face, hiding him completely. No doubt, this acrobat was the star of the troupe, since a sensational entrance had been reserved for him.

He was standing, on a plank, which four men carried on their shoulders, much like an old-fashioned warrior, being honored.

The man, as motionless as a statue, soon reached a hole in the net that floated over the crowd, through the acrobats climbed up to the wooden platform.

A rope, ending in a loop, had been lowered. He placed one foot through it and slowly the rope rose to the rafters.

Jérôme Fandor had, quite naturally, followed the arrival of this acrobat, along with the other spectators. He expected some feat even more surprising that those that had already been presented, some wonder that surpassed the marvels already performed.

Jérôme Fandor was not, however, expecting what he was about to see.

Once he reached the topic of the wooden structure, the man had quietly taken up his position on a sort of small platform, remaining motionless for a moment. Then, just as all eyes focused on him, just as he was the center of everyone's attention, he suddenly slipped one arm out of the sleeves of the robe, brought a silver whistle to his lips and blew it loudly.

Immediately, the other acrobats stopped what they were doing. The spectators, panting, froze in admiring anxiety. The minutes seemed endless. The man did not move.

Jérôme Fandor felt distinctly uncomfortable. He shrieked.

The man had, in fact, removed his robe and was immediately recognizable.

He was tall and slim, with a beautiful silhouette. But, unfortunately, that silhouette was so very tragic. Simply seeing it made the most intrepid, the most courageous of men shiver...

The man was dressed entirely in black. He wore a black, figure-hugging outfit that covered him from head to foot. His hands were hidden in black gloves; his face was covered by a black mask and his hair by a black hood.

Horrific silhouette, frightening silhouette, cursed silhouette!

After glancing at the man for no more than a second, Jérôme Fandor screamed, "Every man for himself!"

Of course he recognized that silhouette. Of course, he could identify it! There was no doubt at all about the man dressed fantastically in black, who crossed his arms scornfully, starting down at the crowd that pressed forward below his feet, separated from him by the large net suspended over the spectators.

"Fantômas! It's Fantômas!"

With all might, Jérôme Fandor screamed the horrible name, the horrific name, the name of blood, the name of death...

"Fantômas! Fantômas!"

It was the Criminal Mastermind, the Frightful Torturer, the Master of Fear who stood above the crows, smiling, amused.

But what was he going to do? What was his infernal plan? What was his audacious project?

"Every man for himself! Fantômas! It's Fantômas!"

Jérôme Fandor had barely uttered those tragic words, which resounded like a death knell, when terror swept over the entire audience.

Faces turned pale. Mouths grimaced. Inhuman, inarticulate cries and groans rose.

The spectators had all stood up. They shoved and pushed in the narrow aisles that separated the seats. They wanted to escape...

Too late!

The Criminal Genius once again blew into his silver whistle, releasing a strident sound.

And Jérôme Fandor, who maintained his composure despite his rage, realized what the terrible monster's sinister plans were.

In a second, the acrobats, who were obviously his accomplices, had performed an abominable feat. They had released the net that hung above the room, allowing it to fall to the ground. They quickly attached it to hooks that had been prepared in advance and then they picked up revolvers, and waited, motionless.

And, under the net, caught in a trap, caught as if in a mouse trap, the spectators, who had stumbled over one another, had tipped over, like a horrible swarming mass of insects, were fighting, tearing at one another, screaming, crying out for help, in the throes of fear.

What was happening?

None of those who have lived through those terrible minutes, possibly not even Fandor, could ever say exactly what happened.

In the human swarm that filled the gigantic net held by Fantômas, the wretch's accomplices fished the prisoners out, one by one.

They were half gagged, three-quarters strangled, then searched and cast aside, stunned, a bit farther off. It was a gigantic roundup. Valuable jewelry, wallets, purses were mercilessly stolen.

No one was able to resist.

And, as the bandits were stripping their victims of their valuables, in the net, where the number of prisoners gradually decreased, nameless chaos continued to reign, as countless human bodies struggled, groaning in fear.

Jérôme Fandor had perhaps been one of the first to be seen by Fantômas' accomplices.

That saved him.

They did not recognize him and searched him as they did the others and then knocked him out with a wicked blow to the head.

When Jérôme Fandor came to, the arena was deserted. Bodies were strewn about him, lying on the ground, motionless. Fantômas and his men had disappeared. No doubt the police were on their way.

Jérôme Fandor, as energetic as usual, got up. He walked ahead, stumbling, with a great deal of pain, yet he walked straight ahead.

"Ah! Fantômas! Fantômas!" he shrieked, "we'll never take our revenge on you! Your boundless audacity leads you into the wildest undertakings!"

And the unfortunate man went on his way, still dizzy, filled with obsessive, unhealthy thoughts of setting out on the bandit's trail, and starting the battle all over again.

When Juve and Mr. Havard, who had been notified by telephone, arrived at Féeric City, with its frightened crowd, they did not find Fandor there.

Like a robot, Fandor kept walking straight ahead, feverish, delirious…

CHAPTER IX
Official Gala

Head bowed low, Juve returned home.

It was 11 o'clock at night and the policeman, had not had a moment's rest since the morning. Yet, it was not fatigue that made him walk that way, head lowered, eyes vacant, hands clasped behind his back, in a gloomy attitude of despair and weariness.

If Juve was frightfully sad, if, all in all, he was prey to a sort of concentrated fury, it was because he had just left Mr. Havard, he had just come from Féeric City, where Juve and Mr. Havard had helped the pitiful victims of the dreadful Fantômas.

Juve was very impressed, even disturbed by the audacity that the Criminal Mastermind had once again demonstrated.

It was true! Fantômas implemented sinister plans which he had stressed in the letter addressed to the chief of police, which Mr. Havard related precisely to Juve!

It was real! The torturer seemed once again to have dedicated himself to cursing the entire city and Paris was supposed to tremble once again under the perpetual threat of his unimaginable, incomprehensible feats, that surpassed the limits of reasonable minds.

Furious, Juve walked up the small Rue de Steinkerque on his way to Rue Tardieu, muttering under his breath, clenching his fists and uttering heavy threats, resounding curses, in a low voice, tinged with madness.

"It was abominable," he grumbled. "In broad daylight, in the heart of Paris, trapping over 500 people in a net, stripping them of their belongings without encountering any resistance, then disappearing, fleeing, hiding in the frightened crowd, mocking the police. That's what Fantômas has just done!"

And the good Juve was so angry that, despite his usual composure, he continued to swear.

"My God! My God!"

Then, suddenly he stopped short, giving a formidable kick to the cobblestone, drumming on it with his foot.

"This has to stop. We can't let this kind of thing keep happening. The Tsar does not have his necklace, the spectators at the Folies-Françaises have been threatened with assassination, the visitors to Féeric City have been attacked. No, no, it can't continue."

Juve started walking again. Unfortunately, despite his anger, despite all his rage, Juve was too much in control of his nerves to be able to forget, even for an instant, the rules of logic he held so dear.

He said that it could not continue... How childish! Had it not been going on for 20 years now? Didn't Fantômas design and implement his abominable projects every single minute? Had he not proclaimed himself the Master of All and Everything? Could anyone deny that the entire universe was under his hand, under his domination?

Juve closed his eyes, as if dazzled.

A hallucinating vision danced beneath his closed eyelids.

Like some gigantic, fantastic allegory, he seemed to see, sitting astride an infernal steed, the Master of Fear, draped in his black tights, hands in black gloves, face covered by a black mask, galloping around the world while everyone fled before him, shrieking in fright, overwhelmed with terror.

I can't stop him!" Juve moaned, in a voice that was almost a lament.

That hour when the policeman once again touched the depths of despair was painful.

For years, he had dedicated his life to this sublime undertaking.

For years, he had set aside his life to fulfill his mission. He had spent years patiently, tenaciously, using his skills as a policeman to oppose the Mad Torturer.

Juve had public approval on his side; he had the law to support him. And that still was not enough to defeat the man who embodied evil, who never retreated, who had no conscience, no heart, no pity and no mercy.

"Ah! The wretch!" grumbled Juve. "How many cadavers will he sow in his wake and why does he not fear drowning in all of the blood he has spilled, which falls behind him like red rain, on his unfortunate victims?"

Juve was allowing himself to be carried away by the dream, to be overwhelmed with the despair that rose from this moment of powerless.

That was just cowardice!

Who is entitled to dream when action is calling? Who can dream when it is time to fight?

"That's enough of that," Juve swore. "This is no time for daydreaming. Fantômas has acted; he must be punished."

Juve was overwhelmed, exhausted. For months, he had been living a mad existence, without stopping for a second, without a moment's respite, without an instant of peace.

It didn't matter that he still wanted to fight, he wanted it now!

The policeman shrugged with that powerful, formidable movement of his shoulders that all his close friends knew.

It was as if he were shaking off the burden of worries that swamped him. It was if he were shaking off his fears.

"Let's get down to work," he murmured.

And he picked up his pace.

Juve was determined. He knew what he wanted to do. He had a plan.

"I'll go home," he said to himself. "I'll go to bed. I need a good night's sleep. Tomorrow, at four in the morning, Jean will wake me up. Then, I'll study the entire file Havard gave me and I will start my investigation... It's up to the two of us, Fantômas. If you want to frighten Paris, you'll find me standing in front of the city. You enjoy hitting France at its heart; I enjoy defending my country."

When he arrived at the door to his home, Juve automatically stopped to buy the evening editions of the newspapers from a paper boy who yelled as he ran.

"This will be useful," Juve thought. "I know from Fandor that journalists are often well-informed. Maybe I'll find something in these papers, some interesting details about the drama at Féeric City."

Juve walked quickly pasted the concierge's booth. He didn't want anyone to know he was in Paris.

Of course, he had no intention of hiding but, in any case, he did not want people to report on his return too soon. It would have served no purpose and could even hamper him. First of all, he intended to search for the necklace he had claimed he would return to the Tsarita; being incognito could be of use and he intended to remain that way as long as possible.

As he walked up the stairs, Juve said, "For example, I hope that, along with my mail, Jean will hand me a letter or a telegram from Fandor. My young couple must be growing worried about what has happened to me... My stupid arrest in St. Petersburg prevented me from joining Hélène and Fandor, but they must have suspected that I was caught up in an adventure and they should have written to me here."

And at that very moment, Juve thought, "Will I let them know I've arrived? Will I summon Fandor?"

Visibly, the policeman hesitated. He had just realized that Fandor might not be of great assistance to him for the investigations he was about to conduct. Moreover, he hesitated to take the young man away from the pleasant hours he must be spending in Hélène's company.

"Good grief, no!" Juve decided, as he reached the level on which his apartment was located. "I won't let Fandor known. The poor boy definitely deserves a peaceful honeymoon. I'll find a way to reassure him about my situation, but I'll tell him that I do not need his help."

And smiling, Juve added, "Let's leave the lovers together, let's leave Hélène with Fandor!"

Juve would, however, have come to a completely different conclusion if he had known about all of the events that had taken place before his arrival, if he had suspected that Hélène had been injured in the attack on the Folies-Françaises, and that Fandor had been involved, that very same day, in the goings on at Féeric City.

Yet, since, he knew nothing of all this, Fandor rang the doorbell of his apartment.

"Jean must certainly be back!" he supposed.

But this was not the policeman's lucky day.

Jean, who was still acting as a nursemaid for Hélène was, naturally, not in the apartment on the Rue Tardieu. Juve could ring and ring, but no one would answer.

The policeman frowned.

"Well," he thought. "This is all a little bit too much. I could accept, at the most, that Jean went to cheer on the Tsar and the Tsarita this afternoon but, my word, I can't believe that he's spending the night out. What can his absence mean?"

Juve stood, for a moment, stunned, in front of the door to his apartment, which remained obstinately closed.

"Now this is stranger," he said. "Even worrisome. I need to look into this!"

And, naturally, Juve decided, "Well, too bad for the owner. I hope I don't cause too much damage."

Juve, like all policeman, could have made an excellent burglar. He was most thoroughly familiar with the means for knocking down a door without making any noise. He had practiced his skill in the past when, after discovering his passion for police work, he was preparing, as a young man, to enter the force.

"One... two... three..."

He placed his shoulder against one side of the door, bent his knees, shoved solidly and, without a sound, lifted the door that was keeping him out, off its hinges.

Juve walked into his antechamber without the slightest difficulty. Without the slightest difficulty and as a result of his prodigious skill, he put the door back on its hinges.

"There!" he declared, in a satisfied tone, "No one will ever suspect that I've entered. Parisian homes are definitely not well built. I will have to get a better locking system."

At that moment, Juve suddenly stopped talking.

It was madness, but a terrible thought had crossed his mind.

Jean had not answered... Jean did not seem to be in the apartment, when he should have been there... Did that mean something? Was it possible that his dedicated servant had been involved in some sort of accident, even that Fantômas, out of cruelty, out his love for evil, had made the poor servant pay for what he felt toward Juve?

At that very moment, the policeman drew on all his resources.

"Jean! Jean! Are you there?"

No one answered, of course.

Nervous, worried despite everything, Juve raced through his apartment.

At every open door, at every room he entered, he feared that he would discover something horrible... his murdered servant!

But, his fear was caused by his fatigue, the nervousness of the moment. Definitely nothing had happened in this peaceful apartment. Juve found everything in order, everything as usual.

"I'm certainly going mad," the excellent policeman concluded, as he took off his hat and coat. "Let's go look at the mail!"

Juve quickly went through the large stack of letters waiting for him and which Jean, naturally, had not forwarded, since Juve had not been able to give him an address in Russia.

"Nothing," the policeman declared soon, wearily pushing aside the letters he had examined. "Nothing of interest. And, what's more important, nothing from Fandor. What could have happened to Fandor on the one hand and Jean on the other?"

This little mystery intrigued Juve, despite himself.

Yet, he could not be all that worried since, it was too obvious that if a catastrophe had occurred, if something had happened to Fandor, to Hélène, even to old Jean, the newspapers would have mentioned it and that was not the case.

"I'll leave the serious business for tomorrow," Juve decided. "At my age, I need to take care of myself at all costs. I'm dead tired, so I'll go to bed."

Juve, in fact, went to bed. He had already prepared his blankets when he suddenly thought about the newspapers he had purchased earlier.

"In fact," he thought. "I'll still take a look at them. They might just contain an interesting piece of news..."

He unfolded one of the papers, quickly read through the report on the sinister adventure at Féeric City and then, despite himself, starting to glance through the columns dedicated to the festivities marking the arrival of the Tsar.

"Well, today there will be a gala at the Opera," thought Juve. "The government came up with the great idea of holding it this very evening! The royal couple must be as tired as I am. In any case, they'll enjoy listening to the music!"

Juve laughed at his own irony when, suddenly he jumped and looked up with the expression of someone trying to remember something.

"But what if I'm wrong? Would I perhaps, fail my word of honor? I swore to the Tsar that I would bring back the necklace Fantômas stole, on the day the Opera gala would be held..."

Juve meditated for a moment.

"Bah!" he said. "Too bad! I'm not going to get in a tizzy about that. Of course, I won't be respecting my word, but I'll do it tomorrow. Moreover, if I haven't returned the necklace it's all the fault of Nicolas II who delayed me in Russia. I figured that I would find the famous missing diamonds rather quickly. I do have an idea..."

As he said those words, Juve smiled with a sarcastic expression. Once again he opened the newspaper in front of him and started to read.

Suddenly, Juve jumped.

"That, for example…" he started to say.

And, no longer thinking about going to bed, the policeman started pacing back and forth in his room.

"What does that mean?" he muttered. "Who could have given that information to the newspapers? Someone is playing a bad trick on me. Someone is playing a bad trick on the Tsar and the Tsarita…"

Juve seemed nervous and preoccupied. The blood was pounding in his head as he crumpled the newspaper in fury, looking most upset.

"That," he added, "complicates my personal situation… If I only knew who wrote that piece…"

And, at that moment, Juve suddenly stopped pacing. He turned pale, chewed on his lips, then spoke out loud, saying, "Could it be Fantômas? If that miserable wretch released that piece of news just to mock me…"

Juve went to pick up a second newspaper, one he had not yet unfolded. He glanced quickly through the columns dedicated to the visit of the Russian royals.

Then, shivering, he said, "Here's the same news item. This is definitely a challenge. It's so stupid in the end…"

And he read a brief news item that all of the evening newspapers had published:

This evening, in keeping with the final program of the festivities, the Tsar and the Tsarita will go to the gala organized at the Opera.

There's no question that the people of Paris will give a triumphant welcome to the two sympathetic sovereigns and their allies. Paris will be touched to see that the Tsarita will put on the famous necklace to attend the gala, the very necklace that demonstrates the full glory of her jewelry case and has been involved in such amazing adventures.

The necklace, in fact, had been stolen, according to the police, by the formidable Fantômas, and Juve, the famous Juve had managed to return it to its legitimate owner.

By wearing the necklace, the Tsarita will honor Paris and provide amiable and spiritual evidence of her appreciation for the famous policeman, Juve.

"Those imbeciles," fumed Fandor's friend.

And he crumpled the second newspaper, just as he had crumpled the first.

Juve paced back and forth. Obviously, he was quite upset by the news item that presented a false situation.

Suddenly, he took out his watch.

"What time is it?" the policeman asked. "A quarter after ten… Damn! It's too late to try anything at all. The performance must certainly have started."

Juve hesitated for a moment, then decided, "Bah! Too bad. Let's be brave! We have to go there. We have to see, we have to know…"

And as he got dressed, Juve sighed, saying, "No rest for me tonight!"

At a quarter to nine, the large personal maid responsible for dressing the Tsarita took a few steps back, clasping her hands in admiration, enthusiastically assessing the ceremonial dress donned by the Empress of Russia.

"Do I look all right?" the wife of Nicolas II quietly asked, getting dressed more to honor Paris than out any sense of elegance. "Will I deserve the compliments that the press will make tomorrow?"

The maid did not hesitate, "Your Majesty is divinely beautiful. Your Majesty's attire is ravishing."

"And my hair?"

"Your hair is perfect, your Majesty. All of the Parisian ladies will be jealous."

No woman could remain insensitive to such praise. Although she was not the simplest of women, the most modest of queens, the Tsarita still shivered when listening to her maid.

"Well," she said. "In any case, I'm ready. His Majesty is as well, I believe?"

The maid bowed, saying, "His Majesty asked me to say that he is ready for her Majesty the Empress."

"In that case, I'll join him.'

As quietly as possible, the Empress Alexandra prepared to walk across the large room in which she had just finished dressing to join Nicolas II who was, no doubt, waiting for in a neighboring dressing room, smoking one of his eternal cigarettes.

And the people of Paris would have been most surprised to witness the simplicity of the imperial couple who looked like any ordinary middleclass couple on their way to the theatre.

The Tsarita had dressed with the assistance of a single maid, she was late, as all women are, and the Tsar was muttering while smoking his cigarette, something all men who take their wives to the theatre do!

Yet, as the Tsarita was about the leave the room, the maid said, "Your Majesty is not putting any jewelry on?"

"No," answered the Tsarita. "The only jewelry I want to wear is the famous diamond necklace."

"Juve didn't return it to you?" the maid asked, curious.

The Empress did not answer and merely nodded her head.

A few seconds later, however, the imperial couple climbed into a carriage.

According to the program for the evening, the Tsarita and the Tsar were to watch the gala performance from a booth where there would be alone. The President of the Republic, in fact, would only turn up to greet the imperial couple near the end of the second act, before the ballet. But that did not mean, of course, that the Russian sovereigns would not be greeted with the greatest pump. The carriages that carried them along boulevards black with people, were gala carriages.

A cavalry squadron surrounded the, and people called out "Long live the Tsar" all along the route.

In the Opera theatre, an ovation was planned. People talked about the marvels of the final program, and the notes of the Havas, the telephone calls from the Prefecture to the sovereigns' secretary, announcing that the hall would be admirably beautiful, that all of Paris would be on hand, and that they would be decked out in all their finery for the imperial couple, wearing fabulous diamonds and all of the finery that could be found in Paris.

"What a superb festivity," said the Tsarita, as she took her place in the official carriage next to Tsar Nicola, who sat tall on his cushion in order to look as tall as the Tsarita.

Yet, Nicolas II shook his head, looking ill-tempered.

"Is your Majesty worried?" asked the Tsarita, concerned as always by the Tsar's perpetual sadness.

The Tsar replied in a dry tone, "A bit."

"About what, sire?"

The Tsar turned to look at he and said, "You should know, madam!"

And, as the Tsarita looked at him, astonished, Nicolas II explained, lowering his voice, so that none of the officials who were naturally seated in the front seats and the impeccable valets standing on the springs could hear.

"Madam, you should understand that I am concerned. All of the newspapers have been saying that you will be wearing your necklace... Yet we do not have that necklace..."

"But we will have it," the Tsarita replied in a concerned tone of voice.

"Your Majesty merely supposes that we will, she can't be certain!"

The Tsarita replied in a surprised tone that she took no pains to hide, "I don't understand what your Majesty is saying. Earlier, your Majesty had one of his chamberlains tell me not to wear anything other than the necklace. I concluded that the necklace had been found, that Juve had brought it back, just as he had promised to do. Is that not so?"

"It is not so at all," grumbled the Tsar.

And in a gloomy voice, the ruler of all the Russias went on to explain, "This evening, all of the newspapers have published an item announcing that you will wear this necklace. I was most surprised. I immediately summoned Mr. Havard, the head of the French police, and he said that the information could only have come from Juve and that, as a result, Juve had to have the necklace. That's all I know!"

The Tsar fell silent for a moment, then added, "It is possible that Juve did not have the time to come to the Palais d'Orsay before you left and went directly to the opera instead. That's where he will give us the necklace that he has taken back from that cursed Fantômas. That's all I can tell you."

A quarter of an hour later, the Tsar and the Tsarita glanced at one another, concerned. The imperials were still in the antechamber and neither had taken a seat on the ceremonial chairs prepared for them.

What was going on?

The problem was that the Tsarita still did not have her necklace.

Juve who was not the author of the information that had been published in the newspapers, had not brought it. Moreover, it was impossible for the Tsarita to break protocol by not wearing any jewelry. What could be done under the circumstances?

The Tsar, who was still convinced that the information had come from Juve, wanted to hear nothing about a rather easy compromise, namely the fact that the empress could put on a few bits of jewelry intended to deceive the public.

"Let's wait," said the Tsar. "There's no reason we have to be in the opera box before the second act and, since Juve has announced that you will be wearing the necklace, madam, that is what you shall do!"

Now, the Tsar and Tsarita had been waiting for about ten minutes, quite put out by the incident, and already the officials on hand were starting to grow concerned when something unexpected, something mad, something fantastic, something terrifying occurred.

Suddenly, while the chorus was quietly accompanying a divine melody, a spectator in the audience stood up. This spectator, as if overcome with madness, jostled all of his neighbors, throwing himself forwards, gesticulating. At the same time as he was fleeing, the man shouted, "Fire! Fire!"

And the most frightening panic washed over the crowded theatre. Everyone stood up at the same time and soon a thousand voices were shouting, "Fire! Fire!"

And then a voice, an abominable voice cried out, "Every man for himself! Every man for himself!"

Chaos reigned.

In vain, in a precipitous movement, the stage manager moved to the controls of the curtain, which slowly started to drop.

In vain, the spectators called out, "Stay calm! Stay calm! There is no fire!"

It was impossible to calm the fear that had overwhelmed everyone.

There was no fire. No flames could be seen. And yet, people shoved, crushed through the doors, while, in the distance, gunshots rang out as the frenzied spectators shot their pocket revolvers randomly.

Paris would only learn the truth the next morning.

It was terrible.

The frenzied panic at the Opera was just another consequence of the formidable cruelty of the Criminal Mastermind, the King of Fear, Fantômas.

Most certainly, it was one of Fantômas' accomplices who had shouted "Fire! Fire" triggering the frenzied panic.

Proof of this came from the fact that, during the panic, when people were trampling one another in the aisles, men, miserable wretches, posted here and there, had taken advantage of the general chaos to relieve women of their jewelry, tear of diamond tiaras, cut the strings of pearl necklaces.

And Fantômas had been seen.

He had been seen, with a dagger in his hand, as he climbed up to the royal box where, overwhelmed with fear, the Tsar and the Tsarita were wondering if they should flee, throw themselves into the crowd, or wait for help that might not come.

Fantômas had been seen!

Witnesses swore they had seen him!

But, they also said that, at that moment, a man had raced toward him, a man had chased him and then disappeared, a man the witnesses swore was none other than Juve.

The panic lasted into the night. Two hours after it had started, the Tsar and Tsarita, were taken out of their royal box, where they had been waiting in terror.

CHAPTER X
Incognito

Fear does not reason, and cannot be calmed or ordered by sheer willpower. That is an indisputable fact and Nicolas II, the Tsar of all the Russias, could perhaps, more than anyone else, support that theory by providing evidence.

Nicolas II was not brave. In Russia, he constantly feared the attacks of the nihilists, he was constantly in fear, he constantly took numerous precautions to avoid death, which was both threatening and imminent.

The Tsar did not dare walk under the large lights at Tsarskoye Selo, afraid that they would fall on his head. He never stood in front of a window, fearing that someone would shoot at him through it. When he wanted to sit down in a chair, he would ask all those around him to sit down in it first, to make certain that no bomb was hidden in that piece of furniture. His precautions extended to his police force. He paid a multitude of secret agents to spy on one another and prepare individual reports on the least significant events, on the small adventures of ordinary life.

Yet, this frightened sovereign, this unfortunate wretch who lived the life of the damned, in constant fear of an assassin's blade, a nihilist's bomb, this Russian who would never dare walk 50 yards alone in the street in Russia, without mobilizing an entire escort, a regime of soldiers, this man who, since he had been in France, breathing freely, suddenly, and for no good reason, found himself freed from all his fears.

Since setting foot on French soil, since detraining in Dunkerque, the Tsar had, in fact, become quite a different man.

What usually terrified the unfortunate sovereign was, in fact, the possibility of revenge on the part of the nihilists. Yet, with childish reasoning, the Tsar told himself that the nihilists were Russian subjects and that, as a result, once he was in France, there was nothing to fear from them.

Perhaps Nicolas II would have felt much less reassured if he had known that the police were terribly concerned about the dangers he could encounter during his official visit. Of course, as a precautionary measure, all of the Polish refugees had been arrested and placed under police supervision. Of course, the august visitor was under the constant supervision of a large number of officers. Yet that did not keep Mr. Havard from counting the hours until the blessed moment when Nicolas II would go back to his home, removing a terrible burden from the man's shoulders.

The events seemed to support the nervous pessimism of the unhappy Mr. Havard.

The panic that had overtaken the Opera had quite naturally caused an enormous amount of emotion. It was a total miracle that it had not had any unfortunate consequences for the imperial couple, it was a true wonder that neither the Tsar nor the Tsarita, panicked by the threat of the hypothetical fire, had rushed into the crowd where, without a doubt, no one would have respected their august personalities and where, as a result, they would have been at the mercy of the common fear, which had resulted in a true disaster.

The tragic night of the official gala was destined, in fact, to remain in the frightened mind of Paris for all time.

The audacity of the criminal genius had caused an abominable catastrophe. People had literally crushed one another in the aisles of the Grand Opera. The panic had degenerated into a frightening crush, causing death and injury. Women had been stomped on, revolvers had been fired and, when the police finally managed to enter the facility, more than 40 bodies were found, horribly mutilated, their injuries, providing evidence of abominable suffering and nightmarish agonies.

Yet, the Tsar and the Tsarita retained no bad memories of that evening. Perhaps the sovereigns did not realize what exactly the savage scene they had witnessed from afar meant.

They were taken out of the opera house, not through the common entrances, but through the corridors used by management. The Tsar had no idea about the scope of the catastrophe. And, since no one mentioned it to him and since he only saw the smiling faces of obliging courtiers, or completely serene officials, the Tsar had no idea that both he and his august spouse had managed to escape from a truly horrible death.

Moreover, the Tsar had other concerns.

While the catastrophe at the opera house seemed unimportant to him, he was truly distraught and even furious at the thought that the fabulous diamond necklace stolen by Fantômas had not been found.

And the Tsar had still had no news of Juve!

That enraged him, drove him into a frenzy of fury particularly since, as the sovereign of all the Russias, Nicolas II was not used to being thwarted, even in insignificant matters.

And for that reason, while people at the Prefecture were frightened, while all of Paris shivered when reading the details of the abominable catastrophe at the opera house in the newspapers the next morning, when the Tsar woke up at the Palais d'Orsay, he simply asked, "Well, why hasn't Juve brought back the necklace since he had sent a note to the newspapers that the Tsarita would be wearing it last evening?"

Naturally, the Tsar could not find any answer to his question since there was no answer and since, in actual fact, it had not been Juve but Fantômas who had provided the information to the newspapers.

Nevertheless, Nicolas II managed to form an opinion that was quite likely.

He thought, "It is very possible, that Juve intended to bring it to us at the Opera but it is possible that he arrived just as people started shouting about the fire and that the panic caused by those cries prevented him from joining us in our box."

Nicolas II, who was still in bed, thought about this for a few moments, yawning, and then suddenly sat up in bed, filled with joy.

"Well, too bad. I'll take the chance," he murmured.

And he burst out into laughter and added, "It's my turn to plot!"

Assuredly, a joyous thought had just crossed the imperial sovereign's mind. He was smiling, in fact. He seemed most amused, perhaps even forgetting the lost necklace which had caused him such concern.

The Tsar reached out his hand and rang the bell.

Almost immediately, the door to his bedchamber opened and his personal valet rushed in and bent over double in an endless bow.

"Bonjour, Provik," Nicolas II said, in a familiar tone. "What is the weather like this morning?"

"May it please your sire, the weather is infinitely fine."

"Cold? Warm?"

"May it please your Majesty, the weather is warm, warm French weather!"

The Tsar rubbed his hands like a man who once again seems particularly pleased.

"So much the better!" he murmured. Yet, a shadow seemed to pass over his face.

"Provik, come here. Listen to me."

"Your Majesty, I'm all ears."

"Swear to me that you will be discreet."

"Your Majesty knows that he can trust me."

"Provik, you will bring me my blue suit and my bowler hat. You will also bring me my cane with the silver handle and my gray gloves. Understand?"

Provik, the valet, listed to his orders with as much emotion as if he were being sentenced to death. He clasped his hands, his lips quivered, and he murmured in a low voice, "May the Holy Images bless you! May the Lord and the Madonna come to your aid…"

Then, shuddering, he took a chance and asked, "Your Majesty has made a decision?"

"Yes."

"Nothing can make your Majesty change his mind?"

"Absolutely nothing, replied the Tsar.

"Does your Majesty know that he is taking a great risk?"

The Tsar jumped out of bed.

"Provik, my old friend Provik," he said. "You are part of the plot. So, you have nothing to say. If I'm taking a risk, then I'll take a risk. Besides, I believe that you're exaggerating. Danger here in France? Did the defunct king of Belgium, did my excellent relative Edward VII…"?

"That's not the same thing," the servant interrupted.

But Nicolas II merely shrugged and asked, "Why not?"

"Because," said Provik, who was obviously far less impressed by the Tsar than a prime minister would be, given the adage that 'no one is a great man to his valet'. "Because, sire, the Belgian king and Edward VII as well, were almost Parisians."

The servant seemed to be reproaching Nicolas II, who suddenly burst out laughing.

"And you do not consider me worthy of becoming a Parisian? Good grief, you've offended me. You should go to the mines. Don't worry, I'll show you mercy. But hurry up!"

Provik must have run out of arguments because he stopped hesitating. He went to get the clothes the Tsar had specified and took charge of dressing his master, an operation that took a fair amount of time, since Nicolas II believed in the effectiveness of medicine, and followed an entire series of treatments that complicated his life enormously.

Provik was part of the plot…

But what plot was this?

The Tsar seemed to grow more and more joyous and the servant more and more concerned, his face darkening with each second.

After a moment, Provik asked, "Does his Majesty not want to change his mind?"

"Never."

"Will his Majesty permit me to accompany him?"

"I forbid it, Provik. I absolutely forbid it!"

The Tsar had just donned his wig and a bowler hat and laughed as he looked at himself in the mirror, since he was obviously not used to wearing a hat and found his attire amusing.

Yet, a few moments later, after Nicolas II had studied himself sufficiently in the large mirror in his dressing room, the imperial personality turned to his personal valet and gave him a specific order, saying, "You will go to the door of my bed chamber. You will open it and you will look down the corridor. There must be no one there!"

"Yes, your Majesty."

As Provik set out to follow his instructions, the Tsar called him back.

"Wait! You're too hasty. It's not just that there must be no one in the corridor, you must also make sure there are no curious onlookers in the service stairway, the stairway you mentioned to me before."

"Yes, your Majesty."

"Wait another moment, Provik. Once you have made sure the premises are deserted, you will rush back here, I will wait near the door. When you give the sign, I'll rush out. God help me! But, I'll run as fast as I can. I expect to get outside without any unfortunate encounters."

This was all rather mysterious and the instructions seemed most unusual. A stranger no doubt would not have understood them, but Provik seemed to understand their hidden meaning.

The servant disappeared for a few moments, then returned.

"The way is clear," murmured Provik.

"Fine," said the Tsar.

And the sovereign ran, he ran on his tiptoes, to avoid making the slightest noise, leaving the room where he had been waiting.

What was the reason for all this? Anyone who would have seen Nicolas II leaving the Palais d'Orsay by way of a hidden staircase, who would have noticed him, a few moments later, leaving the sumptuous building through a low door, hailing a carriage, instructing the driver to take him to the Place de la Concorde, then jumping out of the vehicle at the foot of the Obélisque would have been most surprised.

That person would have sworn that the Tsar was quite simply making his escape. The Tsar would have been taken for an escaping prisoner.

For a long time, in fact, Nicolas had been considering going on an adventure. The most autocratic of monarchs, the most luxurious of potentates, the most ardently defended of princes had experienced a childish desire to walk about on his own, for once, without an escort, without guards, without agents, to stroll about the streets and look at the shops!

The shops. They were a dream come true.

Nicolas II wanted to take the time to contemplate everything at his leisure, to look at the displays, to stroll through the stands. He dreamed of being jostled by the crowd, insulted by some passerby. He dreamed, above all, of setting aside the grandeur of his role for a few moments, of being no more than a common onlooker, unknown, unsuspected, who would be free to spend five minutes in a café, to buy a newspaper for a penny, and to walk into a tobacconist's shop!

Nicolas II desired all of these fantasies, with the same ardor that the little French imperial prince had, a few months before the frightful drama of 1870, asked his tutor, as a reward, to allow him to tour the Tuileries, walking in a creek, getting his feet wet like all children in Paris.

Since Nicolas II knew full well that it would be impossible to fulfill his fantasy in Russia, he had decided to make the attempt in Paris. And, for this reason, he had plotted with his valet, coming up with a plan that would enable him to deceive both the people who surrounded him and avoid the surveillance of the French police, who were responsible for his safety.

Nicolas II had believed that it would be a most difficult undertaking. Yet, quite the contrary, he had encountered no difficulty and was now laughing out loud as he thought of the agitation of his senior advisors when he told them about his escapade.

Nicolas II paid his driver royally and walked over to the Place de la Concorde and from there to the boulevards.

He walked, cane under his arm, one hand in a pocket, looking every which way, turning back to make sure he was not followed, with the joyful satisfaction of a child on his first outing alone.

"How amusing... how very amusing," he thought.

And he decided to take part in all of the activities he had dreamed of in a few minutes.

The Tsar walked into a tobacconist's shop. He drank a glass of beer at the corner of Rue Scribe, he purchased a newspaper near the opera house and, joy of joys, was accosted by a woman near Rue Taitbout!

"Come with my, my handsome blond," the passing woman murmured.

The Tsar, naturally, could not accept the invitation, but his chest did swell with pride. The dubious flattery and adulation of arch-duchesses looking for pensions had never flattered him to such an extent.

Yet. as the Tsar was reaching Rue Montmartre, a man approached him, with a familiar manner. He held a cigarette in his hand and tipped his hat slightly.

"Do you have a light?"

"Yes," said the Tsar, offering the man his cigarette.

The stranger lit his own cigarette without hurrying.

"Thank you."

But, after starting to head off, he turned back.

"In fact, sir," he said. "You don't look like you're from Paris. Would you perhaps need a guide? I'm out of work. For five or six francs, I'll show you some remarkable sights!"

The Tsar smiled at that. The man to whom he had just given a light, the man who was proposing to serve as a guide, was poorly yet cleanly dressed. He was not a laborer, but rather some kind of office employee, wretched and hungry, a child of Paris, obviously, since he had working-class accent, the deep, deep joking tones of those who came from Pantruche.

Yet the Tsar hesitated visibly.

For a few moments, in fact, the imperial personality felt some concern. He had walked straight ahead, without noting the route he had taken and now he did not quite know how to make his way back to the Quai d'Orsay.

To be truthful, Nicolas II was not unaware that he could ask some policeman. But he was afraid of being recognized and then the taste for adventure overtook him once more and wondered what the remarkable sites the man proposed to show him could well be.

"My dear friend," replied the Tsar. "I would willingly accept your offer if you truly had something interesting to show me. What do you propose?"

"Well, well, well," replied the man. "If I tell you, then you will go and see them on your own! Call yourself up another carriage, I give the address and then you scamper off. Is that it, mate?"

The Tsar had trouble following the man's strange talk but he guessed, rather easily, that he was supposed to hail a carriage.

"Fine, let's take a carriage," he agreed.

"Fine, my prince!"

The Tsar's extraordinary guide immediately called a taxi.

"To Montmartre!" he ordered. "Hurry up, old man. Whip up your old nags. You'll carry us up to the outer boulevards.'

Then he jumped into the carriage.

The Tsar did not feel terribly reassured. At that moment, Nicolas II suddenly understood the foolishness of his action. Thoughts of kidnapping, tales of mysterious assassinations came to mind... After all, he had been unacceptably careless by agreeing to accompany an individual he had met purely by chance.

And, as the man had barely climbed into the carriage, the Tsar's concern increased significantly.

The man, in fact, was undergoing a rapid transformation. Far from taking his seat next to the sovereign, he lowered a jump seat, sat down on it, then bowed respectfully.

"Please excuse me, your Majesty..." he started.

"What?" the Tsar said, startled.

"Please excuse me, your Majesty," he repeated. "First for having recognized you, then for approaching you and finally for lying to you..."

Overwhelmed with panic, the Tsar beseeched the man, asking "Who are you?"

But the man shook his head.

"Please excuse me, your Majesty! Time is of an essence and your Majesty must not interrupt me!"

The Tsar, pale with terror, indicated that he was all ears.

Extraordinarily calm, the man continued, "I'm not the wretch I seem to be. Your Majesty will understand that I am with the police. Oh, I'm not a regular officer, just a poor chap who earns his living as he can, by taking on hazardous adventures. But that's not important. I am in a position to give your Majesty the most important of services and I'm convinced that your Majesty will be able to reward me most appropriately?"

There was a question in that sentence.

Embarrassed, the Tsar replied, "What do you want, sir? What service do you propose to offer me? Why have you approached me in this manner?"

The man looked up and said, "Because your Majesty has been betrayed!"

"Betrayed?" the Tsar, replied, livid. "What do you mean?"

"This," replied the man. "I know where the necklace your Majesty lost can be found. I know who has the necklace that was supposedly stolen by Fantômas. I know where it is hidden, I know who has it."

At that moment, the Tsar wondered if he were having a nightmare, if he were going quite mad. Here he was in a carriage, bouncing over the cobblestones of Paris, having a conversation with a stranger and this stranger was offering, to a certain extent, to find the lost necklace, the necklace that was so terribly valuable...

It was unthinkable!

"Talk," said the Tsar.

"Your wish is my command."

And, crossing his arms, the man coldly said, "The necklace your Majesty is looking for is in the possession of that famous policeman, Juve, who is an infamous thief. The necklace is currently hidden in the lining of the vest Juve wears when he is at home."

"Mercy!" shouted the Tsar.

An hour later, Nicolas II, overwhelmed with panic, looking lost, eyes wild, walked down the small stairway on Rue Tardieu, and out of Juve's house.

Of course, the Tsar looked lost. Since the morning, he had experienced emotions so intense, surprises that were so extraordinary, that he felt he was losing his mind.

First and foremost, he had already been somewhat overwhelmed by his solitary stroll through Paris. Then he had encountered the extraordinary police informer who had claimed that Juve was a thief.

Initially, the Tsar had not wanted to believe the man's strange claims. But he had offered proof. He stated, that he had the key to Juve's apartment. The policeman was not at home. They simply had to go there right away and enter the apartment. They would find the vest and in the vest they would find the stolen necklace.

Naturally, the Tsar had refused, out of fear, to take part in such a search. But the man had insisted. He was persuasive, and had subjugated the sovereign.

The mysterious passerby had taken the Tsar to Juve's place. And the Tsar was now leaving Juve's apartment. He had seen the policeman's vest, he had felt the lining, he had felt the stolen necklace hidden in the fabric.

"This is mad. Quite mad!" the Tsar said as he parted ways with the guide, who claimed to be afraid of drawing attention in the neighborhood. "It's mad! Quite mad! So it's true that Juve, the famous Juve is a villain?"

Frightened, the Tsar ran as fast as he could. He wanted with all his being to go to the Prefecture, to sound the alarm. He had found the strength of mind not to take the stolen necklace back. He had left it in Juve's vest, saying that in this way it would be possible to force the policemen to admit his terrible crime.

Yet, as the Tsar was running, the unfortunate sovereign fell victim to the most grotesque of accidents.

The neighborhood in which Rue de Steinkerque was located was not the most luxurious of neighborhoods. As he raced past a fruit store, he stepped on a peel and fell face down on the ground. Naturally, he was hurt, but he had no time to take pity on his fate since a group of people had already surrounded him.

"Your Majesty is not injured?" they asked. "Does your Majesty want to take a carriage? Does your Majesty want to return to Juve's apartment? Your Majesty could rest there."

And the Tsar understood the truth.

Those who surrounded him, those who came in growing numbers to help him, were simply policemen. Of course, he had believed that he was incognito, that he had slipped away from the surveillance of the Sûreté inspectors, but he had done nothing of the kind. The Paris police, quite accustomed to the escapades of monarchs, who liked to go strolling about on their own, had suspected his intentions and followed him.

They had never lost him from sight. He had been under their constant protection without knowing it.

The Tsar was flabbergasted!

An hour later, an epic scene took place in Juve's office.

The Tsar was there, accompanied by Mr. Hennion and Mr. Havard, who had rushed there after receiving urgent telephone calls.

Juve was there as well.

The policeman had just arrived. He was covered with gray dust, he had bags under his eyes and his face was drawn. He looked exhausted.

Juve had, in fact, spent the entire night tracking Fantômas, who had escaped from him in the catastrophe at the Opéra after Juve, revolver in hand, had blocked his way, preventing him from assassinating the Tsar and the Tsarita.

And, when he had returned home, Juve had been surprised to find the police and the emperor there. He listened to the explanations they gave him, nodding his heading, shrugging, occasionally verifying a word, a detail of the account he listened to.

"No," said Juve. "I did not send the note. The person who had announced that the Tsarita would be wearing the famous necklace at the official gala was most certainly Fantômas, and Fantômas had no other goal than to embarrass me. But, please continue, your Majesty. The man who accosted you said that he knew where the necklace was, that he knew who the thief was? According to him, who is that individual?"

The Tsar spoke, while cautiously taking a place behind Mr. Havard.

"You, Juve!"

In response to that accusation, Juve naturally showed no sign of concern, and even smiled.

"Well," he said. "That's amusing!"

Then he asked, "Where did I place the necklace?"

Trembling, the Tsar replied immediately, "Don't try to lie, Juve. The necklace is on you."

"Really?"

"It's in the lining of the vest you just put on."

"More and more interesting," murmured Juve.

The policeman removed his vest, tore out the lining and, initially dumbfounded, took out the superb diamond necklace.

Juve seemed astonished just then.

"Good grief, I don't understand" he admitted.

Then he handed the necklace to the Tsar.

"Is this the diamond necklace that was stolen from you?" he asked.

The Tsar looked triumphant. More than ever, he was convinced that Juve was a thief and the only thing that surprised him was that Mr. Havard and Mr. Hennion had not rushed to arrest the wretch.

"Of course," shrieked Nicolas II. "That's the stolen necklace. The setting, moreover, cannot be copied. Juve, you've been unmasked!"

"Indeed," said the policeman.

Juve was thinking.

Suddenly, he asked, "I imagine you rewarded the honest informer who has unmasked me?"

The Tsar nodded his head proudly.

"I rewarded him immediately," he said. "I gave him a check for one hundred thousand francs, which he must have cashed by now."

"Fine!" replied Juve.

And, suddenly, the policeman turned to Mr. Havard, who did not know quite what to believe.

"Really," murmured Juve. "This is all quite devious!"

And Juve shrugged with impatience, adding, "I have nothing to blame myself for. Honestly, I can't be asked to save people despite themselves!"

And, after uttering these enigmatic words, Juve stared at the Tsar.

"Your Majesty," he advised. "Please place the necklace on the floor.

It was a strange request, yet the Tsar obeyed, curious to see what Juve planned to do.

Juve, quietly took a step.

"A fake necklace," he said. "A fake necklace breaks like this!"

Juve raised his foot and broke the Tsar's so-called necklace.

He continued, "And since it breaks very easily, paying one hundred francs for it was a little steep!"

Juve's action had stunned the unfortunate Tsar.

Clasping his hands, he asked, "So the necklace was fake?"

"Of course," replied Juve, shrugging again. "Your Majesty, I regret to inform you that you have been robbed... robbed of one hundred thousand francs. Good grief! It's a simple matter, your Majesty was sold a bunch of glass for that price!"

Then Juve shrugged again and asked, "Did the man who guided you to my apartment have a small graze on his right temple?"

"He did" said the Tsar, appalled.

"Well," said Juve. "That merely proves that your Majesty spent twenty minutes with Fantômas and that if Fantômas did not kill you that was because he recognized the Sûreté agents who were following your Majesty!"

Juve sat down and crossed his arms.

"All in all," he concluded, "It was all a joke for Fantômas. He found it amusing to make people think, once again, that I am the thief. And he enjoyed his little joke all the more since he took advantage of the situation to steal one hundred thousand francs from you!"

Then, in a judgmental voice, Juve added, "Strolling about alone in Paris is quite dangerous!"

The Tsar was the only one who did not smile.

CHAPTER XI
The Mysterious House

Rue des Irlandais is a small, old street that looks deserted, with grass growing through the cobblestones. It's a street in the Latin quarter, that is no longer frequented by students and even less by the joyous party-goers of Boulevard Saint-Michel, a street that perhaps their fathers knew, fathers who willingly lived at the top of Mont Saint-Geneviève, no longer frequented by young scholars, who are more willing to go to the right bank, than the picturesque regions of a disappearing neighborhood.

Few people go to Rue des Irlandais for the good reason that few people live there. Long, rough walls border each side of it. Here and there a gate carved in the wall or a barred window, indicate to the passerby who has ventured into this place that, behind this wall, there is a dwelling where people live.

No noise is heard in the neighborhood and, at times, people have the impression that they are in the countryside. The few rare people who live on Rue des Irlandais know one another, having occasionally crossed paths when coming and going. Most of them are humble people, who live modestly, away from the spotlight, and who seem isolated in the midst of the hubbub of the capital like dead bodies in a cemetery.

The inhabitants of Rue des Irlandais include one man who, although he does not know all his neighbors, is known to them, even though he rarely leaves his home. He is an old man with a large white beard that reaches down to the middle of his chest and who, judging by his guttural accent and his bronzed tint, must come from some far-off country.

He was, moreover, not very talkative and never exchanged more than a few essential words with his neighbors. He was called Father Saül and that was about all anyone knew about him. He lived at No. 29 and whenever anyone came to his door, for any pretext, they had to wait a long time before the door would open.

Moreover, that door never opened completely. It barely opened and the enigmatic face of the tall old man would be framed by the crack between the door frame and the wall and his lips would utter a question so quietly it could barely be heard.

Saül, no doubt in the manner of the people of his country, spoke plainly to all those who came to ring at his door, while treating them with the greatest respect.

"Good day, stranger," he would say, bowing deeply. "What happy reason has brought you to my door?"

And, if the visitor, either a curious passerby or an unemployed person, believed that he was being encouraged to prolong the conversation following this greeting, he was quickly disabused when it came to the old man's real intentions.

If the unknown visitor did not explain himself in a few seconds, while standing on the doorstep, the door would close, and the tall old man would sigh, saying, "Unfortunately, I don't understand what you want to tell me. Stranger, respect my solitude and go on your way."

However, when the old man went out, which he happened to do about two o'clock in the afternoon, three times a week, he was affable and charitable. He made sure that the neighborhood children respected him, by giving them candy.

The old man's few rare absences were also brief and people wondered what he could be doing in his home where no one ever entered, not even a cleaning lady.

The delivery men, those who brought his daily supplies, were mercilessly condemned to remain at the doorstep, never once entering the building.

How long had Father Saül been living there? People had always known him and the oldest people living on Rue des Irlandais would have confirmed that their predecessors, relatives or past tenants, had already mentioned the mysterious old man.

Father Saül's dwelling covered a rather vast territory.

If anyone chanced to go through the door that opened onto the street with him, they would find themselves in a sort of garden bordered by tall walls, in which weeds, fruit trees and clumps of laurel bushes grew higgledy-piggledy, in complete disorder. It was a delectable refuge for the neighborhood birds, who could build their nests in complete safety, in this tiny virgin forest.

The house stood against the wall. It was a house that dated back more than 50 years, with a single floor and a roof of bricks, that had once been red but had turned brown over the seasons. The windows, which looked out over the garden were rigorously decorated with thick, impassible iron bars.

A small, low door provided access to the interior of the house and once someone went through it they found themselves in a modest bedroom, which resembled a monk's cell. A wrought-iron bed occupied one of the corners of the room; the walls, which had once been white, had taken on a grey hue. In the middle of the room, there was a rough wood table and opposite the bed there was a plain washstand.

That was where the tall old man, known as Father Saül, slept.

There was another room in the tiny house. It had been set up as a laboratory. It contained retorts, crucibles, multicolored sheets, and an enormous fireplace that was constantly lit on which liquids and odd pastes bubbled, giving off violently bitter odors.

In one corner of this laboratory, there was a heap of dirt, mixed with pebbles and elsewhere there were blocks of raw coal that seemed to come directly from the mine.

Most days, and occasionally at night, Saül spent his time in his laboratory where the eccentric man took part in his mysterious work.

The enigmatic hermit's only companion was a tame owl, who perched on an old cupboard, motionless and with its eyes closed, looking as if it were stuffed.

That day, at about four o'clock in the afternoon, someone had seen old Saül walking down Rue des Irlandais and returning home at a pace that was faster than usual. Once he had entered the house, the strange man had locked his door, with more care than usual. Then, he had taken out a series of newspapers from one of the pockets of his long, threadbare overcoat, spread them over the table in his laboratory and started to read them with feverish anxiety.

Yet, the old man did not read all of the pages. His glance stopped on a short paragraph, always the same one, placed on the second page of most of the newspapers.

And this article, which Saül read over and over, without seeming to grow tired or it, said:

Academy of Science

After studying the agenda, the learned members assembled read an anonymous communication which, while initially seeming to come from some hoaxster, contained such claims that a decision was made to ask this far too discreet correspondent, through the newspapers, to identify himself and to provide greater details about the invention he claims to have made.

This was followed by details about the invention which consisted, according to the anonymous correspondent of the Academy of Science, in the discovery of the means to artificially manufacture gold. An old man, a foreigner, living in Sainte-Geneviève, had apparently found an absolute, definitive and certain means for manufacturing the precious metal!

Old Saül read this item over and over. After 30 minutes, he looked up. His face was livid and large drops of sweat pearled on his temples.

He clasped his head in his hands and murmured, "Through the powerful Buddha who presides over the fate of humanity, I believe that, after reading this item, a frightful act of betrayal has just been committed! Who could have revealed the secret of the project I have been working on for close to 40 years and which just now I am convinced I have completed? Lord, protect me and keep the most fearful of cataclysms from falling on my head, which is already bowed toward the tomb, before I have been able to fulfill the sacred duty that was inspired by heaven where our ancestors dwell?"

Then the old man cut the articles that had so deeply disturbed him out of the newspapers, pinned them all together and placed them in a drawer.

And, without a doubt, he found this hiding place not safe enough since he removed them from that drawer and placed them in a chest hidden under the furnace in his laboratory.

After hesitating for a few moments, Saül took them out of the chest and finally placed them in the pocket of his long, threadbare overcoat, murmuring, "That's where they will be hidden the best since that is where I can keep a close eye on them."

Saül cocked his head, believing that he had heard distant noises, but then felt reassured.

He muttered, "Perhaps this doesn't concern me, but someone else was studying the same problem. Did he find the solution? The discovery is much farther away than the anonymous author of this news item claims. And if I only had the resources that could be produced by the artificial manufacture of gold to accomplish my work, I believe that we wouldn't have to wait much longer before the legitimate emperor climbs onto the throne of his ancestors!"

As he uttered these strange words, Saül walked into a neighboring cabinet and raised a trap door in the floor, revealing the top of a small wooden staircase with worm-eaten steps.

He went down into the dark hole and, after a few moments, reached a cellar. Saül flipped an electric switch.

The basement he had just entered lit up. He did not widen his eyes; he did not move s single muscle of his face since the old man was certainly used to seeing the inside of this basement.

Anyone who had found themselves in this basement with the old man for the first time would have been dumbfounded, frozen with emotion. The sight was extraordinary. The entire cellar was filled with crates. The lids were raised, revealing innumerable quantities of gold pieces. They were certainly worth millions and millions.

Yet, was this real gold or the artificial gold the old man had just mentioned?

Someone who had examined the precious content of these crates would soon be convinced that they contained absolutely authentic pieces of gold, which came from various countries: French louis d'or, 30 mark coins, pounds sterling, Italian, Austrian, Russian and American coins.

The old man walked over to one of the crates and, with a trembling hand, lifted a few of the gold ingots, then stood up suddenly and shuddered.

A bell rang twice in the distance. Saül immediately realized that someone was ringing at the door to the house.

Why twice?

Saül quickly climbed back up the stairs that led to his laboratory. He quickly walked through the room that held his bed. The old man took a sort of bulky white robe from a cupboard and threw it over his shoulders. Dressed in this manner, he went to the garden door and, before opening, glanced through the peephole.

On Rue Monge, one of those old houses destined to disappear under the sledgehammers of the demolishers, is occupied by an entire colony of shady vagabonds, for the most part Algerians, Arabs, wretches who had escaped from traveling circuses or freak shows and who, staying in Paris while their families remained far away, make an effort to live in the capital city by taking part in subtle, fishy businesses.

They work as Oriental carpet merchants who, once summer comes, transform into sellers of exotic fruits. Occasionally, they play the accordion or hire on as extras in the suburban dance halls. Jacks of all trades, but masters of none.

This Asian colony lives on Rue Monge in sordid attics at the end of dark, greasy corridors.

Brawls are frequent there, thefts common. And the few strangers who stray into these filthy buildings under the pretext of looking for low-cost hotels leave after losing almost all of their money and their clothing, without knowing who perpetrated such thefts.

On the third floor of this hovel, in a room, the most beautiful one in the entire building, there was a man with an energetic and authoritarian silhouette, with a robust and vigorous body.

He was in shirt-sleeves and, standing in front of a mirror, he was darkening his face with an oily paste. Then he glued short, black sideburns to his cheeks and placed a wig made of long ebony hair, carefully braided, on his head.

Anyone who would have seen this individual, this extraordinary character, put on a long, black silk robe, buttoned on the front from bottom to top and cinched in at the waist by a large silk belt, would have initially believed that the man was some sort of Hindu, some sort of Oriental who had not yet renounced the traditions of his country.

When seeing the individual disguised in that manner, they would never have guessed his true identity, would never have been able to unmask him with a glance.

Yet, someone could have performed this miracle. Someone could have discovered the true personality of this so-called Oriental, simply by noting the dark gleam of his eyes, simply by observing the sardonic and authoritarian grimace of his thin, well-drawn lips. That someone was Juve since the so-called Oriental man with the browned skin was none other than Fantômas!

An extraordinary thing occurred while old Saül was hurrying to his home on Rue des Irlandais. At the very same time, Fantômas was in the hotel room on Rue Monge, completing his make-up.

Newspapers were spread over a red velvet sofa, the filled part of the room, the same newspaper that old Saül had read. Fantômas had even used a blue crayon to mark the passage concerning the Academy of Science, which the hermit on Rue des Irlandais had found so disturbing!

After completing his make-up and putting on his extraordinary disguise, Fantômas wasted no time in the hovel on Rue Monge. He walked down the stairs, encountering, in the narrow and dark, labyrinth-like corridors, a few Arabs on their way to work. These Arabs, who were used to all possible and imaginable outfits, paid no attention to the tenant who was heading out wearing a silk robe like those worn by Orientals.

Fantômas stepped into the street, walking along with the crowd without the slightest concern. With a mocking smile, he looked at the police officers, absolutely certain than none of them, as they saw him go on his way, imagined that this representative of the yellow race, with his woman's clothing, and his long hair tied in a bun under a soft hat, was none other than the elusive, powerful bandit whose name alone made crowds shiver.

Fantômas reached Rue du Cardinal-Lemoine and was walking slowly up the slope when suddenly an ironic smile lit up his face.

Two men were walking toward him, walking nonchalantly in the middle of the sidewalk. Two men with a military look. Fantômas recognized them without displaying the slightest trace of emotion: they were police inspectors, two of the most loyal subordinates of his indomitable adversary, Juve.

The officers were none other than Léon and Michel.

They walked past Fantômas without for a single moment suspecting the man's identity. They had barely glanced at his attire, barely smiled as they elbowed their way past.

Suddenly, the dauntless Fantômas had an idea. He wanted to push his audacity to the limit. He stopped suddenly, retraced his steps, and walked toward the two men, who had also stopped, glancing at the Oriental man, or at least the man they considered to be Asian. They did not dare continue on their way since the foreigner was approaching them.

"Excuse me, gentlemen," Fantômas said, pretending to be amiable and humble, while camouflaging the distinctive sound of his tragic voice. "Could you tell me the way to Rue des Irlandais?"

Léon and Michel looked at one another. They were not familiar with Rue des Irlandais, but a sergeant was passing nearby and they waved at him. The peace officer ran over immediately. He knew the two Sûreté inspectors and cast a suspicious glance at the man talking to them. The peace officer thought he was being required to make an observation about the foreigner.

"It's a man," he said. "But he's dressed like a woman!"

But Michel immediately defended the foreigner.

"It's not a disguise officer. You can clearly see that the man comes from Indochina!"

Fantômas corrected Michel, with a smile, "From India, gentlemen. It's not at all the same thing!"

"I beg your pardon," Michel said, embarrassed.

Then Léon, interrupted, asking the patrolman, "You're from around here, tell this gentleman where he can find Rue des Irlandais."

But the officer had only started working in that neighborhood the day before and he spent five minutes looking through a small agenda, which Fantômas, losing his patience, grabbed from his hands. Finally, the terrible bandit discovered what he needed on his own, something which was relatively easy for him since he knew perfectly well where Rue des Irlandais was located. He thanked the officer as well as the two gentlemen, turned away from them, and set out on his way up Rue du Cardinal-Lemoine.

Fantômas found his little prank quite amusing.

"If Juve plans to work with lads like that to take me down, I do think that I'll be free for a rather long time!"

Suddenly he frowned.

"And those hours are essential for me," he continued. "I need them to complete the work I've undertaken."

"Gold... gold... I need a lot of gold! My reserves from Mexico are considerable, but they are not enough and I need more of that precious metal which will enable me to do whatever I want. For 40 years now, the hermit on Rue des Irlandais, who goes by the name of Saül, has been conducting experiments which I have not been able to follow as closely as I would have liked. I must know what he's managed to do, and if my suppositions have come true. Has he found the means to make gold artificially? I doubt it! But I am certain that he has considerable reserves at his disposal. However, it will be difficult for me to take all of his reserves since he cannot have it all locked away in his basement. He must have other hiding places and I must find out where they are!"

Ten minutes later, Fantômas stood in front of the door at 29 Rue des Irlandais. He rang twice and waited.

That's when old Saül had arrived and had glanced through the people in the door at the visitor who wanted to enter his home.

On the other side of the door, Fantômas' face appeared through the people. Saül looked at the stranger with a certain amount of trepidation.

Slowly, Fantômas uttered a single word, "Bedjapur!"

Saül immediately uttered a cry of surprise and opened the door wide.

"Come into my home," he said, trembling. "Come in, you who know the name of Bedjapur."

Once the door had closed behind him, Fantômas bowed low to the ground, raising his arms over his head, stammering in an attitude of infinite respect.

"Sahib! Sahib! The way to your home has been long and hard!"

Old Saül replied, "I live alone, out of the way, and no one in this western city suspects who I really am. And you, who are you? Why have you come to disturb the silence of my abode?"

Fantômas stood up and stared at the old man.

His glare was so unwavering that Saül grew disconcerted and asked in a quavering voice, "By the great Buddha and his Brahmin princes, tell me who you are, where you come from and what you want to know."

Fantômas objected, saying "This garden open to the winds, this parlor of nature which has no ceiling other than the sky and the clumps of trees for walls, is not a good place for the discreet conversation I must have with you, Bedjapur!"

Once again, as he heard that name, the old man quivered.

"Come in!" he said to Fantômas.

And this time, instead of taking him into the cell-like bedroom or the laboratory, which reeked of chemicals, old Saül brought his visitor into a third room which they entered through a door hidden in the wall.

This room was very different from the others. It was rectangular in shape and had a glass ceiling. There was no other window and all of the light came from above. The walls were covered with rich fabrics and skins of wild beasts. It was furnished in an Oriental style. Small stools, with mother of pearl inlays, were placed randomly around the room. At the back, there was a platform. Three steps covered with red carpet led up to a chair that looked like a throne.

Knowing that his visitor was following him at a respectful distance, Saül walked to the back of the room and sat down on the throne. He bent low for a few seconds and, his face hidden by his hands, he said "Buddha is with us" three times.

He bent low again, closed his eyes and, looking at his visitor who had remained motionless in the room, he declared, "Speak, you who has discovered my hiding place, speak and tell me where you come from and what you want."

Fantômas, who was no doubt familiar with Oriental traditions, bowed three times to old Saül, who was sitting on the throne, then crouched down on the ground, took a deep breath, and said, "Later, we will write on the parchments that relate the history of our peoples, the history which has been transformed over time into legend. The day after the frightful repression of the Indian people by the English torturers, a very young child from the royal family and the last vestige of the heirs to the throne, managed to escape and went to live in the wild in the Gange forests… Bedjapur was his name."

"Surrounded by faithful Brahmins and fakirs with rapturous eyes, this young child quickly grew into great beauty, strength and wisdom and learned to hate the English and love his mother land, India. First, at the age of 20, when the vigor of a young man's muscles occasionally abused the reasoning of the mind, Bedjapur wanted to raise a revolt against the invader and allow the Hindu people to become once again their own masters. But traitors sold his secret to the English and a price was placed on the head of Bedjapur, who had already been vanquished before the battle. Bedjapur confined himself to his hiding place, wandering about in the middle of the forests, meditating amount the fakirs, the dervishes and the Brahmins. In the midst of these wise men, inspired by the great

Buddha, he learned that one thing was stronger than disciplined armies, more decisive than the power of guns, more energetic than cannon balls... He wasted no time realizing that this thing that mastered the work and all of humanity was none other than gold. As of that date, Bedjapur realized that, if India were to become free or if India were to cast off the yoke of England, he needed to accumulate gold and more gold... to the point that the treasures of Golconda would be as nothing compared to the treasures of Bedjapur!"

As Fantômas was speaking, tears rolled down the bony, wrinkled face of the tall old man on the throne.

In an emotion-filled voice, Saül, or at least the extraordinary person hiding behind that name, stammered, "Stranger, what you say is true. That was how Bedjapur thought. But how do you know that?"

Then Fantômas stretched out on the floor, his nose in the dust and in a skillfully camouflaged voice, intended to give the impression that he was touched to the very depths of his soul, he murmured, "I know that, Bedjapur, because I am one of those who are honored to be fakirs. I know that, Bedjapur, because I am no stranger, but your disciple, your subject! I know that because your brothers along the Gange entrusted me with a mission to come and find you in your hideaway, and to ask you when the great deed will be done, when the blessed day will arrive when you will return to the throne of your ancestors, when your throne will be returned to those to whom it belongs."

"Unfortunately," interrupted the old man, "my ancestors are no longer among those protected by Buddha and already my descendants have been called to the celestial paradise. I am alone..."

Fantômas interrupted, "Was it not said, Bedjapur, that if your son is dead it was not without posterity and that he left, a few years ago, not yet far in the past, when the war was being fought on the soil of South Africa, an heir, or better yet and heiress..."

Fantômas paused.

"Stop," shouted the old man. "Those are mysterious things that must not be mentioned out loud! Can we be sure that the walls have no ears? And the secret must not at any price be revealed to those who are interested in knowing it and who would then do everything in their power to kill the one, she who must..."

The old man did not complete his sentence. Fantômas had stood up and, suddenly changing tone, he said, "Bedjapur, you are right and such words will never be uttered among us again. Time is short... Did you read in the newspapers the item about the discovery of artificial gold that seems to refer to you?"

"My son," replied the old man. "It seems that they were referring to me. Could you tell me who wrote that biased and ignoble article?"

A slight small flickered over the bandit's lips. Was it not interesting that he, Fantômas was being asked that question since he was the one who had sent the anonymous note to the newspapers precisely in order to upset the man he had come to see?

Fantômas took on a hypocritical air and said, "Unfortunately, I don't know who wrote that article, but what is essential for me, your disciple, your subject, is knowing, right now for certain, whether you know the secret for making gold?"

Saül, or better yet Bedjapur, stared at Fantômas.

"Why do you ask that question?"

"In the interest of the people of India. Do you trust me or not?"

The old man thought for a moment and then replied, "I must trust you, so I will tell you. For forty years, I've believed that I was on the point of discovering that formidable secret, but I must admit that I don't know the entire secret."

"So," Fantômas said in a disappointed tone. "You have nothing?"

"Yes, I do," declared Bedjapur. "I have lots of gold in my cellars."

"That's nothing!" said Fantômas.

"I have even more in various distant hiding places," Bedjapur continued.

"So little," said the bandit, disparagingly.

"I even have gold in the safest banks of the great European nations," Bedjapur insisted.

This time, Fantômas said nothing and merely shrugged.

"All that gold combined will not be enough," he finally said. "The most insignificant sovereign, the smallest republic could accumulate more gold in 48 hours that you can provide after looking for it your entire life."

"Unfortunately, what can I do?" replied the old man.

"You were supposed to discover the means for making gold," Fantômas grumbled imperiously, gradually losing his humble and respectful attitude.

Bedjapur shivered. Then he seemed to recover from his fleeting dejection.

"I tell you," he said. "I have been looking for the means for over 40 years and I am on the point of discovering it. In a short while, perhaps tomorrow, perhaps later, in a few years..."

Fantômas banged on a stool that was inlaid with white shells, causing Bedjapur to jump in fear.

And, while the old man was growing concerned over the other man's attitude, Fantômas roared, "Tomorrow, you will lie dead next to your pitiful supply of gold and all of India will wait, crushed, oppressed under the English yoke! Is that why you call yourself Bedjapur and why you spent twenty years of your youth living with the fakirs, Brahmins and dervishes, who were counting on you like people count on someone that Buddha has marked with his majestic and immortal finger?"

The old man wrung his hands and sobbed loudly.

"Unfortunately, unfortunately! I have spent my entire life searching, fighting... I have dedicated my mind to the science which I took for my mistress. And now I am approaching the decline of my life and I still haven't succeeded!"

Fantômas interrupted, "Bedjapur, I have something better than the secret you are looking for. You are looking for a way to make gold. Child's play! I tell you, I have something better than that!"

The old man had left his throne. On wobbly legs, he approached Fantômas as if he were fascinated by his piercing gaze.

"Speak!" he begged. "What have you found?"

He fell to his knees before Fantômas, beseeching the other man.

"Speak! Speak!" he insisted. "Now, I'm afraid I will die before..."

Then, Fantômas stood up tall and, taking on a respectful air once again, he looked down to speak to Bedjapur, almost murmuring in his ear, "I have come to bring you the most formidable secret imaginable. I know how to make artificial diamonds! In eight days, you will be the richest man in the world... The man whose wealth will surpass the combined wealth of all the rich people in the universe... But for that to happen, I will need a great deal of your gold in exchange for that secret."

Bedjapur's eyes shone brightly.

"If what you are telling me is true, my son, my gold is yours..."

CHAPTER XII
A Serious Trail

On the banks of the Seine, between the Pont de la Concorde and the Pont de l'Alma, a man walked quickly, following the shore of the river.

He was trotting, bent over. His large hob-nailed shoes stumbled over the uneven cobblestones along the shore. He carried a bag on his back which seemed to be filled with something that was constantly moving.

The man had a hairy face, a bushy white beard. He grumbled as he walked, swearing furiously, although he smiled broadly.

It was none other than the tramp Bouzille.

Bouzille was being followed, from the Point de la Concorde, by a young man who walked quickly behind him. When that man approached the tramp, he placed his hand on Bouzille's shoulder, who cried out in surprise.

"Hey! Help! Someone is trying to kill me! I assure you, officers, I have done nothing! No, no, no I'm not carrying a body in my bag!"

Then he stopped short and turned back to look at the person who had just hit him on the shoulder.

"Mr. Fandor," Bouzille said, bursting out laughing.

It was, in fact, the journalist who had caught up with the hilarious tramp.

Fandor seemed to be in a very bad mood. He frowned as he looked at Mère Toulouche's husband, examining him from head to foot without saying a word.

Ever since the famous day when he had been so extraordinarily captured by Fantômas and had been obliged, like the other unfortunates caught in the net that fell from the top of Féeric City, to hand over his wallet to the thieves working for Fantômas, without complaining, without saying a word, so as not to reveal who he was, Jérôme Fandor, had been furious.

First, he had been terribly concerned over the fate of his beloved Hélène who had been injured during the tragic evening at the Folies-Françaises. Fortunately, he had been quickly reassured about the condition of the woman to whom he had given his heart, Hélène was safe in a small, discreet and comfortable hospice and was recovering rapidly.

That meant that Fandor could act without worrying and set out on his occasionally dangerous searches and wandering, without having to worry that the woman he loved was taking her share of the risks and difficulties.

Fandor was not only furious, but also desperate, considering the turn of events. There was no hiding the fact that Fantômas' acts were growing more and more phenomenal.

Up to this point, the bandit had acted alone or at least in the shadows. He had not declared his power openly and was not afraid, in order to avoid some formidable collision, to turn heel and order his accomplices to flee, to give up the game, and come back another day.

But now, no doubt because he had managed to escape the incessant pursuit of the police for many long years, Fantômas seemed determined to fight face to face with the authorities.

The men who took orders from the bandit were no longer accomplices, they were a veritable troupe, an army, directed by the crime general.

Only the regular police force stood against him and Fantômas, no doubt intoxicated by his successes, did not worry himself about treating the senior officers of the Sûreté as equals, and sending declarations of war to his adversaries at the Quai des Orfèvres, making all of them tremble in fear.

The situation had reached such a point that Juve constantly kept coming up with the most extraordinary and audacious plans to capture Fantômas while Fandor had only one goal in life: to track the comings and goings of the criminal mastermind's accomplices and capture them in order to reach the one who was so truly elusive.

For several days, since the event at Féeric City, Juve and Fandor had been hard at work.

Juve was preparing well thought out, formidable battle plans. At the Sûreté he was organizing a special team that would be responsible solely for Fantômas and for bringing his reign of terror to an end once and for all.

At the same time, Fandor was trying to clarify certain problems. He wanted to determine the secret and mysterious bonds that united Fantômas' accomplices. He wanted to shed some light on the extraordinary matter of the hens that everyone was talking about. Fandor, with his natural perspicacity had moreover come to the conclusion that, under the circumstances, it was important to play a close game. He had the feeling that the absurd tale of the chickens was actually a serious matter and it was important for him to find out just what was going on.

But Fandor felt that, in order to do that, the greatest precautions were necessary and that he had to avoid looking like he suspected the people he might interrogate. Then, Fandor told himself that those who had the chickens in their possession included both the true accomplices of Fantômas and certain naïve individuals who had the chickens without suspecting that they would serve the interests of the sinister bandit.

One of those caring for chickens was Bouzille.

Fandor had learned that under memorable circumstances, but he had not been able to determine the exact role played by the old tramp in the affair.

Bouzille was, as usual, neither fish nor fowl, an accomplice of Fantômas yet not an accomplice, informed about some of the bandit's intentions, but not others.

Fandor needed to determine the truth but he had to do so without revealing his concerns to the old tramp.

After approaching Bouzille, furious, his face dark and his expression concerned, Fandor suddenly smiled and started to laugh along with Bouzille.

"Here you are, old crab!" he said. "I've been looking for you for an hour."

"Really," said Bouzille. "Why?"

Fandor took a cigarette case out of his pocket.

"To offer you a gift."

"Yeah," said Bouzille, trying to look clever, "I guess you've got time to waste! Well, I'd like to believe you. So, where are you headed now?"

"To take a stroll with you," said Fandor, taking the old man by the arm.

"But I'm of no interest..."

"Quite right!" said Fandor. "I wanted to apologize to you for the trouble I caused you when I discovered you in the Moriss column with the theater posters. It is true that you caused me to make quite a serious mistake, after all, by indicating that it was the poster for the Menus-Plaisirs that Fantômas was interested in, while it was really..."

Bouzille interrupted, "That's fine! That's fine. Let's not talk about it anymore. I thought I was doing the right thing. It's not my fault...And, for the rest, I've been punished!"

"Really?" asked Fandor.

"Yes," continued Bouzille. "I've been kicked out."

"Who did that?"

The tramp stood up straight and uttered, "The City of Paris. My landlord."

Fandor didn't understand right off, then suddenly the light shone in his mind.

"Well, that is true. You were living in the Morris column on the boulevard, which belongs to the city. My compliments, Bouzille. That's really something, living in the City's buildings. My contacts don't extend beyond the police prefect and the manager of public assistance!"

Bouzille sighed, saying "The sweepers kicked me out and I've had to move..."

He pointed to his bag and added, "See, I've got my belongings in my bag. It contains a bedroom, the living room, the kitchen, some gardening tools and a few pets..."

"What do you mean by pets?" asked Fandor.

"Good grief! It's Joséphine!" Bouzille replied.

"Joséphine!" Fandor repeated.

"Do you understand," Bouzille whispered. "Joséphine is the hen, Mère Toulouche's hen..."

"Ah, that's true" said Fandor. "And how is the old thing doing?"

"Always the same," said Bouzille. "A bit worse for the wear today than yesterday and more tomorrow than today, as a famous poet said. She works hard until noon and after that she rests until the next morning... a nice gift to give a young man, isn't she? And to think that I've joined forces with a woman like that! There's nothing like it!"

"But you're still living the single life," observed Fandor.

"Sure thing!" replied Bouzille. "And I'd prefer to die…"

He stopped talking.

As he had been talking, two men had climbed onto the docks and were walking toward the vast esplanade that stood next to the Pont d'Iéna. In that area, work was in progress on the large cast iron conduits that stretched under the roadway. Bouzille walked closer to them.

"Well, Mr. Fandor," he said, pointing at the enormous cylinders. "Here's my new address. "When you want to see me, you might just find me in one of these pipes. I'm moving in here."

It was about five o'clock in the evening. Twilight was falling, the docks were deserted and Bouzille, after making sure that there was no peace officer nearby, vigorously threw his bag into one of the pipes.

"Well," he said, giving Fandor a furtive glance. "The move is over. As you can see, it's long and not at all expensive."

Bouzille's bag, however was jiggling about and the chicken's plaintiff clucking could be heard. She did not seem to enjoy being locked up with the unlikely utensils the old tramp used for furniture.

"That damned Joséphine!" Bouzille said. "You have no idea how demanding she can be. There's just no way to keep her quiet. I constantly have to take care of her, to take her for walks… She's almost more work than a woman. If she keeps on this way, I'm going to wring her neck. Either that or give her back to Mère Toulouche!"

Upon hearing that name, Fandor shivered. He would have liked to find out where Mère Toulouche was staying, yet Bouzille said nothing about that.

Fandor asked him, "So, where is the old dear staying?"

The tramp flapped his arms, his eyes grew murky and he replied, "How am I supposed to know? Bouzille goes his way and Mère Toulouche goes hers."

Fandor realized that he would get nothing out of the old tramp.

"Strange!" he muttered as he left the old man, who had retired into his pipe and was arranging his things.

The night passed peacefully and quietly on the deserted docks. The peace officers, who had been attracted by the snoring that came from the pipes that had been placed on the roadway, had discovered an old man sleeping soundly inside the pipes. But they had not felt the need to chase him off and had merely instructed him to move on, without taking care to make sure that he did as ordered.

After noting that the pipes had a lodger, they had gone on their way, failing to note that one of the thickest banks in the Trocadéro garden also had an inhabitant, one who did not snore and who remained quite alert, on the look-out, spying on everything that occurred.

That inhabitant was none other than Fandor who, marvelously disguised as a ragman so that he could go anywhere without being noticed, at least during the early hours of the morning, had sworn to watch Bouzille.

Fandor was starting to despair that the old tramp would ever move when, at five o'clock in the morning, he clambered out of his cast iron pipe.

Bouzille picked up his bag but, no doubt as a precautionary measure so as not to break its wings, he held the chicken, the famous chicken under his arm.

Fandor thought, "If he' carrying all of his belongings, that means he's moving again."

Bouzille head over toward the Passey bridge. Fandor followed him at a distance.

They walked for a good half hour, crossed the Seine and took the left bank. They reached the yarding track that ran along the river where large flat rail cars, loaded with all kinds of waste, stood perpetually.

A filthy being, a shapeless woman, appeared to stand at the peak of the heaps of waste, furiously and frantically searching through it.

It was Mère Toulouche. The journalist had recognized her at a distance and started to take greater precautions in his efforts to find out what was going on.

He was anxious since he had always suspected that, while Bouzille maintained contact with the elderly criminal woman, she was most certainly in constant contact with Fantômas and that by following each of these accomplices, one after another, he would finally uncover their secrets and locate the hideout of the sinister bandit and find the den of the elusive genius.

Bouzille walked over to Mère Toulouche. Fandor took the opportunity to hide under an empty rail car located next to the one Mère Toulouche was searching.

And from there, without being seen or heard, he could see and hear what was going on.

Mère Toulouche, holding a hook in her hand that she occasionally used to scratch her head, had seen Bouzille coming and yelled at him, "You piece of rubbish! Drunk again!"

Bouzille shook his tangled head.

"No!" he replied. "Haven't even had a drop this morning!"

Mère Toulouche placed her hands on her hips and cried out in a hoarse voice, "Are you bringing the hen back?"

"Yes," said Bouzille.

He opened the piece of clothing that served as a vest for him. The chicken could be heard clucking as she tried to escape. She tore herself away from the tramp, flapped her wings and landed on the ground, unable to go any further since her foot was caught in a piece of rope that was tied to the button on Bouzille's pants.

"Gently, gently, Joséphine," he called. "You mustn't run off like that!"

And, since the hen was pulling on the string and clucking with all her might, Bouzille looked at Mère Toulouche and said, "It's unfortunate, isn't it? Such a lack of gratitude. I've been looking after her for eight days now and all she wants to do is escape. Like all women."

"When you've finished insulting the entire better sex..." Toulouche said, as she stood up. "We have all the rights since we're the better-looking ones."

Bouzille grumbled," That remains to be seen. Some samples aren't so bad, but others..."

Mère Toulouche did not insist.

"That makes no difference," she said. "You were called here to return the chicken so hand it over!"

"I'd like to," replied Bouzille. "But who's going to pay me for taking care of the chicken?"

Mère Toulouche had not expected the question.

"At least twenty cents per day."

"Twenty cents per day!" repeated Mère Toulouche. "That's robbery!"

"Well, ten then," suggested Bouzille.

Toulouche replied in an authoritarian voice, "Hand over the hen and I'll pay you a liter of aramon."

Bouzille did not ask to be begged and, with great satisfaction, he got rid of the chicken for a few coins, which Mère Toulouche generously handed him.

"Farewell, Joséphine" he called out. "I'll drink a toast to your health!"

Yet, he did not leave. Before leaving, he wanted to satisfy his curiosity.

"Any news about our buddies?"

"No news," she said.

Yet, after a moment's silence, she added, "Bec-de-Gaz and Oeil-de-Boeuf have no woman."

"I know," said Bouzille, with an understanding expression. "Adèle moved up... she sleeps in silk now."

"Yes," added Mère Toulouche. "She's moving up."

Bouzille shrugged and said, "That's a problem for Bec and Oeil. What will they do?"

Toulouche grumbled, "People always make do in situations like that. They're looking for another woman. That's what they're doing."

A few seconds passed and, hesitantly, Bouzille asked, "And what are you going to do with the chickens?"

In a dry voice, Toulouche declared, "If anyone asks you about that you say you don't know."

And the conversation ended as a result of Toulouche's unwillingness to answer Bouzille's questions

She had not moved from the top of her heap of garbage and Bouzille had remained down below, on the shore and, in order to converse, the pair had to shout. They were unconcerned about this, thinking they were alone. They had no idea Fandor was there and could hear them.

Bouzille had been gone ten minutes when Mère Toulouche, who had gone back to searching through her pile of garbage, had looked around, making sure no one was spying on her, and pulled a large wicker basket, in which she had hidden a half dozen hens, out of the rubbish.

She hurried to add the hen Bouzille had returned to her to the cage. Joséphine mingled with her sisters, who were crammed in the cage, and Toulouche decided to carry them all off.

Fandor's heart was pounding.

He felt that Mère Toulouche knew a great deal about the mysterious story of the hens.

Mère Toulouche must have been put in charge not only of placing the hens in the hands of the various individuals but also getting them back at a given point in time and gathering them all together.

But it was necessary to know why.

While Fandor remained under the rail car, observing what was going on, Mère Toulouche walked over to the Quai de Javel and waited for a carriage to dive by.

The elderly shrew hailed an old carriage, harnessed to a thin horse and driven by an enormous man. As she climbed into the carriage, someone jumped onto the rear springs. It was Fandor.

"Oh!" exclaimed the journalist. "This is getting more and more interesting. Mère Toulouche is transporting her hens in a carriage. This must mean something."

The carriage drove through Grand-Montrouge and Paris. It proceeded past Grenelle, Vaugirard and on to Montrouge, crossing the barrier.

The trip lasted about an hour and fifteen minutes.

Fandor thought, "This is going to end badly. This trip will cost at least three francs and 50 centimes and Mère Toulouche will never want to pay that."

The carriage headed toward Châtillon. The driver did not seem to be familiar with his route, yet the kind, brave man, wanting no doubt to finish his race, asked passersby for directions.

The carriage proceeded and Fandor, who had decided he no longer needed to hang from the springs or to face behind the carriage, held back a few yards and that's how he learned what address Mère Toulouche had given: the Impasse du Moulin.

The Impasse du Moulin was a filthy alley in the middle of unspeakable, tumbledown cottages.

The driver brought the carriage to a stop, saying "I won't go any farther. The road is too bad. Give me my money. You've reached your destination, old woman."

The poor driver looked worried about having let himself get dragged into such a sordid place. Obviously, he expected a discussion with his client, who had just jumped out of the carriage with some difficulty and placed her basket filled with chickens on the sidewalk next to her.

"That will be four francs forty-five," the driver said, holding out a calloused hand and looking at Mère Toulouche, eyes filled with suspicion.

Yet, the coachman's face suddenly lit up. A beautiful five-franc coin had just fallen into the palm of his hand.

He quickly hid it in his fob pocket, saying, "That will be four francs forty-five without the tip!"

Then he asked Mère Toulouche, "Do you want the change?"

"No," the old woman said, generously, "Keep the rest."

This time, Mère Toulouche had earned the title of madam.

After turning his carriage around, the driver respectfully said, "Thank you madam. And good luck. Good day to you!"

He drove off, cracking his whip. Mère Toulouche stayed there alone with her chicken s a few yards from the Impasse du Moulin.

Fandor had just enough time to hide behind a half-open door. Someone was coming to meet the old woman and the journalist felt his heart pound when he saw that person in the distance.

Who was that man?

Mère Toulouche greeted him in a booming voice, "Good day Mathurin!"

And the man replied in the nasal, singsong accent of the Normans, "Good day to you, old woman. Are we going to enjoy some excellent poultry today?"

Pointing at her basket, Mère Toulouche replied, "In case you decided to be generous, Père Mathurin, it would be possible to sell them to you at a good price, while earning a living."

Fandor was flabbergasted by this conversation. Who were they putting on this show for and what was behind these meaningless words?

Fandor said to himself, "I imagine that Mère Toulouche has no more intention of selling her hens than that so-called Père Mathurin has of buying them!"

Fandor did not dare move. Yet, from behind the door, where he was hidden, he realized that there were a few passersby in the street.

"That show was for them," thought Fandor. "Well, things are getting more and more complicated. But what the devil is going on in that terrible street? Is he surrounded by accomplices? Is he alone? That's what I must find out!"

And who was Fandor thinking about when he uttered those words and who was the person he saw disguised as a Norman peasant? Obviously, it had not taken him long to reach a conclusion.

The journalist, in fact, had only looked at the man for a third of a second, but based on his posture and above all his expression, which he had seen for a moment, he had drawn his conclusions.

Fandor, although he was worried about being surprised, was excessively pleased that he had decided to follow Mère Toulouche to the Impasse du Moulin since Fandor was convinced that the man who had joined Mère Toulouche, the fake Norman peasant with the nasal voice, was none other than the sinister bandit that Fandor had been tracking for such a long time.

Père Mathurin was none other than Fantômas!

Mère Toulouche and the man did not remain in the middle of the alley for long. They walked a few yards down the alley and from there nothing else could be heard.

Fandor stood still for a few moments, then raced off.

He did not wish to be caught, or discovered but, above all, he didn't wish to lose sight of the old woman, to remain alert in this neighborhood. Prepared to catch the criminal in one of his many transformations, to locate his hide-out before intervening and to finally arrest the man once and for all.

Just as Juve had promised himself, Fandor had sworn not to act prematurely, not to get involved in a direct fight with Fantômas, once he had obtained all of the information he needed to arrest the bandit and his accomplices.

Fandor spent the entire day exploring the vicinity of the Impasse du Moulin. It was located at one end of Châtillon, in the lower part of the village and extended down to the fields worked by the small farmers. A small thicket of trees lined a brook that flowed, a few yards from there, to mingle with the underground waters of the Bièvre.

The Impasse du Moulin was made up of low houses surrounded by small gardens which must have once been small farms but which now served as housing for the population of shady wretches and loafers usually found in the area.

Since that morning, Fandor had not glimpsed either Mère Toulouche or the so-called Père Mathurin or even the chickens carried by Bouzille's spouse.

Yet, the journalist was convinced that those mysterious individuals had not left the Impasse and decided to continue his observations until he could catch them in the act.

Fandor, who had purchased something to eat from a local wine merchant, was preparing to spend the night on a roof overlooking the Impasse du Moulin when, as night fell, he suddenly shuddered.

A door to one of the oldest cottages in the Impasse had opened. A man stepped out, dressed as a peasant, carrying a cage filled with chickens. That man was none other than Fantômas. He slowly walked out of the Impasse du Moulin.

This time, Fandor felt like leaping on the monster, shooting him with his revolver. Yet, as he set out in pursuit, three or four men stepped out of the shadows, all dressed like peasants, and walked over to the bandit and surrounded him.

Fandor recognized the familiar silhouettes. Oeil-de-Boeuf was there, along with the tall Bec-de-Gaz. Fat Louis was there; he was a newcomer to the gang and already enjoyed a formidable reputation for his ferociousness.

Fandor felt all alone in the middle of all these bandits. It would have been mad to intervene, to declare war. His defeat would have been guaranteed. It was not the right time. But, he could still follow them and discover what they were up to.

Fandor put his revolver back into his pocket and followed the group of wretches surrounding Fantômas, at a distance.

CHAPTER XIII
An Extraordinary Performance

From that moment, Fandor, alone against the gang headed by Fantômas, engaged in a complicated, frantic pursuit.

Certainly, the men accompanying the sinister bandit did not suspect that they were being followed. Otherwise, there would have been twenty opportunities for one of them to rush Fandor and assassinate him without that poor man having time to put up the slightest resistance.

But the journalist, trained by Juve, was a master in the art of hiding when following someone.

Moreover, the circumstances were in his favor. The ragman's disguise, which he had donned the previous day, just by chance, and which made him look like shabby, allowed him to pass unnoticed, particularly in a neighborhood like Montrouge, where he was at this time, a neighborhood that was more popular than elegant and where prowlers were legion.

Moreover, given the falling night and the fact that the poor light cast by the gaslights favored Fandor, no one who approached him or crossed his path would have been able to recognize him without paying particular attention.

Finally, Fantômas and his men were most certainly preoccupied and not paying much attention to the mysterious person who was following them.

The small gang of fake peasants entered Paris through the Montrouge door, then split into three groups.

Fandor was fortunate in that he had identified the vehicle Fantômas had climbed into. He was also extremely satisfied to find a taxi which he ordered to follow Fantômas' vehicle at a distance.

Fandor was both astonished and angered by the bandit's extraordinary indifference and insolent audacity.

While the entire police force was concerned about Fantômas, worrying about where he was, while the Sûreté agents in Paris and the provinces were once again distributing a detailed and precise description of him, accompanied no doubt by rewards offered to anyone who managed to capture him, Fantômas was indifferent to all that, strolling about Paris as he saw fit, peacefully continuing all of his usual activities, organizing thefts, planning his crimes!

Fantômas' colleagues, jammed into carriages, had instructed their drivers: "Take us to Les Halles!"

Yet, the vehicle in which the bandit had settled was instructed merely to follow the others. Fandor's taxi brought up in the rear, some distance from Fantômas' vehicle, which the journalist took pains to keep in sight.

They arrived at Rue Monge and Fantômas' vehicle stopped at the door of a disreputable looking hotel for a few seconds. The bandit got out and rushed into the building.

The vehicle immediately continued on its way, so rapidly that, for a few seconds, Fandor questioned what he had seen.

"Am I seeing things?" he wondered, as he saw the carriage in which Fantômas had been sitting just a few minutes earlier, realizing that it had lost its sensational client.

The journalist instructed his taxi to stop, inviting the drive to part it at the edge of the opposite sidewalk. Then Fandor, perplexed, took up his post behind a newspaper kiosk, facing the hotel on Rue Monge.

"By Jove!" the journalist said to himself. "I do believe he went into the hotel, yet I can't be sure. What should I do! Should I wait?"

Fandor decided there was only one thing he could do: stay where he was.

What else could he do, after all?

Of course, his chances of encountering Fantômas had been compromised, yet that was not the only card in his hand. And he should keep that in mind.

An hour passed. Fandor was starting to despair when suddenly, through the door to the Hotel on Rue Monge, which he had seen numerous, shifty-looking carpet sellers go through, there suddenly appeared an individual with a bizarre silhouette that caught Fandor's attention.

The man, with a very brown face, was wearing some sort of silk robe, much like those worn by the Hindus or the Annamites. His hair, as long as that of a woman, was plaited around his head, forming a sort of turban.

"Yet another foreigner. This hotel is filled with them."

And he would have let that individual walk off, without thinking about following him, if the man had not been carrying a large package that caused Fandor to cry out in surprise.

"The cage with the chickens!" the journalist shouted in his mind.

Of course, Fandor was leagues from believing that the man walking away from him, heading toward Rue du Cardinal-Lemoine, was none other than Fantômas!

The man was so marvelously made up that it would be totally impossible for anyone, even someone who was informed, to recognize the man.

Fandor had the impression that his path was separating in two, that he had come to a fork in his shadowing.

"On the one hand," he said. "Fantômas was no doubt hidden in the hotel. On the other, there is the man with the chickens. Should I follow him? Should I wait for Fantômas to come out? What do I know?"

Yet, time was running out.

Fandor took a 20-franc coin from his pocket. And, as he usually did when he had to make a decision, he tossed the coin into the air.

"Heads I stay. Tails I run after the man with the chickens…"

A metallic clink on the sidewalk announced the landing of the coin.

Fandor rushed over to it.

"Heads!" he said. "In other words, I stay here…"

He hesitated for a second, then picking up his coin, pulling his hat down over his head, he rushed over to his taxi.

"Follow that man!" he said, pointing at the individual walking toward Rue du Cardinal-Lemoine.

Fandor had done the exact opposite of what fate had advised him to do.

At the top of Rue du Cardinal-Lemoine, as he reached an area where there was little hustle and bustle, deciding that his taxi's insistence on following the man on foot could well cause him to be noticed, he got rid of the carriage.

Once again, Fandor let the man get a head start and followed him at a distance of a hundred yards.

The man walked into narrow alleys. Fandor followed him.

"This is truly extraordinary," he murmured. "What are all these people doing carting cages of chickens throughout Paris and what do those hens mean? Are they a rallying sign? Are they some mysterious alphabet that enables accomplices to recognize one another? Are they hens that lay golden eggs? Why are they being handled with such care? I mean, I've been looking into this matter for eight days and I've yet to discover anything!"

But, that evening, Fandor would move from surprise to surprise. First, he observed something that suddenly caused his heart to pound. The random twists and turns of his tracking had led him into the vicinity of Rue d'Ulm, precisely where the small hospice where Hélène was recuperating was located.

Anguished, he wondered if Fantômas and his gang might possibly intend to attack his unfortunate wife yet again, his unfortunate wife who, in Fantômas' eyes, had committed no crime other than falling in love with him, Fandor.

With that thought, he clenched his fists, blood flowed to his brain and Fandor said, "If they want Hélène, then I'll stand in their way."

He had felt overwhelmed since the previous evening, having had no time to sleep, and he was ready for anything.

At the idea that his fiancée, his wife, was in danger, all of his energy returned. The journalist felt driven by a new ardor. He turned into the narrow and deserted Rue des Irlandais, following the mysterious man wearing the long robe. Both men walked close to the walls, hiding in the shadows.

Suddenly, Fandor cried out in surprise, as if the ground had opened up beneath him, swallowing him up. The man carrying the cage filled with chickens, and the cage itself, had suddenly disappeared!

"Good grief!" said Fandor. "Yet, it's not as if there is some kind of trap door in the sidewalk!"

Fandor did not believe that but he did nevertheless look at the sidewalk, the adjacent road, and felt the manhole cover just to make sure that everything was rigorously immobile.

Then he looked up, slapped himself on the forehead and said, "I'm such an imbecile."

In front of him, in the wall, there was a door and, with logical reasoning, Fandor said, "By Jove! That where our man went in. They must have been waiting for him, the door must have been ajar when he arrived and, now he's inside while I'm out here. Well!"

The journalist stepped back.

He was in less of a rush now. He examined the surrounding area and, glancing at a section of a low wall, opposite where the man with the chickens had disappeared, he realized that wall along the street was also the wall for a house that looked over the idle land or gardens that lay behind the wall.

Fandor noticed that it was a very low house with no opening on the street and that the brick roof barely reached one yard above the wall.

The journalist quickly came to a decision.

"I must get into that house and find out what is going on there!'

Although the decision was easy to make, it was more complicated to put it into effect.

And for close to a quarter of an hour, Fandor paced up and down Rue des Irlandais, looking for the place where the man wearing the long robe had entered the building, while trying to go unnoticed and make sure he could retreat in the event of danger.

Fortunately, there was no one else in the deserted street to bother Fandor.

Using a gaslight, he managed to pull himself up to the top of the wall and sit astride it. Fandor, whose eyes had grown used to the twilight, noticed, despite the dark night, that the street was on one side of the wall while a relatively large garden, very dense, lay on the other and, in front of him there was a house, leaning against the wall, the shack covered with tiles, as he had imagined it from down below, in the street, after seeing only part of it.

Fandor did not hesitate.

"That's it," he said. "The man with the chickens entered that shack."

He moved ahead, reaching the brick roof. He stretched out his entire length on that roof and shamelessly yet cautiously started to remove the tiles in order to determine if it would be possible to enter the upper rooms of the house.

But he was unable to move the tiles without making noise and, two or three times, when a tile would fall, he shuddered.

"Good grief!" he grumbled. "I hope no one notices that I'm in the process of demolishing the house!"

Regretfully, the journalist resolved to abandon his dangerous undertaking.

"Poor principle, poor result," he said to himself. "Let's try something else!"

At the end of the house, there was a large chimney. Fandor made his way over to it. Deliberately, the journalist bent down over the opening and, immediately froze in surprise, shivering with joy. He heard people talking, voices rising up the chimney to him. He listened, overcome with an unspeakable emotion.

The words Fandor heard were extraordinary, stupefying. It seemed as if he were involved in some ridiculous adventure, as he had suddenly been transported a thousand leagues away from France. An odor of amber and salt wafted up to him, mingled with the scent of chlorine and hot iodine. Then he heard a metallic, foreign-sounding voice murmur strange things.

"My son," said the voice. "Buddha has finally answered my prayers and, thanks to you, we will possess the rarest treasure in the world, the treasure that will give us infinite wealth, namely freedom for us and ours... Believe in the rod of Bedjapur. When death arrives soon to perform the fatal work on your poor body, your soul will fly to the seventh heaven and take its place among those who accompany Buddha, next to the worthiest Brahmins, fakirs and dervishes!"

"What is he going on about?" stammered Fandor, dumbfounded. "What have I stumbled into?"

He continued to listen. And this time his face tensed and his eyes grew wide with emotion.

A voice answered, filled with respect, "Bedjapur! Bedjapur! Your words are too beautiful for someone as unworthy as me. You are most certainly offending Buddha, by letting me hope that one day, in the eternity of the centuries, his august glance will fall on my miserable soul. But what importance is the reward? That's not what I'm waiting for. If I serve your cause, which is my cause, I do so only to fulfill the duty that belongs to all of us, the pariahs, the Hindus, England's victims, the children of India, bruised and detested by the enemies of the West!"

"Well, well," Fandor stammered. "This surprises me more than I could ever imagine. There's nothing to be said for it, the man who is talking, the man who is replying to that so-called Bedjapur, I recognize his voice. I know who it is... Of course, he's changed his tone and is expressing himself in a language in which is not familiar to him, but I recognize him anyway... It's Fantômas! What can this mean? What comedy is being played out in this shack? Who is the man he is deceiving? Is it Bedjapur? Is it the man in the long robe? Is it me?"

The journalist listened again but the speakers must have gone into another room since he could no longer hear them.

Fandor, desperate, was about to leave the chimney when the voices rang out again.

Fantômas said, "Bedjapur, Bedjapur. Here are the divine birds I thought I must bring to you. You can check the truth of my words yourself. You can make sure that, using the technique I have developed, the vile food consumed by these chickens can be transformed and is transformed within a few hours, and takes on the nature and consistency of the most precious mineral in the world!"

Bedjapur's strident voice interrupted Fantômas, saying, "You've found a means to make artificial diamonds! May Buddha bless you!"

Despite his anxiety, despite his concerns, Fandor could not hold back a burst of laughter which, despite his efforts, rang out through the chimney pipe.

Good grief! This was worse than anything Fantômas had done before. He had convinced the other man that he had found a way to make artificial diamonds and would give the old man his secret!

"Ah!" thought Fandor. "If Fantômas had actually discovered such a secret he would never tell anyone else about it!"

Then he heard the sinister bandit's voice, making an insinuating and gentle suggestion, "Bedjapur, Bedjapur. Soon, when you are alone in this laboratory, you will be able to check the accuracy of my claims. In exchange, as I said earlier, you must help me now. I am poor and wretched. I have many debts. And now that you know how to make diamonds, you who have all the chemical products needed for that, give me some gold in return... give me the reward you promised me."

"I expected that," thought Fandor.

And he waited, curious, to hear Bedjapur's answer.

"In the cellars," the old man said, "The cellars that can be reached through a trap door that I will explain to you, there are crates filled with gold coins. In that place alone, there is more than 10 million. Tomorrow morning, you will go into those cellars and take the crates you want."

Thank you, Sahib," said Fantômas, stammering his farewells.

Silence fell.

At the top of his perch, Fandor waited a few minutes more, ear bent to the chimney opening, then he looked around, resolved to leap down on Fantômas, in the event that he saw the bandit leave the house.

From one moment to the next, the journalist expected to see the tragic and well-known silhouette of the bandit, make its way along a wall, or standing in the frame of the door on the street.

He was prepared to leap down on the other man, revolver in hand.

Ten minutes passed, then fifteen. Fandor heard a slight sound, a silhouette, a shadow was slipping through the garden, disappearing into the thickets of the small park, too quickly to be followed.

Yet, Fandor was not filled with regret. It was not Fantômas he had seen go on his way, but the man in the large silk robe who was disappearing alone, without the cage of chickens.

Yet, Fandor had not identified this man as Fantômas, presuming that the bandit had remained in the house.

Suddenly, he returned to the opening of the chimney, where a pale light rose. He bent over the opening and was dumbfounded. The interior of the chimney was lit by some sort of electric lamp down below and, once his eyes had grown accustomed to the intense light, Fandor understood the exact nature of the fireplace that stood beneath the chimney.

The fireplace was no ordinary fireplace but a sort of brick workbench, on which all kinds of jars, test tubes and retorts stood.

Initially intrigued by this vision, Fandor recalled the words Fantômas had uttered, "Bedjapur, when you are alone in this laboratory…"

And Fandor immediately realized that the chimney he was looking down, was the chimney for the laboratory and that the fireplace was one of the furnaces in the workroom.

Bitter, unpleasant odors rose with the light to Fandor, who had to cover his nose with a handkerchief. Although his eyes suffered from the too intense light, the journalist paid that no heed, focused as he was on seeing what was happening.

Suddenly he heard chickens clucking, not the normal clucking of a peaceful creature, one that was resting, but the hasty clucking of fearful chickens, chickens that were being chased and frightened.

Fandor suddenly witnessed an extraordinary spectacle. Two hands appeared, two very brown, emaciated hands. They held a large black hen that was struggling. Two small wooden vices lay within reach. The two hands, for which no body could be seen, immobilized the unfortunate beast in the vices.

Both hands withdrew and one of them returned, armed with a knife. Suddenly, the chicken was sliced open the entire length of its body. Blood sputtered everywhere while the viscous entrails slowly disappeared into the feathers. The knife was tossed onto the bricks of the furnace and the two hands plunged, without loathing, into the gasping body of the unfortunate beast, carefully searching through the intestines.

Suddenly, a hoarse cry rang out just as a bright shiny object appeared through the perforate gizzard.

Dumbfounded, Fandor uttered a single, "Diamond!"

It was, in fact, a superb diamond, flashing with a thousand lights, that the mysterious hands had extracted from the chicken's gizzard.

"Oh!" said Fandor. "Would Fantômas' prediction come true? Would precious stones now be found in the stomachs of chickens?"

The remnants of the dismembered chicken disappeared, removed by the two agile hands and thrown no doubt into some waste bin. The instruments of torture, the two wooden vices, tinted red, remained victim-free for a minute and then another chicken, more robust, more beautiful than the previous one, took the place of the first…

It too was carved in two. Its blackish blood spurted every which way. The brown hands, covered with blood, dug through the creature's innards. Then two hoarse cries rang out as the emaciated fingers of the mysterious hands pulled out two diamonds!

Fandor did not weary of the extraordinary spectacle. After the two hens were sacrificed, there was an intermission during he heard nothing more. Then, two hours later, three more chickens were sacrificed, each giving the mysterious hands two diamonds.

Fandor remained there, panting, immobile. He was starting to understand Fantômas' interest in caring for the extraordinarily prolific chickens so carefully, chickens who were much better than the chicken who laid golden eggs, since they laid diamond ones.

Day was dawning and Fandor was still on the roof of the small house. Yet there had been no more sacrifices for some time and the laboratory inside had returned to silence and darkness.

"I have to leave," Fandor thought, as he used the gaslight positioned against the house, to quickly climb back down to the sidewalk.

At about nine that morning, Fandor left the small hospice where Hélène was convalescing.

After leaving the strange dwelling on Rue des Irlandais, the journalist, who was very upset, very emotional, had gone to see the young woman.

Initially, not wanting to upset her, the young man had tried to avoid telling her what he had been up to. But, noticing that he was tired, noting his torn clothing, Hélène had grown worried and he had been forced to tell her everything.

And Fandor, who was been terribly upset by the extraordinary discovery he had made wanted nothing more than to talk about it. Yet, when he uttered the name of Bedjapur, Hélène had suddenly grown pale, so pale that Fandor had thought she was about to faint.

She reacted immediately. Swamping the journalist with questions, she made him tell her exactly where the mysterious house that man lived in was located.

Fandor, surprised by her curiosity, questioned her, saying "Why? Why, Hélène are you so interested in this Bedjapur, a man neither of us knows, a man whose name you are hearing for the first time?"

Hélène did not listen to him.

She sat up in her chaise longue, eyes shining as if with a fever and stammered, "Bedjapur! Bedjapur! My God! Could it be possible! After such a long time, I thought I would not be capable of retaining that memory. What a strange coincidence! What a strange adventure! Oh, I'm starting to remember now. Could it possibly be true? Was Laetitia right?"

At the sound of that name, Fandor shuddered.[10]

"Laetitia! Who was close to him and yet far away at the same time. Laetitia! That was the name of the old Negro woman who, in the past, in South Africa, had kidnapped Hélène and whom Fandor had encountered when he met the young woman.

---

[10] See *The Daughter of Fantômas*.

Laetitia knew the mystery of Hélène's birth. She was going to reveal it to the two young people when Fantômas, suddenly appeared and killed the unfortunate woman, no doubt to keep her from talking.

When Hélène uttered the name of Laetitia, Fandor recalled all of the mysteries surrounding the skull he had discovered, and Juve had taken, in the ossuary of the diamond cutting shop that belonged to Hans Elders. An extraordinary skull, in fact, that had served as a hiding place for parchments that could have documented Hélène's origins, if anyone had been able to read the most unusual language in which they had been written.

Ah! The fights and battles that had taken place between Fantômas, Juve and Fandor, over Hélène's famous papers. Each of them had taken possession of the papers in turn and then they had finally remained in Juve's hands and, as of that time, no one seemed to have any interest in deciphering them. And, a few years ago, one man could have had something to say about that and that was Gérard. But Gérard was dead, assassinated by Fantômas.

Why did the name of Bedjapur bring this mysterious memory back to Hélène?

For a moment, Fandor thought his curiosity was about to be satisfied. Hélène, recovering from her initial emotion, motioned him to move closer and took his hand in hers.

"Listen, Fandor," the young girl murmured, panting since she was still quite weak, overwhelmed by fatigue and emotion. "I'll tell you what I know about Bedjapur. One day, when I was just a little girl, there, in Natal…"

But Hélène stopped talking and Fandor did not dare interrupt her. The young girl was obviously exhausted and had fallen into a deep sleep.

That was when Fandor left, postponing his interrogation of the woman he loved more than life, the woman to whom he had promised his soul.

Outside on the sidewalk, Fandor hesitated. First, he had intended to warn the police, to bring the Sûreté officers back to Bedjapur's mysterious house and uncover the secret of the man's existence.

But, after hearing Hélène's words, he hesitated to do that and decided he would not inform the police until after he had listened to what his beloved had to reveal.

Fandor remained perplexed for a moment, then made a sudden decision.

"The building on Rue du Moulin, in Montrouge, is the hideout of a formidable enemy. We must surround it, we must work to capture them all, without wasting another minute, without wasting another second.

CHAPTER XIV
Failed Capture

While these events were taking place along the edges of Rue des Irlandais, in another, more elegant, more fashionable neighborhood in Paris, in the Plaine Monceau area, the wildest incidents and adventures were taking place in a very different setting.

On Rue de Prony, at the house where Adèle lived, Adèle who was the former servant, the former mistress of Bec-de-Gaz and Oeil-de-Boeuf, Adèle who had by a combination of circumstances and high aspirations, been given an enviable, albeit somewhat immoral, role as a luxurious demimondaine.

Adèle's ascension toward her goal had been so rapid and dizzying that everyone who knew her had remained dumbfounded. She was no less surprised and her sudden promotion seemed to have completely unbalanced the poor girl who was not lacking in intelligence although she had been the simple and modest mistress of two criminals and who, since she had become a woman of luxury seemed incapable of making the slightest rational or logical decision.

Adèle had been installed on Rue de Prony by her lover Manoel Palatello, in the superb apartment where he had lived alone prior to that day. Adèle was completely overwhelmed, bewildered, or so it seemed, by the enormous amounts of money Manoel Palatello gave her.

This rich South American seemed to enjoy giving his mistress checks all the time, very large checks for that matter, which Adèle quickly transformed into bank notes and gold coins.

It was organized chaos in her home...

In vain, Manoel Palatello said to her, "I'll give you all the money you want, as long as you don't spend it foolishly, like most of your kind do. Be careful. One day I'll ask you to account for yourself. If ever I find that you have spent your money foolishly, you'll see what will happen to you!

Adèle paid no attention to the Brazilian's recommendations.

"When you give me money," she said, "it's so I can do what I want with it."

And then she added, repeating an old philosophical saying often expressed by Oeil-de-Boeuf and Bed-de-Gas, "You can't take it with you when you die."

From morning to night, there was a perpetual parade of voracious suppliers, indiscrete beggars, people of all kinds, who wanted to grab their share of the fortune the Brazilian was giving the demimondaine.

Adèle, who was a good girl moreover, spent without counting, happy to make the people around her happy, never more delighted than the day on which she spent the largest amount for the least significant thing.

That morning, Adèle got up in a bad mood.

It might have been about noon when she woke up, tired, with a heavy head.

The night before, there had been a party at her place and in the parlor, behind closed doors, the atmosphere was heavy, polluted with tobacco and alcohol fumes.

After eating in a fashionable restaurant, Adèle and her lover returned to Rue de Prony, followed by a dozen party-goers, both men and women, people that they had met in various places, as they made new friends.

They drank, laughed, dance and sang again and then, at dawn, everyone had left, even Adèle's lover who, having started a game of baccarat with three of his compatriots, had decided it would be interesting to keep on going!

Adèle had gone to bed alone, at about four in the morning. She woke at noon, tired and furious. The first words she uttered were violent remarks intended for her servants.

Seeing that their mistress was sleeping, they had not done the least bit of work, particularly, since they had gone to bed late as well. Adèle walked through the messy apartment, wearing only a simple peignoir, her hair floating tangled and curled around her head.

The dining room looked like a culinary battlefield filled with empty bottles and leftovers of the meal eaten by the guests of the previous evening.

Adèle scolded her valet, "How wretched, leaving all this food out in plain sight! Get on with it! Try to make these bottles and food disappear!"

She walked into the parlor, suffocating in the unbreathable air, then scolded her chambermaid. But that woman declared that the parlor was not her territory, that other servants were responsible for cleaning it.

Adèle shrugged, not knowing quite how to respond. She had moved into the position she now held so quickly that she had not quite grown accustomed to giving orders. At some times, her chambermaid was a companion. She was more comfortable with the woman when telling her jokes than when giving orders.

Adèle returned to her boudoir. The room was relatively tidy. It was, moreover, Adèle's favorite place, the room she used when she had a few moments to herself, spending her time there to passionately read all the serialized novels she could get her hands on.

Adèle rang the bell. She was dying of thirst. A servant appeared.

"Bring me a glass of water!" she shouted.

Yet, as she was waiting, she noticed that, here as well, the housekeeping had been sloppy. There was an enormous amount of dust on the furniture and cigarette ashes on the armchair where she wanted to sit.

"Drat!" Adèle grumbled. "The servants are all in on it. They never do anything. I know something about it, I'm…"

If Adèle remembered who she had been, it was not only to say it, but also to prove it to herself. Pushing a sofa with her foot, Adèle had just discovered, hidden under it, a feather duster and a cleaning rag and she automatically rolled up the sleeves of her peignoir and wrapped a napkin picked up from the neighboring table around her head to protect her hair and courageously started cleaning her own apartment.

This strenuous exercise chased away the headache that had been pounding at her temples. She breathed more deeply, she felt more and more rested as the violent exercise relaxed her muscles and brought pearls of sweat to her forehead.

When she needed to rest, she went over to the balcony and looked down at the street, without worrying about the attention she was attracting or the comments of the neighbors, who were quite astonished to see an individual living in an apartment that cost 10,000 francs, doing her own housework while her many servants crossed their arms and lolled about in the armchairs in other rooms.

Adèle was on the balcony and was taking an interest in a dispute involving a carter and a carriage man when she heard herself being called from inside the apartment. The young woman left her observation post and returned to the boudoir. Manoel Palatello had just arrived. The Brazilian seemed dumbfounded at his mistress' attire.

"Have you become a servant?" he asked. "Where is the mistress of the house?"

Confused, Adèle blushed to the roots of her hair and said, "I just wanted to keep active. It's my nature… I have to be on the go."

The Brazilian shrugged. He took a little notebook out of his pocket, wrote something in it, put it back in the pocket and continued his observations, saying "I haven't been giving you 50,000 francs per week over the past month so that you can do the housework! You simply have to pay people to do that. If you want to keep active, get on a horse, do some physical exercise, learn to dance! In fact, what's happening with your dancing lessons?"

Adèle submissively replied, "I started two days ago… and then I stopped."

"Why?"

"Because the instructor ran off."

"Why did he do that?"

"He took a Chinese vase that was on the fireplace mantle. Naturally, he hasn't been seen since."

Manoel Palatello sat down in the boudoir.

"You know what I told you, Adèle. Spend whatever you want, but spend it well, intelligently. And let me know a bit about what you do with your money."

Just then, someone knocked at the door.

"Come in," Adèle said.

A servant entered the room.

"It's the automobile," he said.

"What automobile," Adèle asked.

"Madam knows full well," said the servant, respectfully. "Madam ordered an automobile yesterday morning at 10 o'clock. It's still here and the mechanic is still waiting for orders…"

Adèle lost her temper.

"Idiot! You should have notified me! I forgot all about it. I took taxis all afternoon!"

Impassive, the valet continued, "The mechanic is asking to be paid. He wants 300 francs for renting his car. Since yesterday morning, at 8 o'clock."

Adèle searched through a drawer that held a few spare gold coins. She counted out 25 gold louis coins.

"Here," she said, throwing them at the servant. "Throw these in his face and tell him to clear off!"

Then she turned to Manoel.

"Hey!" she said. "Do you think I know how to do things, that I know how to spend money? Do you like it like this?"

While Adèle's behavior might have seemed a little mad, the Brazilian looked even crazier.

He shrugged.

"It's absurd," he finally said. "You were supposed to give the mechanic 300 francs, not 500. The difference is just being thrown out the window."

The Brazilian took his notebook out of his pocket again, wrote something down, and suddenly ran over to the boudoir door and called the servant back.

"Come back here, you animal," he shouted.

And, when the valet returned, Manoel Palatello declared, "Go and ask that mechanic what his car is worth. I'm buying it from him!"

And as the valet retired a second time, the Brazilian turned to Adèle and said, "Now this is what I call being reasonable. Since a car lasts five or six years on average, no matter how much that man asks for his vehicle, it will most certainly not be 500 francs per day!"

Adèle was dumbfounded.

"Well," she said. "All I can say is that you've got a cast iron constitution!"

Manoel Palatello felt that enough had been said on the matter.

"Let's go into the parlor," he said. "I left some expensive cigars on the table yesterday and I want to see how many are left."

And as he opened the door that led from the boudoir into the parlor. The Brazilian cried out and suddenly stepped back.

At the same time, hasty clucking sounds rang out and, when she heard them, Adèle rushed over to the window and closed it immediately.

"Good grief! The chicken! I had forgotten about it. Drat! If she's run off, that will be a bad business!"

Suddenly, she appeared quite afraid. The she calmed down, seeing that there was no possible way out for the unfortunate hen.

Yet, the Brazilian, who had been very calm up to that point, suddenly grew furious.

"That chicken should be strangled and thrown outside," he said. "I don't want to see it again!"

But this time Adèle, who usually gave in to all of her lover's whims, protested indignantly, saying "Never! It's important to me!"

"And I don't want it," grumbled the Brazilian.

Adèle shook her head obstinately.

"Nothing can separate me from it."

"We'll see about that," continued the South American.

And the two lovers, as crazy and mad as they were, suddenly glared at one another, their eyes casting thunderbolts of anger. Manoel Palatello had picked up his cane and was swirling it about, threatening the hen, whose clucking grew more and more frantic, more and more frequent.

But Adèle insisted on thwarting her rich protector. She picked up her feather duster and prepared to defend the hen.

"You won't have its hide!" she shouted.

And then the threats were followed by blows. An unlikely and grotesque scene took place in the boudoir, concluding with the panic-stricken shrieks of Adèle as she was conscientiously beaten by her irascible lover.

This scene, which had just taken place, had also taken place the previous evening and would take place again the next day.

It seemed as if the two extraordinary lovers were mad about battle, and that they could only be satisfied and peaceful after beating one another. The Brazilian generally came out the victor and, after ensuring the defeat of his victim, he would generously throw a handful of gold on the table and go out to play cards yet again.

When he left, Adèle knew that she would have a few hours of peace.

That morning, like the others, the battle had taken place. Yet, it had lasted longer and had been more violent. Concerned about the fate of her chicken, Adèle had defended herself more rigorously, and responded with more energy.

The shouting, the shrieking, had stirred up the entire neighborhood and the people living upstairs and downstairs had, once again, complained to the police commissioner about the abominable racket made in that house.

It was about two o'clock in the afternoon and Juve was on Boulevard de Courcelles. For several days, the policeman's comings and goings had been mysterious, hidden. The singular adventures that had taken place in the theatres of Paris, the incidents that had taken place concerning the necklace, did not leave Juve any peace of mind.

The policeman had grown grumpy. He would lock himself up at home for hours, receiving no visitors. Old Jean, who had returned to his post, no longer dared to go into his employer's office, where Juve sat, his mind filling with dark ideas. The old man was scandalized when he noted that Juve no longer even thought about Fandor.

Juve was walking along Boulevard de Courcelles, when he suddenly called out to two individuals walking in his direction.

"Hey, you there, good evening," he said.

The individuals stopped, somewhat surprised by this approach. Then, suddenly, as they recognized the police inspector, they ran toward him.

"Well, well, well, Mr. Juve. What a fortuitous encounter. How are you?"

The two men were Nalorgne and Pérouzin, two mysterious lads in whom Juve had a little trust, although they were highly accredited as police inspectors and members of the increasingly compact group of Fantômas' adversaries.

Juve looked at them with a clear and penetrating glance, and asked, "Where are you off to?"

Nalorgne and Pérouzin looked at one another before replying, as they always did.

Juve shook them by the arms.

"There's no point making something up," he grumbled. "Tell me where you're going."

"Well," said Nalorgne, "We're going..."

He stopped, giving Pérouzin an opportunity to continue.

"To investigate a demimondaine," said the latter.

"I know," said Juve. "You're going to visit Adèle, the former mistress of Bec-de-Gaz and Oeil-de-Boeuf."

"Good grief. That's right!" said Nalorgne, "The neighbors have filed a complaint, about all the racket at her place."

Pérouzin continued, "Seems like it was terrible, that they found an entire menagerie in the apartment.... Some people are saying that they were raising chickens there..."

Juve interrupted the two inspectors. He scribbled a few words on a page that he tore out of his notebook and handed to Nalorgne.

"You're going to have to go back," he said. "Give this to your department head and stay quiet. I'll take your place I'll conduct the investigation on Rue de Prony!"

A few minutes later, Fantômas' famous adversary arrived at the demimondaine's apartment. He asked to see her and he was invited into the lobby and then forgotten there. The room was filled with suppliers, shop boys. People were coming and going in the apartment.

For a few moments, Juve enjoyed watching the chaos then, losing patience since no one was taking care of him, he deliberately walked out of the room and headed into the chambers.

Moreover, he deliberately left the antechamber since he had seen, through a door that lead to a staircase, someone walking up the stairs, someone he definitely did not want to meet.

That someone was a caricature with an unforgettable silhouette.

That someone entered the antechamber just a few seconds after Juve disappeared, was none other than Mère Toulouche whose sensational attire as a costermonger disguised as a clothing seller made everyone present burst into laughter.

Juve, however, had headed on his own into the maze of rooms. He opened several doors randomly, walked through a few empty rooms, and finally reached the boudoir where Adèle was nonchalantly lying on a chaise longue, overwhelmed by the beating she had just received.

"Good day," Juve said as he entered the room.

Adèle jumped, saying, "My goodness, you startled me."

"No problem at all," replied the policeman.

But just then, Juve shuddered and stepped back.

The hen, Adèle's famous hen, had just appeared from under the sofa, flapping its wings, clucking in fright.

Juve glanced at the chicken, surprised.

"So, it is true, Adèle?" he asked. "You're raising chickens?"

"How do you know about that?" the former maid said, humorously.

"Everyone in the neighborhood is talking about it," Juve declared. "And that is why I've come to see you."

Adèle glanced at Juve, concerned and suspicious.

"Well, it looks like you've got time on your hands!" she said. "Is there a law against raising chickens? Well, first of all, I'm not raising chickens, and if I were raising chickens it would be the same thing... Everyone does what they want, don't they, and curious people should just mind their own business."

Her opinion was abrupt, categorical and Juve did not insist, realizing that Adèle knew her rights and that she would be more than happy to slam the door shut in the policeman's face.

Juve took another stance.

"My brave little woman," he said, taking Adèle's hand. "Do you think I care about your chickens? I came to see you and for something completely different. People in the neighborhood are saying that your lover is most brutal with you, that he beats you dreadfully. The neighbors are upset. They've complained to the police commissioner. I've come here to look into the situation and tell you that we are prepared to protect you against your Brazilian's brutality."

Although Juve spoke in a sincere and natural tone of voice, Adèle continued to be suspicious.

"Really!" she said. "You've taken all this trouble for me! That's quite nice for the police! When a demimondaine gets hit by her lover or when she hits him back, the most famous and the busiest of all the force's inspectors drops by. I would never have thought they would do this for me! Really, you're going to make me blush!"

Adèle was mocking him and Juve was fully aware of this.

"She doesn't want to say anything to me, so she won't say anything to me," he thought. "Perfect, I'm going to have to take my gloves off with her."

The policeman did not respond to the woman's ironic comments.

"Well," he said, "looking thrilled. "As long as the situation is no more serious than that, I don't think there's any point in disturbing you any longer. You can joke as much as you like, Adèle, but I assure you that at the Sûreté we spare no effort to protect and defend people who are in need. If ever you do have problems, just call me and I'll run over."

Juve bowed, smiling at Adèle, and she smiled in return.

"Don't trouble yourself," he said and he saw that she was preparing to see him out.

And suddenly, the policeman left.

Adèle stayed in the room, listening, to make sure that Juve had truly departed.

She was a bit worried.

"Why did he come here?" she wondered. "Of course, it had nothing to do with my fights with Palatello! It must be something else. But what? Good grief, it's easy enough to see! He wanted information about those chickens. What an idiot! As if I would say anything to him! But it is true that that hen bothers me!"

Adèle hesitated for a second. Then she rang the bell. After a few moments, a servant appeared.

"Go and see if the clothing seller has arrived," Adèle ordered.

"What is her name?"

"Her name is Mère Toul…"

Adèle stopped talking, then said, "I have no idea. I don't even know if there is anyone in the antechamber. You'll be able to recognize her though… she's the ugliest and tackiest of them all!"

Impassive, the servant withdrew.

Adèle murmured to herself, "I just about put my foot in it there. Those stuffed shirts don't all need to know Mère Toulouche's name!"

A few minutes later, the mysterious old woman was chatting with Adèle in the boudoir.

"You know," grumbled the demimondaine. "I'm fed up with your hen! You have to take it away from here. It's causing no end of trouble. You always have to keep an eye on it and it could cause some wicked problems. Do you know who just left?"

"No," said Mère Toulouche.

"Juve!" declared Adèle. "And since he didn't come here to ask me to stick my tongue out so he could see if I was well, I think he may be on the trail of something and that could go badly for us…"

Mère Toulouche assumed an innocent expression.

'Yet there's no harm in raising chickens in your home."

"That's not it," Adèle said suddenly, "You know full well that's there's something suspicious about those chickens. Bec-de-Gaz didn't way what was going on when he gave me the one I have here, the one you gave him for me, but you must know! So, Mère Toulouche, you are going to do me the pleasure of taking this hen away from here. It must be gone from here in five minutes. Otherwise, I'll go and find Juve and tell him that you gave the chicken to Bec-de-Gaz so that he could give it to me and that it was given to you by..."

Mère Toulouche raised her arms to the sky, saying, "Shut your mouth, pretty one! Shut your mouth. You can't talk like that! First, I said nothing but, since you're having problems, I'll get rid of the chicken for you!"

Mère Toulouche bent down toward the chair under which the unfortunate hen, half dead with fear, was hiding. The old woman took a few seeds from her pocket, placed them in the hollow of her hand, and called the hen. After hesitating for a few moments, the hen approached. Suddenly, with the skill of a pickpocket, the old woman grabbed the animal, using her gnarled fingers to grab its wings, tied it up quickly and stuffed it in her large bag.

"Fine," said Adèle, who had witnessed the capture. "Now, get out of here!"

Mère Toulouche wasted no time disappearing. She grumbled as she walked down the stairs, "After all, I did the right thing and Fantômas won't catch me for taking back the hen... all the more so since he's busy liquidating all those that he was keeping in Impasse du Moulin. Have to belief that his plot worked! I'm certain that he will be quite happy to see this one..."

Mère Toulouche, who decidedly had a lot of money, no doubt as a result of Fantômas' generosity, took a car and gave the address to the driver: Impasse de Montrouge.

And, someone behind her was taking a taxi, preparing to follow her. That someone was Juve, Juve who instead of leaving Adèle's apartment when he had taken his leave of her, had hidden behind a curtain and overheard the entire conversation between Adèle and Mère Toulouche.

Just as Fandor had lain in wait for Fantômas and his accomplices in the Impasse du Moulin the previous evening, Juve, who was pursuing Mère Toulouche, was also about to spy on the comings and goings of the street's mysterious inhabitants.

After 45 minutes, they both arrived at Montrouge. Juve, who had sent off his car at the same time as Mère Toulouche was getting rid of hers, followed the elderly woman at a distance.

She arrived at Impasse du Moulin, spent half an hour in the tumbledown cottage from which Fantômas had exited the previous evening, then headed off in turn, after locking the door.

Juve let her leave.

He waited for a few moments and then, taking advantage of the fact that there was no one in the vicinity, he walked over to the sordid dump.

After using a skeleton key to get inside, Juve, his revolver in hand, closed the door and carefully examined the room from which Mère Toulouche had just left.

It was a dilapidated house, a sort of absolutely abandoned shack good, or so it seemed, for storing old tools.

There was only one floor and it contained two rooms, with a dirt floor. In one of the rooms, there was a bench, chairs with broken seats and in the other there was a sort of chicken coop, which housed only a single hen, most likely the hen that Mère Toulouche had picked up from Adèle.

Juve made a quick tour of the unusual dwelling in which he found himself. He crossed his arms and thought.

"What the devil can be going on here? What is going on in this building?"

There was nothing suspicious about the dump and its insignificant, honest appearance intrigued Juve.

"It's hiding something." He thought.

And he wondered if the walls, the large beams for the roof, the chicken cage, were not hiding some secret device, a door, a trap door that led to a basement.

Juve remained on the alert and carefully started to take an inventory of the miserable dwelling, when, all of a sudden, he stopped moving and held his breath.

All around him, he noted unusual sounds, heard strange whispering, observed the characteristic rustling of bodies sliding over a roof, of footsteps surrounding the house.

"Oh!" thought Juve. "Have I fallen into some kind of trap?"

The policeman wondered if Mère Toulouche had perhaps noticed him, if she had drawn him in in order to have him surprised, if she had gone for reinforcements. Juve realized that the dead-end street where the house in which he stood was absolutely isolated. Far from any respectable, honest dwelling.

The shanty and the neighborhood provided a marvelous hideout for bandits. Juve shuddered, and tightened his grip on the revolver's trigger.

"Well," he grumbled. "If I have to defend myself, then I'll defend myself. But I'll have a clear heart and I'll know who I'm dealing with!"

Juve had no doubt about that. He realized full well that that the shack in which he stood was surrounded.

At places, the walls were made of nothing more than plaster tiles. Juve heard someone walking on the other side and realized at the same time that people were settling on the roof. There was no doubt that he had been discovered, that they realized that he was trapped inside and that they were about to give him a hard time!

Juve backed up against the portion of the wall that appeared the most robust to him, leaned against it, gathered the chairs and tables he found in the room in front of him to make a kind of barricade, then waited.

He did not have long to wait. A whistle rang out outside. Then, at the same time, the wall was shoved in, the door was torn off its hinges, a hole appeared in the roof and a dozen men rushed into the shack, brandishing revolvers and shouting.

"Surrender!"

"Never!" replied Juve.

But his cry died in his throat and he burst out laughing.

The policeman was in familiar territory. Before his every eyes, dumb-founded expressions on their faces, stood the Sûreté officers. Mr. Havard stood a little to the side. Suddenly, next to Juve, the familiar voice of his friend rang out, "Juve! Juve! Well, well, well…"

The policeman turned his head and shouted, "Fandor, It's me!"

Once again, Juve and Fandor met, although both had been expecting to face Fantômas. They looked at one another for a moment, astounded, then walked closer.

"I'll explain everything to you," said Fandor, embarrassed.

Juve interrupted him, "I understand. We don't have a minute to lose!"

CHAPTER XV
Silence!

"Do you really feel better, Miss? Do you need me to accompany you?"

Hélène, to whom the nurse was talking, dismissed the woman with a nod of her head.

Yet, the nurse insisted, saying, "You're still quite pale and, for your first outing into the garden, I think it would be unwise to go alone.

Hélène impatiently corrected the nurse, "My good Amélie, I assure you that you are mistaken. First, I am quite hale and hearty. Moreover, this is not my first outing, but my second. Yesterday, I took a stroll in the park, for close to two hours and I was not in the least fatigued. Quite the contrary."

"You weren't alone, madam. A nurse accompanied you."

"I'm much better today," Hélène said dryly. "And I will rest much better if I walk as I see fit, taking small steps, staying silent. Talking wearies me."

The nurse did not insist again. She realized that the patient had made a final decision and that this was not a good time to disagree with her. Moreover, although Nurse Amélie had offered her services, she did so more as an effort to exaggerate her duties than out of any real concern about Hélène going into the garden alone.

The patient had almost recovered. It was true that she had taken a long walk in the park the previous day without experiencing any discomfort. And, she had to get used to going back to ordinary life. In three days, if no complications occurred, she was to leave the convalescent home and return to her normal life.

"Go on, then, Miss," said the nurse who, with a motherly gesture, arrange that shawl that Hélène had thrown over her shoulders. "Come back at 4 o'clock for your snack."

This time, the young woman accepted the nurse's instructions with a pleasant smile and gracefully and slowly walked down the steps of the small porch at the convalescent home that overlooked the park.

And the name "park" was not overly pompous. The building where Hélène had been cared for after her terrible accident had formerly been a hotel and all of the outbuildings had been preserved. In the previous century, that hotel had stood in the midst of vast gardens and wooded areas. Most of the trees had been preserved and the garden had remained intact.

All those who came to the convalescent home were surprised to discover, in the very heart of Paris, a country-like property with lawns, glades and even a small forest and fields of apple trees where a herd of cattle grazed.

The illusion of an immense rural site was enhanced even more by the fact that the facility was not bordered by walls or six-storey buildings, but that it was complemented, on the other side of the palisade, by gardens belonging to other houses.

The previous day, Hélène had strolled in the park with a nurse. She had gone there for the first time. The two women had wandered nonchalantly under the trees, looking this way and that, they then had sat at the edge of the park under a type of bower. Since the day had been very hot, the nurse who had accompanied Hélène had fallen asleep.

The young woman had not roused the brave nurse whose eyelids were heavy following several sleepless nights and had respected her nap time. Moreover, while the nurse slept, Hélène had been kept busy watching a strange and surprising spectacle. Through the fence that separated the garden of the convalescent home from that of a neighboring dwelling, she had watched what was going on at the adjacent property.

And the spectacle had dumbfounded here.

Behind the thick clumps of vegetation that grew randomly in the untilled soil, Hélène had seen a majestic old man with dark skin and white hair, walking slowly. He was wearing a white silk robe and waving his arms, as if praying.

Superb chickens flew all around the man, who kept them close at hand by offering them a profusion of seeds contained in a bag that he held in his hand, dipping into it from time to time to satisfy the voracious appetites of the flock.

Hélène had been surprised by the strange spectacle of the old man feeding the chickens in the private garden. Moreover, the vision had quickly disappeared.

Then the nurse awoke. When Hélène returned to the convalescent home with her attentive guardian, she asked, "Do you know the man who lives in the garden next to this one?"

The nurse looked troubled. "Yes, miss," she replied. "He's some kind of madman, a real character at the very least, that we see from time to time in his garden. And what a garden! A veritable virgin forest that has never been touched by a gardener!"

"What is the man's name?" Hélène asked, more to continue the conversation than to satisfy any sense of curiosity.

"He's called Saül, miss... at least that's what he says. But I think he's hiding his real name. He's a foreigner, an Asian, or so it seems. Moreover, his face is quite brown. He's been in this neighborhood for forever yet no one seems to know exactly what he does. Some say that he's a miser, others claim he's demented, and still others are convinced that he's some evil-doer who is hiding here."

Hélène returned to her room quite cheered by her stroll. She had passed an excellent night and, at dawn, had been pleasantly surprised by a visit from Jérôme Fandor.

But once the journalist left, Hélène felt upset, troubled, concerned.

Had Fandor not given her a detailed description of the strange night he has spent on the roof of the house on Rue des Irlandais? Had he not uttered a name that Hélène found extremely disturbing? The name of Bedjapur?

Alone, Hélène had thought for a long time, extremely agitated.

What a strange coincidence!

The young woman had immediately and easily determined that the old man in the white silk robe who the nurse said was called Saül, and the mysterious individual described by Fandor were one and the same. Bedjapur.

Bedjapur?

Why did that name mean so much to Hélène?

The young woman did not need to confide in anyone. Yet, she got up quickly after Fandor's departure and, as soon as she had eaten breakfast, she indicated her desire to stroll in the park, to stroll alone in the park.

She finally won out. Hélène walked quickly through the shady paths of the large garden.

She did not hesitate. She had a precise goal.

The young woman headed over to the bower from which she had seen the old man and his flock of hens the previous day.

Hélène sat down on the bench hidden under the arbor and spent a half hour there, carefully listening.

From one moment to the next, she expected to see the old man appear and, at that idea, her heart pounded.

But the time passed and no one appeared in the neighboring garden.

Hélène stood up, quite agitated.

"Yet, I must know!" she said. "Bedjapur... Bedjapur... no, it can't be possible! Yet, if I dig into my memory, if I evoke the distant memories of my early childhood, if seems that I recall things that are both terrible and comforting."

The young woman walked along a small path that ran along the wooden palisade that separated the two gardens.

At one point, she stopped. The wooden planks that made up the palisade were broken at that location, as if someone had pushed them over on their way through.

"Good grief! It would be so easy to get to the other side," said Hélène, whose heart had started pounding.

The young woman had no time to think. Spontaneously, her legs carried her to the other side and before she had time to think about what she was doing she was in the neighboring garden.

Hélène walked slowly, taking care not to make any noise, avoiding the dead branches that would have cracked under her footsteps. She walked through dense grass, along banks, around bushes, then suddenly stopped.

She had just heard significant sounds coming from a gravel path: footsteps.

The young woman hid behind a clump of laurels. She pushed the branches aside and poked her head out cautiously to get a look, remaining motionless, dumbfounded, her pretty face framed by the leaves.

Hélène blushed deeply since she had pushed the branches aside just in front of the person who was walking in her direction, the person she had heard walking.

That person was none other than the old man. He was alone, dressed as he had been the previous day in his large white robe. He wore a large amber necklace that hung down to the middle of his chest; a small ivory elephant that had yellowed over time dangled at the end of the chain.

As Hélène observed him, the old man quivered, took a step back, then raised his hands to the sky, dumbfounded, muttering incomprehensible words as he glanced at the graceful apparition.

Suddenly, he bowed down low to the ground, arms outstretched. Then, getting slowly back up, he asked in a melodious voice with a foreign accent, "Who is that peeking out from that bush? What is this human creature that I know, without really knowing, but which I think I have already seen?"

Hélène simply apologized, "I beg your pardon, sir. I'm staying at the convalescent home next door and I stepped into your garden just a moment ago without really intending to. Yesterday, I was sitting under the bower facing your property. Perhaps you noticed me?"

But the old man shook his head, while staring at Hélène, a strange expression on his face.

"I didn't see you yesterday," he said. "But I recognize you anyway, although I have never met you, since there is no doubt a resemblance."

Suddenly, the old man covered his eyes with his hands, saying "Buddha! Buddha! What new trial are you imposing on your disciple? Is your dedicated servant the victim of some spell?"

The old man recovered his composure and, in a trembling voice, addressed Hélène, saying "What is your name? What is your name?"

The young woman was about to give her name when an idea suddenly crossed her mind. Her name was Hélène, but was that what they had called her in the past, when she was in Natal with Old Laetitia... No!

At that time, Hélène was passing as a young boy. She dressed as a young boy, she looked like one, she was educated as one and, in order to complete the subterfuge, old Laetitia and everyone who knew her had called her Teddy.

"My name is Teddy," said Hélène, staring at the old man in order to see how he would react to that statement.

The effect was extraordinary.

The old man stumbled backward. He would have fallen if the trunk of a nearby tree had not stopped him.

"Teddy! Teddy!" the old man repeated. "No, that can't be! It's impossible! Yet..."

While the old man was upset, Hélène was every bit as emotional. She walked over to him, and clasped the bony fingers of the old man in her hands, staring at him fixedly, eyes filled with questions.

"They call you Saül, don't they?" she murmured. "But isn't your real name Bedjapur?"

The old man jumped again. This time he looked at Hélène in fear. His lips trembled. He seemed to want to talk, but the words died in his throat. Finally, after making a supreme effort, the old man recovered some of his composure. He bent toward the young woman, towering over her and in a deep voice he said, "Yes, I am Bedjapur. Who told you that?"

Hélène did not want to lie or to recount the mysterious circumstances under which Fandor had told her the old man's real name. She simply made a vague motion with her hand, then lowered her head, blushing.

The old man was so upset that he did not notice. Suddenly, as if a subtle idea was germinating in his mind. He grasped the young woman's arm and pulled.

"Come," he said. "Let's go inside. Let us hide from the eyes of passersby. Buddha has sent you and I know that now is the time to tell all, to do all... Come in, pure and noble young girl, come into Bedjapur's home!"

Hélène followed the old man, intrigued, curious, and overcome with emotion.

What an extraordinary encounter! What a formidable secret she was about to learn!

Bedjapur was the name of the mystery and emotion that had filled her ears during her very early years, during her early childhood. Before understanding, before reasoning, Hélène had been familiar with the name of Bedjapur, a name she knew to respect, to love more than any other in the world.

Then, as she had grown up and old Laetitia, her nurse, had grown old, the name Bedjapur was only spoken rarely and then always with fear, in hushed tones. The name that had once been blessed, that had been repeated over and over, was then banned from usual conversations.

Hélène had never dared ask old Laetitia for explanations. Bit by bit, she had forgotten Bedjapur. Yet, now, suddenly, purely by chance, her thoughts turned to her younger days, her memory returned liked a desiccated plant that is given air and water.

And Hélène had the instinctive feeling that there were mysteries in her life, that formidable and shadowy secretes surrounded her origins and her birth. Bedjapur was the key to all of the puzzles and through Bedjapur she could learn everything.

The young woman followed the old man. Walking behind him, she crossed through the humble bedroom, which looked much like a monastic cell. She was surprised by the laboratory, with its clay ovens, its test tubes and the flasks from which bitter odors rose.

Then she stopped, dumbfounded, at the threshold to the large rectangular room, lit only by the glass in the ceiling, its walls covered with rich, exotic fabrics and skins of ferocious wild beasts.

She felt as if she were in one of those Hindu temples which she had read about in books and suddenly Bedjapur appeared taller to her, more dignified, more noble, more solemn!

The old man strode majestically across the room. The sound of his footsteps was muffled by the thick carpet covering the floor.

Then he went to the end of the room and, after climbing up the stairs of the podium, he sat down on the golden throne, as he had done the previous day when Fantômas, disguised as a fakir, had come to offer him the means for making diamonds.

Bedjapur motioned to Hélène to sit at his feet. And, raising his arms to the sky while hanging his hands toward the ground, he beseeched Buddha in the sacred language of the Brahmins.

When he had finished, the old man looked at the young woman.

"The time has come," he said. "Listen! Almost forty years ago, Bedjapur, who had miraculously escaped from the ferocious English who were oppressing India, was picked up by poor Indians and raised as the son of a poor man, despite the fact that he was a king. A king! He spent his childhood in poverty, his early years working, but his career is perhaps crowned by the triumph of his dynasty... After studying the history of men and people for a long time, Bedjapur realized that, in order to shake off the yoke, powder that blows up thrones and rivers of blood are of no use unless they are backed by gold coins that calm passions and support legitimate struggles. So Bedjapur came to study, in the very heart of Western civilization, the sciences that would enable him to learn how to make gold. He was on the verge of succeeding, yesterday. Yet, his discovery had not been completed when the shadow of betrayal swept over his books and his work. And Bedjapur was about to despair when Buddha, taking pity on him, sent him an emissary, a fakir who had come to give Bedjapur an even better means for liberating oppressed India than making artificial gold. The fakir gave Bedjapur the means to make diamonds, as many diamonds as he wants!"

Dazed, Hélène listened to this strange speech. But the old man did not notice her dismay. He had opened a chest placed next to him. Hélène glanced at it and cried out in admiration.

The interior of the chest was carpeted with stars that sparkled with a thousand flames, in the dark room. Diamonds of all sizes lay in the chest, sparkling with extraordinary purity.

As he looked at the treasure, the old man who had been so dignified and solemn up to that point, seemed overcome with madness.

He uttered hoarse cries. He smiled sardonically. He plunged his hands into the chest and let the diamonds flow through his fingers.

"Look!" he shouted. "Look! This fortune is immense and I can increase it at will, since all of these diamonds are artificial. They cost nothing to produce!"

Suddenly, the old man got up from his throne, ran to his laboratory and came back, brandishing a hen in one hand and a long knife in the other.

As Hélène watched, he sliced the chicken in two and, paying no attention to the spurting blood, he dug through the creature's entrails. He looked anxious for a moment, then suddenly cried out triumphantly.

"Look!" he shrieked. "Look! Yet another diamond…"

He picked a superb, sparkling gem from the entrails of the beast, despite the blood that soiled his hands.

Then, the old man suddenly stopped shouting, his enthusiasm waning.

"Yet," he said, "Why does a pure diamond need to be covered with this red flow, the bloody flow that soils everything!"

He threw the body of the hen aside and tossed the diamond into the chest, wiping his hands on his white robe.

He turned back to Hélène and in a voice tinged with madness, said, "This treasure, mingled with blood, represents the history of the oppressed, of those who revolted, the heroic deeds and the betrayals. While Bedjapur, the old man, the man on whose head close to a hundred winters had snowed, was always an honest man and the hero of duty, the same cannot be said for his descendants! One son was born, named Sandyck, an unworthy son, a despicable son, who sold the secret intentions of his father to the race of the oppressors, the English! Sandyck is dead, but he left a child behind. That child was to be sacrificed by Bedjapur, but Buddha did not permit that. Dedicated servants kidnapped Sandyck's child, removing it from the just fury of its ancestor and the child was sent far away, to distant lands, where Bedjapur could not join it. Bedjapur had no news for a long time but then, bit by bit, because everyone knows everything here, he learned that the child of his son, that the heir of the infamous Sandyck, was a girl, who must now be a woman. Sandyck had married a marvelously beautiful European woman and Buddha did not want the child to look like her unworthy father, but like her noble mother. Like you, she had golden hair that framed her delicate and pure face. Like you she had pale, deep eyes, she had…"

The old man suddenly stopped, while Hélène, who was quite pale and trembling, listened to the man speak, hands clasped to her bosom. Her heart was pounding.

The old man suddenly stopped as a mysterious voice rang out.

"Silence"

The old man turned around and climbed back up to his throne. He sat down, astonished by this interruption, seeing no one nearby who could have spoken.

"Who dares interrupt Bedjapur…" he said.

He stopped again.

The voice rang out stronger, more imperious than before.

"Silence!"

Thunder roared and then nothing could be heard but Hélène panting as she lay crumpled on the floor.

The young girl was overwhelmed with emotion.

"Bedjapur! Bedjapur!" she stammered. "In the name of heaven, continue with what you were saying… Who was that child? What was her mother's name?"

Just then, Hélène's eyes grew wide. Although the young woman wanted to get up, she remained motionless, on her knees, as if paralyzed with emotion.

A terrifying, extraordinary spectacle took place before her eyes.

The large golden curtain behind Bedjapur's throne opened and a terrifying silhouette appeared. It was that of a man, dressed in black from head to foot, face hidden by a mask. He wore a large, black felt hat pulled down over his forehead. A long knife gleamed in his black gloved hand.

The old man, however, had seen nothing, heard nothing, Bedjapur seemed to have forgotten the order he had just been give and started to respond to Hélène's question.

"You want to know the name of the child," he said. "You want to know who Bedjapur's heir is and the name of the person who may legitimately replace him on the throne of the empire of the Indias, which belongs to his dynasty. Listen to the name of that women whose father was unworthy but whose mother deserves everyone's respect. It's…"

Once again, the order rang out, booming, sarcastic.

"Silence!"

This time, Hélène understood.

The silhouette that had appeared behind Bedjapur's throne was that of Fantômas and the man giving the order to stop talking was also Fantômas.

It seemed that Bedjapur was not about to obey. His lips opened to proclaim the name Hélène was waiting to hear so anxiously. But, instead of that name, a terrible cry rang and a death rattle rose from the old man's chest.

As fast as lightning, faster than a thought, Fantômas' knife stabbed into Bedjapur's chest, plunging deep inside, straight into his heart.

Bedjapur sighed and his arms flapped. The old man's head bent forward and he remained hunched over his throne, motionless, dead…

A cry rang out, followed by a dull thud.

Terrified, Hélène had collapsed on the floor, unconscious.

CHAPTER XVI
The Reconstituted Necklace

"Another one!" shouted Fantômas, who rushed behind the throne, throwing the large black coat he had been wearing, as usual, over his unfortunate victim.

Fantômas had not even spared a glance of pity for the unfortunate old man he had just assassinated.

His joy at having killed him, his satisfaction at getting rid of a wretch he no doubt considered an adversary, an enemy, was pitted against the emotion, the sadness, he felt at seeing Hélène, Fandor's fiancée, the journalist's wife, the same Hélène that Fantômas had loved, with a sincere paternal love for such a long time, lying on the floor, inanimate, just a few steps away.

The sinister bandit walked over to her, and looked down at her for a long time.

She was even more beautiful than ever, a pale, immobile statue. Her fine features, resting, seemed regular, classic, admirable. Yet, when he saw her so pale, so still, Fantômas was overcome with emotion.

"It's as if she's dead..." he murmured.

And, for possibly the first time in many, many years, since the time when Fantômas had stepped out of the shadows and into the spotlight and fame created by his misdeeds and his crimes, for the first time Fantômas saw the tragic image of death, fatal, inflexible, take shape, the death that, despite human will-power strikes randomly, choosing its victims, death into whose arms everyone is drawn, one after another, pulled by an invincible force from which they can never escape.

He sighed as he looked at Hélène.

"I love her like a father," he murmured. "I would have done anything to make her happy, if she had wanted me to. Unfortunately, she has constantly pushed me away. Ha!"

Furtively, Fantômas wiped a tear from his eye.

"It was inevitable," he added. "And how can I ask someone who, despite everything, is not of my blood, to regard me with affection, like those who look at their fathers. Because I am the one who is despised, detested..."

He stopped for a second, then continued talking in a quavering voice, "But I am also the one who is feared, the one whose anger terrifies, whose vengeance sows fear! Come on! Come on! Fantômas, show no sign of weakness, no sentimentality! Continue your work of destruction, vengeance and hatred. Continue! You didn't start so that you could later retreat!"

He bent over the young girl and looked at her, eyes filled with tenderness.

"Her?" he wondered. "No, no, she must be spared, she must live! I want to see her happy! Never, never will I touch a single hair on her head!"

"If I killed Bedjapur, it was not solely to steal his wealth, to take his name, his title his privileges, it was also and above all to keep him from talking, to keep him from telling Hélène about her mysterious and sensational origins... Already, Laetitia, who was able to speak, died under my blows, followed by Gérard, who I caused to disappear just in time. Bedjapur was the only keeper of the formidable secret of Hélène's birth!"

The bandit chortled wildly.

He raised his fist against an imaginary adversary and shouted, "Juve, Juve, from now on you can keep the indecipherable parchment you stole from me, the birth documents for Hélène, who passed for the daughter of Fantômas for such a long time. Bedjapur's lips are sealed forever and no one in the world will be able to find the key that will reveal the text written on those famous sheets of parchment. Keep them, Juve! I have no need for them!"

The bandit turned his head and his eyes, filled with lust, stopped at the chest filled with diamonds, sparkling like flames in the shadows.

Fantômas was about to rush over to the treasure and fill his pockets with it, but a deep sigh caused shivers to run up and down his spine.

It came from Hélène who was still unconscious.

"The unfortunate girl! The poor child!" Fantômas murmured.

Then, suddenly, he rushed over to her, picked her up in his arms and carried her outside.

"She can't wake up here! Fantômas said. "I don't want to have to give her any explanations.... And if she were to see me at her side, after seeing me kill Bedjapur, her hatred and disdain for me would only increase...."

Carrying his precious burden, Fantômas left the room in which the tragic drama, Bedjapur's assassination, had just played out.

He carried Hélène through the laboratory then into the sun-filled garden.

Tenderly, cautiously, Fantômas placed the young woman at the foot of a tree, in the shade, on a bed of soft, green grass dotted with flowers.

Then he attempted to revive her.

Gradually, Hélène roused, opened her eyes, and uttered a few broken words.

"Help! Fandor!" she stammered.

The bandit, who was listening to her, clenched his fists.

"Fandor," he repeated. "Always him! How much she loves him!'

Hélène's lips moved again and in a voice so quite it seemed like a breath, she murmured, "Fandor! Fandor!"

Suddenly, Fantômas stood up, frowned and, automatically, with a nervous hand, looked for the revolver he kept loaded in his pocket.

A cry rang out in the distance, a cry of concern, of anguish... a frightened cry. It seemed as if the cry responded to the young woman's murmur.

Fantômas heard a loud voice call out, in a shattered tone, "Hélène! Hélène!'

The voice was Fandor's.

Fantômas roared and looked around him. He saw no one. But, a few minutes later, he heard rushing footsteps, followed by voices.

It seemed to him that the noises came from the garden at the convalescent center, the facility that stood next to Bedjapur's home.

"So, they've noticed that the young woman has gone missing," he thought. "They're surprised they cannot find her!"

Fantômas glanced at Hélène who was gradually waking without seeing the bandit who stood behind her.

"Farewell," stammered Fantômas, who once again rushed in the direction of the tumbledown cottage where Bedjapur's body lay.

But, as he approached the old house, Fantômas stopped again... He heard voices again, footsteps. He just had time to hide behind a bush. From there he saw men, police officers, enter the building.

"They're coming from all directions! They've no doubt discovered me... They'll hunt me down," grumbled Fantômas.

For a moment, he considered waiting for his adversaries, gun in hand, and killing a few before taking a chance on death, but Fantômas felt that his work was not done yet, that courage was pointless, that audacity was superfluous under the circumstances.

Fantômas assessed the situation quickly. Based on the shouts, the exclamations he had heard, coming from where Hélène lay, he realized that the people who had entered the garden had discovered the young woman and that Fandor was at the head of the group.

At the same time, based on the orders that were given sharply, the meaningful whispering that reached his ears, Fantômas realized that Bedjapur's house was filled with police officers, and probably surrounded, with all exits cut off.

He could still escape through the back of the garden and make his way to the end of Rue des Irlandais, as long as he could climb over a wall that was nine feet-high.

Fantômas did not hesitate.

"I'll see you soon, Fandor," He grumbled. "We lose nothing by waiting. We will meet again!"

Slipping under the clumps of bushes and along the trees, Fantômas reached the end of the park without being intercepted. With uncommon agility and herculean strength, he climbed on top of the wall and then down the other side in a matter of seconds.

But, as he reached that part of Rue des Irlandais which, fortunately for him was deserted, he could not keep himself from crying out in rage.

"Curses," shouted Fantômas. "The diamonds I left behind will fall into Juve's hands! Curses!"

Hélène had been carried into the small room in the facility where she had spent the last few weeks and where she had gradually recovered her health after the terrible accident in the theater.

She had recovered from her fainting spell, but she was still distressed, troubled. Kneeling beside her bed, Fandor clasped her hand in his, while the elderly nurse attempted to explain to the journalist what had happened.

"She wanted to get out, the poor little one. She was strolling all alone in the park, but she was still too weak, she still needs to convalesce. Her strength gave way and we found her in a faint…"

Hélène and Fandor listened to the nurse without paying any attention to her.

They were eager to find themselves alone. Particularly Hélène. She indicated that she wanted to talk with Fandor, in particular, and as soon as the nurse withdrew, she drew the journalist close to her.

Breathless, in a voice filled with terror, she murmured in his ear, "Fantômas! Fantômas is still there! Fantômas has just killed Bedjapur in the house next door… Fantômas…"

The effort was too much for her and the young woman closed her eyes and fainted away again.

"Good grief!" stammered Fandor, calling for help. "What should I do? What does this new adventure mean?"

CHAPTER XVII
Saül

Juve and Fandor's meeting in the sordid cottage on Impasse du Moulin, in Montrouge-Châtillon, had plunged the two men and those with them into deep bewilderment. When Fandor had managed to discover Fantômas' lair in that tragic and dreaded neighborhood, he immediately set off to notify the Sûreté and had convinced Mr. Havard to come and surround the shack with a considerable number of policemen.

The attack on the dump was well organized, well planned and conducted marvelously.

When the signal was given, the police offices, who had been positioned all around the building, had all entered at the same time, guns in hands. There they discovered a man, whom they immediately surrounded on all sides but then they lowered their weapons and shouted in astonishment, surprised, because the man they had just captured, the man they were expecting to be Fantômas, was none other than Juve, a man they had not thought they would see since they thought he was busy taking care of the mysterious and private affairs of the Emperor of Russia, who was only expected to leave Paris the evening following that strange afternoon.

Fandor was just as surprised.

He rushed over to Juve, asking, "How did you get here? By what extraordinary coincidence have you come to be in Fantômas' place?"

After bursting out laughing since, after all, he found the entire situation quite comical, Juve had coldly lit up a cigarette, sat down on a stool, and declared, "It's really quite simple!"

The men formed a circle around him, listening, and Juve started to recount his adventures of the morning to them. Starting with the discovery of the mysterious chicken at Adèle's place, on Rue de Prony, and his shadowing of Mère Toulouche, which had taken him to Impasse du Moulin.

Fandor raised his arms to the sky.

"Juve! Juve! Why didn't we meet and tell one another what we knew! You discovered Fantômas' lair through Mère Toulouche and I…"

And Fandor in turn told Juve about his adventures with Bouzille, his encounter with the elderly criminal woman on the cart loaded with waste, at Quai de Javel, the chase in the taxi, which also led to the house in Montrouge.

"But," shouted Fandor, "We have not lost the match. Just the contrary! And I feel that the longer we go on, the more the chains we add to the human net we are weaving around Fantômas will grow tighter.

"Fantômas has an accomplice, a friend, or possibly an adversary, or even yet some future victim, I don't know what, with whom he has mysterious meetings in a house on Rue des Irlandais. We have to find out exactly what is going on there! Let's go to the house on Rue des Irlandais!"

Along their way, the journalist gave his friend Juve the details of the mysterious night he had spent on the roof of Bedjapur's house, an account that intrigued the policeman considerably.

Mr. Havard, the inspectors of the Sûreté, Juve and Fandor quickly returned to the Montagne Sainte-Geneviève. They walked past Rue d'Ulm and proceeded to Rue des Irlandais. Fandor's heart pounded at the idea that their pursuit had taken him by quite chance close to the facility where Hélène was staying.

But, as he walked past the building, someone waved at him, looking so troubled that Fandor, alarmed, concerned, trembling with an inexplicable sense of foreboding, left his friends, abandoning Juve and Havard to go ahead and obtain information.

The person who had waved at him was Old Amélie.

"There you are, sir!" she shouted. "The good Lord has sent you here and I'm very pleased that I spotted you, just by chance!"

Then she added point blank, "What has happened to the young miss?"

"Hélène!" shouted Fandor, alarmed. "You've lost Hélène!"

"Oh!" stammered the nurse. "We certainly have to hope not... But Mademoiselle is young and she wanted to walk all alone in the park. She set out two hours ago and we haven't seen her since!"

The information, provided brutally, abruptly, categorically, hit Fandor like a hammer. He felt his legs give way and suddenly, he made an agonizing connection in his mind, realizing that the rest home was quite close to Bedjapur's house and that he had heard that man speaking there with Fantômas.

Fandor rushed through the health center, overcome with fear. Unable to master his emotions, he shrieked, throwing caution to the wind.

He called, "Hélène! Hélène!"

That was the call Fantômas had heard. Those were the cries that had alerted the bandit, allowing him to make his escape.

Yet, Fandor found Hélène who had been brought back to her little room in the rest home and bit by bit she had regained consciousness.

But she fainted again and Fandor stayed at her side, worried about her fate, concerned about his colleagues.

While Fandor was in the rest home, Mr. Havard, Juve and the police officers had reached Rue des Irlandais. They slipped along the walls, walking on tiptoe, trying not to make a single sound. Mr. Havard had given his men their instructions.

"Let's do what we did for the Impasse Moulin," he said to them. "First let's surround the house on all sides. Then, when I blow the whistle, head in, revolvers in your hands! If you see anyone, order them to raise their hands and, if they don't obey immediately, shoot them to keep from being killed yourselves!"

The Sûreté officers were brave. They felt safe, not only because their chief was there but, above all because Juve was leading them.

Plus, they had had enough of these perpetual chases, these unfruitful hunts. They were satisfied with the efforts deployed by the higher-ups at the Sûreté. Finally, they had decided to arrest Fantômas, at any cost, and they had to hope that they would manage to do so!

The manhunt started. Juve and Michel had forced the door that opened out onto the street and the first policemen had entered the small garden that stood next to the house. Other officers had climbed the wall, slipping over the rooftops. Mr. Havard, with Léon, was hunkered down behind a bush, watching the entrance to the cellar.

They had surrounded the house so quickly and silently that, if someone had been in the house, it would have most certainly been impossible for him to have the time to escape, let alone see that he had been surrounded.

A whistle rang out in the silence.

As if they had been launched by a sudden pull on a trigger, all of the policemen rushed into the house. They crossed through the room that looked like a cell and hurried into the laboratory. Juve was the first to enter the large rectangular room where the throne stood. The throne on which Bedjapur lay, motionless, curled up, head bent forwards...

Bedjapur was nothing more than a cadaver. Juve walked over to him, followed by Léon and Michel. Mr. Havard, noticing the individual sitting on the large seat, ordered," Hands up!"

Juve imposed silence on the men.

"He's dead!" he shouted. Juve and the policemen all realized that instinctively.

Juve, however, leapt toward the unfortunate man, who was unknown to him. He tried to lift him up, pulling him out from under the large black cloak that had been thrown over his shoulders. Then he shivered when he saw the dagger thrust up to the hilt in the man's chest. He shuddered when he looked at the piece of clothing that enveloped it.

The body was still warm. The assassination had taken place just a few moments earlier.

"Fantômas!" stammered Juve. "Another of Fantômas' crimes!"

Then the policeman glanced at the chest filled with diamonds and other precious stones, uttering a few dumbfounded exclamations. Then, he cried out in joy, calling Mr. Havard.

"Come and see this! Come and see this," he shouted. "Do you recognize these diamonds?"

Havard looked at the treasure, amazed.

"They're magnificent" the chief of the Sûreté said, with a knowing look. "But I don't recognize them at all."

"Good grief!" said Juve, suddenly growing calm and adopting an enigmatic expression.

Havard wanted to ask for explanations.

"There's no point," Jive said, in an abrupt tone. "It would take far too much time to explain it to you, particularly since time is of the essence."

The policeman took out his watch and, looking at Mr. Havard, he asked, "At what time does His Majesty the Tsar leave France to head back to Russia?"

Havard looked at him, concerned.

"You're mad!" he said. "What's that to you?"

Juve grew impatient and said, "Please answer me!"

Michel intervened, saying "We've been ordered to be on duty for eight o'clock this evening at the Gare du Nord. That's where the special train will depart from."

Juve nodded and replied, "Fine."

He jotted a few notes down in his notebook, tore out the sheet of paper and, pulling Havard aside, he gave the other man the paper.

"This document is not very official, but I urge you Mr. Havard, to take it to his Majesty the Tsar right away."

"Have you lost your mind?" the head of the Sûreté asked. "You don't write to the Tsar like that!"

"I know," said Juve. "But he will read it nevertheless and he will be pleased."

"What is this all about?" Havard asked.

Juve explained briefly, saying, "It's about the Tsarita's necklace… the famous necklace stolen by Fantômas, the necklace I've just found, in its entirety or just about! The bandit was so very clever! He knew that he was being pursued for weeks and he sought out the most extraordinary hiding places to stash various components that made up this necklace and which, when complete, is worth more than a million francs. Of course, the setting has disappeared, but the stones are all there…"

Juve walked over to the chest and quickly counted the diamonds.

"Oh, no, there's one missing!"

He thought for a moment then, turning toward Léon and Michel, he ordered loudly, "My friends, do you recall the Impasse du Moulin from which we've just come?"

"Good grief!" said the men.

"Run back there right away," Juve added. "In the little room where I was, in the right corner, you will find a wicker cage. In that cage, there is a chicken. You will wring its neck and bring it to me!"

Léon and Michel, who were accustomed to obeying, rushed out to head back to Impasse du Moulin.

The head of the Sûreté was dumbfounded.

"Obviously, Juve," he said. "It can only be one of two things. Either you have gone quite mad or you're doing everything you can to mock us... Why have you sent Léon and Michel off like that to wring chickens' necks, in a dump that both our adversaries and we have abandoned?"

Juve smiled.

"The chickens, dear Mr. Havard, play an important role in this matter. In the past, the geese on the Capitoline Hill saved the Romans by warning them about the arrival of their attackers. Today, the chickens, after serving as Fantômas' accomplices, by hiding the precious stones from the Tsarita's necklace in their gizzards, have sacrificed their lives to enable the police, and your humble servant, to find the Russian Empress' jewels intact!"

And since Havard was looking at Juve in amazement, the policeman pushed him by the shoulders, forcing him to leave the room.

"I see that you don't understand, but that's not important. I'll explain later."

The two men entered the laboratory at that moment, where they found the other policemen who had spent several minutes searching thoroughly through the rest of the house.

"Nothing! Absolutely nothing" the men declared. "No one."

"Yet," said one, "It seems that large treasures must have been hidden in the cellars at one time. In the now empty crates, we found a few golden louis coins that seem to have been forgotten."

"Good grief," grumbled Juve. "Whenever Fantômas passes by, he doesn't leave much behind."

Havard stamped his feet.

"Juve," he muttered. "I have no choice but to give up on the entire investigation, considering the incoherent manner in which you are behaving. You take over. I'm leaving!"

"And you're perfectly right," Juve replied childishly. "Off with you, Mr. Havard. I'll wait for Léon and Michel here!"

"And my men?" asked the head of the Sûreté. "You know that I need them to oversee the departure of the Emperor of Russia..."

"That's fine," said Juve. "Let them leave with you. I'll wait here alone."

The head of the Sûreté withdrew, leaving the mysterious house on Rue des Irlandais. At the threshold of the door, he called out to Juve, "And that cadaver, that dead man we found with the dagger in his chest?"

"Well, you've thought of everything!" Juve said, voice dripping with irony.

Then, in a conciliatory voice, he added, "Don't worry about a thing, dear man. I'll interrogate the dead man… Who knows, perhaps he has a lot to say!"

Then Juve called out to the head of the Sûreté, "What about the diamonds?"

"Good grief," said Havard. "I don't want to take charge of them. All I can do is take your note to the Tsar."

"Do that then," replied Juve. "And please inform his Majesty that I will be at the Gare du Nord this evening, that I will have the honor or returning the diamonds from the necklace whose disappearance has so distressed the Empress."

Five minutes later, Juve was alone with the cadaver. He looked at it with an astonished, curious look. He walked around it, observing the old man's body. It seemed, tall, noble, dignified, even robust.

Juve had never seen the man before, but he still recognized him. The description Fandor had given him of the hands, the hands he had seen from his perch atop the furnace of the laboratory, looking down the chimney, was all he needed to identify the man.

"These hands," Fandor has said, "These hands were very brown, muscular. Nervous, large and vigorous, but distinguished."

Juve saw the motionless hands, frozen in the rigor of death and murmured a name, "Bedjapur…"

The policeman moved closer. The setting sun cast its red rays through the glass roof. A ray of sun lit the old man's shining, bare forehead. Juve had approached out of respect for the dead man. He wanted to move the body from its crumpled position on the throne, to stretch the man out on his back, to place him on the floor.

And, as he approached, the sunlight suddenly lit up the back of Bedjapur's neck. Behind the old man's ear, Juve saw a sign, a strange and unusual sign. It seemed to have been tattooed in the wrinkled skin of the old man. Juve's eyes grew wide.

This sign, this tattoo, brought back all kinds of memories to him. He had seen it before, a long time ago, on the naked skull of an anonymous dead body that he had discovered in Natal, in Hélène's country. What was the connection between the sign marked on the skull discovered in South Africa and the tattoo on the head of the old man Fantômas had murdered?

Juve repeated the name over and over, "Bedjapur, Bedjapur!"

Then he suddenly cried out in triumph, like a mad man, counting on his fingers, spelling the name he had just uttered letter by letter, "B… E… D… J… A…"

He cried out again.

"These letters… this name… they are the key to the mystery… what I've been seeking for such a long time. Good grief! That was the secret I needed.

Bedjapur is the formula that I had to discover, to know, in order to be able to read and understand the mysterious parchments in my possession, the parchments that contain the revelation about Hélène's birth. Bedjapur!"

Juve sighed deeply with satisfaction.

"It was a good thing I kept those papers, that I protected them from Fantômas at all costs, that I kept them in a secret hiding place where Fantômas could never find them!

"Bedjapur! Bedjapur! Bedjapur! Thanks to you, thanks to your name, thanks to the discovery I've just made, I will finally be able to satisfy Fandor's curiosity and determine if what I've always suspected about Hélène's birth is true…"

Then Juve, overcome with emotion, took out his notebook and furiously wrote down all kinds of things. After an hour, he suddenly stopped.

Léon and Michel entered triumphantly.

Michel brandished the unfortunate chicken in one arm.

"Here's the hen, boss!" he shouted.

And Juve replied, "Slit its gut. There we will find the only diamond missing from the Tsarita's necklace!"

CHAPTER XVIII
Back from the Races

"There's nothing to be said for it, but it's still a fine mess! What misfortune, my old Bec-de-Gaz, that we can't up set up house every eight days! That would be a fine time!"

Bec-de-Gaz, to whom these words were addressed in a sententious and convinced manner by Oeil-de-Boeuf, approved, nodding his head.

Of course," he said gravely. "It's not that it would be difficult to get married once a week, but the hard thing would be finding the cash and then women who would want to go with us…"

"About that," said Oeil-de-Boeuf, growing serious again, "Have you found yourself a good girl?"

"You, Oeil-de-Boeuf?"

"Jaspine first, Bec-de-Gaz."

Leaving the ballroom which was filled with a frightening racket, the two friends headed for a small, neighboring room, where they discovered, on a table, a respectable number of bottles of red wine that had barely been opened.

"That," they said together with sincere spontaneity, "That is for wetting our whistles."

And before starting the conversation, before partaking in any discussion, they started by pouring copious glassfuls, which they downed voraciously.

Then they leaned on the ledge of the open window and looked down on the Seine, that flowed, in the background, in a dark line among the trees of the Bois de Boulogne.

"That's so pretty!" said Bec-de-Gaz. "I think I'm going to wax a little poetical!"

But Oeil-de-Boeuf elbowed him.

"That's not it at all," he said. "See, it's already late in the day. We'll have to reach an agreement about Adèle's replacement!"

Neither of the two men wanted to be the first to start talking, and each waited to hear the other out.

There was a long silence during which they heard, coming from the neighboring ballroom, the deafening blare of an eight-man orchestra, accompanied by a player piano.

In that room, a crowd of dubious-looking but noisy people whirled about ceaselessly, dancing with a sickly passion, more as if they were performing a duty than enjoying themselves.

The room was lit by large windows that looked out on the sidewalk, that ran along the road, a dusty road, filled with automobiles which, barely out of Paris, were already starting to increase their speed to race up the slope that rose in front of them.

They were in Suresnes, at the foot of the famous village, in one of those large restaurants used for weddings and celebrations, which from morning to night, from night to morning, from one end of the year to the other, never emptied.

Early that morning, about twenty individuals had arrived, men and women, stepping out of some sort of large carriage benches, harnessed to horses and driven by a coachman who was already drunk, that had carried them from Belleville to Suresnes.

The breakfast had been ordered, the room reserved for the entire day and they wasted no time settling in for they were dying of hunger.

Obviously, it was a wedding, but a strange and abnormal wedding, for which there was no groom, no bride, in the traditional black suit and white dress. The guests looked more like bandits on a binge, like gatecrashers.

They had an unfortunate impact on the reputation of the Suresnes hotel but, since these people had paid in advance, that same evening through the intermediary of one of their number, they could not be criticized for their appearances.

And, instead of one groom, there were two, and instead of two brides, there were three or four prostitutes who seemed to be candidates.

This was the time, for Oeil-de-Boeuf and Bec-de-Gaz to replace Adèle who had slyly abandoned them, preferring to live, as her former lovers said, in lace and champagne, rather than in the company of the sturdy friends from Ménilmuche and De la Chapelle!

When Adèle had so treacherously disappeared, the two men had initially considered taking care of business and sending her off to the cemetery, in order to teach her a lesson about living, but someone who headed the gang, someone whose advice sounded more like orders, had opposed that execution.

"Each one," he had declared one day while discussing the matter in an abattoir in Belleville where he found himself, "Is free to live their live as he sees fit!"

And then he added, something that was not pleasant for Oeil-de-Boeuf and Bec-de-Gaz: "Moreover, I understand full well why Adèle did not want to stay with two men like you."

And he added again, "I forbid them to cause any harm to the nice little woman, who has done everything it takes to move into higher circles…"

Although, contrary to habit, Fantômas, had shown clemency toward Adèle, and although he was still a general who was not happy with seeing the people in his gang, men or women, leave the group, it was no doubt because he was hoping that, when the right time came, Adèle would help him into the inner circles of the rich Brazilian who she served as a mistress.

That man was covered with gold, from head to foot, and Fantômas always held rich people in high esteem, much like a wolf considers the lamb.

So, thanks to Fantômas, Adèle's life had been spared and no one bothered upsetting the young woman.

As for Bec-de-Gaz and Oeil -de-Boeuf, who were deeply mortified by Fantômas' opinion of them, they were initially angered and had decided to sulk after that and, knowing full well that the Master did not like that, they had changed their minds and decided, on the contrary, to prove to those in their circles that they were not as bad as people liked to say and they were capable of finding a replacement for Adèle, perhaps even two.

Then, they announced that when that rare pearl was found, they would celebrate the fortunate event with a beautiful wedding at Chez Père Korn.

Fantômas got wind of these projects.

And, to the great surprise of the band of criminals, he had, as the good prince he could be sometimes, decided that if Oeil-de-Boeuf and Bec-de-Gaz settled down it would be he, Fantômas, who would pay for the wedding, but that it would be an extraordinary wedding, a fantastic wedding.

That promise had driven up the level of enthusiasm and Oeil-de-Boeuf and Bec-de-Gaz decided to search actively for a bride.

For eight days, they had searched ceaselessly, maintaining a mysterious silence, communicating the results of their efforts to no one.

Then, one fine evening, when they were meeting with Fantômas, they declared, faces straight, "You know, boss, you can set your bomb off now, we're both ready, we're up to this!"

"Show me," Fantômas said, distrustful,

"But the two criminals insisted on reserving the surprise for their friends. Fantômas consented.

The Master of Fear, the Criminal Genius could be nice when he wanted to. They had expected a nice, little party, but the wedding they received was fit for a king.

A carriage had arrived in the morning to pick up the guests, at their homes, at their doors, and take them to Suresnes, where they were informed that they could eat and drink to their fill. Naturally, they had made the most of that situation and imbibed as much as they possibly could. Then they had met the candidates for the hands of Bec-de-Gaz and Oeil-de-Boeuf.

There were three in all, three prostitutes from Belleville, who lacked nothing when it came to youth and charm. One of them, Jujube, a small red-head, a defector from Montparno, seemed to receive most of the votes and people had applauded loudly when, at the end of the meal, Bec-de-Gaz had carried her on his shoulders around the room, showing her off to his colleagues.

But, following that, Oeil-de-Boeuf had shown off an exquisite specimen from Point-du-Jour, called Salsifis, as a result of her slimness and snake-like flexibility. She was well-built, in any case, with superb black hair and wide, deep eyes.

Yet, after these two candidates had been presented, someone called out. It was a woman, who called out from among the guests, someone few of them knew.

In a hoarse voice, she asked, "Would it be possible to join the competition, without having been recommended?"

"Good grief!" someone exclaimed.

And then, everyone saw a small person stand up from her chair and leap onto the table with surprising agility. Everyone recognized her there. It was another prostitute from De la Chapelle who had once, or so it was said, been an acrobat who had performed at fairs.

Her name was La Grenouille, or the Frog, and she deserved that moniker.

She had a broad mouth that ran from ear to ear, flat, colorless hair, and protruding, strange, light grey eyes.

She was nimble and as supple as a grasshopper and her range of facial features was so extraordinary that she both terrified people and made them want to laugh.

La Grenouille was perfectly at ease in the middle of bottles and glasses on the table and her feet, housed in small varnished shoes with extremely high, red heels, moved with extreme skill in the midst of dessert trays.

"Don't step in the jam!" people shouted at her.

Other added, "Don't crush the cream puffs!"

In response, La Grenouille cast incendiary glances at the men, and scornful smiles at the women and, suddenly addressing the musicians in the orchestra, she said in her hoarse voice, "What are you waiting for you idiots. Start the polka!"

The musicians, good guys, burst out laughing then grabbed their instruments and La Grenouille started dancing on the table with remarkable agility and grace.

Oeil-de-boeuf and Bec-de-Gaz were dumbfounded, but they were unable to make up their minds and looked at La Grenouille distrustfully.

"That's certainly not a woman for us!" they thought. "She's far too knowing. Our friends must have put her up to this!"

But it truly did seem as if there had been no prior shenanigans and, moreover, La Grenouille, when she was catching her breath between two polkas, declared "I'm applying! After all, why not? I may be ugly, but I'm foxy and fast... And, moreover, I've got no man at the moment so, if Oeil-de-Boeuf and Bec-de-Gaz want La Grenouille, I'm right here!

Thunderous applause broke out, highlighting the prostitute's open declaration, but her words did not please Jujube or Salsifis.

And the two women, who had been adversaries up to that point, agreed to throw themselves at the new rival.

"First," observed Salsifis, "No one invited you to come here... You weren't chosen by anyone... So, get down from that table and go back to your place."

Jujube approved, saying "That's not how people here behave. Oeil-de-Boeuf and Bec-de-Gaz are free to choose between Salsifis and Jujube, and there's no place for La Grenouille in the room!"

"That remains to be seen," replied La Grenouille who, hands on her hips, was looking at the two other candidates with a challenging air.

And she proudly added, "If either of you wants to, I'll take you on!"

The onlookers were most amused.

"A fight!" they shouted. "Let's see all three of them get into it! This is going to be such fun!"

There was a gambler in the band who was familiar with racetrack betting and he shouted loudly, "Who wants in? I'm playing! Two against Salsifis! Three for Jujube! We pay for La Grenouille!"

La Grenouille, however, had climbed down from her table and jostling the dancing pairs who were forming despite the altercation, she sought to approach Jujube and Salsifis.

As for those two, who were a little concerned by the determined look on La Grenouille's face and fearing they would come out worse for the wear, they were looking about for Oeil-de-Boeuf and Bec-de-Gaz, to come to their aid.

But, at the start of the discussion, Oeil-de-Boeuf and Bec-de-Gaz had disappeared, not wanting to get into this feminine fist fight.

Adèle's two former lovers were in a small, neighboring room, looking out at the Seine flowing by in silence.

Finally, Bec-de-Gaz asked, "Have you chosen, Oeil-de-Boeuf?"

"Not yet," the other man replied. "How about you, Bec-de-Gaz?"

"Me, I'm feeling things out. I don't have an opinion."

Oeil-de-Boeuf, who had discovered Jujube, boasted about her qualities, saying, "She's nice, she has a good personality..."

But Bec-de-Gaz, who had discovered Salsifis, promoted his protégée.

"She's thin, dry, and robust, a real workhorse..."

"I'm not saying no," added Oeil-de-Boeuf, undecided.

Then they looked at one another and said together, "But, when it comes to entertainment, La Grenouille is really great!"

The two men observed another deep silence which they attempted to empty into two more wine bottles.

"All the same," sighed Bec-de-Gaz, "Making your way through life is hard."

"We're too handsome," said Oeil-de-Boeuf. "All the women run after us!"

They listened. A deafening racket came from the neighboring room, drowning out the orchestra and the rhythmic footsteps of the dancers.

There had certainly been a fight; people were shouting and swearing at one another.

The criminals looked at one another, faces glowing gloriously.

"You see," said Bec-de-Gaz. "All of that racket is for us!"

"Well, not to be too flattered or anything," declared Oeil-de-Boeuf, "but it still feels good…"

Just then, the door opened with an abrupt shove. Three disheveled women with gleaming eyes, rushed into the room, panting.

"Oeil-de-Boeuf! Bec-de-Gaz!" they shouted, all at the same time.

"I flattened her!"

"I put her in her place. She doesn't exist anymore!"

"You have to take me, I'm stronger than she is!"

The two criminals, flabbergasted by this feminine invasion, could not tear themselves away from the three women who, somewhat drunk, were throwing themselves at the men, grabbing them by the necks, grasping their hands.

Bec-de-Gaz and Oeil-de-Boeuf found it all very amusing.

"This is so much fun! We're having such fun! Good grief! If only this could start over again every week!"

Suddenly, Bec-de-Gaz shouted, "Oeil-de-Boeuf, I have an idea!"

But Oeil-de-Boeuf interrupted him, shouting, "Bec-de-Gaz, I've come up with an idea!"

And suddenly, they were speaking at the same time, describing the same project that had just popped into both minds.

"What if we kept all three?" they shouted.

The women were stunned, not knowing if they should laugh or be angry and then, since they had drunk copiously, since they had fought and then reconciled, they enthusiastically welcomed the new project.

"Yes! Yes! Bravo!" they shouted. "All three of us will be the wives of Bec-de-Gaz and Oeil-de-Boeuf!"

A formidable din filled the small room, flowing in from the large one, to such an extent that the walls seemed to shake when, suddenly, silence washed over everything like an enchantment.

A man with a hard, energetic face, with a powerful gaze, with a robust frame, had just entered the large room and was crossing through it heading for the small one.

Seeing that the dancers were no longer dancing, he stopped for a second and, in a furious tone, said, "So, what are you waiting for? Go on as if I weren't here!"

Obediently, and without saying a word, the gang members started spinning in rhythm, to the tireless tune of the orchestra.

The man, however, just walked on into the small room. With an energetic wave of his hand, he chased the three women away, retaining the men and, once he was alone with them, he sat down, while they remained standing and struck the table, declaring, "Now let's chat for a few minutes!"

Oeil-de-Boeuf, Bec-de-Gaz, little Louis, a gang member who was coming out of the WC and Fat Alfred, a 50-year-old guy who had spent 30 years of his life in Guyana, surrounded the newcomer, refraining from saying his name in case the walls had ears.

The newcomer was, in fact, none other than Fantômas!

The bandit arrived with the expression he reserved for great days, glaring wildly, looking nervous.

No one dared make a joke, utter a word, move. Fantômas, who tapped nervously on the table, for a few moments, with an empty glass he had picked up automatically, lifted his head, looked at the men around him and asked, "So, you've enjoyed yourselves?"

A few vague approving murmurs responded.

"Well then!" continued the bandit in a deep voice. "The time has come to do a little work!"

He looked at Oeil-de-Boeuf and Bec-de-Gaz.

"Men," he said. "Try not to spend your wedding night in jail"

Bec-de-Gaz attempted a joke, saying "Don't worry Fantômas! We'll go back on our best behavior, like little angels!"

But Fantômas interrupted him, "If you go back now, you'll go back with your pockets empty. But I want you all to be rich this evening. Only, you'll have to apply yourselves.!"

Little Louis elbowed Fat Alfred.

"We're probably going to dip into the cash reserve at the bistro," he said.

Fantômas stared at Little Louis severely.

"You," he said, "Shut up! I didn't ask for your opinion. Shut up and listen!"

Fantômas made sure that the doors were closed, that people were still dancing in the next room, and then he returned to the conversation, without raising his voice too much.

"The races are on at Longchamp today," he said.

Fantômas looked at his watch.

"Five o'clock. The meeting must be over. Fine! We have to let the crowd leave. We still have more time than we need to prepare."

"What are we going to do?" asked Bec-de-Gaz.

Fantômas replied, "It's quite simple. The Société des courses must have taken in a good amount; there was an interesting program and the weather stayed good all day. Well, that money will be ours, that's all! I've decided that it belongs to us now and all we have to do is take it."

Fantômas took a pencil out of his pocket, along with a sheet of paper, which he spread over the table. Then, like a general in the middle of his senior officers setting out a battle plan, he started to draw a brief plan on the blank piece of paper, indicating the paths in the Bois de Boulogne. Then, as his accomplices bent over his work, he stuck his pencil in the paper, at the exact spot where the drawing showed a crossroads.

"There," he said. "That's where we'll take the gold!"

It was seven o'clock in the evening. Night was falling.

The Bois de Boulogne was almost deserted and the Longchamp race track, which had been so noisy earlier, so busy during the afternoon races, was now plunged into the deepest silence.

A white mist rose from the edge of the Seine, enveloping the racetrack, the stands and the surrounding woods in a thickening fog.

Had the racetrack been completely deserted since the last cart carrying horses had driven away from the paddock?

Not quite!

Inside a small office positioned under the weighing station, a dozen senior employees, under the supervision of the treasurer of the Société des courses, were completing the tallies and putting the money away.

Outside, four large carriages waited patiently.

The money earned that day had been placed in robust metal boxes and, once the accounts had been tallied, four racetrack employees climbed into the first carriage, placing a large, very heavy chest between them, containing all of the money.

On the seat of the vehicle, next to the driver, sat two police officers. This first bus set out, filled with agents, followed by the vehicle carrying the chest of cash, followed by yet another vehicle with security guards.

The three carriages did not go far. They were waiting for other similar vehicles, that were also loaded with great caution.

There was the carriage with the silver, the carriage with the gold and the carriage with the bank notes...

The races had been lucrative; the profits were extraordinary, considerable.

The Company's head treasurer, who had attended the departure of the first vehicles, took his place in the one carrying the bank notes, which followed on the heels of the vehicle with the gold. He climbed into the vehicle, along with two other employees, a few police officers. They were followed by another vehicle carrying additional guards.

This veritable caravan, which included exactly nine vehicles, was trotting slowly through the Bois de Boulogne, which was plunged into shadow.

There was nothing abnormal or extraordinary about the trip organized under these circumstances. Every race day, the proceeds were transported to the head office. The greatest precautions were taken to safeguard it and the number of officers in the previous vehicles was a veritable guarantee against attacks by evil-doers.

At this late hour, they encountered few people in the Bois de Boulogne. The trip proceeded unhindered and, after discussing this and that in the vehicles the officers and the Racetrack employees generally found themselves with nothing more to say and thought about their respective affaires, drowsing a bit, tired after their hard day of work.

They were about to leave the forest. They had reached the Pavillon chinois, and the uninterrupted caravan of vehicles loaded with gold and silver was preparing to drive onto the Avenue du Bois-du-Boulogne when suddenly the treasurer who had been staring straight ahead cried out.

"Look there," he shouted. "Look at that racing vehicle!"

The treasurer's exclamation startled the drowsing police officers and guards.

They too cried out, concerned.

A large carriage pulled by five horses was galloping at full speed toward them, clearly giving the impression that the driver was not in full control

In the packed carriage, women cried out, men cried out and, as it drew closer, they realized that it carried people who were late for some wedding at Suresnes and whose joyous day was about to be transformed into tragedy.

People here and there in the vehicle carrying the treasurer cried out as they watched the other carriage race toward them.

What should they do?

What would happen to them?

Up until the very last minute, they hoped that the driver would manage to rein in his horses and avoid colliding with the caravan of vehicles.

They continued to hope, up until the moment when a terrible, frightful, collision occurred. There was a terrifying racket mingled with cries of pain and anguish.

The accident everyone feared had occurred. The carriage pitched forward like a race car and collided with the vehicle carrying the bank notes. Both vehicles cartwheeled, breaking and scattering their passengers every which way.

It was a moment of general panic.

The horses, injured, neighed and kicked, blood flowing everywhere; the men and women had been scattered about, injured as well, by shards of broken glass. A few unfortunates lay under the wheels, half crushed.

The treasurer of the racetrack company had been struck violently on the head and lost consciousness. However, emergency services were being organized...

One of the agents, with an alacrity and dedication that did him honor, had rushed into duty as quickly as possible. He uncoupled the tangled horses, lifted the carriages and took charge of the injured.

Two others had grabbed the treasurer who was lying inanimate, and precisely since an automobile, a luxurious limousine stopped nearby, they wanted to carry the unfortunate employee off into it.

But, just as they opened the door and were planning on telling the owner of the expensive vehicle to carry the injured man to his home, they dropped the treasurer on the ground and cried out in surprise. Inside the limousine, put there by some inexplicable means, but indisputably real, inside the limousine, there was an enormous case containing bank notes, the receipts from the racetrack!

The agents were dumbfounded. Inside the limousine there was a man whose torn clothing, covered with dust, seemed to indicate that he had just been the victim of an accident.

First, they thought it was some company employee, but as they were about to approach him, the man pointed a revolver at them and the limousine started up!

"Help! The thief!" yelled the agents.

A Sergeant appeared and leapt onto the car's running board. But, just then, he cried out. He had recognized the mysterious traveler and cried out in fear.

"Fantômas!"

At the same time, he cried out in pain and fell to the ground bathed in blood. A shot had just rang out. Fantômas had shot him to death!

Meanwhile, the wedding party was spreading out in all directions of the woods, disappearing under the trees.

The wedding party was none other than Fantômas' sinister team.

The bandit had planned well!

The attack had been savage but successful and, while they were trying, as best they could, to lift the demolished carriage, Fantômas' accomplices headed off, one by one, separately, deploying like infantrymen, each familiar with the rallying point where Fantômas, faithful to his promise, would soon share the loot...

CHAPTER XIX
The End of the World

"Well, people can say what they want, but today things are not going well! First of all, I'm feeling a tad nostalgic. It's as if I have a snake in my belly and its plugging my ears... or as if there is a cockroach in my mind that's gnawing away at my heart... No, one thing for sure, things are not going well... My gizzard is trembling and that makes me want to shout out loud, to return to the Arc de Triomphe!"

Bouzille was the one uttering these strong words and Bouzille was addressing them to one of the individuals he had held in the highest of esteem for quite some time.

It was an honest coal merchant who did not actually sell coal, but who did have a small counter made of dirty, spotted zinc on which strong alcoholic drinks flowed.

Quite naturally, Bouzille felt infinitely better in that booth than in a palace. He lived somewhere in the neighborhood, but he left his shack early in order to come and settle in the bar, both elbows leaning on the zinc counter, hands wrapped around a glass, holding forth, chatting, spending his day waiting for buddies who, more fortunate than he was, could order a round, which was not difficult, and pay for it, which was much more so.

Bouzille had grown close to the wine merchant.

This intimacy, moreover, translated in a remarkable manner. The merchant never said a word. He was by nature, deeply withdrawn. And, although he hated speaking, he did know how to listen.

Bouzille, who, on the contrary, was quite chatty, naturally appreciated this listener who let him talk without ever interrupting and who constantly nodded his head in approval.

Yet, Bouzille's soul had been in mourning for some time.

Bouzille didn't understand anything that was going on. He was witnessing, apparently impassively, but deeply touched inside, a complete upheaval of the habits of the underworld.

And Bouzille who was neither a thief nor an assassin, but who had, throughout his entire life, been involved with both, Bouzille, who had a cheerful philosophy, proclaimed it out loud, "It's the end of the world! Nothing is safe. At this very moment, cops are shaking people up for no reason, and no one can be certain of anything, except drinking his glass quietly, without being thrown into the slammer!"

In fact, the police had been enormously active for some time...

Fantômas' latest attacks had really been too much. All of the media had decided to conduct a campaign against what the journalists referred to as "police inertia".

Meetings had been held, public meetings, in numerous public places people had given violent speeches demanding energetic measures and the police were now taking those energetic measures.

"It's no laughing matter," said Bouzille, commenting on the events in a sad voice. "I don't know what's happening, I don't know if there's any connection with the middle class, who have all turned yellow, but one thing is sure, things are not going well in the underworld!"

In fact, no one felt quite comfortable in the shady neighborhoods of Paris. The entire shady population, the Greeks, the thieves, the brothers in arms, were trembling. By stirring up the police, Fantômas had brought terrible reprisals down on all of the miserable wretches.

Every day, there were roundups, raids, and the Prefecture published seemingly impressive statistics.

"They call it a clean-up!" Bouzille continued. "I think they're just getting in our way. Nowadays, when you simply don't have 10,000 francs for rent, when you're not a billionaire, you have to get out of the way as soon as you see a cop... or they'll be on you. It's true. Things always wind up turning sour in the long run."

The wine merchant simply nodded in response to the peremptory remark and took the opportunity to add, "That's true."

Then he seemed to rouse himself from his deep lethargy and asked Bouzille, "What are you drinking?"

Just then, Bouzille grimaced.

Bouzille was an old fox who was familiar with all the tricks barkeepers kept up their sleeves. He knew that that traditional question, when uttered by the lips of a wine merchant, was not an invitation to have a drink. It was simply an order to drink something, otherwise he would have to leave the premises.

The wine merchant was quite tolerant of Bouzille, in fact, and for that very reason Bouzille encouraged all of his buddies to drink, when they arrived.

But this morning, no one came.

Under the circumstances, Bouzille was becoming bothersome. He could not be left alone in the shop, in fact, since he adored sugar. Left to his own devices, Bouzille did not steal bottles, since that would be noticed, but he did like to empty the sugar bowl.

So, in an effort to invite him to take off, the barkeeper asked, "So, what are you drinking?"

"Nothing," replied Bouzille. "I have to go to the bank..."

And he left with a dignified air, raging inside.

"What a clot that guy is!" he thought. "I'm definitely going to take my business elsewhere! Times are so hard that I'll have to join the temperance league!"

Once on the sidewalk, Bouzille hesitated. He looked right and left, he seemed to be inspecting the area, with worried caution. His long white beard floated down over his sweater and he twisted it with a feverish hand.

"Which way will I go?" Bouzille grumbled. "Which way will I go?"

The old tramp sniffed the air for at least five minutes. Then, after checking the wind, he turned to the right and headed in the direction of La Villette.

"It's funny," grumbled Bouzille. "Obviously, when I was sleeping, I must have swallowed a match! My stomach is burning. I have to find some guy to buy me a glass or two, in order to quench the fire!"

Bouzille walked with a most extraordinary little skip.

He was following the arcades in the city and seemed to leap from pillar to pillar, as playing some extraordinary game of hide and seek.

"Hmm!" he said from time to time. "I have to open an eye and the right one. Still, I wouldn't like to get stuck, particularly since it's summer, and I'd enjoy going to the country. It wouldn't be good to get thrown into jail."

Bouzille proceeded in this manner for about 20 minutes. Suddenly, as he was approaching the Lariboisière hospital, he stopped, and hid behind a pillar, from where he observed the leprous façade of an abominable hotel.

Bouzille observed the building for a good 15 minutes.

"Is it quiet?" he wondered. "Are there any cops in the neighborhood? Good grief, it would be stupid to get caught in a mouse trap!"

But the hotel seemed normal. It was unlikely that the police were operating there at the time.

"Let's take a chance," thought Bouzille. "A bottle is well worth a little effort!"

And he headed over to the hotel.

Bouzille had friends everywhere. In this building, he knew a cat burglar, a very well informed man, who wasn't afraid of God, but who seriously feared being arrested. This man took such pains to avoid arrest that he had been nicknamed Fearful.

Bouzille was going to see Fearful, with the hope of asking his brother to buy a round.

Bouzille entered the corridor of the hotel, which was closed by means of an openwork balustrade. He knocked at a low door, protected by a metal mesh against possible attacks. It was the hotel office.

The door opened and Bouzille found himself facing the owner, a giant whose fists were always clenched, ready to strike his tenants.

"Good day," said Bouzille.

And since he was greeted in return, he immediately asked, "Tell me, is Fearful in?"

"No," replied the boss.

Bouzille was upset by this.

"That's strange!" he said. "Fearful never goes out in the daytime."

The hotel owner shrugged.

"Well, he's not here," he replied. "Anything else?"

"Well.... Nothing..." answered Bouzille, who was already retreating. "By any chance did anything happen to him?"

The hotel owner scornfully released this information, "Dear boy, what happens is always what should happen. Fearful is in the country. That's that."

Bouzille, naturally, turned white.

"Drat!" he said. "He was caught?"

"Yes, caught," said the owner. "While waiting for your turn, it was his..."

Bouzille immediately stopped insisting. He uttered a vague groan that could have been taken for either a curse or a respectful greeting, then left the building grumbling.

"Well, that's just dandy," he continued once he was outside. "Life is really going badly... And we all wind up... This is going to wake up my rheumatism... Le Bedeau who went to the cemetery, Fearful who's out in the country in prison, so many others who have been caught, raids every evening, Good grief. It's hard to know who's dead and who's alive."

And Bouzille, who like to flatter himself for having political ideas shouted, "What was the point of starting a Republic!"

Yet, Bouzille did not insist. He even started trotting with all his strength, just as he finished his utterance. Obviously, he was playing with misfortune that morning. Had he not, in fact, just spoken in front of a cop? Well, that would have been fine to be picked up for making subversive comments!

"Not, it's not often," he sighed. "It's not often that I would bring dishonor down on myself for something like that. Republic or no republic, I don't give a hoot. It's friends I want to find!"

At that moment, as Bouzille was at the corner of Rue de la Goutte-d'Or, he had an inspiration.

"What about Korn's place?" he thought. "It would be wonderful if I were to find a little friend there..."

He headed for Korn's place, hugging the walls, a little concerned about the presence of a certain number of individuals who seemed to be strangers to the neighborhood.

"I can smell cops" Bouzille said.

But it was too late to turn back. Plus, he was too thirsty to give up the hope of a free round.

Bouzille continued on his way imperturbable, until he reached Père Korn's cabaret.

The dump had hardly changed.

It was exactly as it had always been and nothing had been changed since it was founded, from the time when, in the past, a long time ago, Fantômas used to recruit his man accomplices there and give instructions to those were now, unfortunately, dead, to Barbu, Le Bedeau and Ribonnard.

Bouzille entered the cabaret and breathed deeply in satisfaction.

"Hey! It's me, Père Korn! How are you, old man?"

Père Korn grumbled. He was, as always, standing behind his counter, sleeves pulled up on his hairy arms, hands hidden in a sink of greasy water in which he was washing glasses.

Père Korn had grumbled.

Inside, Bouzille was flattered since Père Korn only grumbled for those he recognized. Surely, Bouzille must have been pleasant to the barkeeper for the man to show him such perfect friendship!

Bouzille, however, having barely entered the dump, was looking about to see who was there. First, he saw three young criminals who were talking in hushed voices in a corner. Bouzille recognized them immediately. One of them was called Savate, the other Mouche-ton-Nez and the third was the Lutteur.

"Well," said Bouzille. "They look like they've swallowed poison. Business certainly isn't doing well."

Behind them, two women were chatting. One of them was Marie-Salope, who had a ring of grime around her neck. And the other was Marie-Quarante-Sous, a show-off who had a new man every week and who never worked since she was incredibly lazy.[11]

"What's up with them," Bouzille wondered. "Has the cat got their tongue? They're not talking."

And Bouzille, who liked the fair sex, headed over to the girls.

"Hey, Marie-Salope, what did you find in the bottom of the washtub that's made you stop talking? Tell me, Marie-Quarante-Sous, who's put you in such a foul mood?"

Bouzille was joking in a friendly manner. And he was sure of the effect he had. All of the women in the neighborhood adored him. He passed for a dandy, a bit odd, a screwball perhaps, but he wore his heart on his sleeve and he always made people laugh with his tales of the other world.

Yet, Bouzille, who was hoping for an invitation to take a seat since he always authorized women to pay rounds for him, was dumbfounded by his lack of success.

"Get lost!" said Marie-Salope.

"Shut up!" ordered Marie-Quarante-Sous.

Then, pointing a finger at a dark corner of the bar, she added, "First, you shouldn't be making such a racket. You didn't notice your lawful wife?"

---

[11] *Marie Salope*: Marie-the-Slut; *Marie-Quarente-Sous*: Forty-Sous-Marie; obviously two prostitutes.

When he heard those words, Bouzille jumped back.

His lawful wife! They were talking about his lawful wife! That, for example, did not sit well with him. If people were talking about his lawful wife, then he would prefer to leave immediately.

Bouzille, however, inspected the end of the bench that had been pointed out to him, with his piercing eyes. There was, in fact, an enormous, unrecognizable pile of rags there. But Bouzille was not about to let himself be taken in by that heap of rags. He was able to clearly make out a human shape, curled up on the floor, limbs every which way, with an enormous stack of waste, unmoving, clearly a sign of deep drunkenness.

"Yeah!" sighed Bouzille, with a questioning tone. "Is that La Toulouche, then?"

"It is," said Marie-Salope.

Bouzille immediately turned around. He had had an inexplicable thing, in fact, for the abominable shrew. And Bouzille had a terrifying memory of that time. Despite her age, La Toulouche had still been quite strong. As a result, when Bouzille thought back on the time when he was that woman's happy lover, he almost felt like shouting when he recalled the daily beatings he had received.

The worst thing was that Bouzille had regained his freedom through trickery and La Toulouche had never forgiven him. She still called him her man and she was always prepared to swear eternal love for him.

"Yeah," Bouzille said again, tiptoeing away, "This neighborhood is not for me! Not enough women for me. First, since I became a hermit, I've no longer any need for the deceitful charms of that gender!"

At that moment, Bouzille was stepping behind the counter. He gave Père Korn a friendly wink and asked, "Is there anyone down there?"

Père Korn did not answer; he simply spat on the floor.

Bouzille, who was familiar with unspoken languages, interpreted this as a positive affirmation.

So, he went down into the cellars where, he also knew that people could, as a favor, go to drink.

Yet, when Bouzille was barely halfway down the ladder, he had a clear view of three individuals sitting around a table and occupied in a most pleasant manner, judging by the glasses that stood in front of them.

Naturally, Bouzille listened in. Discretion was not his strong point, but indiscretion was his skill.

Moreover, he had immediately recognized two of the individuals at the table: Oeil-de-Boeuf and Bec-de-Gaz.

"Who are they with?" Bouzille wondered. But try as he might to make out the face of the third person, that man was sitting with his back to the light, and was no more than a black silhouette, impossible to identify.

Oeil-de-Boeuf and Bec-de-Gaz, moreover, must have been very drunk. But that didn't stop them from drinking like fish. Bec-de-Gaz stopped drinking, precisely to hum a cheerful song in a slow voice, attempting to keep time, like a funeral dirge.

Oeil-de-Boeuf was obviously trying to express an idea and his drunkenness prevented him from completing a sentence and he had to keep repeating the same words over and over, "Well, you see, that disgusts me. It disgusts me because, well, it disgusts me… And like that, it disgusts me…"

He repeated it over and over!

Bouzille, however, having observed his two friends and realizing what condition they were in, felt immensely satisfied.

"When you're drunk, you don't know what's going on…" he thought. "And, well, if someone steals your glass…"

With that, he climbed down into the cellar.

When he wanted to, Bouzille had excellent manners. With his hand on his heart, he greeted the third individual who was pouring drinks for Oeil-de-Boeuf and Bec-de-Gaz and who seemed to be less drunk than his two friends.

At the same time, Bouzille said, "When there's some for one, there's some for two… When there's some for two, there's some for three… and when there's some for three, there's some for four!"

At the same time, he smiled, a broad smile, reaching out a hand to grab the bottle, since he was profoundly indifferent to the fact that he had no glass.

Yet, Bouzille had not completed this action when he suddenly jumped.

"Oh, good grief!" he said.

And, looking at the face of the man he had not recognized earlier, he said, "Fantômas! Is that you, Fantômas?"

The man stood up.

It was indeed Fantômas. At that moment, he was staring at Bouzille with that extraordinary look, both fiery and filled with shadows, that no one could bear without looking down.

And, voice dripping with scorn, Fantômas said, "Good day, Bouzille!"

Then, as the old tramp was retreating, still holding the bottle he had grabbed, Fantômas rudely ordered, "Put that down, Bouzille. Drop that wine, you imbecile. I'm not going to execute you!"

Bouzille opened his eyes wide, surprised, and said "Eh? What are you saying Fantômas?"

At that moment, the criminal mastermind grabbed Bouzille by the shoulder and pushed him toward the ladder, saying "I said that I have no need to execute you. You have never betrayed me. Not like these imbeciles!"

He pointed at Oeil-de-Boeuf and Bec-de-Gaz.

Bouzille was completely dumbfounded.

"These imbeciles," he repeated. "And you say you're going to execute them? Good grief, Fantômas, I must have grown stupid, but I don't understand…"

Bouzille was most certainly the only person in the world who could talk like that to Fantômas. The Criminal Mastermind allowed the old man to ask questions, even smiling at his distraught expression.

"You don't understand?" he asked. "Well, you will understand."

And, laughing again, Fantômas added, "In an hour Bec-de-Gas and Oeil-de-Boeuf will simply be two cadavers."

This time, Bouzille turned white. He understood what was going on even less. What? Was Fantômas really going to kill Bec-de-Gaz and Oeil-de-Boeuf? What did that mean?

Appalled, immobile, Bouzille continued to stare at Fantômas, who burst into laughter again.

"Hey, do I seem incredible to you?" he asked. "But truly, poor Bouzille, it's just simply because you don't see well."

"I don't see well?" Bouzille repeated. "Why?"

"Because," continued Fantômas, "Because you came here and saw nothing. Get up the ladder!"

Bouzille climbed up the ladder. When he was halfway up, however, he stopped, astonished.

"Well," he said. "Fantômas, someone is knocking at the cabaret door..."

"Naturally!" replied the bandit.

"Naturally what?" asked Bouzille, who was starting the tremble. But Fantômas pushed him from behind.

"Up!" ordered the bandit in a voice that brooked no response. "So, you don't understand, Bouzille?"

Then Fantômas slowly added, "Well, my good friend, the police are arriving. My dear old man, the cabaret is surrounded. There are more than 50 officers in the street. I killed Oeil-de-Boeuf and Bec-de-Gaz by poisoning them while they were drunk, quite obviously, to keep them from being arrested. Do you understand now? Yes? Well, that's fine. So, up with you Bouzille! I'm telling you the police are knocking..."

Fantômas was obviously very calm. Yet, the words he uttered were so abominable frightful. Bouzille climbed up, obeying the order he had received. He climbed up like a robot.

"Good grief," he hissed between clenched teeth. "So, we're all about to get caught?"

And, before he leapt into the cabaret, he turned back once again., saying "Good grief, if the police are knocking then for sure they will come in... and if they come in, you'll be caught, Fantômas!"

When he heard those words, Fantômas burst out laughing.

"Me?" he said. "Be off with you. I don't get caught!"

"It's possible," grumbled Bouzille. "But I wouldn't say so."

Bouzille stopped suddenly, as he felt someone grab his belt.

Behind him, Fantômas had stretched out his arm, pulled him away from the ladder and hurled him with Herculean strength into the middle of the cabaret,

"They take those I allow them to take," Fantômas declared coldly.

And, as he stepped into the cabaret, the extraordinary bandit called out "Friends! The police are here!"

At that moment, for the third time, someone knocked at the door to the bar. A voice, the voice of a police commissioner no doubt, repeated the third legal warning, "Open up in the name of the law!"

"Don't open, Korn!" Fantômas ordered.

CHAPTER XX
Master of All

Fantômas' voice was, as always, profoundly calm, profoundly peaceful, although the minutes raced past and the danger of falling into the clutches of the police was there, immediate, certain, real.

The legal warnings have been slow initially, but the last one was uttered in an imperious tone.

Judging by the manner in which the police commissioner said, "Open in the name of the law", it was easy to guess that, if they did not open in the name of the law, the police would most certainly enter by force. Fantômas had issued a contrary order, in a quiet voice, to the innkeeper.

"Don't open Korn!"

And Père Korn, in fact, was not moving away from his counter, behind which he seemed to be completely devastated, while Fantômas, who was standing in the middle of the cabaret, crossed his arms and looked at those around him.

"My friends," the Master of All and of Everyone said. "We are arriving at a painful moment of a deadline. In recent times, I have had you take part in many interesting tasks, you have made a great deal of money. You should be grateful to me for all this. The police, on the other hand, are furious with you. There are, I imagine, about 50 officers or so on the other side of the door and they are determined to be finished with you. As a result, please pay attention. Every man for himself. I have nothing more to say to you!"

Fantômas was speaking in a half-serious, have scornful tone and his words, naturally, stirred strong, and most justified, feelings on the part of those listening to him.

The Master had never before said, "Every man for himself"! He had never appeared to be so completely, so absolutely disinterested in the fates of his accomplices.

What was Fantômas thinking?

Was he dreaming about a moment of annihilation, of dropping them into the hands of the police, of abandoning those who had been his assistants, loyal up to that time in the paths of crime?

Was it true, as he had told Bouzille, that he had poisoned Oeil-de-Boeuf and Bec-de-Gaz?

Was he going to let Mère Toulouche get arrested?

At that precise moment, the old woman had leapt up from her bench and, pushing Bouzille aside, had thrown herself in Fantômas' direction.

"No!" screamed La Toulouche. "You aren't going to let them arrest us like that!"

Fantômas stared at her and shrugged.

"Why not?" he asked.

"You've always saved us... Save us now!"

In response, Fantômas tilted his head to one side and raised his hand to one ear, like a man prepared to listen.

"La Toulouche," he said. "The officers are gathering at this very moment. In four or five minutes, they will certainly have decided how they will proceed."

"Fantômas! Fantômas! Save us!"

"And," continued Fantômas. "The way in which they will proceed is very easy indeed to determine. They will go to some worksite and pick up a large piece of wood, which they will use as a battering ram. They will smash the door and they will come in..."

He was still speaking in the same calm voice, like a man announcing events that are completely beyond his control. Moreover, his face had not grown pale; his actions showed no signs of nervousness and he seemed as peaceful as if there were not just a single plank of wood between him and the police officers.

At that moment, La Toulouche, haggard and pale, sweat beading on her forehead, literally rolled about on the floor.

"I've got out of prison," she shrieked. "You can't let me get arrested again! Save me, Fantômas! Save me!"

Fantômas pushed her away with the tip of his foot.

Scornfully, with a hint of anger in his voice, the miserable wretch respond to the old woman, saying "La Toulouche, I would certainly have saved you if you had treated me well. Unfortunately, you betrayed me."

"When Fantômas? When?"

"Very recently, La Toulouche. I gave you a black hen to keep and you passed it on to Bouzille. I don't like it when people disobey my orders. I like it even less when people pass on the missions I've given them to others."

La Toulouche, kneeling, twisted her hands in despair.

"Bouzille stole the chicken!" she shouted.

But just then, Bouzille, who had been looking about every which way, said, "Lying woman!"

Fantômas calmed him with a movement of his hand.

"Shut up, Bouzille!"

The Criminal Mastermind placed his hand on La Toulouche's shoulder.

"You don't deserve any pity," he insisted. "You deny an error that you committed and place it on the shoulders of an innocent man. Bouzille did not steal that hen. Let's drop that matter. Didn't you give a hen to Bec and Oeil, who turned it over to Adèle?"

La Toulouche did not want to take part in this discussion.

"Save me! Save me!" she repeated.

But Fantômas continued to look up.

"No," he repeated. "Every man for himself. That's it. I will not turn you over to the police myself, but I will not prevent them from taking you."

At that moment, on the other side of the door, the authoritarian voice of a police official rang out again.

"You don't want to open the door? We'll bash it in… Come on! Once, twice, is that it?"

Fantômas did not appear to have heard.

Now, he was looking at La Toulouche, who, was realizing no doubt that she would not be able to make him take pity on her, and was running about the cabaret like a crazy woman, looking for a way out, looking for a place to hide.

The chaos in the lower room was terrible. The few criminals who had gathered there, had frightened expressions on their faces. Obviously, they all felt that it was a solemn moment, that the battle would be fierce and moreover, brave as they were, they were preparing to pay dearly for their lives.

The large tables had been overturned and the men were kneeling behind them. They held their revolvers and as soon as the police entered they would be welcomed with a volley of shots. Many would die.

La Toulouche, however, who was growing more and more frightened, continued to run about in all directions, like a true mad woman.

Now she was begging Père Korn.

"Do you know of a hiding place?" she asked. "Show me a way out."

But Père Korn remained impassive. He had seen so much, so many brawls break out in his place, he had seen so much, so many police raids, that they no longer moved him.

That evening, however, a flame sparkled in his blinking eyes. Perhaps Père Korn realized that he was about to witness a drama.

Wasn't Fantômas in his place? Wasn't the Master of All and of Everyone about to be captured? Since, in fact, there was no doubt that they were about to capture Fantômas!

Yet, La Toulouche finally had an inspiration. She knelt down quickly, then crawled over to the fireplace and rushed like a mad woman to climb up the narrow chimney.

Unfortunately, La Toulouche was fat…

The miserable woman managed to stuff half her body into the chimney but, since the conduit grew narrower as it rose, she was trapped there, unable to advance or retreat, half suffocated, shrieking abominably….

Outside, the police were still getting organized. Orders rang out.

"Everyone together, eh! One by one! As soon as the door opens, we'll go in! Shoot everyone who resists!"

"It won't be long!" said Fantômas.

The bandit, still standing in the middle of the room, was smiling as he examined the chimney in which La Toulouche was already suffering agonies.

"What a pity I don't have any petrol!" the Master of Fear simply murmured. "I would have enjoyed setting a little fire under that old woman. That would teach her to obey me faithfully!"

Fantômas was still perfectly calm, still peaceful.

Yet, at that very moment, someone approached him respectfully, with such a curious expression, that it was impossible not to take pity.

That person was Bouzille.

Bouzille had a terrible grimace on his face. His old, wrinkled face was torn between fear, hope, anger and deceit. Bouzille held his hat in his hand. He pulled Fantômas by the sleeve.

"Well," he said.

But Fantômas didn't even notice him.

So, Bouzille walked around the bandit. He stood in front of him and looked him in the eye.

"Fantômas! Boss! Hey boss!"

Fantômas saw the old man and smiled.

"What do you want, Bouzille?"

"I'd like to leave."

The answer was simple, but Bouzille was obviously not one for making long speeches in such pressing times.

Moreover, Fantômas did not brush him off.

"Really?" he jeered in a tone that was half pleasant, half ironic. "You'd like to go, Bouzille? And why would that be?"

Bouzille shrugged, saying, "It's just an idea Fantômas. It's just an idea that came to me like that... You see, the police are coming and when the cops and I get together, it's always bad. I have no protection!"

Fantômas did not respond.

Bouzille continued, "When I say that I have no protection, I'm not mistaken of course... I never did anything, Fantômas. So, you are going to protect me. You know, it's not complicated, what I'm asking, it's not rocket science. It's quite simple! I just want to go."

Fantômas seemed to lose his calm.

"Coward!" he said, looking at Bouzille. "Wouldn't you rather have a revolver? You don't like the idea of fighting to protect me? You don't want to take a shot?"

"No, not at all," confessed Bouzille.

And the old man insisted, "Hurry up and save me, Fantômas. The door isn't very solid. Hurry up!"

Then, Fantômas, laughing, grabbed Bouzille by his shoulder.

"Come!" Fantômas said.

It didn't take Fantômas long to do something quite surprising. On the ground, in a corner of the room, lay gigantic wrapping cloths that must have been used to protect some voluminous packages.

"I'll tie you up in that," he said.

And since Bouzille gracefully agreed to the operation, Fantômas did, in fact, wrap Bouzille with the care of a packer wrapping some valuable object. First, he rolled him in the fabric, then he wrapped the bundle in brown paper and finally, he placed a sticker on the outside and tied everything up with rope.

"Bouzille!" Fantômas called out. "Where do you want to go? I'll indicate the address and leave money on the package."

Bouzille's voice, which was a little muffled at that moment, pierced through the thick package.

"Send me to the station, anywhere, to the devil!" Bouzille advised. "I'll get myself out of the package."

"Agreed!" said Fantômas.

He wrote an address on the package then pleasantly asked, "Should I send you by registered mail, Bouzille?"

"Of course!" screamed the old man. "I don't want them dropping 50-kilo trunks on my back!"

Fantômas indicated the instructions.

He was about to walk away when Bouzille once again swore inside the package.

"Fantômas. Hey Fantômas, indicate 'This side up', write 'Fragile' as well."

"Which side is 'This side up' so I can write 'This side down'?" Fantômas asked.

But, in response to this suggestion, Bouzille was wriggling about so energetically in his package that Fantômas had to calm him.

"Now, now, be quiet," he advised. "I'll take care of everything properly. Listen: I'm writing down a new instruction. I'm putting, 'Is afraid of humidity. Keep dry!'"

"Yet," said Bouzille. I'm remarkably dry in here." But that was definitely no time for joking. The battering ram had just struck the door violently and it looked as if it were about to split.

"Shut up, Bouzille!" ordered Fantômas.

The Master of the Terrible quickly threw himself forward. Fantômas wasn't one to hang about. As nimble and supple as ever, he leapt in a single bound, without even taking a running start, onto Père Korn's counter.

From there, the Criminal Mastermind grabbed the cornice of the ceiling, He pulled himself along it with his arms and, under the terrified eyes of the criminals, he reached the precise portion of the wall that hangs over the door through which the police were about to enter.

The cabaret was filled with a most terrible silence, followed immediately by shouting and shrieking. It was no longer possible to hear the panting of the wretches hiding behind the tables. In the chimney, La Toulouche had fallen silent, no doubt suffocated. And quietly, behind his counter, Père Korn gently stirred a glass of sugary water, his spoon clinking.

From the depths of his package, Bouzille asked, "Am I postage due or postage paid?"

Then, suddenly, the battering ram struck the door and it gave way.

"Hands up!"

Roaring, shouting in victory, the police rushed into the cabaret.

As always, they were led by the dedicated inspectors of the Sûreté. Léon and Michel rushed to enjoy the honor to be the first into the danger zone. Unfortunately, their haste to defy the peril was to be fatal for them!

Just as Léon and Michel, side by side, holding their revolvers in their hands, rushed into Père Korn's cabaret, racing through the gaping door, just then Fantômas, who was still clinging to the ceiling beams, gathered momentum and performed a formidable feat.

The Master of Fear, the Criminal Mastermind, the Untrappable, threw himself like a tiger onto the two men who were not expecting to be attacked in such a manner...

Léon and Michel somersaulted and rolled on the ground...

They were not to get back up...

Marvelously precise, abominably cruel, Fantômas had just, in the blink of an eye, struck both men down, planting a dagger in the back of their necks, killing the brave servants of law.

It was a moment of mad confusion.

As Léon and Michel remained motionless, half dead, not even having the time to groan, as the thieves were shooting at the police, the officers, in an effort to take vengeance for their comrades, forced their way into the dump, furious.

Now, Fantômas, had remained hunkered down, stretched out on the floor next to Léon and Michel. He must have guessed that the sight of the two cadavers, would cause the officers to boil in anger. He had guessed that, in order to avenge Léon and Michel, who had been assassinated, all of the police officers would rush into the cabaret as one, prepared for battle.

And Fantômas had counted on that ardent desire!

With marvelous calm in fact, just as all of the officers, swords in hand, revolvers in hand, rushed toward the back of the cabaret to attack the thieves hiding behind the tables, Fantômas, who had remained on the floor next to the cadavers, suddenly stood up.

With a single leap, he reached the door.

"Farewell, Korn," he shouted.

Then he rushed into the street!

Naturally, it was packed with people. The entire neighborhood was terrified, in fact, by the miserable thieves who usually frequented Père Korn's establishment. The announcement of a police raid, of an orderly battle had drawn the entire shadowy population of Goutte-d'Or, La Charbonière and Barbès Boulevard to the scene.

For Fantômas, it was the best possible chance for escape.

"Very well," he said. "I couldn't have hoped for better!"

And he dove into the crowd.

In that mixed population, he was certain to receive an almost enthusiastic welcome.

Obviously, no one recognized him, but they did realize that he was running from the police.

The ranks of the curious onlookers opened in front of him. He ran a few yards, then slowed his pace.

The crowd, like an ocean, had swallowed him up. Very calmly, he took his watch from his pocket and looked at the time.

"Well, well. I'll be late," he grumbled.

When he reached the Metropolitan, Fantômas hailed a taxi.

"Quick. To the Prefecture... to the police prefecture. Yes, my friend!"

Now, as he was fleeing, the battle inside the cabaret continued. First, the officers dragged Mère Toulouche, who was half suffocated, from the chimney.

That one," said the Police Commissioner, "That one is good for life!"

The fate of the others was no better,

Many of the thieves had been injured. In the cellar, Oeil-de-Boeuf and Bec-de-Gaz were dead. Stiff in a posture of drunkenness, glasses in their hands.

Père Korn, for his part, was placed in handcuffs. In vain, he told the police that he was a snitch, that he was on the payroll, and that, as a result, they should let him be.

No one listened to him.

Père Korn might, at one time, have been protected by the police but he had taken far too much advantage of the situation. They hauled him off.

And following that raid, which was to be burnt into the memories of the neighborhood, only Bouzille escaped, Bouzille who was shivering in the bottom of his package.

No one, in fact, had paid any attention to the package that was left to stand next to the wall. They even paid it so little attention that, two hours later, Bouzille found a way to untie it himself and quietly leave the cabaret.

"Well, well," murmured Bouzille. "Paris is worth nothing to me. I'd end up catching some disease considering all my adventures! I came to Pantruche to get a look at the Eiffel Tower and, although I only planned to stay six days, I remained here for two years. Well, too bad! I'm going to return to the country!"

And Bouzille, in fact, abandoned his city life that very night. The old tramp was suddenly overtaken with nostalgia for the open road. He left the Parisian sidewalks without any regrets, returning to the fields, with a vague desire to find chickens that would be lingering along the roadside and whose necks he could wring....

As the police were attacking Père Korn's establishment, informed just by chance by some snitch about the presence of Oeil-de-Boeuf, Bec-de-Gaz and La

Toulouche, no one in the police knew that Fantômas was also there. Meanwhile what had happened to Juve?

Juve was at home. He had been warned that there would be a raid against Père Korn's cabaret but, since he had been assured that only minor accomplices would be there, he had not bothered to take part and this was quite fortunate, since the good man would have certainly the same fate as Léon and Michel,

And, since Juve had not rushed over to Rue de la Goutte-d'or, it was moreover because, that day, he had an important commitment that he could not avoid.

Juve, in fact, was rushing to get dressed, putting on his best suit, and then heading over to the Police Prefecture, where he immediately walked into the rooms that had ironically be named the "school" by staff members.

It was, in fact, in these vast rooms that technical courses, courses organized by Mr. Havard, possibly in order to receive some honorific reward, in order to allow the police officers to perfect their art.

Juve, however, was not about to attend a police course!

Fandor's dedicated friend went to the Prefecture because he knew full well that, that evening, he would meet some very powerful and important people there.

Fantômas' most recent crimes, namely the attacks he had carried out and the audacity he had shown in succeeding, were so outrageous that they had created a strong wave of public opinion and that wave would eventually produce practical results of the greatest interest.

Fantômas had attacked almost all of the countries in the world; he had committed his misdeeds under the most diverse skies, he had covered his trail with blood, throughout the most distant lands, and all of the countries were now joining forces, in their fear.

Russia, England, Germany, Switzerland, the United States, Brazil, Italy, Spain, Portugal, all of these countries had delegated their chiefs of police to meet under Juve's chairmanship, to study the measures to be taken to finally put Fantômas out of action.

For Juve, this police gathering was very important.

Since Fantômas was an international criminal, international measures would be required. And that is why Juve was congratulating himself on having organized this vast police movement, which might result in, which should result in the arrest, once and for all, of the Master of Fear.

When he arrived at the Prefecture, Juve found all of the individuals delegated by the various states on site.

The meeting commenced immediately.

Juve who, naturally, chaired the meeting, since he was the only police officer who could speak about Fantômas in an informed manner, Juve started his explanations.

He provided a description of Fantômas, he described his tricks, his audacity and he concluded his short speech with this simple remark: "Gentleman,

Fantômas is the Proteus of the modern world! He can take on any face and any shape he likes. The reason the police have so much difficulty conquering him is precisely because he is so skilled at disguise, at making himself unrecognizable."

"Yet, over the course of my long career, gentlemen, I have been able to get close enough to this terrifying and legendary individual that I have been able to prepare a description that will enable us to at least try to identify him."

Juve paused, then started speaking again, his voice tinged with triumph, "With the cooperation of several artists and by using photographic techniques which are now available to us, I have been able to do something which I believe, gentlemen, will be of great use to you."

"I have the honor of showing you cinematographic shots that represent Fantômas accurately enough that you will most certainly believe that he actually served as a model for making them."

Juve clapped his hands, darkness fell, and a projector lit up a gigantic white screen located at the back of the room.

Juve had come up with an incredible idea when preparing these movie strips.

It was obvious, in fact, that it was not Fantômas who had been filmed. Yet, as Juve had said, the police were using techniques that were good enough to create a perfect illusion.

Those who wanted to see Fantômas projected onto the screen could be led into error, could believe that they were actually seeing the veritable Master of Fear.

"Roll!" said Juve.

The participants heard the crackling of the projector. At that every moment, moreover, on the white screen, a silhouette stood out.

On the screen, the animated projection had started. And, no doubt in an effort to make it all the more striking, the projection started simply, with Fantômas' silhouette.

Oh! That gloomy silhouette, that black silhouette of a man wearing a mask, swallowed up in a black suit, wearing black gloves, black shoes.

Oh! That legendary and tragic silhouette, that silhouette which had been dictating his own law to the world for 20 years, intangible, unattainable, always driving back the boundaries of ferocity and horror!

When the participants saw that silhouette, they uttered a collective "ah!" in amazement.

Yet, at the very moment, Juve's nervous voice rose out in the darkness of the room.

"Paul" the policeman shouted, calling the projectionist. "What is that shot? Where is it coming from?"

Juve did not recognize the projection!

Fantômas' silhouette, however, turned slowly. It was as if the legendary apparition, dressed all in black, was enjoying the participants' admiration!

On the white screen the silhouette stood out perfectly. Slowly, very slowly, it turned then came to a stop.

"What is that projection? Where did this film come from?" Juve continued to ask. "Answer me, Paul!"

But the operator did not answer...

Juve stood up.

"That's it..." he started to say.

He did not have time to complete his sentence.

The black silhouette stood away from the screen suddenly, holding out its arms.

A hoarse voice shrieked, "You want to project a movie about me, Juve? Go ahead. A trick worthy of you! I've come in person."

Shots rang out.

People cried out in anger, in pain.

Juve leapt forward.

"Fantômas! Fantômas!" he shrieked. "It's Fantômas in person."

It was Fantômas who, driving back the boundaries of audacity, had slipped into the Police Prefecture and, in the luminous halo of the projector, had stood in front of the participants.

It was Fantômas who had just taunted Juve, it was Fantômas who was discharging his revolver at the participants at random. It was Fantômas who, now, slashed the screen with a dagger and then quickly fled.

Juve would arrive too late to block his way.

Mad panic washed over the participants when, after a terrible struggle that lasted a few moments, Juve finally managed to turn on the light and was able to see, unfortunately, face pale, and know that, once again, the Master of Fate had left a bloody trail behind him.

The projectionist, Paul, lay in his projection booth, his throat slashed, and four participants moaned, struck by the Criminal Mastermind's bullets...

CHAPTER XXI
A Great Ship

"Would you like some coffee?"

"Three times rather than two, Juve."

The policeman smiled at that exclamation, then motioned at his elderly servant, Jean, who immediately filled Fandor's empty cup.

Juve turned to Hélène, who was seated next to him, and asked with a smile, "The smoke isn't bothering you, madam?"

With a gracious gesture, the young woman replied that, on the contrary, she loved tobacco smoke and that she might even smoke a cigarette herself.

And Juve, pleased with the pure permission given to him, hastily dug through his tobacco pouch.

The three friends were enjoying breakfast together in the small apartment on the Rue Tardieu, where the policeman had settled after the terrible fire, set by Fantômas, in the building on Rue Bonaparte, had destroyed Juve's former home.

The three friends, who had breakfasted peacefully, were pleased to find themselves in this intimate tête-à-tête. They never mentioned his name, moreover, without emotion, since, although they occasionally commented on their adventures with good humor and enjoyment, they could not help but recall that each step of their adventurous existence, each event in their battle with Fantômas, their implacable adversary, had always been marked by some misfortune, some crime, some murder.

And, as they evoked those memories, their expressions grew darker, their eyes grew wild.

But Juve, making an effort and obviously not wanting that day to bring up sad thoughts, cheerfully scolded Hélène and Fandor.

"Come on! Come on!" he said. "You certainly didn't come here to act like you're going to a funeral. What the devil. You're both young, you adore one another, you're made for one another and, within a few days your wedding, which was interrupted the first time by procedural matters, will be celebrated and you will finally be at peace…"

Juve held Hélène's hand and asked, "So, what are you going to do? What are your projects?"

"Good grief, I don't really know, Juve," Hélène replied, blushing, "I think we'll find ourselves a quiet little place and spend a few happy days there. Fontainebleau, Versailles…"

"In your place," declared Juve, "I would go to Versailles. Versailles with its grandiose gardens, with its large, beautiful boulevards that are always deserted and where you never meet anyone in an inopportune manner, is undeniably charming."

Hélène made a vague movement with her hand, saying that she didn't have a strong opinion, implying that it didn't really matter as long as she was with Fandor.

Maliciously, she added, "I'd go anywhere, but Fandor, I believe, is particularly fond of Fontainebleau."

"Ah!" said Juve, bursting into laughter. "You're already obeying your monstrous husband. You poor women, you always have somebody bossing you around..."

Fandor accepted the joke.

"The fact is," he declared, looking at Hélène. "The fact is that I intend, once we're definitively married, this time, to behave like a tyrant towards my wife."

"I'm counting on that," said Hélène. "It will be one of those tyrannies people love."

And, spontaneously she stood up, to go and kiss Fandor.

Juve protested, "And what about me?"

Hélène turned toward him and clasped him by the neck. The policeman sighed.

"Finally, it will happen and not a bit too soon. You will finally be tranquil and happy, my children. I swear that pleases me greatly."

Fandor, who seemed curiously astonished by Juve's attitude for the past few minutes, finally asked "And you? What will happen to you? Will you come to join us in the country?"

"Of course!" replied the policeman.

"When?" insisted Hélène.

Juve looked evasive and said, "I have a few small matters to settle, unimportant matters, the time it will take, purely for form's sake since no one will refuse me, to ask my superior for permission, and then I'll join you."

There was a moment's silence and then, no longer able to contain himself, Fandor asked, "Look Juve, what does that mean? You invited us to breakfast, you wanted to celebrate with a small, intimate party, which we find most pleasing, moreover, the definitive retour of my beloved Hélène to health, you strongly urged us to leave for the country as soon as the formalities of our marriage are settled and that is all fine and well..."

"On the other hand, you have announced that you will be joining us. That's even better and we're delighted... But, finally, it seems that there is a matter we haven't discussed yet and it seems to be rather unimportant, someone we should not be worried about and who, however, holds a certain place in our lives!"

Fandor fell silent, then looking Juve straight in the eyes, he said, "Fantômas!"

"Well, what about Fantômas?" Juve asked, lighting a new cigarette,

Hélène grew upset. She could never hear Fantômas' name with shivering.

She asked questions in turn.

The policeman frowned.

"Well, what about Fantômas," he said in a rogue voice. "We certainly have to hope than we will be finished with him in a short while and that moment will not be late in coming."

Hélène and Fandor were perfectly aware that Fantômas' most recent escapade had vexed Juve considerably and they could not admit that the policemen would be prepared to give up his hunt for Fantômas, who he had pursued for so long.

Yet, it appeared during the course of this breakfast, that Juve was making plans which did not include the active and rigorous search for the terrible bandit.

Fandor and Hélène could not accept that and, if Juve appeared indifferent, disinterested in what Fantômas was up to, that obviously meant that he had some hidden, secret plan that he did not want to disclose, even to his best friends.

Juve felt, however, as a result of the questions the pair asked him, that he had to satisfy their curiosity.

"Fantômas," said Juve. "Fantômas is certainly in a very perilous situation at this very minute. I told you about the nasty trick he played recently. But that's just one more misdeed that will not bring him happiness."

"His audacious act merely exasperated the entire Sûreté staff even further and people not only in France but elsewhere around the world are determined to do everything they have to in order to capture him!"

Juve then explained the details of the formidable organization he had helped set up.

The Sûreté had been given an enormous budget and all of the police, the agents, the peace officers, the entire gendarmerie and all of the services of the Sûreté Générale were on stand-by. Even the customs officers had been given formal instructions. All police forces everywhere had been mobilized. He was absolutely certain that, at this time, Fantômas had been unable to leave France, since his descriptions, all of them, had been posted everywhere and all of the major routes, borders, boundaries were being watched so closely he could not cross them.

Even the freight trains traveling from one country to another were being watched and specific instructions had been given throughout Europe to inspect balloons when they landed.

"Fantômas cannot avoid capture," concluded Juve. "It's our turn. I can feel it. It's just a matter of days, of hours."

"And what will we do in all this?" Fandor asked.

Juve looked at him for a moment, then said, "You will do nothing, Fandor. You will marry Hélène, that's your right, that's your duty. You have both earned your happiness. Life is short and you have to make the most of it. As for me, I will do very little. I will remain here, at my station, like a general centralizing information at a specific location, without actually taking part in the battle since he has to direct it."

Fandor nodded his head and was about to object that Juve's new attitude did not seem to fit in well with the attitude the policeman had always adopted up to this point, when the elderly Jean entered the dining room, followed by a young man whom he introduced to his master.

"The gentleman comes from the Transatlantic Company," he declared.

"Fine!" said Juve who immediately left the dining room, taking the company employee into his office.

Hélène and Fandor looked at one another, dumbfounded, disturbed by their friend's attitude.

"He's hiding something from us. That's for certain," said Hélène.

"Yes," said Fandor. "Juve obviously has a plan that he is hiding from us and I wonder why..."

"Oh, that's simple," said the young woman. "That's very simple to understand. Juve is so good, that he wants to avoid any little problems and slightest danger for us. He wants us finally to be happy and peaceful and he will assume full responsibility for the battle, for the risks, himself."

Fandor moved closer to Hélène and looked her tenderly in the eyes.

"Will we allow him to, Hélène?" he asked.

Hélène, frankly, without the shadow of a hesitation, shook her head.

"We will not allow him," she declared. "We both have to be Juve's accomplices, his assistants, until the end."

"Excuse me," sighed Fandor. "Juve and I, fine. But you, Hélène? I would be so happy if you would promise to give up your projects and if I could know for certain that you would not try to fight Fantômas..."

Hélène was looking at Fandor, with an expression filled with reproach.

"How can you ask me something like that. I would be so ashamed to stay behind, safe, while you would be in danger."

As the two future spouses were taking part in this generous battle, Juve was in his office questioning the employee from the Transatlantic Company.

"This new ship, sir," said the policeman. "This new ship which will be making its first trip from Le Havre to New York, and which will set out tomorrow, this new ship is a true marvel? It can compete, in all respects, with the enormous floating islands of the English and German lines?"

Yes sir," said the employee. The *Gigantic*, which we will keep armed for its first crossing, is certainly one of the most beautiful ships it is possible to imagine. It measures 250 yards long, rises up to 80 feet above the water line and includes facilities for close to 5,000 people, both passengers and employees. It carries an entire world in its enormous iron shell."

Juve smoked another cigarette,

"The *Gigantic*!" he repeated. "That's a fine name. That ship is extraordinary."

The policeman seemed to be very interested in the details the Transatlantic Company employee was providing.

"Naturally," insisted Juve. "People from the world of fashion and high society are concerned with the first crossing of the *Gigantic*. I've already been shown the first lists of passengers. It includes some very fancy people, Argentinians, Americans, people from the best circles..."

"That's true," acknowledged the employee. "I can assure you that you have to be rather wealthy to pay for that type of crossing, particularly those who want the deluxe apartments!"

"Really?" said Juve. "What are the deluxe apartments like?"

"They are actual apartments, sir... with an antechamber, salon, boudoir, one or two bedrooms, washroom, bathroom, dining room and private kitchen, of course."

"And they cost?" asked Juve.

"The most modest of these apartments costs 1,000 francs per day."

"And the most expensive?" asked the policeman.

"The most expensive is rented, for a lump sum, for the entire crossing, of 30,000 francs!"

"Imagine that!" shouted the policeman. "And have you found a taker?"

"We've had ten requests," said the employee. "There's no shortage of clients!"

Then Juve asked, "And who is the lucky taker?"

"Well," said the Transatlantic Company employee, "I'd very much like to tell you, but I don't know."

"The passenger did not provide his name?"

"He did not provide his name, sir. He paid in advance, by registered mail, then five or six days later we received stacks and stacks of crates and suitcases that we've stored in the hold and which are all designated as being reserved for the passenger who will be taking Apartment No. 1. That's how we refer to the renter of the 30,000-franc apartment."

"Ah!" said Juve. "You don't have any details about him?"

"No details, sir."

"Do you know if he will be traveling alone or accompanied by relatives, family members or servants?"

"We know absolutely nothing. But that doesn't surprise us terribly. We carry a highly-varied clientele on our ships. Frequently princes, people of royal blood coming back from trips abroad, hide their real names and want to travel incognito. Under other circumstances, famous people don't want to reveal their names, imagining as they do that everyone is watching them, which many people do not enjoy. Naturally, we respect the clients' wishes, particularly in the case of a client who pays a great deal."

"And you're right!" said Juve.

The Company employee stood up. Juve was accompanying him to the door when the employee gave him a card bearing this name, handwritten.

"Mr. Juve, you asked for permission to visit the *Gigantic* before it departs. We chatted so long that I almost forgot to give it to you."

"And, yet that's the most important matter," said Juve.

Then the policeman asked, "When can I visit?"

"Starting today, sir and, with special authorization, you can stay on board until next Friday, at noon, at which time the *Gigantic* will leave Le Havre and head for America. The other visitors will be sent off by boat on Thursday evening, to make room for the passengers. The special train from Paris arrives on Friday morning. But, exceptionally, you will be able to remain on board until the *Gigantic* sets off..."

"Please thank the company gentlemen on my behalf," Juve said. "You can tell them that I appreciate the authorization they have given me."

But the employee protested, saying "The honor is ours, Mr. Juve. And I know that these gentlemen are particularly flattered that the famous police inspector, Juve, is interested in the *Gigantic*!"

The Transatlantic Company employee had not been exaggerating when, in eloquent and warm terms, he had, two days earlier, informed Juve that the *Gigantic*, the new boat the company was putting into service, was certainly the most magnificent ship that could be imagined.

The *Gigantic* was, in fact, as large as the largest ships of the company's foreign competitors. But, moreover, the facilities inside were not only sumptuous and comfortable, but they had been arranged with perfect taste, extreme care, that caused delicate and dilettante tongues to say that, undoubtedly, only in France were people so distinguished.

For the past two days, the many people authorized by the Transatlantic Company had been strolling about the immense ship, poking about everywhere, from the deepest holds to the highest deck and everyone was constantly amazed, crying out in surprise and admiration.

The first-class dining room and the deluxe cabins caught everyone's attention, drawing the most admiring and flattering comments.

It was like being in a sumptuous restaurant on the Champs-Élysées or on Parisian boulevards. The ceiling was 25 feet-high and the room was deliciously airy and flooded with electric lighting when evening fell. People could dine there at small tables. A gypsy orchestra occupied a special place in a corner of the room and the meals were served by admirably well-dressed staff, butlers and waiters.

The visitors on the ship included a well-shaved man, wearing a soft felt hat pulled down low over his eyes, wrapped in a large gray cape. This individual, whose attire and silhouette did not go unnoticed, since he stood out from the common crowd as a result of his energetic and martial style, paid particular attention when touring the ship.

He noticed the thousands of tiny details of the inner facilities that were of no interest to the other visitors and he had hired the services of a servant to guide him, as he constantly asked questions.

"This small staircase connects the kitchens to the office, doesn't it?"

"Yes sir."

"And this elevator, where does it leave from and where does it go to? What is the maximum weight it can carry?"

They visited the cabins and the mysterious individual asked about the thickness of the walls and the dimensions of the trunks placed under the bunks.

He checked inside washrooms, he asked if the bathtubs were fixed, namely he took an interest in a great many things that seemed to be completely unimportant.

That man was Juve.

After his meeting with the Transatlantic Company employee, who had come to Rue Tardieu to bring him authorization to visit the *Gigantic*, Juve had quickly taken leave of Hélène and Fandor, promising that he would join them soon, and headed that same evening to Le Havre.

The police had requested permission to visit the company's new ship, saying that he did so out of simple curiosity, a desire to learn more, although he did have another idea in mind.

As the train was steaming to Le Havre, Juve continued to think and convinced himself that it was a good idea to get close to the *Gigantic*.

Thus, as he had informed Hélène and Fandor, the surveillance circle was tightening in around Fantômas.

The police services were organized in a rational matter and it could safely be said that Fantômas had not left France since he had last shown himself to the inspectors who had gathered at the Prefecture.

Juve's investigations had taken him to a fuzzy trail that had been brought to his attention by the Mail and Telegraph department. After thinking about the terms of a telegram from abroad which could have well been sent from abroad by some correspondent or an accomplice, Juve felt strongly that the *Gigantic's* first trip to America would be the object of some sort of attempt on the part of Fantômas. By this time, he had learned the location of the famous deluxe apartment for which someone was paying 30,000 francs for a six-day ocean crossing and which had been reserved in advance by someone who did not want his identity known.

Of course, Juve did not know that it was Fantômas who had rented the apartment, but he wondered if the Criminal Mastermind had something to do with the mysterious situation. Finally, the visitors went to see the famous Apartment No. 1, and when they saw it their admiration turned into amazement. It was impossible, in fact, to imagine anything more elegant, more luxurious. All manifestations of modern art seemed to have been brought together in this apartment. The elegant and graceful furniture was covered with priceless fabrics, old-fashioned wood trim decorated the paneling in the rooms, a few masterpieces were hung on the walls. Superb, sumptuous carpets covered the floor. Everything was magnificent.

Despite the appeal of the apartment, Juve had concentrated his attention on a room next to the apartment which should have only been moderately interesting. It was the baggage room. A considerable number of suitcases and crates belonging to the mysterious stranger who had rented the apartment for 30,000 francs had been stored there. Juve examined these crates and suitcases closely, noting their shape, weighing them, wondering what they could contain. Most bore labels indicating the places from which they had been sent. And they came from the most varied of locations. Some came from Spain, others from Russia, some from England. Some had even been brought over from New York, on a previous crossing, and Juve found this all more and more surprising.

"What can this mean" he wondered. "What is being hidden here?"

Perplexed, Juve left the ship with the visitors on Thursday evening. Then, since he had been given special authorization, he returned to it the next morning and watched the passengers, who had been brought by a special train from Paris, board the *Gigantic*, which was to hoist anchor at noon.

The weather was magnificent. The sea shone bright blue in the distance, an exquisite, fresh breeze caresses the faces of the passengers, making flags and banners flutter.

The ship bustled with activity during the final hours prior to the departure. The *Gigantic's* four enormous smokestacks released large clouds of black smoke, which dissipated in the blue sky. While the enormous floating island was still moored to the wharf, life on board was already starting.

Ship staff came and went, busily making sure that the passengers had been settled in where they were supposed to be. As soon as people went down into the ship, heading for the dining room, they could hear, amidst the clinking of plates and dishes, the plaintiff accents of the violins the gypsies were tuning as they waited for the meal to start. The hallways were filled with passengers perpetually coming and going, wearing colorful hats and clothing, pretty young American girls, elegant French women. And everyone was talking excitedly.

From one end to the other of the floating city, from top to bottom, the scene was filled with uninterrupted movement, like an anthill.

Juve moved through this world, mingling with the passengers, going unnoticed.

Suddenly, a long whistle sounded, plaintive and hoarse, for 30 seconds. It was the first signal announcing the ship's imminent departure. People were filled with emotion at the thought that soon the ropes would be cast off, the gangways would be withdrawn and the *Gigantic*, released from its chains, would start its first trip, its first crossing to America.

Juve walked over to a crew member he knew since they had previously worked for the police, a man who was employed in the company's offices in Le Havre. He was specifically responsible for the passengers.

"Well, Martin," Juve said, clapping the other man on the shoulder. "Will your ship be setting out in 30 minutes?"

"Of course," the employee. "That is, unless it doesn't..."

"Bah!" said Juve. "What's up?"

"Nothing or very little," continued Martin. "But they are still hesitating to give the signal to depart at the required time. We're missing a passenger..."

Bah!" said Juve, laughing. "And they would make 3,000 passengers wait for a single late individual?"

"It's no ordinary passenger,' said Martin, murmuring in Juve's ear. "It's the mysterious stranger who reserved Apartment No. 1."

Juve was already aware that the passenger in Apartment No. 1 had not yet made his appearance. He also knew that the company was confused and did not know if they should give the signal to depart. Yet, he pretended to know nothing and questioned Martin.

"So, the passenger in Apartment No. 1 is someone important?"

"No one knows," said Martin. "They think... They suppose that it might be some sovereign who is traveling incognito, or some important person on an official mission..."

"There's been no news of him?" asked Juve.

"Absolutely none."

Juve walked away from Martin and over to the ship's railing. Bit by bit, he realized that amazement was washing over the passengers. It was five minutes before noon, the sea was high and it was a propitious moment to set out. Yet, the second whistle, which was to be blown fifteen minutes before the departure time, had still not been blown and it seemed as if no one were preparing to cast off the ropes. The tug responsible for taking the ship out past the piers had not even taken up its position!

A few first-class passengers started to complain.

Small groups of people formed around the ship's officers.

"Is there some mechanical problem?"

"What's the reason for the delay?"

"Is there a storm at sea?"

The most extraordinary hypotheses were being formulated. In some groups, which were better informed than others, people were starting to speak what seemed to be the truth, that they were waiting for someone. The passengers seemed to find this unlikely at first, then grew indignant and started to complain.

It was impossible! A transatlantic ship doesn't wait for a single passenger, even a passenger who paid 30,000 francs for his berth! The most unlikely rumors spread.

Juve was starting to wonder what exactly was happening and the policeman seemed to be quite upset, quite disturbed.

Had he discovered something?

Juve went to see Martin again. It was ten minutes after noon.

"Well," he said. "What's happening?"

The other man replied, "The latest news is that they've decided to postpone the departure by two hours."

"That is extraordinary," exclaimed Juve.

"Here's why," said the employee. "We're waiting for the arrival, at 1:35 this afternoon, of a rapid connection with the Nord-Express. They presume, although I don't know why, that perhaps the passenger from Apartment No. 1 is on that train. If that is the case, he will be on board in two hours and we'll leave with him."

"What if he isn't on board?"

"Then we'll leave anyway," continued Martin. The ship can't wait any longer, there's the matter of the tide, the postal service, the wharf that we're blocking and tying up, all the expenses that entails... And to top it off, we'll have to make up for the two hours we've lost, which isn't all that easy."

The expression on Juve's face was most perplexed and he asked, "In any case, Martin, are you certain that the ship won't leave for another two hours?"

The employee smiled, "That's what I'm telling you Mr. Juve. Plus, they're posting signs on the deck."

Juve ascertained that Martin had been telling the truth and quickly noticed that along the walls of the cabins, in narrow racks provided for that purpose, crew members were posting small, hand-written signs announcing that the *Gigantic* would depart at two o'clock rather than noon.

A few passengers murmured and then everyone quickly forgot this setback. They had so much to do to get settled in. Everyone went back to their own activities, no longer concerned about the delay.

Meanwhile, Juve had disappeared. Time was passing. At fifteen minutes before the departure time, the final whistle blew in the midst of general emotion. Workers started to remove the ropes holding the sea giant to the wharf.

As the dock workers were about to remove the final gangway, porters came running, some of them carrying large white crates on which "Apartment No. 1" was painted in white.

When the passengers saw them, and realized that the departure of the ship was about to be delayed yet again, they started to murmur.

Once again, this luxury client was making the *Gigantic* late! Who could that passenger be?

CHAPTER XXII
Apartment No. 1

While the final preparations for the departure were being made and the *Gigantic*, whose formidable equipment was being powered up, was waiting for a signal that was late in coming, Juve had suddenly left the increasingly packed deck of the colossal floating city.

Before going down to the wharf, the policeman first took great pains to make sure that the departure of the *Gigantic* had actually been delayed by two hours.

He had confirmed this matter in the most precise manner, as if he considered it to be very important. Then, when he set foot on the wharf he spied an automobile taxi, waved at the driver and gave him the address for a business street in the heart of the city.

A few moments later, Juve arrived at a carpentry shop. He got out of the car, murmured a few words to the taxi driver and slipped him a 20-franc bill.

The vehicle did not go anywhere. Instead, it parked along the sidewalk. The driver turned his motor off and waited.

Juve went into the carpentry shop, which served primarily as a packing firm.

Père Antoine, that was the name of the honorable merchant, had a vast workshop where mechanical saws snored constantly, cutting planks of work and spreading clouds of sawdust everywhere. The ground was littered with chips and stacks of crates of all sizes, made of all kinds of wood, stood along the walls, some open, others lined with waterproof fabric or even zinc.

Juve walked over to the small office occupied by Père Antoine, a brave old man with curly gray hair, wearing gold-rimmed glasses.

"Do I have the honor of addressing Mr. Antoine?" Juve asked.

"Himself," the carpenter said, looking up.

"Well," said Juve. "I'm pleased to make your acquaintance. I'd like a word with you."

And, Juve took the other man aside so that the young apprentice who was standing next to the boss could not overhear the conversation. And he started to question Père Antoine, who was somewhat surprised by this introduction.

"You are a most enterprising man... A man who knows his business and can do something extraordinary in the shortest amount of time possible?"

Père Antoine looked at the policeman, with a certain amount of distrust, and replied, "It all depends, of course, on the work I'm asked to do and the price one is willing to pay!"

Juve understood.

"The work is not complicated," he said. "And I won't question the bill. The important thing is that it must be done quickly!"

Père Antoine, no doubt with a certain amount of irony, observed, "I'd like to point out, sir, that you have already spent five minutes here and you haven't said what you want."

"That's so!" replied Juve, who did not appreciate such observations. "But I haven't been wasting my time here."

He then pointed at a large crate, lined with waterproof fabric, which a laborer was placing along a wall in the workshop.

"That's what I need," he said. "And while I was making your acquaintance, Mr. Antoine, I was looking all about me, observing the contents of your shop, looking for a crate that would be suitable for me. There it is! How much does it cost?"

"But," said Père Antoine. "It's not for sale. I was given an order for it yesterday."

"What does it cost?" insisted Juve. "I want it immediately!"

"One hundred and fifty francs," Père Antoine replied.

"Perfect!" declared Juve. "Here's the money!"

He took three bank notes out of his pocket and handed them to Père Antoine, who declared, "But you've given me 300 francs…"

"I know that," said Juve. "One hundred and fifty for the crate and one hundred and fifty for packing and shipping. And for the instructions to be written on the crate as well."

"Where does it need to be taken? What do I have to pack in it?" asked Père Antoine.

Juve continued, "This crate must be loaded in the taxi you see out in the street and it must be accompanied to the *Gigantic*, which will be leaving in an hour for New York. You will have the crate placed in Apartment No. 1."

"Fine," said Père Antoine. "That's possible. But what are we to pack in the crate?"

Once again, Juve took Père Antoine aside.

"Don't you have another place apart from the shop which is open to everyone?"

"Yes," replied the carpenter. There's the storeroom in back."

"Well, let's go to the storeroom," replied Juve. "Then I'll tell you what is to be placed in the crate."

"What's the reason for all this?" asked Père Antoine.

"You'll see," replied Juve.

When the two men had gone into what Père Antoine called the storeroom and Juve found himself alone with the carpenter, when the large crate lined with waterproof fabric had been brought to the room and placed on the floor there, Juve, staring into the clear and honest eyes of the dumbfounded carpenter, said,

"It's quite simple what you are going to place in the crate... is a man... a living man..."

"Ah! But I can't," protested the carpenter. "That would be too much. I don't want to get involved..."

Juve insisted, "That living man that you are going to place in this crate will not object at all to being packaged up in that manner."

"What do you know?" asked the carpenter.

"I know," continued Juve, "I know, because that man is me."

This time, Père Antoine was completely dumbfounded. He looked at Juve, then at the door. Suddenly he felt as if he were dealing with a mad man or some criminal.

"No, no," he grumbled. "That doesn't work for me. This is shady business!"

Juve grew excited. Time was passing. He took another bank note from his pocket.

"Here are another five louis," he said.

But the noble carpenter replied, "Not even for 1000 francs!"

"So," continued Juve. "It's all for nothing. It would be to my advantage to make my identity known to you, Mr. Antoine. I'm Inspector Juve, from the Sûreté de Paris. Here's my ID card. Do I have to get a warrant from the Police Commissioner to get you to obey my order?"

The carpenter gradually grew more reassured.

"Ah! You're inspector Juve!" he said. "Yes, yes, I know the name and, no doubt, you're working on something to catch some criminal or thief, perhaps even Fantômas? Aren't you the one who's chasing after Fantômas?"

"That isn't important for you!" replied Juve. "Hurry up and pack me in the crate!"

"Oh! But not like that," shouted Père Antoine. "What if something were to happen to you... I need a paper, a paper written by you, discharging me of any responsibility!"

Juve was stamping his feet in anger. Time was passing and nothing was getting accomplished. Yet, he was fully aware that Père Antoine would obey him if he gave the other man a paper, just as the carpenter asked. So, Juve hastily scribbled a few words on a sheet of paper and gave it to Père Antoine and then immediately settled in the crate, as he gave the other man his final instructions.

"Hurry up and nail on the lid. But, before that, place a chisel and pliers in the crate so that I can free myself whenever I want to!"

"One other thing: it is understood that you will personally accompany the crate and place it in Apartment No. 1. I've given you authorization from the Transatlantic Company to put this crate in the place I have indicated to you. Do whatever it takes. Don't forget that I will be watching you and will be able to hear you!"

Juve had finally overcome Père Antoine's scruples and, a half hour later, just as the last gangplank connecting the *Gigantic* to the wharf was being removed, an automobile taxi raced toward the ship, carrying a large, white crate on which the following words had been painted in black: "*Gigantic*, Apartment No. 1."

Père Antoine, his apprentice and his right-hand man, assisted by the taxi driver then loaded the crate onto their shoulders and carried it onto the transatlantic ship.

"Hurry up to get on and off the ship," people shouted at them. "We're waiting on you to give the signal to depart!"

On the deck of the transatlantic ship, the later arrivers were being hustled and shoved. They had to argue with the ship's officers who did not want to let them pass, but Père Antoine, who heard Juve shouting inside the crater, "Don't give up! Tell him that crate is for Apartment No. 1!" obeyed the policeman scrupulously.

And, in fact, once he mentioned Apartment No. One, all of the rules were lifted and the most rigorous orders were waved. The crate went through, along with those carrying it, and was placed in the apartment. Five minutes later, Père Antoine found himself back on the wharf. He let his employees set out in the taxi and he returned to his shop by foot.

Père Antoine was very satisfied that he had earned 300 francs, plus a tip of 100 francs in the space of an hour. Yet, he was worried, unsettled, wondering if the entire situation would turn against him.

Of course, he realized that he had been dealing with the veritable policeman, Juve, that he had a proper paper, relieving him from any responsibility, but still he was a little concerned that he had locked a man up in a crate and placed that crate in a luxurious apartment on a transatlantic ship!

Père Antoine wondered what Juve's intentions were, saying "When people get caught up in tricks like that, it means they're up to no good!"

Père Antoine left the port and was about to return to his shop when someone tapped him on the shoulder. He turned around suddenly.

"Well, Mr. Charlot," he said.

And Père Antoine automatically shook the hand of the other individual.

The man who had just approached the carpenter, who was called Mr. Charlot, was his colleague or his competitor, the packer who worked on the wharf, opposite the theater. Père Antoine and Mr. Charlot were not on bad terms, both having a good clientele and earning good livings. From time to time, they would help one another, sending clients to one another, acting more like colleagues than competitors.

"So," asked Mr. Charlot. "Is business good?"

"It's fine," replied Père Antoine, thinking complacently about the 400 francs he had earned in less than thirty minutes.

"In fact, business is going quite well," he said, implying that he must have discovered a remarkable way of growing rich.

Mr. Charlot was not jealous.

"Well," he said. "So much the better, I'm pleased to see you happy, Père Antoine, since I've just completed a nice little deal myself. I just earned a large sum without having to do much of anything."

"Really!" said Père Antoine. "How?"

Mr. Charlot placed a finger on his lips. Then, taking his colleague by the arm, he pulled him into a cabaret.

"Let's drink a bottle of cider," he said. "I'll tell you everything while we drink. Only, we must be discreet. The situation seems a little shady to me... But, when clients pay with good money, there's no need to know any more than the client wants to say!"

And then, Mr. Charlot told Père Antoine, who listened very attentively, about the profitable situation that had just occurred.

Someone had come into his shop, two or three hours ago, who had initially asked for an immense crate, one large enough to hold a man's body. Naturally, Charlot complained, saying that that was not his type of business, that the client would have to go elsewhere for a coffin... But the man told him that the crate was for himself, that he wanted to be locked up in it since he intended to travel in that manner. He claimed to be an eccentric and that his physician had recommended lying on planks of wood.

"And you agreed to place him in that crate," Père Antoine asked, interrupting.

Charlot replied, "I tell you that he paid me 200 francs for that!"

Antoine's expression grew mysterious.

"I'm going to tell you what you did with the crate. You carried it one board the *Gigantic* and your placed it in Apartment No. 1, in the back of a small parlor to the right, behind a sofa?"

Mr. Charlot was dumbfounded. His eyes grew round in surprise.

"How did you know that?" he asked

Père Antoine hesitated a moment before speaking, then decided that it was the best thing to do, that it would be better not to hide what he had done, particularly from a colleague, and he confided, "I know because I saw it done. I brought a man in a crate on board the *Gigantic* too!"

And he recounted Juve's visit.

"Only," he concluded, "I was more cunning than you were since I earned 400 francs."

But Charlot was not thinking about that.

"Well, good grief!" he said. "Good grief! Good grief! I believe that we have both done some very strange work... Because, Père Antoine, if you locked the policeman in the crate, then I suppose my client must be the bandit everyone is looking for ... What will those two men get up to on board the *Gigantic*?"

Philosophically, Père Antoine declared, "We know nothing about that and we can do nothing about that. Moreover, there's no reason to be bitter, we both got paid, didn't we?"

In order to calm their emotions, the two men drank another bottle of cider, then peacefully returned to their respective stores.

Two hours earlier, the tugboat that was responsible for guiding the transatlantic ship into open water had abandoned it and the *Gigantic*, whose engineers had been set to work, was starting its trip at a dizzying speed, across the Atlantic Ocean.

The superb ship quickly disappeared off the horizon and plunged into the grayish fog of a cloud-filled sky that merged with the dreary sea. There was a small swell, a short, jerky swell as is common on the English Channel.

Yet, the passengers on board the *Gigantic* did not seem overly affected by the condition of the sea, which did not rock the enormous ship much.

The ship gradually accelerated.

The engines had been set to the maximum as soon as the ship departed, not only to test the boilers, which was a good thing to do while the ship was still close to shore in the event that problems occurred, but also to make up for lost time.

In fact, the ship had set out two hours late and the man at the helm of the transatlantic ship, Captain Blancart, was making it a point of honor to make up for the delay within a day or two. The passengers settled into their cabins or their apartments.

A few phlegmatic Americans had already taken possession of the bar and were sampling iced drinks and smoking enormous cigars while most of the passengers who had finished unpacking, were walking about on the ship, filled with curiosity, hoping to make themselves familiar with the facilities that were completely new to them on the luxurious transatlantic ship that carried them off.

People jostled one another, met unexpectedly, everywhere, on the decks, in the stairwells, in the hallways. Heads peeked through half open doors, amazed, crying out in surprise, when they saw the marvelous exercise room, the fresh water swimming pool where people could swim 30-yard lengths, the tennis court. They found the gypsies in their red vests, their violins under their arms curious as they returned to the tea room, waiting for dinner time, when they would perform in the restaurant.

The general hustle and bustle mingled with the feverish activity of the porters and servants, coming and going with suitcases and bags.

Finally, at times, the whistle blew loudly, making the ship tremble, warning other ships in the distance of its arrival.

The *Gigantic* sailed ahead lightly, rocked by the swell, its entire steel hull shivering under the formidable thrust of its formidable engines.

While everyone was settling in and most of the cabins were filled with frantic activity, in the sumptuous Apartment No. 1, which had been rented by the anonymous traveler people had talked about so much, the most absolute calm and silence continued.

After having to postpone its departure for two hours, in order to wait for this passenger who had paid 30,000 francs for the apartment, the *Gigantic* had left Le Havre, without anyone receiving any news at all about the rich traveler.

The apartment was free and empty and would be used by no one for the entire crossing. But that didn't matter! The company had been paid in advance and had behaved correctly with respect to the luxury client, by postponing the departure of the ship by more than two hours, contrary to the rules and regulations.

The apartment seemed empty but it was, in fact occupied.

One of the rooms, at least, contained a passenger, perhaps two. In fact, there was a large wooden crate in the parlor, standing in the middle of the room, and that crate contained Juve.

The policeman, who had made holes in the wooden walls, glanced around the room, making sure that Père Antoine had installed him where he wanted to be. He was waiting for an opportune time to climb out of his hiding place. Juve, who did not place much importance on premonitions, when they were not supported by precise facts, was nevertheless convinced that Fantômas was on board and was most certainly traveling on the *Gigantic*.

There was no doubt that Fantômas had reserved, or had had someone reserve, the luxurious apartment. Although the policeman had obtained no clues about the bandit, he did have very precise information about the content of each of the suitcases that the mysterious traveler had had carried onto the *Gigantic*.

One of the crates, which had been stowed in the hold and been inventoried by Juve's men, was in fact, filled with gold and, based on the details his subordinate had provided, the policeman had recognized that gold as the gold the unfortunate Bedjapur had kept in his cellars which, it was discovered after his death, had been almost completely emptied by Fantômas and his gang.

That clue was enough to convince Juve that Fantômas was setting out for America and Juve had not been surprised that he had not seen the bandit, since he told himself, "Fantômas knows that he is being supervised, spied on, that all of the borders, all the trains, all exits are being rigorously guarded and, logically, that is why he decided to set off on board the *Gigantic* since the surveillance during the boarding process is not very rigorous."

Juve congratulated himself for his strategy, which had enabled him to get into this apparently empty luxurious apartment where Fantômas would come sooner or later, where he would surely come.

Juve was still thinking, motionless in his crate, determined to climb out only when night had fallen, when, at one point, a small sound caught his attention.

"Oh!" thought the policeman, making sure that he had his loaded revolver close at hand, "Are we, are my adversary and I, already on the point of meeting?"

Juve was not particularly satisfied with that idea since, in fact, he was locked up in his crate and knew that it would take him a certain amount of time to remove the lid. And, if Fantômas arrived too soon, Juve would be locked up while Fantômas would be free. They would not meet as equals and the bandit would have the upper hand over the policeman.

Juve scolded himself.

"What's done is done! I'm such an imbecile... I should have thought about this...I should have arranged things so that I could leap out of my crate at a moment's notice."

Yet, Juve reassured himself.

Listening, he heard nothing more, except, from time to time, strange cracking sounds, the creaking of wood, but he was unable to determine the source.

"How stupid I am!" he suddenly thought. "This ship is new, the wood trim is working, cracking, creaking, nothing could be more natural!"

At the same time, the policeman reassured himself.

"These normal noises will be of use to me and will mask the sounds made by my pliers and my chisel when I open my crate. The sounds produced by Père Antoine's planks will mingle with those of the wood trim that decorates this apartment."

Juve waited a little longer and, since the cracking sounds continued, he did not hesitate to add those of his crate to the series that was being produced.

In 20 minutes, Juve had freed the lid of his crate and was simply waiting for an opportune time to climb out of his crate.

Night had fallen, the apartment was completely dark, and Juve decided to make his move.

"Let's go!" he said. "The time has come..."

But, he immediately stopped thinking, stopped moving. Only his heart was beating, pounding rapidly, since Juve had just heard a new noise, an unexpected noise, but one that was easy to recognize. The sharp clack of a gun being loaded!

"Oh!" though Juve. "This changes everything and complicates the situation a bit! Until now, I willingly believed that the sounds came from the wood trim that was creaking, but I had no idea that new furniture or cupboards were capable of making the sound of a browning that someone is preparing to use!"

Juve felt filled with courage and audacity.

"Well, if Fantômas wants a duel, then he will get one!"

Then the policeman said to himself, "I'll let him know that I'm armed too!"

Without making any attempt to hide the sound, Juve armed his revolver as well. Then he listened.

His mysterious companion had noticed, since a profound silence washed over the room for a few seconds.

"Get up!" thought Juve.

And he got up.

At that moment, the ship was shaken by the sea and the policeman realized that the *Gigantic* was tilting to an unfortunate degree, making it hard for him to maintain his balance.

"Well, that is not going to make matters any easier," he said to himself. "It would be nice to have some light…"

While remaining motionless for the moment, at the bottom of his crate, Juve tried to remember how the room was arranged. His knee brushed against a small sofa and he recalled that he was positioned not far from the wall that led into the corridor.

"So," thought Juve, "By moving along this sofa and then walking straight ahead, I will reach the door that opens onto the antechamber. In all likelihood, the light switch for the parlor should be located on the wall to the left of the door. It might be risky, but it will be better, despite everything, to turn on the lights."

And Juve bravely decided to implement his plan and tiptoed in the presumed direction of the light switch.

Suddenly he stopped and held his breath.

For a few moments, his legs had been brushing against furniture. But now, his shoulder had just struck something. Juve was unable to recall if there was a piece of furniture tall enough to reach his shoulder! Had he just bumped into someone else who was also walking about in the dark?

Despite his bravery, Juve felt emotion wash over him.

"I'm at the mercy of chance," he thought. "It's highly likely that, in a second, my adversary and I will be in each other's arms, trying to perforate the other's chest or skull with a revolver shot! The first one hit will die, unless we are both hit and we fall together, which is also quite possible… Damn! There's nothing appealing about that hypothesis… I would really like to have some light!"

Juve stumbled about, as the ship continued to tilt and finally ran into the wall he was heading for.

He ran his hand along the wall, looking for the light switch. Just as he found it, but before he was able to turn it on, his hand brushed against another hand!

Juve did not withdraw his hand. Quite the contrary, his hand tensed over the hand he had encountered and that hand closed like a vise. Two men, holding hands, each trying to master the other, so that neither could say, "I'm holding", "I'm being held".

Who was the man that Juve felt standing so close to him?

Afraid to move, the policeman waited.

Juve experienced a few seconds that seemed as long as centuries to him. Suddenly, he made a decision. At all costs, he had to tear away from the grasp that held him. He pulled with all his might, but his adversary had had the very same idea and was also trying to free his fingers...

Juve abruptly let go and fell back, collapsing on the floor. At the same time, he heard another body fall, that of his adversary.

"This time," thought Juve. "I have to take advantage of the situation. I have to act quickly..."

He wanted light and leapt for the switch. But he was jostled once again. The other man also wanted light, no doubt. The other man was going to turn the switch as well!

Which of the two men managed to turn the lights on? No one would ever know!

But, barely had the lights turned on, barely had the parlor been lit up with a pale, flashing light, then two cries rang out.

The two adversaries had seen one another. They stood there, dumbfounded, looking at each other. Then they cried out together.

"Juve!"

"Fandor!"

CHAPTER XXIII
Master Stroke

A large ship is like a city. It has its posh neighborhoods, as well as working class and poor ones.

So, the upper decks were filled with a rich and elegant crowd, wearing sumptuous outfits, gleaming jewels and in the lounges piles of gold appeared and disappeared on the green felt of the gaming tables, and people in the places reserved for the luxury, first and even second class, people spent without counting and in exchange received everything modern luxury and comfort could provide. But, the depths of the great ship, the dark holds, the dormitories reserved for immigrants swarmed with misery and poverty in striking contrast to the other spectacle.

And, as it has always been in certain cities, the neighborhood of the rich was off limits to the poor and those who could have helped the unfortunate never set foot in the neighborhood of the poor and this was the case of the *Gigantic* where the people on the upper decks had no idea what was going on beneath their feet.

The 5,000 human beings contained in the single, unique steel hull, were parked, catalogued in veritable superimposed drawers and they were destined to travel together across the ocean without ever being seen.

There was a large variety of passengers in the immigrants' dormitory. Representatives of the most diverse nations seemed to have made a point to get together in these dark, stinking holds, where it was difficult for the air, already polluted by the upper decks, to reach.

The passengers, however, grew accustomed to the crossing. Although a few of the women had been sick when the ship set out, they eventually returned to good health and willingly made the most of the time they were allowed, two or three hours, to stroll on the deck to enjoy the salty ocean air.

Among the immigrants, in the women's sector, there was a young girl, dressed modestly who, although she initially went unnoticed, was later noticed and appreciated for her distinguished air, her energetic look and her determined appearance.

She seemed to have lost her way in the midst of these immigrants and looked out of place, called by her appearance and attire to be somewhere else.

She was charitable, cordial with everyone around her, but, despite everything, not very sociable, seeming to be watching what was going on around her all the time.

One evening, instead of going to bed, as the other women in the dormitory were doing, this mysterious individual had left the vast room, which was plunged into darkness, and walking down poorly-lit corridors, had headed to the baggage room. She found an open door and walked into the black, gaping hold, where mountains of packages were piled.

The sea was rather wild and was shaking the boat.

Yet, there was no danger in walking about in the narrow corridors. And this woman was not walking randomly.

Obviously, she had a purpose and headed into the depths of the ship with the skill and ability of someone who was a member of the staff.

She exited from the other end of the baggage room, walking past a guard drowsing in a small cabin without making a sound and made her way into the area of the transatlantic ship that was reserved for the baggage and boiler room staff.

The zone was filled with the most unlikely and terrifying chaos.

Visitors would have thought they were in a coal mine and feared that the veritable mountains of that fuel would collapse, rolling down, in one fell swoop if they, like the baggage, had not been firmly stowed.

At the end of the coal hold there was a dormitory for the workers. A team of workers were sleeping in hammocks, snoring noisily. Some of the beds were empty. Yet, clothing, blue pants, a jacket were methodically piled at the foot of each bunk. This was the spare clothing that the firemen currently working next to the boilers would put on when they were soon relieved from their work-stations.

What an extraordinary thing! This woman slipped soundlessly in the midst of all these sleeping men who were waiting their turn to go to work. She took off her dress in the dark and slipped into a man's pair of pants and jacket!

She hid her hair, with its golden highlights, under a gray cap which she pulled down low over her ears, then walked into the coal hold and purposely dirtied her hands and face. Anyone who would have seen her would have found it impossible to recognize her as a representative, and even a very fair one at that, of the female gender.

This transformation had barely been completed when a commotion occurred among the sleeping firemen.

A whistle had sounded, a quartermaster had come to give the signal, it was the turn of the starboard firemen to replace their colleagues at the boilers.

The men walked slowly along a long, dark corridor, where dirty water covered the floor, until they reached the boiler room.

That room was filled with the formidable heat of the engines and the intense rods pivoting on their axes.

One by one, the men walked on, heading to replace their colleagues. There were about six in all. And what an extraordinary thing, in the place of one of those they were to replace, they saw an employee they didn't recognize at all.

The man at the head of the line, who had walked on in order to take his usual place, was suddenly struck by the man who had replaced him, with an immense blow to the head. He fell down dead…

This unexpected murder was performed so abruptly, with such speed, that the unfortunate victim had not even cried out and the man behind him did not even realize what had happened. The second worker entered the hold and was in turn struck down!

Then, those that followed were starting to notice that something abnormal was going on. They moved back, then exclamations rang out. They saw the two men lying in pools of blood.

The quartermaster ran over.

"Hey!" he shouted. "What's happening?"

At that moment, a detonation rang out. The officer had just been shot in the chest. The sound of the detonation was lost in the rumble of the machines, but panic spread immediately following this incident.

After hesitating, the four men who remained prepared to retreat. They saw that they were surrounded, that individuals with forbidding faces, with masked faces, were threatening them with knives, daggers and revolvers!

They heard shots, terrible death rattles, then silence fell. Five minutes later, the six replacements and their quartermaster, were lying motionless, swimming in their blood.

Someone had planned this butcherous attack. Someone robust and agile, whose completely black silhouette came and went like a shadow, as light as a ghost.

He had conducted the operation, the multiple murders, with supreme skill.

The man had just murmured a few words and the murderers under his command had quickly picked up the inert bodies then, as if they were used to doing this, they dumped then in the red furnaces where the incandescent coal snored. The odor of burning coal mingled with the scent of roasting flesh. Then, after ten minutes, there was no trace left of the bodies!

Yet someone, a frightened witness, had watched this frightful carnage.

It was the young woman who, a few minutes earlier, had disguised herself as a laborer, who had sought to mingle with the team of men heading for the boiler room.

She had miraculously escaped death. If she had walked into the middle of the group of victims, she would have joined them in their fate, but fortunately, no doubt by chance, she had remained a few yards behind, which spared her life.

Pale, overwhelmed with emotion, fear, the young woman could not tear her eyes from the man with the shadowy silhouette who seemed to have directed the frightening butchery.

Suddenly, her lips moved, weakly stammering a name: "Fantômas!"

She thought she would faint.

"Fantômas!" she murmured again. "I thought so... I was sure, Fantômas is taking over the ship. Fantômas brought who knows how many men here and is gradually replacing the real firemen and engineers with them!"

Then, frightened, the young woman turned back, returned to the dormitory and quickly put her women's clothing on.

But her emotions were so strong, that, barely had she changed her clothes than she swooned, half dead from her emotions, and fell on a pile of clothes.

The ship, however, continued its rapid race across the ocean. Evening fell. The passengers from the first-class and luxury cabins, who had been separated during the day, started to speak with one another. Helped by the music, faces started to smile, conversations started up here and there, and, at the end of the meal, a cordial intimacy reigned among the guests, as they headed into the lounge and the smoking room.

Two charming American women wearing ball gowns suggested organizing a small party. The orchestra, accommodating them, set up in the lounge and performed fashionable tunes.

No one knew what had happened a few hours earlier in the depths of the ship.

They knew nothing of the drama that had taken place in the boiler room and a few officers, wearing dress attire, who were not on duty, had come to mingle with the passengers, no doubt unaware of the butchery for which there was a sole witness, a young woman who had surreptitiously left the immigrants' quarters to go and see what was going on in the holds.

The ball was in full swing when, in the corridors, next to the cabins, someone was walking.

It was a young, blond woman, simply dressed. She seemed to hesitate, not knowing exactly where she was to go.

How did she get there?

This individual was none other than the woman who, a short while earlier, had witnessed the massacre. She had gradually made her way up hidden stairways up to the third deck, then the second. Then the first. She was quite pale and looked haggard.

Most certainly, she had not recovered from the emotions she had experienced.

Suddenly, a sort of guard, dressed in a uniform with braid, asked, "What are you doing here, Miss?"

The young women stammered, not knowing what to say.

"Oh!" said the man. "You look like you're not feeling well... No doubt a touch of seasickness... Is this your first trip?"

"It is," stammered the young woman. "It is my first trip!"

The man, who no doubt misunderstood, took a flask of smelling salts from his pocket and had her breathe in until she wanted to give it back to him.

He declared, "No, no, keep it... You may need it again!"

Then he added, "You are no doubt one of the new maids hired by the company for the crossing?"

Those words seemed to give the young woman an idea, and she bravely replied, "In fact, Sir, I'm one of the new chambermaids and I must admit that I lost my way in this large ship and I don't know where to go."

The man shrugged, saying "Good grief. It's always the same thing. They hire more employees than they need, they don't tell them what to do, they take on anyone, then it's up to us, the supervisors, to deal with things afterwards... So, you don't know if you're in first, second or third class?"

"Good grief, no, sir."

"Well, my girl, it's easy enough to find out. I'm specifically short of people for the luxury class. I found you, I'll keep you! Only, you must do me the pleasure of putting on an apron and a little lace hat. That's the uniform here. It's obligatory."

The young woman submitted willingly.

"Fine, Sir," she declared. "But where will I find such things?"

"In the linen room. Come with me!"

A few seconds later, having donned the small, white regulatory cap and the apron, the mysterious woman, still dizzy from her adventure, was walking beside the supervisor, along a lengthy corridor.

The supervisor gave her his recommendations with a protective air.

"Your role will be very easy and if you perform your duties suitably, I will keep you for the luxury cabins for all other crossings. I warn you though, that the work is hard. The clients are demanding but they pay well. For example, you have to wait for the clients, sometimes late into the night. Some continue to dance until three and four o'clock in the morning."

"I'll do my best!" replied the young woman.

The pair had arrived on the upper deck, close to Apartment No. 1.

"This apartment," said the man to the young woman, whom he took to be a chambermaid. "This room is part of your area. But you won't have to anything during this crossing because the client is not there."

"I'll tell you what happened. Listen well and hold your tongue. There's no need to gossip about this matter..."

The supervisor told her that an unknown individual had reserved this apartment, paid 30,000 francs in advance, but that he had never settled in. He had had crates carried on board but, the situation was most curious, most extraordinary and most surprising, since two hours earlier noises had been heard in that apartment. They had entered and they had found two men, armed with revolvers, who had immediately tried to hide when the staff entered.

The staff had rushed at them, arrested them, and questioned them, although the two individuals staunchly refused to provide any explanation.

As the supervisor spoke, the young woman opened her eyes wide, seeming to take a great deal of interest in his tale.

"What did the men look like?"

"Oh, they didn't look wicked!" replied the supervisor, who most certainly misunderstood the reason for the question.

"One of them was 40 or 45 years old. The other was a young blond man with a small elegant mustache. Distinguished. But, you know, you can't trust appearances. Nowadays, bandits often look like people from the upper class!"

"And what did they do with these men?" the young woman asked.

The supervisor, who definitely found the so-called chambermaid quite charming, smiled at her in a friendly manner.

"Well, you're afraid…" he said. "But there's no danger! We put them in a small unoccupied room."

He pointed at a door.

"That one, over there, Cabin No. 14. They've been locked up there for an hour. The Captain will come down to question them, along with the purser. For the time being, we'll just leave them alone. It's none of our business!"

And the supervisor proceeded to give some more instructions to the woman he considered a chambermaid.

"All you have to do is wait in the linen room until someone rings for you. There's a panel of lights that indicate the cabin to which you are expected to go. This evening, you will be on duty until two in the morning. After that you will go to bed. Do you know where your dormitory is?"

"Of course!" said the young woman, who had no idea where the chambermaids slept, but she couldn't give the impression that she knew nothing at all, to avoid rousing suspicions.

When the young woman was alone in the linen room, she collapsed on a stool and held her head in her hands.

"Good grief! Good grief!" she stammered. "What will I do? What will become of me? It's terrible. How can I prevent frightening tragedies from happening here? How can I reach them, since I'm sure it is them, I'm sure they're the ones that have just been caught and they didn't want to identify themselves, because they certainly suspect something."

The young woman had reached that point in her thinking when a bell rang.

Apartment No. 42 was calling her. She hurried off and met an American couple, a pretty young woman accompanied by her husband, a respectable looking man wearing an elegant suit.

The American woman gave her instructions for the following morning in a nonchalant and scornful manner. She wanted to be wakened at nine o'clock, she would take a bath scented with Cologne water; her husband wanted a whiskey soda and sliced ham when he woke.

Once the orders were given, the young woman withdrew.

But, as she stepped into the corridor she stopped, dumbfounded. Two valets in livery and a chambermaid had just walked past her.

The sight of these servants stirred a deep emotion within her. She stopped to let them walk past, then dragged her heels as she walked back to the linen room, where she fell onto the stool.

"Good grief! Good grief!" It's terrible!" she murmured. "I know those people. They're bandits, thieves... They belong to Fantômas' band!"

"Fantômas! Fantômas!" she murmured again. "That's it! So, he is on this ship. I realized that when I saw him and his accomplices take control of the machines. Then I found members of his gang among the second-class staff as I was walking through just now. And, people dedicated to him are mingling with the luxury cabin servants! But how can I warn them, how can I warn the others who, are no doubt hunting him? Oh! I absolutely must intervene and let them know. Cabin No. 14," she murmured again. "That's where they are!"

At the end of the fancy ball, the corridor for the luxury cabins was filled with people. A large number of people were returning to their cabins, coming and going, joyous conversations rang out. Then after half an hour, silence fell again and all that could be heard was the purring of the engines as they continued their monotonous song without interruption.

The electric lights in the corridor had been turned off, replaced by the pale, wan light of the lanterns. The young woman walked along the cabins, holding the handrail, until she reached Cabin No. 14. She tried to open the door from outside, but could not. Then, with a trembling finger, she knocked discreetly at the panels and listened closely.

Inside the cabin were the two men who had been arrested in Apartment No. 1: Juve and Fandor.

Two hours earlier, they had found themselves face to face, completely dumbfounded by their unexpected encounter. The policeman and the journalist provided their explanations quickly.

"What are you doing here?" Juve asked, frowning.

Bursting into laughter, Fandor replied, "Come on, Juve. Could I let you go off all on your own while I stayed peacefully in Paris or Fontainebleau? I understood full well that you were heading off to track down Fantômas once and for all. I arranged to get on board this ship. A brave carpenter made me a crate in which I hid myself..."

Juve smiled.

"Well done!" he said. "We both had the same idea... Just like me, you supposed that Fantômas was the mysterious stranger who had reserved the apartment in which we find ourselves."

Fandor replied with a laugh, "You're a genius Juve for figuring that out. But I'm also a genius since I had the very same idea. And now here we are together. We'll just have to track down the one who is missing."

"Good grief!" Juve said. "Fantômas is certainly on board! He had his treasure brought on board the *Gigantic*. He never travels without it."

But, at that moment, the policeman stopped talking. Transatlantic Company employees burst into the apartment and rushed over to the policeman and the journalist.

"What are you doing here?" they asked.

Juve was about to reply, to identify himself, to identify his colleague, when his face suddenly turned pale.

In the group of five or six servants and crew members who had just hurried into the room, he recognized two individuals that he knew had worked with Fantômas for a long time. He motioned to Fandor to remain silent.

From that moment on, the supervisor, who was actually a company employee, questioned the two mysterious passengers as forcefully as he might, but he obtained no responses.

"Well!" he declared. "I will take you both, arrest you and you will explain things to the Captain!"

And the supervisor told his subordinates, "Lock these two men up in Cabin No. 14!"

And Juve and Fandor had been in that cabin for two hours now.

Juve had explained to Fandor why he had required him to remain silent. He did not want word to get out about their presence. When the captain arrived, they would explain things to him.

"This matter is serious," said Juve. "I imagine that, if Fantômas has managed to sneak some of his accomplices into the *Gigantic's* personnel, he must be planning something quite formidable. He must not suspect that we're here. Let's try to keep that fact from him until the last moment!"

Juve continued, "It's all the same Fandor. There was no point in you coming here! And when I think of poor Hélène, whom you left behind... That moves me... Does she even know that you've left?"

And Fandor gravely replied, "I told Hélène that I had a duty not to abandon you... She agreed. She's waiting for me in Paris."

At the moment, someone knocked discreetly at the cabin door. Juve and Fandor looked at one another.

"Come in!" they said.

But the door was locked from the outside and, while Juve and Fandor could not open it from the inside, it was obvious that the person on the other side of the door could not let them out either.

Suddenly, Juve and Fandor shivered. They heard a voice calling from the other side of the door, "Juve! Fandor! Are you there?"

Fandor leapt.

"Hélène! It's Hélène," he cried out.

The sound of his voice crossed through the panel and he heard the answer. "Yes, it's me!"

"My God!" said Juve. "How did you get here?"

Hélène's voice replied, "How could I abandon Fandor who, in turn, was unable to abandon you?"

"Oh, what a brave little girl," shouted the policeman as the journalist's eyes filled with tears.

And both men checked their emotions.

Then, in a feverish voice, the young woman said, "Juve, Fandor, things are serious. Fantômas is on board. I saw him. Fantômas has brought a formidable band of accomplices with him. They are terrible people, capable of anything. With my very own eyes, I saw them assassinate seven unfortunate firemen. I imagine that Fantômas is in charge of the boiler room now. He has accomplices among the ship's servants. I recognized a few..."

"Good grief!" shouted Juve. "We know that!"

Hélène replied, "We have to get you out of there right now!"

"Damnation!" grumbled Fandor. "To think that we're locked up in this cabin and Hélène is alone, defenseless, on the other side of the door. If Fantômas were to walk by, he could kidnap her, kill her, and we would be unable to stop him."

"Shut up! Shut up!" scolded Juve, who had suddenly had an idea.

"Give me your knife," he said.

Fandor obeyed. Juve opened it quickly, with uncommon vigor, and he tried to break the lock, applying pressure to the door jamb.

"Daring Juve" shouted Hélène, who had quickly realized what the policeman was trying to do.

Juve grew worried and said, "As long as I don't make too much noise!"

But the young girl encouraged him, saying, "No, no, they can't hear anything and there's no one in the corridor... Be quick, Juve. I absolutely must join you, we must see one another, speak to one another, join forces and sound the warning as quickly as possible..."

"Yes, that's it!" the policeman suddenly shouted.

At that moment, the door gave way. Hélène fell into Fandor's arms while Juve warmly clasped the young woman's trembling hands.

"Finally!" they all shouted. "We're back together!"

Then they looked at one another, with worried expressions on their faces.

Juve said, "We must not waste any time... Time is of the essence!"

CHAPTER XXIV

It was the next day, about ten o'clock in the evening. Lieutenant Blancart, the captain of the *Gigantic*, was leaving his cabin to go to the bridge.

He wanted to be at the helm of the ship himself that evening. Before leaving his apartment, he made a recommendation to Mr. Chatier, the first officer, frowning, "Above all, don't say a word about this matter... Don't mention it to anyone and tell the men who were involved to keep silent."

Mr. Chatier saluted the captain, saying, "You can count on me, Captain!"

Captain Blancart continued, "That should not prevent you from continuing your searches. You have a police department on board. See to it that, as of tomorrow, we have our hands on those two guys."

The police chief, "I'll do my best, captain."

Then the two men went their separate ways. Captain Blancart climbed up to the bridge on his way to replace his second officer who had been directing the operations of the *Gigantic* since six o'clock that evening.

No one had noticed that, during the day which was drawing to an end, a certain emotion, a great concern, had swept over the senior personnel on board. That morning, the captain had been informed that two suspicious men had been discovered in the famous Apartment No. 1, which was still empty, and that when they had been arrested by the crew members and a supervisor, they had not wanted to provide any explanation concerning their presence in the parlor of that apartment and that, as a result, they had been locked up in another cabin.

Yet, when the first officer had arrived, along with his secretary, to question these individuals, they found the cabin empty and the door skillfully broken.

The prisoners had escaped and the personnel had spent the entire day searching for them throughout the ship.

Yet, their searches had been in vain and when evening fell Mr. Chatier, the first officer, had gone to inform the captain about their lack of success.

During the afternoon, Lieutenant Blancart had been busy handling many matters. The section managers, the non-commissioned officers, and even a few lieutenants had presented most singular reports to him. There was less discipline than usual among the firemen and the engineers. The butlers had come to complain that their waiters were incapable of obeying. A few passengers had also complained that money was missing from their cabins, that jewelry had disappeared...

Efforts had been made to calm everyone and arrangements had been made to ensure the silence of the complainants, but the captain, who knew about everything that had been happening, was very emotional, very troubled, since he realized that unfortunate and abnormal things were going on. He presumed that an organized gang of wrong-doers was on board.

Nevertheless, the officer was far from imagining the truth and suspecting that a large number of crimes had already been committed, that the unfortunate firemen had been burned in the boilers and that sinister bandits were using threats and terror to make certain honest people, people who had managed to preserve their lives and remain at their workstations, obey.

Among the servants, the situation was the same. The usual company servants had been joined by numerous newcomers who appeared suddenly during the course of the crossing, as if they had popped up from the mysterious depths of the large floating city.

Yet, anyone who wanted to make an exact account of all this would have had to have nothing else to do and the captain of the transatlantic ship was much too busy with the technical operations of the ship to be able to pay the appropriate amount of attention to the events that were reported to him!

He had been particularly struck by the strange adventure the officer had just reported to him.

Undoubtedly, Apartment No. 1, the luxury apartment that cost 30,000 francs, was destined to provoke the most unusual comments and the unknown passenger that had reserved it and paid for it in advance seemed most mysterious!

Who were the men who had been arrested and then later escaped?

Where could they be found?

Obviously, they were hiding.

After recommending that his first officer remain silent about these incidents, the captain grew hopeful again, telling himself that if they did not find the suspicious men during the crossing, they would certainly be arrested when the ship arrived in New York.

The captain was a professional seaman who loved the sea for itself and, although he performed his bureaucratic duties out of necessity, he was most happy when it came time for him to climb up to the bridge and take charge of his beautiful ship.

He was most familiar with the Atlantic Ocean and it held no secrets for him. He had guided the most beautiful ships of the company, which he had served for fifteen years, and he was overjoyed to be in charge of the he *Gigantic*, which was to be the crowning moment of his career.

Lieutenant Blancart had climbed up to the bridge and, wrapped in his large great-coat, with the hood pulled down over his eyes, since it was very cold, he observed the horizon. The night was dark, but the distant rays of the moon occasionally pierced through the clouds, casting their pale light on the waves.

With the eyes of a seaman, Blancart observed the ocean.

He examined the electric equipment in front of him, which allowed him to transmit orders to guide the ship as he saw fit, simply by pushing a few buttons.

He observed a speedometer and was surprised at the speed at which they were traveling.

"Oh!" murmured the officer, "It seems that the machines are being pushed considerably! The two hours we lost at our departure were made up a long time ago. There is no point in pushing like this.'

He was about to transmit an order to slow, but before he did so, he examined the horizon carefully.

White lines appeared, then disappeared in the distance. The officer wondered if they were simply intermittent reflections of the rays of the moon on the surface of the water, which was excessively calm. Then, suddenly, he shuddered.

"No," he said. "It's not the moon that is turning the ocean silver, it's ice."

And he immediately used the telephone to transmit the order to slow the engines.

Blancart was familiar with the region and knew that, at this time of the year, it was highly likely that they would encounter icebergs floating down from the Arctic Ocean to get lost in the Atlantic.

Like all sailors who have crossed the Atlantic, he dreaded encountering these large, threatening mountains of ice that loomed over the waves and hid their treacherous size under the water.

It was impossible for a ship to make its way through these veritable fields of floating ice and so he decided to give the order to slow. A few moments passed.

The captain looked at the speedometer and cried out in surprise, "But they're not slowing! Did they not understand my order?"

He gave the order again, more forcefully this time.

Then he waited.

The captain's bridge was rigorously closed on all sides. The officer was standing in a glass compartment from which he could see all around him, while remaining protected from the weather. Since he liked the fresh air a great deal and enjoyed feeling the sea breeze on his face, he had opened one of the panels and when the wind struck his face he realized that the temperature had been dropping for some time.

"There's no doubt about it," he thought. "We're approaching the region of floating ice fields!"

Suddenly, as he looked at the speedometer yet again, he swore.

"In the name of God, this is extraordinary. What a lack of discipline. I'll have to give the order a third time if I'm to be obeyed!"

Furious, he picked up the telephone and screamed, "I've already ordered you to turn down the fires, to cut our speed by one-third!"

Suddenly, the captain turned around.

Someone had just touched him on the shoulder, someone who had entered the compartment, without Blancart noticing. He could not make out the newcomer's features. While everything else on the ship was brightly lit, in order for the captain to be able to see at night, his bridge was plunged into the deepest darkness. The devices he had to consult were lit by small lamps that only shone on the dials.

The newcomer addressed Captain Blancart.

"There's no point," the main said gently, "There's no point for you to worry about giving orders. The people manning the engines will not obey you!'

"Really," said Blancart. "I'd like to know why."

"Because," continued the mysterious stranger, "Because I'm the one in charge now and they obey me!"

The captain felt anger wash over him.

"Who are you?" he shouted. "What are you doing here? Who gave you the right to come up here? You know that this place is off limits to the public!"

"Not to me," the man interrupted. "I'm the Master!"

"This man is crazy," thought Blancart, who was about to press on the alarm button to call for help. But his movement was noticed and the mysterious stranger shrugged.

"No point sounding the alarm," he said. "The device no longer works."

Blancart pressed on the button anyway.

Then, furious, he shouted at the man standing in front of him, "Too bad whether help comes or not. I'm warning you that if you don't get out of here in two seconds, I'll throw you overboard!"

The captain's anger did not move the man standing there.

"Just two words, Captain," he said. "Are you prepared to listen to me?"

Blancart hesitated visibly, wanting to get rid of this visitor.

He could not make out the other man's features in the dark, but he did see his silhouette, the silhouette of a powerful man, robustly built, a large black cape swirling about him. Like him, like Blancart, the man's hood was pulled down over his face.

Moreover, the officer realized that, far from slowing, the transatlantic ship was going faster and faster. It seemed that, since he had given the order to slow the engines had accelerated. The speedometer indicated a knot more than previously.

"They're crazy," grumbled Blancart,

For the fourth time, he was about to call, but the other man stopped him.

"You promised to give me your attention for two seconds. I will no longer allow you to keep me waiting. Captain, if you value your life, obey me without discussion. Behind me, I have six dedicated men who will take you and will drag you down into the holds. I want to take charge of the ship."

"And I want to get rid of you," grumbled the captain.

Mad with rage, he rushed at the mysterious stranger, who stopped him short, pointing a gun at his chest.

"Stop there!' he ordered. "One last time, do you refuse to obey me and accompany my men?"

"Yes, I refuse," said the captain, making an effort to hide and avoid the threat of the revolver.

But the barrel of the weapon followed him, implacably.

"Too bad!" shouted Blancart, "I'll kill him or he will kill me, but this has to come to an end!"

And he was about to reach his hand into his pocket and bring out his own revolver. But his movement had been anticipated.

"Don't make a move," shouted the man. "Don't move or I'll shoot you down immediately!"

Then he insisted, "One last time, Captain, surrender! You have no idea who you are dealing with."

"Who I'm dealing with..." stammered the officer, confused.

But he stopped short again, interrupted by the man who said, "You're dealing with Fantômas! Fantômas! The uncatchable Criminal Mastermind! You are dealing with the undisputed master, the man who gives orders when he wants and who desires to be the leader. Nothing will be able to resist me today, just as nothing has been able to resist me in the past. The future is mine. I go where I want and I crush all those who get in my way!"

"Fantômas," stammered the captain.

The name of the sinister bandit, the name of horror and crime was not unknown to the captain. Far from it. Despite his courage, Captain Blancart shivered from head to toe at the thought that he was facing the most formidable bandit the planet had ever known.

"What do you want?" he said.

"For you to surrender to me," said Fantômas.

"Never!"

"Then," said the bandit. "This discussion has gone on too long!"

He pointed his gun at the captain yet again. Shivering, the captain searched through his pocket. He had to defend himself at any cost. He would shoot. But although his gesture had been quick, Fantômas had been even quicker.

"Die!" shouted the sinister Criminal Genius.

A shot rang out. The captain fell, struck by a bullet. Fantômas rushed over to the telephone.

"Victory!" he shouted into the device. "I'm in charge! And now, push the engines my friends. Full speed ahead!"

He had barely uttered this order when a slight tremor occurred, accompanied by a dull noise... It seemed that the ship, the entire formidable structure, had just been shaken, that its hull had shuddered.

"What is that?" asked Fantômas, surprised for a moment.

It seemed to him that the ship was moving off its course. The needle on the compass had just jumped, and the progress of the transatlantic ship had slowed somewhat. Yet, nothing abnormal seemed to happen and Fantômas, picked the telephone back up and repeated: "Stoke the fires! Full speed ahead!"

Someone groaned behind him. Fantômas turned his head and saw the captain, who was dying. His face had grown deathly pale and black blood was flowing from his chest, but his lips smiled ferociously. He laughed as he looked at Fantômas.

"Wretch! Wretch!" he stammered.

The vision of the dying man troubled the bandit. Had he perhaps pushed his audacity too far? Ever since he had taken over the controls of the formidable transatlantic ship, he had been wondering if he really were capable of operating it properly.

But that moment of doubt did not last.

Looking at the dying man, Fantômas declared, "You didn't want to obey my orders and you are dying... Your death will serve as an example for those around you. Because that's how I treat everyone. I am the Master, I do what I want and anyone who gets in my way, who tries to stop me, will be crushed!"

"Anyone..." repeated the dying officer. "Not always! There may be exceptions, Fantômas.... And you may meet your master!"

Fantômas sniggered.

Despite everything, this man, who was so indifferent to the agony of his victims, seemed to be upset by the dying officer's words.

He bent down over the other man, wanting to know what he was thinking and, since the captain did not utter another word, Fantômas shrieked in triumph, "No one can thwart me, this ship is mine, I will take it where I please... It is the most powerful, the fastest ship in the world. I am made for it just as it is made for me, we will encounter no obstacles!"

A hoarse whistle escaped from the captain's injured chest.

"Yes, you will," he said.

"What are you saying?" asked Fantômas, who grew pale despite himself.

'There is an obstacle that will stop both you and the ship!"

The bandit had to bend low, place his ear close to the dying man's lips, in order to hear him. His words already seemed to come from beyond the grave and impressed the Criminal Mastermind most singularly.

"An obstacle? What obstacle?" asked Fantômas.

The captain had grown paler and paler. His lips were turning blue, his eyes were glassy, and blood continued to flow from his chest. He tried to get up, but could not. He tried to speak but the words died on his lips. Finally, making a supreme efforts, as Fantômas waited for his final words, he clearly said, "You will encounter an obstacle and it will be stronger than you... That obstacle is already present. It's the ice!"

The crowd of dancers, in the first-class lounge, rushed at the gypsy orchestra.

"No, no, no more waltzes!" they shouted. "A tango! We want a tango!"

The first violin, a very dark man with a bushy mustache, eyes shining like flames, gallantly bowed to the graceful American woman with her low-cut bodice, and provocative bosom, who had come to him to request a fashionable dance.

The gypsy sighed.

"The Duchess' desire will be fulfilled. My orchestra can play marvelous tangos. But does Madam know someone who is worthy of dancing with her?"

The young American woman, who wore a superb diamond egret in her hair, smiled at the musician.

"Baldini," she said (she knew his name since she had heard him perform all winter in the Parisian salons). "Baldini, you are exaggerating my abilities! I'm not such a good tango dancer as people say!"

Baldini insisted, "Excuse me, Madam Duchess, but in all of Parisian society, I know no one..."

He stopped talking. He had just stumbled and the same jolt had almost thrown the pretty American woman into his arms.

They looked at one another. The incandescent soul of the gypsy was most upset.

The dancers were surprised.

"What's happening?" they asked.

They stopped chatting, a few men left the room and climbed up to the bridge, taking the wide, main staircase.

The dancers included the American woman's husband, the Duc of Vielmar, a young, penniless snob who had married the daughter of a large American industrialist to whom he had given his title in exchange for money.

When he reached the upper deck, the Duc of Vielmar met Charles, the restaurant's maître d'.

"Well, man, what's happening?"

The maître d' was running.

He replied, "Duke, one of my men has certainly dropped an entire stack of dinner plates from China, that we had taken out for the dinner this evening. I've just heard an incredible racket and I'm running over to see..."

"Charles," interrupted the Duke. "Did you feel something, a jolt?"

"Ah!" said the restaurant employee. "Did the Duke hear it as well?"

The two men looked over the railing at the calm sea.

"Well," they said. "It must be some swell or perhaps a wreck that has hit the ship!"

The mild emotion that seemed to have been caused by the incomprehensible jolt quickly faded.

The *Gigantic* continued on its way, steering through the dark of night. the delightful strains of a tango rose from the ball room. The gypsies had returned to their violins and Charles, who listened carefully, heard no sound of dishes breaking.

The duke went back down to the ballroom as two English officers, who were smoking small clay pipes, were talking on the step of the upper deck, returning to their conversation which had been momentarily interrupted.

"My dear Wilding," said one of them, pointing at the horizon. "I've seen the ocean like this before. But it was not during a campaign in South America, it was as we were approaching a polar ice field…"

A seamstress, a French woman, Mme Ménart, was walking along one of the second-class corridors with three young girls, whom she had brought with her from Paris, two models and a designer she was taking to her branch in New York. The four women were returning to their apartments after attending the amateur show that had been performed in the passengers' lounge.

"Ah!" said Miss Germain, one of the two models. "That singer we heard just now was certainly most handsome! "Being a performer is such nice work… and there is so much entertainment on this ship!

Mme Ménart nodded her head, saying, "My dear child. I have a sister who was a performer and she died in poverty… And as for the entertainment on this ship, I don't know, but I must admit, that I've been frightened…. Everything creaks all the time, we hear mysterious sounds…"

Then she added, "You didn't feel the jolt just a while ago?"

"Yes," replied Miss Germaine. "And I suppose it's not important at all!"

They stepped to the side of the corridor, to let a herd of sailors in uniform run past very quickly.

"Good grief! Where are those men going?" asked Mme Ménart.

And, since she did not feel reassured, the seamstress spoke to the quartermaster who was accompanying the sailors, saying, "Everything is fine, isn't it?"

To her great surprise, the officer replied, "Oh, I think it's nothing, but we have to keep an eye on things."

The seamstress turned to the young girls and said, "Did you hear that? What does that mean?"

Miss Germain turned very pale.

"That seaman doesn't look worried!"

The four women were still standing in the corridor when, suddenly, they saw some people they had never seen before appear from a staircase. They were covered with coal dust, soot and grease.

"Good grief!" said the brave woman. "Who are those devils?"

The devils did not respond to the unflattering remark, but one of them, as he was passing close to Miss Germain, whispered in a low voice as he looked at her, "Be careful, miss. Don't go to bed right away… There's water in the holds. Chest high. Things are not fine!"

"What's that?"

"Things are not fine… It might be a small matter, but be careful anyway."

Those were the words that were first murmured in a low voice and then shouted out loud. Most certainly emotion was washing over the ship. The senior officers, the personnel supervisors, tried as they might to reassure people, to put on friendly smiles, but people quickly realized that they were making an effort and their expressions reveal serious concern.

Something was definitely going on, but what?

From inside the ship, three people appeared: Juve, Fandor and Hélène. Since the morning, they had been hidden. In disguise, they had been coming and going everywhere they could go unnoticed, studying the employees. They had come to the conclusion that Fantômas had installed a considerable crowd of his accomplices on board. They had encountered these people among the crew, among the sailors, with the emigrants, people from the bandit's most diverse gangs. They seemed to be waiting for a signal to rush at the honest people and make it impossible for them to defend themselves.

Juve, Fandor and Hélène understood the Criminal Genius' plan.

There was no doubt about it. He had sworn he would grab the *Gigantic*, planning to turn it into an impregnable fortress!

Juve and Fandor knew about the first murders committed by Fantômas and they feared there would be more.

They had kept themselves hidden all day because they initially wanted to understand exactly what was going on and then because they wanted to discover Fantômas. They had searched in vain. The terrible bandit remained invisible.

Finally, as evening fell, and once they knew exactly how many men Fantômas had, Juve, Fandor and Hélène had decided to go and find the captain, to introduce themselves and to tell him everything.

They stepped out of the third door and stopped along the railing, surprised by the activity on board and still not recovered from the emotion of tragic foreboding they had experienced when, ten minutes earlier, they had felt the mysterious jolt.

"What's happening?" they asked.

As Juve walked ahead, the seamstress, Mme Ménart, approached him.

"Excuse me, sir," she said. "Do you know why the firemen have come up from the holds? One told me that there was water chest high in the holds. Is that true?"

"Good grief!" exclaimed Miss Germaine. "We're sinking!"

She cried out in fear. People were starting to notice that the ship was tilting slightly to the left. Yet it was still steaming ahead.

Juve shook his head.

"It's nothing! He said. Perhaps a gust of wind has caused us to tilt… Don't worry ladies!"

He left the women quickly, dragging Fandor and Hélène along with him. He clasped the young woman's hand and leaned close to the journalist.

"Something serious is going on," he murmured in the other man's ear. "Look down there!"

Without the slightest amount of difficulty, Juve, Fandor and Hélène reached the main, first-class deck. They ran into all kinds of people. In particular, they were jostled by the two Englishmen who, a few moments earlier, had been strolling on the deck. And one of the men shouted in a voice that was both fearful and ridiculous at the same time, speaking in heavily accented French, saying "We're lost! The tennis court is under water!"

Juve shuddered when he heard those words.

He reached a sort of balcony that looked over the prow of the ship and pointed the starboard side out to Fandor.

"What?" said the journalist.

"Well, look," said Juve. "Look... everything is plunged into darkness!"

He also had the impression that the engines were pulsing weakly, in a jerky manner. Then there was a tidal wave of humanity, surging ahead in a crazy race...

Officers, seamen appeared from everywhere.

"Attention! Be careful!" they shouted.

A second lieutenant intervened. He stood at the top of a staircase. Pale and furious, or so it seemed, when he saw the sailors, the firemen and the engineers appear like that, from inside the ship.

"What's up with you?" he scolded. "Everyone go back to their stations! I'll blow the brains out of the first man who does not obey!"

Despite his threat, no one obeyed. Of course, he had stopped the crowd of fleeing men, but a junior officer approached him and said out loud, "Lieutenant, there has been an accident, a serious accident, we hit something, an iceberg no doubt. The outer hull has been pierced and water is flowing in..."

The lieutenant chewed on his lip.

"Shut up!" he grumbled. "There's no point in panicking the passengers!"

But the officer's attempt to keep the approaching danger under cover were in vain. Orders were being given everywhere, transmitted by the other officers, shouting.

"To your cabins!"

"Tell the passengers to come up on deck!"

"Seamen, crew members, return to your stations! No one move!"

"Get to the rear of the ship!"

Then, suddenly, rope barriers were set up. A few passengers wanted to rush to the front of the ship.

"We can't get through, we can't get through..." they said.

And since some of them insisted, panicked, wanting to rush where it as forbidden, the officers shrugged and said, "Go there at your own risk. We're no longer responsible for anything..."

Anguished cries, worried murmurs spread through the enormous floating city. People appeared from everywhere, people wearing evening dress, women in low-cut dresses, men in black suits rubbed shoulders with mechanics in blue uniforms, women dressed poorly who had come up from the depths of third class. It was total chaos...

Juve, Hélène and Fandor had been pushed, by the flow of the crowd, to the entrance of the first-class ballroom where people were still dancing.

The vision of this joyous and elegant ball, of the women with their jewels, of the elegantly dressed men, dancing to the thrilling pace of the gypsy orchestras, stood out in stark contrast to the comings and goings on the deck.

But, suddenly, the charm of the ball was broken, because the ship had tilted so much that all of the dancers had slid to one corner of the room, slipping, tripping over one another.

Baldini the gypsy fell at the feet of the pretty duchess and, unable to hide his emotions, intoxicated by the music, by the atmosphere in the ballroom, he stammered, "You are so beautiful! You are so beautiful. If only you would love me!"

At the bar, two men were drinking enormous whiskey sodas.

Juve, Fandor and Hélène ran past them and the journalist, who had no doubt as to the danger they all faced, burst out laughing. He had just overheard one of the drinkers say to his neighbor, "I must be drunk old man! I thought my drink was standing in front of me and here it is on the floor."

The glass had, in fact, fallen to the floor.

As they made their way back up to the deck, they encountered a furious crowd.

Three men were fighting, three men wearing white aprons tied at their waists, three men with pale faces, with terrified expressions.

"They're bandits, thieves!" people shouted. "They searched the cabins, they're stealing things..."

Juve clenched his teeth nervously, frowning.

"Oh!' he said. "Things are going badly!"

The entire front section of the ship was now plunged into darkness and looked as if it were standing on end, slipping into the ocean. People had also realized that the ship was stopped.

A short distance from Juve, there was a sort of small cabin, on which the letters WT were written. It was the wireless telegraph office. The rattle of the telegraph equipment could be heard.

Someone rushed into that office. There was only one employee on duty. The man who had just entered was wrapped in a large black greatcoat and his face was hidden by a hood.

The telegraph operator saw him and thought he was Captain Blancart.

The man questioned the telegraph operator in a deep voice, "What messages have you sent out so far?"

"Captain," said the man. "I'm trying to contact the ships that may be located nearby. I've warned them that we are in distress, that the *Gigantic* had run into an ice field, that there is a hole in the hull that cannot be repaired... I've told them that we may be able to last an hour. I hope they can reach us by then!"

He stopped talking, then continued in a more joyful tone, saying "Captain, listen... Look at this! Someone has answered... I knew it. It's the *Maurania*, on its way to Liverpool. They must be nearby, they've heard our calls..."

The telegraph operator continued to translate the rattles of his device.

"They've answered that they're rushing toward us, that they are still 70 miles from us. We'll have to wait for them to get here..."

The other man had not turned a hair. He listened attentively to the telegraph operator. Then the man the operator presumed was the captain, ordered, "We don't need anyone. Tell the *Maurania* to continue on its way without worrying about us!"

"But, Captain," shouted the employee, dumbfounded.

"Do as I say!" specified the man.

The telegraph operator turned pale.

He looked at the other man and saw his face.

"But, who are you? You're not Captain Blancart..."

"That's possible," replied the man. "But I am the Master, I'm Fantômas. Obey my order!"

"Fantômas!" shrieked the employee. "Help! Help!"

He was unable to continue. With a blow of his dagger, Fantômas stabbed the man in the chest and raced off.

The telegraph operator stood up. The weapon was stuck in his throat. He felt terribly, fatally wounded. His first instinctive movement was to pull the knife out of the wound.

It was causing him intolerable pain, yet the man stiffened.

"If I pull out the dagger," he said. "If I pull out the dagger, my blood will pour out and I will die immediately... I cannot... I have to have time to warn people, to send out a telegram..."

The man dragged himself along the floor, pale, bleeding. He managed to pull himself up onto his chair, while his strength and blood flowed out of him, out of his wound, out of his lips, out of his nostrils, as his fingers were splashed with blood and a fog formed in front of his eyes, the fog of death... He made a supreme effort to communicate with the *Maurania*.

"Hurry! Hurry! We are lost!" he transmitted, as life seeped from his body.

He was almost a cadaver yet he called for help for the passengers of the *Gigantic*.

Just as the telegraph operator was dying, an uproar broke out on the deck.

An order had been shouted, sowing panic.

Someone had shouted: "Lower the lifeboats!"

CHAPTER XXV
Brothers!

As he was returning from an official banquet, the Minister of the Interior was stopped at the door to his personal apartment by his private secretary.

"Mr. Minister! Sir," said the young man. "A frightful tragedy is playing out. Here are the telegrams…"

Mr. Paul Garet, Minister of the Interior walked into his office, reading the document his assistant had given him.

Gigantic. *Telegram. At 10:42 the transatlantic ship, the* Gigantic, *heading for New York, struck a submerged ice berg in the ice field and its starboard hull was pierced. Impossible to staunch the incoming flow of water. The ship is in a nose dive and seems compromised. Rescue operations are being organized. The steamer, the* Maurania *has been contacted and the two ships are in communication.*

"Good grief!" shouted the Minister of the Interior. "That's dreadful! Is there any other news?"

The private secretary handed another telegram to the Minister.

The calls to the Maurania *have been heard but that ship is approximately 80 miles away. Will the* Gigantic *survive until it arrives? Calm sea, foggy, panic on board, courageously put down by the officers… Danger of sinking is increasing, the ship is tilting, the engines have been shut down.*

Paul Garet grew very pale.

"These telegrams are terrible! The *Gigantic* was the company's most superb ship! There are more than 4,000 people on board! Can we save it?"

"Unfortunately…" said the private secretary.

Sounds could be heard in the corridor; the Minister's secretary ran out to see what was happening and encountered a clerk bringing a new telegram.

"Hand it over!" said the minister.

And this time, as he read, he turned completely white and had to sit down. He was terribly frightened.

The employee who sent this telegram has just been mortally wounded by a bandit who says that he is called Fantômas and wants to prevent the Maurania *from coming to the rescue, I am sending the telegram anyway, but…*

The telegram stopped there. The two men looked at one another.

"What does this mean? Do you understand this?" asked the Minister.

"Good grief!" stammered his private secretary. "I don't know what to think!"

The two men looked at one another for a few seconds.

Paul Garet said, "But we have to take action, we have to do something... We have to intervene, to respond to those unfortunate people..."

Then he stopped, realizing just how powerless he was, realizing that there was nothing to be done but wait, hopelessly.

The minister paced back and forth in his office like a deranged man.

"This is dreadful! Unheard of! Not only is an abominable drama playing out, which we must watch helplessly, the death of the *Gigantic*, but the horror of this catastrophe is made worse by the presence of Fantômas on board the ship... no, no, no, that can't be... it's too much!"

The telephone rang suddenly.

The Minister rushed over to the device.

"Hello! Hello! Is that you, Havard? Yes, it's me. What? What did you say? An accident? Two accidents? A fort that has exploded near Paris... a bridge that has been blown up in the suburbs... You're coming? Yes, I'll wait for you!"

He hung up the telephone, stumbling like a drunken man.

"What is it, Mr. Minister? Has something happened?" asked the private secretary, grimacing with the maddest anguish.

"The, the..." stammered the minister. "The greatest cataclysms are taking place at this very moment and we don't know what is going on... Oh! My God! This attack... Apparently, Havard has some terrible things to tell me about..."

The Minister consulted his watch feverishly.

"He should have left the Quai des Orfèvres five minutes ago. He won't be long since he's taking his car."

Someone knocked at the office door.

"Another telegram!" shouted the secretary.

The Minister read it.

The telegram had been sent from London. It announced that the docks were on fire, that the fire had been lit by the hand of a criminal, that an entire neighborhood in the city was about to disappear in flames...

The Minister had no words left to comment on the events. Finally, the Head of the Sûreté appeared. He was pale as well, and his clothes were untidy.

"Mr. Minister!" he shouted. "It's the end of everything... I've just learned about new disasters."

"I know," said the Minister. "London, the *Gigantic*..."

"And Brussels!" shouted the head of the Sûreté. "The Gare du Nord has collapsed, two passenger trains have been crushed under the rubble." The telephone rang again. The private secretary picked up, then announced, "It's the Spanish embassy... It seems that three bombs have exploded in the Palais de l'Escurial. His Majesty is safe, but three ministers have been killed!"

Mr. Havard, Mr. Paul Garet and the private secretary looked at one another, dumbfounded.

What was going on? What was the cause of all these disasters, all these catastrophes, transmitted by telegrams with an un settling brutality, with such cynical thoroughness?

Why was all this happening? Yes, why?

Little by little, the Department had been wakened, clerks, torn from their slumber, came and went in the corridors. Noises could be heard in the yard behind Place Beauvau. Automobiles were rushing in. Journalists panicked by the telegrams their newspapers had received were coming to the Minister of the Interior to get information.

"Another telegram!" shouted the Minister's private secretary.

"Read it," said Paul Garet, who had collapsed onto a couch.

The secretary obeyed.

The Gigantic *is sinking and no one will be saved, not even myself, but I want my death to be dedicated to one final act of vengeances! I have sent telegrams to all my accomplices in all of the capitals around the world, telling them to celebrate my death with some cataclysmic event. You will learn about horrors that have occurred in London, Madrid, Brussels and Paris. Farewell!*

"The signature? The signature? What madman or monster could have sent such a telegram?"

In a quavering voice, the private secretary replied, "The telegram is signed.... Fantômas!"

In the middle of the Atlantic Ocean, under calm skies, on still gray waters, a poignant tragedy was playing out. A formidable ship, the *Gigantic*, tilting slightly to the left, was filling bit by bit with water, threatening to sink. Illusions were no longer possible. Everyone knew what was about to happen. The *Gigantic* was about to disappear in the ice field!

Yet, after the initial moment of panic, relative calm returned. People had been frightened when they heard voices cry out, "To the lifeboats!"

Everyone had wanted to rush, but the seamen, directed by the second lieutenant, stopped the crowd of passengers. The officer waved his gun.

"I order everyone to obey me absolutely." He said. "The slightest sign of rebellion will be punished with death."

Then, a troubling silence washed over the crowd, interrupted only a by a few frightened moans. The officer, very pale, gave orders.

"Women first! Only women!"

Then he turned to the seamen and ordered, "One man for each lifeboat to take the oars, then load the women, in order and silence. Twenty-five people for each lifeboat and not one more!"

The scene was both frightening and heartrending. This way and that, shoving and pushing, the women rushed towards the lifeboats, some wearing ballgowns, others half naked, roused from their beds. There were chambermaids, emigrants, great ladies, young girls, old ladies and cries of despair rang out in the crowd. Husbands, brothers, parents hugged one another as their wives, sisters and daughters were torn from them...

Some did not want to leave. The officers insisted once, and once the women made their decision they were pushed back with the herd of men, toward the middle of the ship...

The first lifeboat was lowered into the water and as it moved away from the ship people heard two cries, followed by the dull sound of two bodies falling into the water.

Two passengers, driven half mad by terror, had jumped into the ocean from a height of 80 feet!

However, on the deck, seamen were reassuring the passengers who were stamping their feet impatiently, some screaming, some weeping, some praying.

"Don't be afraid!" said the men. "Nothing is lost!"

They pointed at a luminous reflection in the distance.

"A ship is approaching," they shouted. "And it's not certain that the *Gigantic* will sink!"

And these encouraging words changed the crowd's attitude. They swept from one extreme to the other and now the most desperate ones were those who had allowed their wife, their sister, their mother to set out in the frail, overloaded lifeboats that looked like shadows in the distance, lost in the immense ocean.

All of the starboard lifeboats were in the water. They could be heard rowing away from the ship, accompanied by shouts, heartrending appeals, as they faded into the distance.

Shouts rang out from the top of the ship. The lifeboats had been lowered into the water, with such haste, in such a rush to escape that three of four could be seen moving away, half empty. Then the sinister sound of a body falling into the water was heard. People were pitching themselves into the ocean, hoping to escape the upcoming cataclysms.

As time passed, the darkness grew deeper on the ship. The electric lights were going out as the water rose. At times, sinister, frightful cracking sounds could be heard.

They were caused by the water which, as it flowed in, broke down walls, gaining ground. Water spewed from the hatches as people felt a large gust of cold air flow from the air shafts.

Yet, in the midst of this chaos and fear, the rousing, radiant music of the gypsies could be heard as they played a terrifying, rough tango quickly and madly!

The lights were still shining in the first-class ballroom, where frightful scenes were playing out.

Hugging couples were spinning desperately, drunk at the thought of imminent death, wanting to finish their lives in a swirl of pleasure. Lovers embraced, exchanging their final kisses of love. Baldini, his eyes wild, had broken the strings on his violin with the brutality of his bow. And, throwing his useless instrument away, he rushed over to the duchess, who was half mad with fear, and took her in his arms.

"I love you... I adore you..." he stammered.

At the bar, the two drinkers had filled their glasses to the top with whiskey.

"I assure you," one of them said to the other. "I assure you that all this is a joke... The ship is not moving. We're just drunk to the gills!"

And they continued to drink. One fell to the floor, dead drunk. While the other, overcome by alcoholic fury and dementia, grabbed a bottle by the neck and, using it like a club, started bludgeoning people all around him, hitting the tables, the counter, breaking glasses, shattering mirrors!

The pale barman was crawling on all fours, having filled his pockets with the cash from the bar. He searched the unconscious drunk man, taking his gold watch and his wallet. An officer running through the room noticed him.

"Wretch!" he screamed. "How can you think about stealing at such a time!"

And, since the barman made an insulting gesture in his direction, the office grabbed a chair and broke it over the other man's head.

Suddenly, the lights went out. The only light in the room was the red glow of a fire burning 150 yards from there, at the rear of the ship, as the nose of the vessel sunk deeper and deeper in the heavy, black water...

It was getting more and more difficult to lower the lifeboats on the port side. A few women who had fainted were packed into the lifeboats, one of them, forgotten, had been thrown into a lifeboat like a package. A voice called out in a frightful scream. The unfortunate woman, had broken both legs when falling into the lifeboat!

Juve, Hélène and Fandor had been separated, then reunited. A seaman wanted to the take the young woman away, but she clasped her arms about the journalists' neck, sobbing.

"No, no, I don't want to leave!" she screamed.

But Fandor pulled her arms away and passed her over to the sailors.

"Fandor! Fandor!" Hélène shrieked in desperation. "I don't want to leave... I don't want to leave..."

But no one listened to her and she was thrown into a lifeboat.

The journalist, whose heart was pounding, bent over the railing to make sure that Hélène was safe.

He saw her lying, unconscious, in the lifeboat a few yards below him.

Then, suddenly, Fandor felt himself lifted by an irresistible force, just as a voice murmured in his ear, "You've done your duty young man. You have to protect her. Leave with her and don't regret anything."

It was Juve who uttered those words!

Fandor did not have time to reply. He felt as if he were spinning in the void. Then he hit the bottom of the lifeboat. His head struck the edge, he felt a terrible pain, and lost consciousness next to Hélène.

Juve wiped a tear from his eye and sighed with satisfaction.

He had completed the plan he had been considering for a few moments. He had torn Hélène and Fandor from the grip of a frightful death.

Now, it was over! Juve crossed his arms over his chest, waiting for the fatal moment. But, just as he turned his head away, to avoid watching as the lifeboat carrying Hélène and Fandor moved away, someone placed a hand on his shoulder.

"We have saved them," said the newcomer.

Juve then recalled that someone had helped him throw Fandor into the lifeboat where Hélène was lying. He looked at the man who had spoken to him, then he shuddered and clenched his fists.

"Fantômas!" he exclaimed.

It was, in fact, Fantômas who stood facing Juve. The two men were about to rush at one another. But a sudden shock, a shudder from the dying *Gigantic* threw both men to the deck!

They fell into a stairwell, rolling down the steps. But the two men got back to their feet and stood facing one another at the entrance to a small corridor lit only by the dim light of a small emergency lantern with a reddish, smoky flame.

Juve placed his hand on Fantômas' shoulder.

"Finally!" he said.

He dug through his pocket, looking for his revolver but Fantômas, who was as quick as a thought, grabbed the weapon and took it from Juve.

"There's no point killing me," he said.

But the policeman, surprised by this unexpected attack, threw himself at the bandit, wrapping his hands around the other man's throat.

"Wretch! Scoundrel!" he shrieked.

Fantômas stumbled for a minute, then stiffened and pulled himself free of Juve's grasp.

"Mercy!" he simply said.

And that word was so unexpected and so extraordinary, coming from Fantômas' mouth, that Juve was dumbfounded...

The bandit continued, "Juve, we only have a few minutes left to live. Death is waiting for us. It will wrap us in the same shroud. Killing me would be a pointless and cowardly crime on your part. Besides, I could kill you and I'm not!"

"Fantômas" shouted Juve. "The death we are about to suffer is far too gentle to make up for your misdeeds and crimes."

"No," said the bandit. "Because physical suffering is not unimportant. Moral suffering is worse. Listen, Juve, time is of an essence, we have to talk. I have formidable things to tell you before death interrupts me..."

The policeman felt fury wash over him again.

"I don't care about your confidences!" he shouted. "I want to kill you... I want to kill you, bandit!"

"No," ordered Fantômas. "Listen, Juve."

And he spoke with such a tone of authority and his face bore such an expression of tragic pain, that Juve listened.

But, just then, the two men had to grab onto the railings along the walls in the corridor because the ship was tilting so steeply. They saw a threatening fringe of foam at the end of the hallway, announcing the imminent arrival of the water.

A door stood half open. Instinctively, Fantômas and Juve entered the cabin and—it was so extraordinary—the ship was tiled to such a degree that, instead of walking on the floor, they were only able to keep their balance by setting foot on the wall, which was now horizontal as the ship fell.

Fantômas said, "Juve, you won't kill me once you know who I am, who we are... You would be filled with incredible remorse if you were to kill me and your life is not long enough for you to have time to regret it."

The policeman, fighting back amazement and rage, shook Fantômas by the shoulder.

"Talk then, wretch!" he screamed. "Explain yourself! What do you mean?"

Fantômas finally said, "Twenty times, Juve, I've had you at my mercy, in the barrel of my revolver, twenty times, I've caught you, twenty times I've let you go... Did you ever wonder why I spared you?"

"Because you couldn't kill me," said the policeman. "Because you were afraid..."

"Of course, I could have killed you!" replied Fantômas. "But I was afraid, in fact, of ending your existence, while knowing your hatred for me... Juve, 45 years ago, a noble, saintly woman gave birth to a son, a son who would grow up to be the most famous policeman in the world. That son was you. You know that I'm not lying when I say that the woman's name was Anne-Marie, that she was beautiful, that she was honest..."

The policeman grew troubled.

"Wretch! I forbid you to bring up the memory of my saintly mother... your words are blasphemous!"

"I have the right to speak," said Fantômas. "What you don't realize is that I have the same rights for respect and love as you do when it comes to that woman. Anne-Marie did not just give birth to the famous policeman, Juve. Her womb, wounded by motherhood, gave birth to another child, the policeman's twin brother, who was quickly separated from him by the hazards of life. While Juve grew into an honest man, the other turned bad, becoming a terrible man, a man feared by all, powerful, formidable... Your brother, Juve, your twin brother, is Fantômas! Me!"

Juve stumbled... He held his head in both hands, feeling as if it were about to explode.

"That's not possible! That's not possible!" he shrieked. "Fantômas, the son of the same mother... my twin brother... Fantômas! Fantômas!"

"Yes," insisted the bandit. "We're of the same blood, we have the same forefathers. Life, which separated us, made us adversaries, has now brought us together, face to face, one on one, as death evens everything out... You have done your duty, Juve, by hunting me. I have done my duty by trying to give Hélène, whom I love, the fortune I stole from her parents and which will be returned to her soon..."

"Hélène" Juve shouted, his voice filled with pain. "Who can tell me..."

Fantômas interrupted again, "Did you not read or understand Bedjapur's secrets? Do you not know, Juve, that Hélène is the grand-daughter of the former emperor of India! That if I killed him it was only to prevent him from telling the innocent and pure young girl, the one who will be, the one who is Fandor's wife, about the terrible crimes committed by her father. Hélène will never know...

At the moment, Fantômas suddenly stopped talking. The foamy, dark water was flowing into the room. The policeman and the bandit felt as if they were being surrounded, locked up in an invading, implacable circle of swirling water.

Overhead, they saw a frightful crack, they heard terrible screams, all at the same time as they felt that the floor had moved out from under their feet, driving them into a bottomless pit.

They expected, from one second to the next, to see the tumultuous water rush into the cabin they were locked on. But they also had the impression that the flood was kept outside the small room by some mysterious, inexplicable force.

The air around them was thick and heavy. They did not understand... They both hung onto the walls of the cabin, looking at one another, wondering about this mystery.

Suddenly, Fantômas murmured, "The air, the compressed air is keeping the water from rushing at us..."

"Yes," stammered Juve. "Like a diving bell."

"Our death," continued Fantômas. "Our death will be slower, crueler!"

Juve looked the bandit straight in the eye. Forgetting that he too was dying, as an innocent victim, he shouted, "That's justice!"

Silence fell, the last silence, the most supremely agonizing silence.

The partitions, the walls of the ship cracked in a sinister manner. The men heard the uninterrupted sound of bells, liked the deafening murmur of a waterfall unfurling.

Despite everything, the water rose, the foam, the white foam flowed over to the feet of Juve and Fantômas... Yet the air, which finally found an outlet, flowed from the cabin in a bitter whistle...

"Let's go!" stammered Fantômas. "It's over..."

Looking at Juve one last time in the pale light of the dying lantern, he stammered, in a voice strangled by emotion, "Juve! My brother... forgive me!"

He reached out his hand.

Juve hesitated for a second, then the frightful cataclysm, the dreadful rush arrived. The two men rolled, jostled, rushed by an invincible force, into the darkness, into the shadows...

An abyss had opened under the thrust of the *Gigantic* as it slid into the water. Then the ocean covered the formidable wreck with a blanket of gray, still water, in which a few ice bergs floated, on their way down into the polar oceans, reflecting the silvery rays of the pale moon.

In the distance, a white line emerged from the fog. The sun was rising...

.

Ill. By Mike Shoyket

A CHRONOLOGY OF TERROR
by Jean-Marc Lofficier
(based on research from Etienne Barillier)

1858. Birth of Edward Beltham of Scottwell Hill. The Belthams are connected to the Royal Family.

1866. Birth of William Beltham, Edward's younger brother. *(Speculation based on our edition of Arnould Galopin's* Harry Dickson: The Man in Grey.*)*[12]

1867. Birth of Carl (the future Fantômas) and Paul (the future Juve) in Brittany to Rocambole and Ellen Palmure. Rocambole perished fighting the Germans c. 1870; Ellen's fate is unknown.

1868. Paul is raised by Anne-Marie Juve, the midwife. Carl is taken to the village of Lyndhurst in Sussex to be raised by Ellen Palmure's former henchman, Patterson, now Reverend Patterson.

1874. Patterson entrusts a seven-year-old Carl to the Belthams; the youth progressively falls under Edward's malefic influence.

1882. Birth of Maud Greystoke. The Greystokes are connected to the Royal Family.

1885. Edward, now Lord Beltham, finances Dr. Moreau's research. The *Matilda Briggs*, which belongs to the Belthams, supplies Moreau's island.
An eighteen-year-old Carl travels to India as the Belthams' agent and claims Rocambole's inheritance. (*Fantômas 32: The Death of Fantômas*) While in India, Fantômas exerted an evil influence over Sandyck, the son of Bedjapur, an Indian king, and caused him to betray his father to the British.

1886. Sandyck had a daughter with an otherwise unidentified European woman. That daughter was Hélène. (*In* La Fin de Fantômas, *Souvestre and Allain claimed that Helen was Sandyck's daughter. But maybe she really was Fantômas' biological daughter. Juve claimed to have found documents that incontrovertibly proved that Hélène was not Fantômas' biological daughter, but*

---

[12] ISBN 978-1-61227-484-3.

there could be lies within lies—Juve lying, the documents lying... Certainly, Fantômas always behaved as if Hélène really was his daughter...)

1887. Sandyck was killed by Bedjapur's followers. To protect baby Hélène from their further wrath, she was taken to South Africa where she was raised by Laetitia. Bedjapur eventually moved to Paris.

1888. The affair of Dr. Moreau and the Jack the Ripper murders in London. *November*. Sherlock Holmes secretly solves the Ripper murders. *December*. As a result, Lord Beltham is exiled from England; the scandal is suppressed because of his royal family connection. The *Matilda Briggs* and her crew are allowed to go free.

1889. The island of Dr. Moreau is destroyed by the British Navy on Mycroft's orders. Dr. Moreau escapes and returns to England under the guise of "Dr. Lionel P. McDuff," under which he operates a private asylum in London.

1891. *Spring*. Carl, now calling himself "Archduke Juan North," operates in the German Principality of Heisse-Weimar. (*Fantômas 5: Un Roi Prisonnier de Fantômas/A Royal Prisoner*). *June*. Birth of Alice, daughter of William Beltham, at Scottwell Hill.

1892. *January*. Carl/Juan North has a son, Vladimir, with the aunt of future king Frederick-Christian. (*Fantômas 5: Un Roi Prisonnier de Fantômas/A Royal Prisoner*). *March*. Juan North is arrested and sent to prison. (*Fantômas 5: Un Roi Prisonnier de Fantômas/A Royal Prisoner*). During that time, Juve grew up, joined the French police and embarks upon a career at the Sûreté.

1893. *March-December*. Lord Beltham (now a serial killer) terrorizes Berlin with Juan's help coining the alias of "Fantômas." (*The Fantômas of Berlin*).

1895. *February*. Birth of Charles Rambert (the future Jérôme Fandor) (*Fantômas 27: Le Cadavre Géant*). *March*. Birth of the grand-daughter of the last king of India, Bedjapur; to save her life, his followers take the baby to South Africa. (*Fantômas 32: The Death of Fantômas*).

1896. The future Fantômas, known as the "Pallid Mask," became involved in a murderous conspiracy and power play amongst the Black Coats. (*Rick Lai's "Corridors of Deceit"*)

1897. *January*. Now in New York, Juan North meets, then partners with, businessman Etienne Rambert. *March*. Juan North ruins Rambert and flees to Mexico. (*Fantômas 29: La Série Rouge*).

1898. *February.* Juan North embarks for South Africa and joins the Boers under the name of "Gurn." (*Fantômas 8: The Daughter of Fantômas*). *April.* Gurn partners with Hans Helder to set up a diamond trafficking ring. (*Fantômas 8: The Daughter of Fantômas*). *June.* In Paris, Lord Beltham marries Maud Greystoke, hoping to use her own family connections to be allowed to return to England. *November.* Birth of Hélène, from Gurn and an unknown mother.

1899. *October.* The Boer War starts. Gurn betrays the Boers, joins the British Army, and becomes an artillery sergeant under the command of Lord Roberts; he uses the war to enrich himself. (*Fantômas 8: The Daughter of Fantômas*). *November.* Lord Beltham arrives in South Africa. He and Gurn renew their acquaintance. Gurn meets Maud. (*Fantômas 1*)

1900. *May.* Gurn leaves South Africa to return to England with the Belthams. His affair with Maud begins on the ship taking them back to England. (*Fantômas 1*). *July.* Beltham surprises Gurn and his wife in bed in his apartment in Paris. Gurn strangles him and assumes the mantle of Fantômas. (*Fantômas 1*). *December.* The new Fantômas kills the Marquise de Langrune. (*Fantômas 1*)

1901. *June.* Fantômas robs Princess Sonia Danidoff. (*Fantômas 1*). *August.* Juve arrests Fantômas who is condemned to death. (*Fantômas 1*) (Juve doesn't realize that Fantômas is his brother.)

1902. *January.* Fantômas escapes the guillotine by substituting an actor in his place. (*Fantômas 1*). *February.* Fantômas blows up the Belthams' Parisian residence. He and Maud leave France. (*Fantômas 2: Juve contre Fantômas/The Exploits of Juve*)

1904. *April.* Fantômas, back in France, murders Jacques Dollon in order to steal his identity. (*Fantômas 3: Le Mort qui tue/Messengers of Evil*). *May.* Fantômas becomes involved in espionage. (*Fantômas 4: L'Agent Secret/A Nest of Spies*). *June.* Maud Beltham finds refuge in Heisse-Weimar. Fantômas kidnaps the King of Heisse-Weimar. (*Fantômas 5: Un Roi Prisonnier de Fantômas/A Royal Prisoner*)

1905. *January.* Journalist Jérôme Fandor (Etienne Rambert's son) frees the King of Heisse-Weimar. Mistaken for Fantômas, Juve is arrested. (*Fantômas 5: Un Roi Prisonnier de Fantômas/A Royal Prisoner*). *May.* Fantômas impersonates the American detective Tom Bob. *(Fantômas 6: Le Policier Apache/The Long Arm of Fantômas*). *July.* Juve is freed. Fantômas escapes to England. *(Fantômas 6: Le Policier Apache/The Long Arm of Fantômas*).

1906. *February.* While in London, Fantômas operates under the aliases of Tom Bob, Dr. Garrick and Sâr Hamashkim. He clashes with Sherlock Holmes, assisted by Harry Dickson who is doing some odd jobs for Nick Carter. (*Sherlock Holmes vs. Fantômas*). *June.* The *Matilda Briggs* stops in London. Dr. Moreau/McDuff moves to Portsmouth. Both Holmes and Fantômas become aware that Moreau's murderous man-ape may still be alive.

1907. *April.* Second encounter between Sherlock Holmes and Fantômas. (*The Grand Horizontals*). Fantômas plots to blackmail Lord Ascott. (*Fantômas 7: Le Pendu de Londres*). *June.* The *Matilda Briggs* stops in Portsmouth. Moreau is forced to move to Scotland.

1908. *April.* Fantômas kidnaps Fandor and ships him to South Africa. (*Fantômas 7: Le Pendu de Londres/Slippery as Sin*). *May.* Fantômas is arrested by Scotland Yard. (*Fantômas 7: Le Pendu de Londres/Slippery as Sin*). *June.* Fantômas is condemned to hang but, with Juve's help, fakes his death. (*Fantômas 8: The Daughter of Fantômas*). *July.* Fantômas travels to South Africa. Juve follows. Fandor meets and falls in love with Hélène. (*Fantômas 8: The Daughter of Fantômas*). *December.* Back in Paris, Fantômas renews his affair with Maud. (*Fantômas 9: Le Fiacre de Nuit*). The *Matilda Briggs* stops in Glasgow. Fantômas finds Dr. Moreau, kills him, takes over the asylum under the disguise of "Dr. Smythe," and moves it to Lyndhurst. There he causes William Beltham to hire the Johnson Brothers and renews his acquaintance with Patterson. Finally, he begins courting Alice, William Beltham's daughter.

1909. *January.* Fantômas challenges Irma Vep of the Vampires gang. ("*A Dance of Night and Death*"). *February.* Fantômas loots the casino of Monte-Carlo. (*Fantômas 10: La Main Coupée/The Limb of Satan*). *March.* The *Matilda Briggs* stops in Dover. Fantômas expresses his desire to meet the man-ape's mate next time the *Matilda Briggs* stops in England. *April.* Fantômas is arrested in Belgium. (*Fantômas 11: L'Arrestation de Fantômas*). *November.* Juve helps Fantômas escape from his Belgian prison. (*Fantômas 12: Le Magistrat Cambrioleur*). *December.* Fantômas robs an American millionaire (*Fantômas 13: La Livrée du Crime*)

1910. *January.* Fantômas returns to New York to plan the theft of the SS *Triumph*. While there, he tangles with Nick Carter. (*Nick Carter vs. Fantômas*). *February.* Juve and Fandor thwart the *Triumph* robbery. (*Fantômas 14: La Mort de Juve*). *March.* Fantômas impersonates Juve. (*Fantômas 15: L'Evadée de Saint-Lazare*). *April.* Juve and Fandor dismantle Fantômas' smuggling ring on the Spanish border. (*Fantômas 16: La Disparition de Fandor*). *May.* Back in England, Fantômas decides to use the man-ape to murder William Beltham. *June.* Fantômas releases the man-ape who kills a woman in Lyndhurst. The *Ma-*

tilda Briggs arrives in Southampton. *July.* Events of *The Man in Grey*. Fantômas escapes. Fandor frees Hélène. Fantômas tries to marry a Spanish princess but is almost captured. (*Fantômas 17: Le Mariage de Fantômas*). *August.* Lady Beltham appears to have been killed by a criminal impersonating Fantômas. It turns out to be Dick Valgrand, the son of the actor guillotined in lieu of Fantômas. (*Fantômas 18: L'Assassin de Lady Beltham*). Juve seeks the identity of Lady Beltham's murderer. *September.* Lady Beltham returns from the dead. She killed Dick Valgrand and his lover, Sarah Gordon. Then, horrified by her crime, she commits suicide (September 21). (*Fantômas 19: La Guêpe Rouge*). *Late September.* Fantômas becomes involved in an insurance scam. (*Fantômas 20: Les Souliers du Mort*). *October.* Fantômas' son, Vladimir, competes with his father to steal a fortune from Hesse-Weimar. Fantômas kills Vladimir's wife, Princess Alexandra. Hélène is arrested in Belgium, but escapes. She joins a circus under the alias of Mogador. *November.* Sonia Danidoff has an affair with Fantômas. Fantômas kills Gérard, a man who knew the truth about Hélène's origins. Fantômas makes Hélène swear to never marry Fandor. (*Fantômas 21: Le Train Perdu*).

1911. *February.* The rivalry between Fantômas and Vladimir continues. Vladimir falls in love with Firmaine, then revolts against his father and tries to kill him, but succeeds only in blinding him temporarily. (*Fantômas 22: Les Amours d'un Prince*). *Spring.* Fantômas, using the alias of Jap, rebuilds his criminal network in Paris. *October.* Fantômas and Vladimir renew their battle. Fantômas kills Firmaine. Vladimir threatens Helene's life. Fantômas blows up the Montmartre reservoir. (*Fantômas 23: Le Bouquet Tragique*). Fantômas and Vladimir reconcile. Vladimir is arrested after Juve thwarts a horse racing scam. (*Fantômas 24: Le Jockey Masqué*). *November.* Vladimir is on trial. Fantômas succeeds in arranging his release. (*Fantômas 25: Le Cercueil Vide*). *December.* Fantômas tries to put Hélène on the throne of Holland. Fandor discovers that his father Etienne has not died after all, but Etienne expires just as he is about to tell his son Fantômas' real name. (*Fantômas 26: Le Faiseur de Reines*). *Late December.* Fantômas impersonates Etienne Rambert one last time as Fandor meets his mother again. Fantômas kidnaps Hélène and sends her to Mexico. (*Fantômas 27: Le Cadavre Géant*).

1912. *January-March.* In Mexico, Helen fights Vladimir for the secret of Fantômas' treasure, which is kept in a hidden lair. Fantômas and Juve arrive in Mexico. Juve kills Vladimir just as he was about to kill Helene. (*Fantômas 28: Le Voleur d'Or* and *Fantômas 29: La Série Rouge*). *April.* In Switzerland, Fantômas tries to kill Fandor. Alice Rambert dies Fantômas convinces Hélène that Fandor is unfaithful to her. (*Fantômas 30: L'Hôtel du Crime*). *April.* In Russia, Fantômas impersonates the head of the Tsar's secret police. Hélène reconciles with Fandor. Fantômas steals a diamond necklace and returns to France.

(*Fantômas 31: La Cravate de Chanvre*). *April*. Fantômas strikes in Paris! He kills Bedjapur just as the Indian king was going to reveal the identity of Hélène's mother. *April 10*. Juve, Fandor, Hélène and Fantômas embarked on the *Titanic.April 15*. The *Titanic* sinks. Fandor and Hélène escape. Fantômas and Juve are believed to have died. (*Fantômas 32: La Fin de Fantômas*).

According to comments made by Allain, the ship was indeed supposed to be the *Titanic*, but the name was changed to that of *Gigantic*, in order to not offend the memories of the victims. (*La Fin de Fantômas* was published on September 20, 1913, less than 18 months after the tragic events.) The authors' intention, at the time, was to have the two protagonists, Juve and Fantômas, die after the ultimate revelation that they were brothers, while Fandor and Hélène went on to live happily ever after.

Due to popular demand, Marcel Allain decided to restart the series in 1925, and produced 11 volumes, the last being serialized but never collected in book form in 1963. Allain died on August 25, 1969. Most Fantômas scholars do not consider these stories canonical, for the most part because the characters (including Lady Beltham, back from the dead without any explanations given) do not age, being just the same in the 1960s as they were in the 1910s. *Fantômas mène le bal*, the final novel written by Allain, has Fantômas and Juve trapped in a rocket and shot into outer space.

Johan Heliot penned a sequel to that novel, entitled "*Vous rêvez trop de Fantômas*" (or "*Fantômas 1970*"), in which both Fantômas and Juve return to Earth as electromagnetic beings, having been transformed by the alien Capellans. Curiously, the Capellans are one of the two warring alien races mentioned by Philip José Farmer in *The Other Log of Phileas Fogg*.

David White is the author of *Fantômas in America*, a novel in which Fantômas returned to America; the main action took place in 1917 New York, on the eve of America entering the Great War. His plot was to capture Professor Harrington, the only man to know the secret of Eldorado and gold-making. His adversary was Detective Frederick Dickson, a cousin of Harry Dickson. *Fantômas in America* is inspired by the long-lost 1920 American *Fantômas* serial written by Edward Sedwick & George Eshenfelder for the Fox Film Corporation, released in France under the title of *Diabolos*, due to Marcel Allain's objections. A mysterious "Woman in Black" might be Lady Beltham, thus reconciling this version with that of Marcel Allain's sequels.

Stories published in *Tales of the Shadowmen* featuring Fantômas are:

#1. Robert Sheckley. "*The Paris-Ganymede Clock.*"

#2. Jean-Marc Lofficier. "*The Tarot of Fantômas*."

Jess Nevins. "*A Jest to Pass the Time*," taking place in 1921, in which an older Fantômas duels with Zenith and competes with various rivals to steal the Moonstone.

Bill Cunningham. "*Trauma*," in which Fantômas returns to Paris in 1916 to murder Vladimir, or a man impersonating his dead son.

#3. Alfredo Castelli. "*Long Live Fantômas*," which recasts the origins of the Lord of Evil.

Travis Hiltz. "*A Dance of Night and Death*," in which Fantômas battles Irma Vep of the Vampires Gang.

#4. Rick Lai. "*Corridors of Deceit*."

#6. Rick Lai. "*Incident in the Boer War*."

William P. Maynard. "*Yes, Virginia, There is a Fantômas*."

#7. Jean-Marc Lofficier. "*The Sincerest Form of Flattery*," in which an incarnation of Fantômas meets Diabolik.

#9. Neil Penswick. "*The Conspiracy of Silence*."

#13. Nathan Cabaniss. "*From Paris with Hate*."

Bibliography

Novels by Pierre Souvestre & Marcel Allain (all published by Fayard):
1911:
1. *Fantômas*
2. *Juve contre Fantômas* (*The Exploits of Juve* / *The Silent Executioner*)
3. *Le Mort qui tue* (*Messengers of Evil*)
4. *L'Agent Secret* (*A Nest of Spies*)
5. *Un Roi Prisonnier de Fantômas* (*A Royal Prisoner*)
6. *Le Policier Apache* (*The Long Arm of Fantômas*)
7. *Le Pendu de Londres* (*Slippery as Sin*)
8. *La Fille de Fantômas* (*The Daughter of Fantômas*) (Black Coat Press, 2006, ISBN 978-1-932983-56-2)
9. *Le Fiacre de Nuit*
10. *La Main Coupée* (*The Limb of Satan*)
11. *L'Arrestation de Fantômas*
12. *Le Magistrat Cambrioleur*
1912:
13. *La Livrée du Crime*
14. *La Mort de Juve*
15. *L'Evadée de Saint-Lazare*
16. *La Disparition de Fandor*
17. *Le Mariage de Fantômas*
18. *L'Assassin de Lady Beltham*
19. *La Guêpe Rouge*
20. *Les Souliers du Mort*
21. *Le Train Perdu*
22. *Les Amours d'un Prince*
23. *Le Bouquet Tragique*
1913:
24. *Le Jockey Masqué*
25. *Le Cercueil Vide*
26. *Le Faiseur de Reines*
27. *Le Cadavre Géant*
28. *Le Voleur d'Or*
29. *La Série Rouge*
30. *L'Hôtel du Crime*
31. *La Cravate de Chanvre*
32. *La Fin de Fantômas*

Novels by Marcel Allain:
Fantômas of Berlin (Brentano's, 1919)
1. *Fantômas est-il ressuscité?* (SPE, 1925) (*The Lord of Terror*)
2. *Fantômas, Roi des Recéleurs* (1926) (*Juve in the Dock*)
3. *Fantômas en Danger* (1926) (*Fantômas Captured*)
4. *Fantômas Prend sa Revanche* (1926) (*The Revenge of Fantômas*)
5. *Fantômas Attaque Fandor* (1926) (*Bulldog and Rats*)
6. *Si c'était Fantômas?* (serial. in *Le Petit Journal*, 1933)
7. *Oui, c'est Fantômas!* (serial. in *Le Petit Journal*, 1934)
8. *Fantômas Joue et Gagne* (serial. in *La Dépêche*, 1935)
9. *Fantômas Rencontre l'Amour* (serial. in *France-Soir*, 1946)
10. *Fantômas Vole des Blondes* (serial. in *Ce Soir*, 1948)
11. *Fantômas Mène le Bal* (serial. in *Constellation*, 1963)

www.ingramcontent.com/pod-product-compliance
Lightning Source LLC
Chambersburg PA
CBHW020826030726
47496CB00001B/109